A SEARED SKY

An adult epic fantasy trilogy

Book 1

JOININGS

by

STUART AKEN

First Published 2014 by Fantastic Books Publishing

Cover design by Heather Murphy

ISBN: 978-1-909163-30-0

DEDICATION

This trilogy is dedicated to Kenneth Burden, who died before I was born: the father I never knew.

Book One is dedicated to Valerie Allison, my loving, patient, and clever wife.

ACKNOWLEDGEMENTS

Any book is the result of more than can possibly be accomplished by the author alone. A fantasy trilogy makes special demands on those who create it. Yes, I wrote this book, but without the help of the following people, I could never have achieved publication.

My thanks go to the members of Hornsea Writers, a supportive group of professional writers who provided constant encouragement, contributed ideas and acted as a set of beta readers for parts of the text.

I give a big 'thank you' to Dan Grubb and the team of editors he keeps locked in his cellars. In spite of their imprisonment, they made the final edit of this book and removed typos and those other errors that manage to elude even the most careful author preparation.

Many thanks to cover designer, Heather Murphy, for her imaginative evocation of the book.

I could try to list every writer who's influenced me over the years, but I've read and absorbed so much wonder and creativity during the centuries I've lived, that I'd be bound to forget someone. So, I'll merely thank all the authors I've read and enjoyed.

Finally, and most importantly, I thank my wonderful wife for her constant support with food and other domestic necessities. But, more than this, Valerie has used her excellent memory, a sound grounding in English language, and the ability to spot inconsistencies, repetitions, clichés and anachronisms at seventy yards to coax me into vital changes. She made the penultimate edit before I wrenched the MS from my computer and sent it to the publishers. For her attention to detail and her dedication in reading this tome, I thank her most warmly.

CONTENTS

Chapter 1

PERILS OF OFFICE

Someone had betrayed him. Otherwise, how had they found him? Aklon-Dji glanced over his shoulder and counted seven in the pack; three were Holy Ones. All bore arms, but only two carried bows. His dipping and zigzagging wasted their arrows. But he couldn't run forever. He must hide soon. The Mire would suffice, with its tall reeds and unreliable tracks through the wetlands. Would they have planned for that? The Holy Ones weren't noted for strategy, so a trap seemed unlikely. More probably, they'd discovered one of The Few and tortured him or her and acted impulsively on whatever details they'd burned and carved from that unhappy flesh. He worried about who they'd broken.

Not the time for such concerns, though the thought of one of his disciples suffering was heart-breaking. He loved them all. But if he didn't escape soon, they'd kill him, or worse, make him captive. Dagla Kaz had increased the price on his head a hundredfold, making it worth the risk of taking him alive.

He jumped a narrow stream. A good sign: slow-running ground water flowed at the edges of the Mire. They'd be reluctant to follow him in there. He glanced again, and, as he turned, an arrow sliced the skin at the top of his left arm. The archer was a female Regular. Would that he could convert her to The Few. He'd have need of such skill come the start of the Cause. He registered her face for the future; a soldier of his father's army. How loyal, though, and how easily converted by truth?

Ahead, a clump of tall rushes promised sanctuary after the chase across the plain. He was beginning to tire after two leagues of swift pursuit. The hunters were strung out; some, a few hundred paces behind the leading pair.

A male Holy One, evidently more pious than usual and intent on glory, put on a burst of speed and passed the two Regulars in the lead. The naked man ran as though possessed, clearly intent on cutting off Aklon-Dji's escape before tall reeds and foul waters concealed him. Already the foul stench filled his nostrils, making breathing difficult. He gulped in deep breaths nevertheless; the sickening stench no match for the threat of death by prolonged torture.

The Holy One was on his heels as he rounded the clump. Two hundred more paces would set him in the first outliers of the Mire itself. Stand upon stand of reeds and rushes, even taller than him, forming a maze where he could truly lose them.

Aklon-Dji checked. He faced the Holy One, sword drawn. The man seemed suddenly perplexed, as if he hadn't considered the consequences of his actions. Aklon-Dji, feeling nothing but loathing for this class of Follower whilst hating the need to kill, skewered him without resistance. He jerked his sword free of the man's corpse. Snatched the other weapon from his assailant's limp hand and ran on before others could fall on him.

He put on a last spurt, fear of torture and its consequences for The Few pushing him beyond even his normal endurance. The original pack leaders, perhaps inspired by hopes of glory, were gaining. Aklon-Dji stumbled over the rough ground and almost fell. He must concentrate. Must keep alert. But there was some intrusion into his body, something working to detain him. He could feel his heart slowing, his breathing becoming laboured. The small wound on his arm throbbed.

Poison. The arrowhead must have been dipped in one of the aconite preparations: the one that killed or the other, which would leave him unable to move but more sensitive to pain? That depended on who'd prepared it. But, judging by the speed of its action, it would soon succeed one way or the other.

'Breathe shallow and fast, Aklon. It'll help. Concentrate. I'm with you.'

The voice in his head was comforting. Surprising but good to know Ivdulon was with him in this danger. Ahead, reeds and rushes waved with more than merely his stumbling gait. He knew he would collapse. And the hunters were close. Close enough for him to hear their calls and threats.

A few more paces. He felt almost finished. The day fading, but his mind alert enough to know approaching dusk alone did not take the light.

'Hold on. I need you, Aklon. Hold on and run. Keep your eyes open. I can see for you, even if your own vision fades. Trust me. Stay with me.'

He had no choice. He must trust Ivdulon; a man he'd never met, a man he spoke to in his mind. A man who lived far away, on the mainland. He could no longer see; his world a blank, black void. But he kept turning, twisting, running still. His legs had lost all feeling, the ground beneath his feet no longer solid. But still he ran. Whether he ran round, or through, obstructions he had no way of telling. Whether they still pursued him, he didn't know. He ran. Blind. Dead, to all intents and purposes. A dead man running for his life.

Something made him slow and turn left. Run. He felt the imperative to turn again. Run a short distance. Turn again. Run again.

From nowhere, it seemed, a familiar voice intruded into his mind.

'Take care, Aklon. I love you, despite your betrayal.'

Of all the women in his life, why his sister? And why now?

Then all was black and nothing.

⚹

Jodisa-Li, silent and attentive outside her father's door, was abruptly aware of her brother in great danger. She hoped he'd take care. The moment vanished as suddenly as it had come; leaving her unsure she'd experienced it.

The present called her back to why she lurked. Anxious to know what brought the Astronomer with his worried look and a message of doom in his eyes, she risked the High Priest's wrath and listened and watched through the gap, silent and still as bone.

'And you are certain, Jhonaht? Utterly convinced of this?'

The Astronomer rubbed his forehead and transferred sweat from his palm to the dun linen of his tabard before he nodded. 'Yes.'

'I'll have the skin scorched and scraped from that fat body of yours if you're wrong.'

'I'm as positive as I can be, Dagla Kaz. We both know the prediction's for next cycle. But I've watched eight nights in a row and can only conclude this is the spark of Ytraa's Skyfire. What else can it be? I might've waited a few more days before approaching you. But you, of all people, know how short is the time.'

Her father strode the hard earth floor of his stark cell in the very centre of the house, circling the entrance to the Pit of Secrets. Purple silk flapped about his thin thighs and his feet slapped the ground, echoing his turmoil; the sound emphatic against the still background of early evening. Only raucous cries of ubiquitous seemeeuws, diving and squabbling for scraps of food on the seashore, filtered through the inner walls, as most of the town sat for their evening meals.

One of the kitchen slaves signalled from the end of the corridor. Jodisa-Li waved her away, welcoming the excuse to intrude. She knocked and opened the door without waiting for a reply.

'Father, your meal...oh, sorry.' She stopped in the doorway, pretending to discover him preoccupied, and made to withdraw.

'Come in, Jodisa. I need a sound, uncomplicated head to help me.'

Jhonaht stared at her with puzzled surprise but snorted involuntarily at the High Priest's insulting implication.

'A fresh pair of eyes and ears, Jhonaht; that's all.'

She saw Jhonaht's irritation subside and he nodded brusquely at her, his eyes scorching her body. She waited for his gaze to return to her face and smiled to set his pulse racing.

'What is it, father? The meal's ready.' She smiled again at the Astronomer. 'You'll stay and dine with us, Jhonaht, of course.'

'Oh…I…well, why not? Yes, I will.'

She nodded and waited for her father.

'Our Chief Astronomer, learned and gifted with sight, declares that Ytraa's Skyfire has appeared. I need your level-headed thoughts to…'

'But it's not due till halfway through the next cycle! It's nine portions early if it's here now. How sure are you, Jhonaht?'

He sighed his frustration at having to explain to her; a mere girl, virgin and untested.

'The last Skyfire ended two hundred and forty two cycles ago, as you know, Jodisa-Li. There should be two hundred and forty three cycles between. However, I'm as sure as I can be that this new brightness is the first spark of the Skyfire. I even had the Holy Ones indulge in some of their unspeakable…I'm sorry Dagla Kaz, but as a man of reason I can't pretend to hold with divining the portents by staring at pulsating entrails drawn from the living belly of some poor unfortunate man or woman. They disembowelled three and declared themselves satisfied the auguries were favourable. I can be no more certain, considering we all accept it's early.'

'Jhonaht's convinced; the Holy One's appear content. I can't see what better proof you could have, Father.'

Her confidence pleased Jhonaht but she stared doubt at him, calculating, so he replaced his beaming smile with the uncertainty she preferred. Dagla Kaz stopped pacing and gazed as though not seeing her, seeming distracted by her comment. He made up his mind, his eyes signalling release from doubt as they firmed with conviction. For the briefest moment, he smiled at her before his features clouded with puzzlement.

Jhonaht couldn't take his eyes off her. They were gaping not at her body this time but what concealed it. Her ceremonial, jade-green silk tabard, belted with a cord woven from threads of rare myllth, mixed with her own red hair, sat well on her. Falling to mid-thigh, it permitted male eyes to trace the green, red and black dragon from its tail, coiling her ankle, up its body to the hem, beneath which, it breathed flame towards the place so many desired. She watched the man of science raise his eyes to the deep V-neck, where bright floral tattoos adorned her breasts.

Jodisa-Li understood their surprise. 'I know it's out of place. But the old woman from the harbour side came to finish the embroidery and I thought you'd like to see how I've spent so much of your coin, Father.'

She gave him a mischievous grin and twirled for inspection.

'Worth every gold crown, Jodisa; it graces the body that graces it, don't you agree, Jhonaht?'

The fat astronomer grabbed the opportunity to study her openly and took his time to agree.

'And, since we must accept Jhonaht's conclusion, you'll wear it sooner than expected. But take it off now I've seen it.' He stared for a moment at the black space below him and, like a man gathering courage to leap a wide chasm, breathed deeply.

'Are you well, Father? You appear troubled.'

'Troubled? I feel like a man condemned. I'll have to call a Special Gathering within days; for the Choosing.'

'So soon?'

'Aware that the Skyfire was due next cycle…' He glowered at Jhonaht as if the early arrival were his fault. '…I've been studying the secret texts again, consigning routes and reports of past pilgrimages to memory…' Again, he glanced involuntarily at the gaping hole at his feet, '… and, if I'm to achieve the exchange of the Virgin Gifts and return with the new Godwood in time, I must set off before the close of the next two sixdays. As you rightly observed, Jhonaht, there's no time to lose.'

'But must you really do this, Father? I mean, it's not as if you actually believe in all that nonsense about…'

'Hold your tongue, girl! Are you trying to…?'

'Sorry, Father.' She bent both knees, until she crouched in an uncomfortable curtsy. The back of her open left hand briefly touched her small nose and generous mouth, in a gesture of supplication. 'I've sent the slaves to bathe in the sea, knowing you needed peace and quiet. There's no one in the house to overhear. Jhonaht and I know how you feel.'

'Nevertheless, it doesn't do to voice such things, Jodisa.' His abrupt anger, born of his fear of discovery, evaporated in light of her assurance and he gestured her to rise again. 'The common people need their faith, my child. Learning that their High Priest's a charlatan might not prove to be in my best interests, it might even seriously undermine my control.'

Jodisa-Li smiled wryly, emboldening Jhonaht into voicing his thoughts. 'Your contempt for the herd and your callous disbelief never cease to amaze me, Dagla Kaz. At least my scepticism's born of study and knowledge. Yours appears to be no more than a general scorn for those who believe in things you don't. It mystifies me how you've never let it slip in public. How many people actually know?'

'We three, and that loathsome betrayer, Aklon-Dji. It's possible Tryonta, bearing in mind the duties he performs on my behalf, may have the merest suspicion. I play my part, as you know, with enthusiasm.'

Jhonaht shook his head, apparently unable to comprehend his relish for the role.

'Why, Jhonaht? Don't be so naïve. I have power, position and wealth. I can order death, life and partnership. I have respect wherever I go, or fear in its place. That garment adorning Jodisa cost more than most earn in two cycles. Her tattoos are the finest available and were three times the price of her tabard. I can cope with a little double-dealing to maintain that level of influence and affluence.'

'It seems your time's come to pay. Think about it, Dagla Kaz, you're going to have to select three unwilling virgins to take nearly four hundred leagues across hostile lands. In Choshinahm, you'll have to persuade those ignorant savages to hand over three of their virgins, if they have any. You'll have to recruit an army of willing labourers there, prepared to bring back a chunk of tree two manlengths wide and more than a manheight deep, knowing they're unlikely to return home. And you've to complete all this before the Skyfire fades. Rather you than me.'

'You think I don't know all that?'

'Of course. I just wonder if the continued pretence is worth the effort. I prefer my lonely watch on the mountain and the loyal service I receive from the Holy Ones and their compliant slaves.'

'Service that would cease if the people knew what we know.'

Jhonaht flinched.

'Come and eat. I've cooked your favourite, Father. It'll get cold.'

She turned and walked narrow passages, between walls of woven redwillow, to her room. Dagla Kaz and Jhonaht continued to the front of the house, from where aromas of cooked food percolated.

Jodisa-Li quickly replaced ceremonial with practical. Though the plain deep red tabard of fine cotton was no more demure. Fastening bone pegs through leather loops, as she returned to the two men, she permitted Jhonaht a glimpse of forbidden flesh. Dagla Kaz moved away from the open window as she entered.

'Making sure no one's lurking within hearing distance, Father?'

He nodded a smile of complicity at her as she busied herself, placing woven rush mats on the wooden surface and collecting knives and spoons for the meal, and turned his gaze on the Astronomer. 'Lust, Jhonaht, for my daughter?'

'She has a fine body, Dagla-Kaz. Is there a man on the island who doesn't dream of sharing it? My interest, of course, is purely aesthetic.'

'Of course.' He released the bronze clip of the belt circling his tabard and indicated Jhonaht should do likewise so they might eat without discomfort.

They sat at the scrubbed wooden table. Jodisa-Li brought the thick shellfish soup her father so loved, ladling the steaming fragrant mix from a glazed earthenware pot into deep bowls of smooth ebony.

Dagla Kaz tasted, nodded his approval and responded, at last, to Jhonaht's challenge. 'I'm ready to pay, Jhonaht. Liar and cheat, I may be, but thief I am not. I wouldn't rob the people of what they consider to be their right.'

'In any case, they'd probably cast us all, stripped, whipped and skinned, from the top of the Monument if you didn't go.'

'That is a danger, Jodisa. They do possess such an unfortunate manner. They will believe everything I tell them as if it's the absolute truth, and follow my directives to the letter. Most tiresome. I did actually consider hiding the reappearance of Ytraa's Fire, you know. I thought I might act surprised. But those pious, self-righteous Holy Ones keep their own records; Keepers of the Mysteries, indeed! Crude and incomplete as their records are, they know now of Ytraa's Skyfire so, of course, they'd never permit it. In any case, its sudden unexplained appearance would almost certainly cause panic amongst the people. And I do so dislike chaos, you know.'

'Just an old softheart, really, aren't you, Father?'

'Soft as ebony, hard as silk, as they say. Though I doubt they comprehend the irony.'

'Don't underestimate them, Dagla Kaz. Ignorant, ill-informed and vulgar they may be but a few show signs of remarkable native intelligence. By the way, talking of ebony, is that new lot seasoned yet? I need a new Staff of Office and I'd prefer one with weight and hardness. It gives an instructive blow such a solid message.'

'You wouldn't hit anyone with your Staff, Jhonaht. I've seen you avoid communal punishments where the victim faces nothing worse than a reed wand.'

'You see my difficulty, Dagla Kaz? Even your daughter denies me the authority of my rank. How am I to control the people in your absence?'

'You won't have to. I intend to appoint that appalling rhaat, Kaz-Ca-Wesdan, as my deputy.'

Jodisa-Li almost dropped the stone slab, with its grilled antelope steaks, in surprise. 'Not that horrible little turd from Morstahn, Father? He's loathed by everyone.'

'Precisely. Enough ambition to make him attempt to replace me in the minds and hearts of the people whilst I'm away but insufficient wit or wisdom to understand that everything he does will make me more appealing to them. By the time I return triumphant, they'll recall me only as a beneficent and merciful leader, gifted with intelligence and wisdom. My occasional lapses of the past will be forgotten under the wave of relief at the removal of such a dreadful dictator.'

'You really are the most awful bowelcreep, aren't you, Dagla Kaz?' Jhonaht clearly feared he'd stepped over the boundary of their relationship, as the High Priest glanced at him with a malevolence that had him trembling.

'What an extraordinary expression for one so educated, Jhonaht. But, I confess, quite justified. Now, Jodisa, what have you done to this antelope? I've rarely tasted meat so tender and succulent. You cook so much better than those good-for-nothing slaves.'

'You shouldn't tease Jhonaht so, Father. You know he's terrified of you. It's really very wicked.'

Dagla Kaz regarded the Astronomer with his penetrating gaze. 'Is he? He's nothing to fear from me but that I might ask too much of him and be seriously displeased should he fail.'

Jhonaht dropped his stare and expelled a loud sigh as Dagla Kaz shifted his gaze back to Jodisa-Li.

'But you're not frightened of me, are you?'

'I was, as a child. I know you better now, Father.'

'Well enough to know that, though you must be in the ranks of those who'll provide the Virgin Gifts, for the sake of appearances, you won't be one of the Chosen.'

Jodisa-Li bowed her head. 'I understand that I can't bring you such honour, Father. I daily pray to Ytraa to forgive my wickedness and beg Ytraa to deliver me from the terrors of eternity spent in the bowels of Mhortag. I now ask your forgiveness for depriving you of your share in the honour my selection would have brought our family.'

To her surprise and, evidently, Jhonaht's, Dagla Kaz laughed at her genuine apology.

'Honour and prestige are of no matter in this, my child. Your grief and remorse at your lapse do you credit but I seriously doubt that Ytraa, or any other deity, would have you suffer in eternity for a transgression not entirely of your own making. Indeed, I applaud the spirit that caused it. But that's not why you won't go to Choshinahm. You, my sweet Jodisa, are my sole heir. To you falls the task of continuing the glorious lie. That is why you won't be Chosen.'

'What if the drummer beats me out?'

'He won't.'

'Father, I'm honoured that you consider me worthy to succeed you, but what about Aklon…?'

He glared at her so fiercely that she quailed. 'Don't even mention his name in this house! He is lower than the dust, less than the smallest nothing. He does not exist.' His manner softened as abruptly as it had erupted. 'You, you are the one, Jodisa. Not that…that renegade.'

Jhonaht glanced at her, frowning.

'You wonder why Jodisa risks my wrath, Jhonaht. But I know her well; she has now confirmed, before a witness, her own position. My children share a distinguished and able father. Their mothers, however, whilst equally beautiful, differed in important ways. Jodisa's dear mother was blessed with pragmatism and common sense. That reprobate boy, who is no heir of mine, was born of a mother whose mind was softened by romantic notions and dreams of tenderness that have no place in those who aspire to leadership.'

Jodisa-Li loved her brother but thought him a fool; his loss was her gain. She smiled as she poured each of them a goblet of the casked wine Dagla Kaz had kept by from the last shipment. Fruity, mellow and clear gold in colour, it had a taste of wild redberry mingled with the sharper flavour of southern grapes.

'Good. Very good. How are the new vines developing, Dagla Kaz? Are we soon to have our own wine from the grapes that produced this nectar?'

'Another season should see a harvest good enough to match even this vintage. I look forward to consuming it on my return from Choshinahm. You'll be part of that celebration, Jhonaht, standing side by side with me as returning heroes from the ancient land of our beginnings.'

A little slow to grasp the meaning of this prediction, he looked at Jodisa-Li. The gleam of humour in her eyes brought understanding and he turned to question the High Priest. 'You want me to go with you?'

He merely inclined his head.

'Why, Dagla Kaz?'

'When it becomes clear that your prediction is wrong, I want the pleasure of demonstrating to you, and the rest of the party, the error of your ways. On the other hand, once it's obvious that you're right, I will enjoy the honour of permitting you to praise my perspicacity in trusting your dubious assurances.'

Jhonaht seemed unable to decide whether he was being serious. 'Surely, I'd be better placed here so I can help calm the populace once the Skyfire is generally known?'

'No, Jhonaht. You will come with me.'

Jodisa-Li sauntered round the room and plucked the hem of her tabard. Jhonaht seemed driven to follow her movement.

'For a man who claims to revel in his rational mind, you seem strangely attracted by the carnal qualities of my daughter. As her father, I'm immune and I'd supposed you to be equally unmoved. But you're as captivated as every male on the island. Perhaps a period of hardship and travel will lessen these desires. For, understand me well, Jhonaht; she is not for you. Come the time, Jodisa will join with many but you will not be one, unless she astounds me and chooses you, of course.'

She stopped before the Astronomer, considering him with that expression she knew drove men wild.

'I…I find her aesthetically pleasing, Dagla Kaz. Lust isn't part of my admiration. I look on Jodisa-Li as I might on a well cut gem, a still lake reflecting mountains, a fall of crystal water cascading over sharp dark rocks. She's an object of pure natural beauty; carnality has no place in my appreciation.'

'Jhonaht begs us believe his eyes make no connection with his loins when he looks at you.'

She took two steps back. 'Really, Jhonaht?' Her fingers curled the hem of her tabard. 'You've no wish to enter where my dragon breathes fire?'

His gaze fixed on her promise, tantalizingly concealed. He licked his lips and swallowed. She giggled, assigning her female influence to the realms of silliness as she released the hem and, with it, his eyes.

'You've grown and matured since I was last here, Jodisa-Li. How many hearts will you break? How many will dream and know they'll never satisfy their want? You know my feelings on the foolishness of women, Dagla Kaz. Your daughter's the exception that proves the rule. If only there'd been one such when I was a young man…'

'But there was.'

Jhonaht breathed in deeply. 'The past is dead, and Jodisa-Li's mother with it, Dagla Kaz. I'd rather not revisit it.'

Her father glanced at the Astronomer with what she thought might be a flicker of sympathy.

'If you'll excuse me, Jhonaht, I'll spend a while in prayer and meditation in my cell.'

'I thought you didn't believe in all that…'

'A man may know God without the irrelevance of religion.' He walked slowly to the open doorway, seeming suddenly born down by the burdens of office.

'Sleep well, Jhonaht. Come sun up I'll need you to send emissaries for me, make suggestions, and contact those we need consult about our trip.'

The Astronomer nodded his acknowledgement and Dagla Kaz left.

Jhonaht turned to Jodisa-Li. 'And do you pray also?'

'I see no reason to adopt that demeaning pose in private, Jhonaht. When alone, I speak with Ytraa in my own way. But, when the eyes of Followers are on us, it doesn't do to disappoint, does it?'

'So sceptical so young.'

'I'm young as a new born babe, Jhonaht; old as the sea. Father's prepared me long and well for my future. Eons ago, I lost what innocence I had. You know well enough my cause for scepticism and you know the suffering…' She stopped, unable to continue her line of justification, struggling to control emotions she was reluctant to display. 'You know much, Jhonaht, but even you're not privy to all my indiscretions. Nor do you know the many secrets lying in the darkness beneath Father's cell. Such reports and accounts might rob a gentle man of his sanity. They turned Aklon to heresy and rebellion. If I'm sceptical, it's because the knowledge I bear makes me wear disbelief as a defence. Come, I'll take you to your room and, regardless of your desires and perhaps my own, retire alone. We've much to do tomorrow, and little time.'

'You seem to delight in making my head swim.'

'I delight in many things.' But she emphasised the natural sway of her hips, as she led him to his room.

Chapter 2

Warrior And Priestess

Aklon-Dji knew his father would torture both of them to death if he and Kaz-Ca-Porlesah should be discovered together. He wondered again whether he should put her to this risk, how he had allowed himself to involve the priestess, knowing how precariously his own life dangled. If they captured him alive, the High Priest would show the islanders how a traitor to the faith would be punished in this life before being dispatched to the bowels of Mhortag for eternity.

He was unsure how the village priestess had discovered him. But find him she had and, somehow, brought him secretly back to her home to recover from the poison and the chase. Ivdulon was behind the rescue; of that he was convinced. For the moment, it was enough that this special woman had saved him from capture and torture. Two days and nights had passed since the chase; time enough for him to recover.

He felt her breathing, and the relaxed pounding of her heart echoing his own. Night revealed form without colour, as a gibbous moon spilt soft light through the small square opening in the eastern wall of her bedchamber. At the far end, the black oblong of the larger window sparkled with familiar stars, many of which they could both name. There lay also the faint new spark, ominous yet potentially liberating, that had urged them together.

'What's Ivdulon say about the Skyfire?' Kaz-Ca-Porlesah raised herself beside him to gaze at that celestial messenger, her voice soft.

He stared with her, inhaling the heady scent of iasomia flowers surrounding the window. Their perfume mingled with her scent and masked the cloying odour from the marshes. Now their breathing had steadied, he listened for danger and drew a picture from the persistent chafing of cicadas, occasional burping of frogs and whine of marshflies, interrupted now and then by the distant howl of a monkey deserted by its troop at the edge of the forest. He found nothing to suggest danger.

Cupping her shoulders with both hands, he lowered his head to whisper with his mouth just touching her ear. 'He confirms what we both assumed as soon as we observed it.'

'He's sure it's false, then?' She lay down again, relaxing.

'He is certain but, like us, unsure how Jhonaht will react. I think I may have given him the impression that our Chief Astronomer is not the brightest firefly in the swamp. Ivdulon knows the new star is not Ytraa's Skyfire. It is a spark that will barely increase in brightness and he predicts it will not leave the western part of the sky, as prophesied, but will fade and die before the true Skyfire appears.'

She wriggled, shuffling the soft bedding beneath her to find a more comfortable position. Aklon-Dji grew suddenly still and alert as a voice gently insinuated into his mind.

'*You're with a woman.*'

'*Ivdulon, this is not the most appropriate time.*' His thoughts travelled soundlessly across the unknown distance between himself and the other.

'*As you appear never to not be with a woman, Aklon, when would be appropriate?*'

'*Not now.*'

'Aklon? You mindtalking with Ivdulon?' She turned to face him.

'I am.'

'*Your intelligence and knowledge are always welcome, Ivdulon but now is not convenient. We are relaxing…*'

'*Naturally. Beats me how you find time or energy to manage that with everything else you do. Still, your choice, young man.*'

'*Indeed, the choice is mine. I seek to live life to the full whilst I retain it. Tomorrow I may be dead or dying and, in any case, one day I shall be too old to indulge in physical pleasure; that will be the signal for me to take on the more cerebral delights you seem to dwell in most of the time. Do you have a complaint relating to that?*'

'*I might wonder at your priorities, but, as you say, youth is your guide. Maturity will bring different rewards. One question, Aklon, then I'll leave you to your carnal delights. Been meaning to ask for a while. When you speak aloud, are you as pedantic as when we mindtalk?*'

'*I use language accurately and precisely. Do you find fault in that?*'

'*Most folk'd think it pretentious. Unless all you island savages talk that way?*'

'*No. I speak as I do and they speak…much as you do.*'

'*Ah, normally. Good.*'

'*One thing, Ivdulon, if I may?*'

The pause was enough to confirm his assent.

'*Was it you who directed Porlesah to the place you led me in the marshes?*'

'*Perhaps. But it's of no consequence. Enjoy your…woman. I'll contact you later, Aklon. Unless you'd rather…*'

'*Yes. I believe it might be to our mutual benefit if I made initial contact, for the moment.*'

'*Not worried you might intrude whilst I'm…?*'

'When have you ever been with a woman, Ivdulon? Farewell.'

The contact broke and he regretted his last comment, fearing it might be taken as an insult.

'Back with me?'

He felt the softness of her skin touching his and kissed her mouth. 'Yours entirely.'

'What did he want?'

'I have no idea. I have arranged to contact him at a more convenient time.'

'I could almost hear him, you know. Sort of awareness; on the edge of hearing. In fact, now I come to think of it, although I believed it was you who led me to the Mire, I think now it might've been Ivdulon.'

'Almost certainly. He has extraordinary powers. He knew I was with you. Ivdulon's abilities are very great. I think he could contact you if he wished.'

'Did you discuss the spark?'

'No. We have said all we need on that matter.'

'I see.'

He heard fear in her voice.

'The spark's the sign you've been waiting for, isn't it, Aklon? That's why you came out of hiding.'

'That depends on my father. If Jhonaht has the wit to recognise it as false, which I doubt, Dagla Kaz will not go.'

'When will you know?'

'You saw it four nights ago, Porlesah; I saw it five. Jhonaht is reputed to have means of seeing denied me, denied even you, though you should hear the result more rapidly than I. He would have seen the spark, perhaps, as many as six or seven nights past; Ivdulon has his own methods and has known of it for fifteen days, at least. Jhonaht has little faith in his own abilities, as you know, and will have asked the Holy Ones to read the entrails. Everything depends on their distorted interpretation of events. Though, if the cabal gathered to make deductions from the unholy gore they usually create is made up of fanatics rather than hedonists, you know how unpredictable they can be about such things. Jhonaht is hardly renowned for his bravery; my father terrifies him. Of one thing we can be certain, my pretty priestess, he will not declare until the Holy Ones agree with him.'

'And then?'

'You know as well as I do.'

'You forget, Aklon, I'm just a village priest, serving in the back of beyond. Unlike you, I'm not party to the mysteries of the Pit of Secrets.'

He found her hand and gentled her fingers. 'If he declares this as Ytraa's Skyfire, Father will have no choice. And he will act very quickly. There will be the Choosing on the Plain of Ytraa and then he must set out on the pilgrimage. Dagla Kaz and the unfortunate Chosen virgins, with a support party, will begin the fool's errand.'

'I hope I don't have to go.'

'He will take your counterpart from the capital.'

'Wendarah?'

'She is much more to his taste. You are far too conservative for Dagla Kaz. But he will go, yes. And, in his absence, I shall begin our work at last. Freedom, Porlesah; freedom for all.'

She was silent for a moment, absorbing this.

'Did Ivdulon say anything else?'

'Just now?'

'Last time you had a chat.'

'A few more random facts; you know the way he is. He is now certain that the world goes round the sun, but not in the perfect circle he was seeking for what he calls the orbit. It moves in something he calls an ellipse, which, apparently is shaped something like a flat drawing of an egg.'

She was silent and he understood she was contemplating this new blasphemy, setting it with the many others he'd related during the last two cycles. 'But that's…Do you believe him?'

'His explanation makes sense, as always. I have rarely known him in error. Would that we had such a mind on the island. If he were here in place of Jhonaht we might even get Dagla Kaz to consider some of the changes I must make in his absence.'

'Told you where he lives, yet?'

'On the mainland, close to the sea. He resides alone, in a tower high on a rock shelf overhanging a city built in white stone and housing one hundred thousand inhabitants. Can you imagine such a place? Our whole island holds only thirty thousand. But he is reluctant to name it. We continue to explore the boundaries of our strange friendship. I wish you could really speak with him, Porlesah; he uses such language and images and his mind is so sharp.'

'Why can't I contact him, like I can you?'

'I do not know, Porlesah. You can contact me only when you are facing me, even if across the distance, whereas I can open mindtalk with you from anywhere. Ivdulon says there are others who mindtalk. Some are as he and I, and others can speak only within the same room or only with specific people. I told him where I was on the second occasion we spoke and he revealed that we are a hundred and seventy leagues apart, as the seemeeuw flies.'

'A hundred and seventy leagues! To talk over such a distance. It's amazing, Aklon. Do you s'pose anyone else on the island can do it?'

'I do not know. I would like to discover others but I feel it best kept secret, for now.'

The question and its answer brought a lull and, in the depth of the warm night, they rested together and fell into sleep at last.

Morning brought brightness, to form a dazzling rhombus on the whitened wicker of the inner wall, beside the bed. It reflected onto their faces and woke Aklon-Dji. He rose on one arm, listened for signs from outside and heard nothing but nature. Looking down at her, blue-black locks shining with health and tumbling wantonly over honeyed shoulders, he felt her vulnerability. He watched her breathing; the slow movement so peaceful in sleep.

He must leave her soon. Too long in one place was dangerous. Too long in her house might be fatal for her. She stirred, as if she heard his thoughts and looked up into his face with eyes that mirrored his own. Lapis lazuli, she called them and he had no quarrel with that. But he thought her eyes softer than the blue rock with its golden specks, brighter than its polished surface. Yet, like his, star-like points sparked within their depths.

'Don't go just yet.'

He glanced out to the clear blue sky, smiled and shook his head. 'In daylight?'

She grinned at him and shrugged off her moment of foolishness.

'In any case, I wish to test some new words of truth on you today. I want you to hear what I intend to tell new recruits to the Few to help them comprehend. Will you be my judge and arbiter?'

'I suppose you'll speak to them in your usual correct and precise way. It's off-putting, you know. Why won't you relax a little, Aklon, and let the words flow into one another, like everyone else?'

'Perhaps I have no desire to be, or to sound, like everybody else. I am not everyone else. I am Aklon-Dji. I am renegade, hunted; worth more alive than the price of my head on a spike to my captor. I have a message to proclaim. Will they hear it better from a mouth that slurs and mumbles or from one that sounds each word as the jewel it truly is?'

'You're impossible.'

'And yet here I am. A paradox, it would seem.'

She rose up, kissed him and pushed him back down, laughing.

Breakfast saw them seated at the scrubbed planks that served as a table, as her loyal house slaves brought peeled fruits on smooth platters, and goblets of turned ebony filled with a steaming infusion of tlathan, its bitter tang awaking their sense of taste after the night. The open doors and windows let in sunlight carrying warm air, scented by the pale yellow and dark blue blooms of the trailing plant that clung to the baked mud of the outside walls. But the heat of day already overpowered that sweet perfume with the foetid rankness of the marsh.

She sent both slaves to collect her gifts of fresh fish, meat and wine from the people and told them she didn't expect them back before noon. They went willingly enough; aware their uncommonly kind mistress was excelling herself in her generosity as she instructed them.

'Buy yourselves new loincloths from the market. Linen, mind you, and bright and good quality; short as well. I want those legs on show. Take coin from the bowl in my bedchamber.'

'You spoil them.'

'No more than you would. Anyway, they deserve it for their loyalty and lack of awkward questions.'

'I imagine he joins with her as often as he does with you.'

'I hope so! Why should she miss out just because she was unfortunate enough to be fourthborn? I don't hold with slavery any more than you, Aklon and I hope we ban it absolutely when we're done.'

'I take it they still think me a messenger from the capital?'

'Of course. Though how you continue to get away with such a thin disguise is a mystery to me.'

'Skill, talent, brilliance of mind, tenacity...'

She stopped him with a thump to his arm. 'Show off. Now, you'd better tell me what you plan to tell new converts, whilst those two are out. They generally keep their mouths shut but you never know what they might say in the heat of the moment. So far, they're happy to believe you're from Chalamamnon. But start spouting blasphemy in front of them and they might wonder why their village priest's consorting with a man of such dangerous and dubious beliefs.'

He opened the discussion they'd held over recent cycles, putting forward new arguments against their religion, giving further instances of Ivdulon's reasoning and more of the appalling truths he'd learned from the texts in the Pit of Secrets. How many, he wondered, would rebel like him when they understood the whole system depended on the lies of a man who, by his own written admission, had abused, raped and murdered?

'I must not only reject all the Followers stand for but destroy the priesthood and the rule of the Holy Ones. And replace this fatally flawed religion with a new faith based on justice, mutual love, respect, tolerance and the worship of a single, omniscient, though unnamed, creator.'

'I know, Aklon. You don't have to convert me. But you're sure we need to abandon even Ytraa in this?'

'Ytraa is fatally contaminated by association with Gadhallah; I am not sure Ytraa can recover from the connection in the minds of the people. And I am sorry, Porlesah. I forget sometimes, in my zeal for justice, that you are truly changed, in spite of your vested interest in keeping things as they are. Forgive my lecturing. I am merely trying out my arguments on you before I use them to persuade others.'

'Why in Mhortag's name you told your father what you planned, I still don't understand…'

'An error of judgement; I admit. But I could not have lived the necessary lie of deceit, as you do each day, Porlesah. Such control and courage.'

'You persuaded me and, as you so rightly say; I've more to lose than most. I don't doubt, given time, you'll persuade a lot more. But we've the army and the Holy Ones to defeat and I've no idea how you expect to do that.'

'I will find a way, Porlesah. My message must get through. If necessary, I will die fighting to destroy the foul doctrines my father holds so dear.'

'You may well do just that. But I, for one, hope we can do it and live. I don't intend to give up my times with you and, whatever we find to replace our religion, I'm sure we'll still find pleasure in the days, portions and cycles to come.'

'I hope so. But that is where Gadhallah was so clever. How do you defeat a religion that gives its worshipers a divine reason to indulge in sex and to do so with anyone who is willing, that encourages it and actually makes frowking an integral part of worship? He created a self-perpetuating lie and it will take a great deal of persuasion to put a stop to it.'

'When they understand we don't want to stop them frowking, but want to do away with sacrifice and mutilation; when they realize we want them to share the wealth that only the priests and Holy Ones enjoy, I'm sure they'll be with us.'

'And if they are not?'

'If they're not, we'll have to admit defeat, leave the island and find a home somewhere else. Perhaps with your friend Ivdulon; he seems a tolerant soul.'

'I must persuade them, Porlesah. I must.'

'You will Aklon. We will.'

Come darkness, he left for an undisclosed destination. 'Safer if you know only what you need, Porlesah.'

'Safer for you, perhaps. I'm already doomed if I'm found out.'

'I know, my sweet priestess. Make sure you are not discovered.' And he was away into the night.

Chapter 3

THE CHOOSING

Kaz-Ca-Wesdan had stopped by Shoarhn's house on his way to the Special Gathering, commanding her to spread the news and get all eligible families on the move.

'Do it now. They must set out tomorrow morning.'

She knew better than to ask, 'Why me?', since he was living with A'ahl, but had to express her irritation. 'It might've been helpful, Kaz-Ca-Wesdan, if we'd had a little more notice.'

'Really?' His tone was brusque and she worried that she'd offended him.

Her winning smile worked as usual on the horrible little man and his anger faded to condescension.

'The messenger from Dagla Kaz came only hours ago. I must go at once. Most are already preparing for First Joining anyway. Off you go, now.'

She set preparations in motion at home. There was precious little information to give friends and neighbours, who would, in turn, pass it on until every eligible family had the news. Shoarhn ended her short tour of the town with a visit to her best friend.

'Can I leave the boys with you, A'ahl, whilst we go? My parents can't manage them for the few days we'll be away.'

'Of course. Bring them on your way in the morning.'

'I'll be very early.'

A'ahl nodded, 'I know. Kaz-Ca-Wesdan actually deigned to explain before he left the house to do his duty.'

On her way home she thought of Aglydron and his insistence on duty. She sometimes wondered why he'd bothered to marry her. He could've managed just as well with sacred slaves.

'All men need a wife, Shoarhn. It's the only safe way to have a partner for worship.'

The house was in uproar on her return. Everyone supposedly making ready for the journey. Aglydron sulked at her prolonged absence but she took control; putting the twins to bed and persuading him to tend the animals, whilst Tumalind helped prepare.

Next morning, they were on their way come sunrise. Three days of hard walking meant her temper was not at its best on the fourth morning of early rising for public prayer.

'Must you always be so pious, Aglydron? The rest are already eating.'

Shoarhn watched her husband replace his tabard and, regretting her irritation, helped him fasten wooden toggles through leather loops to close the side openings. Reaching up, she kissed him, wishing for a smile.

He pulled away from her. 'What're you doing, woman?'

She wasn't surprised; behaving so unconventionally in public.

'Call it piety if you want, Shoarhn. I give Ytraa what's due to Ytraa. It's a pity more don't do their duty.'

She sighed and nodded without agreeing. Her daughter stood patient; holding bowls of crushed grain mixed with fresh fruit for breakfast.

Seventeen weary leagues had brought them south from Morstahn up to the gentle slopes of the plateau. Only the sheer face of Ytraa's Peak, rising some five hundred manheights to its jagged point, broke the skyline ahead. Early morning sun cast an orange glow across the menacing obsidian face that formed the lower half of the mountain. Sparks of brightness scattered from myriad small irregularities and, here and there, dazzling reflections from larger mirrored facets, confused the observer. Yet, there was no life or warmth in that indifferent rock.

Around them, other family groups broke their fasts, talking with excitement or worry of the coming events. Rumour was rife along with the natural exuberance of the young men and women.

'Okkyntalah says he's heard Ytraa's Skyfire has been seen, Mother.'

'He should keep his mouth shut about things a mere boy can't understand.'

'Well what do you think it is, Father? Something must've happened to bring bucks and maidens up from all four townships together when we should've had our separate days.'

'I don't know, Tumalind. I don't pretend to know what the priest doesn't tell me.'

'Okkyntalah's only repeating what others have said, Aglydron. You seem nervous, Tumalind.'

'Only of…in front of so many people.'

'It's the same for everyone. We'll all join.'

'What are you nervous about, Tumalind? You're a Follower. Do your homage to Ytraa. Show your devotion to your creator, your wish to do the will of Ytraa. It's Ytraa you must think of as you join with Okkyntalah; isn't that right, Shoarhn?'

'That's certainly where your thoughts are, Aglydron.'

'And why shouldn't they be?'

Long experience told her argument was pointless. In any case, she was more concerned about the real reason for Tumalind's anxiety. She was confident her daughter was virgin but, as all women knew, the test was a rough tool for its purpose. And failure was too terrible to contemplate.

✦ ⋅✦⋅✦

Tumalind saw anxiety in her mother's eyes and approached her on the pretext of taking her empty bowl, intending to hug her for comfort, but found herself suddenly embraced instead.

'You think of Okkyntalah, my daughter. I know he'll be thinking of you.' The whisper was as much defiance as encouragement.

'I could think of no other.'

'Time we moved. I must be in the front to declare for Ytraa. Come on, you two; and keep that hound of his under control.'

They slung their travelling packs across their shoulders and set off on the final stage of their long march. Tumalind turned and glanced surreptitiously at Okkyntalah who flashed her a smile, full of eager anticipation. He and his family came after.

She looked up after a few hundred paces and saw the very tip of the Monument poking above the ridge; the golden-brown carving glowing.

She said nothing; her father would see it soon enough and be first to acknowledge they were now in sight of Ytraa. True to form, he stopped abruptly, placed his pack at his feet, removed his tabard and folded it within. Before he could berate them for their slowness, Tumalind and Shoarhn made ready.

Okkyntalah arrived, almost at a run. He slowed by her side, glanced at her and turned to face Shoarhn. 'She's so beautiful, bride-mother; just like you. Thank you for such a wonder.'

Shoarhn stretched tall and proud. 'You deserve her, Okkyntalah.'

He bowed to Shoarhn and the silent, disapproving Aglydron and, taking Tumalind's hand, clasped it in love and mutual support against the testing to come.

✦ ⋅✦⋅✦

'Back again? Out o' nowhere, as usual. 'Ow'd you know he'd gone?'

'I have my ways, Lasdilyss.'

'You 'ave. 'An they're worth the wait. But I'll wait no longer now you're here.'

Come noon, Aklon-Dji used the meagre tools of her kitchen to prepare a meal.

'You need to eat more, Lasdilyss; you are too thin.'

She nodded and tore a chunk of tender meat from the leg bone in her hand, devouring it as though she hadn't fed for days. He used a fingertip to take the dribble of stock from her dainty chin to her lips.

'How long will he be away?'

'Forever. Been summoned to go with Dagla Kaz. Doubt 'e'll ever come back.' She used the heel of her hand to wipe the single tear.

Aklon-Dji displayed surprise he didn't feel. 'Him as well; I wonder why? Fool's errand. But he will be back, Lasdilyss. Things will have changed by then, though.'

'We startin'?'

He nodded. 'At last. But I must warn Jodisa how absurd the venture is. I should let her know this so-called Ytraa's Skyfire will make a fool of Father; though she will simply laugh and tell me not to worry on her behalf.'

'When you goin'?'

'Oh, it will be a sixday before they sail and I dare not show my face in the house until he has gone. May I be your guest until then?'

'Thought you'd other interests 'ere in Pampahn?'

'Those with virgin offspring of the right age have gone to the Choosing with the village priest. And I have interests everywhere. I would prefer your company, if you will put up with me. We see little enough of each other. It is a shame your husband is not sympathetic to the Cause...'

'Phildrad's neither for nor agin it. Spends all 'is time mekkin' ends meet for us an' 'is ungrateful parents.'

'One day, you must let me meet him. I know most partners of the Few but for some reason I have never actually seen your husband. No matter. In his absence, may I stay?'

'You're always welcome. I don't 'ave much…'

'I suppose I must play the itinerant pedlar I pretend to be for your sake?'

She laughed with delight when he produced a length of blood red silk; enough to make her a tabard.

'Amazin', you are. 'Ow d'you do that? Like you took it from the air itself.'

'Ah, we each have our secrets.'

'Long as you're so generous, 'specially with yourself. I can't ask for no more.'

'You have my entire attention, Lasdilyss. And I will provide supper, as usual.'

'Just don't get caught. Don't want to see you strung up by your toes with them Holy Ones peeling off your lovely skin wi' strippin' knives before they roast you.'

'I confess an aversion to that fate also.'

Just before dawn, he left her drowsy on her straw-filled mattress.

The abrupt break with Ivdulon had been unsatisfactory and he wanted to know why his wise friend had contacted him earlier. His trance-like state might alarm Lasdilyss and she would never understand.

Aklon-Dji skirted the margin of the smaller marsh on the edge of town and arrived at the pier on the lakeside. He untied Phildrad's coracle from its half-sunken post. Dawn found him kneeling in the tiny vessel, sculling over the quiet surface to where low mountains dabbled their feet in the shallows.

Come daylight, he was hidden from the town, seated on a grassy slope with the boat pulled out of the water. He composed himself; allowing body and mind to relax.

'Ivdulon?'

'Yes. I'm awake and about, Aklon. And not with anyone.'

'Unkind of me. I meant no insult.'

'None assumed. Statement of fact. I suffered a singularly efficient initiation, many cycles ago. As I'd foreseen, energy expended wasn't worth the brief sensation. I've used my time and effort for more fruitful activities ever since.'

'You know not what you miss, Ivdulon. I must introduce you to women who will demonstrate its unique pleasures. You cannot be fully rounded without the experience of many beautiful women.'

'There we must agree to differ. Now, to what do I owe this attention?'

'You contacted me, the other night? I assumed you had a purpose.'

'I mindtalk with many. Now, what did I wish to impart to my friend on Muhnilahm? Yes! Your growing army of supporters; the Few?'

'Making ready for the Cause.'

'Good. You have male as well as female members of this army?'

'Naturally.'

'The women you entice and reward with your prowess as a lover but how do you get the men on your side?'

'How do you know about my renown with women, Ivdulon? I have never made any reference to…'

'Use your head, man. Every time I contact you, you're entwined with a different woman: you must have exceptional skill in that area. Also, I asked Porlesah and she was effusive in her praise.'

'You have spoken with Porlesah?'

'I just said as much! Now, how do you deal with the men in your group?'

'Usually through the woman in the partnership. But those I have cultivated otherwise have generally found my knowledge of certain aspects of life to their advantage.'

'Quite so. You trade knowledge for attention and then persuade them of the rightness of your Cause. Very good. Any potters in your army?'

'One. Why?'

'You might recruit more with what I've learned about a special technique that *makes pots less likely to break.'*

'Some might consider toughness a disadvantage, since they would sell fewer of their wares. However, I am more inclined toward those who have the satisfaction of their customers at heart, since they are much more likely to be in tune with my message of goodwill and justice. What can you tell me?'

Ivdulon described a method, based on a particular mode of firing and the use of a special glaze, which rendered pots lighter and more robust.

'Thank you, Ivdulon. I have no doubt it will secure me the opportunity of a number of converts. How did you come by the knowledge?'

'I was playing with a few ideas and they seemed to work.'

'Another of your inventions?'

'If you must call it that.'

'Ivdulon, you amaze me. You are a man of reason, knowledge, wisdom and learning. You understand history, geography, numbers. You paint, sculpt and design tools to make labour less onerous, and now I find you are a potter. Is there no end to your abilities?'

'It's what I do, Aklon.'

'But you never boast or expect praise. You remain modest, in spite of your extraordinary achievements.'

'What are we but our work? I seek neither glory nor praise. I don't care a leather dorltah whether anyone knows who I am. All that matters is what I do, what I discover, what I can pass on for the good of people in general. Surely that's the secret of happiness and fulfilment?'

'Perhaps, but what about reward?

'Don't worry about rewards, Aklon, I find them in the abstract, in ideas. Nothing delights me more than solving a problem. I'm probably the happiest person alive.'

'Then I am glad for you. Now, do you have any more information for me of the type that can have me skinned and roasted alive for heresy?'

A peculiar sensation overcame Aklon-Dji. The scene before him vanished. He saw, instead, a city of white stone, shining far below him in concentric arcs with a central lane, straight and steep, that led from somewhere out of sight immediately beneath him to the gates of vast walls, defending its outer parts.

Almost at once, the vision changed to the inside of a round stone tower. He saw strange, inexplicable instruments; unfurled rolls of parchment bearing odd devices, numbers, words and complex patterns of lines; and a strange metal object, meaningless in its complexity.

The view changed again as he was taken outside to a still lake of red-stained clear water within a perfect circle. Towering behind and rising to a white peak, a great mountain was reflected in the lake's mirror surface.

'*A glimpse into my world, Aklon. You inhabit a landscape alive with birds, animals and insects. A grove of willow to your left, a small lake below you, a sky alive with gulls; seemeeuws I think, duck and other waterfowl. My world is artificial and, here's the heresy, Aklon: civilised people, who weren't Followers, constructed the city and the lake that sits above it, over ten thousand cycles ago. I leave you with that thought.*'

And Ivdulon was gone. Aklon-Dji knew it would be pointless trying to make contact again for the moment. Ivdulon had left him with ideas and thoughts that needed time to develop and form the right questions. In a few days, he would mindtalk again and learn more. For now, he'd been privileged to see what man might do when freed from superstition, violence and hate and he'd learned that even the history of the world, as told by Gadhallah, was a lie; a limiting, belittling lie.

Okkyntalah stood on the grass beside Tumalind and gentled her hand in his. The High Priest, clad in ceremonial tabard, climbed to the raised dais beside the Monument: a circular platform, a full span wide, reached by a steep spiral of metal spikes driven horizontally into its thick supporting pillar. He stood, three manheights above the ground, where all could see him and spread his arms wide, demanding their attention.

'All be seated as I speak to faithful Followers meeting here at this auspicious time.' He allowed murmuring and movement, following this extraordinary announcement, and then raised his palm for silence.

Okkyntalah squeezed the small fingers of the girl he loved. So close, he could smell her particular scent and hear the soft breathing that caused her chest to rise and fall. He tried to concentrate on the High Priest's words. Tumalind smiled, understanding his difficulty.

'Have no fear; those who should join for the first time will do so, soon. Before they experience that supreme pleasure of worship, however, I have important news and an unusual but vital rite to perform.' He allowed a short spell of muttering before he again signalled silence. 'The noble Lord Gadhallah set out from Choshinahm on the coming of Ytraa's Skyfire, fourteen hundred and fifty seven cycles ago.'

The crowd responded enthusiastically. 'The Lord Gadhallah be praised.'

He raised his arms high over his head and dropped them again before he continued. 'He brought the first Godwood to begin the Monument to Ytraa that now stands five Godwoods tall before you.' He swept his arms in a dramatic gesture at the tall structure towering over them.

'Praise be to Lord Gadhallah.'

Okkyntalah studied the monument, as if for the first time now he was so close, and noted how the fine-grained wood of each Godwood showed its origin as a sculpted portion of the bole of a giant tree. Carved in likeness of Ytraa, each had three aspects; one showing the body and face of a man, one a woman and one the God. The three facets were connected as one so that the figure stood on three legs, spread wide, and had three arms, also spread, and raised to hold the feet of the carving above, and a single great head, crowned with curling hair on top and bearing three faces.

Inspired by the awesome nature of his God, he studied the male with huge erect phallus and bulging scrotum, the female with large breasts and fleshy, open vulva so much less inviting than the dark mystery between the thighs of his beloved. The God aspect bore no features, being sexless, but its face bore a great eye in the centre; a fearful, staring, all-seeing eye that had Okkyntalah unable to hold its gaze. As he surveyed the monument, he understood their arrangement; each Godwood turned one-third to the right of the one below so that all three faces of Ytraa were visible from any viewpoint.

Dagla Kaz bowed low to the Monument before continuing. 'Since that time, when our recording of the cycles began, the Skyfire has been seen four more times, burning in the sky with the wrath of Ytraa and signalling the end of all unless we do the will of Ytraa.'

Okkyntalah joined in with the crowd. 'Ytraa, the great and eternal, be praised.'

The High Priest looked into all the faces staring up at him. 'Our Chief Astronomer has marked a sign in the western sky. I have to tell you all...that Ytraa's Skyfire has returned.'

At the outcries of consternation, fear and some joy, Okkyntalah saw his own fear reflected in Tumalind's eyes. Some denied the possibility whilst others praised Ytraa for sending the sign in their lifetimes. Okkyntalah prayed they might both avoid involvement in the great things he knew must follow this announcement.

'Father will be eager to be involved. Mother will pray we're all spared.'

'Your father's welcome. I want to be with you, Tumalind. Others can do the will of Ytraa.'

Around them, similar whispered conversations took place; some, like Aglydron, desired the honour of service but most were afraid of the unknown that such duty must bring.

Dagla Kaz gave them time to settle once more. 'Not many are privileged to witness the Skyfire, but we shall live to see its glory and face the great test we are set. We must fulfil the promise if the heat of Ytraa's Skyfire is not to scorch us. Already I've put in place the needs and wants of the pilgrimage. Even now, the Chief Astronomer, a captain of the guard, and some of my helpers are preparing for the voyage over the Shylnah Sea.

Now will Ytraa Choose three Virgin Gifts to travel on this most holy of pilgrimages with me. We go to the land of our ancestors, the land where the noble Lord Gadhallah declared the coming of Ytraa's Skyfire to the first Followers, the land between the Wings of the Great Oryol, the far land of Choshinahm. Now you understand why I've delayed the initiation. The three Chosen Virgins must come from amongst those who wait here.'

Tumalind gripped Okkyntalah's hand and he saw her fear.

He recalled Aglydron teaching him this duty during his early instruction in the religion and its history, but some of those about them gasped; fear mingling with surprise.

'The journey will be long and hard. Many dangers face us but Ytraa will protect us whilst we remain true. By sea and land we go. A journey of four hundred leagues and more.

'Know that those who Ytraa Chooses are blessed and honoured above all others. Those they leave behind must accept their fate and find new partners or hope that one of those we bring back from Choshinahm will be for them. Only Ytraa knows the end, except that, if we fail, the Skyfire will burn the world to ashes. We do this in reparation for our many sins and acts of disobedience. It is well that we go forth in humility and pure in spirit to do the will of Ytraa. A new Godwood we will bring back to raise the sacred Monument to greater heights and further glorify Ytraa. The Virgin Gifts we exchange with Choshinahm mingle our island blood with that of our brethren in the ancient land, that we might keep Followers as one great family.

'Time is short. The Chosen must abandon all, this very day, and return with me to Chalamamnon. There, a ship waits to take us across the sea to far lands. Many brave emissaries have ventured there. We will tread in the footsteps of the successful ones and find the safe way with their help and by Ytraa's good grace.

'Where we go, we may find those who bow down to lesser Gods. We may discover wickedness beyond our wildest imaginings. We may encounter evil, cruelty and vile customs. But those who make this journey will remain true to Ytraa. We will be true or die.

'Each pilgrimage must take a tithe to the ancient land in token of goodwill and brotherhood. Each family is to provide a single gold crown. More will be welcomed and will place the giver high in the estimation of Ytraa. The Holy Ones will circulate amongst you and collect these tokens of your faith and devotion. Naturally, the bucks and maidens will be exempt from giving at this time; they're hardly in a position to give what they have no means of carrying.'

Okkyntalah recognised this light touch and felt he should join the short ripple of laughter. It was sparse and slow to come.

'Prepare now for the Choosing. Maidens, take your place in line before the drummer.'

Okkyntalah followed Tumalind's gaze to the huge man who'd emerged from the dark caves behind the Monument.

'Bucks, remain where you sit until the Choosing is over. If your maiden is Chosen, a partner will be found for the ceremony, for you must join at this time.

'Let the Choosing begin.'

Okkyntalah helped Tumalind to her feet and embraced her. 'Come back to me, my love. I can't lose you.'

'I'll return, Okkyntalah. We're meant to be, you and I.' She kissed him, though she shouldn't, and took her place in the file of girls.

Jodisa-Li stepped immediately in front of her in the line. He thought them so alike they could be sisters, but preferred his maiden.

'Please, Ytraa, let Tumalind stay. We'll devote ourselves to you here on the island.' His quiet prayer, he knew, would be echoed through the ranks of waiting bucks.

An enormous Holy One stood before a mighty drum, the thighbones of a former High Priest clasped in his hands. Okkyntalah counted the assembled girls: a hundred and ten, and three to go. The chances against selection were favourable.

The Holy Ones spread themselves along the line. A pair stood, one either side, at the head, their hands clasped. The High Priest, without his tabard now, faced the drummer. His back to the girls, he beat the skin so that it boomed out loud and doom-laden across the plain. When he'd set up a regular rhythm, the Holy Ones at the front raised their linked arms and allowed the first girl to move forward, as through a gate. With each beat of the drum, they lowered their arms, raising them at the next beat, releasing one girl at a time as the line passed through.

The drummer beat steadily, as twenty-seven girls moved through the human gate. Passing Okkyntalah, bright with relief and happiness at their good fortune, they sat with their partners. As the twenty-eighth girl, slender and attractive with a crown of long brown hair, entered the gate, Okkyntalah thought the High Priest winked very briefly. He knew he must be mistaken. The drummer paused, missing a beat. The Holy Ones directed the Chosen girl from the line, amid murmurs and gasps from the Krohtl crowd.

Thirty more girls moved through the gate without pause. And then Jodisa-Li was in place. A brief pause broke the beat fractionally and the Holy ones quickly raised their arms to let her through, as a beat out of time quickly followed. Tumalind entered the gate and there followed a real pause. Okkyntalah watched in disbelief as she was sent to stand with the other Chosen girl. He started; spoke a word of denial, until those around him reminded him with words and looks that he mustn't deny the will of Ytraa.

Mutterings and cries of unhappy surprise issued from the Morstahn population.

Silent and stunned, he took no notice of the remainder of the girls and was unaware of the final virgin being Chosen. His eyes were on his love, his mind filled with despair and grief that he would lose her and never see Tumalind again. But, more than this, his mind rebelled against what he'd witnessed. The pause convinced him that Jodisa-Li, not Tumalind, should be standing with the other Chosen girls and Holy Ones at the cave entrance.

All three maidens, shocked and distressed, were led into the darkness of underground chambers through the cave. The last he saw of his love was her quick pleading glance of hope, love, confusion and despair in his direction.

Chapter 4

THE CHOSEN

Shoarhn was only vaguely aware of Aglydron counting seven crowns into the Holy One's leather pouch. She heard the woman's lavish praise, the blessing and heartfelt thanks of the High Priest she passed on to him. But all Shoarhn's concern was for her lost daughter. Tears welled up and she couldn't stop them falling.

'What's this, woman? Aren't you proud she's been Chosen?'

The Holy One passed out of earshot and Shoarhn spoke her mind. 'Where's your joy, Aglydron, if you're so proud? Why so pale? What made you cry out when she was Chosen?'

Aglydron stared at her for a long time. When he finally found the words, he spoke as if unable to accept their truth. 'Tumalind wasn't Chosen. It was Jodisa-Li. I don't know how, but Tumalind's been taken instead of the High Priest's daughter.' He looked across at the ceremony site. 'I can't allow that.'

She'd seen Aglydron in states of religious zeal many times but his conviction that Tumalind had been Chosen in error brought a determination she hadn't seen in him before. It alarmed her. She knew he might act without thought; do something dangerous and ill-conceived. However, the ceremony ran its course into the next stage and he was forced to remain in place. She hoped the pause would make him think before he acted, but Aglydron's face was set in a mask of stubbornness that frightened her.

'All is now done, according to the will of Ytraa.' Dagla Kaz had donned his ceremonial regalia again and remounted the steps. 'What remains for me, before I lead this momentous pilgrimage and do what Ytraa requires, is to put in order all that is needed for peace, justice and continuity of worship in my absence.'

He gestured for silence again and announced Kaz-Ca-Wesdan as his deputy, named the village priest's replacement and identified the priestess who would accompany him on the journey. No one was surprised at Kaz-Ca-Wendarah's name but her replacement brought as many groans from the crowd as did the deputy High Priest.

'Now to personal arrangements; I must make provision against my untimely demise. Should Ytraa see fit to prevent my return with the Godwood, I must leave an heir to guide and protect you: one of the line of Gadhallah, ready to succeed me.'

A Holy One guided Jodisa-Li to the steps and urged her up to stand close to her father on the small platform. When she was in place, standing proud and rather aloof, her father continued. 'Jodisa-Li is my heir. I declare this publicly so that all may know her new status and afford her the respect her office brings. Because of this elevation, she will not be initiated today.'

Shoarhn saw Jodisa-Li glance at the newly appointed priest of Chalamamnon. Both seemed equally disappointed.

'She will remain virgin and sacrosanct. Let no man penetrate her, on pain of the most severe punishment. She must first be initiated into the rank of High Priest Elect and will therefore return home with me to await preparation. The Keepers of the Mysteries will summon her within seven days of my departure to put her to the test and instruct her in her new duties. I command you to give her your loyalty and ask that you grant her your love. My original heir, Aklon-Dji...' he shut his eyes as if in pain, '...remains under sentence of the most painful death that can be devised.

'Now, I place you in the hands of Kaz-Ca-Wesdan, to be styled Wesdan Kaz, until my return. He will oversee the rest of this ceremony and, with help and guidance from Jodisa-Li after her initiation, act as your supreme spiritual guide. Be loyal and let none gainsay him.

'No ceremony attends our leaving: we fulfil the will of Ytraa and that is our glory. My blessing on those who join for the first time before Ytraa. May Ytraa sanctify your union and may you have that pleasure until your days are ended. Farewell.'

He led his daughter down the steps and into the dark caves, where Tumalind waited with the other girls.

'Are we to be given no chance to say goodbye to our daughters?' Shoarhn's voice muted the scattered murmurs and cries.

Aglydron looked aghast but remained silent as Wesdan Kaz strutted up the steps and signalled for calm. 'As to that, woman, there's no need. Those who go on the sacred pilgrimage are no longer ours. All ties end with the decision of Ytraa. We rejoice in their Choosing and pray for their safety, which, of course, is assured by Ytraa.'

He told the bucks and maidens to reform their circle and required volunteers to join with those who lacked partners. Kaz-Ca-Charrohn, the blonde priestess from Krohtl, strode purposefully toward Okkyntalah, shoving a sacred prostitute out of her way and leaving no doubt that she intended to have the young man.

'Let all gathered here now display their devotion to Ytraa.' Wesdan Kaz almost fell as he rushed down the spiral, intent on fulfilling his own command.

Shoarhn looked across at the cave and saw Tumalind's grief as she witnessed the priestess embrace her beloved only moments before she was ushered out of sight. Her tears for her loss of Tumalind and for her daughter's sadness formed no barrier to Aglydron's devotion to his duty, however.

The tabard the Holy Ones had given Tumalind was too warm, and coarse; it scratched, and smelled as if it hadn't been washed for a long time. In the gloom of the brittle cavern, she saw the other two girls similarly clad in nondescript grey; so different from the colourful embroidered tabards their men would have dressed them in after their initiation. She let a small sob escape her at that thought and tried to turn her mind away from Okkyntalah and his dark green eyes that made her melt. The image of the beautiful notorious priestess enclosing him in her arms, haunted her.

There was no comfort in the coolness of the black-walled cave where the light from the world outside glinted and sparkled like spiked memories from the shattered surfaces. The sounds of joy outside seemed magnified in the silence and tortured her with what she would never know.

'Come, I want to reach the road before darkness. We've many leagues to travel even before we start our proper journey. The sooner we reach Chalamamnon, the sooner we can rest and complete the preparations for our pilgrimage.'

The High Priest's words did nothing to comfort her, as she wandered through the caverns and emerged into sudden brilliance and the heat of late afternoon sunshine, beneath the west side of the mountain.

She'd been snatched from the happiest moment of her life and thrust into a nightmare of uncertainty and hopelessness. Instead of enjoying her first taste of love, she was trudging to a world where everything and everyone was unknown. And the worst of it was that she'd been Chosen in error. The drummer had broken his beat for Jodisa-Li. But she'd been pulled from the line. They'd robbed her of the role of loving wife and mother to the children she and Okkyntalah had planned to make together.

How could this error have happened? And why would no one listen to her? The Holy Ones had dismissed her complaint as irrelevant and irreverent. The Choosing was the work of Ytraa, who was infallible, and therefore she must be in error. Dagla Kaz had merely smiled as if she were a fool and pretended to comfort her with suggestions that her misunderstanding of events was normal and she'd soon adjust to the reality of her situation. Ytraa had honoured her, and she mustn't risk Ytraa's wrath by complaining. Her new life had begun and she must leave her old one behind. She must take her cue from the other two Virgin Gifts.

'They are not suggesting Ytraa has Chosen them in error, are they?'

But then, they hadn't been Chosen by mistake. The mistake of the Holy Ones, the High Priest, the drummer but not, of course, Ytraa, who was perfect and without fault.

The light faded, as long leagues took her further from all that she loved and knew, the grass beneath her feet no longer green but dull, indeterminate grey. Was this her life, now? Everything grey, everything without joy and nothing that was hers?

'It might've been worse, dear. At least you passed the test.'

She looked at the woman who'd walked up beside her. She'd noticed this confident, well-made woman, no more than twenty-five but with an air of authority, amongst the small group gathered to leave with the High Priest. Her sudden concern seemed out of place with her almost frightening sensuality; Tumalind could imagine men being both obsessed and terrified by this woman. She commanded respect simply by her stance. Now, clad in a similar nondescript garment to the one that chafed Tumalind, she nevertheless maintained a sense of one so indifferent to her situation as to make it irrelevant.

'I shouldn't be here, Kaz-Ca-Wendarah. I wasn't properly ...'

'My dear, I've heard your complaint. Take it from me; no one will hear you. The girl you believe was passed over in your stead is Jodisa-Li and I can tell you, with absolute confidence, that she will not be going to Choshinahm. Now, my dear...what is your name, by the way?'

'Tumalind.'

'Pretty name for a very pretty girl. Believe me, I know what I'm talking about; you're stuck with being a Virgin Gift. You can either accept it, and make the pilgrimage with a mind uncluttered by unhelpful and painful memories and "what ifs", or you can wallow in self-pity and live each day of the trip in pain and distress. I advise the former, Tumalind. You can't change your situation but you can make it more bearable by accepting your fate. If it helps you feel better, I've spent many hours of delight with Dagla Kaz and even I have no say about my situation. We may be returning to my home but I won't be staying there. I, too, am destined for Choshinahm.'

'But I love Okkyntalah.'

She nodded; the movement barely visible in the falling night. 'Love. Something I've not experienced, my dear. But I expect you'll do well enough with whoever you find in Choshinahm. For the moment, however, I suggest you accept your lot and make the best of it. Everyone will think much more of you.'

Tumalind had it in mind to reply that that was easy for her to say. But, quiet and obedient as her father had schooled her, she said nothing and resolved instead to remain silent on the subject, keeping her resentment and sadness in her heart and showing the world her brave and dutiful face. Oh, but it was going to be so hard!

'Dagla Kaz. I think these young women have had quite enough to put up with for one day. Can't we call a halt and let the poor dears have a rest?'

'Wendarah, your solicitude does you credit. Another five hundred paces and we'll reach the road and camp for the night. Will that please you?'

'For the moment.'

When they reached the place, the slaves in the party built a fire and cooked. She and the others rested after their long walk.

It was a new experience for Tumalind, to watch and wait in idleness whilst others worked and it did nothing to alleviate her anxiety and despair. She sat with the other two Virgin Gifts, eager to learn who they were, how they felt and where they had lived.

'Who cares where we're from? We're just gifts to foreigners. What's it matter who we are? We're of no importance at all.' The last girl Chosen spoke with more anger than bitterness, a tough edge to her voice and no sign of tears. Tumalind felt she was likely to make trouble and hoped it wouldn't reflect badly on all three of them.

'I'm Tumalind, from Morstahn. I think we might be better…well, it might be best if we try to be friends…'

'Porryh, from Chalamamnon but don't talk about friendship. I'm not sure I'm going.'

'You don't 'ave no choice. None of us does. We 'ave to go.'

'Oh? What's your name, then?' Porryh's question held a sharp note.

'I'm Dilanthas. From Krohtl.'

'That's where that pervert came from, the one they strung upside down and unsexed because he'd been frowking his daughter.'

Tumalind briefly recalled the tests, before the High Priest had spoken. One poor girl had failed and confessed her father had abused her. The man's fate, though just, was something she didn't want to think about. His screams as he was punished had left as deep an impression on her as the simple fact of his exclusion from the afterlife, for no one lacking sexual parts could hope to pass into the Garden of Delights. Criminals of both genders were always unsexed before they were otherwise punished.

'Are they all like that there?'

'No.' Dilanthas glanced at Porryh as if hurt by her suggestion. 'He's a…was an 'orrible man. Nobody liked him. It's 'is daughter I feel sorry for.'

'What about the poor boy who failed the question? Don't you feel sorry for him?'

'Must be soft in the head as well as in his parts. I mean, everybody knows raw tlathan will make the softest prod hard as ebony. Serves the bowelcreep right if he hasn't the sense to use it on a day like today.'

'He was a friend of mine, and Okkyntalah's. A nice, kind and gentle boy. I feel so sorry for him, being unsexed like that.'

'Don't start feeling sorry for anyone else; we've enough to do feeling sorry for ourselves.'

'Kaz-Ca-Wendarah says there's no point in self-pity.' Tumalind told them. 'She says we might as well accept our lot and try to be cheerful about it.'

'She would. She's frowked the High Priest so often she might as well be wed to him. She's bound to stick up for him; he certainly sticks it up her.'

'It's not the High Priest's fault we've been Chosen, Porryh. My father would say it's an honour. I imagine he's trying, right now, to persuade my mother and Okkyntalah that I'm blessed and they should be grateful. But I don't want to be blessed; I don't want go to Choshinahm. I want to marry Okkyntalah.'

'Can't now, Tumalind. This is us. We're stuck an' there's nowt we can do about it.'

Porryh looked Tumalind up and down. 'Okkyntalah your man?'

'He was to be.'

'Wasn't he the one that Kaz-Ca-Charrohn picked out?'

'They say she's a…well, anyway, they say she can't get enough young men.' Tumalind bit back the tears.

'Your village priest, isn't she, Dilanthas?'

'Was. Don't none us of belong to no village now.'

'Well, looks like your Okkyntalah's frowking an expert. He'll soon forget you.'

'Don't say that. I love him. And he loves me. I can't bear to think I'll never see him again. I just can't bear it.' In spite of her intentions and determination, she broke down and wept again. Dilanthas took her in her arms and tried to comfort her with soft words.

Porryh adopted an air of studied indifference. 'My man's a bit of a lad, tell the truth. He'll soon find some other girl. Probably frowking with some tart even now. Tried it with me, you know, loads of times. Wouldn't let him, though. Didn't want my fern and dubbies chopped like they did that poor lass today who wouldn't tell who she'd done it with. I told him he'd have to wait. Well, he didn't have to wait today, did he? Some whoring slave will've given him what he wanted. But I'll have to wait. And you two.'

'I've known my lad for ages. 'E's clever; made me feel all funny inside. I'll miss 'im. Wonder what 'e's doin' now?'

'Frowking your sister.'

'My sister's married.'

'That'll not stop him, will it? Nor her. He was all primed to frowk you today and he never got the chance. He can frowk anyone now. Forget you even exist, he will.'

'I 'ope not.' Dilanthas let her own tears fall silently down her cheeks.

It was Tumalind's turn to provide comfort and she took the girl's head onto her breast and stroked her shoulders. 'Okkyntalah won't forget me. He loves me. He'll always love me, as I'll always love him.'

'Bet he's never given you a thought.'

'No. He'll be true in his heart. He'll not betray me.'

'Use your sense, girl. What's he going to do? Follow us to Choshinahm and steal you away? You're lost to him. You're never going to be available for him. He'll have to find someone else. He's got no choice. Just like us.'

'Cept they can choose who they want an' we can't. We'll 'ave to meck do wi' what we're given.'

The Krohtl girl's thought put a stop to further conversation and the three of them sat near the fire thinking their own thoughts until a slave brought them food.

Tumalind ate simply to keep up her strength. She'd concluded now that she had a stark choice before her. She could either let this accident of fate destroy her, in which case she might as well simply stop living right now, or she could keep herself going in the hope that something, anything, might happen to bring her back together with Okkyntalah.

She knew there was no rational way in which she could expect to be with him; every sensible argument made it impossible. But there was something deep within her that said Okkyntalah wouldn't desert her, wouldn't allow her to be forgotten in some distant land. She was convinced, from that fleeting glimpse of his face as she was urged into the cave, that he also believed her Chosen in error. He wouldn't stand back and allow such injustice to go unchallenged. He'd try to put right the wrong. His love for her was like hers for him. If Okkyntalah had been Chosen to go, she'd have found a way to get him back and she knew, deep inside, that he'd do the same.

So, she would eat, breathe, and find ways to stay alive against all odds in the days and portions to come. Okkyntalah would find her and take her back and they would be together for always. That hope would keep her going, keep her alive, keep her cheerful even, when all else was gone and there was nothing left to hang on to. Knowing Okkyntalah was still there for her would be her foundation and her reason to live.

Kaz-Ca-Wendarah came for them after they'd eaten. Under the rising half moon, she took them along the nearby river to wash and prepare themselves for the night. As a warden, she seemed subtle and kind, even sympathetic. But it was clear she wasn't going to give her charges any chance to run away, as they might in these first hours of strangeness and shock. She remained with them as they bathed and then settled them down with sleepsacks near the fire and set two slaves to watch over them, explaining that they would keep wild animals away. Tumalind smiled grimly, knowing the real reason for the guards.

But escape of that sort was impossible; she would have to spend life constantly on the run, like that dreadful renegade, Aklon-Dji. She wondered, as she tried to find sleep, what had caused such a privileged and fortunate man to turn so thoroughly against his religion and his own father. Unless he was a servant of Mhortag, it must've been something truly appalling.

Chapter 5

TO RIGHT A WRONG

*T*he remainder of the ceremony, the mass joining and blessing of the newlyweds, passed in a haze for Shoarhn.

'It was wrong.'

She heard Aglydron addressing Okkyntalah in tones of profound disbelief.

'Jodisa-Li was Chosen. You saw, didn't you?'

Okkyntalah agreed. 'The High Priest made a sign to the drummer and they took Tumalind instead. Why?'

'I don't know. But I'm going to find out.'

'I'm coming with you.'

'I thought Kaz-Ca-Charrohn had taken you as consort? Seemed impressed with you, for some reason.' Aglydron's tone was all accusation, as if he believed the young man had somehow betrayed Tumalind.

Okkyntalah shrugged. 'She made me a man and I enjoyed it. But she's off frowking some other man now. I love Tumalind and if I can get her back, I'm willing to risk a beating for a bit of disobedience.'

Shoarhn squeezed his arm. 'Thank you, Okkyntalah, but please don't do anything foolish.'

All around them, people were preparing to celebrate the passage of their children into adulthood with food and drink brought specially for the occasion. But Shoarhn and Aglydron felt no joy and Okkyntalah had no cause for celebration.

Shoarhn was anxious that her husband might do something stupid in his agitated state 'The High Priest won't listen to you. What can you do?'

'I don't know. But Ytraa's wishes mustn't be denied. Shoarhn, don't travel by yourself. If I'm not back, go home with Okkyntalah's family. I'll return as soon as I've done.'

Protest was useless with him in this mood and, with a growing sense of unease, she watched him collect his pack. The pair strode purposefully toward the mouth of the cave. Still shocked and sorrowing at the loss of her daughter, she wondered, as she took her place with Okkyntalah's parents, whether she'd ever see her husband again. She knew she should've tried harder to stop them confronting Dagla Kaz: the man wasn't to be crossed. Aglydron would argue and might be punished; even killed. She turned toward the Monument to go and save her husband and the boy from their rash behaviour but

Okkyntalah's mother put a hand on her arm.

'They'll be fine, Shoarhn. Look, the Holy Ones are dealing with them. I doubt they'll get as far as Dagla Kaz. In fact, judging by what he said, I doubt he's still here.'

Shoarhn waited as, all around her, others feasted and celebrated, the newlyweds full of joy. She was alone, a little away from the celebrations, when the sun went down and all fell silent for evening prayer.

Aglydron and Okkyntalah returned as darkness fell. Her husband was silent and morose, a frightening look of stubborn righteousness about his features.

'You can't do anything, Aglydron. We're too small. We have no power.'

'They've gone, just like he said. I thought they'd still be in the caves but there's another way out. The Holy Ones said they went during the actual joining! Okkyntalah and I are going at sun up, to put it right.'

'They'll kill you if you accuse the High Priest of…'

'We're going to bring Tumalind home, bride-mother.'

Shoarhn looked at the two men in the flickering light of the fires and knew she'd get nowhere with argument. Perhaps a night's sleep would make them see sense. Sorrow and anxiety ruled her and dreams were long in coming and brought no relief.

But come morning, they'd gone, taking the dog with them. She was forced, for the sake of the boys, to return home with the others and hope that her husband would soon return to her, with or without Tumalind, as he'd promised.

❖━━━━━━❖

'Look, Aglydron, if we try to find our way alone in this pestilential wilderness, we're going to die. Don't you think we should travel with the families from Chalamamnon?'

The boy's reasoning tone underlined Aglydron's fear and anxiety but he'd have none of it.

'You're a fool, boy. They'll slow us down. Every moment that passes takes the pilgrimage party further away. Can't you see? Any case, families will've set off by now, we'll miss them if we go back. We've got to get on; the party might've already gone by the time we get there, if we don't go after them right now.'

'Maybe. But if we can't find the road in this never-ending grassland, how's that going to help Tumalind? I know it's in the wrong direction but we should've set off for the bridge first. At least we know the road to Chalamamnon runs from there.'

Aglydron stopped pacing and glared at the boy, irritated by his logic. They'd crossed the plain in what he thought must be the general direction of the capital. Since neither of them had ever been more than a few leagues from their village, other than to visit the Plain of Ytraa, they had little real idea where the main town lay. After making an unforeseen detour round a large marsh, they'd reached a point where neither of them had a clear idea which direction to take.

'There might be something in what you say, boy. But we can't go back. We know where the river lies. We'll cross it and travel due west till we hit the road. We can't go wrong once find it; there's only one, as far as I know.'

'I expect so.' Okkyntalah didn't sound any more certain than Aglydron felt.

'We've got to reach Chalamamnon before they set off.'

'You're sure you know how to find the river?'

'It runs close to the road for a few leagues. It's northwest. We'll meet it, eventually.'

Okkyntalah nodded, 'And then try to find a way across.'

Aglydron was minded to curse his pessimism but knew the boy had good cause and held his tongue, this time.

It was near midday when they reached the River Rhyll, only to discover it was wider, deeper and swifter than Aglydron had expected. Northeast, it stretched into the haze without seeming to diminish. Southwest, there were signs it might at least narrow. They went that way, more in hope than expectation.

The sun was merciless and there was little shade this side of the river, though the far bank was dotted with tall, broad-crowned trees that cast wide shadows over the lush illuk of the lowlands. They pushed on through the afternoon, not stopping even for a midday break, urgency lending anxiety to their mission.

At length, after they'd travelled some two and a half leagues along the rugged bank, they reached a broad curve, turning toward the foothills of a small mountain range.

'This is the wrong direction, Aglydron. Carry on this way and we'll end up in that stinking mire they say surrounds Pampahn.'

'The river goes through the hills. It'll narrow up there.' He stated, with more confidence than he felt. Already the plan to do Ytraa's will seemed impossible. But he had to act, no matter how difficult it proved.

Okkyntalah frowned and cocked an ear toward the end of the deep valley, listening intently. 'There's a waterfall up there.'

'Good. River's bound to narrow somewhere near that. We'll cross it soon, you'll see.'

'Or drown in the attempt.'

They'd travelled less than a thousand paces, the water's roar growing loud enough to defeat conversation, when they came in sight of the thundering falls. Spray, in rainbow mist, soaked them as they surveyed the treacherous climb to the top. It was a scramble that needed hands and feet and Shaulah would never make it. Okkyntalah passed his pack to Aglydron with a signal and hoisted his dog across his shoulders, holding her feet together in one hand and using the other to help him climb. It was dangerous and they were both soaked and weary when they reached a narrow, flat space at the top. Shaulah gave Okkyntalah a swift lick on his nose and dashed off to hunt for scents, as they rested on the flat outcrop between the sheer cliffs that forced the river into its thundering torrent.

A short climb upstream from the edge of the fall, the river rushed through a series of narrow channels cut into a huge slab of wet worn rock. On their side of the bank, the flat, reddish platform opened out to form a wide margin beyond which the grass continued in leagues of rising peaks. On the far side, the rock disappeared into a steep rise cloaked in trees and undergrowth. The fast flowing water gushed and gurgled through a maze of narrow channels. Some they could step over but the wider straits they'd have to jump.

'There, boy. See? Told you we'd get across.'

'Maybe. But, fall into one of those channels and you're dead. Look how fast the current's flowing.'

'We'll be all right. Ytraa will help.'

They surveyed the land and found what seemed a possible route across. The steps were no more than terrifying strides over the boiling torrent but the leap across the first wider stream had both of them trembling. Shaulah jumped after them and then wandered off, apparently intent on making her own choices. A few paces upstream brought them to the next crossing point and they leapt this with a little more confidence. Okkyntalah looked round for his dog.

'Look. She's already across.'

She was standing on the far bank, wagging her tail as she watched them trying to find suitable points to jump the four wider streams.

Aglydron walked to the downstream end of the narrow island finger of rock and looked at the gap. The far side strip was even narrower, and pitted. The landing would have to be accurate or he'd overrun and end up in the rushing water. The boy came up beside him and studied the lie of the ground.

'I'll go first and wait to steady you, if you like.'

'I can jump as well as you, boy.'

'My longer legs might make it easier, that's all. Go first if you want.'

Aglydron grunted. 'Go on, then.'

Okkyntalah made the leap, rocking slightly on landing. He braced himself and signalled. Aglydron leapt across and was relieved when the boy's hand gripped his forearm and steadied him. They stood together, water roaring its pent up energy and spraying their legs and feet as it raced through the constrictions. Three more channels to go.

'There.' Aglydron pointed to a place where the next groove narrowed significantly so that the water churned and sprayed the uneven rock on either side. The gap was easy to jump but constant wetness made the surface slippery. Okkyntalah looked at the place and shrugged. He walked upstream and back but could find nothing better. Again, he made the first jump and landed safely enough but slipped and fell on his back. Aglydron waited for him to rise. He did so, rubbing his left buttock and wincing slightly. He held out his hand again to help Aglydron across. The gesture made him feel he got less respect than he deserved but he accepted the help.

The next crossing was a simple long stride over a particularly narrow gap. The water flowed through with such fierce swirls and whirlpools that Aglydron shuddered.

The final stretch was the widest they'd encountered and there was no opportunity to make a run before the necessary leap. Trees and bushes grew hard up against the edge of the steep rise opposite. Shaulah stood on the only flat ground and Okkyntalah shooed her out of the way. She disappeared into undergrowth cloaking the steep rise. The boy glanced at Aglydron, removed his pack and then crouched low and launched himself across the violent, swirling current, landing with one foot in the water and the other on the narrow band of shingle and mud. He started to slide back until he clutched at an overhanging branch. Hauling himself upright, he planted both feet on the soft ground. Aglydron stared across the gap, trying to hide his fear.

Okkyntalah held the branch with one hand and stretched out the other for his pack. Aglydron tossed it, short.

'Quick. Grab it, boy!'

It fell into the river and splashed Okkyntalah as he tried to catch it. Instantly, the water sucked it under and dragged it along. They watched as it was pulled into unknown depths only to be released to bob for an instant on the swirling surface. At the lip of the falls, it rose again before being swept over the edge to disappear forever into the boiling cauldron beneath.

He turned to look at the boy and caught his expression of a fear that, for Aglydron, had been great even before this demonstration of danger.

'I'll throw mine harder. Catch it.'

Okkyntalah nodded. Aglydron threw his own pack and it sailed across the gap too high, so that a shoulder strap caught in the branches and held it, precariously swinging over the water. Okkyntalah made to climb and retrieve it.

'Leave it!' He felt foolish at his failure to secure either of their packs. 'I'll come across first. You'll fall if you try by yourself. Wait till I'm there.'

For a time, he stared at the water and then at the small patch of ground partially occupied by Okkyntalah. He took a step back and looked again. No space for a run. He nodded to the boy and held up his hand as a signal. He crouched and was about to launch himself but suddenly stood and shook his head. Ashamed of his fear, he turned away. For a while, he paced two small steps back and two forward, working up courage. The gap was half as wide again as his height.

If he didn't jump he'd have to return the way they'd already come. The delay in their journey as he worked his way back downstream to the bridge would be too great. In any case, he mustn't lose face in front of the boy. But failure to land would mean certain death as the torrent took him into its churning depths and over the falls.

Shaulah barked from the deep shadows on the slope and Okkyntalah, dappled by sunlight through the boughs overhead, turned to silence her. A bright kylon, blood red beak and talons in sharp contrast to the lime green of its plumage, screeched from the undergrowth and arrowed toward the far bank, dipping into the torrent and catching a fish.

Aglydron nodded at this omen of good luck. 'Give me courage, Lord Gadhallah.'

He crouched and threw himself across the stream. Okkyntalah caught his wrist as he landed with both feet in the water at the very edge of the patch of shingle. For a moment, he teetered between standing and toppling but the boy, still anchored by his other hand to the branch, pulled hard and hauled him upright.

They stood together, panting. The boy nodded at the branches above him and began his climb. Thin boughs bent beneath his weight but he was soon near the place where the shoulder strap had caught. He was out over the torrent before he could reach the bag. The bough curved ominously, dipping its far branchlets and twigs into the river with every move he made. Okkyntalah reached the point where the strap was within his grasp and bent forward to release it. The branch gave a sharp crack and dipped suddenly so that the length he stood on, and the bag, both dropped below the surface. The water clutched at the bag, trying to dislodge it.

'Come back, boy. Leave it.'

Aglydron stood helpless as the boy crouched low, his feet and ankles submerged, and stretched down with one hand under the water.

'Leave it! It's not worth it, Okkyntalah.' The last thing he wanted was to return to Shoarhn and the boy's parents, alone, with news of his death.

His face set in concentration, the boy felt his way along the bough, swaying as the river tried to tear the damaged branch from the tree. He slipped and almost fell. But he recovered and the slip took him a fraction closer so that he was able to reach the place where the strap had caught on a spur. Releasing it, he dragged it, water pouring from the opening, and tossed it to Aglydron. He gathered it to his chest, soaking his tabard, and set it on the ground at his feet as the boy edged his way back along the broken bough.

It seemed to take an age as Okkyntalah slowly crept away from the water, the current still threatening and grasping at the lower branches. He reached the end of his minor branch, where the crack had split the bough along its length for a distance as long as his leg. He caught the major branch and had to put all his weight on the broken bough to lever himself up to the larger one. It was too much. The lower bough split further and finally parted from the tree, as Okkyntalah pulled himself up. They watched it plunge and drop, as the current dragged it until it lodged in a gap a little way along the channel. The boy clambered down and stood beside Aglydron on the narrow spit of shingle.

'Fool! You might've been killed.'

'Got the pack, though.'

Laughing suddenly with relief, they allowed themselves to catch their breath before struggling up the bank and forcing their way through dense undergrowth. It was hard work but, as the ground climbed and left the water, the tangle of bushes, creepers and vines gave way to coarse illuk and they soon found themselves on an easy slope dotted with the trees they'd seen from the other bank. Without pause, they made for the ridge, Shaulah trotting beside them. Neither mentioned the lost pack and its valuable contents, including the tabard intended as Okkyntalah's wedding gift to Tumalind.

The road, when they reached it after a further two leagues across rolling hills, was flat, dusty and deserted. They stopped to rest in the shade of a tree and drank lukewarm water from their shared flask before making their way, with all the speed they could muster, toward the coast and Chalamamnon.

After three days and two more nights of dusty, hot roads Tumalind had come to terms with her new lot in life to the extent that she no longer burst into tears every time she thought of Okkyntalah. She'd developed a fragile mask, which protected her from all but the most brutal of Porryh's verbal assaults and developed a deep-seated defence against adopting the docile acceptance of Dilanthas. She wanted neither to war continuously against her situation nor to allow it to destroy her sense of self-worth or of hope for the future. And, judging by the warmth she received from Kaz-Ca-Wendarah, she was already succeeding in public, whatever her private feelings might be. Whilst the priestess was sharp with Porryh and scornful of Dilanthas, she was kind and almost friendly to Tumalind.

They travelled over countryside quite different from her part of the island. She'd never seen groves of mulberry trees, grown to feed silk worms. Some lower meadows were flooded to grow rice and upper slopes bore great orchards of citrus, whose sharp green and yellow and sweet orange fruits they took to eat as they marched.

'Hey! I make my living from…Oh, sorry Paltrohn, didn't realize it was you. Please, Dagla Kaz, help yourselves to Ytraa's generous bounty.'

The High Priest blessed the farmer. 'May the noble Lord Gadhallah bless your trees.'

There seemed to be few olive trees here and not many fields laid down to flax or cotton. Much about her island home became clear as she saw for herself how different crops allowed trade all over the country. She understood, perhaps too late, her father's place in the scheme of things: how his olive oil, goat's cheese and meat from his cattle might be exchanged for rice and fruit. Okkyntalah's hunting and his father's fishing fed not only their own family and hers but kept others in food exchanged for goods. Things that had seemed simple in the past now became part of a more complex picture and she wished she had more time to understand the whole and talk it over with Okkyntalah. A tear threatened at that and she stopped herself, forcing the emotion to the centre of her where it wouldn't show.

In the town, she saw her first building made of stone. 'Isn't this the High Priest's house?'

'He's rich, Tumalind, but not that rich. This belongs to one of the few foreign merchants who trade with us.' Kaz-Ca-Wendarah told her that these heathen men plied the seas and took away produce to return with exotic goods that the island didn't produce.

'This is the High Priest's house.'

It was large and impressive with its sheltered courtyard and many rooms. But, like her home, its exterior was sun-baked mud bricks coated with oil and pigment to keep off the rain. The pale blue-grey made it seem cool in the heat of midday as they entered at last.

Jodisa-Li, who'd walked all the way with her father, showed the girls to their room and explained where they could wash. But she was eager for different refreshment. 'There's a quiet beach not far away, where we can swim in safety. I go there a lot.'

The others were too tired but Tumalind was keen to feel the freshness of cool water on her skin. 'Can we go now?'

Jodisa-Li nodded, 'I'll get some drying cloths.'

Kaz-Ca-Wendarah seemed willing to trust her alone with the High Priest's daughter and merely reminded her of her sacred duty as they left the house. They walked through dusty streets; slightly broader, but not unlike those in Morstahn. Young children, naked and free, played games. Old people sat in doorways, soaking up the sun, and a blind beggar sat against a wall, crying out now and again for alms. Many of the inhabitants of the town were still on their way home from the ceremony, so the place was quiet.

The deserted beach, hidden from the edge of town by a small grove of palm trees and brightly flowering shrubs, was steep and the colourful shingle slipped under the pressure of her feet. But the clear and calm sea soothed her skin after long marches under the sun with too little shade. The two girls floated and swam and splashed each other, laughing as they relaxed at the end of their journey and came to know each other better. Given time, Tumalind thought they might have become good friends. They left the sea and took the short walk back to the house.

'What's your father like, Jodisa-Li?'

'Do as you're told and you'll find him kind enough. Disobey him and you'll wish you hadn't.'

'Does he hit you?'

'What father doesn't beat his daughter? I've given him reasons enough to chastise me and he's given me plenty of stripes to make me sorry.'

'Your dragon must've cost a fortune.'

'More than your father would earn in cycles. It was a present for my sixteenth nameday, like your bird of paradise. The flowers round my breasts are worth even more but cost nothing; the tattooist owed my father a favour.'

'They're very pretty.'

'Your butterfly's nice. Did you let your buck see it?'

Tumalind blushed. 'I know I shouldn't. But he only looked.'

'And your paradise bird? He's seen where that pecks?'

Tumalind recognized the mischief in this girl who was her age and understood so much, it seemed. 'He was so good. How could I refuse?'

'Funny, aren't they, men? Just looking makes them…have ideas.'

'He was…I knew he wanted to. Obvious, really, I mean, well…but he didn't, we didn't…you know. Well, we both saw what happened to those who failed at the ceremony, didn't we? Not worth it, is it?'

'Not if you get found out.'

'I don't see how you could avoid it.'

Jodisa Li made a face of disbelief but then shrugged.

'No. Anyway, here we are. I'll have to leave you to it, Tumalind. I have to make sure Father gets his meal. The household slaves get a bit lax without an occasional reminder. You'll be eating with us.' And she was off down one of the corridors, leaving Tumalind to find her way to the room she shared with the other Virgin Gifts.

As she was about to go in, a fat woman on her way out collided with her. She glared at Tumalind and seemed about to speak but shook her head and stomped down the corridor. In the room, Dilanthas sat on her bed, pale and alarmed. Porryh face down on her bed, her bare bottom glowing red, was sobbing into her pillow.

Chapter 6

FINAL PREPARATIONS

*S*hoarhn stretched out a leg and found emptiness where Aglydron should be. She turned in the gloom of early dawn, filtering through rush screens, and confirmed his continued absence.

What could he and Okkyntalah hope for from the High Priest? They'd be flogged for their doubts and accusations; hung in beating bags and whipped with pliant redwillow until they bled. And for nothing. Yet, she was proud of their courage; proud they were trying to reclaim Tumalind.

For the fourth morning in a row, she prayed alone. In front of the small effigy, she knelt, placed her forearms on the hard mud floor and her head between her outstretched wrists. Her prayers had never been the devout praises she believed Aglydron gave. But now she begged Ytraa's mercy; begged Ytraa to protect Tumalind on a journey that may have already begun, and to protect and return Aglydron and Okkyntalah. She rose, brushing dust from arms, hands, knees and feet, shaking more dust from the fringes of her jet-black hair, and left the bedchamber. How, she wondered, should she explain Aglydron's continued absence to the boys?

In the marketplace, she spoke with Okkyntalah's father, as she bartered six pale-green duck eggs for a small blue dorado. The sun caught the rainbow colours of the fish darting, bright and nervous, against the deep brown glaze of the wide stone basin. Shoarhn thought of her beautiful daughter, sailing a sea filled with such creatures and with others that, if tales were to be believed, might devour both her and the ship that bore her away.

Okkyntalah's father seemed unconcerned at his son's prolonged absence. 'They'll come to no harm, Shoarhn. Don't fret. They'll both be back soon enough. Aye and with a pair of antelope and a brace of wild duck, if I'm any judge of my lad.' He offered no further comment.

Stroking her fingers in token of the exchange of food, he began trade with the woman waiting behind her and she wondered at his lack of concern over Okkyntalah's inability to make the match they'd all been so looking forward to celebrating.

After the midday meal, she sent the boys to play with other small children, under the watchful eyes of grandparents, and sought Kaz-Ca-Wesdan's advice at the temple. His recent elevation to High Priest-in-trust, however, had already sent him to the capital and she found Kaz-Ca-Uldrad instead. He had little comfort or advice for her.

'Those without office must not meddle in things they are too dull to understand. They should leave them to those of us who have the wit to fully comprehend matters.'

She looked him up and down. The squat, ugly figure of the previous village priest had been replaced by this slender, girlish man with no sympathy and little evidence of concern for his people.

She went to see A'ahl, again, and found her languishing in uncertainty. 'I just hope Wesdan Kaz doesn't call me to the capital. I've had enough as his consort.'

'Still not made up his mind?'

'He's full of his new status and all that it'll bring him.' Her topaz eyes brightened. 'Still, there's younger and prettier than me in Chalamamnon, and without the burden of a lump full of his misbegotten seed. Good riddance! I just wish the puny little rhaat would let me know.'

Shoarhn smiled at her friend's popular insult.

'Caarl was only home one night, Shoarhn, and now he's gone for Ytraa knows how long. For all I know, I'll never see him again! I've got to face life alone. And I'll be forced to surrender this poor little one in my belly to the temple so it can frowk forever with those awful Holy Ones in the so-called service of Ytraa. Don't look so shocked, Shoarhn; I know you feel the same. And don't you think this frowking pilgrimage a waste of time? Oh, don't pretend. Go home to your man and your children. At least you still have them.'

Shoarhn put her arms about her friend's shoulders and gave such comfort as she could. 'I fear I may have only my boys, A'ahl. Aglydron and Okkyntalah haven't returned.'

'Oh, Shoarhn, here's me moaning about a horrid priest who'll probably leave me alone, at last, and a husband who's been absent more often than he's been home and you're worried sick about Tumalind and Aglydron. I'm sorry. What's to become of us?'

'Tell me the truth, will Phildrad ever be 'ome again?'

Aklon-Dji smiled across the rough boards on which they'd shared breakfast. He had no way of knowing what would happen to her husband but he was incapable of lying, even to reassure her.

'Phildrad has as much chance of returning from the pilgrimage as any of them, except the Virgin Gifts, who must remain there. But I will not lie to you, Lasdilyss; my father takes them into peril. They will meet people, lands and other things hostile to them. They go a dangerous route to a land unknown for more than two hundred cycles. And, on the last pilgrimage, there were signs that the people of Choshinahm no longer held Followers in high esteem. But Phildrad is resourceful in his own quiet way; he is brave, from what you have told me, and I expect he will return to you at the end of the pilgrimage. Of course, he will be away longer than Dagla Kaz intends, since this spark is not Ytraa's Skyfire. But I can make one prediction, Lasdilyss: the Phildrad who returns will not be the same man who left.'

'What d'you mean?' She paused with the rib close to her mouth, stock running down her fingers to her hand, unnoticed.

'Travel and association with different cultures inevitably changes people. He will encounter strange and outlandish ideas. He will visit places where people never show a thumbswidth of skin and others where they never wear any covering. He will find people who believe in gods so strange that you and I would not recognise them as deities, some where their god requires human sacrifice. He will cross rivers so wide that the far bank is not visible, sail seas with waves higher than the Monument of Ytraa, walk mountain passes where rain falls as a soft white solid so cold it can kill a man.'

''Ow d'you know all this, Aklon?'

He smiled at her use of his real name instead of, Phildrad, his alias when with her.

'Beneath my father's house, in the Pit of Secrets, lie parchments, carved tablets of stone and other messages telling of the first journey that brought us to this island and of all the pilgrimages that have taken place since. I have read them all, Lasdilyss. It is why I reject our religion. I know what all High Priests before me have known and accepted. The difference is that I have had a unique influence in my life. I have the advantage and burden of knowing truths denied others. Whether any of my predecessors would have responded to the secret knowledge as I have, had they known what I know, I cannot tell. But my father would not hear me when I tried to explain. That is why I am a danger to him, and renegade.'

'Never a one word answer from you, is it?'

He smiled and nodded his agreement, resisting his usual urge to explain why he was so particular about what he said and why he felt the need to give reasons for his actions and beliefs. Instead, he made do with a gentle stroke of his fingertips on her cheek; a gesture she would take as one of concern and care.

It was enough for Lasdilyss and she rose from their meal, slipped her rough tabard on and went out to care for her husband's dependent parents.

Aklon-Dji took advantage of her absence to commune with Ivdulon to see if the wise man knew the answer to a puzzle.

'As ever, you seem busy, Ivdulon. Do I intrude?'

'Not in any way that will stop me. What is it, Aklon?'

'May I ask what you are doing at present? I have a picture of some process that has no meaning for me.'

'Ah. Not familiar with a shower?'

'A shower is something that involves rain.'

'Shower is just the term we've adopted. You allow water to run over your body in a series of fine streams rather like rainfall. It's directed and has some power behind it. Used with mixes of animal fat and vegetable juices, it takes away dirt and stinks and leaves the skin clean and fresh. I don't doubt that you wash?'

'In common with most, I take a dip once a week. More if I can. But naked is sacred, and that makes regular bathing difficult without the luxury of a personal home in which to conduct it.'

'So, you'd welcome the idea of a shower such as this?'

Aklon was abruptly aware of a stream of water flowing down his skin, the scent of some substance rubbed in and a feeling of freshness and lightness.

'As ever, Ivdulon, you amaze me with your talents and your abilities to perform difficult things with ease. If this is a shower, I would welcome it. How is it achieved?'

'The how seems quite simple but is not of my doing. Those who built my home, made structures that feed running water through the whole city. How they achieved these things is something we don't understand, since almost all the work is hidden. We're reluctant to uncover it in case we disturb it and stop it from working, as happened with a different system centuries ago. It seems to rely on the natural propensity of water to fall downhill. I can tell you no more. Now, since I suspect you didn't come into my mind to witness my ablutions, perhaps you'll let me know what you want to either tell or ask me?'

'Fascinating. Yes, water is apposite. I have long wondered about the story of the flooding of the world. Do you think it is true or is it some sort of parable intended to warn us against certain acts?'

'The tale of Swerriflomihl and his boat constructed to escape the deluge. I'm sure such a flood happened in one part of the world at some time. But I doubt it happened all over the world. Just think about the height of the mountains and you'll know that much water simply doesn't exist. No, I believe it was a local affair. Perhaps the world trembled, as it will sometimes, and disturbed some natural barrier in such a way that it broke open and allowed the sea to pour into low-lying land. Storms often accompany such events and the people wouldn't know what had hit them. I suspect Swerriflomihl happened to have a suitable boat; perhaps there was a lake in the area and he was a fisherman. It would make sense. So few people would survive that sort of deluge that it would take a long time to return to any level of civilisation. And, in a time before written records, the story would be embellished and altered by each generation as it was handed down. No, I think, on balance, *it's probably a real event exaggerated by the passage of time.'*

'And you came to this conclusion simply by long thought and consideration of the elements contained within the story?'

Ivdulon laughed; a sensation passed to Aklon-Dji for the first time and one in which he felt compelled to partake.

'I've never given the matter a thought, to be truthful. But that's my opinion, for what it's worth.'

'You came to this conclusion just now, even as you were describing it to me?'

'I have all the information. I have experience of many different cultural beliefs. You lack my advantage and hindrance of mindtalk with many people, so you won't know that every culture has its own myth of a flood. Some are very similar but others bear little resemblance to the story Followers tell their children. I suspect there have, over the ages of the world, been many instances of sudden local deluge and, as terrifying events, each has spawned its own tale in an attempt at explanation.'

'Ivdulon, as always, you astound me. I will leave you to your thoughts and creative doings until the next time I need some stimulation for my mind. Thank you, friend.'

'A pleasure to share your thoughts, Aklon. Now, if the lady is your current paramour, I'll leave you to engage in the physical activity you seem to be at every time I try to contact you.'

The link broke and Aklon-Dji became aware that Lasdilyss was frowning at him. He smiled a welcome.

'You're a funny one, Phildrad. Always on about 'ow you've got to stay alert so they don't catch you. An' 'ere's me, a simple village woman, able to come in and find you daydreaming and ready to be caught by anyone.'

He rose and took her in his arms and reassured her that he would remain more alert in future. He must never risk contact with Ivdulon under such circumstances again.

⚬──✢──⚬

The day after their arrival in Chalamamnon, a house slave roused the girls early for prayers and breakfast, explaining that the High Priest and Jodisa-Li would be busy all day with final preparations. On returning to their room, Tumalind discovered the fat woman waiting. Porryh skirted round her with her hands behind her back but the woman just nodded and Tumalind saw that, far from the fierce being she'd first encountered, this was a face more familiar with laughter than any other emotion.

She smiled at them. 'I'm Corphanda from Pampahn and I travelled with Phildrad; who'll be our cook. Now then, let's see: Porryh, with her sharp tongue, who already knows it's best not to cross me; Dilanthas, who always does as she's told; and Tumalind, who thinks she was wrongly Chosen. Right. We'll all get along just fine if you speak your minds with me, 'cos that's what I'll do with you. I don't take to no pretendin' or carrying on nor nowt like that. I like things out in the open. I've a ready smile an' a good ear what hears and a tongue what don't repeat no secrets. I've a good brisk slap for any pretty bum that thinks it's cleverer'n me. Haven't I, Porryh?'

The girl nodded and defended her posterior.

'Right, now we understand each other, let's spend some of his lordship's coin on some nice new clothes.'

In spite of her rough and ready manner, Tumalind liked her at once. 'Are you our guardian, Corphanda?'

'That I am, Tumalind. Now lass, you can either let this thought o' yours spoil you wi' longing what won't be settled or you can just take it as the will of Ytraa and…'

'It's all right, Corphanda. I'll keep my thoughts on that to myself and I've decided already to make the best of a bad job, so please don't worry about me on that score.'

'You'll do. Now, young Porryh, you've a sharp tongue. Well, mine's sharper an' longer and got more to say, so just keep yours from flippin' an' flappin' an' we'll all be that much happier.'

'Doubt I'll get a chance to say much with you about.'

'That's the way of it. As for you, little quiet one. You're obedient and good, an' that's fine, 'cept I like some spirit, so if you feel like soundin' off, do it to me. Right?'

'Thanks, Corphanda; I'm a bit shy and frightened, that's all.'

'Aye, well, happen shy's fine for a virgin. An' we're all scared, even yon high and mighty, if the truth's known. Come on, then. Let's get shot o' those dull bags an' dress you fit to be seen.'

They followed her from the house. For a small, portly woman, she moved with surprising speed, kicking up dust with her small, bare feet. She quickly had the girls lost amongst winding streets down by the harbour. There, small fishing boats lay at anchor in the early morning sunlight, bright sparkles flashing amongst the dark reflections of hard, wet wood. Seemeeuws cried their melancholy calls and a gentle wash of water on shingle announced the soft state of the sea. The ubiquitous smell of fish and seaweed hung in the warm breeze, mixed with spicy cooking aromas from a waterside inn. Two large ships, bigger than any Tumalind had ever seen, were moored on the quay and one, a two-masted vessel, was being loaded with supplies.

'That's the Nupraxyss, an' we'll be sailing on her in the morning.'

The announcement brought a lump to Tumalind's throat and threatened tears but she resisted and remained silent.

Corphanda brought the girls to a market stall where the merchant was laying out his goods for display. She looked him up and down. 'Well, young man, I hope the clothes you're sellin' are better'n those on your back, that's all I can say.'

He was about to remonstrate when he caught the mischief in her eye and shook his head. 'Mother, you're a wicked tease. You'll get the finest available here. There's none better on the island. Nothing but pure silk for these pretty girls; embroidered in silver and silken threads and…' he whispered for effect, 'gold. So, what can I tempt you to conceal these lovelies in?'

'You've a curtain for privacy? An' a shiner to see themselves?'

The merchant, a youngish man with roving eyes and lank hair under a soft wine coloured cap embroidered with sea shells, displayed an alcove inside his canvas stall. Within, a thin sheet of polished iron hung from ceiling poles on bronze chains so that it swung gently.

'Right. No peepin'; I'm the prettiest sight you'll be seein' from this little show. I want one special and two workaday for each of them. Show me what you've got.'

Tumalind, who'd worn linen all her life, felt the luxury of pure silk and, after the coarse tabard the Holy Ones had given her, found cause at last for some small pleasure in her changed circumstances. The shiner reflected her image as she'd never seen it before and she stood, both with and without the new clothes, seeing how she appeared to others, and discovering her remarkable similarity to Jodisa-Li.

She chose dark blue, falling to mid-thigh, with a waistrope of plaited kid and four carved bone fastenings through kid loops on each side. She wore this as they left the stall. Over her arm, she carried a deep green tabard with similar fastenings and one in paler blue, embroidered with a red and green kylon and with silver fastenings and a waistrope of auburn maidenhair. All had the medium diamond cut neck, giving a v at front and back. Tears spilled briefly as she recalled that, on her return home with Okkyntalah, they would have cut each other's hair to shoulder length and sold the long tresses, keeping enough back to weave into a waistrope for her.

Tumalind was surprised at the brevity of Porryh's black tabard with its toggles of senglar tooth and silver weave waistrope. She carried another of pure white, trimmed with gold, and a third in scarlet, embroidered with a serpent in seven different colours. All three fastened at only two points along each side and had deep square necklines, displaying as much of her breasts as was permissible. Corphanda frowned but let her to have her way.

Dilanthas chose knee-length pale pink, rose and lemon, embroidered with flowers. All three waistropes were plaited kid and the fastenings bronze. She'd chosen the close-fitting, rounded neckline and five side fastenings.

'Much better. Proud to be seen with three such lovely young things. Those horrid items the Holy Ones give you can go back for slaves, since that's all they're fit for. Now. Hair. You'll have to keep it long, of course, but it needs to be easily looked after. Best if it's braided.'

She took them to an open stall where a hunched old woman sold the girls beads made from coloured woods, small pierced pebbles and the rounded teeth of various animals. They bought fine leather cord and dried gut to thread the beads.

Shopping concluded, Corphanda led them back toward the house. 'Now, whilst we're on about such things, I want you clean and fresh. I'll have no nasty, smelly misses about me or you'll feel the sting of my hand. Understand? And tell me when you're bleeding. There's ways of dealing with moontimes you'll likely not've 'eard of and I can make you more comfortable. Now, you'll all be missing the fun and pleasure your young lads gave you with their fumbling and tickling under your hems. Oh, don't pretend to be shocked, Dilanthas. And I've nowt against a bit of comforting; mutual or single. Talking of fingers; keep your nails clean and short. You can't do nothing sensible with long nails. Teeth is important. Keep 'em clean; no one likes stinky breath. Feet. You're all used to walking good distances but any cuts or swellings, bites or stings, anywhere at all, tell me. I know me 'erbs and roots and I've a good supply of what keeps a body healthy. But it's got to be caught quick. Poison's not no problem if you get shot of it fast. I want you healthy and pretty when we get to where we're going. Got all that? Good.'

She shepherded them into the house in time for the midday meal. Afterwards, she had them wash each other's hair and braid it in tight plaits that could be washed without having to be undone every time. She supervised as they oiled each other with scented unguents to keep their skin soft and supple in preparation for the days to come at sea. And she showed them how to use special stones to file their nails into soft curves that would look attractive whilst retaining practicality.

Kept busy and occupied, Tumalind was surprised to find that the day had passed so quickly and it was time for their last evening meal on the island. Corphanda put them in their most decorative tabards and led them to the largest room in the High Priest's house. She had timed it so they arrived last. Those already assembled stopped chatting and voiced approval as she presented her three Virgin Gifts.

Even whilst receiving the plaudits, Tumalind realized that Corphanda had been very clever in the way she'd dealt with them. Three young girls, with little experience of life, were easily impressed with such a reception and, as they basked in admiration, bound to have their minds taken off the real difficulties ahead of them.

Chapter 7

INTRODUCTIONS

Dagla Kaz, splendid in red and gold, greeted the girls. A vivid Tree of Life adorned his chest. Wiry arms and legs stuck out, incongruous and ungainly, but his severe face and fierce eyes of bright lapis lazuli prevented any insult. He made Tumalind feel uneasy, as he stood at the head of the table, though he asked the girls to sit before he introduced the party. At mention of their name, each member stood and introduced themselves.

'Kaz-Ca-Wendarah, our priestess from Chalamamnon, comes as my personal aid and consort, and spiritual guide for our Virgin Gifts.'

Graceful and tall, the deep diamond cut of her tabard displaying her figure, she rose slowly. Two serpents, red on black and green on blue, coiled around each other and her breasts, to hide beneath the rich purple fabric. A fine chain of silver linked the sides of the wide v. Three obsidian beads fastened each side of a tabard as scandalously short as Porryh's. Tumalind saw a third serpent, gold on violet, spiralling her near leg.

'During the pilgrimage, please neglect my title. We'll be living close and rough and I'd prefer to be treated as one of the group.'

'Opposite her sits Jhonaht, of Krohtl. He spends his life meditating, considering and learning in his high cell on Ytraa's Peak. As Chief Astronomer, he is responsible for starting this momentous voyage. He comes as navigator and because, as discoverer of the Skyfire, he should not miss the full joy his keen eyes have brought us all.'

Jhonaht, tall, fat and going to seed, stood and bowed a little self-consciously to each of them in turn. His eyes lingered on Tumalind and, though she felt uncomfortable, she lacked the confidence to stare him out. He wore no finery and his knee-length tabard was dull brown with a high-cut circular neck and a simple leather strap round his ample belly.

'I apologize for the unfortunate timing of my observation but we all bow to the will of Ytraa. The Holy Ones have confirmed my sighting of Ytraa's Skyfire.'

'Next; Phildrad, from Pampahn. His reputation, that he does wonders with food, had better be deserved: he'll be our cook, making what we find along the way enjoyable or, at least, edible.'

Nondescript and average, brown haired, brown eyed and brown skinned, even his expression said this man wished not to stand out. Tumalind, persuaded he was as dull by nature, failed to register what he wore. He stood, bowed and sat again.

'Tryonta, from Chalamamnon, is my personal assistant and a hunter of exceptional skill.'

Tumalind stared. He might be Okkyntalah's elder brother. Tall, good-looking and well-muscled, he was what her lover would be in a few cycles. But his dark hair was too well groomed, his dark eyes cold and hard. This was a man not to cross; a man with dark secrets. His short, brilliant yellow tabard, embroidered with an emblem of the rising sun in deep crimson, fastened with boar's teeth through fine gold chains, and belted with a broad band of multi-coloured woven leather, spoke of a man too concerned with appearance. For all his superficial resemblance to Okkyntalah, Tumalind instinctively felt she couldn't trust him.

'I serve willingly and travel this long road with you in joy that I have lived to experience the light of Ytraa's Skyfire.'

There was insincerity in his tone and she knew she'd find it hard to like him.

'Dilanthas; our hazel-eyed gift from Krohtl. Be kind to this obedient young lady who is modest, shy and unhappy to leave her betrothed. I expect the rest of you to protect her and her two companions with your lives if necessary.'

Dilanthas stood and nodded briefly to Dagla Kaz before sitting down again. The waistrope gathered her tabard tightly into her narrow waist and, against her intention, emphasized her small breasts and slender hips. Tryonta stared at her.

'Corphanda, from Pampahn, will look after our Virgin Gifts. Beware her tongue; its lash can cut a man's boast to a tenth its size.'

Corphanda struggled to her feet beside Tumalind, her copious pale green tabard tied roughly round her girth with a narrow band of dark leather. She stared hard at each of the party in turn and then laughed.

'My tongue'll keep you lot in order, my hand'll check my three charges. Anyone else lays a finger on these girls and they'll answer to me. And regret it. I'm as fair as I'm fat and tough as I'm round. So, you got any complaint agin any of these girls, see me and I'll deal with it. You got any advice about any of them, tell me, and I'll ignore it, probably. Glad to be along.'

Dagla Kaz rose once more and nodded at the girl opposite Corphanda.

'Porryh, also from Chalamamnon; a blue eyed beauty with charms to undermine the will of any red-blooded man. Do not be tempted. She is for our brethren in Choshinahm and must arrive there whole, as she is now. Beware her tongue; it will make trouble.'

Porryh stood abruptly and climbed onto her seat. The tabard flapped around the tops of her thighs, attracting the men.

'I don't want to be here. But I won't make trouble. I'll go to Choshinahm as a sacrifice, for the sake of Ytraa. But don't look to me for fun or pleasure. I'm unhappy and I'll stay that way.'

She jumped down, the movement lifting the hem and exposing a stripecat, leaping from her knee, to bury its front claws in shadows. Tumalind saw Tryonta lick his lips. But no one chastised Porryh and she sat down again, sulking.

Dagla Kaz stared at Tumalind for a short while before he spoke and evidently found whatever sign he sought in her face, for he nodded and smiled.

'Tumalind is from Morstahn and their loss will be Choshinahm's gain. This copper haired beauty, with eyes that mirror my own and looks that match my daughter's, is a pleasant, kind and good-natured young woman of intelligence. She also shows good judgement. Her initial belief, that she was Chosen in error, she has locked away with a determination to do as required by Ytraa. She is an example to us all and I envy the Follower fortunate enough to win her when we reach our destination.'

Tumalind felt such mixed emotions at this description, she was unsure how to reply. She clutched the sides of her tabard, parting the edges until she felt what she was doing and clasped her hands in front of her instead.

'I'll try to behave well. I'll try to do as I should. I can't make promises, as I don't know what we face, together or alone. Ytraa will guide us to what is right. I leave behind a dutiful father, a loving mother, mischievous brothers, and a partner without equal. I hope you'll forgive my tears; I'll try to control them. We three girls go to a strange land, knowing we'll never return. I ask you to be patient and help us make the pilgrimage with courage and grace. Thank you.'

She sat, brushing the tabard beneath her and feeling the rough grain of wood through soft silk. In the short silence she looked up to see unshed tears in Porryh's eyes and admiration on other faces. Dagla Kaz nodded at her and rose once more.

'Caarl, also from Morstahn, is our guide. He stands second only to me in rank on this pilgrimage. A captain with the Holy Guard, he has skills in tracking, planning and leading which will prove invaluable.'

Tumalind smiled at him. Very tall, well-built and solid, he stood at the end of the table, opposite Dagla Kaz. His fiery hair contrasted with vivid green eyes. He'd been away on duty more often than he'd been with A'ahl.

'I'll do my best to lead you well. We take a road not travelled for many cycles and with knowledge less accurate than we'd wish. I'll protect and guide you. But I'll punish anyone, and I do mean anyone...' He stared into the eyes of each, impressing them with his authority. '...anyone who places another in danger or disobeys a direct order; the Virgin Gifts included. I'll stripe the skins of any. The girls I can punish without leaving marks. Do not make me demonstrate.

'Tonight's our last on the island for an unknown period, our last in real comfort, maybe for the whole trip. We face danger, distance, trouble and hard walking. I ask no more than you can give but I expect your best.'

Dagla Kaz rose and raised the palm of his hand to Caarl, who nodded, smiled at Tumalind, and sat down.

'Thank you all. There is one who has yet to arrive. Tarruss, from Krohtl, wasn't at the joining ceremony and has the furthest to travel. He was last to be informed.' He glanced at Jhonaht and Tumalind saw the fat man wince. 'I expect him to arrive for our sailing on the high tide, early tomorrow. He will be an extra guard due to his strength and skill at arms. Finally, another who will be with us aboard ship. Baklan, the master and owner of the Nupraxyss, is an unbeliever and a seagoing merchant I've known many cycles. He does this for coin, nothing else. He has no understanding of spiritual matters and is an adventurer with little regard for convention. He'll try to seduce our virgins, though I've warned him of dire consequences, but he won't take a woman against her wishes. We must all be vigilant over him and his small crew, for they will see the girls as fair game.

'You all understand the great importance of our mission and I've nothing to add but a final reminder that we do what we do in the name of Ytraa. Let that be at the forefront of your minds, in the depths of your hearts, in the very centre of your spirits.

'Now, to lighter things. We have a feast prepared to mark our departure. I suggest we make our prayers before we eat so that we have no need to interrupt our enjoyment. Come, sundown is but moments away. Let us pray and then let us feast, perhaps, as Caarl put it, for the last time.'

⁕ ⁘

Aglydron's insistence that they travel as long as their legs would carry them, took them part of the way in darkness so they missed a fork in the road. They spent that night in an old stone quarry, its enclosed shelter turning the usual warmth of darkness into oppressive heat. It took them much of the morning to return to the road. Having lost Okkyntalah's pack, they had to break their journey to find food. Walking only in daylight, after their mistake, hunting at need and camping at night, they arrived in sight of the town just after sundown on their fourth day. They slept under fruit trees and were on the last leg by sunrise.

Mid-morning found them wandering the streets of a town larger than they'd expected. Their search for the High Priest's house proved fruitless until, eventually, an elderly and very deaf woman emerged from a dilapidated house. After much misunderstanding, she directed them.

'Won't be no one there, mind. They're all down the 'arbour. Off on that there pilgrimage.' And, with that, she returned indoors, giving no clue as to why she'd come out in the first place.

'Where's the harbour?'

But she either didn't hear or couldn't be bothered to return.

'Where's the sea?' Okkyntalah scanned the horizon and saw seemeeuws swooping and diving to the southwest.

They threaded through dusty streets until they were on a shallow cliff above a wide, sandy beach. The harbour lay some twelve hundred paces to the north and, even from this distance, they could hear excited voices carried over the calm bay. As they watched, a large two-masted ship sailed into view from behind the buildings lining one side of the harbour, its canvas catching the light breeze as it navigated the narrow entrance to open sea.

They dashed over shingle and sand, intent on stopping the party leaving with Tumalind. Okkyntalah arrived just as the small crowd of spectators, mostly children with grandparents, started to disperse. Aglydron was a few paces behind, and sweating from the exertion. It was clear the sailing ship held the pilgrimage and they fought against the tide of the crowd. Sheer volume delayed them on the narrow quay and when they finally reached the furthest point of the stone wall, the ship was already leaning into the wind, its wide sails pushing it over the waves.

'Tumalind!' Okkyntalah stood forlorn and hopeless, able to make out the face and figure of his love as she stood in the stern and gazed back to land. He saw her grief, waved, and then watched her joy grow at seeing him there.

'Tumalind!'

She raised her arm in a loving hopeless farewell, as the ship turned, adjusting course and hiding her temporarily behind rigging and woodwork.

'We're too late.' Aglydron seemed lost in despair now that the pilgrims had set out. He sank to his knees and wept.

Okkyntalah watched Tumalind, waving until he could no more discern her. He turned and looked about the harbour, where a couple of fishing boats were making ready to go to sea. There must be something they could do. They couldn't let her go like that. He wouldn't lose her so easily. One of the fishing boats cast off, its two-man crew steering with oars for the narrow gap between the steep harbour walls. The single mast had the sail still furled, awaiting the wind on the open sea.

'We need to get out to that ship. Can you take us?'

The fishermen looked up quizzically at Okkyntalah's call and stopped rowing, the slight swell making them bob slowly up and down just below where he stood.

'I must talk to the High Priest. Will you take me out to him?'

The fishermen glanced at the distant ship, looked at each other, shrugged and shook their heads. 'Landlubbers.' They took to their oars and continued on their way.

But Okkyntalah wasn't defeated. He dragged Aglydron to his feet. 'Come on.'

He all but pulled him round the harbour wall, where the other fishing boat was about ready. Urging Aglydron on, he reached it just as the boat was untied.

'Will you take us out to the ship carrying the High Priest and his party? I've an urgent message for him.'

The fisherman scratched his dark beard and stared up at him as if he were mad. He glanced across the calm water of the harbour to the mouth, through which the twin masted vessel could be seen, nearly a league off. 'Your message'll 'ave to wait, lad. Urgent or no. Tha'll no catch yon wi'out you can fly.'

'Will you try?'

'I've a livin' to get, lad. Yon ship's gone to the likes on us. You'll not catch it in this little ketch, nor in no other in this 'arbour.'

He pushed away with his oar, the young lad beside him rowing mechanically whilst staring open-mouthed at Okkyntalah and Aglydron.

'We'll take a boat ourselves, Aglydron. Row it out until we catch up with them.'

Aglydron shook his head. 'Too far. We've not the skill nor the strength to catch it.'

'Then we'll follow them across the sea and catch them on land.'

'You're dreaming, boy. We've tried and we've lost.'

'Mhortag's balls! We can't give up like this. I want Tumalind back.'

'Tumalind? She what you think this is about? Doesn't matter what you want, boy; it's more important. It's about saving Followers from Ytraa's wrath.' Aglydron's previous fervour returned with his declaration, as if voicing his thoughts gave them purpose as well as meaning. 'We'll just have to do what we can. You're right, boy. By Ytraa's will, we'll do what we must.'

'You just said it was hopeless.'

'Thought it was. But you've made me hope. And given me an idea. Remember how to find the High Priest's house?'

'More or less. Why? What good will it do us?'

Aglydron merely urged Okkyntalah forward to find the house. For a short while, they walked in silence, Aglydron studying everything with concentration.

'There. That must be it. It's the biggest place around. But what good will it do us?'

Aglydron stared at the house, lost in thought. The streets were starting to fill up with townsfolk returning from the ceremony. But Aglydron remained where he was, eyes fixed on the house.

'There! There she is!'

Okkyntalah followed his gaze and saw the beautiful girl who should've gone to Choshinahm instead of Tumalind. She appeared to be on her way to market.

'We've got to take Jodisa-Li with us and make Dagla Kaz see sense; swap her for Tumalind. It's the only way.'

'You're mad. She'll never come with us. And the High Priest would kill us. You said yourself it was impossible. Anyway, we've no boat, no idea how to get there. We can't do it, Aglydron.'

'We can. Ytraa will provide. We must! This is a test. Ytraa's trying us to see how strong our faith is. We've no choice.'

Okkyntalah shook his head; the very idea too big to contemplate, in spite of his original proposal to do just that.

'You any coin, boy?'

'Not now. Why?'

Aglydron dug in his pack and extracted a couple of crowns. 'Go to the harbour and find a boat that'll be easy to get out, but say nothing. Buy some girba, three should do, and food for the voyage. Fill the skins with fresh water and hide them near the boat, where we can find them in the dark.'

'Aglydron, I don't know what you're…'

'Putting right the wrong done by the High Priest. I must. It's my destiny. I know it. You want Tumalind back. If you won't do it for Ytraa, do it for her. But do it!'

Okkyntalah was uncertain of his best action in light of Aglydron's sudden madness.

'Meet me back here just before sunset. And don't let me down, boy. Ytraa is depending on us. I know what we've got to do and how we can do it. Trust me, and trust Ytraa. Now, go. And don't make no one suspicious.'

He was about to argue but, to his amazement, Aglydron crossed the wide square to the High Priest's house and just walked in. No one seemed to notice and nobody stopped him. For a while, Okkyntalah stood, astounded by the man's audacity, and then, still unsure of what he was involved in, returned to the harbour to do as Aglydron had asked.

Finding a boat was easy enough, but the thought of stealing it was so foreign to Okkyntalah that he had difficulty accepting even the idea. The ox-skin water carriers were no problem and filling them, at a trough with a flow of clear water issuing from a stone spout, was easy. He found a handy place, above the high tide mark on the outside of the harbour wall, to store the full girba, the bread and the dried meat he'd bought and wrapped in cured dorado skin. It was out of the way of rhaats and shaded from the sun but close to the boat. Though, exactly what Aglydron proposed was unclear and whether he'd actually go with him on whatever mad scheme he'd devised, Okkyntalah wasn't sure.

He ate at a waterside tavern where he attracted attention as a young stranger alone, until he explained. 'Lost my partner at the Choosing. Just seen her off on the pilgrimage. Thought I'd spend the time we should've had, as newlyweds, travelling. See some of the island before I go back home.' It astounded him how easily the lie came and how those he told readily believed.

The capital was so different from Morstahn; the people, less friendly but with a more varied population. He saw some very dark-skinned men and others with yellowish skin and oddly shaped eyes.

He left the tavern and, at a loose end until he was due to meet up with Aglydron, walked the beach with no particular purpose. He was prizing open a large clam with his knife, for Shaulah to eat, when a shadow fell across his hands. He looked up from where he crouched to find a young girl smiling at him.

'Lonely?'

'I was…I'm just…'

'Heard what you said in the Merchant's Maiden. 'Bout your girl bein' sent on the pilgrimage, like. Bad luck, that. Must be missin' her, I reckon.'

'Well, yes. I am but…'

'I can teck your mind off it, like. If you want.'

'Sorry?'

'Nothin' like a bit o' fun to teck your mind off your troubles, you know.'

'Fun?'

She laughed and raised the hem of her short, gaudy tabard to display one thigh to her hip. 'Country boy, aren't you? Like to see the rest?'

Okkyntalah was dumfounded. This young maiden was offering herself, apparently unconcerned at the consequences. His memory of the defiled girl they'd punished at the ceremony made him shake his head in wonder at her offer. She must be a simpleton.

'You'll get yourself in trouble asking men like that. They'll split you. I know. I saw it at the…'

'Oh. Don't worry your 'andsome head about that. I know I look younger, but I'm no virgin. 'Less you think a girl can't do it with who she likes once she's done it in sight of Ytraa?'

'Well, of course you can. You just seem too young to be…anyway, I mean, it can't be long since your first. Doesn't your man mind you offering yourself to strangers so soon?'

'Mind? He sends me out for it. Easier than fishin', isn't it? For him, anyroad.'

'Why would he want you to…?'

'I'll have to spell it out for you, country boy. I do it for money. You pay me an' I pay him, an' he lives a life of ease on his fat backside while I work on me back. Get it?'

'You join for money?'

'Straw for brains. Worth a couple o' crowns, aren't I?'

'You could be worth a thousand: I've got a girl, and there are…'

'On her way to Choshinahm.'

'Anyway, I've nothing but three dorltahs to my name.'

'You just ate at the Merchant's Maiden.'

'And spent the last of my coin.'

She laughed and looked back toward the harbour, searching for someone. Evidently, she found him. 'Drinkin' away my earnings, you lousy prod. I'll show you.' She returned her gaze to Okkyntalah and took his hand. 'You've talked me into it. I'll do you free an' you can tell your cousins to visit Syylvah when they come to town. Tell 'em what a good time I give.'

She led him, curious and unsure but vaguely excited, up the beach toward a stand of trees, Shaulah trotting at his heels. Okkyntalah wanted to explain but, by this time, they'd reached the trees and she was ready.

The priestess at the ceremony had been more concerned for her own enjoyment than his. This girl seemed eager to please him, and did.

'Mhortag's balls! Wish you was mine, Okkyntalah. You're nearly as good as…Oops, nearly named someone as I shouldn't. Let's just say there's a man gets to my place every time. Trouble is, he's always on the run. You'll do for me in the meantime. If you're still 'ere tomorrow, be down the harbour. No charge. But I've got to go now.'

He watched her slip her tabard back on. She'd taught him what it could be like and he was certain that what he'd share with Tumalind would exceed even what this girl had shown him, in the same way as the sun outshines a candle, the sea shames a pond. And then he laughed, knowing such comparisons were meaningless.

'What's funny?'

'I couldn't begin to explain. But, thank you, Syylvah. You've done more for me than you'll ever know. You might even turn out to be the cause of my untimely death.' He reached out and embraced her. 'Thank you. I wish you joy in your life. But, before you go, will you answer a question?'

She shrugged.

'Why would a man pay?'

'If you was ugly, old or fat, or partnered with a dry drudge, you might think me worth a couple of crowns, mightn't you?'

Okkyntalah shook his head at the strange ways of city dwellers. 'Can't see it; plenty more olives on the tree, as they say.'

'You're right. Followers mightn't do it for coin but this is a port, Okkyntalah. Sailors and merchants ain't Followers and they pay good for fun with a girl like me. I get by. Still prefer to do it free with you, though.' She moved away, smiled invitingly and sauntered off.

He wondered whether she expected him to go after her. But he let her leave. He knew, now, that he'd risk whatever Aglydron had in mind if it would get Tumalind back. For, with her, those amazing physical sensations would merge with what lay in his heart and, together, there could be no purer love, no more heightened expression of delight. This must be what Ytraa had meant all Followers to share.

He returned to meet Aglydron but he wasn't at the appointed place. There was time enough, and he sat with his back against the low embankment surrounding the house behind him. The sun was still hot, he'd eaten, quenched his thirst, and shared pleasure with a pretty girl. Now he was set to restore his love to him. He was young, able and in good health. Life stretched before him full of promise. He relaxed and let the heat of early evening seep into him with Shaulah, alert to passers-by, at his side. As his eyes closed, he wondered exactly how Aglydron was doing with his plan to get them killed.

Chapter 8

CRIMES OF DESPERATION

Somehow, he'd found her. Tumalind gazed across the waves until Okkyntalah was so distant he merged with the town as they left the island behind. But he'd been there, seen her; tried to reach her. Now she was convinced he would try to get her back. How he'd manage this, she'd no idea, but that he would try, she was certain. It was enough: hope in a sea of despair.

Until they'd boarded ship, and the crew, with bawdy comments and leering looks, had cast off with the cheers of the crowd sealing her fate, until then she'd hoped she might, perhaps, escape the trip. It had seemed possible that something, anything, might happen to spare her. But they had set sail and she'd still been with them so that all hope was gone as they left for a world entirely strange.

Then Okkyntalah had appeared and, with him, Father. There on the harbour; waving. She knew he'd come after her, would save her from this injustice and take her back home to Morstahn.

Porryh, whose man came from Chalamamnon, had seen nothing of her buck. He hadn't been there at her parting and neither had Dilanthas seen her man. But Okkyntalah had managed it and she loved him the more for his effort.

All that was behind now. She must face the unknown and keep that promise buried deep; a flicker of light in the darkness of her soul. The town had vanished over the horizon, along with all sign of the island. The sailors had scorched her flesh with their eyes. Dilanthas had already fallen sick with the motion of the boat and had taken to her narrow bunk in the tiny cabin they shared with Corphanda. Porryh had been smacked for her cheek to the ship's master: she'd shown the red palm print to Tumalind, letting half the crew see. Had Corphanda been about, she'd have earned a matching mark on the other side.

As they were casting off, a giant of a man had run along the harbour, weaving deftly between knots of townsfolk. He'd leapt on board, spear in one hand, bow at his back and long, polished sword at his belt. Tarruss from Krohtl had made it just in time.

Tumalind stood now, at the front of the boat, the place the crew called the bows, and felt the wind ripple her tabard and the slight spray from the waves dampen her skin. That was what she would do now; look to what was coming, not what she'd left behind. She'd face her future with courage and tell any who asked that the tear on her cheek was just the wind in her eyes.

A rough hand stroked her shoulder and dropped to the curve of her bottom, as she turned round. The crewman grinned at her with broken, blackened teeth and squeezed where his hand cupped until she slapped it away.

'No call to be uppity, lass. Jus' come to tell yer there's food if you wan' it.'

'I'm virgin and not for the likes of you.'

'Ay, an' fish fly wi' seemeeuws an' sleep in the clouds. Yer'll be beggin' for a length o' this afore we've sailed a dozen leagues. Allus is; lasses. Can't get enough on a sailor.'

'Not this one. Where do I eat?'

He pointed down but she refused to look and pulled away from him. He tagged along and it was only on the flat deck between the masts that she shook him off. She complained to Corphanda about his behaviour and was pleased to see her have words with the sailor, though the pair parted in ribald laughter.

⁘

Aglydron had slept little. He woke Okkyntalah for morning prayer, though they had no need to move until much later. The young man had shown him the boat and the stash of water and food, which they must now replenish, since they must delay their departure.

'How do you know she'll be home tonight?' Okkyntalah seemed to question everything.

'Heard her talking to a friend.'

They'd been right above him when he was in the dim cell in the middle of the house; a place he'd escaped to so he wouldn't be discovered.

'I expect I shouldn't have been down there. Maybe Dagla Kaz will execute me when he learns of it. Unless Ytraa strikes me down first.'

'Is Ytraa likely to kill us when we're risking our lives to do the will of Ytraa?'

'You and me are nothing, boy. Tools. D'you think Ytraa can't set the wrong to rights without us? We're but…'

'Why are we risking death, then? Why don't we just let Ytraa do whatever's needed to put things right?'

Aglydron swiped the back of his hand across the boy's face. 'Show respect, boy! You talk like we've a choice. We do Ytraa's will, whether we live or die. Ytraa guides us and we do what we must.'

Okkyntalah wiped his hand across his mouth, taking away a thin smear of blood, which he examined through slitted eyes. 'Nothing you say makes sense, Aglydron. Don't hit me again; I'm a man now, not a child to be beaten. Next time, I'll hit you back.'

'You think joining once, with a priestess, makes you a man? You're unmarried still, childless…'

'I've frowk…joined with others. Anyway, the ceremony makes us all…'

Aglydron glared. 'Who? When?'

Okkyntalah shrugged. 'I have, that's all.'

'That how you show your love for my daughter? Joining with every girl who lifts her hem? I thought you loved Tumalind…'

'I do love her. I'm willing to risk my life to get her back. Why should frowking with another mean I don't love Tumalind? You join with others, so does Shoarhn. We all do. We're supposed to, aren't we?'

Aglydron fumed, knowing the boy was right but reluctant to confess he felt differently about Tumalind in this respect and surprised he should feel this way. He must, however, restrain his temper; the anxiety of doing what they had to do making him tense and quick to anger.

'Sorry, boy. Shouldn't have struck you. We need to work together to do the will of Ytraa. Forgive me. You're still a boy to me; the lad who was to wed my girl. Just need time to adjust to your new status.'

'It might help us both if you stopped calling me boy and used my name. You were telling me about what you heard in this secret chamber.'

Aglydron surveyed the boy, who had already grown in experience. Their journey to the town had been a source of new deeds and knowledge for them. Their planned crime and pursuit of Dagla Kaz was an event that would make more than mere men of them both.

'For one fearful moment, I thought she'd bring her friend down there. But she told her the chamber was sacred. Only the High Priest's allowed. She was just showing her where her father prays.'

'What made her spend last night away from home in the first place?'

'Didn't want to be alone in the house the first night after her father set sail. Alone! Three slaves in the place. Nearly got caught twice.'

'But you saw these drawings, these…maps, you say they're called? I never heard of such. Pictures of the world with places shown on them? Do they really…I mean, how can they show the routes across the strange lands?'

'May Ytraa spare my soul; from what little I heard from Jodisa-Li, we're not even supposed to know they exist, Okkyntalah. Just that knowledge is enough to have us stripped and hung in beating bags. There's stacks and stacks of rolled up scrolls and tablets of stone down there. If I'd had time, I might've read some. Locked chests and sealed containers, too. Might wonder what's so secret it has to be kept so well hidden. But the drawings of the routes and land, the maps, was laid out on a table. Looked like Dagla

Kaz had been copying them, if the parchment and spilled ink is any guide. Took all my nerve to read them.'

'Good job the Holy Ones taught you your letters, Aglydron. But do you know where they've gone and how to get there?'

'Know where they're bound. But they might've gone by any of three different routes. She'll tell us, once we're out to sea and she's got no choice.'

'They'll kill us. You know that, don't you?'

'Of course I know! We must do Ytraa's will. No choice, Okkyntalah. We must do this and there's no other way, is there?'

Okkyntalah shook his head. 'Perhaps you getting sight of the maps and not being caught is a sign we're doing the right thing.'

Aglydron hadn't thought of this. 'Course it is. Doesn't mean we won't be punished.'

They spent the afternoon in the town, abandoning their temporary camp on the outskirts and keeping within reasonable distance of the house so they might learn if the girl left again, or whether her friend remained with her. They knew she was back; saw her talking to their old village priest. For a while, it looked as though he was going to take up residence in the house himself but Jodisa-Li wouldn't let him through the door and he went off in a fit of anger.

The day dragged, as the hour for their dangerous scheme drew closer. They checked their water and food stocks and Aglydron sent Okkyntalah off with some of his dwindling coin to buy a new sleepsack and spare tabard to replace those lost over the falls. The young hunter still had his knife, bow, and a small quiver of arrows but everything else had gone.

They ate at the Merchant's Maiden and Okkyntalah made eyes at a striking and immodest young woman sitting with a sour-faced portly drunk; she made equally obvious eyes at the boy. Aglydron put two and two together but remained silent.

As darkness fell, they stashed the food, water and their other belongings ready in the boat they'd earmarked. It had been so difficult to make this move.

'Stealing, Aglydron.'

'I know, I know. But what else can we do? D'you have coin to pay the owner? He'll share in the glory of the duty we do for Ytraa and he won't be punished, as we will.'

'Doing him a favour, really, I suppose.'

'Might look at it that way. But we've no choice.'

No matter how they tried, neither of them could think of another way to put right the wrong. And the theft of a boat seemed almost trivial when compared with what they intended for the High Priest's daughter.

They waited for the townsfolk to empty the streets. Waited, in the dark of this strange place, for the quiet of night. As they made their way through silent streets to the High Priest's house, Aglydron started at the sound of a dreamer crying out in sleep, Okkyntalah was disturbed by the sudden distress of an infant waking hungry, both jumped at the angry shout of a wife castigating her drunken husband.

'Ready?'

Okkyntalah was silent in the pitch dark.

'Ready?'

'I...sorry, forgot you couldn't see me nodding. Yes. Oh! Ytraa bless this thing we do and bring us success.'

Aglydron heard the tremble in the boy's voice and wondered if his own sounded as strained. They crossed the wide, empty square; Shaulah silent as the men, as if she understood the need for secrecy. The door to the house opened with ease and Aglydron took Okkyntalah's hand on his shoulder to guide him in the near pitch darkness. They spoke in softest whispers. His previous survey of the house, carried out while the girl was away, had revealed all he needed to know of location and route. In the dark, it was more difficult but he traced a hand along internal walls and found the first door, then the second and the empty space that opened as a corridor.

Silent as bare feet on mud floors allowed, they stalked a short way down the corridor and found the door he'd identified as hers. Outside, he came to a sudden halt and Okkyntalah collided with him, cursing softly as he hit his knee. They froze in the darkness, listening for signs they'd been heard.

The door to her room opened with ease. Her perfume and the soft sound of her breathing confirmed she was there and asleep. Aglydron unclipped his belt and made it ready as he crossed the room to swing the rush blinds away from the window. Starlight filtered into the room. There was no moon visible.

They'd practiced on each other, knowing they must work swiftly in the dark and not make a mistake. If they were caught, they'd die without a chance to explain what they were about. No one would believe them in the absence of the High Priest and they would be executed by the most painful means the Holy Ones could devise. Capturing someone was unheard of; to subject the daughter of the High Priest to such indignity would surely induce the most terrible wrath of authority.

Aglydron knelt beside the raised wooden platform on which she lay in her sleepsack. His outstretched fingers sought the side and found it. Slowly, he worked his fingers along the seam to find the top or bottom of the sack. He found thin air. And touched skin. He pulled away at once, afraid she might wake.

'It's this end.'

He waited in the dark. Heard the young man move slowly beside him. Okkyntalah would have but one chance. If he failed, she'd scream. She'd bring the whole town around them. Aglydron felt the wooden frame move slightly. Heard the quick rustle of fabric. A sudden dull knock of bone on wood. Okkyntalah's stifled moan of pain. The girl made a muffled sound as through a gag. Okkyntalah silenced her with whispered threats. They peeled the sleepsack down and found her flailing arms. She made more noise than they could risk and Okkyntalah quieted her with dire threats he obviously couldn't mean. But he convinced her and she lay passive. They bound her wrists and pulled her sleepsack back up her body.

All remained quiet. Aglydron, found the candle he recalled, and the flint beside it. He had to strike three times. The sound was magnified to frightening proportions by the silence. In the flickering flame, they gathered some of the girl's belongings and lay them on top of the sleep sack. She watched with eyes as full of anger as they were of fear.

'Enough! We go now.'

They'd spent almost all of Aglydron's coin. He'd come upon a small stack of coin in the house and, conscious of their perilous position, decided to take it. He went in search, leaving Okkyntalah to bind the girl's belongings to her for the journey to the boat.

Aglydron returned and extinguished the candle. Somewhere from the back of the house came voices. The slaves had woken and were arguing over who should go to see if Jodisa-Li was all right.

'The window.'

Okkyntalah moved in the darkness. He headed for the oblong where the sky was a patch of spangled indigo in the blackness. Between them, they lowered the girl onto the dust of the road. Anxious leaps took them beyond her huddled body. A soft whistle brought Shaulah from her place beside the front door of the house. Hefting the girl, still in her sleep sack, over his shoulders, Okkyntalah set off at a run along the narrow lane at the side of the house. Across the square, the dog and Aglydron on his heels, they didn't stop to see whether they were pursued. Or even seen. They ran through the narrow streets. Down to the harbour.

Aglydron had to guide Okkyntalah back onto the right track with rough words as they came to narrow streets and he took a wrong turning.

The boat they'd chosen was almost at the mouth of the harbour. Tied beside another two. They had to balance across these before they could settle in the one they'd prepared. Okkyntalah dumped the girl, like a bundle, on her back in the bottom of the boat. Aglydron helped him untie the ropes that held the boat to those beside it. Jodisa-Li, perhaps realizing this was her last chance of help, tried to scream. Her muffled moans sounded loud in the silence of the calm night.

'Quiet! Another sound and I'll knock you senseless.' Aglydron's muttered threat silenced her.

She lay struggling ineffectually as they loosed the boat, rowed out of the harbour, and into the unknown of the night.

⁂

The small boat rocked in the cradle of soft swell formed by winds a hundred leagues distant. Aglydron gazed down at the girl, sleeping at last after her struggles.

He left the tiller, hoping the current might steer them in the absence of any breeze. Stooping, he eased her head up from the roll of bright clothing they'd used to pillow her, and slipped his free hand beneath long, deep chestnut tresses to the nape of her slender neck. She moaned as he unknotted the linen but didn't stir when he removed the gag. It didn't matter now if she woke; no one would hear her screams this far from land.

Back at the tiller, his weary eyelids drooped over sore eyes, threatening to deny him the dawn. Exhaustion loosened his neck muscles, dropping his head forward and merging his red beard with chest hair in the square neck of his tabard. Nothing invaded his moment of uneasy rest, but some instinct warned him he was falling asleep. He snapped his head upright, forced his eyes open and checked that Okkyntalah, curled in the bows, hadn't witnessed his lapse. He mustn't appear weak in front of the boy.

The lazy swell lulled and calmed but Aglydron remained tense and anxious. Above and about him, the sky paled as it lost more stars. The Eyes of Ytraa had already closed overhead and the tiny radiant spark of Ytraa's Skyfire, seen at last and now never absent from his thoughts, faded at the glow of approaching sunrise even as he sought it. Low cloud marred the clear amber of the northeast horizon, marking the position of the bulk of the island. But over The Point, the harsh peninsula sealed from the rest of the island by the precipice they called The Scar, there was no sign of cloud. No land was visible and Aglydron sighed his relief: the boat wouldn't be seen as it drifted slowly on the current, following the length of the dagger-shaped point that lay just below the horizon.

His tired eyes again scanned for pursuit and found empty sea. The amber glow brightened, heralding the coming day and habit and piety brought devotion to the surface of his mind.

'Okkyntalah, the sun.'

The boy woke at once, stretched, glanced about and noted the lightness in the sky. Shaulah uncurled from the small space behind him, cocked her head sideways and wagged her tail. He scratched her ear as she, too, stretched and yawned silently.

'Shall I wake her?'

'Sun up.'

Okkyntalah shrugged his body free of his lightly quilted sleepsack and knelt on one knee beside the girl. 'Jodisa-Li, the sun.'

She moaned but his soft litany didn't rouse her. He grasped her covered shoulder, shook her, not roughly. Waking, she shied from him at once. 'Take your evil hands off me!'

'The sun, Jodisa-Li.'

She glowered at him. 'So?'

'You'll want to make morning prayers.'

'Untie me!'

Okkyntalah sought guidance from Aglydron.

'We'll have to. She can't be any other way for prayer. She can't escape now.'

Okkyntalah opened the neck of the bag and slipped his hands under her arms.

'How dare you touch me!'

Ignoring her protest, he pulled her upright. On her knees, she glared defiance at him as he peeled the padded sack down her body. Trying not to look at her, he loosed the belt that held her wrists. The men took up position at once in the bottom of the boat and, in silence, made their obeisance to Ytraa.

Aglydron rose, replaced his tabard and the belt he'd used to tie the girl's wrists, and regained the tiller. The girl was still rubbing her wrists and hands, bringing back the life they'd been denied in sleep. The young man, shuffling further from her, pushed boar's teeth pegs through leather loops before fastening the bronze buckle of his hunting belt. Neither looked at the girl.

She caught them off guard when her time with Ytraa was done. 'I need to make water.'

Aglydron looked at her, captivated by her extraordinary beauty, then collecting himself, nodded at the gunwales.

She rose unsteadily to her feet, grasping the rough wood of the mast for support and glancing toward the signs of the island. Venom fed her voice as she spat at their backs. 'Mhortag's spawn! My father will blister you over the embers of justice, and I'll be first to lash your quivering flesh with tnetsi thorns.'

'We'll not use you that way, Jodisa-Li. As a Virgin Gift, you're sacred. We'd sooner die defending you and your chastity.'

Aglydron glanced and saw her squat over the narrow wooden board, clinging to the gunwales for balance. He turned away.

Okkyntalah, broad back to the girl, knelt to roll her sack and stack it with the others. Aglydron manned the tiller, his face turned determinedly away from her, his head drooping and his eyes closing again with weariness.

'Don't take too long, Jodisa-Li. The nazzakks have teeth that can take off your bum with one bite.' Okkyntalah's jest found no response from her but Aglydron managed a smile and assumed the girl was still sulking.

He felt himself dozing again. The dog barked, shattering the silence and reminding him uncomfortably of his difficulty in staying awake. 'Quiet, Shaulah!' He glanced at her and understood her excitement. Jodisa-Li was in the sea, already sixty strokes from the boat, swimming strongly for the unseen coast.

Chapter 9

ESCAPE ATTEMPTS

Aglydron saw Okkyntalah stare, open-mouthed, as Jodisa-Li moved away across the open expanse of water.

'She's terrified, or mad.'

'What you waiting for, boy? Get her!'

He woke up then; stripped and dived into the water, rocking the vessel with the force of his leap. Aglydron dredged oars from the bottom of the boat. Fitting them awkwardly onto their thole pins, he began to row with difficulty; the width of the boat intended to take two oarsmen sitting at either side. But, by stretching his arms out wide, he could manage short strokes. Wearily, inexpertly, he made his way toward the girl in the water; zeal warring with exhaustion.

The girl was fast and strong but Okkyntalah hunted in the small lake south of the village and was an experienced swimmer. He gained on her rapidly. When he tried to grasp her, she lashed out, winding him. Encouraged by his struggles for breath, she struck out again for the unseen coast.

Aglydron watched him float and relax. 'Get her!'

Okkyntalah gestured for patience and gave chase again only when he was ready. Aglydron hauled on the oars, taking the boat in roughly the right direction. Jodisa-Li's escape attempt was futile and he was confident the boy would catch her long before they came in sight of land. He'd give her a sound beating for wasting their time and effort.

She was tiring; driven by fear but unused to swimming any distance. When Okkyntalah caught up with her again, she was exhausted. Still she struggled as he tried to return her to the boat.

Aglydron strained with the oars, slowly closing on the swimmers. He was a dozen strokes away when he saw pointed fins. Dark and ominous, they arrowed for the pair in a tight group of five, approaching from the west. A vision of the girl taken by the vicious killers flashed across his mind. How easily their task might end before it had begun. The girl still struggled, arms and legs flailing as Okkyntalah fought to control her.

'Look out, Okkyntalah, nazzakks!'

At Aglydron's warning, Okkyntalah struck the girl to subdue her. She yelled as much in anger as pain as the blow failed to stun her.

'Bowelcreep!'

He turned her to face the danger. 'Nazzakks. Still; or we're dead.'

She followed his gaze across the calm water. The closing fins stopped her struggles at once. Aglydron edged the boat closer, between the fish and their prey. Okkyntalah cupped Jodisa-Li's foot in his hands and thrust her over the gunwales. Aglydron hauled her, none too gently, into the boat. He hung low to grasp the young man's arms and was startled to see fear erupt into a smile of pleasure as one of the company of dolphins nudged him upward with its snout between his legs, hoisting his trunk clear of the water. It squeaked its message of joy and friendship as Okkyntalah slipped sideways off the creature's nose and splashed back into the water to play with them.

'Okkyntalah!' Anger made him bellow. 'This isn't a game. We do the will of Ytraa.'

The young man stroked the helping dolphin with gratitude and it again shoved its snout between his legs and hoisted him clear of the water so he could haul himself back into the boat.

'The fishermen say they understand human speech.'

Aglydron frowned at the creatures. 'Thank you.'

The five bowed in unison and dived beneath the surface until they faded into the depth of blue.

Okkyntalah wiped water from his skin with his hands before he moved to retrieve his tabard, only to discover it absorbing a pool of fresh water.

'Aglydron.'

Jodisa-Li was emptying the last of their three water skins over the side; the other two flaccid girba lay at her feet, their stoppers floating in water trickling from their opened necks. Triumph lit her face as she rose to her feet, dropping it with a gesture of contempt to make a small splash in the bottom of the boat.

'Mhortag's whore! I'll skin your seat. Hold her, whilst I teach her some respect.' Aglydron unclasped his belt and swung it so the air sang with its threat.

Okkyntalah reluctantly forced her onto all fours. 'You can't beat the naked.'

Swaying with exhaustion and the motion of the boat, as fresh water sloshed about his feet, Aglydron was in no mood for mercy. 'Allowed or not, she'll learn to behave herself or suffer.' He lashed her with his belt, raising wheals across the perfect skin and causing her to cry out in pain, humiliation and outrage.

'Enough.' Okkyntalah released her after the sixth stroke so Aglydron was unable to deal the other half dozen he'd intended.

She drew a blood red tabard quickly over her and clutched it to her body; the embroidered gold and silver emblems of the Tree of Life distorting as she crushed the silk against her skin and knelt in the bottom of the boat. Tears coursed down her face but she glared defiance at him.

Aglydron plucked a wooden goblet from the stores and tossed it at her. 'Refill them with what you can.'

'We can't drink that; it's full of dead fish scales.'

'Do it, or suffer another beating.'

'We'll fall sick if we drink that, Aglydron; she's right.'

He rubbed his eyes. Shrugged. 'We'll have to go back for more water.'

Anticipation brightened her eyes even through her distress.

'Don't think you'll escape. I'll bind and gag you. And there's no one to help you on The Point, less you want to live and die an outcast's whore. Nothing to eat. You'd be dead in days.'

'What's the use of going to The Point, Aglydron? No water there.'

'We won't make Ylcrat without water, let alone Rophan. There'll be a spring. We just have to find it.'

'Easily said.'

'We've no choice, Okkyntalah. The mainland's too dangerous.' He saw the challenge in the young man's eyes and issued his scornful return. 'There'll be signs a hunter like you can see.'

Okkyntalah raised his eyebrows but said nothing.

Resigned to the risk of being sighted, Aglydron struggled to raise the small sail and let the gentle breeze push them toward the coast.

'It's impossible to get up or down the cliffs, Aglydron.'

'Nothing's impossible when you do the will of Ytraa.'

The girl closed the side openings of her tabard. She toyed with the goblet in her hand, sullen and uncooperative, and watched Shaulah lap at the liquid without concern.

'I can beat you, Jodisa-Li; starve you, keep you thirsty, keep you bound, gagged and blindfold. If you want better treatment, help us and don't hinder Ytraa's will. Whether you like it or not, you're going to Choshinahm. You can travel free or tied; I don't care.'

'Choshinahm?'

Aglydron, the emergency over, let weariness overcome him. He shook his head. 'I'm too tired to play games, Jodisa-Li. We're putting right the wrong done by Dagla-Kaz, as you must know. You'll take your rightful place as Virgin Gift to the lost brethren.'

'My father; wrong? How dare you, a commoner, question the High Priest? Dagla-Kaz is beyond reproach. How can you presume to suggest otherwise?'

'Dagla-Kaz swapped Tumalind for you at the Choosing. We both saw it. May the Lord Gadhallah's memory fade forever and Lake Qonahn dry to a desert if I'm wrong.

Take the tiller, boy. I must sleep if I'm to stay alert when you go for water.' Aglydron stepped past the girl and curled up on the boards in the bows.

He was asleep even before Okkyntalah had taken the tiller.

'You're mad, both of you. Mad and evil.'

Okkyntalah nodded. 'Mad; but not evil. I'd have spared you the beating, Jodisa-Li. I'm sorry for the pain and indignity. Try to understand we're only doing what we must to put right the wrong. We saw your father take Tumalind in your place. We've got to do Ytraa's will. You were Chosen, Jodisa-Li, not Tumalind.'

'I'll have you both unmanned, skinned, roasted and beaten with tnetsi thorns.'

'If that's the will of Ytraa.' He tried to keep the terror of that fate out of his voice; the girl must be frightened, not him, if he and Aglydron were to control her.

'What do you, a village lad with no education, know of Ytraa's will?'

'I know what I saw. I know what should be.'

'Fool. You'll die in agony. And for nothing. Even if we find my father, he'll not take me to Choshinahm in place of your precious...betrothed. I'm right, aren't I? Yes. She's the Virgin Gift and there's nothing you can do about it.'

'We'll see. If it's the will of Ytraa...'

'The will of Dagla Kaz is more likely...' She stopped as if she'd said too much.

'The will of Dagla Kaz?'

'Nothing. I spoke in anger. I'm hungry.'

He stared at her until she looked away, in spite of her declared superiority.

'When you've bailed out the water you spilled, you can eat.'

'I'm thirsty.'

Okkyntalah nodded at the water lapping her legs as she knelt. 'That's our drinking water.'

Shaulah chose that moment to add volume and pungency to the fluid. Jodisa-Li moved quickly and straddled the pool, staring with disgust, the wooden goblet in her hand.

'When the bottom of the boat's dry, you can eat and maybe have a drop of wine. As Aglydron said, it's up to you. Now, I'll say no more. Work quietly or you'll get nothing. Aglydron's been awake all night and needs rest.'

'Think I give a rhaaht's fart for his sleep?' She shouted loud enough to wake the dead but Aglydron didn't stir.

'Do I have to take my belt to you as well?'

She sneered but replied in a soft firm voice. 'I'm the daughter of the High Priest; I'm the High Priest Elect and...'

'You're a Virgin Gift, Jodisa-Li. Your old life of privilege, rank and luxury is over. We'll feed and water you; die if we must, to keep you virgin. And I'll do my best to save you from Aglydron's temper. You'd better do as you're told or suffer. No more talk now.'

Okkyntalah breakfasted on fresh fruit and pale-green sour wine from the hard leather flagon, as he steered the small craft toward the island, the sail flapping in the slight wind. Already, the low hills of the peninsula were creeping above the horizon.

For a while, the girl just stared at the bottom of the boat. She seemed as much perplexed by her situation, as frightened. Eventually, hunger perhaps persuading her that obstinacy would get her nowhere, she began bailing. By the time the cliffs were in sight, the bottom of the boat was merely damp.

Okkyntalah scanned the coast for a place to beach the boat and scale the cliffs. The land seemed to rise sheer from the waves, climbing between four and fifteen manheights in a harsh, forbidding wall. What little beach he could see was narrow and rock strewn with no place to land. On his approach, he'd spotted a dark cleft in the cliff face half a league south. The current flowed slowly in that direction, whilst the gentle breeze blew onshore. He struggled to control the direction, trying to avoid the rocks and eventually had to lower the sail so the boat drifted parallel, about two hundred paces from the cliffs.

'Some sailor.' Jodisa-Li's scorn was all too obvious but he ignored her taunt.

As the dark rent in the cliff face came within sight, he called Aglydron. The older man didn't wake. 'Rouse him, Jodisa-Li.'

'I'm not your servant.'

'Wake him, please.'

'Why should I? I'll do what I must to keep you mad men from harming me, but I'll not be your slave.'

'Wake him up! Mhortag's balls, it's clear you've been spoilt.'

She relented, poking Aglydron none too gently in his ribs with her toes. He woke with a start and gripped her ankle tightly. She cried out in alarm and he released her.

'What?'

'Likely place to land, I think.'

A shingle beach, strewn with pebbles of every colour, shape and size, formed a wide band immediately below a rock face striped in shades of red, orange, brown and black. As they drew nearer, a small cave came into view within the far wall of the deep split. Aglydron took the tiller and sent Okkyntalah up front to check the depth of water.

'Why did you lower the sail, Okkyntalah?'

'Your idiot friend can't sail. Some voyage this is going to be. Hoping Ytraa will send the wind you need to take you where you want to go?'

'Quiet, girl, or you'll feel my belt again.'

As they reached the shallows, Okkyntalah leapt from the boat, painter in hand, and landed knee deep in near silent surf. Running up the beach, he hauled the boat up until its bows rested just free of the small breakers.

He climbed back on board and bent to examine the empty water skins; at least she'd only uncorked them and they remained undamaged. A foot on his rear shoved him hard against Aglydron and he heard the girl jump into the shallow water and run up the beach. Struggling to disengage from the older man, Okkyntalah sent Shaulah to follow Jodisa-Li.

Aglydron screamed at him. 'Get her!'

Okkyntalah dashed across sand and pebbles after the girl. He studied the deep cleft, which cut a dozen paces inland with sheer sides and no place to hide. Moving into the mouth of the cave, he could see nothing ahead, darkness almost total after the bright sunlight. Adjusting to the gloom, he moved toward a faint lightness ahead. Almost at once, he heard a scream of terror. Shaulah's angry barking followed. The girl screamed again. He inched forward in the darkness, unwilling to risk his head against the uneven rock of the low roof, yet concerned to rescue the girl from whatever terror had caused her to cry out. Deeper in the cave, he rounded a sharp corner and saw daylight through the low tunnel ahead. But there was no sign of the girl and Shaulah's barking ceased abruptly.

'Jodisa-Li!'

Her answering cry was stifled. 'Help me!'

Okkyntalah crouched low and sped for the entrance. He emerged, squinting, into reflected daylight. Before him, a narrow stretch of red sand and mixed shingle divided the cave from another cliff ahead. Part way up the opposite face, climbed a huge naked man. Under one of his massive arms he gripped Jodisa-Li. Shaulah lay stretched on the sand.

'I'm here, Jodisa-Li, hold on…'

The giant turned at his voice, looked down and let the girl go so suddenly she almost fell headlong to the sand below. Balance and agility helped her find her feet and she half scrambled, half tumbled down the rough steps nature had riven in the cliff. She flew past Okkyntalah back into the cave, her face a mask of terror. Okkyntalah looked up at the giant, who stared down at him, more anxious than threatening. Neither moved.

'I need drinking water. Can you guide me…?

The big man frowned, then turned and scaled the rest of the rough natural staircase with a speed that belied his size. He disappeared from view after a swift backward glance that suggested he feared pursuit.

Okkyntalah looked about him. The girl was secure. She'd returned to the cave and, from there, could go nowhere but the beach where Aglydron waited. Cliffs rose all around him so that he stood in the shaded base of a yawning, narrow hole with the sky a deep azure lozenge above. The cliff at his back mirrored the stone face in front of him. In some distant time, an unknown God had split it from the main face of the rock to lean away and form this craggy hollow. The torn face to his right was bright with sunlight at the top. A fringe of dry vegetation rattled in the breeze a dozen manheights above.

He considered climbing to make a sortie but, instead, gathered his unconscious dog and returned to the boat.

Aglydron had bound the girl hand and foot and beaten her soundly. She was weeping but the gag prevented any sound. He nodded at Shaulah. 'She all right?'

'Stunned. He must've hit her with something.'

'Who?'

Okkyntalah explained and Aglydron glanced at the sobbing girl with a nod of satisfaction.

'Take care of Shaulah whilst I go for water.'

'They'll know we're here now. I'll keep the boat offshore at anchor and be ready to leave as soon as you're back. The renegades and perverts will be after this bitch as soon as they know she's here. Might be safer to try further down the coast.'

'It was hard enough finding this place; there may be no other. It's supposed to be impossible to get on or off The Point by sea, Aglydron. And there must be water close by, else he wouldn't be living here. Anyway, he was more scared of me than I was of him. Big as a hut but a noman. Probably lives alone.'

'What'd a noman want with her?'

'Who knows? Maybe to sell? Use as a slave? Eat?'

Aglydron nodded. 'Criminal or sagger?'

'Sagger; still had ears. I'll risk it. Saggers are generally harmless.'

Aglydron smirked in spite of himself. 'Harmless to women, anyway.'

Okkyntalah echoed his derisive laughter.

Jodisa-Li watched through her tears and wondered whether she might've been better with the giant. Mute and tongueless he may have been, but he'd tried not to harm her, in spite of her struggles. It had been the sheer size and sight of him coming on her so unexpectedly that had made her scream and struggle. And why was he there, waiting? It suggested more than mere coincidence.

Why had she run from him? Aglydron had been cruel, tying her wrists painfully, binding her ankles with rough rope that cut into her flesh and using his belt on her again until she feared he'd skin her backside. If the boy hadn't returned when he had, the madman might've beaten her forever. And now she'd destroyed any chance of escape before they left the island. Frustration, as much as pain and humiliation, made her weep.

'Be swift, Okkyntalah. We can't afford more than today. If you're not back by sundown I'll have to go on without you.'

'With no water?'

'I'll have to trust to Ytraa. I've got to catch Dagla Kaz. The more leagues between us, the less hope of catching them. My knowledge of the route grows less the further we go. If we don't find any sign of Dagla Kaz on the mainland at Shakahnl, I'll struggle to know which way to go.'

Aglydron was completely mad. The boy seemed to have some sense and had been less unkind to her. But she'd see both punished for their evil.

'I'll be back before sundown. With or without water.' Okkyntalah frowned at Jodisa-Li, wincing at her obvious discomfort and pain. 'Don't forget she needs to be fit to walk.'

'I'll worry about the troublesome bitch. You get fresh water.'

Okkyntalah nodded and gave her a look of sympathy. He stroked Shaulah and was gone at a swift lope up the beach.

Aglydron looped a noose of rope around her neck and fastened the free end to the mast. 'Run now and you'll hang yourself.'

As if she could run with her ankles bound so tightly that she was losing feeling in her feet. Her knees hurt from the pressure of the hard wood but she couldn't sit after his beating. He jumped from the boat and pushed against the prow with all his weight. Slowly, the small craft moved into the water until it was afloat. He waded after it, hauled himself back on board, rowed out a short distance and dropped the small anchor. The boat bobbed and tugged at the rope on the soft waves. She'd been to sea before and was unlikely to vomit into the gag from the motion at any rate. It was small comfort as she tried to work her hands and feet to make the blood flow.

Aglydron busied himself around the boat for a short while before tending the dog. He surprised her with his gentle attentions and she was impressed, in spite of herself, as the dog's eyes flickered open and she struggled to her feet. Unsteady and clearly still dazed, Shaulah didn't seem to be seriously injured. She sat and worried at an itch on her foreleg before settling down in the bottom of the boat to sleep off the effects of the attack.

Jodisa-Li moaned involuntarily when she overbalanced and placed too much weight on her swollen hands to stop herself falling on her face and being strangled by the noose. Aglydron turned at the sound and looked her.

He hadn't looked at her properly since they'd bundled her aboard.

The rumours of her beauty were not false. Chestnut hair, loose and free, fell to the middle of her slender back. They must let it grow, now. Her high forehead spoke of intelligence and eyes identical to Tumalind's stared at him with a direct challenge. The small nose was just short of pert in her strong face and the mouth…But the gag prevented study of that. He considered.

'If I take off your gag, will you swear by Ytraa to be quiet?'

He was surprised she took her time to decide. She stared at him for so long that he was forced to withdraw his gaze.

'Will you?'

When he looked back at her, she nodded. He released the silk band he'd tied too tightly in his anger.

'You make me hurt you; not doing as you're told.'

'I make you do nothing; unless you're incapable of exercising your own will, fool. If you were captive, vulnerable, held against your will by someone cruel and insane, wouldn't you try to escape?'

'Okkyntalah and me aren't mad and I don't mean to be cruel.'

'Don't you? Is that why you beat me so hard you broke the skin? Is that why my feet are swelling with the tightness of my bonds, my hands have lost all feeling?'

The evidence was clear and he undid the rope at her feet with difficulty, leaving her legs free, now that the boat was afloat and the noose held her captive. Her wrists he untied and then bound loosely, with soft strong kid, so she might use her hands but would be handicapped if she tried to escape again.

'You brought all this on yourself. Do as I say and you'll find things easier.'

'Do as I'm told? By you? What? Let you invade and despoil me and sell me to some vile slaver when you've used me all you want?'

'We won't use you, Jodisa-Li. Don't you see? You're a Virgin Gift. We're not going to sell you. We really don't mean you any harm.'

'Then let me go.'

'If it was just for me, I'd never have stolen you away. Try to understand; Okkyntalah and me are in this with you. Ytraa wills you go to Choshinahm. None of us dare go against Ytraa; you of all people must know that.'

'I was not Chosen.'

'Okkyntalah and I saw your father sign to the drummer. He passed over you and took Tumalind instead. But that was the wish of Dagla Kaz, not the will of Ytraa. The High Priest can do many things, but he can't go against Ytraa's will.'

'You say. Did others see this sacrilege you accuse my father of, or was it only the father and the betrothed of Tumalind?'

'You might want it different, but we saw what we saw. D'you think I'd risk Ytraa's wrath just to stop my daughter going? I've a girl serving the temple, fourth-born and given freely from her mother's womb without ever taking suck from her swollen breasts. I'm proud to serve Ytraa. Why would I stand in the way of my daughter's honour if she'd truly been Chosen?'

'You accuse my father of doing just that.'

'But you're his heir. He wants to make sure the line of Lord Gadhallah survives and I don't blame him. Whatever reason your father had, Jodisa-Li, I know Tumalind wasn't Chosen and you were. Dagla Kaz will have to decide when we catch up with him, but he must know it's death to all Followers if he breaks the holy oaths to Ytraa.'

'What do you know of the law? What are you? Fisherman? Hunter? Ploughman? Dagla Kaz has spent his life interpreting the signs and sacred texts. He's read the secret books and knows....'

'There are secret books, then? I thought it blasphemy, a legend.'

'I said it not. You're mistaken.'

'You can't unsay it, Jodisa-Li, no matter how much you might want to.'

'You heard it not. I know nothing of these things.'

But he was incapable of silence. 'They're the scrolls and tablets in the chamber under your father's cell, and in the locked chests under the maps.'

'That knowledge sentences you to a beating and the removal of your tongue. But, since you'll die a most horrible death, perhaps that small taste of justice won't matter.'

'You've admitted they exist, Jodisa-Li, and that means the same punishment for you. You'll lose your tongue. We're as guilty as each other.'

She considered his words. He thought her unlikely to speak of this to her father, in the hope that Aglydron wouldn't mention her slip.

'I would eat now, please.'

'A lesser man might starve you till you revealed all. But you'll eat, aye and drink, even though you should go thirsty after the trouble you've caused.'

He gave her fruit and a small bowl of wine. She ate delicately, drank slowly, taking small sips and he admired her behaviour, aware she must be very hungry and thirsty. 'You're your father's daughter, Jodisa-Li. Proud but civilized and genteel. Those who you honour will be fortunate indeed.'

'You're jealous. You want me yourself.'

'Any man would. But I'm husband to Shoarhn for eighteen cycles; mother of my children. She may not have your astounding beauty, Jodisa-Li, but I've been with her for that time and I join with others only as Ytraa requires. As long as you're the only woman with us, Okkyntalah and me will be celibate as a noman.'

'You really believe every word of the village priest, don't you? Who's your Kaz?'

'It was Kaz-Ca-Wesdan, but …'

'Wesdan! As stunted in mind as he is in growth. My father only put him in temporary charge because…anyway, that doesn't matter. He'll relinquish his post as soon as Dagla Kaz returns with the Godwood from Choshinahm. But if you listen to the words of such a man and believe them all, you're a fool, Aglydron.'

'I Follow. I do as I must and as Ytraa wills.'

'Fool. I'm the daughter of the High Priest and will be the next to hold that office. Your village priest must obey me. You must obey me. Unbind me! Release me, Aglydron.'

'You're not heir now. You're Jodisa, Virgin Gift and you've no power over anyone. You're sacrifice and servant to Ytraa and must do Ytraa's bidding.'

'Idiot! I can have you killed, tortured, cast unmanned into the endless dark of Mhortag's bowels. Release me and take me home!'

'You can't do nothing, Jodisa, but submit to your fate; to join with one or many of the lost brethren so the link doesn't break and Ytraa can return them to the true way before the end of time. As I see it, you'll be partner to some wealthy man or live as a sacred vessel in one of their temples.'

'You'll have to watch me every step of the way, Aglydron. If I can escape, I will. If I can kill you or the boy, I will.'

He looked into her eyes, saw hatred behind their brightness and knew she meant what she said. The journey, hardly begun and fraught with risk and uncertainty, looked even longer and harder.

Chapter 10

Dangers Faced

For Tumalind, the first two days at sea proved a time of growing knowledge, the forming of relationships and some barriers, and the acquisition of various skills for survival in the wild.

The living quarters were cramped and crowded, so that many of the party slept on deck whilst the weather held. The food was adequate but tedious and unvarying, prepared by the ship's cook.

'I'd cook for us, but Dagla Kaz says the sailors won't let me.'

Tumalind was astonished at Phildrad's offer but not surprised the High Priest had turned him down. The crew were very touchy about their duties and made a clear distinction between themselves and their passengers, as far as work was concerned. It was a shame they failed to use the same demarcation in social matters.

There was too little room for any proper movement and the constant rolling made many of them queasy, though only Dilanthas and Jhonaht suffered enough to take to their beds. Corphanda prepared various potions, to no avail. Her limited experience, treating fishermen on the quiet lake near Pampahn, was little use on the high seas. One of the crew traded a recipe for her favours, which she'd have given freely, but swore her to secrecy over its contents. In spite of her vocal doubts, the sailor's cure quickly had the desired effect.

They sailed under clear blue skies and a broiling sun, or warm black velvet nights, studded with more stars than the sky over land had ever displayed. The spark of the Skyfire, a dull smudge, lay low in the western quarter.

It was never cool, even with the wind blowing, and their small cabin was unbearable much of the time. The girls prayed anxiously, their posture exposing them to lechery from the sailors. But, true to the word of Dagla Kaz, the crew never tried to force any of the girls to lie with them and took no more advantage than a bawdy interest, licentious looks and occasional groping.

Tumalind was first to risk a dip in the barrel on deck, in an effort to cool down as much as to be clean. Sailcloth surrounded her as a screen.

'The heathens have climbed the riggin' to watch.'

'Shame the sea's so calm, Corphanda. A bit of rough weather might pitch them from the yards and booms.' She ignored their taunts and ribald remarks.

'Scrub yer back, darlin?'

'Rather do 'er front.'

Back in her tabard, she continued to suffer vulgar invitations until she accurately mocked their paunches, their baldness or their stink. They soon left her alone and teased the other women instead.

Porryh let them touch her without comment, though whether from pleasure or indifference, Tumalind couldn't decide. Dilanthas, once off her sick bed, was forever clutching her tabard protectively round her.

But, in the middle of the third afternoon, threats of a more serious nature took their minds off tormenting sailors. Dark storm clouds built to the west. The sea, rising and falling with a soft slow swell until then, became rough and choppy.

Tumalind's experience of the sea was as swimmer and fisher for shrimps with a net in the shallows. Okkyntalah's father, who took his small boat into the waters close to Morstahn, had told her the sea could be more dangerous and unpredictable than a wounded stripecat. She'd stood on the shore and watched dark clouds cover the sky and grey the blue waters. She'd seen the far swell froth with white manes as wind scooped the tops off crests. She'd listened to the angry roar of breakers smashing hard on the beach, ripping out trees near the water's edge and piling great banks of shingle and sand under the cliffs.

'Will the storm hit us?'

Baklan didn't even glance in the direction of the cloud but studied her instead with the eye of the practised womaniser.

'It will. But, with Tryhnn's help, I'll keep you out the clutches of Taniwha. He'll not drag us under to have us for mermen and mermaids. Have no fear, my pretty; I'll look after a treasure like you. We'll weather the storm.'

Rain sent them to their small cabin; hot and humid with only a narrow gap at the top of the ill-fitting door to bring in fresh air. They sat in the dark; the pitching of the boat making sleep impossible and rest uncomfortable as they clung to the uprights and waited for the increasingly angry sea to drown them. The storm lashed, pounded and soaked all. Even the sailor's recipe had little effect on Dilanthas in this turmoil and Porryh began to suffer as well so that Tumalind was soon nursing two sick companions. Corphanda had gone to the crews' quarters to care for a man whose fingers had been crushed by a flailing spar, and the weather had trapped her there.

The wind howled and raged, whistling with spite through gaps in the superstructure. Timbers creaked and groaned. Men yelled in anger at their companions' incompetence. Baklan shouted obscenities at all and sundry. The air in the cabin grew foul and foetid as the two girls vomited into the darkness and all sweated with fear in the confined space.

At last, Tumalind could stand the stifling shadows no longer. She opened the door onto the night. Wind snatched the flap of wood from her grasp to crash and splinter against the outer wooden wall. Waves, solid and streaming with phosphorescent flame in the thick darkness, crashed over the deck and washed across her feet. She swallowed her scream of terror. Wrestled to reclaim the door. Howling wind drove sheets of rain and spray to soak her from head to foot. Dilanthas screamed from the darkness. Porryh pleaded with Ytraa to save them. Tumalind fought against the power of the weather. Swamped by the edge of a falling breaker as it washed the deck, and almost swept her off her feet, she struggled to find the door handle. Gasping for breath, she battled against wind and water. And won, at last. The door slammed shut again. But the top half had splintered and rattled as it hung loose, forming only a partial barrier.

Now, wetness added to their miseries. But it seemed the sheer fright of exposure had worked where the sailor's remedy had failed and Porryh was no longer sick.

'Stupid bitch! Trying to kill us all?'

'I just wanted some air. I'm sorry.'

'I'm frowkin' soaked. And my bed's sopping wet!'

'Everythin's soaked. Stop complainin' Porryh. Tumalind wasn't to know what it were like outside.'

'We're going to die! I know we are. We're going to drown! We're going to end it all in this godforsaken pitching, frowkin' darkness.' Porryh's voice grew increasingly sharp and strident as terror overtook her. 'I don't want to die! I don't want...'

Tumalind acted without thought. She'd seen her mother deal with a hysterical young woman and followed her example. Porryh calmed instantly after the slap and then began sobbing, as much for all she'd lost as in fear for her life. Tumalind held her, soothing the girl with soft words of comfort and fellow feeling.

The storm raged unchecked and seemingly without end. Wind howled through rigging and tore at the few sails still unfurled, ripping one canvas to flap and smack the air above them. The ship lurched and dipped, bucked and shook, as waves tossed it and sought to drown it. Loud over the background of screaming and groaning timbers, came a report sharp as the crack of a whip. A fearful, groaning creak followed, to end in a crash that shook the whole vessel. Men yelled and screamed in the dark. The girls in their cabin were rigid with terror.

The night without end shrieked and wailed. Blackness and water. Timbers that groaned and threatened to splinter. Frightened, angry voices of helpless men. These were all they knew in their fear.

⋆

Aklon-Dji slashed at the undergrowth with the well-honed blade of his sword, raising yet another cloud of the tiny infuriating bees that buzzed about his ears and eyes and made his skin itch wherever they landed. They were harmless enough but drove him wild with their insistent crawling all over him. He'd been in the jungle since the early hours; having left Lasdilyss so he could spend a couple of nights with Kaz-Ca-Porlesah, following her return from the Choosing. He'd learned much from the priestess and was now on his way to inform Jodisa-Li of the possible consequences of their father's mistake.

Already, he was regretting his route through the edge of the rainforest instead of skirting the lake and travelling cross country to Chalamamnon from there. But this way had an advantage: none of the trackers, who tried to shadow him everywhere, had ever dared hunt him in the jungle.

Here it was at its narrowest; a stretch no more than a league or so where it left the mountainsides and passed close by the lake. Behind him, to the south, lay the broad tongue of land that was believed to be uninhabited, even by the last of the Caboceer; the tribal peoples who'd settled the island long before Followers had arrived. Aklon-Dji had been told that the entire peninsula was covered by rain forest and, since game was thought so hard to catch and the terrain difficult, no one ever ventured there. But, in his many searches and wanderings, he had recently discovered a number of small valleys devoid of the closely packed trees and full of lush grassland where herds of large deer-like creatures grazed. He was still pondering which of these isolated valleys might make the best home for the people of The Point to escape to once he was ready to make his move and start the Cause.

He slashed again, sweat dripping off his arm and hand so that he stopped for a moment, removed his tabard and wrung it out. It was the third time he'd squeezed the sweat and water from it since he'd entered the forest and he was weary with effort and heat. Jodisa-Li didn't deserve this degree of risk and sacrifice. But he would do it anyway.

Above, the dark underside of the canopy cut out the sky completely so that he had to find direction by other means. He'd once spent several days completely lost in the jungle and had emerged very hungry and dehydrated only a few hundred paces from the place he'd entered it. After that experience, he'd persuaded one of the Caboceer to travel with him as guide. It had been a mutual learning experience; the small, black skinned woman had spent her entire life on The Point but she'd proved an invaluable teacher.

'My ancestors never lived in the trees, you know, Aklon.' Mkolo-ti had reminded him as they'd climbed the Scar.

'I know. But your people were on the island for centuries before we came and chased you onto The Point. You must have some knowledge of the jungle.'

'Only what's been passed down to me by my ancestors. And it's over thirteen hundred cycles since my people wandered our homeland freely. I doubt I've much in my memory of real help.'

But she'd recognized plants from descriptions she'd learned from her mother. Her knowledge had expanded as they'd actually entered the trees, as if the forest had awakened memories she never knew she retained. So many of the plants were poisonous it was as well that Mkolo-ti had been with him or he might have died very quickly. Apart from teaching him to identify the few plants he could eat, she'd taught him how to hunt and to gauge direction and distance in the dense jungle.

Ahead, he saw brightness at last and wondered whether he was approaching the small clearing he knew existed close to the place he intended to exit the trees. Instinctively, he became more wary; the clearings were home to longnoses. Unpredictable, huge and armed with great curving tusks, they could kill a stripecat with ease. A man stood no chance against them. Yet, they could be docile or totally indifferent. He'd once fallen out of a tree as one of the huge beasts had lumbered by and shaken the trunk so violently he'd been unable to keep hold. He'd landed on the creature's broad, leathery back and expected to be killed instantly. Instead, it had raised its long serpentine nose, sniffed at him and used it to pick him up. It had inspected him with tiny black eyes before setting him gently on his feet and lumbering off through the undergrowth.

Aklon-Dji gripped his forked stick tightly as he approached the light. Here, near the sunlight, was also the danger area for some of the more poisonous snakes. He'd spent four days half paralysed on the floor of the jungle after being bitten by one and had always carried a forked stick since. In his pack were the remains of another small snake he'd killed and cooked earlier. Once free of the trees, he'd rest, eat, and give the sun a chance to dry his skin and his tabard.

The light grew as he approached and the land sloped down and away from him. He slashed at the undergrowth and came out of the trees onto an open hillside. Slightly out of reckoning, he'd reached the edge of the forest sooner than expected and was relieved to be free at last.

He scanned the area in front of him but saw no sign of human life. The hill sloped down into a shallow valley with a stream glistening in the bottom. The other side of the valley was steep and rocky with occasional stands of tall trees and small areas of low bush. The grass cloaking the slopes was waist high and he'd have to keep his eyes and ears alert for stripecats, at least until he was in sight of the coast.

After filling his girba in the stream, he crested the ridge of the next hill before looking for a resting place. Under a spreading magrana, he stopped and removed his backpack. He stripped off his tabard and wrung it out before draping it over the hot stone at his feet. The overhanging branches of the fruit tree afforded shade if he should want it but, for the moment, he needed the sun to dry his skin. He took the meat from his pack, the chunk of sweet, malted bread and the hard leather flagon with the rest of the sour green wine that Porlesah had given him, and ate as he sat on the baking stones. A ripe fruit from the tree completed his meal, its juicy sweet pulp quenching his thirst and leaving a slightly bitter aftertaste.

'Alone? You're slipping, Aklon.'

'Ivdulon. Greetings. You find me relaxing after battling through the inhospitable rainforest. How stands it with you?'

'I knew you were on your way to your small capital town. Porlesah told me. Is she beautiful? She sounds so to my mind.'

'Carnality, Ivdulon?'

'Curiosity. I like to know whether my instincts for such things are accurate.'

'If she seems to you like the sweetest of fruits mingled with mature wine and leaving an aftertaste of honey, you have her.'

'Good. I must see her through your eyes next time you're together'

'Do you see my view as we speak?'

'The hill slopes away from you and I see a faint line on the distant horizon that suggests sea lies beneath sky there. Above you, ah, wide branches of that wonderful tree, the pomegranate. Excellent fruit. Do I taste the flavour lingering in your mouth?'

'You surprise me each time we meet. You can savour all my senses as well as my thoughts?'

'Why else would I detach my mind from yours when you're... with a woman? There are some things that should be shared only with those we touch, don't you think?'

'So, you could indulge in such things if you wished?'

'If I wished. Now, to loftier matters. Porlesah's confirmed that your idiot father has taken the word of that fool, Jhonaht, and has set off for Choshinahm. I wonder what will happen to the High Priest when the people discover his error. And I wonder what'll happen to his offspring?'

'You find me on my way to warn Jodisa, though the exercise will be pointless.'

'She lacks your rebellion and sacrilegious nature, of course.'

'But then, she also lacks my contact with you and your knowledge, Ivdulon.'

'Mmm. I might change that. It could be useful to have her on our side.'

'Are you able to do that?'

'I found Porlesah through you, Aklon. Sometimes I come across folk by accident, sometimes by searching but there are others I can't reach unless I'm introduced to them. Perhaps, Jodisa-Li is one such. I take it her eyes are the same colour as yours and bear the tell-tale gold flecks?'

'So, that is the mark? I did wonder. Do all who bear the flecks have the power?'

'Potentially, I believe, though the gift varies immensely. I've yet to come across anyone with my facility for wide searching. Still, that's a burden I must suffer for the benefit of the knowledge it brings.'

'Burden? I wish I could do as you can, Ivdulon.'

'Only because you've no idea how it can take over your life. If I wasn't selective, I could spend all my days and nights in contact with others. I could spend a half hour with each and not speak to the same person in three wakeful days, Aklon. Would you really want such intrusion into your life? They're not all as sensitive or well-mannered as me. Would you welcome intruders when you lie with your many women?'

'You have a point. But I still envy your variety and scope.'

'Enough idle banter. I came to warn you only to take care. Porlesah gave me information that makes me fear for you. You're too valuable to my scheme to lose. Take special care just now. She tells me Wesdan Kaz is ambitious and without mercy. Be wary of him, Aklon. I'll need you in the future I have planned.'

'I am always wary, Ivdulon. Caution keeps me breathing. But what is this plan you wish to involve me in?'

'You're already involved. When we've overthrown the wicked rule of Gadhallah on your island, I'll take you further into my confidence and let you know the next stage of this war against the evil we share. For now, beware. And I think I should warn you there's a rather large beast a few hundred paces to your left. I'll leave you to deal with that, as you are undoubtedly able.'

The contact broke and Aklon-Dji studied the stripecat Ivdulon had pointed out. It was basking on a rocky outcrop a good distance from him. He dressed slowly, picked up his gear and kept his sword unsheathed as he slipped silently down the slope and out of sight, heading for the coast. When he looked back, the stripecat was no longer sunning itself. He would have to be extra cautious until he reached more open ground and could see all around him.

⚬ ⚬

Okkyntalah slung the water skins over one shoulder, grasped the new spear he'd bought in Chalamamnon, and gazed over the dry, dusty ground. A trail of light dust marked the lumbering progress of the giant mute as he headed for a small, unexpected group of trees poking their heads over the distant ridge. A league and a half to the southeast, they were the only sign of ground water in the desolation. No matter how hard he looked, Okkyntalah could see no other indications of life and he set off towards them at a steady trot.

The sun, climbing now, was already hot on his face and threatened to bake him dry as the earth beneath his feet. Neither shade nor shelter relieved the rocks and scattered thorny bushes of this desert. His quarry had already vanished over the ridge when Okkyntalah ran into a brood of venomous sand snakes. They hissed but slithered off listlessly at his approach. Apart from the wide wings of a troop of buzzards, hunting high for carrion, he saw no signs of animal life. When still half a league from the ridge, he stopped to listen at what he thought was the call of a horn. But there was no repeat. In fact, so silent was it in this desolate place, he could hear his heart beating its regular rhythm.

The slope masked the trees as he approached and he came on the small wood abruptly, as he crested the ridge. For a moment he stood and collected his breath, stilled himself to listen, aware he was likely to be close now to any human habitation there might be in this forsaken place. From the trees, the light rasp of cicadas invaded the silence.

Unmistakable, in the near distance, the sound of children laughing and screaming in play made him smile with pleasure and then grow anxious as the presence of other people was confirmed. He froze at the sudden sound of a woman's anguished cry; silence fell from the children and a man's voice called something unintelligible. A call that seemed like that of an animal, though not one he knew, came from above. But he could see no sign of it in the trees. The short spell of quiet slowly filled again with children at play as if nothing of import had occurred. Nearer, the soft breeze through the copse formed a background to the songs of tree-dwelling birds. And, there it was, the sound of water tumbling over rocks a short distance away.

Cooking smells filtered through the soft brown dampness of the wood, bringing moisture to his dry mouth.

Cautious; every tale since childhood priming him to expect great danger and cruelty at the hands of the rejects, criminals, renegades and savages who'd been banished to The Point, he crept forward. Deep shadow lay beneath the lush bright-green canopy of trees whose roots lay in well-watered ground. He half crouched, half walked to the wood, ears, eyes, nose and feet alert to danger. There were footprints in the earth here: some, the small feet of children, others the soles of men and women and, amongst them, the unmistakeable prints of the giant.

The sickly sweet, almost overpowering scent of tshu-tshu filled his nostrils as he entered the shade beneath the solid cover of the trees, its trailing blue flowers decking the trunks it climbed. Behind and underneath the scent another aroma, uncomfortably familiar yet unidentified, made him cautious, anxious.

Glad to be out of the baking sun, he rested his back against a broad, black trunk to allow his eyes to grow accustomed to the shade.

Nothing moved in the trees nearby and only cicadas sang; the birds now silent.

The very stillness warned him he was not alone. As his sight adapted to the gloom, he saw a small clearing to his left. Little grew on the dark damp floor of the wood and only beetles and ants moved amongst small patches of bright sunlight that speckled the ground as he stepped into the space.

He stifled the forming cry before it reached his lips and turned away from the horror until he could be sure of facing it again without voicing fear and revulsion. What was left of the body, pierced by the pole, was so distorted by the agony of death it was impossible to know whether man or woman had ended life amid flame and blade and lash. The mask of pain still clung to the skull. The mouth wide in a scream without end. Smashed teeth, stark with coagulated blood. The left eye was gone. Its socket writhing with worms. But the lidless one survived to stare blind hate at any who dared live in its presence.

Okkyntalah backed out of the clearing and circled the gloom with growing dread. All outside sound seemed to have ceased and he heard only his own breathing, the snap of small, dead branches beneath his feet, the gentle rasp of his tabard against his thighs as he walked.

The sound of water was below and right. He wondered what had urged him to the site of that too recent punishment sacrifice. Alert and cautious, he moved down the slope through trees to a ribbon of silver that sparkled below in dappled shade and sunlight.

Still no one challenged him. He followed the flow upstream to a small pool, where water gurgled and splashed gently from blood red rocks into a shallow natural basin of blue-black obsidian. He knelt and filled the first skin, stopping it securely with the cork bung and cross strings. Only then did he drink from the pool, cupping his hands and draining them until the cool, clear water quenched his thirst. Dripping from face and hands, he filled the other two skins, re-attached leather harness and hoisted all three onto his shoulders. He plunged his hands again into water and sluiced his head, face and arms with clear, cool liquid before he rose to his feet again. The journey back would be slower with the added weight but it was barely noon; plenty of time before sundown.

The giant was standing above him on the bank when he turned, holding Okkyntalah's spear in his hand: he'd heard nothing of the man's approach. Beside him stood a small bony man, also unmanned, carrying a battered unsheathed sword. The young hunter considered the knife at his belt and the weight of the skins on his back. Flight was impossible. When the big man nodded toward the lower edge of the wood, Okkyntalah moved as directed.

Chapter 11

LIFE AND DEATH ON THE POINT

All the rumours, and the stories told by lay preachers like Aglydron, said the people of The Point lived and died, but mostly died, as savages; without rule or purpose. They were wild, uncouth, ignorant and brutal; possibly cannibals. Here dwelt those whom Ytraa had rejected, punished or condemned, and those unforgiveable ones who'd deliberately turned their backs on Ytraa.

The small village, under the eaves of the wood, spread out bright and colourful with painted mud brick walls and windows shuttered with blinds of woven leaves. Not a plain surface in sight. Everywhere was decoration. Animals, flowers, men, women, children, active and at rest, playing, working, sporting, loving, living, dying. He was so entranced he stopped without warning and the bony man walked into him.

'Sorry, young man.' The voice was cultured, the tones well-modulated.

Okkyntalah turned and nodded his acknowledgement. 'My fault.'

The bony man pointed his sword to the gap between two of the dwellings. Okkyntalah moved along a narrow footway paved with crude slabs of stone, beneath which water flowed, carrying waste, if smell was a guide. At the far end, a wide square opened, planted with trees shading rough benches. Every seat was crowded: the people all sizes but uniformly thin, and every shade of brown, from Jodisa-Li's pale honey colour, through his own olive, to a shade so close to black it was almost indistinguishable from the deepest shadows. There were many of these dark people and none was scarred or painted. He'd heard talk of island people with such black skins but he'd put it with the tales used to frighten naughty children. Yet, here they were.

He found himself unable to look away from the people, talking in quiet tones and glancing at him with interest rather than staring in open curiosity. Children were generally naked of course, but here, no shred of clothing concealed adults. Such display shocked him, for they weren't at prayer. Many bore designs of various types in bright colours, painted on their bodies. And many carried hideous scars inflicted by the Holy Ones; slashed breasts, castrations, brutally gashed mouths. Okkyntalah looked on the victims of the God he worshipped and wondered how a loving deity could permit such things.

'We've few flies in our village, young man, but you'll find them if you keep your mouth open.'

Okkyntalah blushed at the man's reminder of his obvious shock and closed his mouth. The gathered people stilled as the small party made their way across the square. A small girl limped across, deformed feet making her movement ungainly. She tugged at his tabard, a puzzled frown marring a pretty face. He bent and tousled her curly hair and she smiled at him. He watched her respond to a call and make her way back to a small group of youngsters, many of whom were deformed in one way or another. Amongst them was a young man of about his own age, who seemed vaguely familiar. Okkyntalah stared at him but the boy made no attempt to engage with him. It was only as he turned away again, that Okkyntalah remembered him as a boy he'd played with until he'd disappeared shortly after losing his sight. This, then, was one of the rumoured Defectives abandoned at the foot of the Scar by parents unable to accept imperfection. He had no time to speculate, however. The bony man had brought him to where, side by side in rough, wooden chairs, sat a man and woman.

She spoke in a voice of absolute authority tinged with humour. 'We, who are denied by Ytraa, have no need to adhere to Ytraa's rules. We feel no shame about bodies gifted us by our Creator.'

Okkyntalah found so much around him at odds with the tales he'd heard. With no guidance but manners he'd learned from parents and priest, he dropped to one knee with his head bent and the palms of his hands held forward at shoulder height.

'Forgive me, I intend no insult.'

'You do well, but stand. You have a name?'

He stood and kept his eyes on her face. 'I am Okkyntalah and hail from Morstahn.'

'Well, Okkyntalah of Morstahn, you speak with Chellyth of Mhalinhum.' She gave a wry smile as she pronounced the place name and Okkyntalah felt mockery somewhere, if only he could find it. 'Por-Kildu is, with me, The One.' She nodded at the man beside her. Okkyntalah nodded his greeting and took revulsion from his face before it fully formed. He'd never seen a man so scarred.

'Yes, the beauty you find in me is a fitting prize for the marks of torture he bears. You may look, Okkyntalah of Morstahn. Allow your eyes to travel where revolted curiosity and natural lust direct. We are honest here.'

Okkyntalah nodded. Politeness and custom drove him to respect what he believed were the wishes of his captors. He allowed his eyes to stray first to the man and his multiple scars that disfigured body and face, and discovered he felt more pity than revulsion. Instinct warned him against showing that it and he merely nodded at the man. He, in turn, stared back at Okkyntalah through eyes that seemed to penetrate his very soul. He released him with a swift glance at his lady and Okkyntalah felt relieved to be free of that scrutiny. But it was both difficult and fascinating to look where Ytraa and

Chellyth's partner alone should look. A band of leather, a thumbswidth deep, passed beneath, and was partly concealed by, her breasts. And she was decorated with patterns of orange, yellow and vermillion, suggesting flames that seemed to live as she breathed in and out.

'What causes you to invite most painful death by trespass here?'

He looked into her dark orbs. 'My companion and I are on urgent business to the mainland but our waterskins were breached. I came to fill them; nothing more.'

Chellyth leant across and whispered in Por-Kildu's ear. The man nodded and seemed to smile at her. 'Because you know us not, I give you a second chance. The truth, Okkyntalah of Morstahn. Truth in Mhalinhum is neither partial nor distorted. Tell all why you are here.'

Okkyntalah glanced about him at her gesture. Every eye was on him from the benches under the shade of the trees. Even the few children were silent, waiting. Chellyth's face was blank when he returned to seek a clue from her. Por-Kildu looked right through him. He could describe the reason for his plight or tell a tale. He chose the whole truth.

Mention of Dagla Kaz brought gasps from some and a flicker of anger and hatred in Por-Kildu's eyes. Jodisa-Li's name caused a stir and murmured approval as he explained the reasons for her kidnap and their planned journey.

Chellyth consulted with Por-Kildu and called the giant to them. Much seemed to be explained by signs and facial expressions from the big man.

'You speak with the voice of a minstrel, Okkyntalah. Do you sing?'

Okkyntalah shrugged, feeling again the weight of the full girbas that still rested on his shoulders.

'Show me.'

He hesitated, feeling exposed and uncertain in this crowd of strangers.

Por-Kildu addressed him for the first time. 'Chellyth will be obeyed.' His voice was deep and powerful; laced with menace.

Okkyntalah sought a song that wouldn't offend and might amuse. He began the newly popular Round of Wine, singing clearly and proudly of the harvest of green grapes and expecting them to join him in the raucous chorus.

'Enough. Your voice is good, Okkyntalah, but your choice offends. We lack grapes.'

He bowed. 'I didn't know. I apologise.'

Chellyth gave a curt nod and beckoned the bony man. 'The boys that have been born?'

'They live, Wise One.'

'Have the mother bring them.' She turned again to him. 'A test of your true mettle, Okkyntalah.'

The bony man bowed and ran to one side of the square where he stopped before a dwelling and struck the wall four times with the hilt of his sword. All the women rose to their feet and spread their arms wide, tipped their heads back and ululated with such sorrow that Okkyntalah felt tears start in his eyes. Por-Kildu beckoned him.

Up close, the scarring was hideous and terrifying, as if the skin had melted and been sliced and left to heal unaided.

'When Chellyth bids you act, hesitate and your death will be more agonising than that in the punishment grove. Do as you're bid, at once, or spend a portion in agony before you're granted a death you'll crave.'

His tone of voice, choice of words, and the explicit threat made Okkyntalah dread the coming ordeal. The women's ululation had become a keening of such despair that he wanted only to stop his ears and flee. From behind him, the giant grasped his arm and urged him to the centre of the square.

The weeping mother, milk still wet on dark breasts that had fed the infants, carried her new-born sons and presented them to Okkyntalah as she knelt before him. For a moment, he was torn between the traditional greeting to a nursing mother and the requirement to receive the babes. He took the gurgling infants in his arms and held them, fearful of what was to come. All sound halted abruptly and he saw that Chellyth had moved to stand a short distance behind the mother, where she held her hand up high. She nodded at him and he turned to find three men a short distance behind him with swords drawn.

The mother, on her knees, looked up into his face with such pleading that his heart turned over with fear at what they might ask of him.

'What am I to do?'

Chellyth lowered her arm and stepped closer. The giant had withdrawn to one side. The men with swords menaced his back.

'We have too many men. We have too little food. We have no cotton for cloth, no ores to make metal, no escape from this, our prison. Our ways are hard but just. Our ways are not soft and easy like Muhnilahm with its pastures and its mines, its fishing and its silkworms. We are here with nothing. Dry stones we till for food. The sea is denied us, but that your arrival brings welcome news of a way that might take us down to catch fish. For that, I thank you. Silent Giant tells me we may reach the water at the foot of the cliff you climbed?'

'Yes. We found it by accident. It's not easy but you can climb up and down. The small beach leads to the sea, through the cave.'

'That is good news indeed. But nothing is ever by accident.'

To his utter astonishment, she stepped up and kissed him on both cheeks. 'I thank you, Okkyntalah.'

She stepped back and continued. 'The few swords we win, we preserve and keep sharp until the blades grow thin and fail. On the whole of The Point this is the one place with water. Near starvation threatens the life of a mother who must raise more than one infant at a time. We do what we must. Judge us not, Okkyntalah of Morstahn, for the priests and Holy Ones of Ytraa leave us without choice.'

'One infant must die.'

She bowed her head with the burden of her decision and returned to her place a couple of paces behind the mother, but would not leave the scene of the coming murder.

Por-Kildu stood a little apart, so that she stood alone. He glanced at the mother and then at Okkyntalah.

Okkyntalah recalled Por-Kildu's words and laid the babes in the dust at their mother's knees. He knew what was required and was both disgusted and torn by the need. Bending, he selected the bigger of the two boys and handed him to the mother, who took him eagerly but remained crouched and weeping. The smaller he left on the ground, still gurgling and content after his recent feed.

He took his knife from its sheath and placed the honed cutting edge against the skin of his arm as if to test the blade. 'It's a poor piece, with no proper edge. I would do the deed swiftly and without unnecessary pain.'

He sheathed the knife and approached the men with swords, his hand outstretched. Chellyth nodded as the men made questions. Okkyntalah touched each blade in turn, feeling for the sharpest. He nodded and took the sword he chose.

With heavy heart, praying that Ytraa would guide him, he approached the mother and her baby. 'Let the child be moved away. I would not harm the mother and the other child.' He hoped the tremor in his voice didn't betray him.

Raising the sword high over his head, he braced his legs in preparation for the downward slash. As the mother bent low to move her child forward, Okkyntalah leapt across her and grabbed Chellyth, clasping her to his body. At his back, the water skins overbalanced him so that he had to lean on her to prevent himself falling over. He held the blade against her throat.

'Move; now! Or I'll cut your throat.'

'You'll never leave alive.'

'You'll die with me.'

She moved forward awkwardly as he urged her from the square, the people poised to rush him at the first sign of weakness.

'Chellyth dies if anyone follows.'

Por-Kildu signalled silence as uproar broke out. He took Okkyntalah's spear from the giant's hand and raised it in threat. Okkyntalah let the sword draw blood at Chellyth's neck to trickle and drip into the dust at their feet. Por-Kildu threw the spear hard and fast, at the ground before the mother's knees. Blood pooled on silent land. The people raised their voices in lament for the dead infant but made no move toward the retreating pair.

Okkyntalah gritted his teeth at the abomination and urged Chellyth roughly from the village. Through the trees, he glanced over his shoulder to check that no one followed too closely. A man dropped from the trees, landing close to Okkyntalah and threatening him.

'Stay your hand unless you'd lose The One.'

The man bowed at Chellyth's silent nod and let them pass unharmed.

All across the plain, he held her wrist with one hand as he dragged her, protesting, toward the distant cliffs. Men and women followed at a distance, armed and menacing but unwilling to risk her life. For all that his pace was slower than his outward journey, his heart pounded at twice the speed.

At the cliff, he approached the edge until he located the boat, some two hundred paces to the south. He urged the woman before him.

'I'll kill you as you go down.' She promised.

'You won't.'

He reached the place where he could descend the natural staircase. 'I'm sorry. I must do this.' He forced her to the ground on her face and sought those who followed. Still three hundred paces distant, they were moving forward. 'Forgive me, Chellyth, I have no choice.'

'No more have I.'

Sticking the sword into the ground beside her throat, he untied the bow fastening the band of leather and sliced it in two with the fine, honed blade of his hunting knife. He tied her wrists behind her, bound her ankles and pulled her to lie on her face with her head and shoulders overhanging the edge of the cliff. 'Struggle and you'll fall to your death.'

He called to those waiting to capture him as soon as he moved away from her. 'I have The One bound with a rope around her neck. If you approach the cliff before I'm gone, I'll pull her to her death. Turn now, and move back or I'll cut her flesh.' He knelt beside her with his knife in the space between her shoulders. The people turned and slowly backed away. At once, Okkyntalah began his descent of the cliff. He was no more than three manheights down when she began to scream.

'Kill the boy!'

The water skins made the going difficult but he reached the foot of the cliff before the first hunter appeared above to pull his leader to safety. More followed and some threw rocks and wooden spears as others started down the cliff in pursuit. Okkyntalah sped into the cave and through to the beach as fast as he could.

'Ready, Aglydron. They're on my heels!'

He dashed across the pebbles and waded into the water. Aglydron began to raise the anchor and Jodisa-Li slipped free of the noose.

'Aglydron, the girl!'

Okkyntalah was waist deep as he shouted his warning. The first of the hunters emerged from the cave. Aglydron grabbed the girl's arms. He forced her to the bottom of the boat, one foot in her back, as he hauled on the anchor rope. Okkyntalah struggled on through water up to his shoulders.

'Jodisa, they'll rape and kill you. They hate you and your father.'

His warning interrupted her struggles with Aglydron long enough for him to raise the anchor and unship the oars. From the shore, the hunters, now joined by Chellyth, aimed their spears at the boat and at Okkyntalah. One, Okkyntalah's own, thrown by the giant, barely missed Jodisa-Li and lodged in the bottom of the boat. Another sliced a girba, releasing its weight of water and aiding Okkyntalah's escape. A third grazed Aglydron's head and stuck fast in the wood of the mast. He pulled it free and threw it, more in anger than hope, at the men on the shore, finding a target. Okkyntalah swam the last strokes to the boat. Aglydron took the water skins and helped him in.

Aglydron's lucky hit had caused them to stop throwing their spears. They picked up the wounded man and carried him between them, waiting at the edge of the surf. Chellyth remained in the water, up to her thighs.

'Return to The Point, Okkyntalah of Morstahn, and I will kill you with my own hands, slowly and painfully.' She remained in the sea, watching their escape for a long time.

But, safe in the boat, and sailing away, Okkyntalah had no reason to believe he'd ever return, and treated her threat with scorn and a gesture of rude dismissal. He soon forgot her warning, for the clear blue sky was clouded ahead. Already, the wind splashed waves over the bows. Neither he nor Aglydron had sailed alone and they must now travel toward that towering anvil cloud, bright as sun-bleached cotton above, dark with storm below.

※

Aglydron pondered the far horizon, where the storm already raged, and prayed that Ytraa would help them through. Jodisa-Li had tended his small head wound, washing away the blood and patting at the cut with a gentle pad made from one of her plain tabards. She'd been silent since their escape and he wondered what she thought now that the island was far behind them. But he had more urgent concerns. Choppy waves, churned up by freshening winds, were confused by the deeper swell from violent distant gales. Already, they shipped water when the bows broke the crests. A wave, topped with flying white foam, poured over the side of the boat as they broached to in the changing winds.

'Bail! Bail both of you, or we're nazzakk food.' Aglydron's shouted order had the girl plunging into the slopping brine with her wooden bowl to throw out the water.

Everything was wet. And, despite the warm climes, the fierce wind cooled their wet skin. The rain hadn't yet started.

'We'll drown. You're going to kill us, you fool!'

'Save your breath to bail, girl. Ytraa will protect us. This is a test of our faith. Bail, girl; bail!'

Okkyntalah worked silently and swiftly with the canvass bucket he'd emptied of fisherman's tackle. He fell sideways as an errant gust tugged at the slack sail and tilted the boat at a crazy angle.

'I'll drop the sail before it upends us.'

'No! You'll lose control if you...'

'Do the job I've set, girl. I lead here.'

Another gust shook the mast and flapped the loose, slanted sail as it drove the boat in the opposite direction. Aglydron gazed at the sea, seeking guidance. He left the tiller and reached for the halyard that held the sail aloft. He'd tied it with a landsman's knot, and water and motion, tightening it, had made it impossible to untie. The girl knew nothing. The boat was shipping more water because the sail was making them pitch uncontrollably in the fitful wind. He must get it down at once. Unsheathing his hunting knife, he attacked the knot.

'Fool! If you lower the sail, you'll have no control over the boat and...'

'Quiet! What does a pampered girl know of the sea?' Aglydron parted the rope.

The heavy wooden yardarm, released from the halyard, crashed down the mast, its lower end smashing into the boom and sending it flying forward. Okkyntalah and Jodisa-Li escaped serious injury only by diving flat into the bottom of the craft. But the boy took a hard blow to his shoulder and the girl scraped her elbow as she ducked out of the way.

They had no time to complain or protest. The boat swung wildly against a steep wave and shuddered upward until it seemed almost vertical. Stores and equipment slid noisily down the floor of the boat, to crash into the stern as Aglydron tried to furl the sail.

The three of them clung on with their hands. Shaulah could find no purchase for her claws. She fell from the bows down the length of the boat toward Aglydron. For an instant, he was uncertain whether to regain the tiller and try to restore control or catch the dog before she fell irretrievably into the boiling waters. It had been his idea to bring her along so she could recognise Tumalind's scent and help lead them to her. He reached out. Caught the dog by the scruff of her neck, as the boat began to drop back to the horizontal. She yelped at the sudden tug on her pelt and he dumped her into the bottom of the boat before he set about rolling the flapping sail atop the spar.

The water in the hull had flushed some of their precious supplies out of the stern before the craft righted itself again. There was a brief spell of comparative calm and all three desperately tried to secure everything in readiness for the next upset. Aglydron, finished with the sail, grabbed the tiller and fought to turn the boat into the waves so that it met them with the bows rather than side on. But they were making no way now, from either sail or currents, and he was hard pressed to alter course in any useful way. His efforts made a small difference, however, and they managed to avoid shipping more water from the larger seas. The smaller waves continued to splash enough water into the craft to keep Okkyntalah and Jodisa-Li busy.

As the storm grew, so night fell, and with it, the rain. At first, it was a torrent. Later, it came down with such force that it calmed the sea and, instead of bailing seawater, they scooped rain from the boat in a desperate effort to keep afloat.

In darkness relieved only by the phosphorescent glow that ghosted the waves, Aglydron joined them as they bailed until their arms, backs and knees grew numb. The night surrounded them with hopelessness. It took away all sense of direction and time. Drained them of all but their will to survive.

Aglydron dreamed waking dreams as his arms moved mechanically to shift water from the boat. Dreams of sunlit dry land. Dreams of days of quiet joy in silent countryside. Dreams of gentle hills and pastures full of blooms.

The black night and the rain had no end. They bailed. They moved in silent rhythms dictated by their places in the boat and the nature of their bailers. Aglydron lost all sense of time. Place had no meaning. The three of them were tools in the hands of a harsh God. Ytraa had set them to move water forever. Why? Ytraa was punishing them with an impossible task. A task without end. A task without hope. Until death should take them.

Chapter 12

AFTER THE STORM

*T*he ship continued to lurch, though the rain stopped in the early hours when the wind died to a mere gale. Tumalind risked opening the door again and found the eastern horizon aglow with crimson, purple and gold. Shimmering between dark ragged edges of cloud and chopped lines of gold crested waves, it promised a fine day. Emerging from the wet and dark, the girls stepped onto a deck patched with soaked shadow and oblique skylight.

Corphanda dashed over to check on them. 'How'd you come by that, lass?'

Porryh put her hand to her bruised eye and glanced at Tumalind. She muttered something to Corphanda but Tumalind heard only 'bumped' and 'dark'.

Corphanda looked from one to the other but nodded. 'Ay. Well, if that's the worst the storm gave you, you've done well enough. Come on; get your clothes and your paillasses out on deck, let sun and wind dry 'em. There'll be food when you're done. I'm away to see if yon lad needs a splint or a shroud.'

They followed her nod to the shattered forward mast where it had broken. It was lying across the deck, protruding over the side, and a crewman lay trapped and unmoving amongst the tangle of ropes beneath.

The men were trying to raise it enough to pull him free, but the weight of canvas and rigging hampered them and they had to cut sails and ropes away first. At last, they were in a position to use bars and hoists to lift the great length of timber. The injured man was silent and still. Tarruss put his huge shoulders to the mast and added lift that allowed Baklan to drag the sailor free.

Corphanda dropped to her knees by his head and examined him. She rose, shaking her head, blood dripping from both hands. Tumalind watched the sailors shroud their comrade in sailcloth and take him aft.

Under the gaze of the passengers, the crew bound both ends of the shroud with stout rope, enclosing lumps of dark stone from the bilges into the package to help the body sink. They lowered it over the stern of the ship to drop into the quieting sea, where it sank quickly out of sight in the clear blue-green water.

Baklan stood at the bowsprit and watched. 'Jeklyzhon was a good sailor, a brave man and a loyal friend. We mourn his loss. Tryhnn, take our companion and care for his soul, if you will. He alone of our company failed to come through the tempest Taniwha sent. Our proud Nupraxyss has also suffered. But good seamanship, fortune, a well-built vessel and your kindness, Tryhnn, have spared the rest of us.

'Farewell, good Jeklyzhon. May Tryhnn keep your mortal soul safe.

'Taniwha, you got one more merman, but the rest escaped your clutches, this time. Be content with that.'

It was all the master said and the crew returned to their duties, cutting free the broken mast so it could be laid along the deck until they could replace or repair it. When they had rigged the sails on the remaining mast, the ship slipped through the water again and its movement became less erratic.

Dagla Kaz called a meeting later in the day. They stood with their backs to warm wooden railings, or sat on the dry deck and felt hot sun dry salt onto their clothes and skin.

'We were to travel directly to Kamakq, a town straddling a narrow band of land between the Shylnah Sea and Ka'la Bay in the great Southern Ocean. But we must now put into a port in Niphralon to effect repairs. Some of you may know Rhonholoah has a certain, shall we say, fierce quality? Baklan assures me that, provided we don't excite the local people, we'll be safe. There is, however, something you all need to know.'

Dagla Kaz paused and stared at the ends of his fingers, as if unsure how to impart his next piece of information. Tumalind wondered what bad news was to come.

'The inhabitants of Niphralon are not Followers. Indeed, Baklan, who's travelled extensively, knows only their customs. Their religious practices they keep secret. They will, however, think our women's tabards scandalous and an invitation to join with them, even the Virgin Gifts. Women in that city must be covered from head to ankle, including their face and hands. Only their feet may show.'

'But our tabards allow us to be always ready for worship, Dagla Kaz. Full covering must surely insult Ytraa.'

'A valid point, Tumalind, but they'll consider any woman contravening their rules available. Odd and arbitrary, I know, but we have no choice. We'll be visitors in a strange land and we must conform to their rules. I'm sorry, but I see no alternative. The men, apparently, go naked above the waist but covered to the ankles, and armed. Carrying weapons indicates manhood; their lack, weakness. It'll be difficult, but Baklan assures me it's the only way to prevent trouble, if we're to venture off the ship.'

He looked around. 'The men and women in Rhonholoah live in separate halves of the same building. Each house has two blocks facing one another across a walled square, divided to keep the sexes apart. Baklan thinks the walled areas aren't considered public and women shed their cowls within. I don't like it; it's peculiar and illogical and there may be a risk...'

'If we'll only be safe in public when covered from head to foot, I'd be happy to risk taking it off amongst other women. It'd relieve the intolerable heat of such garments.'

'I agree, Wendarah; my concern was about how the men of the country...well it's totally nonsensical, if you ask me. But such is the way with foreigners, I suppose. I'm really more concerned for our Virgin Gifts. I hope and pray no harm befalls any of you because of these strange customs.'

'Suppose a Virgin Gift falls foul of this rule and someone has a go at 'er, Dagla Kaz, what then for the pilgrimage?'

The High Priest was silent, considering his answer. 'It's an absolute and inviolable condition of the pilgrimage that the Virgin Gifts remain intact, Tarruss. Guardianship of their chastity is a test of our determination to protect the Chosen of Ytraa on their journey. We must ensure we keep them...safe, at all times. Our choice here now lies between temporary shame for our party, or eternal burning of Ytraa's Skyfire for all; I see no option.'

'So, we're not just robbed of our loved ones and taken to foreign lands to be left with barbarians, but we're forced to hide from Ytraa and bake in their streets. Why can't we just stay on board whilst the mast's repaired, Dagla Kaz?'

Before he could reply to Tumalind's question, Porryh spoke her mind.

'If all I've got to look forward to is danger and a life with strangers, I might just go out there like this and let the foreign bowelcreeps frowk me. If I'm not virgin, there'll be no point taking me to Choshinahm, will there?'

Dagla Kaz controlled his temper and glanced at Corphanda. Seeing his struggle, she dragged Porryh to her feet from the deck with her hair and slapped her bottom hard. 'Wicked girl.'

Tumalind was shocked to receive similar treatment.

'I'm surprised at you, Tumalind; thought as you'd know better.'

The High Priest held up his hand to stop the matching smacks she was about to inflict.

'Tumalind, I understand your concerns and your request is justified. Unfortunately, the ship's unsafe whilst under repair; Baklan says the shipwrights are the worst of the lot and will see all women aboard fair game, regardless of their wishes. I'm sorry, but we've no choice. Even I can't overrule the customs and beliefs of foreign lands, no matter how ridiculous they are. And you won't be alone; Wendarah and Corphanda will have to do the same.

'As for your suggestion Porryh, let me make it absolutely clear. It rests with all of us to protect your chastity and we'll do whatever we must to ensure it. Should any of you, however, place yourselves in danger of violation, Caarl will show you the meaning of pain. And, should a Virgin Gift actually be ruined through her own fault, I will personally put her to death by the most painful and lengthy means I can devise. Do you understand?'

Porryh paled and nodded.

Corphanda put her arm about Tumalind. 'Sorry; seems I was hasty. Have that one in hand agin the next time.' She turned to Porryh. 'As for you, young miss, be glad the High Priest saved you from a second and a third. Such badness! I can make your bum so sore you'll not sit for a week, you know. So, just watch your step.'

Porryh lifted her hem, attempting to see the mark. The sailors took advantage but she made no effort to hide herself until Corphanda's expression made it wise to do so.

Tumalind rubbed tingling skin through her tabard as she made her way to the bows to look for signs of land, wondering what other degradation and trials this pilgrimage had in store.

Just as Aglydron reached the place where he knew they would spend eternity moving water to no end and they should give in and let the sea take them, the clouds cleared to the southwest and the sky brightened. The sun emerged into a bright blue patch and a great bow of colour arched over the quieting waves, rising from the water and curving across the sky to dive back into the sea. He gazed on this sign of a new beginning and wondered what good news it might presage. The rain stopped as abruptly as it had begun and the rainbow slowly faded.

Only then, exhausted but preparing from lifetime habit for prayer, did he recall they hadn't prayed at sunset.

'Ytraa was displeased with us. That's why Ytraa sent the storm. Nothing must interfere with prayer again. We've had our warning. Ytraa spared us this time. Next time we might not be so blessed.'

Jodisa-Li gazed, incredulous. 'The storm was on us by evening prayer.'

'It wasn't raining until after dark. If we'd prayed, we might've been spared.'

She shook her head but said no more and made her token obeisance. Aglydron and Okkyntalah, stretching with difficulty, spent more time with their devotions and, by the time they'd done, the girl was ready to face the day.

All three were exhausted after their frantic night. Nevertheless, Aglydron made them remove the remaining water. They each took a drink from one of the skins and breakfasted on some fruit that had survived, though it was contaminated by salt. Shaulah made do with a small flying fish that had fallen into the boat.

The sea, calm now but for the long, regular swell of the retreating storm, lulled their exhausted bodies into drowsiness as the rising sun heated and dried them. Aglydron struggled to stay awake as the other two fell into the sleep of the spent; the boat drifting with the current and a warm steady wind toward a point Aglydron could only hope was their chosen destination. Darkness and cloud had robbed them of any sense of direction and they might be sailing anywhere but that the sun told him they were heading more or less the right way. How far off his intended course they were, he had no way of knowing.

※

Jodisa-Li woke to hot sun baking her salted skin. She sought shade she couldn't find. With the sail still loosely curled where Aglydron had tied it, there was nothing to protect them from the midday sun. The men were fools. She thought to wake Okkyntalah, lying at her feet, to help her. But she wanted no arguments, no fights about what must be done. Her father had seen that she was versed in many skills and she knew how to survive, even if these ignorant landsmen didn't.

The few clothes they'd brought for her were soaking still. She wanted something soft and dry to wear against skin irritated by the stiffness of the tabard she'd worn through the storm. She surveyed the bottom of the boat and the remains of their supplies and goods. A long drink quenched her but she resisted the temptation to use any of their precious supply to refresh her skin. There was no way of knowing how long it would be before they could collect more fresh water, though the storm had provided plenty. To her surprise, someone had apparently had the presence of mind to funnel rain into the partially used girba and filled it to the top. She guessed that was Okkyntalah and allowed a small point in his favour.

From the bundle of hide-wrapped food, she took a couple of plantains and a mango. They were wet and tainted. It was little enough but it satisfied her immediate hunger. She could've eaten more and deprived her captors of food. But Aglydron would as soon beat her as look at her.

He murmured when she slipped an oar from between the sleeping men but he didn't wake. She lashed it upright to the bows with some of the finer cord. Cutting more of the same twine with Okkyntalah's hunting knife, she made a line between the top of the oar and the mast. Briefly, she was aware she could kill them as they slept, but she knew she couldn't handle the boat alone back to their island. Her wet tabards and sleepsack she draped over the line for sun and wind to dry. Still the men slept, though Shaulah woke, stretched, and watched her.

All around the horizon was only sea and sky, with a vague suggestion of darkness in the direction the storm had vanished. Jodisa-Li considered the night they'd sailed through and decided she'd stand more chance of living through as captive of these fools if she helped rather than hindered their progress. Their stated intention was to find her father and, if they caught up, she'd have him to protect her. He'd have them put to death most painfully; a punishment she'd enjoy. Then she'd go with the pilgrims on a trip she couldn't otherwise have undertaken. On balance it seemed more sensible to ensure the success of the early part of their misguided mission. She clearly couldn't escape the men now; especially since she had no idea where they were.

She crept to the mast and examined the remains of the halyard that had held the yardarm and sail in place until that fool had cut it. Coils of rope, cord and twine lay amongst the fishing gear in the bottom of the boat. She found a length of the right thickness and, using the marlin spike that Okkyntalah had replaced in the canvas bucket, set about splicing the new length to the cut halyard so that she could hoist the sail again.

By the time Okkyntalah awoke, she was at the tiller, in a dry tabard of emerald silk with silver fastenings, her hair tied back in a practical tail. The sail was back in place, trimmed and full of a breeze that skimmed the craft across the waves.

'The sail will give us shade and we'll be able to steer a course of sorts.'

'You managed that on your own?'

'I manage a lot, boy. And I know better than you and that fool how to sail.'

'What can you know? A girl who's lived in luxury and ease all her life.'

'I know you aren't sailors, not even fishermen. I know enough to raise the sail that Aglydron so stupidly struck last night, almost sinking us. I know enough to give the boat speed so it can be steered instead of drifting helplessly. Aglydron says Ytraa kept us afloat last night. I tell you, boy, it was either Ytraa or supreme good luck. It certainly wasn't anything your foolish companion did. I've sailed. I've some skill that might yet save our lives when we reach the reefs between us and the island of Ylcrat. Though why you want to go to that godforsaken place I can't imagine. It's the haunt of evil people who eat each other and are partial to the fresh meat of strangers. Still, why should I care? I'm dead whichever way I look at it. If I don't drown, I'll die of starvation. I might just as well be eaten, I suppose.'

'Ylcrat's just a stopping off place for fresh food and water. We're not staying. And Aglydron says the tales of cannibals are rumours. D'you really know about boats, Jodisa?'

'Jodisa-Li to you, boy.'

'We've been through all this, Jodisa. Your title's meaningless now.'

She gritted her teeth and put his lack of respect with the other faults and crimes to be punished when they found Dagla Kaz.

'Father had me spend time with a master fisherman. He believes the High Priest Elect should have many skills.'

Okkyntalah examined her splice in the rope. 'Impressive. I'm a hunter. Aglydron's a farmer with oxen, hogs and goats and a fine grove of olive trees but he's a teacher too; shows the children their letters and helps them master the lessons. He's only been in a boat once before. My father's a fisherman but I didn't want go to sea. Mother always frets when he's away and she wanted me to work on shore. I've been out with him a few times, but I know only basic things. I was to learn more, once Tumalind and I were betrothed, so I could...'

'Tumalind. What's she like, this girl you're risking our lives for?'

'Tumalind is modest and pure, untouched and truly virginal...'

'And you think I'm not?'

'That tabard says all that's different between you and Tumalind.'

Jodisa-Li looked down, expecting to discover some unseemly exposure or display but found none. 'I wear what's expected of my rank and status. Do you object to the length of my garment? It's acceptable to others. Does the fabric offend you; the colour? I like silk against my skin and this green suits me well. Perhaps you think the neckline impure, revealing too much? I enjoy the freedom of the deep diamond cut. My father encouraged me to display the quality of the workmanship in my flowers.'

As she knew he would, the boy gazed at her tattoos. It was clear she could use her wiles to get the young oaf on her side. Defeating the older fool would then be easier.

⋯

Okkyntalah studied her as she protested her innocence of a crime he hadn't suggested. She was right; the garment suited her very well indeed.

'I meant no criticism, Jodisa, just that it shows the difference between you and Tumalind. Her hem's a little longer. Her fabric's linen; the ties, four instead of three and of kid, with wooden pegs. She chooses the smaller V-neck so her tattoo is unseen; it's nowhere near as fine as yours, of course. And her colour's invariably grey, to set against her copper hair. She suits her style as much as you suit yours, but she's less displayed, more covered, that's all.'

'Is she tall or short, fat or thin, this paragon? Do her teeth shine? Describe her to me, this cause of my discomfort and abduction.'

'She didn't cause your plight, Jodisa, your father did.'

'So you say. I don't accept that. I don't believe you.'

'Ytraa will show you, when we catch up with Dagla Kaz.'

'Perhaps. Is she beautiful? I hope so. I'd hate to be abducted for a frump.'

'Tumalind's as beautiful as you, Jodisa-Li. Very similar in many ways, but different. Her hair's glossy like yours but its colour is more like burnished copper. Her eyes are wide and bright, like yours and, by Ytraa's holy cleft! Sorry, I've just realized, your eyes are exactly the same colour as hers; like that precious stone...I can't recall the name...'

'Lapis lazuli, my father says.'

'That's it, even down to those amazing gold flecks. You're a thumbslength taller than Tumalind but I doubt there's a feather's weight between you. And her skin's a slightly deeper shade. Her feet and hands are small, again, like yours. She's serious but she laughs as well. Clever, but silent until she has something sensible to say. I've loved her since the time of proving and I intend to have her back.'

'Sounds too good for you, boy. In fact, she is too good for you. But I agree with your description; you've a good eye for the details so many men miss. You forgot to mention the paradise bird that pecks where you'd like to enter. And you never mentioned what a good swimmer she is. Yes, she's a beautiful and intelligent girl; I wonder what she sees in you.'

Okkyntalah gaped at her.

'You'd catch flies, were any to be had.'

'You've met Tumalind?'

'The Virgin Gifts stayed at my father's house before they set sail on the pilgrimage. Tumalind was very pleasant. I could've been friends with her under different circumstances. By the way, when we catch up with her, if we ever do, you'll find her taste in tabards more sophisticated. Last time I saw her, she was in silk, and enjoying its soft touch. Yes. I liked Tumalind. She's far too wise for a verigreen like you.'

He refused to rise to her taunt. 'We've a long and dangerous journey ahead of us, Jodisa. It'd be better for all of us if you could be civil.'

'I should respect my kidnappers, give them an easy time, and admire them for their courage in stealing a defenceless maiden from her bedchamber in the middle of the night? Is that what you mean?'

'We had no choice.'

'I'll aid you where it'll make me safer and more comfortable, boy. But don't expect respect or gratitude from me. Neither of you deserves it. You're brigands and criminals. I relish the thought of watching you dangle upside down, as your skin is pared away in strips. I shall personally scrape your lovefruits before I sear them from your living bodies with a flaming brand. And I'll be first to lash your tortured bodies with thorns of justice. My father knows what to do with those who violate maidens.'

'We've told you, you're sacred in that sense. I promise you, you needn't fear sacrilege from Aglydron or me. Don't you see, if you're not virgin when we find Dagla-Kaz, our whole mission will be for nothing?'

She tilted her head to one side, considering. 'Then your mission's already failed, boy. My father passed over me as Virgin Gift for the very simple reason that he knows, without any doubt, I am not a virgin.'

Chapter 13

Taken

'Don't gawp like a startled gaarbel, Okkyntalah.' Aglydron's sudden interruption surprised Jodisa-Li, who thought he was sleeping. 'She's lying.'

'Believe what you will, Aglydron. You've already proved yourself a bigger fool than anyone could imagine. But I know I'm not virgin. I know what it's like to join. I know what joy and ...' She faltered, finding difficulty controlling her emotions, cursing her inability to recall the deaths of her baby and her lover without tears springing to her eyes and her voice breaking.

'I saw the blood; proof that you're still intact and....'

'Fool! You think a show of blood can't be arranged?' His ignorance allowed her to turn sorrow into anger. 'You think all who bleed at the test are virgin, all who don't are violated? Men! Idiots. No doubt, you believe your wife allows your seed to make her swell with new life every time you join. Men are fools. Why should we grow children to have you tear them from us and ...'

'Stop! I'll hear no more of your blasphemy, girl. Silence, or I'll stop your tongue with rope and only free it to eat.'

She glared at him. But she'd already said more than she intended.

'Ignore her, Okkyntalah. She's lying to make us take her back to Chalamamnon. We won't.'

'Take us to Ylcrat, then, and let them dine on us, if you will, Aglydron the Wise.'

'D'you believe every tale you're told? I thought you'd have more sense than to hear stories made up to frighten children.'

'Father gives them credit. Father, who's travelled and seen foreign lands, traded with Yellowskins, bought lapis lazuli and myllth from merchants out of Balagaaq; he believes the tales. What do you know, cowman from Morstahn?'

'Less than I would and more than you believe.'

She saw doubt on Aglydron's face and wondered what drove this troubled man who'd irrevocably altered their lives with his zeal. 'Why have you taken me?'

'I've told you. You were passed over...'

'No. The real reason.'

'Ytraa's will must be done.'

'Or what?'

He looked at her with incomprehension.

'What'll happen if Ytraa's will isn't done?'

'Don't sport with me, girl. You know what happens if we fail.'

'I know you'll die when we meet my father. I know I can't be a Virgin Gift, and that my father knows it. I know Tumalind will go to Choshinahm to satisfy the needs of ritual and tradition.'

'Ritual and tradition? You make the will of Ytraa into mere ceremony? How can you talk like that? How can you lead if you don't truly Follow?'

'Stories for the rustics, and they believe them.'

'What do you mean?'

She knew her anger, frustration and the residual fear she felt as a captive would betray her into saying things she should not. 'I would sleep a little now. I've repaired your dangerous handiwork. If either of you have the wit and skill, I suggest you catch some of the fish that keep us company. What little is left of the fruit and dried meat won't last long and I'd prefer not to die of starvation.'

'I'm leading this mission, girl. I'll decide what we do.'

'As you wish, fool. I prefer to stay alive but, if you'd rather kill us all…' She shrugged, took her sleepsack from the line, laid it under the shade of the sail, and settled down without another word.

⸻

Aglydron looked from the insolent girl to Okkyntalah. 'Can you fish?'

'Of course.'

The boy sat in the bows and examined the gear left in the boat. He brought out a wicker creel, several coils of different types and thickness of line, a broken oar with a barbed spearhead and light line spliced to it and a small box, worked from shells, containing three barbed metal hooks and some small metal weights with holes to take fishing line.

Aglydron took the tiller and tried to determine their direction of travel. Watching their wake, he estimated they were moving roughly southwest, with a following wind. But, since he had no idea where they were in relation to Muhnilahm or Ylcrat, nor what distance or course they'd travelled in the storm, he could be reasonably sure only that they were travelling away from their island.

Okkyntalah knelt in the bows, knees apart for balance, and leant out over the clear water to fish. In his right hand, he held the makeshift fishing spear, the line attached firmly to his wrist. He remained motionless, watching.

'What are you waiting for?' The girl demanded imperiously.

'Working out their patterns of movement, so I have a hope of hitting one.' He spoke without turning round, his concentration on the task.

Aglydron admired his determination and attitude to the job. Jodisa-Li tilted her head slightly as she rested on her sleepsack, facing the bows. He noticed the turn of her head and the direction of her stare and understood at once. In spite of his disapproval, he smiled. The girl had spirit and it was difficult to condemn.

'Jodisa, I don't think that's…very ladylike, do you?'

She jerked her face toward him and had the grace to blush in spite of the mischief in her eyes. 'Not accusing me of sacrilege, this time? I'm pleased to see a sign of humanity beneath your piety Aglydron. It suits you better than righteousness.'

Okkyntalah, leaning deep from the hips, poised to strike, was oblivious to his exposure and remained a statue. Aglydron, in spite of himself, gave her a grin of complicity and she indulged in a cheeky smile back, like a child caught in a minor act of naughtiness. The exchange was so unexpected that he felt sudden sympathy for this poor girl they'd captured and taken from all that she loved and knew.

'Any idea where we are?'

She shook her head. 'Night and the stars might help. The storm was too violent; our attention taken with bailing and survival. We might've travelled in circles through the night for all I could tell. Some storms, they say, can drive a boat in loops. But I guess we're sailing more or less southwest, if that's any help.'

He admired her honesty. She could've pretended knowledge she didn't have and given a position that would send them off course. 'Thank you. What you did with the rope; it's very good. You hauled up the sail alone?'

She nodded.

'You're stronger than you look.'

'Many things are not as they appear, Aglydron.'

He studied her again, as she lay on her back, her feet stretched out toward him and her face turned away; still trying for the best view of the boy. Without realizing he was doing it, he followed the red and green dragon from her left ankle up and around her leg to where it vanished into shadow.

'Is that the way of a gentleman?' As if she'd known he was observing her, she turned her head and looked him in the eye.

He stifled his quick anger, recognising her taunt as a rejoinder to his earlier dig, and smiled at her question, which carried no more than mild revenge. 'The workmanship's so good. Such detail and form. When you move, it could be alive.'

'It took Franorahl seven weeks. I felt only the final part, the head and fire that my partners and my… and Ytraa alone should see.' Again, there was the sudden sadness, a hint suggesting at great loss still keenly felt by this strange young woman.

'When you say Franorahl, she designed it and chose the colours. One of her helpers did the work, of course.'

'Franorahl worked alone. She did my beast herself. But she only designed my flowers.'

Aglydron glanced, in spite of himself, at the gold, scarlet, blues and emerald of the floral display. The piece was exquisite and, judging by what was public, the design must range over her upper body. The back he'd seen when beating her. That memory filled him with remorse he wouldn't show.

'Dagla Kaz must be richer than I thought.'

'You'll never see the gift as it should be seen. He gave it mostly for Ytraa, a little for me. I wear it for those I'll join with, when I find them, and for me. Ytraa may look when Ytraa will, I suppose.'

'You amaze me, Jodisa. I don't see how a girl raised as High Priest Elect can be so disrespectful of Ytraa. You must've given your father many reasons to beat…'

'Yoohaar!' Okkyntalah's shout of triumph took them both by surprise.

The girl sat and faced him. Aglydron watched the boy land a large, flapping gaarbel in the bottom of the boat, the barbed blade of the spear buried in the flesh behind its bulbous head.

'Toss it back, boy!'

'It's food, Aglydron. Are we so pious we can afford to throw away good food?'

'Food, girl? It's prohibited. Toss it back, Okkyntalah.'

He tossed the carcass overboard and bent again with his spear. Almost at once, he plunged the point into the sea again. This time he caught a good sized dorado. He filleted and skinned the fish with easy expertise, clearly relishing the chance to impress the young woman. The bones he tossed overboard, the guts he gave to Shaulah and the skin he laid out flat to dry. He handed the girl the liver on the point of his knife, apparently unsure how she'd react to uncooked flesh.

'It's tasty and good. Try it.'

To their surprise, she ate it with enjoyment. 'Good. Very good. But I'll need a drop of water to take away the effect of the salt.' She took a mouthful and washed her mouth round, swallowing the precious fluid rather than spitting it out.

Aglydron accepted a long strip of flesh and chewed it rather gingerly until he discovered it tasted as good as any fish he'd eaten. Okkyntalah gave the girl a piece and set about another strip himself, fed more scraps to Shaulah and looped the other lengths over the line to dry. A good mouthful of water and a single plantain each completed their meal and left them in better spirits.

'Will you tell me what route you plan to take to Choshinahm, Aglydron?'

He could think of no way in which the knowledge could help her escape. 'I looked at the maps your father left, as you know…He must've took copies with him. I'll have to use memory. After Ylcrat, we'll sail to Rophan-Ra, missing that sewer of Mipahnhil, and keeping close to the coast as far as Shakahnl so we can land from time to time for supplies. From there we'll go overland through Cushlanah to Pastroahn in the Great Forest and on…'

'You're following the Old Route? Father indicated he might go a different way. He mentioned Kamakq, actually.'

'Kamakq?'

'It straddles the border between Niphralon and Kabalyt. Obviously, he wanted to avoid Mipahnhil but he was considering taking one of the other outlets of the River Sure so he could sail as far as Mistahn and then…'

'Dagla Kaz was going to sail to the Lake of The Lost? I can see he'd want to take the boat as far as possible, but to risk Mount O'bo? He'd really take that gamble? The Old Route's proven, isn't it? The notes on the map say it's been used three times. Why break with tradition and risk everything?'

'I don't know that he will, Aglydron. I merely tell you what he told me; that he was considering the idea. I can't tell you which route he actually took, because he never told me and, whichever way he planned, he'd have to set off from Muhnilahm in the same direction. But I know he intended to visit Kamakq. He was most insistent about that when he was discussing the journey with Baklan.'

Aglydron was silent for a time. 'You're trying to put us off course, trying to make us think our journey's a waste in the hope we'll turn back. We won't, Jodisa. We'll go on, with Ytraa as our guide.'

'Again you accuse me of a crime I haven't committed. I'm not trying to divert you. The sooner we meet up with Father, the better for me. I'm simply telling you what he said, warning that you may find no evidence of him at Shakahnl. Now, I think I'll sleep, since the boy, who's rather more man than I'd suspected, seems unlikely to offer further sport. If I sleep now, I might help discover our position come nightfall. And find we're on our way to Rhonholoah, where the savages will take me as a bed wench and slice you two into pieces to feed their hunting dogs.'

Okkyntalah puzzled over the girl's comment about him but couldn't fathom her meaning. He'd heard the names of more places than he knew existed, yet Aglydron seemed as familiar with them as the girl. His memory of those secret maps must be very good.

The older man sat at the tiller and tried to make the wind fill the wide canvass, losing it again so that it flapped and the boat juddered in its course. His inexperience seemed to mingle with fear, stopping him taking full advantage of the wind.

Jodisa-Li sneered at his efforts but made no move to help. Okkyntalah gazed down into her face as she relaxed at his feet. 'Won't you guide Aglydron?'

'Since we've no idea where we are or where we're headed, there's little point in speeding anywhere.'

He felt in awe of her, as he did the Holy Ones with their arcane rituals, their strange appearance and their single-minded pursuit of Ytraa's service. They practiced a form of magic that could make people do things normal mortals would find impossible. They lived lives as far removed from his and ordinary folk as those of fishes or birds and they created a feeling of deep unease in everyone.

But he found himself drawn to Jodisa-Li, almost compelled to look at her. And he knew it wasn't simply her beauty that drew his eyes. Some mystery in her made it difficult to control his feelings. It wasn't like the love he felt for Tumalind; that was deep and mingled with care, pride and a longing to be with her all the time. What he felt for Jodisa-Li came from something he couldn't comprehend. It frightened and excited him and he was convinced he must resist it or be lost in some way he couldn't explain.

He determined to look away and find some task or other to concentrate on. At that moment, as the thought became real enough to turn into action, she looked into his eyes and he was convinced she read his mind. Her smile was as engaging as it was terrifying. He couldn't look away and felt himself drawn into those eyes of sumptuous blue with their promise of something extraordinary yet undefined. She brought her hand up to her face and brushed her fingertips along her small nose. Took them to her mouth and down over her throat. He followed, compelled, as she stroked to where the mounds of her breasts rested in shadow. She paused briefly and led him down her body to the hem of her tabard, touching the tattooed dragon. She laughed silently and he shook himself. He lifted his eyes along her length to her face. The expected scorn wasn't there. Instead, he found a look of deep sorrow and had to turn away.

Aglydron stared at him with concern and he wondered how much of what he'd felt had passed across his face to make his companion so anxious.

'Take the tiller, Okkyntalah. I've things to attend to whilst it's calm and bright.'

This wasn't true; Aglydron merely wanted to separate him from the girl, and he knew it was better that he did so.

'I also have things to do.'

Aglydron bristled and seemed about to rail at him but nodded and looked down at the girl before he turned his attention to sea and sail. 'Do them quickly. There's things I must do before night.'

Okkyntalah avoided looking back at her. He tidied his gear, checked the fishing spear, scratched the sleeping dog behind her ears, hung his own and Aglydron's sleeping rolls on the line now that Jodisa-Li's clothes were dry, and only then made his way aft.

He changed places with Aglydron. Concentrating on the little he'd learned from his father, he tried to fill the sail with wind. He was more successful than Aglydron and they skipped across the waves and slowed only intermittently. Where they went mattered less than his display of skill and ability to the girl now resting with her feet close to his.

The Nupraxyss limped thirty leagues, taking two days to reach Rhonholoah and arriving late in the afternoon. Tumalind leant on the wooden rail as they approached the harbour, her braided hair rippling in the fitful offshore wind. Baklan had been truthful about the women.

'How can they bear to walk covered like that?'

'They've no choice, is 'ow. An' neither 'ave we. We'll just 'ave to get on with it.' Dilanthas shook her head as she stood beside Tumalind and watched the women float across the dusty ground.

'How do they see where they're going?'

'Who knows? But we'll find out soon enough.' Porryh, arriving on her other side, echoed their gloom.

Once the boat had docked, Dagla Kaz and Caarl borrowed loincloths and headbands, strapped on swords and accompanied Baklan onto the great stone quayside as he went to arrange for repairs. The rest waited on board.

The land smelt strange after the clean air of the sea. Animal dung, spices, wet jute and the inevitable fish and seaweed smell of any harbour assaulted Tumalind's nose.

'Can't smell any flowers, or green things.'

'Big city, ain't it? All dust an' muck an' shit.'

'And strong virile men; just look at them!'

Tumalind, conscious of Corphanda's eyes and ears close by, tried to distract Porryh from the inevitable consequences of her fantasies. She looked along the dock and found what she sought.

'I thought the Nupraxyss was big but look at those!'

They followed her pointing finger and stared in disbelief at ships with three, four and even five tall masts; some vessels so big they could have held their own ship half a dozen times. In the noise and bustle, no one seemed to have noticed them. Ships unloaded grain; their crews clad in dusty loincloths and their hair turbaned in bright colours. Others loaded some hard brown material that one of the crewmen told them was iron ore.

'You've none on your little island, so we'll pick some up on the way back. Baklan knows 'ow to trade for a good profit. An', if one o' you three lovelies wants some profit, I'll give you a good time an' a fistful o' coin for your pleasure.'

'Thank you, but we're saving ourselves for clean men whose breath smells better than stripecat's squitter.'

'Cheeky cooch!' He stumped off.

'I'm glad you dealt wi' 'im, Tumalind. They scare me.'

'No need to be scared. Let them, I say. It's the only pleasure we're going to get before we're given to some stranger in Choshinahm.' Porryh's grumble sent them into silent contemplation as they stared at the scene.

Tumalind wasn't going to dwell on what she couldn't have or control. Instead, she kept to her determination to learn what she might wherever she found herself.

This city dwarfed Chalamamnon and she realised again how limited and incomplete was her experience. She turned her attention to the men and noticed they were mostly very dark skinned but that some were paler, some yellowish and others more red than brown. All displayed their torsos and walked tall. Nowhere did she see a belly stuck out like Jhonaht's. Though, his was beginning to shrink with the rigours of their journey.

She watched a group of women threading along the quay. The men hardly seemed to notice, passing them with barely a glance. One strikingly tall woman balanced a large pot on her head, hands invisible by her sides, as she walked gracefully along and turned down a narrow road. Beyond, she noticed a plain but buxom girl with a short red wrap about her ample hips; a red band barely concealing her breasts. Tumalind looked on with fear for the girl's safety, as a man approached and placed something in her hand. She smiled and led him off, followed by coarse catcalls from other men. It struck her as an odd sort of meeting.

At length the High Priest and Caarl returned and handed out black, brown and grey shrouds, loincloths and headbands. Tumalind examined her cowl for signs of a front or a back. Close-up, it was just a wide tube of harrateen, stitched together at the curved top with long, wide sleeves set in. To her relief, a small oblong of fine gauze allowed a restricted view of the world.

As they were examining these unwelcome costumes, cries and shouts from below attracted them. Men formed a ragged circle about two others who were shouting and squaring up to each other, the spectators egging them on with jeers and insults. The taller of the two combatants made a clumsy attempt to punch the stockier man in the midriff. He grabbed his assailant's hand and, to their horror, plunged a dagger into the tall man's belly. The group of watchers jeered as the injured man went down. When it was clear he wasn't going to get up again, most walked away. The man with the dagger bent, wiped his bloodied blade on the fallen man's loincloth, and replaced it in the sheath. He left the injured man bleeding on the ground. Two onlookers helped the victim up and half dragged, half carried him toward the town.

Such sudden and fierce conflict was unheard of on the island and the women were pale with shock as Dagla Kaz prepared to lead them to their quarters.

'Such is the way of things here. Make sure you don't fall foul of their customs and laws. Stay close.'

They crossed the quayside into dusty streets. As custom required, the men led; the women following a few paces behind in single file. The three girls held hands through their shrouds. Tumalind, reeling from the violence, followed the party through the tangle of winding narrow streets, her view restricted and her head swimming.

Some streets were crowded with men and women and others almost deserted. The small viewing panel made the rough roads, with large cobbles sticking up here and there and deep potholes, dangerous. She stubbed her toe trying to avoid a ragged hollow, staggered and, as she put out her hands to save herself, became detached from Porryh. She fell on her knees and briefly stopped to rub the pain away.

When she rose and looked about, she'd lost sight of her companions. Spinning wildly in a desperate attempt to find them, she was soon disorientated. Which way should she go? She cried out in alarm; alone in this strange and violent place. She cried out again, her voice muffled by the cowl.

'What is it, deary?'

She turned, instinctively suspicious of the oily voice. Another woman stood close, eyes glinting sharply behind the black gauze panel.

'Lost, are you?'

'I'm a stranger. I was with a party and they've gone on...'

'Left you, have they? That's all right, deary, I'll look after you. Come with me.'

'No! No, I must find my friends....'

'Friends? But they've left you to fend for yourself, deary. You're alone. I can tell by your voice you're a young girl. Come with me and I'll see you're taken good care of.'

'I don't want taking care of, thank you. I want my friends. They haven't abandoned me; I'm simply lost. Can you show me where visitors might stay, please?'

'Visitor, eh? Stranger? Come with me, deary. I'll help you.'

The woman grasped her arm with a grip of iron through the fabric. Tumalind was frightened now; in the hands of a woman she felt instinctively meant her no good.

'Come along, now. Can't stay out here on your own, deary. Never know what might happen.'

'Let go of me!'

'Don't be afraid. Just making sure you don't lose me like your friends. Wouldn't do to be wandering in a strange city all alone, now, would it?'

'Please, tell me where I might find them. Just show me which way I should go.'

'But that's what I'm a trying to do, deary. Isn't that what I said? Just don't want you losing your way again. Come along now; it's this way.'

She felt no trust at all for this stranger but no one had come to find her and, perhaps, her suspicion was more to do with fear than common sense and was a little unfair. What, after all, could an old woman want with her? She allowed herself to be led, reluctant, and scanning through her patch of gauze for anyone she knew.

They came to a plain wooden door in a white wall. The woman opened it and pushed her in, barring the door behind them.

'Now, let's have a look at you, shall we?'

In one swift movement, the cowl was dragged over Tumalind's head. Standing before her was the naked old woman, her cowl already abandoned. The crone tossed Tumalind's cover on top of her own and circled her, sucking on her teeth.

'Where are my friends?'

'I'm your friend. Just do as I say, and you'll have a friend. Yes, I'll help you.' She lifted the tabard, pulled at it. 'What's this? Take it off. Folk'll get the wrong idea.'

'I think I'd better go, thank you. I'll find my friends on my own.'

With remarkable speed, the old woman dashed between Tumalind and the door. 'They've left you. Left you alone in a strange city full of danger. Do as I say and I'll look after you. Don't you know it's against the law to keep that on? Off with it, less the man gives you a good thrashing.'

'I want to go back to my friends.'

'Do you? Well, I want you here, and I've got you, haven't I?'

Chapter 14

CHANGING RELATIONSHIPS

*H*igh above Chalamamnon, Aklon-Dji rested under ancient olives long since abandoned, and awaited nightfall so he could visit another of the Few. Troublesome and dangerous, with her insatiable longing, she nevertheless kept her ear to the ground and was willing to undertake difficult and dangerous missions. He hoped to discover information about Jodisa-Li from Syylvah.

'*My young friend, again without female company?*'

'*Ivdulon! You find me awaiting the cloak of night. I must thank you for your advice relating to stripecat fur. I did as you advised, and continue to wear a small tuft of it bound into my neck chain. It seemed to ward off the creatures.*'

'*Scent's a powerful influence on wild animals. I'd every reason to expect it to deter attack.*'

'*You didn't know?*'

'*I don't know everything, Aklon. But some things are clear by deduction.*'

Aklon-Dji could think of no response to this comment, other than to accuse his adviser of possibly placing him in extreme danger. And he was sure that hadn't been the wise man's intention. He decided instead to ask what had brought him into his mind.

'*Idle speculation: you intend to overthrow your father in his absence and make changes. I wonder, have you thought about consequences?*'

'*You mean, I assume, that there will be bloodshed and conflict and that many people may be hurt as a result? I see no way of accomplishing what we need to do without causing damage to both individuals and society. What is your point, Ivdulon?*'

'*Merely this. Such actions are often taken without thorough planning. It's one thing to remove a power that deserves to be purged but it's entirely another to successfully replace it with something worthy. Have you plans for the time after the rebellion?*'

'*Plans? Hopes only. It is difficult to plan without foreknowledge of the outcome.*'

'*It is. But you should consider all possible outcomes, Aklon. Many will be happy to join your cause during and after the uprising, when they see the real advantages. But there'll be diehards, intent on damaging your new society. Consider how you'll tackle such disruption and, perhaps, indiscriminate violence. You'll be in danger long after the dust settles, you know. And many of your helpers will remain vulnerable. Think about it. Form plans. Have schemes ready to deal with the disaffected. Or you may find your rebellion*' *brings only civil war, bitterness and death to your community.'*

'As ever, full of advice and startling thoughts. You remain a comfort to me, Ivdulon. I shall sleep easier for having to consider your ideas and predictions. Thank you.'

'Think nothing of it. I leave you to stew, in the knowledge that you'll prevent the worst effects of your changes. Farewell for now.'

Aklon-Dji smiled wryly and sat in the shade with his mind now engaged on the problems Ivdulon had raised. As if he hadn't enough troubles already. But the wise man was right. If the Cause was successful, he'd need arrangements in place to maintain the peace. If he failed...

Aglydron fully understood the attraction of the girl but worried that Okkyntalah's admiration might become something more. Beautiful, graceful, vivacious and sensual, Jodisa-Li was also clever, skilled and brave. She was everything a man might want in a woman, but that she was proud, scornful and lacked respect. Such defects, though, wouldn't discourage a boy. Her small praise of a youth eager to impress might easily turn his head. He wanted the youngsters to get on but couldn't risk Okkyntalah taking sides with her.

Aglydron must reveal her as the menace she was. Her lack of reverence for customs and her scant regard for proper observation of ritual signalled her truly dissolute nature. Show Okkyntalah her real character and he might put the boy on his guard against her wiles.

Without preamble or warning, sure Okkyntalah would listen without interruption but that the girl would betray her impatience and voice boredom or drift into inattention, he embarked on the First Great Knowing.

'Before Ytraa, nothing was. Black and Empty was all.'

Okkyntalah paid attention at once. But, to his surprise, Jodisa-Li also sat up to listen. He continued, using traditional words taught him by the Holy Ones, confident she wouldn't last the lesson.

'Then came Ytraa. And Blackness and Emptiness rose up against our God in great anger. And Ytraa fought the Blackness and filled it with light. Thus was there darkness and there was light. And all was void and empty. But Ytraa took the Emptiness and filled it. And Ytraa saw Ytraa and desired Ytraa and our God did join the male part of Ytraa with the female part of Ytraa and did send forth the First Great Seed and did plant the First Great Seed in the womb of Ytraa. And Ytraa was the mother and the father of the First Great Sapling that was born of our God. And Ytraa did plunge the First Great Sapling into the Emptiness and it grew, spreading its roots into darkness and its branches into light. Thus came the First Great Tree. For Ytraa brought forth the First Great Tree and all other trees came from this one; from the First Great Tree.

'Now, when the Tree was grown, it bore many fruits. Ytraa found the fruit was good and blessed the Tree, calling it Av-Qijjahn and Zephystryss, meaning First Born and Last To Die. And some of the fruits Ytraa made into stars to shine in the outermost Blackness. And some of the fruits Ytraa did eat, for they were good. But the greatest of the fruits Ytraa did make into the World. Even the very world on which all things that are, do live and come into being. And upon the World did Ytraa make the water and the land, the seas and rivers. The oceans and lakes did Ytraa make, for they were beautiful in the eyes of Ytraa. The mountains and valleys, the hills and plains Ytraa made. And all the World was beautiful for it was made by Ytraa and was perfect.'

He glanced up to find Okkyntalah rapt but, to his dismay, Jodisa-Li was also paying full attention. His brief look, however, barely interrupted the narrative.

'There came a time when Ytraa looked upon the world and thought to people it. And Ytraa again grew desirous of Ytraa and again the male part of Ytraa joined with the part of Ytraa that was female. Thus was born the First People. And the First People was born of our God in numbers beyond count and all were in the likeness of Ytraa; being both man and woman in one. But the fruit of Ytraa, though they were like Ytraa, they were yet unlike Ytraa. For Ytraa is God and Ytraa is Man and Ytraa is Woman. But the First People, they were Man and they were Woman only; the First People had not the part of Ytraa that is God and is unknowable and mysterious and terrible beyond imaginings. And Ytraa was well pleased with the fruit of Ytraa's womb.

'Then did Ytraa see that the World was barren and bare and Ytraa did join again and again and again in passion. And with each joining was born a new plant or a new animal or a new insect or a new fish, such as was the desire of Ytraa. And Ytraa did join with Ytraa more times than can be counted and the First People did see the joining and rejoice and they also did join and did multiply and increase until their like was over the face of the world. And Ytraa was greatly pleased with all that Ytraa created and all that our God did. And all was peace and harmony in the World.

'But one fruit of the Great Tree hid in the Blackness. This one fruit was not good and was not made into a star nor yet into a world, nor yet eaten to sustain Ytraa. And that fruit grew sour and bad. And its seed put forth maggots. And the maggots did grow and burst forth from the fruit and did devour it. And they grew wings and did become as hornets. And amongst them and over them was the Great Hornet, Mhortag the Cruel. And they did fly down and did sting Ytraa and hurt our God sore. But Ytraa killed them not, feeling pity for their state.

'And Mhortag, seeing how Ytraa did love the World, settled on it and marked it. And all that is ugly and unclean was made by Mhortag. The plagues were brought by

Mhortag and the wild beasts that devour flesh and the snakes that bite and the creatures that sting. And the fish that devour the people did Mhortag make after his own likeness for he was jealous of Ytraa and of Ytraa's people.

'And Mhortag did the greatest evil known, for he took the people that were man and woman in one and did split them asunder. The men he took from the women and the women he did divide from the men so that they were one no more but were two. And the people did cry out in lamentation for that they were become divided and were whole no more.

'When Ytraa saw what Mhortag had done, Ytraa was wrath and did banish Mhortag to the outermost depths of nothingness, saying, "Go! Leave this world I have created and never return or I will surely kill you." And that is where he dwells to this day. But before Mhortag fled, he set poison in the World. Some he put into beasts so that they were fierce and some he spread amongst the people so that they might not live forever, as had been the will of Ytraa, but would grow wicked and would die.

'Then did Mhortag flee into the Blackness, but he rent the covering of the darkness and did release it so that night came all around. But Ytraa made the sun in the likeness of a golden ball of flame, glowing with light and heat, and set it in the sky over the World, where it spins a circle round the world, so that there is time for sleep and time for activity. And the sun gave life where the darkness would destroy it. And Ytraa caused the stars to shine also that the people might know the ways to travel over the World in the darkness. And the Moon made Ytraa, in the form of a disc of light to brighten the night sky and defeat the darkness.

'And so was the World made by Ytraa, a thousand cycles before Gadhallah came into being. And Ytraa keeps the people and protects them always from the evil that is Mhortag. And the Eyes of Ytraa gaze down from the sky and see the World that Ytraa did create. And the Eyes of Ytraa are like stars in the sky, yet they move not like other stars, being always in one place above the World. And this is the end of the First Great Knowing.'

Okkyntalah nodded and made the sign, gathering and accepting the essence of Ytraa and clutching it to his chest.

The girl, silent and attentive throughout, also made the sign. She turned to Aglydron, her face shining with the passion of a true Follower. 'I don't know why you chose this time to remind us of the wonder of Ytraa, Aglydron, but I approve your telling of the First Great Knowing. You spoke with more truth and fervour than I've heard in many a telling; much more moving than some village priests I've had to listen to. You're a better teacher than I'd imagined. Thank you.'

Aglydron was both astounded at her praise and puzzled by her devotion. She'd shown scant regard for aspects of the faith that he held dear, yet seemed genuinely moved by the fundamentals of their religion. He had to revise his opinion of her again and recognise she was more complex than he'd thought. Looking up from her serene face, he found Okkyntalah staring at her with renewed esteem.

Experience warned him against open opposition to their friendship: still enough a boy to fly in the face of reason, Okkyntalah might find her more than he could resist. A clumsy attempt to keep them apart could simply push them together.

On Muhnilahm, the task would have been difficult enough: he'd seen many cases of attraction between the wrong bucks and maidens to know the problems. Here, in the confines of a small boat with no other people to distract them, his task in keeping their relationship merely supportive, rather than intimate, would be hard indeed.

⚬

'Tumalind! Tumalind! Where are you?' The distant voice called in concern.

'Here! Behind the door! See; they haven't abandoned me. They've come back.'

'Tumalind?' The voice, close enough now to recognise, made her sigh with relief.

'Yes. I'm here. Wait.' She went to unbar the door.

But the old crone was determined. 'Not so fast. I've plans for you.'

'Help me, Tarruss!'

'Tumalind?' He was just the other side of the door.

Another call came from beyond the far wall that crossed the yard behind her. She turned to see a heavy man making for her from an open door. At once, she knew she must gain freedom now or be lost forever.

'I'm here, Tarruss!' She dragged the old crone by her wiry arm and spun her into the man's path. Grasping the wooden bar, she lifted it, opening the door a fraction just as he reached her. He grabbed her wrist. Pulled her from the door. Tried to shoulder it shut.

'Help me, Tarruss! Help me!'

The big man pushed hard as her captor tried to close the door. The fat man seemed to be winning, his foot wedged against the wood. She'd be lost. She lifted the wrist he held and bit his hand, hard. He struck her. Tarruss took his chance and shoved the door wide. Tumalind, on her knees from the blow, struggled, as the screeching old woman tried to hold her down. Tarruss slammed a fist into the man's face, dropping him. Tumalind fought free; pushed the old woman over the man. They fell in a heap. She dashed into the street. Clutching her tabard protectively to her, she watched, ready to run. Tarruss hit the man again as he rose, sending him sprawling. This time he didn't get up. The crone wailed for help. Another man entered the yard but saw Tarruss and stopped. The old woman screamed at him but he wouldn't move.

Tarruss grabbed both cowls, returned to the street and gave them to Tumalind.

One stank; she tossed it to the ground and dragged the other over her head.

The old crone shrieked. 'Prime goods an' you let 'er go. Cowards!'

Tarruss put an arm about Tumalind. 'Come on, little lass, let's get you to safety.' He guided her swiftly along narrow winding streets, the screeches of the old woman fading. Other people they passed stared with curiosity and Tumalind felt threatened in spite of Tarruss at her side. It seemed an age before they reached two wooden doors in a long white wall that rose well over a manheight.

The left hand door was carved with a repeated design of stylised, rampant male parts. Blushing, she turned to the other. This bore oval hollows and stylised breasts.

Tarruss knocked on both. The male door opened, allowing a glimpse into a small anteroom where Dagla Kaz was talking with Tryonta. The High Priest turned his back but the other man, just returned from searching for her, made no move to hide. Tumalind was grateful Tarruss had found her; to be beholden to Tryonta would be unthinkable.

The other door opened and Corphanda peered round it and glared. 'Why'd you let go Porryh's hand, girl? You was told to keep firm hold.'

Tumalind explained and watched Corphanda's face alter. 'It wasn't Porryh's fault, Corphanda. I'm sure she thought I was still with them.'

Corphanda was unconvinced. Tumalind wasn't entirely certain about Porryh's actions herself.

Tarruss quickly related to Corphanda and Dagla Kaz what he'd found, making it clear that Tumalind had been taken against her will and had helped in her own rescue.

'Well done, Tumalind.' Dagla Kaz called. Tarruss made sure she was safe within the women's side before he entered the male door, just as Caarl returned from his search of a different street.

Corphanda helped her remove cowl and tabard. 'The others are over there. Your clothes go on these pegs in case you need to go out. But you'll not be doing that.' She looked her up and down, frowning. 'No one, no man's...you've not been... touched, have you?'

Tumalind shook her head, tears threatening now the danger was over.

'You'll be fine, lass. Safe. We'll be fed an' looked after till the ship's ready to leave.'

Tumalind, trembling, nodded her thanks. Corphanda hugged her close and, with some prompting, she told her guardian exactly what had happened, the tears escaping.

'Why would the old woman want me? What for? I don't understand.'

Corphanda comforted her with hands on her back. 'Best you don't know, dear. Come on, let's find the others.'

'I'd rather you told me, Corphanda.'

'Well, some places, heathen places, men pay to join with women. But women won't sell themselves, so they capture them and make them do it, see?'

'They were going to force me, for coin?'

'I know; wicked isn't it? But, don't worry, you're safe now.'

'But that's terrible, Corphanda; imagine what would've happened if Tarruss hadn't found me when he did! The whole mission would've been ruined and…'

'I know. Don't bear thinking about, do it? Still, you're safe now. Come and have a nice soak.'

They crossed the wide square, paved with cracked stone overlain with fine brown dust that stuck to their feet. Tumalind, her breathing returning to normal at last, heard the sound of water tinkling somewhere close. Recovering, she took in her surroundings.

In the centre of the left wall of the open square, a large pool reflected the sky. Its wall in black, white and red, matched a high screen, pierced with narrow, serpentine holes, which split both the pool and the whole open area in two. Through the small gaps, she could just discern movement. Women populated the half they occupied and she guessed the other side of the screen was for men.

'Not naked together, then.'

'No.' Corphanda urged Tumalind to the pool. 'Nearly though; you can see as much as you like if you're wicked enough to peep through them there 'oles. Porryh knows better now. I'll be havin' words wi' her about what happened to you.'

Tumalind turned from the wall, understanding the other girl's curiosity. She wondered if she should defend Porryh against Corphanda's suspicions but said nothing, unsure exactly what had happened.

A fall of clear water spouted continually from a sculpted muscular man, filling the pool. Women sat on the stone edge and in the water, bathing or just relaxing under the sun. Here and there, palm trees grew from great earthenware pots decorated with colourful scenes of men at work and leisure. In the shade of these, others lay on rugs or couches, drinking from small stone vessels or nibbling dainties and fruits from glazed earthenware disks. At the far side of the pool ran a long arched gallery of open cubicles where women lay on cloth covered benches in the form of naked men on their hands and knees, being oiled and massaged by others.

Tumalind saw Dilanthas in the pool near the fountain and sat with her in the cool clear water as Corphanda waddled off to one of the cubicles.

'Where's Porryh?'

Dilanthas nodded toward the arch where their companion lay on her back as a dark skinned woman massaged oil into her legs. Corphanda made straight for her. They watched the pair engage in conversation, Corphanda's manner and stance making it clear this was no casual exchange. Porryh sat up, scornful; said something. Corphanda pulled her off the bench, turned her round and bent her over. The ten slaps were loud enough to stop all sound in the square. Some local women cheered and others laughed. Porryh yelled and then bowed her head and nodded at Corphanda. Gingerly, she lay back on the massage bench, face down. The woman continued the massage and Corphanda waddled away to get something to eat, rubbing her hands together.

'What's she done now?'

Tumalind could guess. She'd speak to Porryh later.

'Where'd you get to, anyway? Porryh never said you'd let go and I couldn't see, what with those silly gauze things.'

Tumalind explained, but the idea of women joining with men for coin was something she couldn't grasp and Tumalind felt Dilanthas was sure she must be making it up.

Wendarah paddled across, smiling. 'I was so worried. No one realized you were missing until we got here. Those stupid shrouds just don't let you see a thing, do they?'

She had to tell her story all over again and this time, taking the horrified lead of the priestess, Dilanthas believed her.

'Well, thank the Lord Gadhallah no real harm befell you, Tumalind. I take it you're not injured or hurt? Just your lip where he hit you? Good. We're stuck here, I'm afraid. Once the mast's repaired, we'll be on our way again. But, until then we'll have to put up with massages in scented oils, sweetmeats to eat and good quality wine to drink, whilst doing nothing at all in return. I really don't know how I'll stand it.'

Tumalind laughed. 'I suppose we'll just have to do the best we can and try not to complain too much. But it'll be hard.'

Dilanthas frowned and then smiled uncertainly. 'Well, I don't care what you say; I think it's very nice.'

Tumalind looked about her. The place had an air of having seen better days but was clean and comfortable. There were worse ways to spend three days and, after the fate she'd escaped, there was little for her to complain of for the moment. She looked back at Wendarah and smiled at a sudden thought.

'Dorltah for them?'

'Just remembering; the last time I was with so many women with no men present was my initiation. Seems cycles ago now; another time, another place. It was on the way back I decided to declare for Okkyntalah. Wonder what he's doing now.'

∞

'What's that?'

Aglydron and the girl followed Okkyntalah's pointing finger toward the western horizon. Emerging from the sea, where sky met water, rose a series of irregular black shapes with narrow gaps between. Beyond, to the west, a small patch of darkness marred the blue of sky where it met sea.

'The Great Reef. We should go closer, then keep it to starboard and follow it to the end. There, a course due north will take us to the island, where the cannibals will enjoy us.'

Aglydron felt his temper rising at her presumption. Knowing she was right about the reef made it hard for him to bear her confidence and display of knowledge. He swallowed his pride, accepting that was what drove his resentment, and nodded. 'The Great Reef's like a crescent moon, east of the island. You've studied the ancient maps, Jodisa?'

'I entered the Pit of Secrets with the knowledge and blessing of the High Priest.'

'I did it for Ytraa. If I die for that...' He shrugged. 'I've gone with my conscience. What else could I do?'

'Surely Dagla Kaz will understand we had no choice, Jodisa? He won't condemn Aglydron for trying to put right a wrong.'

Jodisa-Li's look said everything and Aglydron knew that, in her eyes, they faced certain death when they met up with her father. For him, it was enough that their actions would fulfil the will of Ytraa. Okkyntalah might have other views.

'You seem to know about boats, Jodisa. Will you guide us so we can avoid the reef?'

'I'll do what I must to preserve my life, boy. No more.' She looked at them in turn as she considered her next remark. 'I was taught by a fisherman. I know of no way to teach what I know other than by example. I shall have to touch you. But only because that's how I can show you how to respond to the moods of wind and water. Don't fool yourselves that I'll find any pleasure from it or that it invites any response.'

'We both respect your status, Jodisa. You seem overly concerned that we'll abuse or violate you. Haven't we already shown ourselves honourable in that way?'

'Alone in an open boat, with two condemned criminals who've nothing to lose? One a young man who lusts for me and the other a brutal madman who's already abused my flesh; how can I feel safe? You've already violated the laws of Ytraa. How can I be sure you won't rape me? I'll need a lot more proof of your good intentions before I even begin to feel safe.'

Chapter 15

Lessons At Sea

She smoothed her tabard close as she sat next to him at the tiller. Okkyntalah felt warm skin where her leg touched his and, in spite of her stated intent, was surprised when she passed her arm about him and rested her hand on his forearm. He was conscious of her female smell; the softness of her skin and form where she touched him. She guided his arm to move the tiller as Aglydron watched closely.

'Concentrate on the boat, boy. I'm not yours to command or persuade, though the craft may be.'

He blushed at the accuracy of her observation and determined to turn his mind to steering the craft, though her closeness almost overwhelmed his senses. She put gentle pressure on his arm and he moved in the direction she indicated. He followed with the tiller when she twisted her arm to the right, the boat heeling over as the sail filled with wind to push it swiftly across small waves.

For five or more leagues they sailed as one, her hands guiding his, her words slowing or quickening his pace at need. She taught him to move the sail with ropes at boom and yardarm, moving the boat forward even when the wind was not behind.

'Good. But try to feel wind, currents, waves and swell through the boat. Make it part of you.'

He concentrated on the changes, felt them as he did the subtle influences that guided his hunting and, understanding how they affected the boat, used them to keep on course. She showed him how to tack across the wind, making for a specific spot, using one of the broken teeth as a target.

'I'm uncomfortable, sitting like this. You're good, Okkyntalah. Your father's blood runs through your veins: perhaps you should've been a fisherman, after all. You handle the boat like a good man does a woman.

'I'll rest now. Aglydron, I'll teach you later. Or the boy, Okkyntalah that is, might show you; he's an easy pupil and has the necessary skill.'

He moved to release her, watched her rise. How he wanted this woman who was sacrosanct and inviolate; her very inaccessibility increasing his desire.

She crouched low, spoke in tones too soft for Aglydron to hear. 'And Tumalind?'

He had no reply. Had she read his mind, heard his thoughts? Or had his hunger spoken from his face? He glanced at Aglydron, seated in the bow fashioning a leash to give Jodisa-Li some freedom with control once they were on land, but there was no sign he'd seen their exchange. Relieved, he watched her lower herself gracefully back into the bottom of the boat, moving her sleepsack into the shade of the sail again.

She stretched out and closed her eyes. Would he be able to resist the temptation to watch her next time she prayed? Once, he'd blasphemed by opening his eyes when Tumalind was praying. Her form had captured him and only with supreme effort had he looked away, but Ytraa hadn't blinded him as Kaz-Ca-Wesdan had warned. He'd told no one; shame and fear preventing him admitting a sin that should've seen him wear the bronze hood of repentance for a sixday and, thus temporarily bereft of sight, be pelted with dirt, stones and dung. But the vision of Tumalind presenting herself for Ytraa remained a potent image in his mind and he longed for the day when she offered herself to him.

The speed of the boat dropped and waves tossed them uncomfortably. His lapse in concentration had moved them closer to the reef. Finding the wind again, he filled the sail to take them from danger. The jagged faces of the rocks, devoid of vegetation or colour, looked like the rotting black teeth of some aquatic giant. Now they were closer, he could see that the rocks varied in height, some reaching twenty manheights. The gaps they'd seen earlier were now shown to be filled with smaller, lower rocks. And, behind them, far away yet menacing, a cloud of smoke rose from a shape breaking the distant horizon; the legendary mountain breathing the fire of dragons on Ylcrat.

'Let me take a turn, Okkyntalah. I need to know how to handle the boat before night falls. We'll have to work in shifts and I want to be sure of what I'm doing before sundown.'

Okkyntalah moved to let Aglydron sit beside him. He adopted the position Jodisa-Li had taken and guided the older man in the ways of tiller, sail, wind and waves. For the time it took the sun to approach the horizon and settle behind the reef, he taught what he'd learned at her hands. Though, he was less adept as a teacher, or Aglydron was a poor pupil.

Jodisa-Li appeared to sleep throughout. But she rose as sunlight stained the timbers at her side a fiery orange. 'If you treat women as you do the boat, Aglydron, I pity them. You're too swift and abrupt. You should caress and be gentle. Firm at need, but persuading rather than imposing.'

'What do you know of the ways of men and women, girl?'

'More, it seems, than you.'

Okkyntalah, sensing tension might spill into further conflict, pointed to the sun. 'It's time.'

They prepared themselves and Okkyntalah was incapable of resisting temptation. But, lying in the bottom of the boat, he couldn't view Jodisa-Li and tried to give himself to his devotions instead. But he hoped a real opportunity would come.

Darkness fell quickly, as the sun left an unblemished sky soon bright with a myriad stars. Low in the west, the smudge of the Skyfire glowed like dull gold dust against the darkening sky, reminding them of the reason for their journey. The black rocks of the reef, their bases wreathed in pale green phosphorescence and churning sea, broke against stars on the horizon. They kept their course half a league from danger as they sailed through the black quiet night. The only sounds were distant surf, breaking against those ancient menacing teeth and the closer slap, slap of small waves on the wooden hull as it cut through them and rode the gentle swell.

As they sought their way past the end of the reef, Okkyntalah saw flickers of dull red patch the underside of the dark cloud, as if the smoke were bleeding. What might that ominous sight truly mean?

Taking first watch after sundown, he was at the helm when the end of the reef came in sight. Reluctant to wake Aglydron, he was unsure what course to steer. 'Jodisa.'

To his surprise and relief, the girl responded. 'What is it?'

'The end of the reef. What course should I set?'

'Fool. Make for the island. Can't you see the fire mountain?'

'Yes.'

'Take a wide arc away from the reef and then turn for the cloud of smoke issuing from the mountain. I think you'll find the island lies beneath it.' Her heavy sarcasm stung, as she clearly intended.

It was as well that darkness hid his blushes.

Okkyntalah kept course until the last rocks faded into blackness aft, before he swung the tiller and trimmed the sail to take them toward a growing pall of smoke obscuring stars many leagues to the north. He had to tack to maintain course in a wind that varied from east to northeast. Fair weather kept the night clear. He relaxed a little, the worst of his watch now over. If nothing else, he might redeem his earlier stupidity by handling the boat well.

Breaking surf sounded over the slap of waves. Perhaps the wind played tricks with his hearing, blowing noise from the reef, now behind him, over the sea to torment him. He nodded: all was well.

Haughty, proud and unkind, the girl lay at his feet. In a creature of such loveliness these things were unimportant. He played with an improbable future where he traced her dragon from its tail to the very tip of fire he imagined it breathed into the heart of her womanhood and she urged him on, praising his loving and giving him the joy she told him he richly deserved.

Waves crashed close. Too loud to ignore. Under the faint light of a rising crescent moon, the dim phosphorescence marked where the sea smashed against low rocks. Too late, he realized he hadn't steered far enough from the reef before turning. They were almost on these last outriders and facing certain disaster. He cried out in alarm.

Jodisa-Li awoke and struggled upright to discover the reason for his concern. Recognising the danger at once and with collision imminent, she slipped from her sleepsack toward the tiller.

'Let me take the…'

Desperate to show his prowess and save them, Okkyntalah wrenched the tiller and pulled the ropes to move the sail. He avoided the nearest rocks but the boat heeled over abruptly, swinging the yard into the girl and pitching her into the boiling waves.

Aglydron woke as the girl yelled and splashed into the sea.

'Get the tiller! Jodisa's in the water!' Okkyntalah, with no thought for anything but her life, plunged after her.

The boat, uncontrolled, swung wildly in the small choppy seas. Okkyntalah could see no trace of the girl. 'Jodisa!'

No answer. He spun round, searching frantically for her in the darkness. 'Jodisa-Li!'

Far on the horizon, dragons breathed bright, fierce plumes of flame into the air. The orange and red tongues reflected on the sea around them. He saw the girl. Face down in the waves. No more than a few strokes distant. As he raced toward her, she began to sink. He swam to the place he'd seen her. Plunged below the waves. He rose for air and looked about. No sign. He dived again.

'Ytraa guide me!'

Once more he came to the surface. Gasping for air, he saw her rise nearby only to sink again as he approached.

⁂

Aglydron, only partly aware of what was happening, found the tiller. At Okkyntalah's call on Ytraa he became fully awake and tried to turn the boat toward the boy. It was more than his skill could manage. The boat tossed and heaved, making no forward progress. In panic at potential disaster, he dropped the sail and let it flap. He took an oar from the bottom of the boat and sculled. He'd seen boatmen move their shallow craft across the calm waters of the island lake in this fashion. Slowly, almost imperceptibly, the boat moved toward his target.

The dragons' flames diminished and died. Only a sullen red glow from the distant mountain, and the moon's feeble light relieved the darkness. But still he fixed his eyes on the position of the swimmer as he frantically tried to close the distance.

⁎

Aklon-Dji approached his father's house with stealth in the darkness. He circled three times and learned only that the domestic slaves were now all female. He could find no sound or sign to show that Jodisa-Li was home. But, from her bedchamber, he heard another female cry quietly at some hurt. For a while, the evidence of his ears and eyes puzzled him. When the woman called out the name of her tormentor, he understood that Wesdan Kaz had taken up residence in the High Priest's house. But where was his sister?

Even as the question formed, he was overcome with a feeling of such deep distress, a sense of such imminent danger to life, that he fell to his knees and had to remain still, his breathing hard and fast. Without understanding why, he reached out with his mind and found himself in water, drowning, taking water into his lungs and choking on the salt taste of brine.

'Kick your legs. Kick upwards or you will perish. Fight it. Fight the darkness. Move upwards to the surface. Hold your breath. Kick. Kick. Kick.'

The weight of water broke above him and the blackness of the night was bright with stars. He breathed in deep draughts of fresh air and coughed and choked as water surged up through his throat and spurted from him. So real was this sensation that he felt the ground to discover if it was wet. He tried to form the link again but it was gone, leaving a sensation as troubling as the previous moments had been extraordinary.

He'd been in the sea with, impossible as it seemed, Jodisa. And she'd been drowning. Of that, he was certain. But he wasn't with her now. And what was she doing in the sea? He regained the use of his legs and rose unsteadily to his feet on the dry mud. Did that mean she was now safe or had she drowned and he'd lost connection with her because of her death? Before he had time to reason, he was almost in the house, ready to demand answers about his sister's whereabouts. Instinct and his habit of survival stopped his hand, even as it pressed the door. He shook himself and knew his own death would be certain if he went inside like this.

Breathing deep and silent, he gave himself time to calm and recover before he left his father's house. He set off down narrow streets toward the harbour, in search of the source of information he'd first intended to visit. Maybe Syylvah could explain some of what he'd experienced.

⁎

Okkyntalah forced himself toward her, thrusting through the sea until he found the spot. But he couldn't dive again. Not now. He was exhausted. And then she was with him. Suddenly on the surface, coughing, choking. Relieved, he held her head above the waves, as she vomited water back into the sea.

143

Calling Aglydron's name, he swam toward the boat. But he was tiring after so many dives, his soaked tabard impeding him. The girl was unconscious and he must keep her face out of the water. Twice, waves overcame him. Twice, he pushed himself and his precious load back to the surface. But he could hang on for only moments. If Aglydron didn't come right now, he must drown and lose the girl. Their journey was for nothing. Aglydron must return to Muhnilahm alone. Face an agonising death for his blasphemies. All was lost.

Something solid nudged his back. The boat? Almost with his last strength, he turned. In the dim light, he saw a grotesque shape moving with him. He grasped the nearest part. Found a broad, wooden beam beneath his hand. Fighting, now the chance of life was so close, he struggled to lift and drag Jodisa-Li onto the floating debris. Heedless of her skin scraping against timber, he forced her onto curved planks of wood that rose above the surface from the beam. Too exhausted now to even kick his legs, he clung on with his hands and watched the girl as she lay prone above him on the ruined planks.

Aklon-Dji stood in the open doorway of the small house and listened. Outside, the noises of the harbour; ropes slapping masts in the gentle breeze, waves washing the beach, loose sails flapping listlessly, contrasted with the quiet in the house. Only one person breathed in sleep, indicating it was safe to enter.

She was on her back, her hair tumbled wild and soft across the pillow. His lips found her mouth as his hand enclosed her hip and she moaned and shifted as dream mingled with reality and sleep gave way to slow awareness.

"Bout time too.'

'Where is he?'

"Im? Who cares? Long as you're 'ere, at last.'

'I need to know, Syylvah.'

'Time is it?'

'A half past the mid of night.'

"E'll not be 'ome now, then. Either in some drunken woman's bed, else on the floor of the inn. 'E'll not be back tonight.'

She was his most dangerous but possibly his most devoted and well-informed recruit and she frequently risked more than she should on her own behalf as well as his. She'd know something of the fate of his sister. But, for the moment, the young woman had concerns other than the High Priest's daughter. And he knew he would get no sense from her until she had her reward.

'Okkyntalah! Jodisa!'

Aglydron sculled across the broken waves, surf still loud at the starboard side, foaming waters now all too clear against the blackness of night. He reached them as the boy was losing his grip and in danger of going under for the final time. Leaning out, he grasped Okkyntalah's wrist and pulled him back above the surface, dragged him over the beam and onto the wooden flotsam that scraped and ground against the boat. He could do no more without leaving the vessel, and that was too dangerous.

Shaulah, who'd barked just once as her master plunged into the sea, put her paws on the gunwale and looked down into darkness where he lay half in, half out of water.

With no alternative, Aglydron made a makeshift noose and tossed it at the wreckage supporting the boy and girl. Three times he found no purchase, but the fourth throw caught on something strong enough to hold and he allowed a little slack before attaching his end of the rope to the boat so they wouldn't part in the night.

Tired by his efforts, he knew he couldn't rest yet. The two on the flotsam weren't secure and low sharp rocks of the reef remained too close. He must first get them away from danger and then devise a way of hauling the pair into the boat.

With the added drag of floating wreckage, the boat was even more sluggish. As he sculled slowly away, he continually scanned the raft to make sure they weren't in danger of falling off or drowning where they lay. For what seemed hours, he pushed the oar back and forth in the water behind the boat until the surf was no more than a distant memory, the choppy seas a slow soft swell. Only when he felt there was no further danger of grounding or capsizing did he stop. Then, he raised the sail once more, to flap inconsequentially in the still air of fading night. He fixed the tiller to steer them on a direct course toward the smoking mountain and the island.

Too exhausted to move, Aglydron watched as Okkyntalah finally stirred out of his own exhaustion. The boy moved slowly and pulled himself further on to the uneven surface of the wreckage that had saved them and bent over the girl's still form.

Chapter 16

MYSTERIES

*O*kkyntalah placed a hesitant hand on Jodisa-Li's chest and closed his eyes in relief at the slow rise and fall. Shallow and weak, her breath at least declared she still lived after the near calamity. The touch of her skin recalled his fruitless dream, cause of this mess, and he lifted his hand, determined to avoid carnal thoughts of her and concentrate on Ytraa's will. Again, they'd experienced the wrath of Ytraa and, again, they'd been shown Ytraa's mercy when they relied on their God.

He stroked her head and eased his hands beneath her to raise her from the wooden planks. She moaned and he wondered if she might have some injury he couldn't see. But, upright, she coughed and retched. More seawater and the contents of her stomach splashed her lower half and Okkyntalah's thighs. He urged her to sit and spew the rest of the seawater. She coughed and gagged; moaned as she rested against him.

Slowly she came to.

Pain, at the side of her head. Sickness in her stomach. Jodisa-Li felt aches in her body, soreness on her skin. Gradually, she realized parts of her were wet whilst others were dry. Her mouth tasted foul. She coughed and retched. Salt water, mixed with the remains of her last meal, slopped into her lap.

She was naked. The boy's arm was round her shoulders, his skin touching hers. His other arm was beneath her knees and his face so close she could feel his breath on her cheek. She ought to feel outraged, but her body and mind allowed no emotion and no action.

'Is the girl all right, Okkyntalah?'

'I think so.'

The men called across a distance far greater than the boat. She felt too weak to move. Too weak even to protest, too weak to denounce the boy for daring to touch her. Yet, part of her found the touch reassuring, comforting, even welcome. She was soiled and that mattered more.

'I must clean…'

'Time enough when you're recovered. We thought we'd lost you.'

What had happened? How had she come to be this way? Everything was dark. She could feel but could see almost nothing. Her head hurt. The boy stroked the sore skin of her back, talking softly and apologising. But his words blurred, like colours seen through moving air above a fire, without edges, shifting, forming and dissolving so they made no sense. The darkness had a noise inside it, pulsing, fading and pounding until it ceased abruptly.

'She's fainted, Aglydron. I think we ought to get her into the boat, if you can help?'

'I don't think I've the strength just yet.'

Okkyntalah retched at the acid stench of vomit in his nostrils. He moved his head away to seek fresh air and scented something far worse, nearby. That smell made him recoil and want no more to do with it. He rejected what it told him. He must do something, anything to keep it from his consciousness.

'I'm going to wash her. She'll not thank us for putting her in her sleepsack covered in sick. Perhaps, when I've done, you'll help me move her.'

'Maybe.'

Okkyntalah gently let her slide onto her back. He surveyed his surroundings and, under the light from moon and stars and the flickering radiance of the cloud, he guessed they were lodged on part of a wrecked ship. Broken and curving, it seemed to be a portion of the bows of a vessel much larger than their own. Odd sparks of unexplained green came and went about the edges of the flotsam. The wreckage floated well on the calm surface of the sea, though it was constantly awash and would afford no protection in rough water. A long beam, broken at the end, protruded from the planks and ribs of this makeshift raft. He recalled clinging to it when he thought he might drown.

The rising curve towards the remains of the prow lay in deep, impenetrable shadow. But the thing he'd nosed lurked within that blackness, like a nightmare, and he wanted nothing of it.

Kneeling over the girl's prone form, he cupped seawater and sluiced his own body and hers, washing her with his palms to wipe off the soiling, rinsing her again and again until they were both cleansed. He turned her to face him as he washed her back, holding her close to his own body and feeling the wonder of her skin against his own now he no longer feared for her life.

She moaned again, waking briefly as he turned her again onto her back and away from him.

'What…?' But she fell back into unconsciousness.

'Pull us close, Aglydron; help me get her in the boat.'

Aglydron heaved on the rope, pulling the wreckage until it scraped the stern of their own craft. He secured it with a clumsy knot and reached out to gather the girl from

Okkyntalah as he carried her toward him on his knees across the planks.

With care, the boy transferred her to Aglydron. He took her weight and felt her lightness, the slightness of her form. He thought of Shoarhn at home, so lithe and slender. He laid the girl gently on top of her sleepsack so the air might dry her skin before he covered her.

Okkyntalah stepped into the boat and laid his own sleepsack beside hers. Without a word, he lay down to sleep.

'I'll release the wreckage.'

'Let it be. We'll free it when there's light enough to see what saved us. It's better we don't cut rope if we don't have to.'

Aglydron agreed. He let the wreckage float behind them, tugging now and then, as the boat moved slowly through the dying night. Dawn came softly as they drifted in a quiet sea. He trimmed the sail again and put into practice some of Okkyntalah's lessons, coaxing the small craft and its bulky follower toward the distant island with its mountain of fire.

⁂

Aklon-Dji woke to the sound of argument in the next room. He was dressed in an instant, his back to the wall, just within the doorway, hand on the hilt of his sword. The words and voices caught up with his survival instinct and told him Syylvah was scolding her man, Wurrt. He relaxed a little. Syylvah was more than equal to her feeble waster of a husband. She'd married him only because of the wealth his father had promised. The old man had changed his mind after he remarried a younger woman, who wanted her own children and all his wealth for their futures. This loss had persuaded Wurrt to send his wife out to tease coin from gullible foreign sailors.

'I don't spend me life partin' me thighs to anyone wi' a few dorltahs just so's you can chuck it down your useless throat! You're a worthless squitter. A waste o' space. Get out an' earn some coin o' your own if you want to fill yourself with fallin' over juice. Go on! I'm sick o' the sight o' you.'

The man's whining, mumbled reply was too indistinct for Aklon-Dji to make out but it was clear he left the house.

'An' don't come back unless you're sober!'

He waited a moment and stepped from the bedchamber into the other room to find Syylvah standing at the open door, her fist raised to the back of her disappearing husband.

'Is he ever sober?'

She turned and studied him. Her face reformed the scowl into a smile of pleasure, and she closed the door. Stepping up, she wrapped her arms about his neck before she spoke. 'I s'pose you want breakfast.'

'The idea is not without appeal.'

'Afore or after?' She pushed him backwards, laughing and giving him no choice.

Over food, as the sun climbed higher and the hot air of mid-morning wafted the smell of the harbour through the open door, he asked what she knew of his sister.

'It's all the talk, Aklon-Dji. Thought you'd 'ave 'eard by now.'

Morning began poorly, with prayers strained by Jodisa-Li sulking over her state on waking. Okkyntalah, with the strong memory of his cause of the accident, avoided looking at her and busied himself with an examination of the wreckage that had saved their lives.

In the clear light of sunrise, the reason for his fear during darkness was plain. The smell, now rank in their nostrils, arose from the horror lurking within the curved section of broken bow. The corpse was bloated, eyes gone and skin taut over swollen flesh. Scraps of fine fabric clung to parts of the dead woman.

'Cut it loose and let it drift to haunt some other place.' Jodisa-Li's shudder of fear surprised Okkyntalah, who felt less afraid now he knew the source.

'I'll see if I can free her and let the sea take her. She can rest in peace instead of providing pickings for the seemeeuws.'

'Would she be better as nazzakk food?'

'Rather the sea have her than she drift endlessly, to be picked piecemeal until her bones bleach in the sun. No, I'll cut her free, then we'll release the wreckage.'

Aglydron hauled the floating pall a little closer to allow Okkyntalah to step aboard. He knelt beside the corpse and mastered his revulsion at the stench of death, his repugnance at rotting flesh already invaded by small sea creatures. His knife sliced the strange net that had caught her. She wasn't bound but the net that draped her had wrapped itself beneath keel and planks, and twisted around the broken beam. At regular lengths along its outer edges were green, egg-shaped objects, about the size of a human head. On closer inspection, Okkyntalah saw they were hollow and transparent. He cut one loose and tossed it to Aglydron.

'Any idea what it might be?'

The older man shook his head, baffled.

'Let me see.'

Jodisa-Li held it up and looked through it, her face a frown of deep concentration. 'It's glass. A merchant told father about a solid material you could see through. Of course, we laughed, but he insisted it was true; said it was called glass. I think this is it.'

'Do you suppose it's worth anything?'

Aglydron shrugged. 'We've no room for treasure.'

Okkyntalah nodded and freed the body. She slid toward him, tearing rotten skin and releasing more of her putrid stench into the air.

He was about to let her go, when he saw the bangle and knew he must retrieve it. Her ankle was swollen and he had to force it over her foot, scraping skin and flesh with it. He held the ornament for a moment in wonder. With care and tenderness, he eased the corpse along the planks to the broken edge. Gently, he let the water take her. Even before she'd sunk into the clear blue, fish were at her, tearing, ripping, devouring.

'Take this woman, oh Lord Gadhallah, and though we know not her name nor whether she was a true Follower, may Ytraa allow her into the Garden of Delights, where she will know happiness and rest forever.' He stood on the wreckage and sang a short lament he'd last sung at the burial of his grandmother.

Okkyntalah stood for a moment of silence and then bent and washed the smell of her from his arms and hands, and the bangle. Curious about the strange glass ovoids, he released more of them and watched as they floated freely on the waves. 'I think they must've helped keep this wreckage afloat, you know. I wonder what they're for.'

He cut the final tie that held the net to the wreckage and, slowly, the sodden wood began to sink. At once, he released the noose of rope from the rusted iron bracket that Aglydron had caught blindly in the night and, stepping into the boat, watched the wreckage disappear beneath waves. The remains of the rope, with its glass floats, bobbed along behind them in the water.

As he turned, he caught Jodisa-Li staring at him with a look of wonder and knew he'd impressed her in a way he didn't understand. He smiled and shrugged, passing the bangle to Aglydron.

'Amazing. Solid gold; encrusted with rubies and emeralds. Not a slave, then. A hostage?'

'You surely didn't rob the poor woman?'

'It's no use to her. A trinket like this might feed us for portions to come on the mainland.' Aglydron nodded at Okkyntalah. 'You did well to save it.'

'Hand it to me.'

Aglydron passed it to her. She examined it and nodded before passing it back to him. 'Not gold. Myllth. Worth a fortune. I wonder who she was.'

Okkyntalah caught the tone of concern in her voice but Aglydron seemed not to have noticed.

'Doubt we'll ever know.'

'Is that my destiny? The anonymous hostage, the nameless plaything of fate? Is that my future?'

'Whatever Ytraa decides. That's your future, Jodisa.'

'You care nothing for me. I'm not a woman, not a person. I'm just an article of exchange. One piece of property to be swapped for another.'

'I care for you as much as any true Follower. I might not care for you as much as I do for Shoarhn, or Tumalind. But I care as....'

'Care enough to scrape my skin raw and leave me naked for the world to see. Care enough to shame me. Enough to let this boy lie beside me uncovered and close enough to...'

'The boy, as you so rudely call him, saved your life! Okkyntalah nearly drowned saving you. And we left you uncovered so you'd dry off. You were wet! We were exhausted and you were covered in sick. It was as much as we could do to get you back into the boat. I'm sorry you're upset, Jodisa, but we didn't leave you uncovered out of disrespect; we were just too tired to do anything else. Any case, it was dark, so we couldn't see you.'

She glared at Aglydron but said no more. It was possible they were telling the truth. The humiliation of such involuntary display before men like these roused her anger and she was in no mood to be conciliatory. It was the man's fault. Okkyntalah at least cared for her and she couldn't blame him for what had happened.

He leant over the side of the boat and caught the net with its glass floats. She could see his mind working as he examined it. Slowly he nodded and set about the net with his hunting knife until he'd reduced it to a long length of rope with the remaining floats attached. To her amazement, he then drew the rope around the outside of the boat, up under the gunwales, asking Aglydron to hold the loose end as he spliced the rope to form a complete loop about the boat, which he then attached at various points with more short lengths of the cut netting.

'Might help keep us afloat in another storm.'

Aglydron just grunted and she was still too angry to say anything, but her admiration grew, as it had with his unexpected song for the dead woman.

All morning, through their silent midday meal of strips of dried dorado and of fresh tonyina, caught by Okkyntalah, washed down with tepid water, she fretted. In the afternoon, she took a turn at the tiller, trying to ignore her sore back. She handed over to Okkyntalah and lay on her front to ease the pain of her salted grazes.

Still she rankled over her exposure in the night but she remained silent, turning over in her mind their behaviour and realizing at last that they hadn't violated her, though they could have. She'd let it drop for now, but it was another crime to add to the list she'd give her father when they found him. If they found him.

And how likely was that? Would she spend the next few cycles, her best, tied like a slave to these two fanatics who only wanted her as a virgin, searching fruitlessly for her father in all the lands between here and Choshinahm? They wanted only to swap her for a common girl who could have no concept of what she was missing by being a Virgin Gift. But she, Jodisa-Li, as High Priest Elect, should be free; free to indulge in the pleasure and fun her office conferred, and with any man she chose. Once she'd had the necessary days on the Plain of Ytraa, indulging those dreadful Holy Ones, she would've been free to make sorties into sexual freedoms conferred by her rank and position.

Had she risked blindness and blistered skin from the potion for nothing? Had she let those crones probe her very centre with their instruments of mystery, hurting her and cackling as she cried in pain, testing her and declaring her suitable for the delaying treatment, had all that been to no purpose? She was secure now. Could have any man she wanted, take the pleasure she'd been promised in return for all the pain and risk, and know she would begin no new life within her womb until and unless she chose.

And now these imbeciles, these cretins denied her her reward. They'd keep her pure for some undeserving Follower on the mainland. She hadn't been reared for that. As leader of the Followers after her father died, she could and would join with as many as she wished. It was her destiny. That Ytraa remained man and woman and God in one being was still true, in spite of everything else Gadhallah had admitted in his secret journals. She must make herself one with man as often as she could and thus be as close in form to Ytraa as was possible for a woman. Only in the ecstasy of joining, could man or woman know the joy of oneness with Ytraa. That's what she must display to the fools she would rule. It was what she'd been raised for, it was why she was. And it became too much to stay inside her, silent and unsaid.

'Fools! You know nothing of my life and purpose. You deprive me of my sacred duty, my very reason for existence with your petty adherence to rules that are meaningless for such as Dagla Kaz and me. We transcend the ways of mortal men and women. We, who are direct descendants of the line of Gadhallah, don't obey common rules. Through Vaarkil and Mythanpho to Gadhallah, we can trace our line back. We're not like you. I'm not like you. I don't belong within your narrow definitions of what's right and wrong. I'm outside such considerations. I'm High Priest Elect, chosen by Ytraa to show the way to all Followers. You can't deny what I am. You can't deny me my sacred right and duty. You must let me be what I must be, what I am.'

They looked at her with surprise at her sudden outburst. Okkyntalah bowed as though he understood her plea but said nothing, deferring to the older man, the teacher, to decide what response was due.

'What you might've been doesn't matter, Jodisa. Ytraa Chose you. You were Chosen, whether you like it or not. You're not High Priest Elect. You're a Virgin Gift.'

'I'm not a virgin! I'm not!' Her carefully directed anger, controlled and aware of certain untruths as she'd made her initial plea, now broke down under a combination of fear, desperation, rage and frustration. 'I've had more men than a temple prostitute, more than any Holy One, more men than that whore, Kaz-Ca-Charrohn. I've frowked ten men in a day. I've even had an infant torn from me before it could...before he...' She faltered; tears springing to her eyes and undoing all the doubt her lies had spread.

The single truth, that grief so absolute she couldn't think of it without the deepest sorrow, destroyed all her tales and, with what they would see as its utter impossibility, brought into question every lie she'd spun in her attempt to shock them into believing she wasn't virgin so they'd abandon their quest and let her go.

Aglydron seemed moved by her display of emotion in a way she hadn't expected. He embraced her, as a father might an errant child, in forgiveness.

'See, Jodisa, you're too good, too honest. You try to make us think you're wicked and unclean; unworthy. But you can't even bear the idea of that final blasphemy. I should beat you for your wicked words, but I won't. It's clear your heart's pure and you said all that just to make us take you back to Muhnilahm. We can't. You must accept your lot, as I have, as Okkyntalah has. We've a long road together, Jodisa. It'll be easier for all of us if you just accept the will of Ytraa.'

She should've burst with sheer frustration at his reasoning. She should've shouted that he was wrong, wrong, wrong. But her profound grief at the recent loss of her child and the cruel death of its father, mingled with Aglydron's concern and compassionate embrace to make her weep instead. She let him hold her as she sobbed for lives passed out of knowing, for a future that would never be, for a past steeped in wickedness, for a life ahead that must be all she'd been raised to despise, that must reject the whole of what she'd been educated to expect.

Chapter 17

THE VANISHINGS

*O*kkyntalah roused them from their separate, exclusive reveries. 'We've reached the island.'

Practical considerations overcame whatever thoughts and feelings Aglydron and Jodisa-Li had shared in their prolonged embrace. Okkyntalah remained excluded and knew that they were closer for their mutual experience. Because he perceived that what they shared wasn't sexual, he felt no jealousy.

'We've made good time. I didn't think we'd get here before nightfall.'

'Good wind. It changed mid-morning; been a following wind since our meal. This boat's quite good when handled well. Better than the one I learnt on, anyway. Whose boat did you steal?'

'Don't know. We took the easiest one to get out of the harbour.'

'That may make sense, Aglydron, but some poor fisherman's lost his livelihood as well as a fine vessel. I hope you're both proud of your thieving.' The condemnation in her voice and on her face seemed reduced, as if something had changed in her.

'As proud as we are of taking you against your will, Jodisa. We did what must to fulfil the will of Ytraa. Nothing else matters.'

She sighed. 'The will of Ytraa. Yes. I see. Well, let me take the helm, Okkyntalah. Oh, and thank you for saving my life. I've nothing to reward your bravery, since you won't have me even were I willing. But I'll tell my father, if we ever find him; it might spare you some agony. Aglydron, sit in the bows and watch for reefs and outcrops. The coast around the island is supposed to be dangerous. They say it's impossible to land here except for one small cove.'

'And where's that?' Aglydron's voice betrayed annoyance at the way she'd taken over, but he said nothing of it.

'I don't know. I've never been here.'

'You seem to know a lot about the island.'

'My father taught me much, Okkyntalah, and I'm a quick learner. As High Priest, you need to be clever, quick-witted, sharp and wise.'

'As a Virgin Gift, you should be obedient, graceful, humble and accepting.'

Okkyntalah saw resentment in her eyes as she took the tiller and sat down. He wondered what more trouble she'd give before they handed her to her father. Beautiful and tempting she may be but, when he stopped daydreaming, he still yearned for

Tumalind with her uncomplicated love and simple needs. And, whilst Jodisa-Li might be honey for the eyes, he understood that his attraction to her was no more than lust. What he felt for Tumalind was love; a deeper and more satisfying need.

'She'll do very well for you, Okkyntalah, if we ever find her.'

He looked up at her and saw her laughing silently at his surprise. How could she know? Could she read his mind? He tried a question in his mind, asking would she join with him if it were allowed, just to see if she responded. The smile on her face and the single nod, as she looked into his eyes, left him uncertain. And the proximity of the island left him no time to dwell on it.

The coastal approaches were littered with small, jagged rocks and shallow shoals. Rocks lurked just below and jutted through the surface in a few places but elsewhere the water was deep and untroubled under cliffs as steep and precipitous as those on the Point. In other places, the rock looked as though it had once been liquid but had solidified in strange shapes; grotesque, cruel and dangerous. They sailed the eastern coast and found nowhere to land. At the northern tip of the small island they could see the slopes of the fire mountain, where sudden bursts of flame and steam, awed them. Slowly moving streams of red-hot viscous matter, like the molten metal from the smiths' furnaces, and clouds of thick black smoke issued from the summit. The rumble echoed across the water as deep-throated growls.

'Are there dragons?'

'Here? Or in general?'

Okkyntalah stared at her. 'Both.'

'No such things. Tales for children's bedtime. Nonsense.'

She shook her head at Aglydron. 'Denying the existence of what frightens you doesn't make it cease to exist. There are dragons in the mountains between Cushlanah and Choshinahm. But not here. This is just a fire mountain. Fierce, cruel and without mercy, it has a spirit the people placate with blood. Perhaps, if they don't eat us, we'll be sacrifices.'

'Take no notice, Okkyntalah; she's trying to frighten us with tales because she fears the island. She thinks we'll turn back for Muhnilahm for want of food and water.'

'Wrong, Aglydron. I expect you to seek a way onto the island and attempt to find food and water to continue your journey with me as captive. But you'll find no hospitality here. We're more likely to end up roasted for the table or in the mountain's jaws.'

'Look! A cavern; between those outcrops. I'm sure I can see a beach inside.'

Aglydron followed Okkyntalah's pointing finger. 'Much good it'll do us. D'you think there'll be a stairway through solid rock, up to the surface? It's hopeless. We'll try the western shore before nightfall.'

They moved with difficulty now the fitful wind blew directly against them. Lowering the sail, the two men rowed the boat, as the girl became lookout for rocks and other dangers.

At the northern end of the western shore, the rocks and cliffs were all of the molten type; in places splintered, craggy and sharp with teeth that would rip the bottom from their boat should they go too near. They rowed two leagues and still the cliffs were unassailable.

Jodisa-Li saw the beach, just as Aglydron and Okkyntalah were growing tired of pulling the vessel through the choppy waves. She guided them toward dark grey sand gently sloping out of the water into trees and dense low shrubbery, beneath a sheer scowling cliff. They beached the boat and rested, relieved to be on land again and free from constant motion. Shaulah ran across the sand to nose amongst the vegetation.

Okkyntalah left Aglydron with the girl and, calling Shaulah, made off into the trees to search for a way up onto the island. When he returned, he discovered Jodisa-Li had gathered driftwood for a fire and Aglydron had caught two good-sized pagurya, with red shells and large fighting pincers, from the rock pools.

The girl started a fire with her burning glass before the sun was too low. She brought a water skin and an unglazed, open pot from the boat to cook their evening meal. Their first cooked food since they'd left home.

'Next cooking fire we see will probably be the one they roast us over.'

By the time Okkyntalah returned from his second sortie, in the other direction, the pagurya were almost ready to eat.

'The smoke from the fire's visible from the foot of the cliffs, Aglydron. I hope it's not too obvious from the top of them.'

'Is there a way up?'

'There's a fall of clear, fresh water that drops into a pool. I'll collect fresh supplies there after we've eaten'

'Can I bathe there, to wash my skin free of salt?'

'We all should.'

'The water falls sheer from an overhanging lip and there's no way up beside it. I travelled the length of the beach from where the sea meets the cliff to the other end, where it meets the cliff again. There's no way up.'

'Did you see any sign of people?'

Okkyntalah recognised thinly veiled fear in her voice. 'There's a pile of bones close to the far end of the cliff. A man, I'd guess. And I found this nearby.' He showed them a wooden stave, broken at one end and carved at the other in the likeness of a man's face, screaming in agony. The workmanship was as fine as it was alarming.

'Perhaps he was carrying it and fell over the cliff.'

'Or he was pushed.' Jodisa-Li's fear showed in her face.

'We can't do nothing just now. Let's eat and spend a night on dry land. We'll decide what to do in the morning.'

'Or we could fill the waterskins and sail on, living off Okkyntalah's fish.'

'I don't believe they're cannibals, Jodisa-Li. Do you, Okkyntalah?'

'The skull was cloven in two. I'd say he was killed and pushed over the cliff. I don't think anybody tried to eat him.'

'Perhaps not. But someone killed him, didn't they?'

Unsure what had woken her, Jodisa-Li lay still, feeling relaxed after a good sleep, listening to soft surf on the beach, foreign songbirds in nearby trees, wind sighing through broad leaved shrubs. The ever present rumble from the fire mountain, so deep and penetrating it felt as if the ground itself grumbled, reminded her of where she was and why. She sat and eased herself from her sleepsack, reached for her tabard and put it on, wondering where her waistrope had gone.

The leather leash connecting her to Aglydron, to prevent her escaping in the night, had vanished. She wondered when he'd decided to allow her such freedom. Judging by the paleness of the sky, the sun was already above the horizon on the far side of the island.

'Sun up.' Okkyntalah rose on her far side and she turned at his movement.

'The boat's gone!' Instinctively, she checked again that both men were still with her, one either side. Only the dog was missing, and she could hardly have taken the boat.

The men were wide awake at once. All three rose to scan the sea. But there was no sign of their vessel. Reluctantly, Jodisa-Li joined them as Aglydron, in this moment of fear and near panic, insisted they all pray.

'Nothing must stop our prayers or we risk Ytraa's wrath.'

She made a perfunctory act of worship, and stood again as the men donned their tabards, which also lacked belts. It was then that Aglydron turned on her.

'What have you done with the tether?'

'Nothing. I thought you'd removed it whilst I slept.'

'Don't try that, girl. Give me it or I'll stripe your hide.'

Okkyntalah called the dog but there was no response.

'It wasn't there when I woke up. Just like our other things and the boat; it's gone.'

He glared at her but said nothing. They searched the nearby space but found only their sleepsacks, the tabards they were wearing and the ashes of the fire. Everything else had gone. Okkyntalah's hunting belt and knife, the cooking pot, Aglydron's short sword and scabbard, Jodisa-Li's waistrope, fashioned from her own hair, with its gilt clasps and small kid purse containing her burning glass and a few gold rounds, all had gone.

When they examined the sand where they'd beached the boat, there was no trace of its ever having been there. No footprints in the sand. It was as if they'd been cast up on this beach just as they were. They wandered aimlessly, calling for the dog and unsure what they should or could do.

'Follow. All restored will be.'

The disembodied voice came from the trees. Jodisa-Li searched for the speaker but could see no one.

'No harm befall you will. Unless be you not what seem you.'

'Can you see him?'

Okkyntalah shook his head.

'Come.'

'Who are you? Show yourself.' Aglydron's voice sounded oddly harsh compared with the gentle coaxing from the trees.

'Come.'

'We stay here till we can see you.'

There was a long period of silence in which the fire mountain grumbled loudly and spewed hot ash and billowing smoke from its crown. No one moved and there was no motion in the trees.

Aglydron broke the silence. 'We're not moving till you show yourself.'

'So wish you. I reveal myself not. Only can be had food as I please.' The voice made this a statement rather than a threat.

They had no choice. Aglydron led Jodisa-Li toward the trees, Okkyntalah following.

'Come.'

A narrow path, which none of them had noticed the previous evening, wound through the undergrowth. Just barely, under the rumble of the fire mountain, the breaking of the surf and the sighing of the wind, Jodisa-Li thought she heard the soft fall of feet behind her. But when she turned, the noise, such as it was, stopped at once and there was no one to be seen. It was not Okkyntalah she heard.

The narrow track took them to the foot of the cliff close by the waterfall.

'Wish you may to refresh after your sleep yourselves.'

Jodisa-Li knelt and splashed cold water on her face before cupping her hands to wash out her mouth and quench her thirst. The men both scooped water to their mouths to drink and flush away the taste of sleep.

'First will travel the woman.'

She turned to discover a wooden structure; no more than a frame of branches lashed together with vines, hanging close to the rock face, suspended on a thicker vine that disappeared over a protruding stay at the top of the cliff.

'The bottom beam step on. The top hold with hands both.'

'Show yourself. This young woman's sacred to us. We can't let her go if we don't know who's taking her.' Aglydron's voice sounded flat and, in spite of his effort to sound authoritarian, his words rang hollow. There was no reply and all was silent for a space that seemed to last forever.

'First go will the woman.'

Jodisa-Li shrugged and stepped toward the frame but Aglydron put out his hand to stop her. At once, a small white pebble whistled from behind and struck his hand with enough force to make him cry out in pain and surprise.

'Not be prevented will the woman.'

<hr>

Aglydron watched Jodisa-Li place herself on the frame as instructed, stretching her arms to grasp the top pole. At once, she was pulled silently aloft until she came level with the cliff top. He was amazed when the stay turned sideways and swung the frame so she vanished from view. At once, the frame dropped back, stopping a hand's breadth from the ground.

'The man hunts who.'

Okkyntalah followed Jodisa-Li, his progress as rapid as the girl's in spite of his greater weight.

Aglydron went up last to join his companions on top of the cliff. The swift rise was alarming on the open frame but he made it without falling, not looking down as the ground flew away from him. He landed at the top and was surprised to find no sign of those who'd hoist them; no indication of how their movement up the cliff face had been achieved.

'Clear is the track but winds it. Pain or death find you will if from it deviate you. Lie in the trees traps and dangers.' It was the same voice.

'Where are you taking us? Who are you?' Jodisa-Li's normally confident tones fell like drops of fear from her lips and carried only to the nearest tree before they failed.

Aglydron looked at his companions in the silence that followed. 'We've no choice.'

They took the trail, walking single file between trees and dense undergrowth as it led them snaking up the sloping hillside under dappled sunlight. Again, the fire mountain grumbled, making the ground tremble.

Birds with brightly coloured plumage flitted in the upper branches of tall trees. Small, bright granota in rainbow colours, hopped along the ground on their long back legs, their webbed feet incongruous out of water. Some climbed trees as they croaked their melancholy chorus. Shrubs bright with flowers of every colour, size and shape, decorated the floor of the forest and leant their heady fragrances to the still air. Timid creatures, like antelope but smaller and more delicate, peered curiously from the shadows before returning to feast on leaves and flowers in the undergrowth.

They climbed to a wide flat treeless ridge with a shallow hollow along the centre of its length. Here, the forest opened north to give a clear view along the spine of the island to the fire mountain. Thick black smoke flowed from the top of the cone and flashes of red and orange glowed and died within and underneath the billowing dust and fumes. The ever-present rumble made the air vibrate. Aglydron could smell the mountain's evil breath; even feel the heat of it on the breeze. A great roar issued from its throat and the very ground split at the cone as he watched, releasing a slow, thick flow of glowing matter that moved inexorably down the hollow of the ridge toward them.

'What in Ytraa's name...?'

'You're sure these aren't dragons?'

'Not dragons, Okkyntalah. The mountain vomits fire from the belly of the world itself. Like a festering boil, when lanced, pours forth its poison, so the mountain spills the heated blood of the world in sickness. This is the work of Mhortag and we do well to fear it.'

They looked at Jodisa-Li with respect as she spoke with such confidence about this fearful danger.

'Come. Short grows time.'

They forced their gaze from the spectacle and sought the path, only to find it failed out here in the open. Instead, the ridge sloped down to the south, the central hollow growing deeper and the sides steeper so it formed a channel down toward the southern tip of the island. There, less than half a league away, a village lay cradled in the bottom where the channel widened to a flat plain between the steep tree-lined walls of the elevated valley.

As they approached, walking abreast along the broad stony way, Aglydron saw houses of mud bricks, thatched with long leaves. A small spring broke from the ground a hundred paces from the nearest house and flowed swiftly down the dark grey ground in a rocky bed. It fed a small lake where children, playing naked in the shallows, stopped to stare in silent wonder as the visitors passed. Of adults, there was no sign.

Closer, the round huts looked crude and makeshift, as if they were of no importance; mere shelters against inclement weather. No pride or design had formed them. The entrances were rough open spaces in the walls, uncurtained and without doors. There were no openings for windows.

They walked on, driven by a compulsion they could feel without naming, until they reached what must be the centre of the settlement; a wide rough circle devoid of buildings and unpaved but with a surface worn smooth by the passage of many feet. In the centre stood an object none of them expected in this place. Without pause or thought, they prepared for prayer and prostrated themselves before the faces of this strange manifestation of their God.

This was Ytraa in a shape and form they hadn't known. Each, having made the prayers that seemed most suitable and right, rose from the dust and stood in wonder.

Here, in this small village, far from Ytraa's chosen place, these Followers had carved the trunk of a great, living tree into a likeness of Ytraa that was as wonderful as it was strange. The figures of Ytraa as man, woman and God intertwined and linked like mortal men and women striving to join and become Ytraa so that it was impossible to tell where one figure ended and another began. Man was wrapped in woman, woman coiled round God, God embraced man and woman as the figure rose up, reaching for the open skies above.

'Naked worship you?'

Aglydron reluctantly removed his rapt gaze from the God and turned to find many people had gathered silently to stare at them. The voice, that which had urged and guided them to the village, issued from behind a mask set on the shoulders of a man who stood an armslength taller than the rest. He moved forward and apart from the crowd. Leaves and flowers intertwined with living snakes around a frame of woven twigs that hid the man's head completely. From a fine leather band around his neck an exquisitely carved wooden five-pointed star hung, the fifth point uppermost. A thick kidskin belt at his hips, strung with flowers, leaves and feathers from brightly plumaged birds, formed a loose skirt that hung down his thighs.

All the men in the crowd were dressed in like manner, except they wore no mask, only coloured devices painted on their faces, each different. The men were fat and indolent, though the tall man with the mask was almost gaunt. The women wore skirts of flowers and feathers about their hips and kidskin bands around their shoulders, also strung with fresh flowers and feathers, partially concealing their breasts. Their faces were not painted but their hair was braided with fine cords and starred with small flowers. They were all lithe.

Jodisa-Li retrieved her tabard and covered herself.

Okkyntalah picked his up and hesitated. 'It makes no sense. We mustn't look at each other when at prayer but we stand naked in public before Ytraa…' He shrugged himself into his tabard.

'Now isn't the time for such questions, Okkyntalah.' Aglydron, unconcerned about others' opinions, held to his respect and devotion in the presence of Ytraa and replied to the man. 'All Followers of Ytraa worship uncovered. How can we be like Ytraa if we hide from the gaze of Ytraa? How can Ytraa know our worth if we don't show our whole selves to Ytraa? How can we hope to join with Ytraa if we're not open and available to Ytraa? Don't you know this?'

'Nothing of this know Ittrah we. Your god to do with our Pillar of Life has what?'

'This isn't Ytraa?'

'A celebration of life this is. A tree this is; carved it is in likeness of men with women. Your god wooden is?'

Aglydron looked again and saw what was really there rather than what he'd hoped and wished to see. The profanity appalled him and he quickly clothed himself.

'I made a mistake. Our monument to Ytraa is built from five Godwoods, carved in the likeness of Ytraa. Soon there'll be six. I see now that this is an obscene mockery….'

'Trespassers here you are. Not invited you were. Worship our Pillar of Life we not do but venerate it we. Shows us it what is in life good. Nothing we bad see. With narrow mind and ways foreign your not insult us. Not of the Core you are?'

'I don't know what the core is. We're Followers, from Muhnilahm.'

'Unwelcome to island our are you. Leave you now must. Or die.'

'Why bring us here, then? We didn't ask to come but we can't leave without…'

The people gasped at Jodisa-Li's abrupt question and Aglydron quickly gathered that on this isolated island, women were not treated as equals.

'Jodisa, be silent. The men speak here.'

His tone of voice was enough, though he expected a lashing from her tongue later.

The masked man grunted approval.

Okkyntalah spoke, softly and without rancour. 'We're your guests, I think. But we don't understand what you require of us.'

At his naming of them as guests, the crowd murmured and the masked man bowed very slightly.

'Stay not you may. Know we now that not of the Core you are. Permitted only the Core is to remain. Go you must. Or must die you.'

Chapter 18

FIRE MOUNTAIN

The words and stance of the man in the mask gave ample warning and Aglydron knew they'd lose all if he didn't placate this strange and apparently magical person. 'Sorry, Paltrohn. I meant no offence. Your monument looks a bit like ours but it's not Ytraa. It's a work of great craft and skill, for all that.'

'Of great beauty is it. With us will die it in days three if wills Krakgragog it; if acceptable not our sacrifice is. Unless powerful more than Krakgragog Ittrah is and to stop the destruction act he will.'

'I don't think Ytraa will interfere.'

'Not will or not can?'

'I think the mountain will have its way.'

'All-powerful Krakgragog is. Sacrifice to him must we. Than sacrilege you and your companions worse as a sacrifice are. Not of the Core are you. For sacrifice suitable not those without value are. This place leave you must.' With this, the man turned his back and approached the crowd, all of whom looked away.

'How can we leave? We've none of...'

The man in the mask stopped but didn't face them. 'Not of the Core are you. If of the Core were you, sacrificed would be you. Leave must you. Witness what to appease Krakgragog we do may you not. Or die must you.'

'We'll gladly leave. We'd go now, but all our belongings have been stolen.'

The crowd gasped as if Jodisa-Li had said something profoundly shocking. The man in the mask began to shake from head to foot. He dropped to his knees, facing the crowd, which had stopped as one and turned as one to stare at them. Thrusting his right hand out at shoulder height, the masked man swung it in a wild, swift arc. When he stopped, his finger pointed at a young woman. Curling it, he moved her toward him as though attached to a cord. Seeming without volition, she lurched forward and stopped in front of him. He rose again. Stripping away the flowers and feathers, he exposed her chest. From his mask, he drew a small black and green striped snake by its tail. Holding it above the woman's head, he slowly lowered it down over her face until his hand reached her forehead. The snake stared at her through red eyes. It dropped and swayed over her heart, mouth wide to display long curving fangs, its forked tongue flickering like a small bright flame.

The crowd made no noise, no movement. The woman stood still as stone, silent as the sun. The snake waved and brushed her skin. It turned, hissing with a sound of death but then coiled up and around the wrist of the masked man. He released its tail at once and it slithered along his arm, back into his mask.

The crowd cried out in exultation and the woman closed her eyes briefly. When she opened them, she seemed released from outside control but fell to her knees before the masked man. Kissing his thighs, she stretched her arms sideways and lowered her head. He raised his left foot, placed it on the back of her head and slowly forced her to the ground until she lay prone, her arms still outstretched. He stepped lightly onto her back and uttered a short burst of ritual words. The crowd made a sound of agreement. He leapt high into the air and landed soft as a fallen leaf between the woman and the crowd, his back to her.

The people made a long slow sigh of loss, as one, and melted into the spaces between the huts behind them. Never turning, the masked man followed. In moments, the space about the Pillar of Life was empty of all but the three Followers and the woman, still lying on the ground.

Jodisa-Li ran across and knelt at her head. 'Are you hurt?'

Okkyntalah and Aglydron arrived in time to hear her say she wasn't. Jodisa-Li tried to help her to her feet but she wouldn't move.

'Come, we won't harm you. We want to get off the island and be on our way. Will you help us find...?' Aglydron's words had the required effect and she rose to her feet, her front dusty and her face streaked with the trails of tears.

'Help. Yes. No longer of the Core am I. Come. Please.' She plucked two long feathers from her skirt and turned to face the fire mountain. Shaping the feathers into a cross, she blew on them and called 'Krakgragog' three times. Thrusting her arms before her, she let the feathers fall to land in the dust. For a moment, she studied their positions until the wind shifted them.

'It is over. Come. Now, or we die.'

Aglydron began to question her about what had happened and whether she'd been chosen to help them.

She put her finger to her lips and shook her head. 'No time for explanations. Your questions must wait. We must go now. Follow me. Please.'

They looked at each other, puzzled.

'You speak normally but the masked man speaks...'

'Yatukon knows all. I am but a woman.' The woman stepped back into open space behind her, raised and pointed her forefinger, and turned on the spot, drawing an invisible circle round herself and then walking around all of them, speaking words meaningless to them. She walked swiftly out of the open space in the direction they had come, making for the southern end of the island. Aglydron and his companions watched her, unsure what she expected of them.

She stopped and turned to face them, her face full of pleading. She frowned with concentration until, suddenly visited by inspiration, she found the words. 'I know it's hard for you, but unless you come with me right now, in the next few moments, we will all die.'

They began to move and, as if to underline her words, a hail of stones and missiles rained toward them from the trees. They ran to their guide and followed as she led them toward the tongue of molten rock that flowed inexorably down the channel, making for the village. Feeling they had no choice on this strange island where nothing was explained but much happened, Aglydron encouraged the other two to keep up with her.

On the outskirts of the village, Okkyntalah spotted Shaulah strung upside down on a pole by her legs, a strap around her muzzle. He ran and lifted her from the branch on which she was hung. Okkyntalah had no knife to release her and returned with her as she was. He and Aglydron slung her between them like a hunting trophy. He paused to untie the gag.

'No time.' The woman glanced anxiously at the huts and pleaded with them. 'Now! Or we'll be too late!'

She began to trot toward the tongue of molten rock and, having no alternative, they followed, wondering what escape was to be made by running toward certain death up the slope.

As she ran, the heat and dust choked Jodisa-Li and dried her throat. They halted but the woman pulled at them desperately, appealing to Jodisa-Li, as if to a sister, to help her convince the men of the urgency.

'Please, tell them if I fail, we all die most horribly. Please make them see.'

Jodisa-Li could feel real terror and the sense of impending doom carried by the woman and she urged her forward, knowing the men wouldn't let her go without them.

So, they ran; coughing in the smoke and fumes, scorching under the heat of the sun and the fire from the mountain. When Jodisa-Li thought they must all be lost, consumed by the molten rock they approached, the woman halted and gazed about, clearly seeking something. The red-hot flow was now less than a hundred paces away, moving steadily forward, faster than a man could walk. The heat was almost unbearable this close. The woman nodded as if confirming her thoughts and led them to the low steep western wall of the channel.

Hidden within a narrow cleft in the face of the dark grey cliff, was a small black opening, wide as a broad man's shoulders and a little taller than Okkyntalah. She slipped into the gap and Jodisa-Li followed without a second thought. She sensed the men, with the dog slung between them, hard on her heels.

The darkness was almost total after the bright dusty sunshine and a cool draught replaced the stifling heat as fresh air blew from below. Jodisa-Li was tempted to stand and catch her breath in this sanctuary of peace and calm but the woman urged them on.

'Hurry. But take care. There's nothing to stop you falling and many hard steps lead to the bottom. I beg your leave to lead, for I know the way.'

Jodisa-Li followed, discovering well-cut stairs carved into the rock and leading down, steep and winding. No light came from behind after they turned the first corner in this black tunnel and none from below. She stepped in total darkness down a staircase she could feel only with her feet. Gave her trust to this unknown woman whose place and purpose she hardly understood.

'Put your hand on my shoulder; I'll guide you.'

Jodisa-Li placed her right hand on the woman's right shoulder and found her movement helped her understand the gradient and spacing of the steps so that she descended more certainly.

'You'd best do the same, Okkyntalah. I don't want you tumbling on top of me.'

She felt his hand softly discover her back with his fingertips, trace the skin in the V-neck of her tabard and caress her shoulder to rest there. In the darkness, the contact was more comfort than she expected.

A space of time, where there was only an unending descent into thick enclosing darkness, passed. The air ceased to cool them, no longer flowing from below but now following and overtaking them, in a hot foul stream, as if the mountain blew at them down the tunnel. There remained only the urgency of placing feet on stone, of feeling for step after step in a world blacker than night.

At last, as slate replaced jet, silence became soft sound that she identified as breaking waves. They came, quite suddenly, out of the tunnel onto a narrow ledge cut into the rock wall of a cave. Ahead, the blinding brightness of sky and sea blazed through its small mouth, reflecting in brilliant moving points of sunshine on broken water. Below them, in the calmer black water, two boats lay at anchor. One, a simple two-man craft without mast; the other, their own small fishing vessel.

The woman led them along the ledge and down a final shallow flight of stairs onto a sloping beach of coarse black pebbles. Their boat was a few paces from the shore. Still not pausing, with her face set in fierce determination, she walked into the sea. It was clearly not her element and, with water up to her shoulders, she was floundering before she gained the ship. Unaided, and as if driven by a fear beyond mere death, she thrust herself out of the water and onto the boat. They followed, helping each other to board.

At once, Okkyntalah sought a knife to release Shaulah but the woman, crouched in the bottom of the boat, shook her head. 'Your fresh meat can wait. We must leave the cave now.'

As if to give meaning to her warning, the tunnel they'd descended issued a loud gasp and a cloud of hot air, laden with smoke and ash, roared out at them.

'Already we may be too late. The boat must go now.'

The gust of foul heat combined with her urgency and insistence made Okkyntalah and Aglydron take to the oars after the boy brought up the anchor. Jodisa-Li, conscious of the dog's discomfort, discovered a knife in the bottom of the boat and released her limbs and muzzle. The poor animal couldn't stand and made no sound, looking very sorry for herself. Jodisa-Li moved to the bows, past the woman who seemed terrified now the boat was moving and there was no more for her to do.

Jodisa-Li guided the men but realized at once she'd be better at the tiller. She returned aft and spoke to the woman. 'Sit in the bows and look out for rocks and other obstructions.'

The woman looked at her with incomprehension. Jodisa-Li indicated the place she'd vacated and pointed, urging the woman to take her place. The woman seemed incapable of moving and Jodisa-Li understood she was terrified of the water.

'We followed you toward fire and death. Now you must trust us and do as I say or the boat will hit the rocks and sink and we'll all drown.'

The woman crawled and, when she reached the bows, remained on her knees, resting her arms on the prow so she could look out.

They were quickly in the mouth of the cave and met the choppy sea where it broke against cliff and land. Behind them, another roar issued from the tunnel and the cloud of smoke became a blast of hot ash, followed by a tongue of molten rock that heaved down the steps and onto the beach. The men rowed more urgently, aware of the danger that followed them. But their task became more difficult just at the time when they must keep an accurate course between the edges of the cave's mouth. Jodisa-Li struggled with the tiller. She called instructions to the woman. Asked her for information about rocks in their way. The woman called back, her voice soft with terror.

'Louder! I can't hear you. Shout!'

'Rocks, a manlength left.'

Jodisa-Li threw herself against the tiller. Aglydron stroked for all he was worth.

'No, Aglydron! Use the oar to push us off the rocks if we get too close. Okkyntalah, you pull harder.'

They did as she urged and missed the rocks by an arm's length as a wave took them nearer. The men used all their strength to fight the flow of water. They emerged into sunshine from shadow. A cloud of hot steam pushed at them. The molten rock had found the sea.

Ahead, Jodisa-Li saw an arc of jagged rocks with a narrow gap about twice the width of the boat just paces away.

'Pull hard, both of you. There's no time to set the sail until we're through those rocks.' From the stern, she steered as best she could, hoping the men understood how to row between rocks.

The stern passed under the face of the cliff. Another loud roar issued from within the cave. The sound of quenching came as water hissed and boiled behind them. More steam billowed from the cave mouth. Heated air pushed them from the cliff. It scorched their skin. Blew them closer to the rocks.

Okkyntalah guided Aglydron, telling him when to pull hard and when to ease on his oar as they approached the narrow gap where water swirled and churned. Jodisa-Li corrected their errors with the tiller. The woman in the bows held out the fishing spear, ready to push against rocks, should they come too close.

At last, the bows were through the gap and heading for open sea. One last effort with the oars was all they needed to be safe. Behind them, the mountain burst open with a huge explosion, shooting ash, smoke, burning boulders, stones and pebbles high into the sky.

'Krakgragog is angry. We must die or the Core will end.'

The woman turned her fishing spear into the boat and jabbed at the men with it. Still in the dangerous channel between rocks, Jodisa-Li daren't abandon her post at the tiller. Okkyntalah bled from a deep wound to his shoulder but rowed on valiantly, dodging the point of the spear. She moved to attack Aglydron but, as Okkyntalah lifted his oar to swipe the woman, Shaulah, with an enormous effort, got to her feet and bit her wrist so she dropped the spear into the bottom of the boat. She cried out in alarm; gasped as if she realized she'd done something unforgivable. Bending to retrieve the spear, she used it to push them off the rocks again. The mountain roared. But they were clear. Through the gap. In open sea at last.

Jodisa-Li raised the sail, heaving on the halyard until the yardarm was high up the mast. Adjusting the ropes, she caught the wind until the sail was full. The boat sped from the island, sailing northwest with the wind full behind.

The woman dropped the spear again and fell to her knees before Okkyntalah and Aglydron, her head in her hands in utter shame. 'Let me heal your wound.'

But, within moments of their escape from the turmoil of cave and rocks, they found themselves in more danger. Ash and small red-hot rocks showered down on them and into the boat. Closer inshore, along the north-western edge of the island, huge boulders splashed into the sea, roaring steam and hissing as they hit water. They must deal with the hot rocks or the boat would catch fire.

'No time.' Okkyntalah told her.

The woman, concern over her God's anger gone as swiftly as it had come, scooped seawater with a wooden goblet and doused the red-hot rocks that smoked in the bottom of the boat. With a marlinspike, she cupped them in the goblet and tossed them into the sea, where they hissed as they dropped beneath the surface. The rest followed suit, using whatever they could find to jettison the dangerous hail.

One falling rock caught in the ropes and rigging where the yardarm crossed the mast. The ropes and sail began to smoulder. Shaulah barked until Jodisa-Li, still at her post in the stern, saw the cause of her distress.

'The sail!'

Okkyntalah looked up and gauged the distance to the top. It was too high for him to leap. He scrambled up the mast, his injured shoulder making a hard task more difficult, and only making it to the top on his third attempt. By this time, the sail was beginning to burn and flames licked at the wooden yardarm and mast. Aglydron knelt on all fours. The woman clambered onto his back and passed the canvass bucket full of seawater to Okkyntalah.

Hanging on with one hand in the choppy seas was almost impossible. He missed completely with his first bucket, soaking Jodisa-Li instead. She flinched, her hands still on tiller and yard. They tried again. Passed the empty bucket down to Jodisa-Li to refill. This time Okkyntalah doused the flames. Soaking himself, the woman and Aglydron. But the hot rock still smouldered against wood and rope.

Chapter 19

Knowledge Of Strangers

Entering the darkness of the house after working in the fields under bright sunshine, Shoarhn was momentarily blind. She didn't notice the figure lurking there until he moved forward, shadowing the window. Without knowing why, perhaps half hoping it might be Aglydron, she stifled the cry of alarm that came involuntarily to her lips. But she knew a moment later this very tall man was not her husband.

'Who are you?'

'My apologies. Please, allow me to help you. I may be a friend. You are Shoarhn?'

'Yes. What are you doing in my house?'

'I need to speak to your husband.'

His manner of expression and his great size leant an air of authority to him that made her respect rather than fear him.

'So do I, Paltrohn.'

'Paltrohn is an unsuitable title for me. Your husband is absent?'

'I don't know where he is.'

The man stood, deep in thought.

'I still don't know who you are and I don't like finding strange men in my house.'

'I understand that. It seems to be as I feared. When did you last see him, Shoarhn?'

She studied him and decided that, in spite of the sword hanging from his belt, he was unlikely to attack her. Hands on hips, feet apart, she stood tall and challenged him. 'I said I don't know who you are. I would like to know.'

'Yes, of course. It could be quite important to know where he was last time you saw him, you see.'

'Who are you?' She made her voice full of authority, hoping she'd judged rightly that he was no threat.

'Oh, I apologise, forgive me. My name is Aklon-Dji. You may have heard of me.'

'The High Priest's son? But you're a wanted man. A renegade...'

'So I understand. I shall tell you what I know; then, perhaps, you will tell me what you know?'

'I could be hung upside down, split and beaten to death for having you in my home.'

'Yes, I suppose so.' He sat at the table, almost as if he would fall if he didn't rest.

She saw, then, his exhaustion. 'I have children.'

'Yes. Take them next door. They will be safe with their grandparents. I shall wait until you return.'

'Aren't you worried I'll tell someone you're here?'

His extraordinary eyes seemed to puncture her flesh and see right inside her. 'I think you know I present no danger to you, Shoarhn. No one saw me arrive. No one will see me leave. And it is possible, though unlikely, I might be of help to your husband.'

She nodded and left, not sure why, let alone if, she should trust the most reviled man on the island. But he seemed so entirely different from the man his father described as the worst heretic ever known.

The boys were playing chuhck-chuhck, tossing the cross-shaped stick to one another and seeing who could make it fly highest. She waited for the catcher to collect and then took them, protesting, to her parent's house, where she left them with her mother. 'Keep them for tonight, please, Mother. I'll collect them in the morning.' She gave no explanation and her mother, fixing her with a knowing look, asked for none.

Aklon-Dji was preparing tlathan for them when she returned. He placed a goblet each on the rough table and sat behind it as she seated herself opposite.

'I am not as evil as my father and his cronies would have you believe. I merely wish the people to know the truth, as he has demonstrated and explained it to me. My mistake was in telling him how I feel about that knowledge. Unfortunately, you see, my disclosures will ensure not only the end of power for my family and all who currently enjoy rank within the system, but the end of the reign of Gadhallah himself as our Lord and intercessor with Ytraa. You will understand, I believe, that my father is a little unhappy about that.' His smile was open and trusting as he gazed at her across the narrow scrubbed boards of the table.

She felt curiously drawn to this handsome, cultured, and singularly dangerous young man who'd entered her house uninvited and yet who clearly posed no physical threat to her. 'You're very candid.'

'I can be honest with those who have an honest nature, Shoarhn.'

Confused by his declaration, she hardly knew where to begin with questions. The simple fact of his presence was a threat, yet it held more danger for him than for her, though he seemed at ease. Nevertheless it seemed sensible to get him out of her house as soon as possible, in spite of his great physical attraction. 'What's this about Aglydron?'

'Your husband, and as far as I can ascertain, the promised of your beautiful daughter, Tumalind, a gifted young man called Okkyntalah…?' he raised his eyebrows in question and she confirmed with a nod. '…believe that Tumalind was substituted for Jodisa-Li, my sister, in the Choosing?'

'Yes.' She wondered how he knew.

'They are both missing from home?'

She nodded and gained the impression she was merely confirming what he already guessed. His knowledge intrigued her and she decided to risk having this handsome stranger in her house, if only to learn the fates of her husband and Okkyntalah.

<hr>

Jodisa-Li stared at the smouldering rock. 'You can't leave it there. It'll set the sail on fire again.'

'Pass me an oar.' Okkyntalah clung on with both hands until they lifted the oar to him. Leaving go with his injured arm, he poked and prodded until he dislodged the rock. The woman gathered it in the bucket and dropped it into the sea. Okkyntalah lost his grip and fell, landing half on the woman's legs and half on Aglydron, too slow to move out of the way. There was a brief moment when anger and hurt threatened argument and discord. But the woman laughed and the others joined in, hysteria and relief taking the place of fear and rage.

'I'm soaked!'

They all looked at Jodisa-Li as they struggled to get up. When they laughed at her, she couldn't help but join in, realizing that, like them, she must be streaked where water had splashed the ash covering her.

Smaller stones continued to hail down on them and they quickly returned to avoiding fires, until they were clear of the shower. By the time they could relax, the island was below the horizon, with only the angry mountain visible. It still breathed great clouds of black smoke, grey ash and red showers of rocks.

Out of sight of her god, at last, the woman began to weep silently. Now the tension and activity was over, it seemed she could no longer deny her feelings.

Aglydron was ready to berate her for her attack on them but Jodisa-Li wasn't willing to let her suffer at the hands of this unreasonable man.

'She saved our lives, risking her own, and now she's got to leave her people and her land to go with strangers into strange lands. Give her time to spend her grief, Aglydron.'

The woman cried out to her god in anger and despair.

Okkyntalah removed the remaining stones, discovering their belongings all stowed there when the boat had been taken. He took his hunting belt from within his sleepsack.

'How did they…?' He looked at the sleepsacks they'd abandoned on the beach and shook his head at yet another mystery. Fastening the hunting belt around his waist, he placed the knife back in its scabbard. He passed Jodisa-Li her missing waistrope. Aglydron left his short sword but belted his tabard. All three stared at their retrieved objects with wonder.

The woman, tears spent at last and face now set in grim determination, held her hand toward Okkyntalah. 'Please. I need your knife.'

'Not until you explain your attack on Okkyntalah, woman.'

She looked at Aglydron. 'I'm sorry. Forgive me. I'll do no more harm and, in a moment, I'll heal you.'

Okkyntalah was obviously convinced. He gave her it, handle first. Careless of her flesh, she cut the kidskin belt from her hips and tossed it, flowers, feathers, and all into the sea. She thanked Okkyntalah, and handed the knife back. But when she began to tear at the braids and flowers in her hair, Jodisa-Li left the tiller.

'Take over, please Aglydron.' She went to comfort the woman. 'What are you doing?'

'I must have nothing from the Core. Nothing. What is not me must go. I am not of the Core. I must bear nothing of the Core.'

'Then let me. You'll tear your skin. Let me do it for you.' She noticed the rocking of the boat. 'One of you trim the sail, please, or we'll bounce like this forever.'

Okkyntalah adjusted the ropes and soon had the craft skipping across the waves.

'You'd do this for me?'

'Of course.'

The woman seemed amazed but accepted Jodisa-Li's help and sat calmly at her feet as she undid the many braids and carefully removed the bright flowers from her long, pale hair. Everything she removed, Jodisa-Li gave to the woman, who tossed all into the sea until there was nothing left but herself.

Calm, she knelt before them and bowed her head. 'I am become yours. As woman of the Core, my words may not show more mind than man of the Core. Women of the Core speak as Women of the Core. I am not of the Core now, therefore I have nothing and I am become nothing. What I am is yours. If you beat me, I am yours. If you bed me, I am yours. If you devour my flesh, I am yours. If you throw me to my death in the waters, I am yours.'

Jodisa-Li took a spare tabard from her bag and passed it to the woman but she merely knelt, hands hanging loose, head bowed.

'Come, put this on.' She helped her, showing how the finely turned bronze pegs slipped through the loops of braided hair. The woman accepted the cover as a duty, without gratitude and without protest, simply as something required of her.

'You're not ours. You're…'

At Aglydron's words, she became animated and distressed. She began to undo the fastenings as if she would reject Jodisa-Li's gift.

'If I'm not yours, I'm less than nothing. I've been provided for you. If I displease you, punish me. Please, I beg of you, don't spurn me or I'm less than nothing and must wither until I'm insubstantial as the breath of flowers, ethereal as the smoke that rises from the fire.'

Jodisa-Li took the woman's fingers from the pegs and put her arms around her in an attempt to comfort her. The woman slipped her hands into her lap and sat on her folded knees, awaiting their judgement.

'You're free. We don't reject you. We welcome you as our equal and our friend.'

Okkyntalah and Jodisa-Li nodded their agreement with Aglydron.

'You saved our lives. Only those in Ytraa's service have no life of their own. They're Chosen or they serve by choice. You're not like them. You're free, like us. We don't own you. We don't own anyone. But you're welcome as a friend.'

'I don't understand. I'm rejected by the Core. I cannot be equal with you. I'm lower than the sole of man. I'm nothing. What the Core spurns, no man values. I don't understand you.'

Aglydron shook his head and Jodisa-Li moved aside so he could be close to the woman. He knelt on one knee before her and took her hands in his. He took her face in his strong hands and kissed her forehead.

'You're one with us. You owe us nothing and we expect nothing from you. We don't understand the Core or how you were selected as our help. But now isn't the time. We're hungry, tired, thirsty. We'll drink, eat what we have, rest and let tomorrow be soon enough to ask and answer questions.'

Aglydron's behaviour with this stranger amazed Jodisa-Li, so she had to adjust her judgment of this odd man who'd captured her. He was a puzzle, but in this mood of uncharacteristic kindness, she might find some solace for herself.

'Aglydron, I can't bear this ash on my skin and in my hair. I'd like to bathe in the sea, if I may.'

'Good idea.'

She helped Okkyntalah lower the sail so that only the gentle current moved them slowly away from the island.

'We'll bathe in turn. We'll need to keep a look out for nazzakks and we ought to be tied to the boat in case we get into difficulties.'

Jodisa-Li nodded and removed her waistrope, then unfastened the side openings of her tabard and turned to the other woman. 'Will you keep lookout for me, please?

Then the men won't have to watch me as I bathe.'

The woman nodded but seemed unsure what was required of her. Jodisa-Li slipped Aglydron's rediscovered leash round her wrist and handed the free end to the woman. She dropped into the sea in her tabard, letting the sea wash it clear of ash. Once it was clean, she handed it up to the waiting woman. Okkyntalah, meanwhile, made an ostentatious show of not watching her by sluicing the inside of the boat with water from the canvas bucket and dredging the blackened liquid out over the other side of the boat.

She ducked under the waves a few times, allowing the sea to wash ash from her hair and scraping her skin clean with her hands. Finished, she swam back to the boat. 'I'm done. I'm coming back aboard.'

The men turned away and the woman helped her back in.

'Your turn now.'

The woman looked at the water and at Jodisa-Li. She shook her head. Jodisa-Li squeezed excess water from her hair and tied it into a tail behind her head as she sought a dry tabard. 'Off you go. I'll watch out for you.'

'I cannot.'

'Why not?'

'She can't swim; can you?'

The woman nodded at Aglydron. 'Is that what you call this dancing in the water? Is that swim?

'Swimming, yes. You can't do it, can you?'

'No. On the island, none of the Core does this swimming. I am not of the Core. I'm sorry. I will try it if you say I must.'

'Tell you what. Me and Okkyntalah will bathe, then you can wash inside the boat.'

The men took their turns and then the woman stripped without any show of shame or modesty and washed herself with water drawn from the sea in the canvas bucket. Okkyntalah and Aglydron, though fascinated, had the grace not to stare too directly until she was finished and dressed again.

'We don't approve of nakedness, except for worship.'

'I'm sorry. I offend you. My body is not worthy. How do I displease you? Tell me and I will change until I become worthy in your eyes.'

'There's nothing wrong with the way you look. You're very pretty, beautiful, even. We just don't make ourselves naked in public, that's all.'

'Not naked? Even the women? Why, please?'

'Well, naked is sacred and for the eyes of Ytraa.'

'A man takes a woman and they go not naked together?'

'Oh, yes, of course, when we join. Or it'd be blasphemy. How could Ytraa witness our worship if we weren't naked?'

'I don't understand. I'm simple. Forgive me. I should be beaten for my act.' She began to remove the tabard again. Jodisa-Li stopped her.

'If I'm wrong, I must be punished. Please, beat me that I may learn. Please don't make me go away.'

Okkyntalah smiled at the woman. 'Peace. We won't harm you.'

She seemed desolate and anxious. He took her in his arms and stroked her cheek, placed an arm about her shoulders.

'You've done no wrong; you have a lot to learn, that's all. We'll accept you as you are until you've had time to understand what it means to be a Follower. For now, we ask no more from you than your trust and loyalty whilst you remain with us.' He glanced at Aglydron and received a reluctant nod of approval. When he turned to Jodisa-Li for her agreement, she felt moved to be truthful.

'Aglydron and Okkyntalah, you amaze me. I thought you brutal, insensitive and unfeeling. I was wrong. This woman offers herself in a way that lesser men would use to their advantage. You're kind, caring and understanding toward her. I must conclude that what you've told me of your reasons and intentions for taking me is the truth, after all. I still believe you're wrong, but I can at least accept that your reasons are honourable.'

'Your woman speaks to you as an equal. Am I permitted to ask questions?'

Okkyntalah nodded. 'How else will you learn about us?'

'Is your woman an equal?'

'I'm his superior, actually, but he won't admit it.'

Aglydron glowered at her until her smile of mischief softened him. He turned his attention to the woman.

'Ytraa created us all. But Mhortag split man from woman, woman from man. At first, we were all one and all with Ytraa. Now we're divided, it doesn't mean man's better than woman or woman has more value than man. We're equal. Though, there are men and women who have more power because of their status. Before she was Chosen as Virgin Gift, Jodisa-Li was one. She was the High Priest Elect. And the High Priest is the most powerful person in the world.'

Jodisa-Li pulled out one of the water skins. 'And I'm not his woman. Or his.' She nodded at both men in turn.

'You share your body with both, of course.'

'We don't, as you so delicately put it, share Jodisa-Li's body. As Aglydron said, she's a Virgin Gift and therefore sacred.'

'The term has no meaning for me. Gift I know. What is virgin?'

Jodisa-Li offered the girba to the woman. 'A person of either gender who hasn't joined, had sex, that is. I keep telling them I don't qualify but they choose not to believe me.' She turned to Okkyntalah. 'When did you refill the water skins?'

'Whilst you were bathing in the pool, under the waterfall. I filled them from the fall. Why?'

It took a short time for the import of his reply to reach her. 'You watched me bathe?'

He laughed at her outrage. 'I'm teasing, Jodisa-Li. I filled them before you bathed, before you were even ready. Though, if I'd wanted to, I could've watched. You seemed completely unaware of me even though I was standing in the open.'

'That was Yatukon. You are woman and must be observed by man always. Yatukon has power over all. You, as a woman, would not see him or any other man, if he did not want you to, even if he were that close to you.'

Jodisa-Li glanced at the woman's hand where the space between her thumb and forefinger would not have held a braid of hair. 'A magician?'

'I don't understand the term. Yatukon is Yatukon, the one who is, the one who has been, the one who will be. Yatukon is Core of the Core. Without Yatukon the Core is not.'

'This Yatukon was the man under the mask?'

'Yatukon wears the Crown of Krakgragog. No one has ever seen his face. If you look on him you'd be blinded by the vision of perfection.'

'And what's your name?' Okkyntalah, steering in the stern, was looking at her with interest. 'What do we call you?'

'I have no name. I was of the Core. I am not of the Core. I take nothing from the Core. I am nothing. I have no name. I am no one.' The sadness in her tone was such that they all felt it.

'But you must have a name. Everyone has a name.'

She looked at Aglydron and shook her head. 'I have no name.'

Chapter 20

The Naming Of Strangers

Shoarhn waited as Aklon-Dji stared into his steaming cup of tlathan and sighed, apparently collecting his thoughts.

'Jodisa-Li is also missing from home. I am not normally welcome there, you know? My father has made an inconvenient threat to have my skin peeled from my body in thin strips and my quivering flesh roasted alive, should I show my face. It has persuaded me to keep away. But, when I heard that he had set off on this preposterous return to the land of our forebears, I thought I should risk a short visit to see my sister. She, you understand, has a marginally less rigid attitude to my blasphemy and truth-telling than Father. However, at the house, I discovered only that the domestic slaves had increased in number, augmented in service to that rhaat, Wesdan Kaz, now in residence. And my sister, along with some of her belongings, had vanished.

'I made discreet enquiries from friends here and there. The signs were that Jodisa had not left voluntarily. Two strangers; a man of your husband's description and a younger man, enthusiastically drawn with great praise, by a young woman of my acquaintance, were seen in the vicinity. They and a fishing boat have disappeared. It took little time to discover the origin of the two men after my friend told me of Okkyntalah. I knew, of course, about the way my father had rigged the Choosing; he could hardly let Jodisa go, since she is not virgin. So, I put three and three together, concluded I may have arrived at a dozen, and decided I had better confirm my calculations.'

Shoarhn found this powerful man fascinating, rather than frightening. That he spoke so lightly and jocularly of matters of great moment was somehow a comfort. 'What made you think it was Aglydron and Tumalind's Okkyntalah?'

'The descriptions. One of them very detailed indeed. The young woman was quite explicit and he had rather incautiously provided her with his name and place of origin. When and where did you last see them?'

Any doubts she might have harboured about him vanished. There was something open and honest about his manner, in spite of his odd way of speaking, that made her feel she could trust this man with her life. He wouldn't put others in peril for his own sake.

She described events on the Plain of Ytraa after the Choosing. 'I thought, at first, Aglydron had gone by himself and Okkyntalah had gone off with that...with Kaz-Ca-Charrohn. But she came looking for him and raged like a wounded stripecat when she discovered he wasn't waiting for her.'

He nodded. 'I heard he had decided against her favours, following the ceremony. She would be a little upset. Once that wanton has her mind set on a man, it is not wise to deprive her. I am now quite convinced about the two men. It makes sense. What I guess is that they kidnapped my sister and stole the fishing boat to follow Dagla Kaz, in the vain hope of persuading him to swap her for Tumalind. Fool's errand, of course. In the unlikely event they find the pilgrims, my father will have the pair tortured to death. I am sorry. Insensitive of me. I did not intend to cause you anxiety, Shoarhn. I have this unfortunate need to tell the truth and it sometimes gets the better of me.'

'You seriously believe they've kidnapped Jodisa-Li?'

'Everything points to it. Of course, I cannot be certain. But, in view of the facts, I think my assessment is probably fairly accurate.'

'How in Mhortag's name do you know all this?'

'Information is readily available if you have the means to collect it, Shoarhn.'

'Will Dagla Kaz really kill them?'

'Unless Jodisa persuades him otherwise. And whether she will after the way they must have stolen her away...It is pure conjecture, of course. But the facts do rather fit.'

Shoarhn wasn't certain how she felt. She knew she should be devastated but discovered she was more concerned for Okkyntalah than her husband. 'Mhortag's balls! Aglydron's such a pious fool. I told him to leave it be.'

'Out of curiosity, why do you suppose he would do such a thing? Okkyntalah I can understand; Tumalind is rather a rare beauty, a quality she clearly obtained from her mother, and I can appreciate why he might not want to lose such a gem. Aglydron, however, was not normally so concerned about the fate of Tumalind.'

'You seem to know a great deal, Aklon-Dji.'

In spite of the pause she left for explanation, he remained awaiting her reply.

'Aglydron wanted to right a wrong, that's all. He'd have done the same even if it hadn't been Tumalind. Aglydron always leans towards the fundamental in religious matters. Do you really think she was wrongly Chosen, then?'

'No doubt. It was a choice between her and Jodisa and my father would not let my sister go, under any circumstances. Nothing to do with her not being virgin, of course; that would be a minor concern. But she is his sole heir since he disinherited me. He would not want her married to a stranger in a far land. Who would carry on the family blood line then?'

'She's really not virgin? But she bled at the...'

'Shoarhn, you are an experienced woman. Surely, you have employed a little subterfuge yourself, from time to time? How long since your last child? Eight cycles?'

How could he know so much? 'But that's different. I'm not the only one and...'

'I am not criticizing. You are very sensible. Apart from the dreadful risk of having a fourthborn to be sent off... Oh! I am so sorry, Shoarhn; that I did not know. An appalling sacrifice and one I would end. But a woman as lovely as you would not want the ruin of constant pregnancy. Any husband worth his seed would shield you from that, anyway.'

'No wonder your father's frightened of you if you say such things.'

'An accurate observation, but there is worse than that, as far as he is concerned. I gather you are not quite as pious as your husband?'

'I do what I must. But, to be honest, I find some of what we're expected to do difficult and sometimes downright cruel.' It staggered her that she was so honest with this stranger whose very association was a death sentence.

'Good. The virginity, by the way, was a trick with a thin membrane full of senglar's blood. It is an old deception that the family has used for generations. He had the unfortunate young man discretely killed, of course.'

'I'm sorry?'

'Oh. The one who took her virginity? I believe she loved him in her own way and Father will probably have told her he was sent to The Point, unless, of course, he wished the lesson to be a little more potent. Of course, Father could not allow him to live to tell the people that he had delved deep where most men on the island desire to venture. No doubt, Tryonta killed the poor lad. It would not be the first time. A most unpleasant man.'

Shoarhn could hardly believe what he was telling her but couldn't consider him a liar. His candid honesty certainly explained why he was a wanted man. She wondered how he managed to evade capture and remain so well fed and fit.

'Might I trouble you for a bite to eat before I go, do you think? I have neglected to eat for a little while and may be forced to go a little longer before I am in a position where...'

'Do you have to go straight away? Why not spend the night here? I've asked Mother to have the twins overnight.'

'A comfortable bed would be a blessing. I have no pressing need to go, other than to reduce your danger. In any case, I would be ill-advised to leave during the hours of daylight.'

'How do you avoid capture?'

'I move, Shoarhn. I move a lot. And change my looks. My hair is not this colour.'

'But your eyes. They're so beauti...so distinctive.'

'From Father. Jodisa's are the same.'

'So are Tumalind's, actually.'

'Really? From her father, then?'

'Aglydron has light brown eyes.'

'Ah. Naming ceremony, perhaps? A spot of variety?'

Shoarhn smiled. 'I've no objection, to that, of course. But, to tell the truth, though I've never told anyone, I suppose it might even be your father. He was there when Ytraa… took me, at prayer on the Plains of Ytraa. The right time, as well.'

Aklon-Dji nodded. 'That might explain a few things. It might be why he chose her. You do not believe it was actually Ytraa, then?'

'It's one of the things I've often been suspicious about. I once saw our village priest take the part of Ytraa; I wasn't peeking. I never said anything, of course; who'd risk having their tongue torn out and being blinded? But it's an easy way for the priests to use any woman, or man, they desire, isn't it?'

'That, of course, is why it is taught. You are a bright woman, Shoarhn. There is much else I could tell you. But I would do it better on a full stomach.'

She nodded and opened the flagon of wine Aglydron had reserved for a special occasion. For her, this was such a moment. The young man was attractive, desirable, and as fascinating as he was dangerous.

⁂

The problem of the woman's name weighed heavily on Aglydron. He was conscious of what they owed her. She'd selflessly rescued them from a situation that would have ended their mission, and probably their lives, there on the island. More than that, she'd healed the wound she'd inflicted on Okkyntalah.

Once they'd all bathed, she'd seen the injury and been distraught. 'I'm sorry I pierced you. I was frightened and thought Krakgragog desired us all dead. I forgot, for a moment, I wasn't of the Core and Krakgragog had no further interest in me. May I heal you?'

Okkyntalah had shrugged the tabard off his shoulder and let her examine the cut. She'd spent time in gently feeling over and around the laceration with her fingertips.

'It's deep but not serious and your flesh is young and healthy. You'll heal well. I must prepare for the healing.'

To their amazement, she rose to her feet in the boat, ignoring her own fear of the motion and the sea, and stripped off her tabard. With the pointed forefinger of her right hand, she drew a circle to encompass herself and Okkyntalah. Kneeling, she stretched her arms high and wide above her, threw back her head and sang a pleading litany, to the sky.

Aglydron moved to cover her but Jodisa-Li stopped him. 'She's communing with her god, Aglydron, let her be.'

Reluctantly he let her continue. She opened her fingers, spread them wide and then clutched, as if drawing power from the very air, and pulled the invisible force in toward her body, releasing it again over her heart. Trancelike, she cupped the wound with both hands and placed her mouth over the gap between them. Blowing softly, she murmured more words of supplication into the space. Okkyntalah winced and then looked astonished.

The woman groaned and fell into the bottom of the boat, apparently exhausted. Jodisa-Li covered her and held her head in her lap until she recovered, only moments later.

Okkyntalah and Aglydron examined the wounded shoulder and, in total disbelief, showed it to the girl. The intact skin held only a faint white scar where the wound had been.

They watched the woman's recovery with concern and wonder. When she rose, her first concern was the healing and she examined the skin, probing and asking Okkyntalah what he felt.

'No pain; just a tingling sensation.'

Evidently satisfied with his replies, she placed her arms about his neck. 'Excuse me; I must complete the healing now.'

To Okkyntalah's evident delight, she kissed the wound and then his mouth with a passion that clearly affected him. She rose again into her first position of supplication and again sang the words, this time seeming to withdraw the power from her centre and offer it back up to her god. She chanted again and replaced the tabard.

This experience had left the three Followers stunned and full of fearful admiration. They'd heard of certain types of magic but healing of this sort was unknown on the island and Aglydron was unable to decide whether what they'd witnessed was entirely wholesome or the manifestation of some heathen spirit.

'Does the healing power come from Krakgragog?'

'Oh, no. Krakgragog is powerful, dangerous and unpredictable. But he has neither healing power nor any wish to do anything positive and helpful. The healing is from the air around us. Anyone can do it. I just draw out power and, when I've used what I need, give it back.'

'But you sang strange words we didn't understand and ...'

'Sang? I sang nothing...to no one. I merely took the power that's there. Nothing more. There's no mystery or secret about it. Surely some on your island can do the same, otherwise how are people healed?'

'You don't know you sang?'

She shook her head, clearly unwilling to believe him.

'We've never seen anything like what you just did to Okkyntalah. Can others do it on your island?'

'Women. Some of the women can do it. The men, of course, don't…'

'Is it from the Core, then?'

'I'm not of the Core.' She cried openly at this and they let her express her grief without further probing. But there was clearly more to the healing than she could explain.

Following her gift of healing Okkyntalah, the party felt even more respect for this remarkable woman and again tried to discover her name. But she was adamant that she had no name and no amount of reasoning or persuasion could tempt her to say what she'd been called before the island community had rejected her in that extraordinary fashion.

Questioning over the last two days of calm and soft winds, with little progress toward their next destination, had answered some questions about her former life and the society she'd left.

The island was populated by three groups, with the other two villages based one on the northern plain and the other on the eastern slopes of the fire mountain. Yatukon was their leader. The men subjugated the women, though the woman didn't describe it this way and seemed unaware she'd been a slave. Even small boys took precedence over grown women and could demand anything they required of them.

It was small wonder to Aglydron that the woman had no concept of virginity: from her answers, it was clear that women were sexual slaves as well as domestic skivvies. The men did no work or any activity, other than a type of game of hunting, which she couldn't describe in any detail.

'Do they ever actually catch anything?'

'Rarely. They celebrate with drink and feasting and much lying with the women.'

The women farmed the land, gathered fruit from the forests, built shelters, hunted for real food, raised the children according to strict rules issued by the men, and provided sexual entertainment.

There was no pairing, a man simply deciding which woman he wanted when and for how long. Sometimes a woman was used by a man once and then discarded; other women spent long periods with one man, indulging other men at his behest, whilst he used other women also. Several men publicly used some in the space of a night at celebrations. Women were beaten for small misdemeanours. Only Yatukon made no use of women. He was unique.

'He knows all there is to know. Yatukon can tell when the fire mountain will be angry, days before it happens. He can walk on the fires without harm and he alone knows how to make blades from the shiny, hard, black stone that comes from the belly of the fire mountain. Yatukon is everywhere and always. No one knows when he began and he will end only when the Core is gone.'

'The Core is the name you give the people?'

Her eyes filled with tears but she answered, even as the drops spilled down her cheeks. 'The Core is the Core. All who live on the island are the Core. The Core is all life and Yatukon is Core of the Core. I'm not of the Core. If I'm not yours, I'm less than nothing.'

Aglydron embraced her awkwardly in the boat, feeling her sorrow and distress. 'You are ours. We value you. Haven't we shown you, with our gifts, our talk, our laughter and concern that we care about you? Now, you can't go on without a name.'

'I have no name.'

They'd travelled this road before and it was clear she wouldn't alter her mind.

'If you've no name of your own, we'll have to give you one. Will you accept that?'

She looked at Aglydron as if he'd offered the Moon. 'You'd name me? You'd give me my own name?'

'If you'll have it.'

'Oh, you are more generous and merciful than I believed possible. To have a name once more. How will I repay such a gift?'

'With your loyalty.' It was out of Aglydron's mouth before he fully understood what he was asking but he couldn't withdraw it. If she'd sworn service and obedience before, she now promised her all to Aglydron for as long as she might live.

'You have my life and my self; I have no more to give you. But I will die before I see you harmed.'

It wasn't what he sought or wanted but he knew by now there was no retreat from this. She'd do as she would do, no matter how much he might try to dissuade her. He found himself unable to say, with absolute honesty, how he felt about her devotion. To take his mind off what struck him as an unworthy feeling, he asked his companions, 'What can we call this lovely lady who's come so unexpectedly to us?'

Okkyntalah studied the strange healer. She was different and beautiful in a way he couldn't define. Perhaps her pale hair or the light tone of her skin singled her out. Her form was all that man could want from woman yet she carried herself with modesty and dignity. There was no pride in her but no shame either. It was as if she stated with her being no more than the facts of what she was, without opinion, without exaggeration, without false modesty. Her eyes, so pale as to be almost devoid of colour until they caught the hue of sky or sea, seemed to promise everything when they looked at him, though he felt that what she offered was for him to determine. Her mouth was wide and full but rarely smiled, as if she were constantly sad. Yet, when she laughed, as she did in the right circumstances, her smile lit her face with vitality and joy.

Jodisa-Li's heliotrope tabard, with its gilt fastenings and belt of auburn hair braided with myllth, fitted her well, though she was taller and more slender than the girl. He glanced across, saw Jodisa-Li watching him and wondered what was in her mind. She smiled at him with a warmth that hadn't been there before they'd shared their escape from the island.

Aglydron sat waiting, wanting answers to his question as the woman sat beside him, patient and still as ever.

'Nothing to suggest? What about Stellanyl?' He turned to the woman, who was still smiling at the mere hope of a name.

'Not Stellanyl, Aglydron. That means "stranger" or "one who is different". I don't think she wants to be reminded that she's not one of us every time she hears her name.'

Aglydron considered Jodisa-Li's comment and seemed to agree that his suggestion was not well chosen.

'Her hair's like myllth. Why not call her Myllthlan?'

'Precious as myllth. That'll do very well. Excellent suggestion, Okkyntalah, don't you think, Jodisa?'

'I think it shows remarkable judgement. I approve. What does our friend think?'

The woman was unaware that she was speaking to her at first until Aglydron indicated that was the case.

She looked up at Okkyntalah first. 'You judge me the value of myllth. I don't know what it is, so I can't say whether I'm worthy of the name. It has a sound about it that I find comfortable. What is this myllth?'

Aglydron touched the bracelet, still amongst their things. He suddenly understood the horror felt by the islanders at their accusation of theft. If they hadn't stolen this valuable item, then theft must indeed be foreign to them. He nodded as the woman formed a question with her eyes. 'See? It's the colour and lustre of your hair. What else could we call you?'

'This is a piece of real craft and skill; almost beautiful. It's of high value?'

'It's the most precious thing we know of. Nothing has more worth than myllth, the colour of pale gold but more beautiful and a hundred times more rare.'

She looked again at Okkyntalah. 'Yet you select this name for me? I who am without worth.'

He took her hand in his and tried to convey how seriously she impressed and attracted him. 'You've proved yourself more valuable than anything we own; you saved our lives.'

⚬ ═─┼─═⚬

Aglydron could see she was doubtful but knew she'd accept it if he said she should. 'I give you the name, "Myllthlan" and declare you known as such for as long as you dwell beneath the Eyes of Ytraa.'

Okkyntalah took his cue from Aglydron's use of the naming pledge and left the tiller to embrace the woman. He kissed her forehead, took her hands in his and knelt before her. 'Welcome, Myllthlan. May the Lord Gadhallah bless and cherish you. May the Skyfire burn within your soul but never scorch your being. May you live and die as well as Vaarkil and Mythanpho. May you be loved by all and love all in return. And may Ytraa be your guide in all you do, in all you think, in all you feel.'

He kissed both her cheeks and rose to return to his place at the tiller as Jodisa-Li moved forward and performed the same ceremony. Aglydron then took his turn but, as namer of the newcomer, claimed his right and kissed her lips before he bowed and moved to sit beside her once more.

Her eyes were wet with tears as she accepted their welcome. She rose to her feet and stood with confidence in the becalmed boat. Her voice was strong and full of joy as she made her declaration. 'I am Myllthlan. I am Myllthlan. I am Myllthlan. I live forever in your debt, Aglydron the kind and the noble of bearing. I live forever in your debt, Jodisa-Li the compassionate and the wise. I live forever in your debt, Okkyntalah the generous of spirit and the…beautiful.'

That slight stumble, showing something close to shyness, lifted the solemnity and let them laugh a little, especially as Okkyntalah blushed beneath her praise.

Chapter 21

Dangerous Words

'I promise you I shall be back, Shoarhn. No. Please stay where you are; the memory will sustain me. It is best you do not know where I go or when I hope to return. But, return I shall. I have many women who protect, nurture, feed, shelter and serve me. I always promised never to allow a single woman to become important to me, for my sake and hers. You have forced me to reconsider.

'My life is full of danger but there is no reason why yours should be. Please keep this meeting to yourself Shoarhn. I look forward to our next, hoping I may stay longer than one night.' Aklon-Dji kissed her soft sweet mouth again and moved, silent and swift, into night.

On the edge of the village, he slipped into an olive grove and waited in the deeper darkness behind an ancient gnarled tree. It wasn't long before the tracker arrived. The man had been waiting on the road and followed him this short distance. Aklon-Dji was certain the man didn't know where he'd spent the night. Even so, he shadowed him across the dry grass.

'I wonder, might I trouble you to explain why you are tracking me?'

The man spun round, drawing his sword. Aklon-Dji disarmed him with a swift upward stroke that took the weapon from his hand and flung it in an arc to land in the trees.

'And, why, a traveller such as I might ask, should you draw your sword in answer to a simple question?'

'You're…I…you startled me. Anyone'd be the same, taken by surprise like that. You wanna be careful, you'll get yoursen killed one o' these days.'

'And the reason you came after me?'

'I never. Why'd I want to come after the likes o' you?'

'Precisely my question.'

'You're touched. I wan't going after nobody. I were…'

'So, you admit you were going after somebody. If not…'

'I wan't. I just said not, didn't I?'

Aklon-Dji sighed; the world was deeply disappointing. 'You declared that you were not going after nobody. By logical and linguistic extension, you must, therefore, have been going after somebody.'

'I don't know what you're …'

'Enough badinage. Let us retrieve your redundant weapon and be on our way; together for the moment. Please, do precede me. I believe we shall discover your blade in that direction.'

He led the protesting man across the dark ground to a space between two large olive trees. The sword lay on the ground, reflecting starlight and the faint glow of coming dawn on its polished blade.

'Er, no. I believe I will be safer if I carry the weapon. Perhaps you will relinquish your belt and scabbard so that I may more easily bear it?'

The man was reluctant. Aklon-Dji demonstrated the superiority of his position and blood trickled down the man's biceps. He did as he was bid and Aklon-Dji fastened the belt around his waist with the other man's sword hanging from it.

'Now, let us take the way together, since you were clearly travelling in the same direction as I intend to go. I suggest this in expectation of confirmation of the fact, no more.'

'You talk frowkin' rubbish. I've no idea what…'

'Oh dear. How tiresome. You agree that this is a blade? You feel the keen edge? Notice how readily it slices through the outer layers of the man to expose the inner being?'

'Mhortag's bowels! You'll bleed me to death. What you..?'

'What I require is truth. Do excuse me, but I prefer not to follow the road; we will turn off the path here and approach the sea to walk wondrous cliffs, which, here, fall in sheer steeps to the water below.'

'Why you wanna go that way?'

'That will shortly become clear, though I doubt you will appreciate the message. I have little enough time to spend on important things. I beg you not to waste the resource in prevarication. Tell me, do you do this for my father or for the Holy Ones?'

'Don't know who your father is.'

'Dagla Kaz, of course. So, you admit to working for the Holy Ones?'

'I admit nothin'. You're mad. I've no idea who you are but it's time you let me go on my way.'

'You do not know who I am?'

'Why should I?'

'I have presently informed you.'

'Mad frowkin' fool…'

'You are the fool. There is not a soul on this island who would deny knowledge of Aklon-Dji. Your feeble attempts at trickery outwit you. I hope they have paid you well for what you do; your family will have need of whatever coin you have so far been given.'

'Pay? Think I need paying to do what's right? Vermin. Bowelcreep. I'd turn you in for no more than the satisfaction of seeing you hung and skinned. Renegade!'

'Ah, more educated than we first appeared. That gives you less excuse, not more. It pains me to end your life. I apologize for the necessity. But if you will take up with such as my father and the Holy Ones for the purpose of ending my life, you must accept the consequences. You may make supplication to your creator before I kill you, if you wish.'

'We'll catch you. In the end, there's no escape for you. Kill me. But there'll be a hundred others to seek you out and put you to blade and flame. The evil you purvey will bring the wrath of Ytraa on your head soon enough.'

'Please do me the favour of removing your tabard and falling to your knees.'

'If you're going to kill me, just get on with it.'

'I thought you would wish to honour your God before you meet your God.'

The man was trembling but unwilling to voice his fear. He considered the suggestion for a moment, looked him in the eye in the growing light of early morning. Aklon-Dji admired the man's courage, though not the conviction behind it, and placed a gentle hand on his shoulder. The man dropped to his knees on the edge of the cliff and pulled the tabard over his head. Aklon-Dji prevented him tossing it over the cliff. He allowed the man a short time for prayer.

'I must, unfortunately, release your life from your body. I wish I were not obliged to do so. Forgive me.'

A single blow took his head from his body and made the killing as silent and clean as possible. Hating violence, he was aware he would long ago have been killed had he not killed first. He rolled the body over the cliff. The head he bundled into the garment and tossed as far out to sea as he could. The man would be missed soon enough but it might take them longer to discover his fate.

It was clear they knew he was back in circulation. He'd spent too much time and trouble on the business with Jodisa-Li and the two missing men. He must be lost for a while again. The Point beckoned. It was a long way from Morstahn and the woman who'd taken such a hold on his heart, but there, at least, he might rest without the need to hide.

Practiced and skilled as he was, it would nevertheless take him four days and nights to cover the thirty leagues without being seen and without visiting others for shelter and help. Enough of the Few had been placed in danger by this abortive venture. He only hoped he could make it to the convict colony without further bloodshed.

Three days for repairs had stretched into four, then five and, in the end, Tumalind and the rest of the party didn't return to the ship until the seventh night after they'd left it. Baklan wouldn't sail from the city that night, in spite of Dagla Kaz's impatience.

'Most of the crew's drunk. Would you have me risk leaving harbour with my men full o' fallin' down juice?'

So, it was on the midday tide of the following day that they finally sailed away from Rhonholoah.

'About ruddy time an' all. Thought we were goin' to be stuck there forever. There's only so many oilings and massages a body needs. Still, your skins should be grand now; stand you all in good stead for the days to come at sea.'

'Where to next, Corphanda?'

'Two days up the coast to Kamakq, then mebbie through the straights into the Sea of Llahkan. Not sure where we're bound from Kamakq, Tumalind, but it'll all be overland if we stay ashore there. Mebbie we'll sail up the wide river afore we get to the Sea of Llahkan, I don't know. Dagla Kaz knows where he's going so I'd not worry. Baklan says this bit of the voyage should be simple if the wind don't back to west of north, whatever that might mean.'

'One o' the crew says there's pirates on this coast. Said we might be taken to be sold as slaves, mebbie even eaten!'

'Take no notice of 'em, Dilanthas, they're just tugging your toes. Pirates, indeed! What d'you say, Phildrad?'

They were on deck, sitting in the sun and enjoying the refreshing breeze as they sailed a softly rolling sea at an easy pace.

'Never bin out o' Pampahn. Know nowt about pirates.'

Tumalind wondered if Phildrad was the dullest man alive. Corphanda and she had tried several times to bring him into conversations but he rarely said more than a few words and they were generally to deny an opinion. She knew their chaperone had travelled up from Pampahn with this boring man and wondered how she'd managed with his morose manner all those days alone on the road. But he was definitely preferable to the next speaker.

'I think you'll find that Dagla Kaz is unlikely to allow us into waters where there are known dangers, ladies. He's a man of great wisdom and experience and the ship's master is familiar with this coast. I believe you can, as Corphanda suggests, take it that this talk of pirates is the crewman's rather childish idea of a joke.'

She'd instinctively disliked Tryonta on sight, and further experience of the man had done nothing to change Tumalind's opinion. Asked why she didn't like him, she would've been hard put to give a reason beyond her first impression of a man who rarely said what he meant and whose smile, extending only to his lips, she believed hid a nature both cruel and evil. She'd wondered from the beginning why he was one of the party and had yet to discover his special talents.

Tarruss, his massive back to her as she looked across the deck, had already proved his worth. He was a gentle man for one so huge. She'd seen him mend the tiny links of one of Wendarah's gold chains with his great thick fingers, making her wonder at the delicacy of one so big. His touch, when he'd rescued her and again when he'd lifted her back on board the ship before they set off, had been soft and careful, as if he thought her liable to break. Yes, Tarruss was a man she liked and trusted.

Jhonaht seemed to have found his sea legs at last and had stayed on deck after spending much of the previous sea voyage in the cabin he shared with Dagla Kaz. He was a little less round than when they'd set off and looked better for that. She watched him as he pointed a strange metal contraption at the sun. He appeared to be making measurements but she couldn't tell why or what use he would make of them. She'd caught him watching her from time to time and wondered if his interest was entirely carnal. Certainly, he hadn't looked away when she'd faced him and hadn't worn that face of guilty contemplation she'd often surprised on Tryonta.

She went back to the tabard she was embroidering. In Rhonholoah, Corphanda had asked each of them if they wanted something to do whilst they were at sea and she'd decided to add designs to her two everyday tabards. Corphanda had supplied her with silks and needles and she was now busy fashioning a picture to remind her of her village home.

Dilanthas had opted for a similar pastime and was embroidering a fair copy of a paradise bird but Porryh had scorned such work as tedious and was playing tahk-tahk with Wendarah and, judging by her pile of blue and yellow tiles, winning for once. She jumped four of Wendarah's premier tiles in a zigzag with one of her own minors. 'Hah! I win!'

The priestess shrugged and collected the tiles back up in her hands and returned them to the bag to shake them up before starting another game, whilst Porryh reconfigured the five fields of the board into a different order.

Caarl and Dagla Kaz were aft with Baklan, poring over parchment sheets bearing strange devices. She'd heard them talking about a group of small uninhabited islands that lay between Rhonholoah and Kamakq and she supposed they were deciding which route they should take.

The crew were busy at those duties they performed when the wind was steady and the course required them to alter the sails only every now and then. Tacking, Baklan called it. The wind, he'd told her, was blowing northeast and, since they needed to travel northwest, they had to make a sort of crooked line across the sea to get the best in both direction and speed. Baklan had been gratified by her interest and had shown her, with his finger on a piece of marked parchment, the way they sailed first north and then due west then north again to take them where they wished to go. She'd put up with his hand fondling her hip, his rough fingers stroking her skin through the gap in the side of her tabard, so that she might learn something from him. She'd no idea what use such knowledge might be but she was curious about everything and had discovered she enjoyed learning simply for the pleasure of understanding. Since she'd been with the pilgrimage party, she'd had more opportunity to occupy her mind with things beyond religion and she was acquiring many intriguing facts and managing to see how some of these were interrelated.

She'd already determined to cultivate Jhonaht and learn from him about the stars and, especially, the Skyfire. She'd seen it now; a tiny fuzzy spark, low in the western sky just after sundown. It seemed so small and insignificant a cause for all the disruption it brought and she waited with impatience for it to come into its glory and fill the sky with fire and flame as it had in ancient times. As long as they were all faithful and true, the Skyfire wouldn't burn them; she knew that.

The small boat drifted on the slow current under quiet air, hardly scending on a sea so calm it reflected the growing bank of cloud on the northern horizon and the plume of smoke rising, even yet, far off to the east.

'Bad weather on the way.'

Okkyntalah looked at the cloud still leagues away and moving slowly east. He shook his head at Aglydron. 'I doubt it'll come this way. But it'll be wet and windy on Muhnilahm come tomorrow morning.'

'May I speak? I'm sorry; I forget I'm no longer bound by the rules of the island.' Myllthlan gave a smile of apology. 'I think the storm will probably reach us before light tomorrow. There'll be wind but no rain at first. It'll blow from east of north for a day before it leaves us.'

'You study the weather?'

'Ylcrat's at the mercy of the storms and relies on them to fill its streams and small lakes with water. All know the weather.'

'Do you have an opinion, Jodisa?'

'Me? I leave the weather to herdsmen and those who fish. I never had need to know when rain would come or if the sun would shine ten sixdays on end.'

Aglydron looked at Okkyntalah. 'You know the weather well enough on land. I think I'd trust Myllthlan's predictions at sea, though.'

'As you will. We can't do anything about it, whatever comes our way. But this time we should be prepared for the worst.'

'We don't seem to suffer storms this frequently on Muhnilahm. I wonder why we should come across them more often out here?'

'Perhaps you don't get the rains in Muhnilahm, when it pours without end for days and days?'

'Never known such weather. Did you get that on Ylcrat?'

'Most cycles. And in the days before the rains, storms were always more frequent.'

'My father said something about the rains. Pours down for three or four sixdays on the mainland, he told me. Perhaps we're going to arrive ashore in time to be drowned there after just escaping it at sea.'

The cloud seemed nearer as night approached and they felt uneasy knowing they might have to face another storm. Myllthlan, in particular, was anxious. She feared the sea and showed her amazement as the others dropped over the side of the boat to wash at the end of each day. In her turn, she kept clean with a thorough strip wash in the boat. Okkyntalah wondered how long it would be before Aglydron gave her grief over this blasphemy. For himself, he was happy at the view.

◆ ══◈══✦

Tumalind heard Baklan shout his orders and knew the crew would change the sails to turn the ship due west again. Porryh and Wendarah put their hands protectively about their respective piles of gaming tiles so they wouldn't tip as the ship heeled over onto its other side. The ropes sang as they played through their iron blocks, the sails slapped as they lost the wind, then thumped as they filled again with air. The motion of the ship changed as they ploughed across the swell instead of sailing with it. Now the wind blew across them, bringing a freshness to subdue the heat of late afternoon. The only cloud was on the left hand side, marking the invisible coast of Niphralon, which, Baklan had told her, lay four leagues off. Otherwise, the sky was deep azure and unmarked. Seemeeuws had followed them from the harbour; reluctant to leave, they soared and called and sometimes landed on the water, sometimes dived beneath to come up with silver fish wriggling in their beaks.

'Sail ho!'

The crewman on the sighting platform almost at the top of the forward mast pointed directly ahead. The sail he could see wasn't yet visible to those on deck, so they remained in place and continued with their interests and games. All continued, calm and peaceful, as they maintained course for Kamakq.

The sailor in the lookout again shouted but she didn't catch his words. Baklan shaded his eyes and looked out to the far horizon, where sails were now just visible. Talking with Caarl and Dagla Kaz, an anxious frown formed beneath his grey curls.

Something worried them but Tumalind couldn't guess what.

Baklan gave the order to turn the ship so that the wind was full behind them. This, she knew, would take them away from land and, ultimately, off course. But, once the ship was moving with the wind, the master ordered all sails set to increase their speed and she knew then they were running from some threat.

Thinking to capitalize on her cultivation of the ship's master, she made her way to where he stood with Caarl and Dagla Kaz, intent on finding out what was happening.

'Stay back, lass! Get down and out of sight!'

She stopped but didn't move, puzzled by his strange concern to hide her from something she couldn't see. Baklan spoke rapidly with Dagla Kaz and Caarl and she waited to see what might happen. Caarl, firmly but gently, took her by the shoulders and propelled her back to the lower deck and her companions.

'You must all, all the women, go below decks, now. And stay out of sight.'

'Why?'

'Please just do as I say. If I catch a woman on deck, I'll punish her severely. Now, below decks, all of you. Now! And remain quiet.'

A'ahl looked at her with eyes full of knowledge as Shoarhn entered her small house, her whole body still alive and vital after her night with Aklon-Dji. 'Who's been prodding your fern, and with great skill and passion by the look of it?'

'That obvious?'

'There's a message written on your face, Shoarhn. It says you've been frowked so completely and so well you think you've gone to the Garden of Delights.'

'He was rather wonderful. Young, tall, broad, strong, passionate and so tender and caring. And, even if he does talk in the most peculiar way, those eyes! Oh, A'ahl, he's so… His eyes are exactly the same colour as Tumalind's and so…'

A'ahl looked about her fearfully. 'Enough!' She went to the open door and checked for neighbours, glanced out of the window to make sure no one was close by. Only then did she start to relax again. 'Do you want to get us skinned? Speak softly of him if you must speak of him at all. And how did you know it was safe to tell me, anyway?'

Shoarhn was puzzled by her manner but alerted by her words and suddenly recalled Aklon-Dji's request that she say nothing. 'I've no idea what you're talking about, A'ahl. Who are you trying to protect?'

A'ahl dragged her to the table and sat her down but remained standing herself. 'This is too serious to make light of, Shoarhn. We both know there's only one man who fits your description. Tell me what you know.'

'I've no idea what you mean. I spent the night with a young man I've never met before and he was very good, that's all. End of story. What else is there to know?'

'That's better. How do you think he's managed to stay alive for so long? Certainly not by having his frequent converts yell it from the rooftops. Oh, yes, I've had him as well. He believes in spreading his bounty and I, for one, am happy and proud to have had my share. But you must be careful. Suppose I wasn't one of the Few? I can't believe he told you?'

'Few? I've no idea what you're talking of, A'ahl. I just had to share my joy with someone who I knew would understand. That's why I came to see you.'

A'ahl grabbed a long knife from the shelf behind her and held the sharp point against Shoarhn's throat. 'I'll slit your throat if you don't answer my questions, Shoarhn. He's too vital to the Cause to be lost by careless talk. Now. Why did he come to see you?'

Shoarhn gulped. A'ahl was a lifelong friend, a gentle and caring woman who showed affection and care for everyone. But the look in her friend's eyes, the knife threatening her throat, the way she stood over her, all made her understand she was in real danger. She gathered her thoughts together. She'd clearly allowed emotional excitement to overcome common sense. It hadn't occurred to her that she might be placing either herself or Aklon-Dji in any danger. As A'ahl so rightly pointed out, she was lucky her friend was also one of his friends. She might've been the cause of his death otherwise.

'I'm sorry, A'ahl. I didn't think. It's all right. You don't need that. I was just excited and lost my mind for a moment. You obviously know a lot more about this whole business than I do. I'll tell you what you want to know.'

'How do you know you can trust me?'

'It's obvious. The way you threatened me, for a start...'

'Oh, that boy and his prod! It's going to get him killed one of these days. Look, I could be working for the other side. I've been frowking with the squitting village priest for the past six portions, for Ytraa's sake! How do you know I'm not a spy for their side?'

'You couldn't be, A'ahl. I know you too well. There's not a cruel or dishonest bone in your body.'

She flashed the knife. 'I would've used this, you know. I'd risk my own life and yours rather than his. But remember from now that no one knows about him. No one ever sees him. He's invisible and never discussed. The less we each know, the better for him and the better for us. But be ready, Shoarhn. Be ready for the day when he leads us to the change.'

'Does this make me one of the Few?'

'Perhaps. But always remember that the distance between death and life for us is less than a word. I wonder why he came to you, when I'm so close...? No. I don't want to know. He had his reasons, no doubt.'

'He had his reasons, A'ahl. He's beautiful, isn't he?'

A'ahl smiled and nodded. 'The most beautiful man I've known. And you know how I feel about Caarl.'

'Mmm. I have to admit Aglydron's not a patch on him. Too concerned with pleasing Ytraa rather than me or even himself.'

'Aglydron. Of course. He and Okkyntalah are still missing, aren't they?'

'He thinks they've kidnapped Jodisa-Li and taken her with them to find Dagla Kaz.'

'And what do you think?'

'I'm sure of it, now.' She explained all she'd learned from her husband, Okkyntalah and now Aklon-Dji.

A'ahl listened intently. When Shoarhn had finished, A'ahl returned the knife to her throat. 'On the floor, hands behind your back. Believe me; I will use this.'

'A'ahl, I....'

'Do it!'

She felt A'ahl's knee in the small of her back as she quickly lashed her hands together behind her with the waistrope wrenched from her tabard.

'I never meant any....'

A'ahl slapped her legs hard. 'Quiet! Whore!'

She rolled Shoarhn onto her back, cut a strip of cloth from her tabard and gagged her with it. She cut off another strip for a blindfold and then cut through the side fastenings and stripped the torn tabard from her. Lifting her to her feet by her hair, she thrust her across the floor and out of the room.

'You can sit or I can push you down; either way, I want you on the floor.'

Shoarhn sat as A'ahl bound her ankles together. Her friend pushed her over and fastened her ankles to her wrists so she lay curled backwards on her side, exposed and vulnerable.

'When I come back, you traitorous whore, I'll bring others with me. I'll watch them rape, burn and slice you until you tell them everything you know. Such is the fate of those who befriend that foul renegade.'

Chapter 22

Darkness And Threat

The women went reluctantly and only because Caarl's threat was clearly meant. Down, into the foetid bowels of the ship, to rest on dirty sacking in the dank darkness amongst crates and bags of cargo, the eyes of rhaats peering like dim furtive points from the darkness around them. Outside, the sun continued to shine and the wind blew fresh and clean.

'Why are we down here?'

'Something to do with that sail the crewman saw, I think.'

'What do you know, Tumalind?'

'Only that they altered course after they saw the sail. We've increased speed and they've told us to get out of sight. I think we're being chased.'

'Pirates.' Dilanthas voiced her fear so softly that only Tumalind seemed to hear and she just looked at her friend and nodded agreement. Neither of them voiced their concern to the others.

For what seemed time without end, they all remained where they'd been sent until Porryh grew restless and climbed the ladder toward the deck.

'Where you going, Porryh?'

'Can't stand it down here. I'm going to see what's up.'

'Caarl will punish you. He meant it, you know.'

'I can't stay down here!'

'You will stay down there. And you will remain absolutely silent, if you wish to live in freedom. I'll send someone down to explain. You must be quiet.' Dagla Kaz halted her at the head of the steps, his tone suggesting fear as much as concern.

Moments later, Jhonaht fumbled his way into the belly of the ship to give them an explanation, his voice so quiet they had to gather close.

'It's pirates. Baklan says there are two bands. One is led by Ryglan from Kabalyt; made up of thirty-five to forty hardened criminals. They trade in anything they can steal and, if they catch us, they'll kill everyone over forty and sell the rest as slaves. Women suffer most at the hands of this lot; apparently they don't care that their abuse lowers the value of their captives. They enjoy inflicting pain, laughing at the screams of terror. They make bets on how many men a woman can take before she starts to bleed.'

There was prolonged silence at this news.

'And the other lot?'

Jhonaht drew breath. 'If possible, they're worse. Led by a woman, Ni-Dehla, they select younger men for sex slaves; they're considered the lucky ones, though Baklan says they treat them cruelly if they don't come up to expectations. The older ones they whip until they bleed and hang just above the waterline as living bait for nazzakks, which they worship. They watch the killer fish bite pieces out of the poor unfortunates, until they bleed to death, and then dump them in the sea. Some men they castrate and seal the wounds with hot pitch. They sell them as slaves for the harems of the potentates in Balagaaq and Tohltaz. Young women they circumcise, brand, and sell as sex slaves for the same harems. Older women get to feed the nazzakks along with the men.'

'How do you circumcise a woman?'

Tumalind thought Wendarah would know such things but was glad the priestess asked, as she was curious.

Jhonaht looked uncomfortable.

'Well? Do you know, or don't you?'

He shrugged. 'They cut out the pleasure nodule. Leaves women still able to join but makes them less likely to seek enjoyment for themselves, so they say. Don't ask me why. I've no idea. Seems as foolish as it does barbaric.'

'So, what are harems, Jhonaht?'

He brightened at Tumalind's question. 'The world isn't full of Followers. Some religions see women as less than men. They treat them as goods and chattels. A harem's a collection of women kept for the sexual use of a single man.'

'What; one man and lots of women? What use is that to anyone?'

'Good question, Porryh. But I have no logical answer. No answer at all in fact. It's a mystery to me.'

'So they keep them in these harems forever and just frowk with whichever one they want? What about the women?'

'Precisely. But they don't keep any of the women for long. Once they're thirty or so, they take them, naked and unarmed, to a walled arena and watch half-starved manecats and stripecats feed off them. Same fate awaits male slaves over thirty. Such wonderful, civilized people.'

'Mhortag's balls! I don't want to go into no harem!'

Dilanthas started to cry and Tumalind held her for comfort. 'Will the pirates catch us, do you think, Jhonaht?'

'Their ships are moved through the water by sail and by slaves chained to rows of oars. They use whips to make them row faster. We've only the wind to propel us. That's why Baklan's set the wind behind the ship, to give us best speed. We hope to outrun them until it grows dark and then lose them in the night. Pray for a moonless one and a steady wind, for they're gaining on us. And, though I've made little use of my personal parts, I prefer to remain attached to them.

'You'll understand why you're out of sight now. Potential female slaves drive them into an even more frenzied pursuit. That's also why we need your silence. Voices carry well over water and we want to give them no clue to your presence on board.'

Jhonaht returned up the ladder and left the women in stunned and fearful silence in the humid darkness. They waited and waited, hoping and praying all would be well, since they could do more.

◆ ─────

When Jodisa-Li had finished her prayer session, which she actually spent thinking about her lost lover, she discovered Myllthlan watching her with curiosity.

'Ask me. No harm in asking questions, after all.'

Myllthlan seemed a little taken aback by her directness but welcomed the chance to learn.

'It seems odd that you're all so concerned not to look at each other or be watched when you're washing or doing other things without the coverings you use, but you expose yourselves so utterly when you worship. Especially you, Jodisa. On the island, any woman in that position would have a man inside her straight away.'

'I notice you have no such scruples.'

Myllthlan studied the men as they lay prone in the bottom of the boat. She moved closer to Jodisa-Li and whispered. 'I've known many men and seen the different shapes and sizes in their bodies and manhood. What about you?'

'I've had only one man and I loved him.' She didn't want to revisit that grief and found herself curious about the way this more experienced woman viewed her captors. 'What do you think of these two?'

'Well, I haven't had sex with either yet, though Okkyntalah's eager. Aglydron's a mature man who looks as though he's used to hard work. There weren't any like him on Ylcrat; they eat too much and don't do anything. Aglydron's firm and strong but sex with him would be like most men I've had.'

Jodisa-Li stopped herself giggling at this candid talk. It wasn't something she'd experienced much at home, her upbringing and social status keeping her away from such contact. She wondered if women on her homeland indulged in the same sort of chatter.

'So, what of the younger man?' She kept her voice low now the men were up from their prayers and going about their various tasks.

'Okkyntalah's still growing and developing. He's lithe and strong. I bet he can run for hours without tiring. Make love like that, too.'

'You talk of sex with Aglydron but of making love with Okkyntalah. Is there a difference?'

'Of course; you're young and inexperienced. Sex is just a man thrusting with his prod until he's satisfied. Most men do this. Making love is when a man cares about you in other ways and leads up to the act with tenderness, wants you to enjoy it as much as he does, and brings you that wonderful feeling of ecstasy that only a loving man can give a woman. It's a pleasure I've known only once. Okkyntalah seems to me to be such a man.'

'So, you'd enjoy joining with Okkyntalah, but it would just be a sort of duty with Aglydron?'

'That's right. You can tell by the way they are. They're both strong and healthy but Aglydron has an air of duty and piety as well as a brutal side that makes him hard to really like. I expect he frowks as if he's doing what he must. Okkyntalah's very different. Apart from his appearance...' she studied him openly and candidly so that Jodisa-Li felt she could do the same. 'Broad shoulders, firm long limbs, good height and just a little hair on his chest; his is the sort of body that just begs to be shared. But it's his eyes, really. Look into those deep pools and see the promises he makes and wants to keep.'

'I've no doubt he'll frowk with you, Myllthlan. Perhaps, he's waiting till we're off the boat. You'd enjoy joining with him, then?'

'I hope so. The men of Ylcrat use women when and how they want. But these men of yours are different. Both look at me with desire but neither has taken me and, true to their word, they leave you untouched. Okkyntalah I'd welcome and enjoy teaching ways to find and give delight. Aglydron I'd serve with experience and duty, willing to please him as I might. He's a man of contradictions and, in spite of his generosity to me, I can't feel at ease with him. The younger one, though, excites me and with him I might again experience the pleasure I had from just one man on Ylcrat. A pleasure so rare it might've been a dream, yet I feel it in my memory even now.'

'So, you do have desires of your own, Myllthlan? I'd begun to think you existed only for the men. But you know Aglydron is husband to Shoarhn in Muhnilahm and Okkyntalah's promised to the girl they want me to replace as Virgin Gift?'

Myllthlan smiled. 'Your men have one woman only?'

'No. But they'll join with others only at need. You may find them less willing to indulge you than you wish. Tell the truth, I'd have Okkyntalah now if I thought I'd get away with it; he's rather fascinating, isn't he? But Aglydron would whip me if I tried; might kill me if I succeeded. He believes me virgin and is determined to keep me that way.'

'But I thought you said you were afraid they'd take you by force? Though I can't say I understand that fear; women have no say in such things, surely?'

'I did worry when they first kidnapped me, but not now. It's one thing to have a man because you want him. But it's unthinkable to be used against your will, isn't it?'

'I never had a choice. I take it the women do in your home?'

'We're equals. Rape is punishable by a very painful death at home.'

'Rape? You have a word for something I cannot comprehend and a word for a state of being that is foreign to me. Why? Why are they so concerned about this virgin thing?'

'It's the decree of Ytraa, brought down through the ages to us by Gadhallah, from whom I'm a direct descendent.' She wondered if her pride showed but Myllthlan made no comment. 'It's the will of Ytraa that young men and women remain chaste until the ceremony of the First Joining. After that, they're free to have sex, as you put it, with others. Some do choose to join only with their chosen partner for life, though most don't. And everyone's available for any of the priesthood at any time and for as long as the priest or priestess chooses. But that first joining is sacred because it symbolizes the reunion of woman with man whom Mhortag split asunder at the beginning of the world.'

'So the men must worship this Mhortag. He made sex better for them, didn't he?'

'Myllthlan! Never let Aglydron hear you say such a thing! He'd whip you for your blasphemy. Mhortag's the source of all that's evil. Mhortag causes death and destruction and disease. Please don't say such a thing ever again, even in jest.'

Myllthlan stripped at once and knelt on all fours at Jodisa-Li's feet. 'Beat me for my wickedness. I must learn to hold my foolish tongue. Beat me so I learn to do your will.'

Aglydron and Okkyntalah looked across, the older man asking, 'What's she mean?'

'She made an error of judgement over something she's ignorant of, Aglydron. It wasn't as wicked as she seems to think. Let me deal with this. It's a matter for women, you understand.'

'As you will, Jodisa. And cover her up.'

Jodisa-Li knelt and drew her upright. 'Put it on. I won't beat you. In any case, no one's supposed to be beaten whilst naked. That's sacrilege. Remember, naked is sacred.'

Myllthlan followed her glance at Aglydron and saw her frown as he looked away. Jodisa-Li helped her with the fastenings, which were still strange to her.

'I must atone. What would you have me do?'

'Nothing, Myllthlan. You've much to learn. We won't teach you by punishing accidental errors. But learn from your mistakes and don't repeat them. As a start to your learning, I'll ask Aglydron to recite the First Great Knowing. Pay attention. He teaches it better than most I've heard.'

They all listened as Aglydron retold the story, Jodisa-Li again finding his narration captivating; something to do with his fervour and use of the old language, she supposed. By the time he'd finished, the boat lay in darkness with stars above and to the west and south. Behind them, all was black as cloud built, obscuring moon and stars. The quiet of the sea slowly changing to motion as an increasing swell raised and lowered the boat.

'I'll take first watch.'

Aglydron agreed with Okkyntalah's suggestion. 'It'll be well, if bad weather comes, for you to be fresh to face it in the morning. Wake me when the belt of the Hunter reaches the horizon. The women should sleep for now. I'll wake Jodisa for the last watch.'

Myllthlan whispered to her. 'I know it's not my place, Jodisa, but I think the stars will be hidden behind clouds before that time.'

She nodded absently and looked at Okkyntalah, wondering how he controlled his obvious desire for the new woman. Would Myllthlan offer herself in the darkness and quiet of the coming night, whilst Aglydron slept?

They'd eaten fresh dorado, caught by Okkyntalah, and drunk sparingly from the water skins. The night air remained warm enough for sleep without need of cover and they spread two sleepsacks together in the space in front of and around the mast for her to share with Myllthlan. The older woman silently signalled she wanted to be closest to Okkyntalah as they settled down and Jodisa-Li accommodated her. Aglydron curled in the bows, with Shaulah at his feet. Jodisa-Li fell asleep wondering about the different life Myllthlan had led on Ylcrat.

❦

'We'll not outrun the scum before dark.'

Dagla Kaz saw certainty on Baklan's face and agreed.

'But dusk will fall soon. Surely we can find a way to hold them off until then?'

'I'm open to suggestions, Caarl. Speed alone won't do it. Look. You'll soon be able to see their ugly frowkin' faces, they're so close. Once we're in range, they'll fire off arrows to soften us up. Then they'll close and loose grappling irons to attach us together and slow us down.'

'Do you have any pitch on board, Baklan?'

'Of course. It's a ship!' The master's eyes narrowed with suspicion. 'What you got in mind?'

Caarl pondered for a few moments, watching the pirates. 'Tryonta, fetch my bow and yours and as many arrows as you can. Baklan, have the men set up a cauldron of pitch and a source of fire, here on deck. And send some spare canvas down to the women. Get them to cut it into thin strips, as quickly as they can.'

Baklan seemed unsure. 'I don't like fire on my ship. The timbers are soaked with pitch to keep them waterproof. A naked flame could make the ship a torch in no time.'

'Exactly, Baklan. We have the advantage. The Sun's behind them and the sky will remain light in their rear long after it's become dark from their direction. We'll be hidden in gloom at a time when they're visible as a silhouette against the dusk. It's then we shoot flaming arrows into their ship. We can see them but we're almost hidden. Even if they have time to retaliate in like manner, we'll be more difficult to hit.'

Baklan scratched his head and seemed uncertain.

'Do you have a better plan?'

He turned to Dagla Kaz. 'I admit, I haven't. We'll try it.'

Even as they made the arrangements, darkness was falling. By the time all was ready, the sun had gone and the sky they sailed into was already black, cloud obscuring the lower stars as it rolled in from the northeast. But behind them was clear, their pursuers silhouetted exactly as Caarl had predicted and growing close enough for their voices to be heard. Dagla Kaz felt proud of his man.

'Have the crew stand by with buckets of water, in case they fire back. We should catch them unawares.'

When all was ready, Tryonta, Caarl and Tarruss readied their bows and wrapped pitch soaked lengths of canvas around their arrows. Together, they lit them from the small, enclosed fire set in its metal and stone hearth, and released their missiles over the short distance toward the following boat. Tryonta's hissed into the sea close by the bows but Caarl's stuck in the mast amidships as the one from Tarruss overshot and landed in the waves beyond. Cries of dismay rang out from the pirates and, before they could retaliate, three more flaming missiles all found their mark. Tarruss hit a crewman, who fell amongst the slaves rowing below and Caarl struck the wall of the cabin, aft. Tryonta's second arrow stuck in the bows, just out of reach of the crew but well above the waterline.

Darkness was almost complete by this time but the flaming arrows had caught and made the ship an easy target with the dusk sky behind it. A dozen more arrows hit the following ship before they felt their task was done. The pirates tried sending a few of their own missiles across but, in the darkness, only one found a target, on deck right at the feet of Tarruss. He quenched it with one of the standing canvas buckets of water, putting it out almost at once.

The pirate ship, its rowing slaves disorganized by fire and the fallen and panicking crewmen, slewed off course and came broadside, aft. Flame licked sails and rigging, catching in rope and fabric and roaring as heated air and wind fanned the fires. Flame danced up the superstructure, turning the whole of the cabin into a wall of fire. Flame scorched the flesh of sailors and oarsmen so that those who were free leapt from the ship in their panic to escape. The masts quickly became blazing torches, lighting up the sea all around the stricken ship.

In the flickering brilliance of the flames, Dagla Kaz caught sight of the pirate ship's master; a woman, half naked and wielding a vicious, curved sword as she fought for control of the desperate crew, slicing the flesh of those who disobeyed her. A man holding a flaming whip of fire in one hand, lashed at the oarsmen and then jumped overboard. Men in the water, some still on fire, cried out for help from those they would have captured and tortured.

Baklan spat at them. 'Drown, scum!' He turned to Dagla Kaz. 'The laws of the sea mean nothing to such as them. I'll do nought to save rhaats.'

'Come on up, ladies. You're safe now.'

At Jhonaht's behest, they came back up on deck in time to see their pursuers sinking into the waves. As Dagla Kaz watched, the female leader, Ni-Dehla, with hair and skirt alight, drew her sword across her own throat.

'See the dangers of domineering women?'

The intrusive voice had visited him before, so that he no longer started at its presence in his head. Much of what it said was true and he merely nodded his agreement.

The blazing ship sank beneath the waves, hissing with the violence of a huge angry snake.

For a long time, they looked back to where a few plumes of isolated flame and smoke rose against the backdrop of the darkling sky. All sounds of pain and terror had ended and they sailed the sea alone again, in peace.

'Those poor men.'

'You'd not have said that if they'd caught us, Tumalind.'

'I meant the slaves. They had no choice, did they?'

'That's the lot of slaves, though, isn't it? Lose your freedom; lose all your rights. Just like us.'

Dagla Kaz glared at the girl and Porryh shifted to escape the smack Corphanda threatened at this accusation, but she failed to move quickly enough and yelped. He smiled. That woman had proved a brilliant choice as guardian for the Virgin Gifts.

Baklan laughed at the girl's yell of outrage. 'Dowse that fire, you lot and make ready. We've defeated that scum; now let's see if we can avoid the frowkin' storm.'

Chapter 23

CONSEQUENCES

*O*kkyntalah heard the breathing of the sleepers as they settled in the quiet of the falling night. Over to the west, he frowned at what looked like a fine plume of smoke, low on the horizon and marring the pale glow of dusk, where he thought only water abounded. Tumalind came to mind, unbidden, and he smiled at the picture he formed of her.

As stars turned and the night grew older, fresh sounds arose. Waves splashed and lapped against the boat. Wind filled the sail and flapped loose ends of ropes; a warm wind carrying the deep-sea smell of the wide eastern ocean on its breath, though it blew from north of east and, from time to time, held a faint reminder of the fire mountain.

In the darkness, against the following clouds of black, he became aware of a figure close to him.

'Myllthlan?'

'I've come to you, my handsome one, to give what you desire.'

They spoke in whispers and she knelt at his feet so she could be closer to him.

'What do I desire?'

'To be with me as a man is with a woman. I've seen it in your eyes. I've seen you follow the curves of my body with hunger. I'm here to feed you, lest the hunger make you mad. I'm prepared.'

The awkwardness of the small seat at the stern, the rocking of the boat, the paraphernalia of steering and sail, were nothing to her. Her experience brought joy and his care brought pleasure.

'Thank you, Okkyntalah; you have the way. I thought you must.' She lifted from him.

He sensed her moving back toward the mast to sleep away the rest of night. Waves crashed and wind moaned in the ropes. He felt the memory of her. She'd shown him wonder and he would want her again and again and again. If joining meant this, let it be his life from now. For a time he dwelt in that fantasy.

'You were supposed to wake me, Okkyntalah. And we're off course. Look. Can't you see the Eyes of Ytraa? Don't you know which way we should be heading? Can't I trust you to keep alert even for a small part of the night?'

'I'm sorry Aglydron, my mind wandered in…'

'I know. Your mind was on Tumalind. Shoarhn and me have been one for cycles yet I sometimes yearn for her like a youth. But we've got to concentrate. If we fail, Okkyntalah, you won't get those delights. We won't just die; we'll dishonour Ytraa, bring disaster to all Followers, and cause doom to the world of men.'

'It's a heavy burden, Aglydron. Can we bear it?'

'Ytraa will help us. Keep faith, and all will be well.'

Okkyntalah left the tiller to the older man and took his place on the sleepsack he'd vacated. As he lay down to sleep, his mind dwelt again on the pleasure of Myllthlan and moved him to dreams of Tumalind. Distant and unattainable she may be, but Tumalind was still the woman he'd have for life if he could. Myllthlan gave pleasure but he had no wish to do more than join with her. Her attraction was physical, like Jodisa-Li's. He went to sleep wondering what it would be like to join with the High Priest's daughter. His emotions and desires had been stirred by Myllthlan's experience and he hungered for more of that pleasure and knew he'd take everything she offered him.

◆·····◈·····◆

As Myllthlan had predicted, the storm hit around dawn. Prayers were difficult but Aglydron insisted. As usual, Jodisa-Li found her attention on anything but their god. Myllthlan made her first obeisance to Ytraa, expressing the hope of helping save all their lives.

Their control of the boat made passage through this wild weather less hazardous than the earlier storm. However, even with four against the elements they were exhausted by the end of the day when the wind at last abated. Although less rain fell this time, it still soaked everything they had.

Clouded skies and strong, erratic winds had taken them far off course so that they had only a vague notion of their position on the wide Shylnah Sea. The rain had replenished some of their drinking water but they hadn't been able to catch fish during the foul weather and their supplies of food were very low. Okkyntalah fished again as the others went about their own duties. Aglydron took the tiller. Jodisa-Li and Myllthlan set about trying to dry out their clothes and other supplies.

'Are you hurt, Jodisa-Li? I notice you seem unable to sit still, and move as though in pain.'

Jodisa-Li scowled at Aglydron. 'He beat me for trying to escape. I'm bruised and sore.'

'Let me see. I may be able to…'

'It's my bottom.'

'I can't mend what I can't see.'

'Turn away, you two.'

Aglydron turned reluctant eyes toward the deepening dusk of the far horizon, where the sun would soon leave sky for sea.

Jodisa-Li knelt on all fours and raised her tabard.

'I thought you weren't supposed to beat people when they were naked, Aglydron? These stripes came from a strap on bare skin.'

'She made me angry.'

'I see. The bruises and stripes are simple enough, Jodisa, though Aglydron must've used some force for them to last so long. But your skin's cut here, and here, where two or more blows have crossed and broken the surface. I must prepare to heal as I did with Okkyntalah. Is that permitted?'

'She's suffered enough. Heal her if you can, Myllthlan.' Okkyntalah didn't look up from his fishing but Jodisa-Li heard the care in his voice and smiled with satisfaction.

'Easily said, Okkyntalah. She deserved those stripes and might learn better the longer she wears them.'

'Or be scarred for life and maybe even made sick.' Okkyntalah's comments warmed her and she smiled though he couldn't see her.

'I'm sorry to contradict you, Aglydron. You know I'd follow your command. But, Okkyntalah's right. If the skin's left broken this way, she may well be scarred and she may take in poison from the rough wood of the boat, giving her a fever and making her ill. Do you want this?'

'Heal her if you must.'

Myllthlan prepared herself to heal and again drew the power she used from the air. Jodisa-Li felt a mild sensation of heat as the healer passed her fingers over the bruises and the stripes. As she blew on the open wounds and knit the skin together again, she felt a tingling sensation that penetrated deeper under her skin and left her feeling slightly numb for a few moments. When she stood again, she felt no more pain.

'Thank you, Myllthlan. I can sit at ease for a change.'

'That's all to the good. Make sure you earn no more stripes and then we'll all be happier'

His continued carping disappointed her. After all they'd been through, she'd hoped he might be less her enemy.

'Ah, but to be good enough for you, Aglydron, I'd have to be almost perfect and I'm sure I'll never manage that.' She hoped he heard scorn in her voice. When she saw that he had, she relented, considering their situation and close confinement. 'Perhaps, we could meet in the middle? I could become a less troublesome prisoner and you could be less cruel?'

'For my part, I'll try.'

'That's settled, then.' She stood and turned her back to the young man now hauling his catch into the boat. She bent over. 'See Okkyntalah? I'm smooth and unmarked again, am I not?' She flipped up the back of the tabard to expose Myllthlan's healing.

Looking over her shoulder, to gauge his reaction, she saw the spear and newly caught fish slide from his slack hand as he stared at her, open-mouthed. A small splash marked his surprise.

'You're perfection, Jodisa. I'd see you unmarked till the end of your days.'

At the same time, Aglydron got to his feet in the stern. 'I'll stripe you again for that; shameless whore!'

Okkyntalah realised he'd lost both fish and spear and, without warning or preamble, jumped over the side to retrieve them. His movement rocked the boat precisely as Aglydron rose, and the older man, unbalanced and overly concerned about visiting retribution on Jodisa-Li, toppled into the sea.

Shoarhn lay huddled in the dark; wrists and ankles burning from tight bindings, fingers and feet growing numb, mouth dry with fear. On her side, she could only wriggle, and the rough floor grazed her skin as she tried to worm her way from the room. She came up against a wall and wept with frustration as she trapped herself in a corner.

Time passed without measure. Sounds from beyond came through woven walls but gave no clue to the time. Where had A'ahl gone and who would come to torture her? Why had she been so foolish, so full of pride at her experience as to tell anyone? Even her trusted friend, A'ahl. And now she'd be burned and cut and they'd rape her again and again and again until their brutality split her and she became all pain and torment. But she would say nothing; of that, she was determined. They could hurt her all they would but she'd tell them nothing that could endanger the handsome young man. She must protect him at all costs.

But, A'ahl: how could she have been so wrong about her friend? Could she really be on the side of the authorities? For answer, she had only to consult the bindings, the fear, the captivity, and her bursting bladder.

It must be true. A'ahl had deserted her to be tortured, shamed, destroyed. Left her until dignity no longer mattered and brief relief mingled with shame and discomfort as she lay in her own cooling wetness and waited.

Footsteps approached, at last. They had come. How many? Impossible to tell. Men's voices amongst the women. They turned her roughly onto her front and cut the bindings of her ankles to release them from her wrists. They hauled her to her feet and held her there, on legs that wouldn't support her.

'I'm going to release the gag. Utter a sound and I'll cut out your tongue. Nod if you understand.'

She nodded.

The gag tore her lip and she ran her dry tongue across the wound.

A hard male voice, close and cold, asked a question. 'Who were you with last night?'

She remained silent, terrified, awaiting the hot bite of a whip, the cold slicing of metal blades, the searing agony of burning wooden embers.

'Who did you join with last night?'

She said nothing, her bowels churning with fear.

An unknown female voice, further but still close, informed her. 'To make it clear, you may speak to answer our questions. Do you understand?'

'Yes.' She felt the urge to speak so strongly that she almost told them everything without further questioning but she held her tongue and told herself it would soon be all over. Death would bring an end to the fear that almost overwhelmed her and the pain she knew must come. Who would take care of the boys? But terror and despair lurked in that and she wouldn't countenance it, yet.

'The man who came to your house, what did he look like?'

'I had no visitor.'

'He was seen.'

'I spent last night alone.'

Something cold and hard touched her skin just below her right breast. She felt it drawn across and up her flesh to the base of the nipple where it rested, the point sharp against sensitive skin.

'Tell me who you were with.'

'I was alone.'

The point circled her nipple and then crossed her breast to the other and circled there, not cutting but threatening, cold, and terrifying to her flesh.

'Who parted your thighs and entered your fern?'

The point dropped down her body and rested against the place he'd pleasured so well.

'I was on my own last night. My husband's not home.'

The point left her and she waited for pain. Waited.

In the silence something must happen to her. She waited.

The silence grew until it felt intolerable and she thought she would burst if she didn't fill it with her confession. But she said nothing.

Waited.

Those who supported her let her go and she staggered and fell to her knees and let out an involuntary gasp of pain. She waited for the hand to grasp her throat. Waited for the hands that would force open her mouth. Waited for the blade to cut out her tongue.

'I was alone. Really, I was.'

Soft sounds she couldn't identify left her. She remained on her knees, waiting; terrified. Alone. Vulnerable.

'I was.'

Time passed.

'What do you know of Aklon-Dji?' The cold female voice came out of the silence like a shock and made her whole body jerk with sudden stiffness.

Her mind reeled with fear and desperation but she willed herself to stillness and breathed in deeply to calm her trembling limbs and torso. Only one answer she could give.

'He's the renegade son of the High Priest. To be captured alive or killed on sight.'

'What of the Lord Gadhallah?'

'He is our saviour, our founder, the link with Ytraa the great God who created us.'

'Why do we join with each other, man and woman?'

'The fourth Great Command; that man and woman join when they will and when they might to become as one in the sight of Ytraa who created woman and man as one being.'

'Who did you join with last night?' A new female voice.

'I joined with no one.'

'You were seen.'

'The witness made a mistake. I spent the night alone. My husband is away.'

'Where is your husband?'

'I don't know.'

'Where is he?' The man again.

'I don't know.'

'Where is your husband?'

'I don't know. He'd gone when I awoke on the morning after the Choosing.'

'Where did he go?'

'He didn't tell me.'

'You're lying.' The point of the sharp, cold metal touched her cheek and traced a line to the corner of her mouth, where it rested a while. 'Tell me the truth and I'll release you.'

'I'm telling the truth. I am. Aglydron went in search of Dagla Kaz, that's all I know.'

Silence again for the longest time. Had the torturer gone? Did she kneel alone? Were they all watching her and sneering at her as they decided how they should make her suffer before they killed her?

'I hold in my hand a blade heated red by flame. If you fail to answer my next question correctly, I shall draw the hot metal across your breasts and burn your proud nipples away. Do you feel the heat?'

She felt the searing heat pass slowly, close but not touching, across her middle. She nodded.

'Who did you speak with last night?'

When was last night? Was it still the same day that A'ahl had bound her? How much time had passed since she'd been blindfolded?

'I spoke with no one.' It was the only answer she could give.

She waited. Silence.

Soft sounds approached and she listened for clues but found nothing other than fear and the image of men with sharp, hot blades to pierce and cut and mark her skin.

A hand moved behind her, undoing the blindfold and releasing it. She could see. Blinked at the brightness of candlelight. A'ahl stood before her, her face full of sorrow, pain and concern. They were alone in the room. She released the bonds at her wrists, untied her ankles, bathed her soiled skin with warm water and a scented cloth and dabbed her dry before she helped her to the bed in the corner of the room.

'I'm so sorry, Shoarhn.' She held a goblet of sweet pale yellow wine to her lips and allowed her to take a sip or two. 'I hope you'll forgive me. We have to know, you see. If you wish, you're now one of the Few. If not, remember we all know who you are but you know only me.' She passed her the goblet of wine, held it again to her lips. Tears coursed down her friend's face as she looked at her.

Shoarhn wept quietly. She understood the danger had passed but she puzzled over what she'd suffered. She drank again and rubbed at her wrists and her ankles.

A'ahl bent low and plucked a small earthenware bottle from the ground at her feet. She unstoppered it and poured a few drops of aromatic oil into her palm, replaced the stopper in the bottle and rubbed her hands together. She took Shoarhn's near wrist between her palms and softly, lovingly, gently soothed the pain away with the oil. 'I'm sorry, Shoarhn. We have to be sure. I didn't want to be cruel but there's no other way.'

'I don't understand.' Recognition of truth in what her friend said tempered the outrage that rose in her. Exhaustion denied her the anger she felt she'd earned. 'Explain it to me.'

'You were tested, that's all. Of course, if the others, Holy Ones, had got hold of you, you'd have told them all they needed to know. They're not so kind as we are. You were tested, Shoarhn, and you passed. That's what happened.'

'Tested?'

'To discover your loyalty.'

'Loyalty? To who?'

'Me, basically. But essentially to me and…others.'

'How do I know I can trust you now?'

A'ahl turned and slipped a sharp dagger from beneath the bed, handed it to her handle first. 'Use it, if you think I deserve it. I'm unarmed and alone now.'

'It was all so…it seemed so real. You terrified me. You can't know the terror and anguish I…'

'I've been tested, Shoarhn.'

'You have?'

'We all have.'

'All?'

'All who were here tonight. Just the seven I know. There are more but we keep our known contacts low to avoid losing too many if one is caught. You'll eventually get to know more, of course, as time progresses.'

'A man threatened…'

'Yes. A man tests the women, if possible. A woman tests the men. We have to make it as close to how it would really be. That's why I bound you so tight and left you so long. You have to know what you might face. Of course, it's only a taste, really. The Holy Ones have ways that hurt forever. We can't do any damage or we'd lose more than we gained. But we have to at least make a real test of all who might become members of the Few and be ready to fight for the Cause.'

'Are there many?'

'More than you'd expect. Not enough yet for when the time comes; but there will be. Rest for a few days and then I'll begin to explain all the lies and tell you the truth of this faith we all follow like ants.'

'Why are you naked?'

'We test in that fashion. It's a reminder to us of your vulnerability. I stay like that now so I'm in the same state as you. You've been tested and passed. You deserve kindness and equality now.'

'Suppose I hadn't passed, A'ahl? Suppose I'd blurted out the truth?'

'The knife you felt was real, Shoarhn. The sea is deep.'

'You'd really have let them…kill me?'

'Just as you'll let them kill the next man we try, if he fails. There's no other way, as long as we struggle against an enemy so vile and corrupt. Bend your mind to the consequences for others who make the Cause their own and you'll see it's the only way. Rest now, Shoarhn. The boys are still safe with their grandmother. Sleep; I'll remain with you. In case you have nightmares.'

She fed with A'ahl's help. As her friend massaged away the pain and tension of the binding and the torture, she began to relax, at last, and let the questions recede to the back of her mind as sleep took her.

One of the Few: soon she'd know what that meant. Her life would never be simple or safe again. Somehow, she'd become part of a force for change without fully knowing what she would change or why and what would result from the change. But she knew, without question, that the leader of this Few was the young man who'd stolen her heart so short a time past and that, for him, she would do whatever was required of her. Even if the cost was her death.

•───┼───•

Aware of the dangers to both men in the water as dusk fell and light faded, Jodisa-Li took the helm and shifted the sail to bring the boat round. She headed first for Okkyntalah, well aft, passing Aglydron on the way. 'Throw the fool a rope, Myllthlan. And hang on to the other end.'

Myllthlan uncoiled a length of rope from the bottom of the boat and tossed it toward Aglydron. It fell short and he continued to splash toward the boat, now moving away from him. She threw it again, just as Jodisa-Li came round so that Okkyntalah could grab the gunwales at the side. He chucked his spear, fish still attached, into the boat and grabbed the side. She left him to his own devices and turned again to make toward Aglydron, who'd just missed grabbing the rope and now struggled in the water. Okkyntalah, climbing aboard, saw the older man in trouble and flung himself back into the sea to help him.

Myllthlan stripped off her tabard to join the rescue.

'Stay where you are. You can't swim and you'll only cause more trouble. Help me to pull them aboard when we reach the fools.'

She knelt at the side of the boat, arms outstretched and waiting. Okkyntalah reached Aglydron at the same time as the boat caught up. Jodisa-Li brought the vessel to a halt with the sail and he and Myllthlan pulled and pushed the older man on board. Okkyntalah swiftly followed.

For a moment, all was still and silent in the boat as the two men caught their breath and both women watched, horrified by what might have been. Shaulah stopped barking and stood on her master's shoulders so she could lick his face.

Jodisa-Li took the tiller again and sat down to try to set the boat back on course. But she had no idea which way they should be heading after their detour; she could only let her memory and wind take them at best speed and hope that was the right direction. The sky, almost a uniform black by this time, held the merest suggestion of pallor marking the place where the sun had set. It gave her vague guidance. Myllthlan took Okkyntalah his tabard and helped him into it.

'Thank you, Jodisa. You did well.'

'You have your reward for your kindness. But you'll see no more, whether I remain unmarked or not.'

'I meant your seamanship, not your naughty display.'

'Why did you show Okkyntalah?'

'As evidence of your powers, Myllthlan. What other purpose could I possibly have?'

Aglydron sat in the bottom of the boat and coughed up seawater. 'To show how wicked you really are, girl. I'll have a strap to your skin as soon as I'm recovered.'

'No, Aglydron. Enough. We almost lost you and I nearly lost the fishing spear.'

'I'll make the whore sorry!'

'Enough!'

'You saw what Ytraa thought of her wickedness, how Ytraa made us pay for her blasphemous act and…'

'No. I saw how my stupidity and your anger combined to make a harmless prank into near tragedy. Let it go, Aglydron. There's nothing to gain by making more of it than it really was.'

Myllthlan stared at the young man with admiration.

Jodisa-Li felt the same. 'Okkyntalah's right, Aglydron. I know I shouldn't have done it but I meant it in fun not as insult or blasphemy. I meant no harm. As I said, I rewarded his caring. You I excluded because you caused the injuries; nothing more.'

Aglydron looked at her in the fading light and she knew she'd made her point clear to him; knew he felt foolish and snubbed. Whether Okkyntalah fully appreciated her gesture she couldn't know. She believed he'd been too impressed with the view to consider the invitation she'd intended.

Chapter 24

GODS AND HEROES

As before, calm followed the storm. This time, the sea grew still as the wind died to nothing and the swell became an undulation that rocked the small craft like a mother trying to sooth a fretful child into sleep.

Day broke still and heavy, with a mist that blocked the horizon in all directions and no wind to move them. Captive to current, they moved sluggishly where the sea would have them go, with no knowledge of how near or distant was the shore.

At her suggestion, Okkyntalah taught Myllthlan to use the fishing spear and, between them, they caught three fish. They fed on choice parts before hanging the rest in strips to dry in the sun, if it ever shone again. Silence enclosed the boat all morning. Bored, Jodisa-Li asked Myllthlan why she hadn't collapsed after she'd healed her, as she had with Okkyntalah.

'I don't collapse.'

'You did after you healed me.'

She looked at Okkyntalah. 'I did?'

They all nodded and she shrugged. 'I never did before. I don't think I did.'

'And you kissed him full on the mouth after you'd kissed his wound but you only gently brushed my wounds with your lips. Why?'

Myllthlan smiled and lowered her gaze. 'The kiss is needed for full healing; how it's given is up to the healer.'

They laughed at her confession and it lightened their mood again.

Jodisa-Li suggested they use the time to instruct Myllthlan in the ways of Followers. Trying to persuade Aglydron that she was more pious than he thought her, she was delighted when he readily agreed.

'Tell the tale of Vaarkil and Mythanpho, Aglydron, so our new member understands some of the roots of our faith.'

⁎⸺⸺⸺⁎

Aglydron, flattered by the girl's suggestion, was happy to impress the newcomer, with whom he hoped to join as soon as opportunity allowed. Okkyntalah took the tiller from him, though there was little enough need. The girls made themselves comfortable before he began his tale.

'I'll tell you the story as I first heard it, Myllthlan, from my father when I was a child, but I'll include parts he left out as unsuitable for one so young. He taught me in words used by the ancients and I'll apply the same style.'

He pictured himself in the distant past, in Choshinahm, and found the words and mood to let him tell the tale as the truth he knew it to be.

'On a day so distant that even the ancient calendars do not name it, came Vaarkil into the world. Pah-Llon, Master Fisherman of Qolahn by Lake Qonahn in Choshinahm, being in his one hundred and ninetieth cycle of that office, was emptying lobster pots with two young pupils in the early morning.

'All was still on the waters of the lake. As Pah-Llon drew up the last pot, he gazed down through clear waters and saw that it was full. But his pleasure at the catch fell to dismay when he emptied the contents into the boat. For, amongst living lobsters, lay a naked, new born man-child. And he must surely be dead. But Pah-Llon held the babe aloft and showed it to Tryhnn of the Lake and asked, in a loud voice, for the infant's deliverance. And though there was no wind that day, the waters of the lake became a turmoil and tossed so that the small boat might be overwhelmed. The young men with Pah-Llon were afraid and begged him stop, that the waters might calm but Pah-Llon paid no heed, begging Tryhnn for the life of the babe. And then, since that seemed not to please the Gods, he called on Ytraa to be merciful and save the infant. At once, the waters quietened and the babe breathed and gave a cry. And they returned to Qolahn.

'All the village came out to greet their return for they thought the boat lost in the turmoil of the waters. And with those who came was the woman of Pah-Llon's house, Tihldha. Ancient she was, being near in age to Pah-Llon; and he could count four hundred and twelve cycles in the caves of his memory. Tihldha took the child from Pah-Llon and held him in her arms. She bared her breasts, though she had been barren and dry for countless cycles. Yet, the child sucked there and grew strong on the milk he had and the whole village was amazed. But Tihldha said it was a sign that the child would be a great hero in the world. She named the child Vaarkil, meaning 'one who was found', and blessed him before Tryhnn and before Ytraa. Thus were she and her man blessed so that Pah-Llon and Tihldha grew to be of great age but knew not a day of sickness even until the day they departed this life.

'The child grew strong and straight and tall and was of noble appearance. Vaarkil became a man of proud bearing, true and kind, and generous of spirit. The village of Qolahn gained much from his presence and they loved him well.

'It happened that on the same day as Vaarkil was found in the lake, so was conceived the fair maiden Mythanpho. In a desert region north of Lake Qonahn, where none now dare venture, lived a solitary people. One of these, Valorysta, was a widow who lived with her only child, her daughter, Poliphri. It was their custom to dwell alone as small families and come together in groups only at times of suffering or celebration.

'Poliphri was a maiden of great beauty, a prize amongst her people. Yet, she knew no man in all her life, though many greatly desired her. After the middle of the day, when it was pleasant; for in those parts, the nights are often cool but the days are ever warm, she took herself into the hills to lie under the sun in praise of her god, as was their custom. As she lay, it happened that the spirit of the sun, Ulkhon, came upon her as he rode the air above. Seeing her unadorned and alone in worship, he was overcome with passion for her.

'Ulkhon took Poliphri and fell on her and filled her with his light and life. Poliphri was dazzled and afraid. But Ulkhon soothed her and spent his lust and she was quieted and made brave and worshipped him for his act. He blessed her and gifted her with beauty to live till she lived not. So it was that Poliphri lived five hundred and sixty three cycles yet aged not a day from that time.

'The child that Ulkhon made in her womb he blessed also saying, "This is the child of the Sun Spirit Ulkhon. She will grow to be the fairest maiden the world has ever known. Gold will not match the burnish of her hair...".' Aglydron glanced at Myllthlan. 'In those days, they didn't know about myllth; or they'd have used that instead.'

Myllthlan smiled her pleasure at his compliment.

'Ulkhon continued, "...polished ivory will envy her skin and the blue of the evening sky will live in her eyes. The child will be born without pain to her mother and no troubles will her mother have from her. Know that you and your babe are blessed, Poliphri, and fear no living creature."

'Ulkhon left her and Poliphri returned to her mother, Valorysta, and told her all that had happened. When the child was born, all was as Ulkhon had foretold and the people marvelled. For the people of that land were of olive skin and sable hair and hazel eyes, yet the child was beauteous fair and she was called Mythanpho by her mother, meaning daughter of the Sun.

'Yet, as she grew, some of the people loved her not, envying her beauty and her grace. And in her sixteenth cycle came one who would use her, for he lusted after her because she was more beautiful than any woman in the land. Mythanpho was brave and fought him off so that all he had of her was her robe. And Mythanpho ran into the desert and escaped and dare not return for fear that any man who might see her thus might violate her.

'For many portions, she wandered clad in wild flowers that she wove into garments for her modesty. Vaarkil, hunting for wild boar, came upon her bathing in a stream. Her beauty stole his heart and his noble bearing captured her so that they fell in love at once and she felt no fear nor shame at his approach. He did cover her with his cloak and took her home to Qolahn and they became one at the evening ceremony and all the village did rejoice that Vaarkil had found one so fair to be his wife.

'Many were the love songs that they sang together by the lake. Many were the sons and daughters that she bore, seed of Vaarkil, offspring of Mythanpho, and all were fair and strong and well-loved and blessed with eyes the colour of lapis lazuli, which was the colour of Vaarkil's eyes. And they dwelt by the lake many cycles in great happiness.

'Now, in those days, a tale was told of the monster, Na-Dagun, that dwelt at the bottom of the lake. The serpent of great size, and with two heads, caused the waters to boil and sank fishing boats, devouring the crews. But Na-Dagun had not been seen for many long cycles, even by the elders and they were ancient beyond the cycles of modern men. Pah-Llon, named guardian of Vaarkil, had eaten the grain of more than five hundred harvests when he lived no more.

'Some of the young men of the village were disrespectful and made fun of the tales of Na-Dagun, saying it was no more than a story made up to frighten children. But the elders nodded sagely to one another and told the youths that time would tell the truth. Some of these young men were idlers and headstrong and went to find Na-Dagun and wake the serpent, if it be real, and cut off its heads for a wager. The village elders were wrath and said that they must not jest about Na-Dagun nor wake the serpent from sleep lest it take the village fishermen, as it had in the past. But the young men just laughed and said the serpent was no more than a worm grown fat on the imaginings of old men.

'They searched the lake and prodded the bottom with long sticks and returned to Qolahn laughing that they had killed the great serpent with pointed sticks and that all could sleep safe in their beds again. Three days after this a fishing boat returned with two men missing and a tale of a great two headed serpent that had devoured the others and almost wrecked the boat. The serpent, they said, had eyes like red hot coals and scales of yellow and green and teeth as long as a man's forearm.

'The young men laughed at this and declared the tale to be the result of too much strong spirit in the flagons aboard the boat. They said they would go into the lake to see the serpent for themselves for they believed not the fishermen. The elders forbade them go. So it was, at night, the young men took a boat and stole, from her bed, Lesythemis, one of the fair young daughters of Vaarkil and Mythanpho to use for sport on their voyage...'

Aglydron caught Jodisa-Li's pointed stared, but she gave no argument, no voice to the thought that he saw pass through her mind, and he went on. '...and they departed the shores to find the serpent.

'In the morning, there was great anger in the village at what they had done and great sorrow for Lesythemis. The people and elders promised that the young men would be most grievously punished on their return if harm came to the maiden. Vaarkil and

Mythanpho swore an oath to avenge the dishonour the youths had brought on their daughter and strife grew in the village, for the parents of the youths were full of guilt at what they did.

'After two days, the boat returned. Sixteen young men and Lesythemis had set out but only three young men came back. They were sore afraid and fell on their knees before the people to beg forgiveness. All the others in their party had perished in the jaws of the serpent Na-Dagun. The elders questioned the young men who returned and discovered that, of the sixteen who went, only the three who returned had not made sport with Lesythemis. They told the elders they had tried to stop the others, for the maiden was terrified and suffered great torment by what they did but the other young men heeded them not and used her cruelly and laughed at them, casting doubt on their manhood. Still, these three had not used Lesythemis, pitying her in her distress and anguish. The elders punished the survivors lightly and the village people were content and Vaarkil and Mythanpho did not press for further punishment of these youths.

'Then a law was passed so that others might be saved from death by the serpent. Na-Dagun dwelt in the deep part of the lake, so it was decreed that no boat must fish beyond the sight of land. And so it was. But the fish catch fell and hunger haunted the village that had once been the home of laughter and plenty.

'So it was that Vaarkil, being at this time in the spring of his life, having seen no more than ninety nine cycles, was vexed by the sadness of the people and did wish to end their suffering. Three times, he went to the council of elders and asked permission to go onto the lake and destroy Na-Dagun. But they were loath to let him go for he was just a man against the two headed serpent and they feared he must be killed.

'Then Vaarkil told them he would avenge the death of his daughter, Lesythemis. And the elders met again and said that in all the village, Vaarkil was the most blessed of men. He was the best swimmer, the surest diver, the most fleet of foot, the strongest with bow and sword and spear. This, they said, was because of the manner of his birth in the lake. After much talk, they let him go, blessing him and saying many prayers to their Goddess of the lake, Tryhnn, that she might deliver him, and praying to Ytraa who, in those days, before the revelations of the Lord Gadhallah, was considered but a minor God. But Vaarkil put his trust in Ytraa as well as in Tryhnn, worshiping both Gods, as was his way.

'He took a small boat and lade it with provision for the voyage and with weapons to defeat Na-Dagun. But Mythanpho would not let him go alone and must go with him. The people of the village and the elders did not wish it but they were starving and they let them go onto the lake. And they provided them with armour, a breastplate and shield of burnished bronze for Vaarkil and a pinafore of linked bronze chains to guard his manhood. For Mythanpho, twin cups of figured bronze in likeness of coiled serpents, linked by fine gilt chains, to protect her breasts, and a lap cloth of bronze links in the shape of a serpent's head, that her fruitful loins might be protected. And these they wore but nothing more for they would not be weighed by clothing should they have to fight Na-Dagun in the water. The village people praised them with great song and watched the small boat sail out on the lake until they could no more see it.

'Two days and two nights passed and none knew what happened on the lake for none was there to see. As the sun rose on the third day a great cry came to the village. The people left their houses for the call roused them from their sleep. And they came from their beds and went to the shore and waited.

'Out of the mist that hung over the still waters of the lake came a swimmer who pulled a heavy load. As she drew close, they saw it was Mythanpho and they waded into the water to help her. She was naked and her hand held the hand of Vaarkil and he was naked and much wounded and was dead, for the serpent had deprived them of their armour, so he might devour them. Yet, in each dead hand did Vaarkil grip one head of the serpent and these were huge and the teeth were many and mighty.

'Mythanpho waved the people from her that she might speak to them. And she stood in the shallows and they saw that a great gash ran from her neck across her breast to her thigh and blood spilled from the wound. Yet, she stood and held the body of her man with her as she spoke. "Know that this day have Vaarkil and Mythanpho slain the beast with two heads. Na-Dagun is no more. But the monster wins even this day, for Vaarkil, the greatest man who ever lived, is dead and so am I. Mortals cannot fight with monsters of the dark world and hope to live. Do not forget Vaarkil the brave and the noble nor yet his woman Mythanpho. This day have we done great deeds and have shed our lives that you might live in peace. Bury us well and care for our children."

'And then did Mythanpho fall to the ground and with her Vaarkil and she breathed no more. Those two fair people were not seen again walking after that day and they were covered in mantles of great worth, being woven in fine strands of pure gold and silver, and were laid to rest in the lost cave chambers of the high mountains, side by side forever. And the great heads of the monster were raised on pointed stakes that all could see them and know what deeds had been done.

'Some say that Vaarkil and Mythanpho did not die that day but that they are resting after their great toil and that they will return one day in an hour of great need and will once more free their people from great evil and terror.

'And from that day, the custom of naming children after the great heroes began as a way of remembering them.'

Aglydron's tale ended and both Okkyntalah and Jodisa-Li thanked him for the telling. Myllthlan, wiping away a tear, seemed full of questions.

'It's a wonderful tale, but I thought Followers believed in only one God?'

'Tryhnn and Ulkhon were early gods. Ytraa gave them power over certain aspects of the world. Tryhnn's the spirit of the waters and we venerate her, but we don't worship her. Ulkhon, as the spirit of sun, moon and stars, holds the same sort of place in the hearts of Followers. Vaarkil was the son of Ytraa and Tryhnn, else how could he have survived the depths of the lake? Mythanpho was the daughter of Ulkhon and the mortal maid, Poliphri. As part human, part God, they have special places in our worship. They're held up as examples of what a man and woman could and should be. They're also the known ancestors of the Lord Gadhallah, who revealed the truth of Ytraa; that Ytraa is the God who created all.'

Jodisa-Li wore a strange expression but said nothing. Myllthlan absorbed this information and seemed to gain an answer to a question.

'I still don't understand your funny ways about being naked. But I suppose the heroes, being naked when they fought the monster, must've had some effect on the later worshippers. I mean, you tell this tale to children and so they learn that being naked isn't just for sex but also for other things. Is that right?'

Aglydron had always accepted what he was told and had no answer. He floundered but Jodisa-Li stepped in.

'You're right, Myllthlan. We consider nakedness a state of higher being. Joining is an act of worship, so we make ourselves naked for that, as we do for prayer and, of course, for more practical things, like defeating two-headed demons in the water, where clothes would cause too many problems. We're not prudish, you know. It's just that we understand the power of the naked human body to make men and women more aware of each other in a sexual way and we prefer to leave that sort of connection for times of worship. Does that answer your question?'

'Thank you, Jodisa-Li. It does. For now, anyway.'

Aglydron was grateful to the girl for her reply but a little troubled by Myllthlan's indication that she'd have more questions in future. She was the first non-Follower he'd come into close contact with and her view of his faith was that of the outsider with no concern about doubting things that he readily accepted. He wondered how many questions she held and whether he'd be able to answer them all satisfactorily.

<hr />

This beauty fascinated Okkyntalah. She represented many strange things for him and her intelligent questions set him thinking. He wanted to learn from her as well as have her learn from them.

'Did you worship only Krakgragog on Ylcrat, Myllthlan?'

'The Core believe only in the Core and Krakgragog. We didn't worship Krakgragog but paid homage to him in fear and terror of his anger and unpredictable power. But I can see now that this must be a mistaken belief. Krakgragog resides in the fire mountain and seems to hold no sway beyond the island. Yatukon had me believe that even if I succeeded in saving you, as I was duty bound to try, Krakgragog would take me back and kill me before I was out of sight of the island. You saved me; you didn't let that fierce God destroy me when he might have. I think your Ytraa must be more powerful than Yatukon and the Core.'

'Is that why you attacked us when it looked as though the waves might take us as we escaped the cave? You thought you might appear better in the eyes of your God?'

She rose at Okkyntalah's question and moved to sit beside him, pulling the tabard clear of his shoulder and examining the site of the wound she'd cured.

'Not so I'd be looked on more favourably, no. In any case, Krakgragog is not easily appeased. I forgot, for a moment, that I was no longer of the Core. I believed my God wanted me to perish and you with me. I was bound, as Core, to do the will of Yatukon and the Core. You were brave and strong and prevented me. You showed me that my God was not all-powerful, but that Ytraa cares for those who Follow truly. I am of Ytraa now, I am a Follower.'

The skin on Okkyntalah's wound bore only a soft white mark. She nodded and kissed the place before closing her eyes and making a quiet prayer of thanks to the power of the air around her.

They were still unused to the way she freely touched them, without embarrassment or ceremony, tending their cuts and bruises, liberal with her kisses to their minor wounds. But, though she betrayed their custom and habit by her attentions, Okkyntalah couldn't blame or condemn her. He actively enjoyed the care she lavished on them, and he noticed even Aglydron found it easier to be relaxed as a result of Myllthlan's care.

Night drew upon them as a darkening of the grey that surrounded them. They'd eaten more fish, drunk more of their water but no wind had come to blow them anywhere and, as night descended, they had no stars to guide them. The current pushed them where it would and they could do no more than ride with it to whatever destination it would have them go. They could only hope that destination proved welcoming and helpful to their journey.

'I just hope we don't end up in that cesspit called Mipahnhil. They say sailors never leave their ships when trading there, or, if they do, they're never seen again.'

Okkyntalah was unsure how to respond to Jodisa-Li's fears: her warnings about Ylcrat had been wide of the mark. But she spoke with such confidence he felt concerned in case they drifted helpless to this feared destination.

Chapter 25

In Muddied Waters

Dagla Kaz fingered the small block of hardened paste. An elongated teardrop, hanging from a thin cord threaded through the inside of his tabard, it fell against his manhood. Only alone or in darkness could he touch his diminishing source of solace. In Kamakq he must revisit the remorseless, nameless beauty who had hooked him on this pernicious spring of agony and ecstasy. There, he would renew his supply and pay the price. It was why he'd insisted they travel this route. His secret: the means by which he restored flagging mental and physical powers to levels undreamed of even when young. But utter dependency made this substance a cruel master, robbing him of reason, peace and rest as its effectiveness reduced. He must have it; continue to feed off it. Or lose his sanity, his strength and his potency.

Once, Wendarah had asked its purpose as she undressed him. 'My token superstition. We each have some silliness we'd rather others didn't know, Wendarah. I'm sure you keep your secrets. Let me have mine, if you would.'

He'd lied easily enough, self-deprecatingly concocting a tale of a family heirloom with supposed secret powers to rejuvenate the older man. Close enough to the truth to prevent further questions. And, since she was a frequent benefactor of his potency, she'd asked about it since only to ensure he still possessed it. He stroked it again, for comfort.

Darkness, pitted with sparks of distant tribal fires, faced him as he leant against the rail, looking to the south, where Kamakq lay hidden in the night.

'We'll dock tomorrow, Dagla Kaz. Will you see her?'

Baklan's sudden question, springing from the silence of the night, startled him but he covered his surprise well enough. 'What do you think?'

'Too austere for my tastes. Oh, she's a stunner, all right. But I like more meat and down to earth fruitiness, myself. Still; no accounting for taste.'

'She possesses more than mere physical beauty, Baklan, though I confess that, for me, her appearance would be attraction enough.'

'Still don't know her name, though.'

'And never will. No one does. In fact, I know almost nothing about her.' He felt unequal to confiding the real reason for his obsessive need to visit her, even to his long-term go-between.

'You're all a bit, well, taken up with frowking, aren't you? All you Followers seem to need to be forever…'

'Don't trespass on our friendship, Baklan. I know you're just an ignorant and wicked heathen, but don't overstep the mark. We believe what we believe. Joining is utterly central to our faith and not the topic for vulgar jest you heathens make it. We put together what Mhortag split asunder and, in joining, pay homage and worship our God. Ytraa made us one; two join to make one again. Is it any wonder we relish every opportunity to create together the one that Ytraa first made?'

'Spare the religious rot, Dagla Kaz, it's wasted on me. I like to frowk as well as the next man but I'd not be putting myself into her clutches just for a moment's pleasure.'

'You speak of what you don't understand. In some things choice is not a factor.'

'Well, she's obviously got something special, to make you take a detour when you're in such a squittin' hurry.'

Dagla Kaz looked about them in the faint lamplight on deck and relaxed as he saw they were alone. 'It's not the sole reason, Baklan, though she'd be enough for me. There are things I need to know, privy only to some in the city.'

'If you say so. Think I'll turn in. Busy day tomorrow.'

Dagla Kaz remained on deck for some time, staring into a darkness that seemed to increase when the sparks on shore slowly died.

'Are you wise, to let a mere woman rule you?'

The voice spoke the truth, but he was powerless to resist her appeal.

Dark heavy clouds obliterated the stars. The boat rocked gently at anchor and, here in the sheltered bay, close to land, they should be safe from the other gang of pirates and could rest easy in their narrow bunks. He considered Wendarah for a moment but thought again of the woman he would visit in the morning, and went alone to his cabin.

Night brought no relief from the mist and Aglydron had no stars to steer by. He could only allow the current to take them where it would.

With morning, the water appeared cloudy and tinged with streaks of muddy brown. In spite of the murk, Okkyntalah caught another mutsuuh and Myllthlan tried with the spear, bringing a gaarbel aboard; its foolish expression making her laugh as it struggled ineffectually in the bottom of the boat.

'Throw it back! It's not permitted. Throw it away!' Aglydron stared at the fish with horror.

'Why? We ate it on Ylcrat, Aglydron, and the flesh is very good. Though you must leave the head alone, as it's full of poisonous barbs.'

'It's forbidden. Throw it away, woman. Now.'

She looked at him and he thought, for one incredible moment, that she would laugh at him.

'Forbidden food? A strange idea. On Ylcrat we ate everything. Surely, at sea, it's unwise to reject such bounty?'

'We're not on your heathen island now and I'm telling you to throw that aberration of nature away. Do it! Now!'

She shook her head in wonder. 'It may be forbidden for you but I can and will eat the fish I caught.'

Shaulah had the gaarbel's guts along with those of Okkyntalah's fish and the rest of them ate fresh raw steaks from that. Aglydron watched Myllthlan deliberately slice her fish into strips and feed three of them into her sensuous mouth as she looked him in the eye.

'If you expect me to die of poisoning or to be struck down by your god, you'll be disappointed, Aglydron. I'm sorry to disagree with you over this matter but I won't waste good food when it's provided by the bounty around us.'

Okkyntalah and Myllthlan both sliced strips of flesh from their separate fish and hung them on the makeshift line that Jodisa-Li replaced for that purpose.

Aglydron watched her for signs of illness, wondering at her lack of concern at breaking this taboo.

'Myllthlan isn't a Follower yet, Aglydron. Perhaps it's only Followers who may not eat the flesh.' Jodisa-Li's observation might have comforted him had she not made it in a tone of distinct scorn.

Around midday, the mist began to dissolve and, an hour later, they relaxed under bright hot sunshine over calm water that ran brown and impenetrable beneath the boat. The reason for the muddy water was obvious at last: less than a league off, the low coast ran east to west as far as they could see, dotted with trees and cut by the outlets of many streams and rivers. In the east, smoke rose from domestic fires and the tip of a slender wooden tower showed above the gentle slopes of mud flats where a village stood on a stilted platform. The stench of sewage was heavy. Across the still water, the distant squealing of children at play carried to them.

'Where are we?'

Aglydron looked at Jodisa-Li for confirmation before he answered the young man's question. 'I can't be sure, but I think we must be close to Mipahnhil.'

'We should avoid it.'

Okkyntalah nodded his agreement with Jodisa-Li.

'We've been guided here by Ytraa. I don't think that place is the city; just a village.' Still smarting from Myllthlan's disobedience over the gaarbel, he was determined to have his own way and increase his diminishing authority. 'There's a reason for us coming here that we don't understand. Ytraa's cared for us so far. We have to trust Ytraa and see what's here for us. Maybe Dagla Kaz came this way after all.'

Jodisa-Li's face was serious and full of concern as she stared at him. 'I'll not argue with you, Aglydron. There's little point. But, should evil befall us here, let it be remembered it was your decision that we stray into this dangerous place where they have strange customs and from which, it's said, none escape.'

He wouldn't permit any further erosion of his authority and must show them he was leader. 'We go ashore. That is my decision.'

Still no wind, and the water was a millpond under the hot sun. Okkyntalah wondered if there was any real danger as he and Aglydron rowed for the shore.

'Kill us all if you will. I'll have nothing to do with it.' Jodisa-Li sat in the bows and refused to help, so Myllthlan took the tiller to help steer the small craft toward the village on stilts. Okkyntalah wondered if she acted from a sense of obligation to Aglydron after her extraordinary disobedience over the fish. He admired her stance even though he couldn't help thinking she'd taken a risk in eating something forbidden.

As they drew closer, the village emerged as a large town with signs of dilapidation at its edges. A harbour, surrounded by wharfs built on stilts, lay at the eastern edge with a long jetty protruding south on its western side. Ladders led from below the surface of the sea to its top. And, around the end, a group of small children splashed in the sea, diving and jumping without fear into the muddy waters. One of them, about to dive, spotted the boat and pointed, shouting excitedly to his friends. The activity ceased at once and all turned to watch the slowly approaching craft.

A long, undulating yodel reached them across the water and Okkyntalah spotted a tall thin man standing atop the wooden tower with his hands to his mouth to funnel the sound. He faced each of the four compass points in turn and repeated his call.

'See? They know we're coming and will gather to meet and capture us. We'll never leave this place alive.'

The children were close enough now to be individuals with smiling faces of welcome, eager to greet the strangers.

'Like the cannibals were going to eat us on Ylcrat?'

She glared at Aglydron but made no reply.

'Cannibals?'

'A rumour, Myllthlan, and clearly not true.' Okkyntalah told her.

'Oh, there's truth in it; but a long, long time ago.'

They heard no more from her because the children who'd swum out to meet them were shouting and calling as they closed on the boat. Others, less skilful or more timid, remained near the jetty. The children near the boat asked for their names and gave their own in exchange. There was no atmosphere suggesting the danger Jodisa-Li had predicted. All seemed friendly, welcoming and excited.

As they approached the place where they hoped to tie up their boat, before asking permission to enter the harbour, Okkyntalah noted a small brood of highly coloured water snakes, emerging from the shadows and moving across the surface where the children played. He took a hand off his oar and pointed to them. The children followed his finger and warned their friends near the jetty.

The lad who'd first pointed out their arrival, a youngster of no more than seven cycles, prepared to show the visitors his prowess as a diver. As those below him scattered to move away from the snakes, he was about to launch himself into the water. At exactly the time he bent forward to perform his dive, he learned of the danger. Struggling to pull back, he overbalanced and plunged in an ungainly fall to the water, hitting it with a loud splash, amidst the writhing snakes.

All was silent as the water stilled and they waited for him to surface, hopefully some distance away. He came up not far from the approaching boat and it was clear he was in difficulties, though whether because he'd been bitten or because the fall had winded him wasn't clear. Aglydron plunged into the water to help him.

'Isn't he in danger of drowning like before?'

'He's fine, Myllthlan. It's only in choppy seas he struggles. He swims well enough in water as calm as our lake at home.'

But Okkyntalah kept his eyes on him, all the same.

The watchtower in the trees wasn't hidden to Aklon-Dji and he called a greeting to the watcher. The man laughed down at him and shook his head. 'You know us too well, Aklon-Dji. We're never goin' to be able to hide from you.'

'Would you wish to conceal yourselves from me?'

'Course not. But it's good sport tryin'. Welcome, friend. Go on down, they're expectin' you.'

'Will you not come down with me? I have gifts.'

'I've to stay up 'ere. Seen you comin' two leagues since. Precautions, The One calls it. See your presents after I'm relieved.'

Aklon-Dji nodded his acknowledgement of the man's obedience to orders and trotted down the slope through the woods into the village. Children ran to greet him, gathering round and begging him for tales of his doings and adventures.

He laughed. 'I will tell you stories later. First, I must see The One.'

Chellyth sat with Por-Kildu in the shade of the overhanging roof of their thatched hut, awaiting his announced arrival. Her deep brown eyes greeted him with a smile of welcome that failed to hide the sorrow behind it. Por-Kildu, as usual, stood and took Aklon-Dji's hands between his own in greeting and welcome.

Aklon-Dji removed the spare belt and sword he'd acquired and handed them to Chellyth. From the pack at his back, he withdrew a skin of pale sharp wine, a dozen citrus fruits and the remaining haunch of the antelope he'd killed on his way to The Point. He laid these offerings at her feet.

'As always, you bring gifts of great value, saviour and friend. We've precious little to give in return. But a bed is yours and the company of all the women you want.'

'But not the woman I most desire.'

She stood and held him close to her. 'I am for Por-Kildu only, as you well know, you wicked man.'

'A man might try, might he not?'

'And waste his time, Aklon-Dji.' Por-Kildu shook his head in mock reproof, the moving shadows filling and emphasising the wounds marking his face. 'What brings you this time? I'd have thought the absence of the High Priest would mean you were safe enough on the other side.'

'Ah. You have heard, then? Your reach grows ever longer, Por-Kildu. I commend your skills and....'

'No. Aklon-Dji, I'd not misinform you. We discovered by pure chance. We had a visitor; one who'll be wise to stay away unless he seeks a painful death at Chellyth's hands.'

They told him of Okkyntalah's visit and his news, hiding nothing in their account.

'You must do as you see fit, of course. For myself, I would see the young man spared, if indeed he survives his journey and his challenge to my father's authority. All I have heard of him makes me believe he would be good for us. However, that is a choice you must make.'

'I have spoken it aloud.'

'Words are capable of retraction, Chellyth. Words may be unsaid when deeds may not be undone. But I leave that, as ever, to you and thank you for your news. It confirms what my investigations have uncovered. And they sailed from here, when?'

Chellyth counted on her long, slender fingers. 'Eleven days ago they sailed from our shores.' She looked out to the northwest, her face an enigmatic mask.

'I have an intimation, an inkling, an instinct that many threads are drawing close together. I believe, and I can be no more definite, that this Okkyntalah and his companion, Aglydron, may be movers of a greater cause than they espouse. It is my belief that wheels we set in motion when we first met, Por-Kildu, are moving with a speed and force that might soon become unstoppable. Sooner than we hoped, your people might find freedom. There might be food and clothing, shelter and provision for all. And, at last, a real escape from the fear and isolation of The Point.'

'What more do you know than you have spoken, Aklon-Dji?'

He let his eyes dwell very obviously on her breasts in the hope he might distract her from questions about his words. 'I know more than I can speak of and less than I would know. But then, I see more than I should and less than I would.'

She shook her head at him. 'You're incorrigible. The man, Okkyntalah, used my breast band to bind me. It provided no concealment anyway. And you see what you may, since I remain unhidden.'

He grinned in apparent resignation at his loss but gave no hint of his gratitude at the success of his small subterfuge. He'd managed to tell the truth without betraying knowledge he was certain must make them think him mad. Who, after all, would believe he could speak with someone many leagues away, occupying a stone tower overlooking a fabulous city of white stone in a foreign land? But, if Ivdulon's words were true, then the whole world was a different place from that which he understood.

And changes would come soon, to overthrow the tyranny of the priesthood. Until then, he must continue to work and build up his network of trusted helpers and fellow-believers. One day the Few, and those on The Point, would rise up against the evil of his father. And that day was fast approaching.

Aglydron reached the boy in time to recognise that he'd been bitten by one of the snakes and was dying in front of him. He gathered the small body and struck out for the base of the nearest ladder with his free arm. The snakes had scattered but the rest of the children were scrambling to get out of the water amid much panic and commotion.

Aglydron held onto the ladder with one hand and kept the boy's head above water with the other. Okkyntalah sculled the boat to the jetty and Jodisa-Li made fast to a beam above, leaving slack in the rope to allow for tidal changes. Okkyntalah took the boy as Aglydron mounted the ladder. He climbed after him with the child slung over his shoulder. The women came last.

'Let me see.' Myllthlan examined the child and shook her head. Nevertheless, she prepared herself for healing and made the gestures and supplication to her power, using her fingertips to draw out the venom from the twin pinpricks on the boy's side. She rose after a while and shook her head in sorrow, indicating that Aglydron should lift the child from the boards where Okkyntalah had laid him.

'I can't save him. I doubt any can. He's almost gone.' Oblivious of the many eyes upon her, she dressed.

The man atop the tower stared down in their direction and raised his hands to his mouth to direct a series of short, sharp calls to all four compass points.

All talk from those gathered on the jetty ceased at once and the growing crowd of townsfolk formed themselves into a barrier. Aglydron studied them for hostility and intended violence but found only determined indifference.

The men were bare-chested and clad in plain natural linen aprons of various lengths, attached to bands circling their waists. Some wore a triangle of coloured linen, tied at the neck with a knot and allowed to flap loose between their shoulder blades. Most wore conical hats woven from reeds.

The women's clothing varied in length. Their tops were covered, more or less, by triangles of linen tied at one shoulder, leaving the other bare. The size of the cloth determined the degree of concealment. Around their hips, they wore a second triangle as a skirt, tied on the opposite side to the top piece. These also varied in length; some barely reaching mid-thigh but others falling to the ankle on the long side, with every variation in between. The women's hats were shaped like upturned boats, sticking out ahead and behind. No one wore any adornment.

The people moved silently and arranged themselves so that a narrow pathway led between their ranks from the jetty into the centre of the town. It was clear Aglydron and his party must follow the open path. There was no menace from the crowd, only a sense of single purpose that was palpable.

Aglydron, the child held in his arms, moved first, feeling he should lead. Jodisa-Li came after, with Myllthlan behind her and Okkyntalah at the rear. Shaulah, left in the boat, was sensible enough to remain quiet.

As they passed through the throng, more and more townsfolk gathered from the narrow paths and roadways that divided the small wooden houses from each other. Aglydron felt compelled to move with slow dignity through the constricted pathway. The scents of men and women, burning spices and raw sewage battled with one another as he breathed evenly to control his anxiety.

As he approached the tower, a broad man wearing a yellow neck scarf and long loin cloth, and a slender woman, breasts partly concealed and skirt ending halfway down her left thigh, detached themselves from the crowd and stood before him so that he had to stop at the foot of the structure. They examined the child in turn and Aglydron made to pass the boy to them but neither would accept the body.

'I am Doklas. My woman is Chislanda.' The man bowed briefly, stepped back a few paces, and then knelt upright with his hands hanging loose at his sides.

'I am Chislanda. My man is Doklas.' The woman bowed only her head and then raised her face to stare with grief at the child in Aglydron's arms for a few moments before she moved to kneel beside her man.

The man from the tower descended. His brief triangular apron, barely concealing his manhood, was decorated with ornate stitching in orange, green and blue, forming patterns and shapes without meaning to Aglydron. On his head was a tall version of the conical hat, also coloured, and his neck was bare. He stepped between the kneeling man and woman as if they were of no consequence. He touched the boy's face, wrists and neck with two outstretched fingers and held his ear against the silent mouth before he closed the eyelids with his thumb and finger.

'The boy fell into the water at the end of…'

The crowd gasped as one. The man from the tower faced Aglydron with an expression of deep sorrow on his lined and weathered face and held up a hand for silence.

'Death you bring to Mipahnhil. Life you must give before you go.' He clicked his fingers behind him and the boy's parents moved to stand either side of him.

'I didn't cause the lad's death. I just took him out of the water after he'd been bitten by…'

'You bring death. You must bring life.'

'Look, I don't know your customs…'

'You will be silent. If you do not, you will be punished.'

'I'm sorry, but you're…'

The man struck Aglydron across the face with the palm of his hand, so hard he almost knocked him off his feet. Okkyntalah stepped forward but the crowd held him back. They also restrained the two women and Aglydron wondered what new danger he'd led them into merely by trying to help these strange people.

Chapter 26

CUSTOMS STRANGE AND DISTURBING

'You will not speak but to answer my question.' The man glared at Aglydron and waited until he nodded his understanding.

He gestured at the man named Doklas to rise, unknotted his apron and passed it to the woman, Chislanda. She bowed her head, accepting it. He turned the knot of her triangle to the front and did the same with the skirt. The crowd murmured and lowered their faces.

Doklas stepped between the man and Aglydron. He took his woman in his arms and kissed her with passion but she made no move to embrace him, merely standing with her arms loose at her side.

He turned eyes full of pain to Aglydron. 'Chislanda is warm as sun on reeds, more graceful than the young tree weeping into still water, lovelier than iasomia blooms, generous of heart, kind to all and a perfect flower of love. Oncemother was Chislanda. She who has me for all time has you until she bids you leave. Obey her and return to her the respect she richly deserves. Harm any part of her and I will see you die.'

Aglydron felt he should protest, ask questions, demand explanations, but it was clear he was embroiled in some religious rite and he daren't offend these people who crowded so close. His face still stung from the blow and he felt his vulnerability. At all costs, he must preserve his life and those of his companions; to fail would be to destroy his mission.

Doklas looked once more at Chislanda before turning to the child in Aglydron's arms. He kissed the boy's forehead, throat and genitals, stroked his hand along the length of his body and then moved away to lose himself amongst the crowd.

The man from the tower held his hands up again. He unknotted Chislanda's breastcloth and tossed it at her face. 'Weep for shame, woman. Your firstborn was your only born and is no more. Fill your belly with new life or live in shame and die unbred.'

He turned to Aglydron. 'This woman will guide and instruct you. Do as she bids. You bring death and leave her without honour until you fill her with life again. Hold your questions!' The man glared at Aglydron with such fierce arrogance that he felt unable to speak. 'I am not yours to examine. You are less than any slave. Chislanda will instruct you. Go; do as she decrees!'

Aglydron looked to his companions for support and help but they could do nothing, pinioned as they were. The whole crowd turned away and behaved as though

Aglydron and the woman didn't exist.

'What am I…?'

'Hold your tongue, bringer of death, or the Galhta will cut it out.'

Aglydron, at a loss what else to do, remained still and silent.

'Come.'

He took a few steps after her but found he couldn't accept his fate so easily. 'My friends. What will become..?'

She turned and struck him across his face with the back of her hand so hard that she cried out with pain. 'Be quiet! They will be taken care of. Come. And say no more.'

As she passed through the crowd, the people kept their backs turned. Aglydron, confused, frightened and alarmed by events, followed her until they were clear. For a short time they walked in silence, quite alone.

She halted by a narrow stair, leading down through the boards of the street. Turning, she displayed, at last, her grief for the dead child. He waited, the child in his arms, until she calmed a little.

'I'm sorry I had to hit you but another word would've brought the fury of the Galhta on you. I probably spared you a public beating. I can't explain everything now. You're a stranger and must be anxious about your own fate and that of your friends. Trust me. I will tell you all. But first, we must tend to my son. All will be well. Your friends will be treated as guests and will have their liberty in the town. None can leave until you've made me with child. Come. We must place my lost son where the waters will take him.'

'Why do I have…?'

'Now isn't the time. If you won't trust me, I'll have the Galhta beat and humiliate you before all. Do you want that, or will you do as I say, without further question, until we're alone in my house?'

Aglydron considered all that had happened since their arrival in the town. He recalled the strange events with Myllthlan on Ylcrat and the overpowering impression of single-mindedness from that crowd and the one here. He'd no wish to suffer shameful and painful punishment in public. For the moment, it seemed the sensible course was to do as this woman bid and find answers when, as she put it, they were alone in her home.

'Lead on. I'll do what I must. But I've questions you'll answer when we're done.'

'When all we must do is done, I'll tell you all you need know. Come, then, to the place of dedication. Once we reach the foot of the steps, do not speak. Talk in the Hallows and you lose your tongue. Do you understand?' She stared at him to make sure.

He nodded and she led him under the town. At the foot of the ladder, she removed her hat and, with enormous effort, threw it away. For a moment she gazed as though at a lost love. She finally nodded and beckoned Aglydron after her.

The stench of human waste filled still air. A forest of wooden posts supported the buildings above. Underfoot all was damp, dim, slimy and putrid. This part of the river delta was too far inland to be washed by high tides. All the waste from above lay undisturbed, except by clouds of flies that rose and buzzed to torment them as they passed. Small gangs of rhaats sneaked amongst the foulness.

Aglydron carried the boy down the soft descent to the edge of town. Closer to the sea, the ground sloped away from the buildings but the piles of waste did not diminish until the point where daily tides removed the filth.

Chislanda took him within a few paces of the very edge of the raised platform, well into the tidal zone. Here, she fell to her knees in wet mud.

Aglydron waited for her to complete her silent prayer. Looking about him in the gloom, he saw seaweed clinging to the lower parts of the pillars and small and large pagurya scuttling here and there, scavenging for food on posts and in mud. Casts left by large red globworms marked smooth mud flats. The stench was less intense close to the sea, but still powerful enough to make him wonder how people lived with it.

Chislanda was still for a long time before she rose and faced Aglydron. The weight of the small child was beginning to tell and his back and arms ached.

The boy's mother kissed her son on his eyes, lips and genitals and then stroked his full length with both hands until the whole of the front of his body had been in contact with her palms. She stepped back and ripped strips from the garments the Galhta had removed from her and her husband. Each strip she draped over Aglydron's shoulders. She untied her skirt and tore that into more strips, heedless of mud and filth that soiled the hem after her prayer. When she had ten lengths of material, she bound two round each of the child's limbs and one about his neck, leaving loose tails on all. With the final strip she gently blindfolded him.

She looked up to the underside of the floor. Aglydron followed her gaze and was horrified to see the decaying remnants of other bodies suspended from the wooden beams that supported the flooring boards. He wanted to ask how they were to get the child almost two manheights above the mud but Chislanda placed a finger on his lips. She crouched and pointed at him. He copied her and she climbed onto his shoulders, seating herself first and then struggling to stand, holding herself in balance with a hand on his head. She made him understand that he must rise until he was upright. They tried three times before she managed to stay on his shoulders and by this time, they were both fouled with mud.

She touched his face with her toe to make him look up and then indicted that he should lift the boy to her. It seemed an impossible demand; his arms aching from bearing the child for so long. But he managed; stretching his arms as high as he could above his head. When he felt her take the weight of the child, he immediately transferred his hands to her legs to help her keep balance.

He couldn't understand how she would hold the child and fasten him to the boards above her at the same time. Looking up the length of her body, he saw she had the boy balanced on her head, held with one hand whilst she used the other to feed the first strip around one of the narrow horizontal beams above her.

Embarrassed by the exposure of her position, he turned to stare at the ground and, shoulders and legs screaming from the strain, waited until she indicated she was done. Releasing her legs, he braced himself as she jumped down beside him, reaching out to stop her falling headlong into the stinking mire. They both looked up at the boy suspended by strips of cloth close to the boards.

Chislanda raised her hands toward her child in a gesture of parting and said a few soft words. She led Aglydron up the gentle slope from the sea. They walked until the base above them touched the tops of their heads and still she went forward, stooping and dodging aside to avoid the protruding wooden pipes that were the source of the waste. Aglydron skidded as a fresh load dropped to the ground at his feet. The reek became so powerful that they both retched, but still she led him on, through clouds of flies.

At length they were forced to crawl on all fours as the ground rose to meet the floor. Here the stench overpowered Aglydron and the woman waited as he emptied his stomach contents onto the mud. At last, they emerged, almost on their bellies, into clear sunlight.

Filthy, sweating, nauseous and weary, they moved from the landward edge of the town across a meadow full of flowers where cattle grazed.

'Come, we must wash.'

'We can speak again, then?'

'I may. You should stay quiet until we're in the privacy of my house.'

Aglydron, too weary to care anymore, went with her over meadow grass up a shallow slope. As they gained slightly higher ground, he was amazed to discover a complex, sophisticated water supply that fed the town.

River water flowed along an uncovered wooden causeway that stretched out of sight along the banks. A steady stream of muddy water flowed from the channel into a large, curved, man-made lagoon. The water drained down over many walls, each less than a handbreadth deep, forming an arc of wide shallow steps, each bearing a lagoon of water in the space between. In alternate steps grew stands of reeds and other water plants. Finally, crystal clear water fell into the last of eleven of these arced ponds.

From this reservoir, the broadest, largest and deepest, the clean water was collected in leathern and canvass buckets by men and women. Aglydron noted that most were naked, though some women wore a short wrap across their hips. All were hatless.

A couple of small falls fed two minor reservoirs, oblong in shape and below the main lagoon, one at either end of the last pool. It was to the nearest of these that Chislanda led him.

'We can wash here.'

She undid his belt and pulled the tabard over his head. Aglydron was conscious others could see him but Chislanda shoved him unceremoniously into the clear water, following him in with his soiled garment. She was his height and the water rose to their waists.

Abandoning the tabard, to float free and the belt to fall to the hard floor of the pool, she set about cleaning the filth from her skin, using the palms of her hands. Aglydron followed her example. Once clean, she washed his tabard and belt free of the dirt he'd collected from beneath the town. She rung the garment out and laid it with the belt on the wooden boards beside the pool. Finished, she took him in her arms and turned him to face away from her.

'Kneel.'

He complied, his chin just above the surface, and she massaged his shoulders with a skilful touch that took away the ache of his prolonged efforts beneath the town.

'When we leave the water, replace your garment if you wish. Walk beside me without a word. Look neither left nor right and say nothing. You mustn't speak in public. If you don't do as I say, I'll strip you and smack your bottom, hard and repeatedly, as I would a naughty child. Understand?'

Aglydron turned to look at her and nodded but let the question show on his face.

'If you think I can't do it, by all means talk and look. Those close by will hold you whilst I humble you.'

He nodded; this time without qualification.

The walk through the town was uneventful but difficult, anxious as he was to learn all he could. He did as she'd demanded, however, and was relieved when she indicated the door of a hut, close to the seaward edge of town, and urged him in before her. He noted the looks of scorn her nakedness drew from those they passed, though no one said or did anything to either of them. Although it was difficult to gauge in this strange town, he estimated that they had placed the body of her son directly beneath the house.

Once inside, she drew a rush curtain across the doorway and immediately removed his tabard. 'You will remain thus whilst inside. And you may now speak.'

She draped his clothing over the back of a wooden chair that sat opposite another at a small wooden table. A third chair lay newly broken under the table. From a round wooden tub, she collected a pinch of small, sharp crystals and tossed them into a clay bowl, containing smouldering coals, in the corner farthest from the door. At once, a sharp spicy fragrance filled the room, eliminating the background smell of sewage so that the air was pleasant to breath, at last.

'I've many questions.'

'I have answers. But first, lie with me and fill me with your seed so I can grow a life to replace the one I lost today. Come.' She led him by hand to a dim space in the far wall. Within, a small room housed a wide flat bed of fresh dry reeds covered in several layers of soft pale cloth.

Dagla Kaz knew the city of Kamakq lay athwart a narrow band of high rocky ground separating the Shylnah Sea from Ka'la Bay. This natural harbour formed an almost landlocked intrusion of the Southern Ocean into the long, curved peninsula of Kabalyt and Niphralon. A border city, Kamakq housed the cultures of both countries; so diverse and contrasting, it was hard to understand how they existed in harmony. Yet, Baklan told Dagla Kaz, there was rarely any tension or trouble. The two different peoples mixed and traded, ate and drank together, occasionally sharing beds and even marriage.

'They don't talk about their beliefs in public, Dagla Kaz. Mebbie that's how they get along together.'

Whilst Baklan revictualled the ship and gave the crew a night off, Dagla Kaz found a guide to take him to Her. He'd visited the woman only once; the first time he'd sought the potent stimulant she traded. He usually obtained fresh supplies, expensively, through Baklan, who claimed to have no idea what the small sealed silver cask contained each time he handed it over.

'She says nothing; just looks at me with eyes that strip me to my soul. I'd never dare stay.' And he declared he had more sense than to ask about that small cargo.

Dagla Kaz had promised, and begged, Her for further contact only when his duties permitted. She'd agreed but had warned that his payment would be greater because of his infrequent personal attendance.

The guide demanded more than was properly due for the short journey, knowing Dagla Kaz had no choice. He must go; and only female guides could lead. From the noise and smells of the busy docks, she took him up steep winding cobbles to the southern edge of the city. At the crown of the rough hill, where the lane turned and began a steep decline to the second dockland area, sheltered by the bay, she took him on a dusty way to the southeast. It was almost a league but the route never descended. At last, they reached the high stone wall and arch with its closed gate of ebony, studded with two wide eyes in bronze rivets.

The guide turned her back to him, stood proud and raised her long dark skirt to reveal a scrip dangling from a strap round her hips and lying between her buttocks. He unlaced the soft kid pouch and placed coin within. The woman wouldn't touch it unless she could immediately wash her hands. Haughty, her gaze fixed ahead, she waited until he retied the lace before allowing her skirt to fall back into place. She faced him abruptly, contempt and scorn on her face as she thrust her breasts at him. Supported and divided by embroidered open cups, and painted in concentric circles of blue, gold and red, they were crowned with gilded nipples. She waited for his lips to touch each in acknowledgement of trade now done. He kissed lightly and stood back to admire her, as required. She bowed with heavy sarcasm and turned back to the city without a word.

Contempt was expected but it retained the power to make him feel small and undeserving, as intended. He watched her saunter away, hips moving with the fluidity of a practiced sensualist, and wondered how many other men she'd brought to this dark portal to life and death.

When he faced the gate, it opened silently, the space filled with sky beyond. Stepping through, he moved rapidly to the left side, his back against the wall, as the gate silently shut behind him. Ahead and below lay the dark calm waters of Ka'la Bay; the mountains that formed its narrow confluence with the Southern Ocean, no more than a deepening of the mist on the far horizon. And there, a hundred manheights beneath his feet, crouched Her house.

Steep and tortuous, the path clung to the cliff face below the gateway, plunging in precipitous gradients and narrow flights of near vertical steps down the purple brown rock. Never wider than his shoulders, the path narrowed here and there to little more than the breadth of a single foot. Without handholds or barriers, it was a descent to test the most courageous, or desperate, of spirits. And, at its end, was the price she would extract for the reward he craved.

※

When the woman hit Aglydron, Okkyntalah and Myllthlan moved to protect him but the crowd prevented intervention. Once she'd led Aglydron away, however, and the man they called the Galhta had climbed atop his tower, the crowd dispersed and left them alone.

'Please come, Paltrohn, Paltra. I show you where you stay.'

Okkyntalah turned to the dark skinned young woman waiting a short distance away. Bare headed, clad in a worn coarse linen band wrapped about her hips, she stared only at him.

'I Malarhah. I do what you want.'

'Well, Malarhah, perhaps you'll do me the honour of explaining why our friend's been taken prisoner and tell us how we can find and talk to him?'

She smiled briefly. 'I delight tell you all. Please to come. I refresh you and set you at ease. Paltrohn speak most fine from very fair face.'

He was so taken with her compliment and manner that he allowed her to lead them without further questions. That Jodisa-Li followed without demur was a surprise, though Myllthlan's acquiescence was expected. It wasn't until they reached the hut, where she told them they might stay undisturbed, that he recalled the urgency of his questions.

'Our companion. What's happening..?'

'All be well. I tell all, soon. First to comfort.' Malarhah made to draw the rush curtain over the open doorway but Jodisa-Li stopped her.

'Let it be. I prefer the light.'

'As Paltra wish. But I not please Paltrohn and spice not so good.' She bowed her head to Jodisa-Li and turned to Myllthlan. 'You wish also, Paltra?'

Myllthlan nodded.

She turned to Okkyntalah. 'And you, Paltrohn?'

He didn't care whether the curtain was drawn or not, though her suggestion that she might please him sounded promising. He shrugged, however. She took brown shiny grit from a small wooden bowl and tossed it into a burner in the corner of the room. The fragrance of burning spice soon masked the stink of sewage.

'You eat?'

'I'm starving.'

'Is there anything to drink?' Jodisa-Li scanned the room for food and drink.

Okkyntalah did likewise but found only a clean rush floor scattered with rugs made of scraps of linen woven together, six wooden chairs with rush seats around a rough table and two long low settles with soft cushions along adjacent walls. Two openings in the wall opposite the door suggested other rooms but these were too dim for him to make out what might lie within.

'I bring. Please stay till I back. Men will stop you to leave.' And she was gone.

'Strange.'

Myllthlan agreed with Jodisa-Li's observation.

'Pretty, though.'

'You could hardly keep your eyes off her.'

'Jealous, Jodisa?'

'Jealous of a boy's attention when I could...?'

'Shouldn't we be thinking of a way to help Aglydron?'

'I doubt he needs our help, Myllthlan. The place seems to be full of women only too willing to please men.'

'But she hit Aglydron and he was forced to go with her. That man from the wooden tower said...'

'The Galhta; he said Aglydron would have to give life to replace the boy who died.'

'I know. Did he really mean...?'

Jodisa-Li raised her eyes to the ceiling.

Myllthlan suppressed a giggle. 'Shall I tell him, or will you?'

'You've given him practical instruction, Myllthlan; you might as well tell him what results, since he doesn't seem to have the wits to work it out.'

Myllthlan looked at Okkyntalah but addressed her comments to Jodisa-Li. 'He's young but his needs are a man's. It's my place to satisfy his needs. Do you object?'

'Not at all. Frowk all you like. Just keep it discreet. We object to public performances, unless they're for Ytraa.'

'The woman has lost her son, Okkyntalah, and Aglydron brought the body to her. It seems the custom here is for him to make her pregnant again. You understand?'

'Of course, but, well, do you really think he's got to...?'

'Would it be such an imposition, Okkyntalah? Most men would find her desirable. You have an eye for beautiful women. You've joined with Myllthlan, ogled me shamelessly, and now...Oh, don't look so put out! Be honest, Okkyntalah. I wasn't complaining; I only wish you'd turn your desires into action, now I know you better.'

Her admission was welcome news to him until he recalled her status.

'Much as I'd love to, Jodisa-Li, you know I can't.'

'An intriguing puzzle. Tell me; does incapacity, custom, or some other impediment prevent you giving this beautiful young maiden what she desires?'

They turned as one at the deep, resonant tones of the man who stood in the doorway. Sufficiently tall to bend to enter a space even Okkyntalah had managed without stooping and broad shouldered enough that his arms brushed the edges of the entrance, he was a man of presence and power. Confidence oozed from him and humour lurked ready to spring from his startling eyes as well as from his mouth.

'Good day to you all. I see I have company at last in my lonely prison.' He appraised the women with open admiration before turning a slightly mocking smile on Okkyntalah. 'So, young 'un, do you lack the means or does something else stop you satisfying your desires?'

Okkyntalah felt on his guard against this commanding stranger; wary rather than afraid. He wondered what his presence here meant and worried he had designs on the women, in particular, Jodisa-Li.

Chapter 27

Exchange And Advice

As the High Priest crossed the strip of level ground, She appeared in the entrance, even more breathtaking than he recalled.

'Dagla. What pleasure.'

'A pleasure that is all mine.' He dare not add the condescending, habitual 'my dear' that hovered in his mind.

So much in that short greeting, though no more words were spoken. She moved into the building, pale violet gossamer flowing gracefully, tantalisingly, about long shapely limbs and sweeping the smooth dark stone She glided over.

He followed, incapable of other, as She floated along wide corridors decorated with panels of intricate geometric shapes in many colours and with a significance he felt he should appreciate but couldn't understand. Hovering on the edge of his awareness were figures, moving and observing; all women, hidden in all but suggestion and guarding their mistress and leader against any unwanted action.

In a small square courtyard, sudden brightness outlined Her through the fabric and he gasped. She slipped her hand through the simple fountain playing in the central pool, as She passed, briefly turning the water the colour of her covering. On, to Her private chamber with its broad divan beneath the expanse of open window overlooking the bay. Though he'd descended so many manheights to this point, the sea lay an equal distance below the broad shelf on which the house rested. She stopped at the foot of the sleeping platform, against the low-silled opening, to look toward dim mountains clouding the horizon, twenty leagues distant.

As he approached, She faced him, gazing through wide eyes that mirrored his own. Her mouth made a promise greater than any mortal could possibly keep. Details of Her flooded his vision; diminutive, exquisitely formed ears laid bare by the sweep of pale golden hair that fell in a flowing shining sheet to Her waist; small straight nose, strong and narrow, nostrils lightly flaring as She drew vitality from the air around Her; small firm chin of resolute demeanour; full lips of moist warm invitation turned into a knowing smile.

She took a silver flagon, tall elegant and plain, in slender fingers, and poured purple wine into slim goblets of polished blue black obsidian with mouths narrower than their bases. He watched the soft fabric slide along Her pale slim arm as She raised Her chalice toward him and beckoned him with Her free hand. Her fingers touched his as he took the proffered drink and a hint of the passion that would follow passed between them. They raised their goblets, the ringing of their touch a sweet surprise in the silence of the room.

Close now, he inhaled Her perfume; the scent of woman incarnate mingled with a perfume redolent of forest flowers and another fragrance hinting at the very root of the living world. Her eyebrows, delicately curving in lines of lustrous gold, rose with question as She gazed deep into his eyes. The skin of Her cheek, soft as breath, smooth as dusk, invited his caress, though he knew better than to attempt such intimacy.

Without a word, he undressed and stood before Her, waiting. At Her nod, he knelt and touched his forehead to the ground at Her feet. She put a foot lightly on his shoulder and he rolled onto his back, gazing up at Her in growing need.

Her face played with his emotions, promising and scornful in turn, raising hopes and kindling his desires only to dash them with contempt. He knew he was the cause that twisted Her beauty into disgust and he longed to smooth Her features into the serenity of acceptance. He cried out wordlessly, begging Her forgiveness, pleading for Her understanding and Her sympathy.

She pointed and he wriggled on his belly to the tabard She'd kicked delicately to the far wall of the chamber. He removed the tear-shaped pendant of hard, jade green paste and, trembling, held it up for Her to use or discard. She took it, placed Her bare foot under his midriff, and turned him on his back again. She stepped between his skinny thighs and raised one lovely foot to threaten or arouse.

The pendant, source of his desire and need and want of more than Her and almost more than life itself, She crushed in slender hands and scattered over and around him. Surging power, as freshly exposed stimulant coursed through his body, prepared him for what he now must give. He rolled to coat his skin with the dust that lay about him, writhing in an ecstasy of want that threatened to unhinge him.

In a frenzy, need mastering his terror, he gripped Her robe and dragged his aching body upright, tearing the fine gauze in his passion. Risen, he dared touch Her skin and She moved, it seemed, as he directed. But, on the bed, She laughed and pushed him from Her easily as every muscle in his body cramped with tension and desire. She turned him on his back again, set alight his skin with magic fingers, made his very bones ache as every muscle fought to be hardest and most rigid.

Paralysed, but feeling every particle of his being, Her skin burning his, he watched Her rise above him. He knew what was to be: that now would come the pain, the hunger, and, only at the last, release. He was terrified of what he would become, but must go through with it. She would take everything. Even hope was gone. His very soul would shrivel as She took what She required.

He knew the moment, knew the price. Passive; rigid with desire so strong it ruled his very being, he watched Her straddle him and closed his eyes.

She placed a first finger on each of his eyes, the tips of Her little fingers stopped the entrance to each ear and Her thumbs joined on his parted lips. Her remaining fingers drove hard against his forehead and temples. She dipped, enclosing him. Her hands held still, though She moved Herself to rhythms without care for him. The moment he welcomed and dreaded approached. And though he knew he must control and hold back, he had no volition beneath Her authority. She tensed and Her hands gripped; fingertips digging into him as She drew from him all he was, all he knew, all he felt. This was Her reward: nothing less than the whole of his experience flowed from his body, mind and soul through the tips of Her fingers into Her. Even as he felt the hot release, his very self flowed into Her and left him a shell devoid of knowledge or thought, without past or future.

Spent with the effort of absorption, She collapsed on top of him, Her breathing stentorian, Her heart beating hard and fast against his. An echo of a thought intruded into his empty mind, meaningless, unconnected and unexplained.

'Ivdulon will be most pleased with this.'

His muscles relaxed and the burning decreased as he suffered Her lightness upon him, Her need to be still and at peace. The emptiness retreated as echoes of what he'd known and thought and felt began the long process of refilling him. He was no longer complete. He was a shadow, a half being, a container to take what would be. Later, he would become aware of all he'd known before She'd taken him, all he'd felt before She'd sucked out his experiences. Yet, these would be shades, mere reflections of reality.

Slowly, he came to; became his separate self. She lifted free of him, stood and brushed Her fingers through Her hair, moved to the window with Her back to him, Her face to sunlight and sky. Feet apart, arms outstretched at shoulder height, She made obeisance to a God without meaning for him. Done with Her worship, She faced him, calm and peaceful, Her eyes now drenched in knowledge of him. She bent to the silver casket beside Her and drew out Her debt. Threading the new source of power and pleasure on the old cord, She wrapped it in his tabard and had both vanish in Her hands. His gold already stood in three equal stacks on the table.

Without a glance, She sauntered from the room, Her indifference to their shared experience more insulting than anything he'd ever known. He stumbled through the deserted house and clambered up the path, gasping with effort, desperate to reach the place in time. At the top, the gate swung open only long enough to let him pass, slamming shut as he stepped onto dust. His crumpled tabard lay abandoned on the ground, the precious source concealed within its folds. He knelt and gave thanks to anyone or any god who might care to receive them; certain only now that he'd gained the prize for his endurance and his sacrifice.

He returned to the city in a haze as the power of the new source slowly flowed into him. Over time, he would experience new ideas, deeper feelings, as it filled him with perceptions more potent than his native wit. And he would go back to Her, again and again and again, to give everything he had, to relive his humiliation and fear, when She required him. And he would pray for the moment, knowing he would dread it when it came. For now, he had just enough within him to cope with the remains of the day.

❊

'I am Okkyntalah of Muhnilahm, and I request your name, Paltrohn, before I reply to your question.'

'Spoken well; Okkyntalah. Of Muhnilahm, eh? The jewel in the Shylnah Sea. I am Feldrark of …but that's not important at present, since I'm captive here, like you. I've never travelled to your island but I believe we share a faith in the one God, Ytraa.'

'You're a Follower?' Jodisa-Li was as amazed as she was pleased by this revelation.

Feldrark nodded so that the reddish brown curls on his head shook. 'Yes. And I've been stuck in this godforsaken backwater for almost a full turn of the sun. I see Malarhah's absent. Has she gone for food?'

'You know her?'

'This has been my home, she my servant, almost since the day I had the misfortune to founder on the shores of this unholy midden.'

'If you're so unhappy, why don't you leave?'

He looked Jodisa-Li up and down appreciatively. 'Would that it were so simple, my lovely. You will see. Give it a few days, and you will see. But enough of that.' He turned back to Okkyntalah. 'You haven't answered my question, young 'un.'

'Question? Oh. Jodisa-Li's a Virgin Gift and therefore sacred and inviolable. Myllthlan's an entirely different matter, though. And Malarhah has gone for food, yes.'

Jodisa-Li had to turn away when Feldrark put his chin in his hand and gazed steadily at her. 'I see.'

She was unsettled by a feeling of gentle, unintrusive probing, though she couldn't identify the source of this or understand how she came to feel it. She knew, almost at once, however, that the stranger was not a man she could ever tell a lie. Before he let her be, she experienced a different, warmer sense contrasting with his almost academic scrutiny and leaving her with a feeling of security and trust.

He turned to study Myllthlan, who stood proud and confident before him.

'Ah, a vessel of pleasure, with other, more important, secrets as yet undisclosed.

You have no pretensions to virginity.'

Myllthlan made a small curtsey and looked into his eyes with a directness that Jodisa-Li didn't miss.

'I hope we have an opportunity to discuss your desires and wishes in full, Myllthlan.'

Okkyntalah seemed unafraid but wary of this stranger and content to let him take the lead in this introductory process.

There was about Feldrark an air of leadership and confidence that made Jodisa-Li feel protected and at ease. She was fascinated. That he was used to authority was clear, yet he was a prisoner here. Were they, also, prisoners?

He was fit, healthy and vibrant with life. A man who liked women. A well-made man. His face spoke of noble ancestry, with its fine features and high forehead. Clean-shaven and with short curling hair, he was handsome. His open, honest eyes, with her colouring, seemed to see inside her very soul, and were disturbing and inviting. About his neck, he wore a multi-stranded chain of myllth; its links finer than any she'd seen. From the gathered chains hung a solid figure, also in myllth, of the worldly form of Ytraa. Exquisite, it expressed majesty and potency. Feldrark's broad chest was bare and almost hairless, as were his arms. But he wore an open kidskin jerkin, embroidered in scarlet, gold and violet with intricate designs of beasts and flowers and edged with minute woven strips of dark glossy leather. At his waist, a deep belt of the same leather, embellished with silver roundels and studs in diamond shape, was buckled in a bright metal she didn't know. It supported kidskin aprons at front and back, falling to mid-thigh and leaving hips uncovered. His feet were bare but a solid myllth bangle, studded with green and ruby gems, circled his left ankle.

'I don't normally care what people, men or women, think of me, Jodisa-Li, but your approval is welcome. Thank you.'

He said this in such a manner that the blush she would've expected for being found out in her frank appraisal never materialised. Leaning very close to her, he whispered in her ear. 'When we are more than friends, I'd dearly love to follow your dragon into the lair where its fire merges with yours.'

'You'd feel my heat but I wouldn't burn you.' Her frank reply surprised her and she felt glad Aglydron couldn't hear and hoped Okkyntalah wouldn't blame her.

Malarhah returned, bearing a wide wooden board piled with platters and food. A quartet of flagons, dangling from kidskin straps, bit into the flesh of her neck and shoulders. Feldrark and Okkyntalah relieved her of the burdens at once and she bowed her thanks before setting the table to eat.

The intense heat of midday had passed, leaving a sultry warmth in the still air.

Fine incense smoke curled from the pot. Sunlight angled through the open doorway, casting deep shadows against sharp highlights. Sounds of everyday life emerged from beyond rush walls; people going about their business, gossiping, greeting one another, passing on news of daily events. From a distance, the muted cries of children at play again suggested the earlier tragedy was forgotten. Sellers announced their wares as they walked the streets. Insects buzzed and hummed outside but not within the hut; the burning spice deterring them. Raucous sea birds fought and scavenged in the harbour. Closer, a man cursed in anger and a child yelled.

Feldrark nodded at Malarhah and then the doorway.

'Paltrohn say no, Feldrark.'

'For the moment, Malarhah, I have the power of decision, here at least. We'll go on as we did before our guests arrived.'

Malarhah nodded and drew the curtain across the doorway, dimming the interior and creating a cooler feel. She removed her band of linen at once and laid it on the ground by the entrance. Jodisa-Li saw Okkyntalah stare at the dark girl and silently denounced his lack of piety. But Feldrark removed his jerkin and his belt and aprons and hung them on the pegs that stuck out of the wall beside the doorway and she revised her unspoken criticism as she realised she was equally incapable of turning away her gaze.

'I've adopted their customs. Easier. The heathens uncover in private. I've no idea why. But, be warned; they don't take well to questions about their habits and they're not welcoming of custom that disapproves of their own. I leave it to you whether you comply.'

Myllthlan conformed at once, placing her tabard next to Feldrark's clothes and earning his approval.

'Naked is sacred.'

Feldrark nodded at the young man. 'But life is more sacred than custom.'

Okkyntalah reluctantly complied. Jodisa-Li decided to maintain her modesty, for now. Feldrark glanced a question at her but made no comment.

'Shall we eat? And I'll answer questions you've asked, and some you haven't.'

They sat at the table and Malarhah placed food at the ready, unstoppered the first of the flagons and stood behind Feldrark, apparently waiting to serve.

'Help yourselves, please. Malarhah, when I said we'd go on as we did before, I meant in all things.'

The servant girl bowed her head and sat, though she clearly felt ill at ease and waited for the others to fill their platters and goblets before she served herself.

The plain food was fresh and sufficient. Fish of a kind Jodisa-Li didn't recognise, a coarse stringy green vegetable that tasted salty, and a whitish round vegetable with soft flesh and a creamy texture. The wine, if that was what it was, tasted harsh but was curiously quenching. Its pale blue colouring surprised her and only after she'd taken her second goblet did she understand its potency. She glanced at her companions and noted Myllthlan was careful with the drink though Okkyntalah appeared unconcerned. Malarhah hardly touched it but Feldrark drank deep and without apparent effect.

✦─────✦

Okkyntalah, full of curiosity and concern for Aglydron, was about to question Feldrark about their situation when the stranger spoke.

'I think it best you understand the customs and beliefs of this place before any more time passes. Our various tales we can tell at our leisure; we'll have plenty of it. It's important you do nothing to cause offence here or their petty rules will see you publicly stripped and beaten in the most humiliating and painful fashion. I speak from bitter experience. I had no tutor when I arrived and have had to learn for myself. I can at least spare you that.'

'We need to know about Aglydron, first. He's been taken from us and…'

'There's another in your party?'

Okkyntalah, with occasional interruptions from Jodisa-Li and a couple of observations from Myllthlan, told him the story of their arrival. Feldrark listened without a word until they'd finished.

'Jodisa-Li is correct. Aglydron must make Chislanda pregnant before you'll get the opportunity to take the leaving test. You won't pass. No one does. But more of that later….'

'What do you mean, Feldrark?'

'I'll tell you, but not now. No, please don't try to force me. Let me first explain how things stand here, so that you won't fall foul of their ways to find yourselves abused, hurt and ridiculed. Believe me, it's best you let me do this my way.'

'Can you speak so freely in front of Malarhah?'

Feldrark glanced at Okkyntalah with respect and gently stroked the servant girl's arm. She smiled and cupped his hand against her skin.

'This little lovely isn't a citizen. She's a slave. She has no rights, no property, no protection from the law. I could kill her and no one would care as long as I paid the price she's deemed to be worth. No, Malarhah poses no danger to us. She is pretty, servile, ignorant and willing. But she's no threat. One thing, Okkyntalah; I see your want of the girl, and don't blame you for that. She'll freely give anything you demand but won't enjoy it. She gives because she has no choice, but gains no pleasure; she's been rendered incapable of such enjoyment. Use her if you must. I have not, since I understood the reality after our first coupling. She may, however, enjoy your more gentle attentions. I leave it to you and her, should you wish to make the attempt.'

Okkyntalah was surprised Feldrark cared so deeply for the slave girl. He clearly didn't see her as a mere chattel to do with as he would and that made him look at the man with more respect. It was clear that Malarhah was devoted to him.

'Now, to your protection. Listen well. What people wear denotes status. A man with a neckcloth has fathered at least two children. Smaller aprons, as worn by the Galhta, indicate he's fathered four or more children. Fecundity bestows rank. Status in Mipahnhil depends entirely on the ability to produce children.

'The women here are uncommonly fertile but there's something wrong with the men. They can make a stand well enough, but their seed's poor. Here you might be king if you make children.'

'I take it you've not fathered many offspring, then, Feldrark?'

'An interesting observation, Okkyntalah. Logical but untrue. At the last count, I'd fathered fifty four children…'

'You count Visyllyth? Toadwives say she with boy twins.'

They all turned to look at Malarhah who nodded to add emphasis to her news.

'Fifty-six, then. Thank you, Malarhah. But I don't figure in their scheme. Neither will you, Okkyntalah, nor Aglydron. We're strangers, non-citizens, non-believers. Unless a man abandons his faith, his ties with family, everything from his past, he can't be accepted here.'

'But you've been here for almost a cycle. Haven't you been tempted to accept your fate and…?'

He smiled at Myllthlan. 'I've more to lose than most. But that can wait. It's important you understand about status and the rules of this society. Listen and learn. Back to the men. Shorter aprons mean higher status. A neckcloth and short aprons are higher than no neckcloth and longer aprons. But no neckcloth and a front apron only is the highest status under the Galhta. The exception is a completely naked man; such is a slave, kept that way to ensure no weapons are hidden.

'The women are different. Malarhah is a slave and would go naked under normal circumstances, for the same reason as a male. She's allowed her token wrap only because she's borne children, taken from her by other women. However, her status remains lower than any free woman as indicated by that mockery of cover. Naked women are slaves who haven't given birth. On the other hand, those free women with breasts fully covered and the long skirt have more than three offspring living.

'The death of a child brings shame on its mother. The Galhta uncovered the woman's breasts and turned her skirt as a public shaming, and she'd feel it keenly. She's been used to walking the streets with respect, as mother of a child. Now she's childless and must revert to her former status and be publicly humiliated with only the short skirt until she becomes pregnant again. I hope your friend has energy, for she'll give him no rest until the toadwives declare her with child again.'

'How soon can they tell if she's pregnant? The midwives on Muhnilahm can only be certain when she's been carrying for four Moontimes. We can't wait that long. We have to…'

'The toadwives have some secret way. I don't know what they do, or how. It's a business only women know. But they'll see the woman your friend is servicing every day. They can tell the sex and number of babies she carries, with certainty, when the infant's been growing only three sixdays in the woman's belly.'

'That's still nearly a Moontime and we can't spare the delay. We must leave in days or our mission becomes more difficult, more hopeless. If we don't find Dagla Kaz soon, I may never see Tumalind again.'

Feldrark stared at Okkyntalah. 'Ah. Frowking's all well and good. The fun a young man or woman should have. But Tumalind is the one. I see. If she's the reason for your mission, I wonder why Jodisa-Li and… But, no, I must stem my curiosity. For now, you need to know as much as I can tell you if you're to avoid punishment.

'This matter of status is crucial. You must give high status women and men priority in every matter. And I do mean every matter. Whatever you're asked to do by a person of higher status, you must do without demur, without question. Hesitation or reluctance will bring punishment.

'Myllthlan and Jodisa-Li, you're safe to walk the streets as you wish. Women rule here, under the Galhta. No man will opportune you. Women make all sexual invitations. If a man dares even to try to take a woman against her will, he'll quickly discover he's without the means to please a woman or himself ever again. That excludes slaves, of course; they're subject to abuse and usage wherever they go, regardless of gender.

'The Galhta is law. He's spiritual leader, guide, mentor, judge and executioner. You cross that man at your peril. He's fathered at least eight children; a unique achievement in this stinking hole, until I came along in my innocence. He hates me, of course, but I'm too valuable to the community to kill or release.

'Oh, and Okkyntalah: don't spill your seed unless within a woman. Anything else is punishable by blinding.'

'No mature Follower would do otherwise.'

Feldrark nodded his agreement.

'I don't know if you're in the habit of worshipping Ytraa in your natural state…You are? Good, it's the way of the true Follower. You may do so here without fear. They think the ritual odd and amusing and will not show due deference by averting their gaze. They'll peer and closely examine you. But they won't touch you or try to take advantage. Though, Okkyntalah, you may find yourself approached afterwards to perform.

'And that brings us to their God. They worship what can only be described as a descendant of Tryhnn for which they have no name: Tryhnn they deem too important for daily worship, calling on her only in extremis. They refer to their God simply as She Who Is, Is. If you hear that phrase, stop whatever you're doing, face the river, and bow your head until you're aware of those about you moving on. They take a dim view of anyone showing disrespect for their deity. I can tell you; you feel pretty vulnerable strapped face down on the beating frame with your legs spread and your bum in the air. And, after the first three hundred citizens have given your buttocks or thighs a hefty slap, or beaten the soles of your feet with the stick of pain, you learn just what a painful and humiliating punishment it can be. Does no lasting damage, but by Mhortag, you can't sit or walk for a week. No one will carry you and this is a wicked place to wander on hands and knees.

'Malarhah will take care of your needs for food and water and she'll wash clothes and that sort of thing. Don't worry about letting her do it. She feels valued and, in any case, only slaves go to the washing stones and only slaves are permitted to collect food and drink for the likes of us. I don't even know where she gets the stuff, to be honest.

'You're free to wander the town alone or together. But don't try to leave, or take a boat out of the harbour and don't…'

'Shaulah!'

They all started at Okkyntalah's sudden exclamation.

'I've left Shaulah in the boat. And all our stuff. I'll have to go and get her.'

'There's another woman with you, and you left her in your boat? Is she as interesting as Jodisa-Li and Myllthlan?'

'Shaulah's my hunting dog. I must go and get her.'

'You've brought a dog on this inexplicable quest of yours? I begin to be intrigued.'

'I must go for her. She'll be thirsty and hungry and…'

'Malarhah, guide him, please. He'll be lost a dozen strides out of the door.'

Malarhah stood and waited for Okkyntalah to approach the door. She opened the curtain and ventured out.

'Wait. Because Malarhah's going with you, she needs your permission to dress. I'm sure you wouldn't have her go naked.'

Okkyntalah nodded to the girl and she stepped back inside and re-emerged, fixing the band of cloth about her hips. He went with her into a world strange and full of dangers.

Chapter 28

Vengeance And Revelations

*T*umalind thought they'd been unwise to go to the inn. Dagla Kaz had returned from some secretive mission distracted, uncommunicative and frankly not much good for anything. After buying provisions, Baklan had led them to the tavern to celebrate their escape from the pirates. All seemed well, though the proud women, scandalous in their simple covers, and with dark eyes outlined in green, gold and blue were as disturbing as the villainous looking men in their outlandish garb.

The tavern was noisy and crowded; smoke from long-stemmed white pipes filling the air with its pungent sweet smell. The tavern pot-girls, dressed in soft, full skirts of bright colours, tied at hips to expose one leg and falling to their ankles, their multi-coloured hair braided into four or more long tresses, exchanged ribald comments with customers. Unlike the women from across the border, they covered their tops with bands of soft silk, though this did little to stop the men's eyes following them as they wandered the spaces between the tables, carrying flat bronze discs bearing flagons and goblets. The landlord held sway in a railed enclosure raised in the centre of the room, collecting coin and conversing with those he thought worthy of his time.

At first, the women had been objects of curiosity; their paler skins and short tabards exciting comment. But the locals had been content merely to stare appreciatively. As the evening wore on, drink loosened tongues and heightened inclinations, so all of them were approached by men who made their feelings too obvious.

Tumalind studied these strange men with their very dark skins and odd mode of dress, their open displays of weaponry, and wondered how much of what they said indicated bravado and how much they actually meant. They wore only a broad leather belt round their waist with a band of coloured linen tucked in at back and front, passing loosely between their legs. The impression of cover made it difficult for the girls not to eye them. With Dagla Kaz lost in his own thoughts and Caarl occupied with the landlord, Corphanda was left to ensure the moral protection of her charges. When one of the local men lifted Porryh's tabard and planted a hand in her lap without complaint from her, their guardian decided it was time to take them back to the ship.

As she stood, a roar of approval broke from the corner, where the crewmen were bragging to locals about their defeat of the pirates. They told how they'd fought off the attack, crediting Baklan with the idea of fire. Tumalind saw Caarl turn from his conversation and smile at this deception but he showed no interest in correcting the claim. Baklan, however, basking in the admiration of local women and men was happy to retell the tale. He embellished it with improbable details and gained as many laughs of disbelief as he did stares of admiration. Tumalind doubted he'd have to seek a companion for the night.

Porryh, seeing Corphanda's interest in the discourse, removed the man's hand and pulled her tabard down. She gave their guardian a pleading look and earned a reluctant nod.

'Just another half and then back to the ship.'

Time passed quickly in the atmosphere of action and humour and Porryh took advantage of Corphanda's apparent relaxation to allow further intrusion. Tumalind wanted no such contact from strangers but would welcome Okkyntalah's gentle attentions again. How she missed him and wondered where he was at this moment.

The door to the tavern burst open just as Caarl agreed to Corphanda's suggestion they leave. A fierce man, followed by a gang of brigands clad in black belts and loincloths, and adorned with necklaces of nazzakk teeth, strode into the inn and straight up to Baklan. The man frowned down over the ship's master, a scar on his forehead wrinkling into an ugly 's'. All conversation halted and the pot-girls stopped where they were. Even the landlord ceased his chat to gaze warily at the newcomers.

'You sank Ni-Dehla and her crew?'

Baklan, somewhat the worse for wear, leant back on his stool and looked the man up and down. 'And if I did?'

'Did you or didn't you?'

'Any law-abiding ship's master would've done what I did to those filthy pirates. The evil whore'll take no more sailors for slaves.'

The man drew his sword and drove it hard down through Baklan's neck, deep into his chest, killing him instantly. Blood spurted over those closest. Tumalind looked away, her mouth masked. Some women screamed. One of the pot-girls dropped her tray of empty goblets. None of their party moved, other than Caarl, and his action seemed likely to cause trouble rather than to stem it.

'Stay, stranger. He who killed my sister is repaid.'

Tumalind was relieved that Caarl stood still as the brigand pointed his bloodied sword at him.

The killer surveyed the room. 'Let all this poxy town know that anyone as aids this murderer's crew or passengers loses their own lives and ship.'

Caarl took another step but stopped when three of the brigands drew heavy, curved swords. The gang turned and left without another word, their leader last out of the door.

Uproar broke out and, to their consternation, the Followers were the target of the people's anger. They hustled and herded them from the tavern, telling them to leave their city at once. Dagla Kaz seemed oblivious to the seriousness of their situation. Caarl gathered them together outside the tavern and led them away with calls, threats and occasional missiles following them. Out of sight of the inn, he halted them beneath one of the flaming torches that lit the dark streets.

'What now, Caarl?'

'We seem to have no choice, Tumalind, but to go to the dock, collect the rest of our party and belongings and leave.'

'And where do we stay tonight?'

'On board, can't we?'

'I doubt it, Porryh. But whatever we do, we must do it now. To the docks first. We must let Jhonaht and Phildrad know.'

They straggled down the cobbles. The crewmen tagged along, carrying Balkan's body. As the party climbed the gangplank, the sailors' leader told them to leave the ship at once; they couldn't stay, even for that night. They must go now. They packed quickly.

Dagla Kaz seemed a little more aware of their situation as the frenzy of activity grew round him. 'We must leave.'

Caarl merely nodded at the High Priest's statement of the obvious. One of the crewmen took him and Dagla Kaz to one side to explain the true nature of the threat against them. Tumalind listened, anxious to learn what she could.

'Ni-Dehla's brother's the leader of the other pirates. It's Baklan's bad luck, an' ours, that the bastard were in dock today. Killing 'is sister an' her crew were right enough at sea, but braggin' about it were frowkin' stupid. There's folk who'll tell tales to such as Ryglan if they think it's worth their while. Pirates think they're invincible, see? They'll kill you lot if you go to sea again. No ship's master's gonna risk havin' you aboard now.'

'Why don't the people get together and fight him? He's only got a small band of brigands. They could easily defeat the gang if they joined forces.'

The crewman shrugged. 'Not their problem. They'll not risk their lives to 'elp you here in Kamakq. You've got to get out an' you can't sail. You'll 'ave to walk to Rophan-Ra. Shorrannon you're making for, aren't you?'

Dagla Kaz nodded; the odd, dreamy look falling from his eyes as the urgency and depth of the crisis concentrated his attention.

'Have to walk through Kabalyt, far as Slophrahn, at any rate. Might get a ship there. They don't let no pirates roam in the Sea of Llahkan. Might take you to Litkala.'

Dagla Kaz shuddered visibly at the mention of this place and Tumalind wondered what made him react with such repulsion.

'Else, the only way is by the Bituhn Crofts and I'd rather stick me 'ead in boiling oil. Still; up to you.' The crewman wandered away to join his mates and consult with them over their own problems.

Dagla Kaz and Caarl rejoined the rest of the group and explained matters. It was dark and they had no idea what they would do or where they should go. They were all frightened by events and couldn't believe they'd lost their only means of transport and their shelter for the night in one fell swoop. Alone and friendless in a hostile city, they had no obvious means of help or escape.

'Why don't we go back to Rhonholoah and try to get another ship from there?'

Tumalind watched to see if Dagla Kaz regained the mantle of leader. The High Priest turned and struggled to answer Wendarah's question.

'We might do that, yes. We might. But, you see...you see, it's a journey of some fifty leagues. Much of it over arid land. If we make it...make it through and...and then find rumours of our enmity with the pirates have already reached the port...well, we'd get no ship there...and then, well then we'd have to walk the whole way back to be where we are now. No. No. No, I think on balance we'd best walk through Kabalyt. If we reach Slophrahn and can get no boat there, we're in the right direction. Yes. Yes, we'll go that way. Yes.'

'And tonight?'

Dagla Kaz had evidently recovered his wits enough to be mildly amused to hear such a succinct question from Corphanda. He even smiled rather thinly. 'Tonight, dear lady, I think we'd better...yes, better make for the western edge of town and find a place to sleep.'

'Won't the pirates just follow us and kill us on the road or where we sleep?'

'I don't know, dear lady. They've not attempted to kill us yet. I can't understand them. Perhaps the crew can throw light on the situation.'

Caarl and Dagla Kaz approached the small band of sailors, huddled about the gangplank. They were discussing what to do, since they'd get no passage aboard another ship from Kamakq and daren't risk sailing Baklan's boat with the pirates after them.

'Will the pirates follow us if we go overland, do you know?'

'No.'

'You're sure?'

'Only on the sea. That's their place, see? They think they rule. But not on land. They only butchered poor Baklan 'ere in port to send a message to everyone. Long as they've killed the man they think's responsible, they'll not trouble you, unless you go to sea. Now, sorry, mate, we've our own problems. This ship's marked now.'

'Why not come with us?'

A few murmured at this suggestion but they quickly decided they'd rather trust their luck alone. Dagla Kaz shrugged and turned away.

'Keep out the Wormstalls of Glahynne, mind.'

He turned for clarification of this warning but found the men glaring daggers at the sailor who'd raised it.

'Why? Tell me why.'

They shook their heads and looked away. When Dagla Kaz moved close, to question the man who'd given the warning, he took out his dagger and threatened the High Priest.

'I just want to know what....'

'Leave it. Squit off, go on! Frowk off an' leave us be! An' get off the ship, now.'

They picked up their belongings and set off along the route Tumalind had watched Dagla Kaz take earlier that day, this time avoiding the tavern.

Fear had her look over her shoulder and start at every sound as they climbed through a city now strangely deserted, as though rumour of their passing had preceded them and they were to be shunned and avoided. Even the torches that had lit the streets no longer burned. Only the silhouetted shapes of the houses, cutting against the deep azure of a spangled sky, showed them where to go. The slapping of bare feet on cobbles echoed eerily about them as they walked in silence, anxious their voices might call down some further calamity.

At the fork, they rose above the houses and a gibbous moon emerged to give more light. Dagla Kaz turned to the south and stopped. He muttered under his breath, 'Too late my beautiful tormentor. I have no more to give.'

'Sorry, Dagla Kaz?'

He gave Caarl a strange, detached look, as though he were in another place. For a moment, he looked as though he might travel on up the hill but he shook himself and, staring toward some unseen point with longing and despair etched on his face, turned west instead, down the steep slope that led to the smaller dock on Ka'la Bay.

'Are we bound for another ship, Dagla Kaz?'

'No, Tarruss. But there's hope of a different tavern down there, where we might spend the night at least.'

The docks were quiet, no one on the streets, all lights extinguished even though the night was young. The first tavern door they knocked on remained shut and when they called for service, a voice yelled at them to go.

'Frowk off! Get out or you'll regret it.'

They received the same response at other taverns.

Out of town, dispirited and confused, they settled in a grove of fruit trees for the night, not lighting a fire in case of further trouble.

⋆ ⋆ ⋆ ⋆

'It'll be some time before Okkyntalah returns. He's a good-looking boy. Many of the women will want his seed. I hope he remembers all I've told him.'

Feldrark suggested they gather on the settles, now the food was finished, and take more wine. He drew the curtain full across the door, where Malarhah had left a small gap.

'Tell me how you come to be here and the purpose of your strange mission. There's more to it than that lad's lust for the girl he loves.'

Jodisa-Li, with a brief interruption from Myllthlan to explain aspects of the Ylcrat incident, told her tale in its entirety. They'd all made their evening prayers and were listening to Feldrark's tale by the time Malarhah returned, carrying their goods and holding the dog as distant as the leash would allow.

Feldrark took Shaulah from her and stroked her back; she licked him and settled near the door. 'Where's Okkyntalah?'

Malarhah shrugged. 'Paltra took him to house near harbour. Thricemother. I wait. Her man come home, go away. Paltrohn stay. I come back. I go for him in morning.'

Feldrark laughed. 'That'd be one of the fishermen's women. We'll not see him for a day or two.'

He noted disappointment on Myllthlan's face.

'And, if you ladies have no objections, I'm for bed.' Feldrark saw the question in Jodisa-Li's beautiful eyes. 'Alone. The Mipahnhil women do nothing by halves. I'm in need of rest, for now, at least.'

'And if you hadn't been so well used?'

'I'd seek your company, of course.'

'Even though I'm a Virgin Gift and therefore sacred to Ytraa?'

Feldrark studied this young woman who'd come so unexpectedly into his life. She wanted him as much as he desired her. But his deeper feelings about her were complex and disturbing and there were many reasons why he should indulge neither her nor himself at present.

'If that's the case, I must reject what I expect to be the most wonderful experience of my life. Is it true, Jodisa-Li, or does some secret make you available to mere mortals?'

'Feldrark not mere mortal. Feldrark Wharhll of Litkala and mighty man of power.'

Malarhah's announcement had a startling effect on Jodisa-Li. She blanched and stared at him with something like revulsion, yet her feelings were mixed if her manner was a guide.

'My father, Dagla Kaz, High Priest of Muhnilahm, would stripe my hide simply for talking to you, Wharhll of Litkala. He holds your country the domain of all that's wicked in the world. He says your version of the Followers is evil, cruel and deviant. That wickedness is practiced daily and men join with men, women with women and mothers with sons. He told me there's no worse place in the world than your land and that many of the abominations your people commit are so vile that he couldn't even describe them.'

'And what does the daughter of this High Priest think now?'

'I'm my father's child, Feldrark. Not always obedient, not always good, not always ready to believe every tale I hear. What I think will wait until I know you better. What I feel, however, is too strong to be given voice until I know I can trust you with my life.'

Feldrark looked at her with respect; her honesty touched him and her admission of strong feelings toward him, in spite of her father's advice, was brave.

'Here, in this comfortable prison cell, Jodisa-Li, you'll find all the time you need to learn what you wish to know of me and, through me, my people. In the meantime, I'm for my bed. Perhaps, when I feel the rise of energy, I should try sweet Myllthlan?'

Myllthlan smiled agreement and displayed no concern that she was second choice.

'Or, bearing in mind the abominations of my land and my faith, should I rather lie with the dog?'

To his huge delight, Jodisa-Li's laughter showed she felt this suggestion too ridiculous to contemplate. He bowed to her, kissed Myllthlan gently on her cheek, and moved to the left hand chamber. 'When you're ready, Malarhah. I'll need your gentle comfort.'

Malarhah got to her feet at once, as expected. He sighed and took her hand. 'Will I ever impress on you that you don't have to obey my every whim?'

She merely shrugged and went with him. In the darkness, she lay with him, simply embracing. Her tenderness defending him against nightly terrors, he passed into sleep.

Sun-up found Dagla Kaz fully recovered. He took Caarl to one side at once. 'I make no apology, offer no explanation for yesterday, Caarl. Understand merely that what overtook me was unique, unavoidable and will not be repeated. For now, we must set an example to the others and make firm decisions, quickly and with what wisdom, wit and experience we have between us. What do you know of this country?'

'Nothing. I've travelled most of Muhnilahm, but I've never been off the island.

You?'

'I came some cycles ago, but I visited the port on the other side and only looked down on Kala Bay from...from a place on high. I ventured only a short way along the coast, and an inhospitable place it was. Let's see what the land charts can tell us.'

'Land charts, Dagla Kaz? I know of charts Baklan used to navigate the seas. Are there reliable charts of this land, then?'

'Maps. The like of which you've never seen. I have access to information you will not be aware of. What I'm about to share with you is secret, sacred; knowledge given only to the select. I need your expertise to make the right decision, otherwise I wouldn't risk disclosure. Come.' He led him first to his pack, from which he drew a roll of parchment longer than his forearm, and then away from the group.

Caarl had helped construct rough maps of Muhnilahm, and updated them. But he would never have had the chance to see a map of such a wide area as that which Dagla Kaz unrolled before him.

The soldier studied the scroll with amazed curiosity. 'I thought maps were unreliable and not to be trusted when it comes to measuring distances. But this one seems drawn by a hand with greater knowledge than man alone could possess.'

'Perhaps you'll understand the sacred nature of this parchment and all its information. The detail and scope are, I know, well beyond your experience, Caarl.'

'By the cleft of Ytraa, I never knew such things existed!' He bowed his head at his unintended blasphemy.

Dagla Kaz was merely amused and pointed out what he believed to be their location. Caarl, reading the fine script, confirmed his opinion.

'This makes my attempts look like the scribblings of a child.'

'It is rather startling, I suppose. I've become used to the work, having studied it closely for many cycles. It is, I suppose, a clever piece of work.'

'It's brilliant, Dagla Kaz.'

The High Priest twitched with impatience.

'Apologies, but the work is miraculous.'

'Quite. Can we get on with what actually matters?'

'Do you know anything at all of the country between here and Slophrahn?'

'Nothing. I made no enquiries. I'd intended to cross to the mainland of Rophan-Ra, avoiding the cesspit of Mipahnhil, of course, and sail up river as far as Shorrannon. There, we should be able to find a smaller riverboat and a guide to take us right up the Sure, across Mistahn and up the River Mehrrhyph as far as the city that gives its name to the river. Beyond there, it's unnavigable for many leagues and I'm undecided whether to cross the Mountains of Geldakq through one of the high passes or go by foot to the low pass at Aagtaz. Time and local advice will determine that when we reach there. That's my intended route.' He traced the route with his finger as he described it.

'Why did we come to Kamakq instead of going straight to Rophan-Ra? We could've reached Shorrannon by...'

'My reasons are the province of our spiritual welfare and could not be denied.'

'You seem very sure of success with a boat if we get to Shorrannon.'

'I sent people out, knowing the Skyfire was expected. They had instructions to make what discoveries they might about the countries and people we would meet. One returned from Shorrannon only a few sixdays before we set out. Her fellows are still under way and we're unlikely to get their reports now. If the Skyfire hadn't come early, I'd have been better prepared but...'

'Why wasn't she included in our party, Dagla Kaz? Her first-hand knowledge would be invaluable.'

'She, er...died, Caarl. I'd better be brutal and let you know some truths I've born alone. The scout died a short while after she imparted her information. She'd picked up some evil sickness on the journey. You'll know Followers have made pilgrimages to the homeland almost since we arrived on the island. You may not know that, after the first few return pilgrimages, not many came back. The last to make it home was a Holy One who set out in 1307 and returned, heavily pregnant and with three others in attendance, in 1312. No one has returned from Choshinahm since that time. No one. You will, I'm sure, be sensitive to the need to keep this to yourself.'

'More unknown trials face us.'

'Undoubtedly.'

'So be it. For now, we should get a local guide. The city folk won't help. We should follow this road to the nearest village and pick up a guide, or at least some directions.'

'I've no faith we'll find such help but I can think of no better scheme for the moment. The road takes us from the coast, though, and our shortest route lies northwest and across the Wormstalls of Glahynne, here.' He pointed to the broad tongue of land dividing the Shylnah Sea from the Sea of Llahkan.

'Didn't the sailors advise against the Wormstalls?'

'Superstition. Probably believe its haunted or the realm of witches or some other imagined evil. Sailors are very superstitious, you know. Not level-headed like soldiers.'

Caarl smiled a little wryly and nodded his agreement. 'The villagers will no doubt tell us what lies on that route.'

They returned to the small encampment and breakfasted on what small supplies they had. Water was the main problem as only Jhonaht and, to his surprise, the young beauty, Tumalind, had thought to bring water skins with them. They drank a small amount each; not knowing when they'd find fresh supplies, and stuffed their belongings into their backpacks. Caarl offered to carry the water skin Tumalind had brought but she declined.

'I'd feel safer if your hands were free for your weapons, Caarl.'

Dagla Kaz watched Tumalind as Caarl approached with praise. 'She's a deal of good sense for a young woman, that one.'

'And a willingness to do what she must even though she believes she was wrongly chosen.'

'Pretty, too. You know, Dagla Kaz, she's a real asset.'

'Certainly less irritating than some.' He watched her movements as they set off and noted how close they were to those of Jodisa-Li. From behind, she could almost be his daughter. Except that he felt no carnal longing for Jodisa-Li. *Loins to entice every man. Take her, why don't you?'*

Oh, that he could! He shook his head to clear the thought. He must complete the task.

Cloud sat, a dark grey band, far over the sea to the north but the sky overhead was clear and blue, the sun bright and already hot. Birds sang about them and insects buzzed and droned nearby. The trees bore fruits that looked similar to the magrana and, judging by the activity of one of the larger azure and tan birds, they were edible. Dagla Kaz directed Phildrad who, shrugging his resignation, plucked one of the dark purple globes and sniffed at it. He sliced the outer skin, revealing a mass of transparent red, orange and yellow kernels of pulp surrounding small white seeds. He speared one of the coloured corns and tasted it gingerly. Nodding approval, he chewed it and his face broke into a broad smile.

'Like magrana, but sweeter.' Without further hesitation, he bit into the fruit and filled his mouth with the flesh. 'Very good.'

The rest of the party followed suit and then picked as many of the fist-sized globes as they could easily carry.

They set off, emerging from the trees onto the road, the city at their backs. The brick and timber houses clung to the steep side of the hill, climbing to the summit, faint wisps of blue smoke wavering here and there to declare the rising of the citizens. It was time to be gone.

The way was ill made and dusty and Caarl advised they should walk abreast, so that no one would have to walk in dust raised by those in front. In practice, they had to walk in two groups with a short gap between. Tarruss and Jhonaht acted as guards to the rear party.

Either side of the road, fields harvested of crops, awaited ploughing or seeding. They passed by a second grove of the trees that grew the purple fruit, already laden with as many as they could carry. Beyond, the road wound up a steep incline before it levelled onto a dusty grey plain studded with huge black boulders and small patches of low dry scrub. Fine tough grass grew sparsely on the thin stony soil and there was no sign of animal life on the ground.

Soaring high above, a troop of black-winged green vultures provided a constant reminder of their new and precarious state in this hot, waterless land.

Chapter 29

GUIDANCE AND LOSSES

Four dry leagues along the road, Dagla Kaz at last recognised signs of civilization, though these were few and mean: unfenced fields that had given up their produce and lay full of dry weeds and encroaching prairie grass. The road, such as it was, had not branched along the way and now curved to the east as it dropped into a shallow valley. A muddy stream lay turbid and moribund as it drained what was left of a small lake, where bony cattle stood up to their knees as they drank.

They followed the track as it breasted a low hill and saw that the stream flowed into one of the broad fingers of Ka'la Bay. At the edge of the water, a cluster of mud and thatch huts stood in no order or design around a patch of flat ground. Two young children tended a small herd of goats grazing the sparse grass, but of adults, there was no sign.

The children watched, full of suspicion, and backed away as Caarl approached.

'Is there anyone here we might talk with?'

They stared, silent and wary.

'I just want directions.'

The children looked at each other and said nothing. One of them, the smaller, raised an arm and pointed to the coast through the houses.

'Thank you.'

Caarl led the way along tracks between the dwellings where they found a group of twenty or so men standing in a line up to their knees in the sea. Their women, waist deep, approached the men, smacking the surface with the palms of their hands as they moved forward in a wide arc. Ahead of them, the sea bubbled and boiled with fish that leapt and dived as they tried to escape the shallows. The men caught those fish that came near, scooping them from the water to toss them onto the shingle, where they flapped helplessly.

The Followers stood at a short distance, waiting for them to complete their harvest. Few took notice of them and, as the group of women reached the men, they all left the water, tossing out the last of the catch. Dagla Kaz and Caarl approached and the villagers stood, waiting to meet their visitors. An older man shouted an unintelligible command and the women ran, giggling, to retrieve their skirts from above the tide line.

'We're trying to get to Slophrahn. Does anyone know the best route to take please?'

The older man emerged from his fellows and waved them and the women behind him. He walked to within five or six paces, looked them up and down, but said nothing.

'We'd like a guide, if one of the men here would like to earn some coin, that is?'

Still the elder said nothing but a couple of the men showed interest.

'And could we buy some fish?' Dagla Kaz hoped commerce might elicit a response.

'Fish?' The elder's voice was strangely high and his pronunciation made the word sound like a question.

Caarl pointed to the fish still struggling on the shingle and the man nodded without turning round. 'Fish.'

The women of the party made their way down to the sea, to cool off. Dilanthas splashed her face and arms with water and then turned to the village women and conversed with them readily. Dagla Kaz shrugged and returned his attention to Caarl's slow discourse with the elder.

'Is this possible? We will pay well.'

'Fish.'

'Yes, fish. And a guide?'

The elder nodded. 'Fish. Fish good.'

Caarl seemed to be getting somewhere at last. 'Yes. Fish. Good. We buy some?'

The elder seemed unmoved by his enthusiasm and merely nodded again but said nothing more.

Dagla Kaz was losing patience at this slow, apparently fruitless negotiation. 'I think we've established that we want to buy some of your fish. But is there one amongst you who would guide us?'

There was laughter from the women and he looked up to see the girls enjoying their dialogue with the villagers. They seemed to be getting somewhere, at least. But his question to the old man received no answer.

Dilanthas trotted up the shingle with one of the village women, both laughing as they approached. He thought they were going to talk to him but they stopped near the elder, where the woman dropped to one knee and the girl quickly followed suit. The elder touched the woman on her shoulder and she rose, placing a restraining hand on Dilanthas, who remained where she was. Soft words passed between them and the elder looked up at Dagla Kaz and back at the woman and down at the girl. He nodded slowly and called out. A younger man stepped forward from the small crowd and stood with his head bowed before the elder. More soft words were exchanged; the younger man raised Dilanthas to her feet again and took her back down the shingle. Dagla Kaz watched suspiciously. The village woman remained in front of the elder, her head bowed.

The man and girl selected several fish from the beach and he threaded them onto a fine line. They walked back up the shingle and showed the chosen fish to the elder who nodded and spoke to her. She nodded, bowed and came up to Dagla Kaz.

'They want three crowns for the fish but I'm sure I can beat 'em down to two. The man'll teck us to Xythonl, wherever that might be, for three crowns. What am I to say?'

'*Beat the savage down, man. Beat him down.*

'Well done, Dilanthas. Yes. We'll pay for the fish and the guide.' He put his hand out to Caarl for the coin.

'Er, no, Dagla Kaz, if you'll excuse me. I'm sorry, but that won't do at all. We'll 'ave to eat with 'em and talk so they know who they're dealin' with. They'll not send one of their men off wi' strangers wi'out knowin' summat about us first.'

Dagla Kaz turned to Caarl for guidance and the soldier shrugged his agreement. Dilanthas returned to the elder and spoke quietly with him, her head bowed and her arms behind her back.

All seemed settled, then. The people welcomed them into the village and the men, who seemed to live naked, set about coaxing a fire from the ashes that smouldered at the top of the beach as the women collected the fish and strung them by their tails on frames under the palm trees. The fish selected by Dilanthas were placed in an open reed basket and left in the shallows under the shadow of a palm overhanging the sea.

A feast of fish, split grain, chopped seaweed and slices of a pale golden root vegetable was served as a stew in hollowed gourds, eaten with fingers easily burnt by the hot, sticky liquid stock. Dagla Kaz noted that Phildrad at last seemed to be taking an interest, asking questions about the ingredients of the meal. There was much laughter as misunderstandings arose about names and customs but no bad feeling emerged from these good-humoured folk. Satisfied that the strangers meant them no harm, they welcomed them into their village like lost family returned.

Dagla Kaz and Caarl sat either side of the elder, cross-legged on the ground, and ate their meal with their fingers, following his lead. For a while, he quizzed Dagla Kaz about their journey but showed little interest in his replies. He nodded to Dilanthas, sitting with the other women who'd served the men first and were only now starting to eat. 'Valuable young woman. Good flesh, obedient, modest. Make a good wife.'

'I believe she will, but it'll be far from here. She's one of the girls I told you about, the ones we're taking to Choshinahm.'

The elder looked surprised. 'You give away such women? Never will I understand the ways of strangers. If she were ours, the men, they would fight for such as her. And that other one, the one with hair that shines like sunset on the surface of the sea.'

'Tumalind? She's a mind to match her looks. Even our man of science has more than merely an eye for her. And what of Porryh?' He nodded to where she sat, unconcerned or perhaps unaware of her exposure from the posture she'd adopted to eat.

The elder glanced and looked away. 'That one will give her man trouble. She's no modesty. Thinks she's as good as a man.'

The meal over, a wide shallow bowl of milky liquid was passed to the elder by one of the women, who held it out to him with her arms outstretched as she knelt before him, her forehead touching the ground. He took his time removing it from her hands and Dagla Kaz was struck by the difficulty she must have had in keeping it steady and level at such an uncomfortable stretch. She, however, made no complaint and merely waited until the elder had supped from the bowl and took it back. She repeated the process to each of the men in the circle. He noticed his companions, except Tryonta of course, relieved her of her burden as soon as they could, but the village men all took their time, concentrating on their talk and laughter, before lifting it from her.

The liquid was strongly flavoured with aniseed, burning as it drained down his throat. A second woman with another bowl repeated the round, followed by a third. By this time, Dagla Kaz was acutely aware of the strength of the liquor and hoped he'd be able to get back to his feet without stumbling. The village men, however, seemed unaffected.

The event had been a welcome break in their journey but they were eager to get on their way and Dagla Kaz sympathized with Caarl when he grimaced, as two of the village women began to dance. One of the men beat an accompaniment with a stick on a hollowed log, varying tone and volume as he struck it in different places and producing a hypnotic tempo that soon had the watchers swaying in time.

The women wove and twisted, snaked and stepped in an intricate pattern that seemed to suggest a tale. Dagla Kaz recognised certain aspects of the dance and put together a story of a woman caught by a great fish, swallowed whole and finally spat out, alive and well, on this shore. He wondered if it was a re-enacted history, commemorating the arrival of these people in this land. And the elder confirmed this eagerly.

The dance done, the villagers accepted their applause but clearly expected a reciprocal demonstration. Again, Dilanthas came to the rescue, swiftly recruiting Tumalind and, after rapidly whispered instructions, pulling a simple wooden flute from her pack and beginning to play. Tumalind, graceful and unselfconscious, performed a simplified version of a dance learned by most children. It told the tale of a young girl lost in the forest, scared by a beast and befriended by another until she was eventually restored to her family, amid much rejoicing. The villagers enjoyed the demonstration so much they asked her to repeat it so that their own women might join in and learn to perform it in the future. Porryh, evidently feeling left out, joined in the second rendition, adding words in a song that told the tale in a series of simple verses as the dance progressed. Her voice, clear, full and tuneful, surprised them all, and the villagers were so delighted they asked for another repeat so they might learn the words of the song as well.

At last the celebration and entertainment was done. Dagla Kaz haggled with the elder over the price for the fish, ending up paying the two crowns Dilanthas had predicted.

The elder called for the young man who'd helped Dilanthas collect the fish. 'This is Grahtl. He will guide you.' He held out his hand and tested Dagla Kaz's coins with his teeth before passing them to another man to hold.

Dagla Kaz and Grahtl nodded to each other and the High Priest put a hand on his shoulder in gesture of friendship. The young man, startled, copied the gesture but seemed unsure of its significance.

Grahtl then nodded again and moved to where a woman stood, waiting. He parted her skirt, drew his hand up between her thighs and then under his nose and nodded at her. She bowed her head. He turned to retrieve the fish, then led the party from the village amongst much waving and calling.

On the road, Dagla Kaz consulted the map with Caarl once again and their guide was invited to have his say. It was clear the drawing had no meaning for him, however.

'Can you guide us through the Wormstalls of Glahynne?

Grahtl rolled his eyes and trembled. 'Not go there. No one go there.'

'Isn't it the most direct route to Slophrahn?'

He looked at Dagla Kaz as if he were crazy. 'I take you to Xythonl, not other place.'

'But that's on the west coast and we need to be on the east.'

'Xythonl only place I go. Not…not other place.'

'What's so bad about the Wormstalls?'

Grahtl shook his head. 'I go to Xythonl. Not go there.'

Dagla Kaz looked to Caarl, seeking support in his chosen route but he was no help.

'This is the second time we've found real fear about the Wormstalls, Dagla Kaz. If you hire a local guide, I for one, believe it makes sense to take notice of his directions. At least if we go his way, we pass two more cities, where we might obtain food and the other supplies we'll need for the long march to Slophrahn. There's no sign on your map of any habitation if we go by the Wormstalls of Glahynne. Who knows what sort of terrain lies that way? My inclination is to follow this man's advice.'

'If that's the case, we might as well not bother with a guide. The road takes us there.' Dagla Kaz turned to the man. 'Does the road go all the way?'

Grahtl looked at the dusty track at his feet. 'Some. Not all. Other roads go to places you not want go. And the forest will get you lost.'

Dagla Kaz shrugged his resignation and they set out on the road with only two hours to sun down. A walk into entirely unknown lands with a guide who gave little cause for confidence.

◦ ⋄ ◦

The day after his arrival on The Point, Aklon-Dji walked into the deserted dry hills and set his gaze toward the west. His mind sought and reached for the tower and found his mentor, busy but alone and willing to speak.

'Ivdulon, it is Aklon-Dji. I need your wisdom.'

'You've been silent a while. But I expect it's not easy for you, living the life of a renegade and a rebel, bedding all those willing women in between your other adventures. Ask me what you will, but first tell me a little of what's been going on in your island.'

He told him of his journeys and the reasons for them, explaining what he'd learned along the way, filling in the gaps when Ivdulon requested further information.

'Something else troubles you, Aklon. I feel it without understanding its source.'

'I experienced a connection, very brief but strong and vivid, with my sister. She was in the sea and I think she was drowning. I tried to coax her back to the surface and to life but I am not certain I was successful. The connection broke as abruptly as it was made. Can you advise me?'

'You've never mindtalked with Jodisa?'

'I was not aware she could do it.'

'Perhaps she's one of those with the gift and doesn't know it; like your father. I've come across others who connect, as you so appropriately describe it...yes, I like that, connect. It's apposite. However, I meander. Yes, she possibly only connects, and possibly only with siblings or parents, when she's near death. I wish I could reassure you, Aklon, but I can't. Such subjects are often difficult to reach until they become aware they have the gift. But, tell me, did you feel fear, panic or any other strong emotion at the time she cut the connection?'

'Nothing. The connection was there and I seemed to experience what she was experiencing. I made my attempt to take her to the surface. She...ah, yes, she breathed fresh air. And then she was gone again.'

'That, at least, is a good sign. I suspect she either recovered or was rescued and removed from the water.'

'I hope so. She may have been corrupted by my father, Ivdulon, but I love her as a

sister. How do you know about my father's gift?'

'Ah. Dagla Kaz spent a brief but torrid time with a particularly adept...er, connection, of mine. A woman in the city of Kamakq, who purveys a...'

'So, he did go to Kamakq! I had heard he intended as much but could see no reason.'

'The lady, or rather the peculiar enhancer she purveys...or, perhaps, both she and her product. Anyway, she appears singularly alluring and she provides a type of...I suppose you'd call it a stimulant. She's able to absorb not only the thoughts of her victims and beneficiaries but their feelings, experiences, indeed everything they've known and encountered in the period prior to their joining with her. She's then able to live their lives, vicariously, feeling and experiencing everything they've suffered and enjoyed. And I, because I'm the sink, the receptacle of everything that travels through the air in mindtalking, I also experience, feel, understand and empathize with those she's succoured and used in her ravenous search for life.'

'Every time I talk with you, you manage to surprise me, Ivdulon. Is there no end to your abilities and talents?'

'I won't dignify that with an answer. Your father's a deeply troubled man who, in spite of appearances, isn't entirely evil. His basic problem is a fear of the unknown. He's troubled by doubts about the faith you and I are so eager to destroy, he's troubled by his own insistence on its adherence by the Followers of Muhnilahm, he's troubled by the power of the Holy Ones...you must tell me more about them, by the way. Your father's impressions left me slightly confused as to their purpose and practice. But that can wait. He's terrified of his fate at the end of life, which is why he succumbed to the dubious allurements of my...er, contact, in Kamakq. Her concoction provides both stimulus and a degree of slowing of the aging process. Though, Ytraa help her devotees, they'll suffer agonies on their deathbeds in exchange for the added cycles. Nothing is without its price.'

'I called on you for a specific purpose, Ivdulon and, as so frequently proves to be the case, you deflect me with information of a fascinating and mind altering quality.'

'It's part of my mission; to improve the thinking of those I speak with. What did you want, specifically, Aklon?'

'Jhonaht has declared this spark to be the Skyfire and my father...'

'Your astronomer's a man with little brain. What will your father do when he discovers he follows the false trail?'

'I do not know. I expect it depends where he is when he discovers it. But it is a sign for me to act, Ivdulon. When will you send the help we need?'

'You must be patient. We've lost our spiritual leader and, though I know his *whereabouts, until he returns, nothing can be done for you. But, I've every hope of his return soon, especially as new minds have recently gathered with him. When he comes back, with a bride and the Staff, he'll be ready, I think, to begin a mission to your island. Then we'll see what will be. You must prepare, organize your people, Aklon. The day approaches, but rush nothing, or you'll stumble at the door to victory.'*

'Are you ready, yet, to reveal your whereabouts to me? Have I earned such trust?'

There was a spell of silence, in which he was conscious that Ivdulon was pondering; considering. Abruptly, his mind filled with the scene that met the eyes of his contact. He saw the walls of the white tower pass, a fleeting glimpse of a framed but moving image of a dark skinned woman, and then a flight of stone steps, which ascended to emerge onto a floor above. He looked from a window, aware of the sounds of seemeeuws, the distant breaking of surf, the gentle murmur of activity so many manheights below as the scene took in the city spread out beneath.

'I've shown you before, Aklon. Gaze on the wondrous city of Litkala.'

For a brief spell, he had the view along with the name and then Ivdulon broke contact and he was alone on The Point again.

The fabulous scene, with the city laid out, white, bright, and beautiful under the hot sun, faded from his mind. Litkala. Aklon-Dji knew its name. His father talked of it with terror and disgust. It was the haunt of a sect of Followers who had so distorted the truths of Gadhallah that their acts and beliefs were abominations. In solitude and despair, he drowned in this newfound knowledge and pondered why he'd asked such a question, when the answer must end all contact with his source of knowledge and wonder.

＊

Feldrark settled himself comfortably between the two women and ensured their goblets were full. Malarhah, returned from her duties and, free for the rest of the day to serve them, was comfortable on the other settle and relaxed in the space she made, weary after her demanding chores.

'Tell us, Wharhll of Litkala, what keeps a clever, resourceful and strong man pent up in this turdhole, when a little courage and wit would allow an easy escape?'

Jodisa-Li's contempt cut him. He knew it wasn't personal loathing but a puzzling hatred of his home for no reason he could comprehend. It would take careful probing to discover her beliefs and he'd no wish to force her into declaring why the name of his beloved Litkala made her wonderful mouth sneer and her glorious eyes widen with fear. For the moment, it might serve him better to answer her question and cultivate her understanding of his unique situation. He'd been a lone captive too long. Perhaps, with the help of these newcomers, he might find a way to escape this dreadful prison, at last.

'You think I haven't tried, Jodisa-Li? Three times I've suffered the humiliation and pain of their peculiar form of punishment; my next failure will bring painful execution. But you're right; if there wasn't a very pressing reason for me to stay, I would've succeeded long ago. My attempts have been half-hearted because, in the very centre of my being, I know I can't leave without something they've stolen from me. Until I retrieve it, I won't be able to return home with honour.'

'What have they taken that's so important you'll put up with such imprisonment?'

'Oh, come on, Myllthlan, the man's hardly suffering, is he? There's more incentive for him to stay than leave.'

'It probably seems that way. But I'm weary of it, to tell the truth. I left my home in search of a partner for life. I'm tired of this endless serving for the purpose of others.' He took a deep draught of wine and studied the women in turn. 'Beautiful women. How often is man trapped by such temptation? I set out from my home city more than a sun's turn ago. Come the new moon, I'll have been away for thirteen Moontimes. There was sorrow and pride at my departure. My people didn't want me to leave. My mother and father were loath to let me go. But tradition and faith set me on the road from Litkala.

'I had to go from the city with nothing but the clothes I wore when we met, my sword and dagger, and the Staff of Ytraa. It would be inconceivable, ignominious, impossible to return without the Staff. I'm also bound to have with me a woman suitable and willing to be my life's partner. And she must be from outside the borders of Litkala. Thus is the line of rulers made strong and diverse. My own dear mother, a beautiful maiden when father won her heart and beautiful still in her middle cycles, hails from Rhonholoah in Niphralon many leagues from home by sea and land.'

'Your mother's dark skinned, then, like Malarhah?'

'Not as dark, but darker than you. You know the country?'

'My father knows of it. The merchants there trade myllth and emeralds from the Prolanq Mountains for the colours we use in our tattoos and for our olive oil, which is the best available.'

'Your father won't know, for they're very secretive about it, that they're a race without a god. They do magic and believe that the spirits of the dead wait in a place of trial until a new child is born for them to inhabit. It's a strange and dangerous belief. Malarhah doesn't come from Niphralon but from Balagaaq, over the mountains, on the very edge of a dessert region where she was sold as a child of six cycles. The selling of girls is common there. I intend to return her home when I finally escape, if she wishes to go.'

'I glad come with you. But not want go home.'

Feldrark nodded at this piece of news, wondering why she hadn't mentioned it before.

'But you'll never escape if you can't get back this Staff of Ytraa. You've said you'd be shamed to return without it. What does it look like? Perhaps we can find it whilst we're stuck here in this midden.'

'I've searched every day and never found a sign of it. No one will tell me anything of its whereabouts. But I know it was with me when I was found.'

'Found? How were you found, Feldrark?' Myllthlan seemed deeply curious about the way he expressed this fact.

'First describe this Staff for us.'

'The Staff of Ytraa was taken…passed down to the people of Litkala by Lord Gadhallah himself, at the time of the Great Division. It's a relic of great value; priceless and irreplaceable.'

'Yet they send a man out into the wilds alone, bearing this treasure?'

'It's part of the test, Jodisa-Li. And part of our faith, that Ytraa will protect the Staff. Its loss would signal the utter destruction of Litkala. You understand why I must retrieve it?'

Chapter 30

A Lost Staff Is Key

Litkala. Why had he asked? Now he must end all contact with Ivdulon, his soul mate, his mentor, his friend. Litkala: a forbidden place, a foul, polluting pustule on the squitter of the world. It was the worst place imaginable; his father had told him of its evils and its…His father! Aklon-Dji cried out in anguish and relief; that his father still had such a hold, and that he recognized that what his father said about Litkala was invalid. The views of Dagla Kaz were irrelevant: the opinions of a man incapable of knowing truth and honesty and love.

He breathed again, drew in the life-supporting knowledge that Ivdulon showed him the truth, dispassionately and without attempting to convert or sway him. And he knew that, of the two men who'd influenced his life, it was Ivdulon he trusted and admired, Ivdulon whose words and ideas most closely echoed his own.

Litkala.

He laughed aloud as he recognized the irony. Dagla Kaz had so reviled the place that it must, by definition, be the haven of moral, ethical, and intellectual perfection. That was what his father loathed; its wondrous qualities that put Muhnilahm a thousand cycles back in history, relegating his island home to a time before true civilization had sprung forth.

He knew the location of the city, in relation to the island, from the maps his father had shown him at the start of his real education. The maps, perhaps more than anything else, had started him on his long and dangerous road in search of truth. When he'd stumbled, almost by chance it seemed, upon Ivdulon in Litkala without knowing his location, and learned of the different route other Followers had taken, his doubts and his ambitions for change had grown and fired him to action. He wondered, would he have so readily heard Ivdulon's words had he known, at the beginning, they came from Litkala? Shaking his head at the wisdom of his mentor, Aklon-Dji accepted that such knowledge would have formed an insurmountable barrier to his early education. It said something of his journey from then to now that Ivdulon had let him know the truth. Perhaps he'd come of age in the eyes of the wise man on the mountain.

He gazed at the barren Point. How could anyone, any so-called civilized religion, banish folk here? How could his father, knowing the reality that lay behind their faith, continue to wield his power, continue to deal out vile and cruel punishments he knew were without justification? He'd tried to reason with the High Priest but had failed. Soon would come the time for action. Then he would be pitted against his own father and, so that others could live in freedom, might even have to kill him. Assuming, of course, Aklon-Dji could manage to stay alive long enough.

But, by Mhortag's balls, he was impatient to start. Desperate to end the island's version of Followers as a religion.

＊ ＝＝

'What does this staff look like?'

'It's not very special to look at. A branch of ebony torn from a tree by…by our leader, to help him walk the many leagues from Choshinahm. But, after the Great Division, it was cleaned and mounted at its head with a likeness of Ytraa, made of gold. The figure is but a handbreadth tall but the Staff itself reaches my shoulder. Hard as iron and black as the hair on Malarhah's pretty head, it's without bark and polished, though not smooth, so that every crevice and twist gleams. A simple iron ferrule protects the end. And it was with me when I was found; that much I know.

'It hasn't been lost or destroyed but the people of this place have hidden it to make my imprisonment more certain. They know I can't leave without it. Once I know its whereabouts, I'll escape and find a worthy woman to be mine. Though, now, that may be easier than when I set out.' He glanced at the women either side of him and both looked at him with surprise. His grin of mischief made them incapable of deciding how serious he might be. It wasn't yet time.

'To my tale!' He drank deeply, and Malarhah, who seemed unusually thoughtful after his statement, sprang from her settle and refilled his cup from one of the flagons. He smiled at her, stroked her arm tenderly and indicated she should sit again.

'I set out on foot for Shorrannon, though, in truth, I never expected to take a wife from there; too close to Litkala. Shorrannon's reputedly the home of the most beautiful women in the whole world. Though, having met you, Jodisa-Li, I have my doubts as to that.'

'Flattery is charming, Feldrark, but it won't tell your tale.'

'Flattery's falsehood mostly. I spoke only the truth. But you're right; I'll keep to the matter.'

'Oh, you can flatter me whenever you like. I shan't object.'

He smiled at her, pondering her ability to separate her loathing of his land from her clear attraction to him.

'I left the city by road, the people cheering and wishing me a safe and successful journey. The first night, I ventured off the road into the forest we call the Greenreald, in search of shelter and food. I'm an experienced hunter and found both easily enough. I slept and woke to put more leagues between my home and me. Two more nights and I was close to the eastern edge of the forest when I stumbled on the thing I most feared. I came upon Mhortag's Dread at dusk without knowing where I was…'

'Mhortag's Dread? I've heard the name. It's a place of legend, a place of horror and infamy.'

'It's a relic of the Great Division, Jodisa-Li. A shameful reminder of unspeakable acts that happened at that terrible time. It's the site of great slaughter and dreadful acts, where brother fell on sister, mother tore the living heart from son, father dishonoured and strangled daughter, husband violated and mutilated wife, child unsexed and sliced parent. Hundreds died or were despoiled, hundreds were left desolate and dying for the beasts to devour and none were buried. That place is still haunted by those tortured souls.

'Warriors have fled screaming from the margins, men and women have gone mad just passing through by day. It was a road at the time of the disaster. Now, the trees tower close overhead but nothing grows along the length, though the dust and bones of those who perished there drown the paving stones. It is always dark but never without the ghostly light of the undead. Nothing moves in that long strip of dread. I entered it at dusk and nearly lost my mind trying to escape its malevolent grip.

'I'll speak no more of it. It's a horror I would forget, except that I can't. I still relive that loathsome walk when I'm alone in bed at night.' He glanced toward Malarhah and smiled his gratitude.

'Then, between us, we'd better see that you're not alone.'

The echo of terror left him as he smiled at Myllthlan's offer, stroking her face with his fingertips and thanking her with his eyes.

'I came out of that place a different man. Wiser and, I think, more compassionate, more understanding of the evil that dwells within man and awaits only blindness and prejudice to escape and devour him. I wandered lost and bereft of sense for days I can't count, and missed my place of seeking. I ate nothing and drank only the rain that fell on me or the puddles I fell in as I collapsed from sheer exhaustion. When I came to the river; wide, deep, and fast flows the Sure at that place, I came to myself and knew where and who I was again. I was weak with hunger and constant movement. Though it's less than twenty leagues as the oryol flies, I must have travelled three times that distance as I wandered witless from the terror of Mhortag's Dread.

'Weary beyond description, I came back to my senses and knew I must survive. By Ytraa's grace, I still had the Staff and hadn't met with any brigands to rob me as I wandered lost in that wide, empty land, where only the Bruxa dwell. I came to a small village, an outpost of Shorrannon, though I didn't realize that until too late, and asked the way to the city. They seemed scared, as if some evil dwelt in me. But I bribed one of the men with my hunting knife, bejewelled and precious, for his boat. I stepped aboard that small craft and it took me down river, and I looked upstream and saw the edges of the city and knew I was sailing away from the place I sought. I had no strength to turn and row upstream. I lived on water from the river and the small fish I caught with my hands as they swam about my unguided boat.

'At length I strayed into the great Mire of Rhoshe, though I knew not then where I was. I won't bore you with the days and nights I spent being eaten by flies and shifting the boat off mudflats. Near death, I floated from the Mire to the open sea. It was there that fishermen from Mipahnhil came upon my boat.

'I've been here ever since. They said the price for my life was the creation of a new life here. I've created many but still they keep me prisoner.

'It's a sorry tale for an adventurer who set out to win a woman for his partner. I've had more women than most men could dream of but not one worthy to sit beside me in my home. So, here I stick, frowking day and night with different women, making sons and daughters that the men of Mipahnhil claim as their own. But I can't discover the Staff of Ytraa and, without it, I'm sunk in this stinking cesspit.'

The night closed about them and they made their prayers, belatedly.

'Malarhah doesn't pray?'

'As a slave, she has no faith, Myllthlan. Her own has long since melted away into the nothingness that is her memory of her heritage.'

'Is there God? I am used. Abused. Insulted. Work hard for nothing. Feldrark gives me care alone. I know no God.'

Feldrark comforted her, wondering at this uncharacteristic outburst.

'Feldrark not know but I make promise. I find way to help him if I able.'

He became acutely aware that the change in her resulted from this influx of strangers into the small house. They, like him, treated her with respect and kindness and this seemed to have made her more open.

'You not tell me story of Staff, Feldrark. You not trust Malarhah?'

Feldrark had been kind to her; held her close without using her, as soon as it became obvious she derived little pleasure from joining. He'd cared for her and shown affection for her as a fellow captive. But he hadn't thought her interested in him or his plight.

'It just never occurred to me, that's all.'

'Feldrark. You only good thing in my life. You good man. I do anything to help you.'

He'd told her that he'd take her with him if he could escape. At first, she hadn't believed him. But his treatment of her seemed eventually to convince her.

'What's going on in that pretty head of yours?'

His question surprised her out of her reverie. 'I was just wondering, if I discovered this Staff of Ytraa, could we all escape this awful place and…?'

They stared open mouthed; no one more surprised than Feldrark at the revelation of her secret.

'Don't be alarmed, Malarhah. I've long suspected there was more to you than you displayed. Your secret's safe with us. I don't know why you act the dull fool, although I might guess. But it's safe with us. Keep up your act outside, Malarhah. There are many who'd see you dead rather than allow you to shine brighter than themselves.'

'I do what always did. No one know Malarhah got brain. I do what you say. You tell what I do.'

He looked at her and smiled as he shook his head with wonder. 'You don't have to keep it up with us, Malarhah, unless you feel it would be easier.'

'To tell the truth, Feldrark, it's such a relief to speak normally, to express ideas I've always confined to the realms of my own mind. The sense of freedom is tremendous. If I find the Staff, will you get us out of here?'

Feldrark looked at the other two women, as if seeking their support. 'I think, given the help of our new friends, we might escape. Six of us stand a better chance than a man alone. Do you think your men will want to leave this place?'

Jodisa-Li considered briefly. 'Okkyntalah would frowk his way to exhaustion given the chance. He joined enthusiastically with Myllthlan in the discomfort of our open boat, so he'll be in paradise with a willing woman in privacy and comfort. But, once we get him back, we'll remind him of his devotion to Tumalind; once he understands there's a chance of leaving here, he'll come back to reality. It might help if Myllthlan and Malarhah make it clear they'll satisfy his needs on the way.'

Both women nodded, Myllthlan with enthusiasm.

'Aglydron will be more difficult to reach and find. But, no matter what pleasure that woman gives him, he'll leave her. He's dedicated absolutely to the cause of our expedition.'

'Good. Malarhah, just one thing, my beautiful and clever girl, if you do discover the whereabouts of the Staff, you mustn't retrieve it. I must reclaim it myself. Understand?'

'As you will, Feldrark. Though it might be safer if a dull-witted slave trespassed on the Galhta's tower, perhaps in pursuit of some young wag's practical joke, intended to get her publicly beaten for failing to satisfy his perverted desires.'

'You know where it is?'

'Oh, yes. I overheard the Galhta telling one of the women when you first came.'

'And it's still there?'

'I expect so. I'll check, tomorrow.'

'He is, though, isn't he?'

'Who is what?' Tumalind resumed her washing of Porryh's hair, the brief pause no doubt the cause of the comment.

'Oh, come on, Tumalind, don't play the innocent. I've seen you watching that lovely bum of his. You're no different from the rest of us.'

'No, I'm not. But I wasn't thinking of Grahtl.'

'Not still thinking about lover boy; what's his name?'

'Okkyntalah. Yes. I think about him all the time. Don't you miss your intended?'

'No. Can't say I'm any keener than you about being stuck with some heathen bloke in a foreign land but I don't think of the one I left behind. He'll have forgotten me; not much point me remembering him, is there?'

'You don't really mean that, Porryh. I've seen the look in your eyes.'

'Maybe. Waste of time, though, isn't it? We're not going to get what we want, so we might as well forget it.'

'I can't. I know he'll wait for me. I just know it.'

'Wait? What's the point?'

'I…it doesn't matter. That's just the way I am. Ignore me.'

Porryh turned round to stare at her and shake her head before plunging it beneath the water to rinse away the froth from the crushed flaglilies Tumalind had used to wash her hair. She pushed her head back up and Tumalind watched the current slowly take the bubbles downstream, popping silently as they floated on the clear calm water of the river.

'You'll break your heart, you will, Tumalind. Forget him. Think about Grahtl. I do!'

Tumalind laughed in spite of herself. 'Much good it'll do you. Have you seen the way Caarl keeps an eye on you? You'd not get within a pace of that young man before he'd be between you.'

'Looks at you a lot, Caarl.'

'Does he? I hadn't noticed.'

'Good looking fellah in an older sort of way, isn't he?'

'Caarl? I've always thought so. He's married to a friend of my mother's. Certainly looks after himself.'

'Tryonta's handsome, don't you think?'

They changed places, Tumalind seating herself between Porryh's thighs and tipping her head back so she could massage the cleansing sap into her hair.

'Handsome enough. Don't trust him, though. There's something mean and dark in those eyes.'

'I know.'

'He looks a bit like Okkyntalah. 'Cept Okkyntalah hasn't a mean bone in his body. He's kind and loving and gentle and…Oh, Porryh, I love him so much!'

Porryh twisted her round and held her in her arms as the water flowed over and around their waists and legs. She held Tumalind's head against her chest and stroked her back, trying not to cry herself. They remained together in their embrace of comfort until Dilanthas came and jumped into the water beside them, splashing them out of their reverie.

'What you two up to, then? Bit o' girls' togetherness, is it?'

'Oh, don't be horrid, Dilanthas. I was having a weep over Okkyntalah, that's all. It's you and Wendarah who get up to that sort of thing, not us.'

Dilanthas shrugged. 'It's not horrid. Anyway, summat's better'n nowt, as they say.'

'It's all you'll be getting, anyway, till we get to Choshinahm.'

'All any of us'll get till then. Know what 'appens when we do get there?'

'I don't think even Dagla Kaz knows, to tell the truth. It's two hundred and forty cycles since the last Skyfire. No one alive can remember anything about it. I think he's just hoping there'll be someone in Choshinahm who knows what's supposed to happen.'

''E's teckin' us all that way an' 'e don't even know what to do wi' us when we get there?'

'That's what I think.' Tumalind dipped her head beneath the water to rinse her hair and glanced up at the bank when she raised her head again. 'Cross your arms and legs, girls; creepy Tryonta's come to spy on us again.'

They watched him walk along the bank, giving sidelong glances in their direction and trying to pretend he didn't know they were there.

'You watch. He'll say he never saw us; dirty prod.' Porryh stood up, so the water flowed round her legs, and turned to face Tryonta, her hands tidying her hair.

Tryonta stopped in his tracks no more than ten paces from the girls. He stared at Porryh with his mouth open and then remembered to turn away. 'Sorry, girls; didn't know you were bathing here.'

Porryh made no move to cover herself or to sit back down, in spite of the other two giggling and scolding her to get herself covered. Tryonta couldn't resist another look at her before he moved back the way he'd come.

'Shameless hussy.'

'I know. Showed him, though, didn't I?'

'Showed him exactly what he wanted to see!'

'Don't you care, Porryh? I mean about 'im seeing you?'

'Not especially. I'd rather it was Grahtl, though. He's a man worth displaying to.'

'You're wicked, you are.'

'I know. Never get to the Garden of Delights, will I?'

'You shouldn't joke about it. It's forever, you know?'

'I know, Tumalind. I'm sorry. I just…well, it's all so unfair, isn't it? I thought men and women were supposed to be equal before Ytraa?'

'So we are.'

'Why aren't there any male virgins along on this jolly, then?'

Tumalind had no answer, but it set her wondering. Dilanthas just shrugged.

When the sun had dried them, they returned to the small encampment upstream to find Phildrad busy with his pots and herbs, a delicious aroma greeting them. Tryonta turned away as they approached and Tumalind was unable to resist making a comment.

'What's the matter, Tryonta? Only like to look at us without our clothes?'

He turned and glared at her, seemed about to retort when Dagla Kaz interrupted his discussion with Grahtl and fixed Tryonta with a stare that had him considering his feet.

'Didn't know you were there.'

He opened his mouth to speak but Porryh's comment sent him into the trees.

'Like last time? An' the time afore that?'

'What's cooking, Phildrad?'

He looked up from his pot and smiled at Tumalind, glanced at the other two girls with a satisfied expression. He put his finger to the side of his nose. 'That's for me to know and you to eat.'

'Rhaat again, then?'

He shook his fist at her but they all knew the gesture was good-humoured and they left him to the job he was happiest at and went to sit with Corphanda and Wendarah in the shade under a spreading tree.

'What's Jhonaht doin'?'

'Ytraa only knows, Dilanthas. He's forever fiddlin' with that thing. When I asks what it is, he looks at me like I'm just a stupid woman and won't understand.'

'I don't know exactly how it works, Corphanda, but he can tell how accurate the map is by pointing that thing at the sun and reading the direction of the pointer.'

Wendarah was startled. 'You know about the map, Tumalind?'

'Dagla Kaz dropped it when I was walking past. I picked it up. I thought he was going to hit me but he just shrugged and shook his head. I didn't realize it was secret.'

'It's not, now. How come Jhonaht explains things to you, Tumalind, when he clearly thinks the rest of us are too dumb to understand?' Wendarah seemed serious.

'Got the hots for Tumalind has our Jhonaht.'

'Jhonaht? The hots? Come on, Porryh, Jhonaht's only ever shown interest in one woman and that was Jodisa-Li's mother. Even then, his interest was mostly aesthetic. He's the only man I know who doesn't like frowking.'

'Is there summat wrong wi' 'im, like? Not a sagger, is 'e?'

'Dilanthas! You just scrub your tongue; using words like that about the Chief Astronomer. I never heard the like! Gettin' far too familiar, being on this trip and on the road. I'll be taking a hand to your naughty little bum if I hear any more o' that sort of talk from you, young lady, that I will and no mistake. Sagger, indeed. I never did.'

'Looks like Corphanda's got the hots for him, anyway.'

'Cheeky young madam. I'll be marking your wicked bum too if you're not careful, Porryh. I've got respect, that's what. Respect for a man so clever an' informed. Jhonaht's got more knowledge in 'is tiny toe than you've got in the 'ole of that over-developed body of yours.'

'Not jealous, are we, Corphanda? Not just a bit envious 'cos my curves are so fetching and yours are…?' Porryh stood and backed away as Corphanda rose and moved toward her. 'Have to be faster than that, Corphanda. You'll not catch me so easily.' And she trotted away over the sparse grass, totally unaware that Corphanda was hard on her heels.

Tumalind and the others watched as the unlikely pair, hunter; ungainly but surprisingly fleet, and prey; graceful but inattentive, closed. They heard the smack from where they sat and had to laugh as Corphanda waddled back rubbing her hands together with satisfaction, followed by Porryh, rubbing her bottom with regret.

'Might've warned me she was on my tail.'

'No more than you deserve, Porryh. You should know by now that Corphanda's bite's worse than her bark.'

They all laughed at Wendarah's remark.

Phildrad rattled a stick against his cooking pot and they moved toward the fire, eager to eat. He served them himself, ensuring each got a portion of all the ingredients. But, no matter how they pressed him, he refused to reveal exactly what they were eating. They knew, of course, there was meat from the spiny creature that Grahtl had speared during the day and that the wild garlic they'd dug from the shadows near the riverbank trees was in the pot. But what else he'd included, he wouldn't say.

They sat in two rows on the fallen tree trunks that Caarl, Tarruss and Jhonaht had rolled into place either side of the fire. The meal was welcome on this, their third night out of the village. Grahtl and Tryonta had kept them reasonably well fed on the journey but this meal was the best they'd managed so far and was helped by the trees that gave welcome shade.

Dagla Kaz held up his hand and they stopped their conversation and waited for his announcement. 'I have to tell you that Grahtl will set us on the road tomorrow and then return home to his village.'

'I thought he was taking us to Xythonl?'

'He was going to, Wendarah, but he tells me the rains are on the way and Jhonaht agrees. They're early and both our forecasters believe the rain will start either tomorrow night or the following day. Grahtl obviously must go home before the road becomes impassable. The river, apparently, will be a raging torrent once the rains set in and he'd have to wait three weeks before he'd be able to cross back again.'

'What'll we do, Dagla Kaz? We can't expect these girls to walk through that sort of weather. I take it the rains must be 'eavy and we can expect everythin' to be soaked. And, if I know anything about such things, and I do, there'll be the danger of fever. That sort of thing always comes wi' bad weather and we can't afford to have the girls fall sick whilst we're travellin'. This should've been planned for, you know. It really is too much to expect...'

'Yes, Corphanda. Your concern for your charges does you credit, but let me explain. First of all, I've no intention of walking through the rains. It would be impossible anyway. But there's a town called Qlentz a little over two days easy walk from here. We'll be setting off at sun up to make our way there. If we don't dawdle, we should cover the ground in a day and a half. We'll stay there until the rains end. As for planning, I could hardly be expected to have forecast the problems with the pirates, could I? Though our astronomer might've read the auguries a little more accurately....'

'My calculations failed to include a long stay in Rhonholoah. Had that visit, as I said at the time, lasted only three days, we'd have avoided the pirates and been in Shorrannon by now.'

'Perhaps. In any case, I agree that had all gone according to plan, we would by now be in Shorrannon, the northern limit of the rains. But, Ytraa has decreed we should have a more difficult journey, for reasons we'll all come to understand in time, no doubt. We can't travel in the rains and Grahtl tells me that Qlentz is the nearest place we can expect to find shelter, so, I suggest we all get some sleep and hope to wake up refreshed and ready for a long, swift march in the morning.'

Chapter 31

An Unforeseen Delay

'At last!' Jodisa-Li tried to hide the amusement in her voice at his obvious sheepishness.

Okkyntalah had the good grace to look a little shame faced as he explained his absence of three days. 'I couldn't get away. Every time I left one and tried to find my way here, another took me in. It's more by luck than judgement that I'm here, at all. I ran into Malarhah as I was leaving a hut. She brought me most of the way and directed me the rest, otherwise I might've wandered lost and been claimed again for more days and nights.'

Feldrark nodded his understanding. 'Well, you're here now, young 'un. We've things to plan; and at once. How important is Tumalind to you?'

'What do you know of Tumalind?'

'What Jodisa-Li told me. Do you love her as you've declared?'

'We're betrothed. She's the one I want to spend my life with.'

'But you're happy to lie with others meanwhile.'

'Tumalind's not here. For all I know, I'll never see her again. We're stuck in this stinking mire till Aglydron completes his task with that woman, anyway. You've been with the women here. We're all Followers; it's what we're supposed to do, isn't it?'

'I don't have a life-long partner yet, Okkyntalah. When I do, I'll see no other.'

Jodisa-Li saw he meant exactly what he said but wasn't sure how she felt about his declaration or, indeed, why she should care.

'If that's the way of it with you. I only know what we're Commanded to do by Ytraa.'

Myllthlan stood and put her arm about his waist. 'I understand, Okkyntalah. So do they. We just need to know how much you'd like to leave here.'

'I'd leave right now if I could. What they offer is like the fruit of the shyltharn; a picture of delight with a promise of wonder but with flesh that cloys in the mouth and leaves a taste more bitter than gall. No. Give me freedom, a forest full of game, the liberty to move at will and the promise of my Tumalind waiting at home. I've frowked for three days and nights and I still see only Tumalind in my mind. But we can't go until Aglydron's free.'

'We can free Aglydron'

'We don't even know where he is.'

'We know where he is. We know where the Staff of Ytraa is hidden. We know where the boat's lying at...'

'Staff of Ytraa?'

Feldrark explained. 'And Malarhah found the Staff, as she predicted, on the Galhta's tower. Our escape won't be easy but I've planned it all as...'

'Malarhah? Won't she betray us? I mean, isn't she...?'

'I'm taking her with me, as a free woman, to Litkala. She loathes these people and has already proved herself an invaluable ally. Malarhah can be trusted. What do you think Aglydron will do? We've no way to warn him of our plans.'

Okkyntalah looked askance at Feldrark. 'I don't wish to be rude to a stranger, but if you're from Litkala, I'll have nothing more to do with you. It's a place we've been told to avoid because of the cruelty and corruption of the Followers there. Why should we...?'

'I'll forgive your insult, young man, because your native stupidity makes you speak of what you know not. Litkala is civilized, educated, generous and tolerant, as you'll see for yourself, if you live long enough to reach it.'

'Our priests say the Followers there are evil beyond imagination and that cruel acts and foul abuses go on daily. They say the name of the Lord Gadhallah is reviled there and...'

'They speak from ignorance. There's been no contact between our peoples for over fourteen hundred cycles. If I were to believe all I've been told of Muhnilahm I'd have to give you black skins and wild eyes, and have you constantly naked whilst eating your children. The fact that I don't believe a word of it merely shows I've more intelligence than you display and that the words of our ancestors are clearly false.'

'You insult easily for a man alone. I'd have you take back your affronts unless you'd feel the edge of my blade.'

'Stop it! Both of you. Like squabbling children. It's perfectly obvious we've been told a pack of lies about each other. Let's rely on the evidence of our eyes, shall we? I was schooled by my father to believe all sorts of evil about Litkala. Feldrark's their spiritual leader, Okkyntalah, and everything I've learned from him tells me that his people are good, kind and tolerant.'

'Maybe, but you're influenced by the fact that he wants to frowk you until the end of time. He hasn't touched you, has he, Jodisa?'

'Unfortunately not.' It was out of her mouth before she knew it. A quick glance at Feldrark confirmed her slip was welcome and she relaxed again, not caring what the boy might think.

'Jodisa-Li's right. I apologise for my shortness, Okkyntalah. Perhaps you'll accept her word about my restraint with her as well? It's hard to be given a reputation you don't deserve. I've learned things from this beautiful young lady that make me believe I've been equally misinformed. We have each other to test in the flesh, isn't that a more reliable measure of our worth than the prejudice of centuries of ignorance?'

Okkyntalah glowered but then nodded, sullenly. 'I accept what you say, for the moment. But I withhold my judgement until I've seen things for myself.'

'That'll do, for the time being. Now, can we talk about the things that really matter?'

Jodisa-Li again reviewed her opinion of Feldrark. He was a much more complex and likeable figure than she'd originally been inclined to admit. She found him increasingly interesting and attractive.

Okkyntalah asked Feldrark for his plans. He nodded his approval and agreed the plan was basically sound. 'But they'll pursue us. What can we do about…?

'We've that planned also. All is covered.'

'Aglydron will give trouble if Jodisa goes to free him. He'll think she's trying to betray him. It's best I release him. He'll trust me.'

'I need you to get your boat into free water. It's stuck in the middle of their reed boats and I need someone who can sail to free it.'

'Jodisa's a far better sailor than any of us. She's brilliant. She can handle the boat. Let her take Myllthlan, so they can carry the supplies. Best if Shaulah goes with them, as well.'

Jodisa-Li was delighted to hear her skills described to Feldrark.

'Will your dog behave and be still?'

'She'll be quiet at need. Trust me, she's well trained.'

'She's a good animal to have around in a crisis; I speak from experience, Feldrark.'

He looked at Jodisa-Li with curiosity but she wasn't prepared to interrupt with other tales. 'Very well.'

'Malarhah and you can get the Staff and I'll get Aglydron.'

Malarhah swept aside the curtain with one hand and entered with food and drink. 'You'll never find your way to him or the harbour on your own. I'll have to take you both to get the Staff and then all three of us can get Aglydron.'

Jodisa-Li laughed at the surprise on Okkyntalah's face and explained Malarhah's deception to him.

'You give a good act, Malarhah. You fooled me.'

'I've fooled them most of my life here. I'll be so pleased when I can be myself again.'

Malarhah's idea made sense. The four of them would return to the harbour together.

'Won't the townsfolk be suspicious?'

Malarhah smiled at Myllthlan. 'You haven't ventured out after sundown, have you?'

She shook her head.

'No one's abroad once darkness falls. They've a morbid fear of the dark, encouraged by the Galhta for reasons I've never fully understood. But I often walk the streets at night and see not a single soul. Barefoot, you can pass without a sound.'

They planned the escape for the following night to give Malarhah time to collect food and drink for the first part of their journey. In the middle of the night, Jodisa-Li woke to a roaring, rushing noise that filled the air about her.

Malarhah reassured her in the morning. 'The rains. They've come early. Every cycle, they come. There'll be no one on the streets now unless they have urgent business. I'll be kept busy carrying food and drink. It makes no difference to our plan. At least no one will abuse me whilst the rains fall. This could be our saving. Everything will be easier now.'

'Except for you, Malarhah. You'll be exhausted.'

'It's only for one day. I've had to work the whole rains before and they last for three sixdays most cycles. I'll be tired, but I'll be all right.'

Whilst they were at prayers, Malarhah left them and didn't return until their midday meal was due. Soaked and dripping, already she was tired; her shoulders marked with stripes where she'd carried heavy flagons on their straps all morning. She brought them food and drink. Feldrark kissed her forehead as she left and begged her to take care.

'I'm fine. I'll be back this evening with our last meal in Mipahnhil and supplies for the journey.'

The day proved long and they used the time in swapping tales; Feldrark explaining to Okkyntalah how he came to be a prisoner and Okkyntalah telling Feldrark the whole reason for their mission. Feldrark looked at Jodisa-Li with mild disapproval and shook his head at her deception.

'What do you expect? I've no wish to go to Choshinahm. I'm of the blood. I've been schooled to lead; not serve. For all we know, the people there might be savages now. Who knows what's happened since our last visit?'

'I understand your apprehension, Jodisa-Li, but I wish you'd trusted me enough to give me the whole tale. I'm not a savage and I have power as a Follower. All may not have to be as Aglydron and Okkyntalah deem.'

'How else could it be? She's been Chosen. Tumalind was substituted falsely. It can't be any other way.'

'It might. But now isn't the time to discuss it.'

No matter how Okkyntalah pressed him, Feldrark refused to be drawn further on the topic. Jodisa-Li considered his words and pondered why, given the opportunities he'd had during Okkyntalah's absence, he hadn't even tried to seduce her. She wondered exactly how the Wharhll of Litkala might alter her future.

⋆──⋆──⋆

Sundown came with no more than increasing darkness. The Followers made their obeisance and waited for Malarhah. Nervous and apprehensive, now their escape was close, they fell to bickering until Feldrark reminded them their lives were at stake in this enterprise.

'What we plan is more than just a simple leaving. Some may be hurt by our departure and they don't forgive such injury in Mipahnhil. None of us wishes to harm another soul but we must be prepared to shed blood if necessary. We need calm, now; and steady nerves. If you can't rest your tongue, Okkyntalah, find what relief you may with Myllthlan. I need you in control and brave, not nervous and unsteady.'

The rebuke was enough and the boy took the woman into one of the bedchambers almost at once, leaving Feldrark alone with Jodisa-Li.

When they emerged, Feldrark was growing anxious. 'Malarhah should be here by now. We're lost without her. Not that I'd leave her behind. She should be here.'

'She told you; she's others to cater for in the rains. We must be patient.'

Feldrark nodded at Myllthlan and saw how serene she appeared. The boy must be good with women.

'You're right. Perhaps I should follow my own advice and take you back in there?'

'I'll willingly serve you as I might, Feldrark. But might you not need that energy for other things this night?'

'I've energy and enough; it was but a jest.'

'Perhaps.'

The flash of jealousy that stuck an angry mask on Jodisa-Li's face was justification enough for his comment and provided more evidence of her strong feelings for him. That was better than good: he intended to have Jodisa-Li as his bride. Not even her father could prevent it. She was eager to join with him. For her, it was only a question of opportunity. For Feldrark, there were other considerations that meant he'd do nothing until the right time.

'I will, however, take a rest; alone, if you don't mind.'

He made himself comfortable in the dim bedchamber and focussed his thoughts.

'Ivdulon, I have need of your counsel.'

'Feldrark! At last. You've been silent too long. I was considering breaking your command and making contact with you.'

'I'm pleased you didn't. Nothing to report until now.'

He explained about the new arrivals and their plan to escape.

'Should I send a party to meet you?'

'No. I need to impress the young woman, Jodisa-Li, as I intend...'

'Jodisa-Li? Her companions are Okkyntalah and Aglydron of Muhnilahm...'

'You know of them?'

They exchanged the information each knew and Feldrark spent longer with Ivdulon than he'd intended.

'I'll keep you informed of our progress. But under no circumstances are you to send help unless I specifically request it, as before.'

'Ever the stubborn independent lad.'

'Too many things of import hang on me getting this exactly right, Ivdulon. Fortunately, Jodisa-Li's very beautiful; the chase and capture will be that much more rewarding. Her relationship to Dagla Kaz makes her even more important to us, especially if she's a potential mindtalker; wonderful. We must ensure the High Priest isn't alerted to his own gift yet. His susceptibility could well be crucial in our plans.'

'I agree. But I wish you'd allow me to set some help in motion. You're far too important to lose in some act of bravado.'

'Not bravado, Ivdulon. Without courage and independence I'm nothing. Stop fussing like a mother hen.'

'I can't help but care, Feldrark. You're like a son to me.'

'Just as my father was. You're a sweet and loving woman, Ivdulon, but please don't smother me.'

'I don't know who worries me most these days; you or that philanderer on the island, Aklon-Dji. Both essential to the greater scheme and both reckless. Please don't contact him yet; the interaction might encourage a competition in which both of you will be even more rash than you are already. Take care, Feldrark; much depends on you staying alive.'

'I intend to live a long and full life, Ivdulon, never fear. But I must go; they may come upon me in this state at any moment. Let my parents know I'm well and will soon be free. Farewell.'

He cut the contact before his mentor could argue more with him and returned to the company of the others.

They all waited in darkness, hearing rain pounding the boards outside, barely masked by the thatch and the woven rushes at door and window. But Malarhah never came.

Morning found them weary, hungry and anxious. An old crone brought sodden food and one flagon of poor wine and would have left without a word had Feldrark not stopped her.

'Where's Malarhah?'

'Eh?'

'The girl who's been my servant all the time I've been here. Where is she?'

'Dunno.'

'Tell me where she is, old woman, or I'll have you beaten.'

The old woman backed away, cowered and whimpered. 'Young Paltrohn hurt her, they say. She'll 'ave to rest a bit afore she's well enough to work again.'

'Where is she?'

'Slaves' quarters. Where else?'

'Take me.'

She flinched and dropped to her knees. 'Daren't take you there, Paltrohn! They'll skin my backside. No.'

'I'll skin every filthy morsel of you if you don't. But, if you do, I'll give you this.' Feldrark showed her the jewelled empty scabbard that had held his sword.

'I'll take you, Paltrohn. Don't want no present. They'd say I stole it an 'ang me upside down on the tower till I rotted away. I'll take you. Onny don't tell no one.'

Feldrark nodded. 'I'll be as quick as I can.'

And he was out into the rain with the old woman, buckling his belt as he walked streets running with water. Already, the river beneath the town was flooding and washing away the gathered detritus of the past cycle; flushing it into the sea, raising the stench afresh.

They walked a tortuous path to the harbour and across the small wharf, where occasional merchant ships tied up. The sailors, suspicious of the reputation of the town, usually remained aboard to be entertained by some of the more desperate women from the town, hoping for a child, and by slaves, earning money for their masters. But the wharf was deserted now and would remain so until dry weather returned and the level of the river dropped again. The old woman led him in sight of an area of dilapidated huts on the edge of the town. She wouldn't take him nearer.

'There. I'll not go in. I've work to do.'

'Thank you, mother. I'm sorry I had to bully you. Take this for your trouble.'

She gave him a toothless grin of surprised gratitude for his kind words and for the small coin he took from his scrip. Leaving him, she hobbled back the way they'd come.

The thatch was poor and rotting, the walls bowed with age and disrepair, the huts small and crammed together. There were no reed curtains, no windows, merely crude open entrances into dank interiors.

Feldrark entered the only occupied hut. Three slaves huddled on the floor, uncovered and apparently abandoned to their fate. A small man lay whimpering in a fevered sleep. An old woman, scabbed and so thin that her ribs poked hard against her skin, lay dying for want of care. And Malarhah, still and uncomplaining, lay curled like an infant in the corner of the room. Her eyes were closed and she gasped as if in pain.

'Malarhah?'

She started, winced and opened an eye. The other, he could see now, was closed with swelling where she'd been hit. 'Leave me. Let me die in peace.'

Feldrark knelt at her side and touched her, feeling for signs of fever and finding chill. He probed gently for places she was damaged. She tried to bite back her moans of pain but he discovered she was hurt in several places, and bleeding between her legs.

He cradled her and lifted her from the floor. 'Your skirt?'

'Gone.'

He took her into the rain, held in his arms like a baby, and walked back to the hut he shared with the others. They were drenched when they arrived but the downpour had washed her skin clean of the fouling.

'What happened?'

He laid her on one of the settles. 'I need cloths, something to dry her with and something she can wear when I've attended to her hurts.'

Jodisa-Li emptied their packs onto the floor and took stock. Clothing was their only fabric.

'There are enough tabards for us to have one each to wear and a spare to wear when one's in need of a wash.' Jodisa-Li handed him a fine tabard of expensive violet silk. 'Let her wear this. I'll cut the other to a shorter length and take a portion for cloths to bathe and dress her wounds. It'll leave a scanty garment, better than going naked, but not much.'

'There's no need to ruin our clothes, Jodisa-Li. Tear some strips from the bedding in there. And let me attend her.'

'Of course, Myllthlan. See what you can do for her, please.'

Jodisa-Li urged Feldrark out of the way and Myllthlan made her preparations.

She touched Malarhah's swollen eye first, drawing out the bruising and allowing it to open again with surprise. The bruise beneath her left breast was clearly tender to the touch but Myllthlan was gentle as she eased it with her fingertips and brought the flesh back to normal as Feldrark gazed in amazement. There was a gash open under her right buttock and she closed this with her fingers, blowing on the wound until the skin repaired itself. The man who'd attacked and used her so savagely, had kicked her before and after raping her, so that she was bruised and cut. The damage wasn't, however, as great as it first appeared. Her forced walk from the scene of the attack had kept the wounds open and the rough floor of the slaves' quarters had made her restless, preventing the flesh from healing. The healer placed her mouth over the wounds and blew softly. Feldrark turned his head away, embarrassed by this intimacy. When he returned his gaze to the slave girl, it was to find her seated and examining herself with amazed delight that she appeared whole and unhurt.

She moved to stand and winced with pain.

'Internal damage. What did he put inside you apart from his prod?'

Malarhah looked at Myllthlan with wonder. 'A reed stem. How did you know?'

'I'm a healer. I'm sorry. I must make sure there's nothing left inside to cause poison and give you fever. I might hurt you. Are you ready?'

Malarhah nodded. Myllthlan asked Okkyntalah to kneel with the girl's head in his lap and relax her with gentle touches whilst Feldrark and Jodisa-Li held her legs apart. She investigated quickly and efficiently, recovering two long splinters of sharp stalk, bloodied and bent from the force of their intrusion.

'I can see nothing more but there are internal injuries I can't reach to heal. Time will cure them. You'll be in pain and you'll bleed for a while, Malarhah. It's best if you lie still for a day or so.' She turned to Feldrark and Jodisa-Li and smiled. 'You can let her legs go now. But stay where you are, Okkyntalah; you're attentions are helping her.'

Myllthlan finished her healing process, passing back her energy and power to the sky before taking her place on the settle again. She looked weary and fell asleep almost at once.

'Incredible. Has she done that sort of thing before?'

Okkyntalah and Jodisa-Li explained their experiences, the girl hiding nothing of the cause for her injuries. Feldrark glowered and determined that Aglydron would pay for his cruelty when the opportunity arose.

'You're whole now?'

She turned and displayed to him. Malarhah smiled at the delight on his face.

'Jodisa! It's one thing to accept this heathen practice of communal nakedness, it's quite another to go showing your all to Feldrark.'

She turned to Okkyntalah. 'Sorry, didn't know you wanted to look as well. Oh, sorry, I forgot. You already have.'

He blushed and said no more.

Feldrark, reassured of her good health and unspoiled skin, turned his attention back to Malarhah. 'What happened?'

'I was on my way to get our meal when he called me into his hut. I had no choice, of course. He was alone. I told him I was busy getting food and drink but he made me lie across the table. His seed spilled before he entered me and he fell into a rage. He punched and kicked me. Said it was my fault. I don't know if it was the hurting or the blood or what, but he was stiff again and he shoved and thrust until his seed was planted. Then he kicked me again and used the stick until I begged him to stop. He pushed me out into the rain.'

'Before we leave, show me where his hut is. I'll make certain he never treats another woman that way.'

'Oh, he won't, Feldrark. No one treats Malarhah that way and gets away with it. I went back inside. He was crouching at the waste pipe and I hit him on the head with his stick. He never even cried out. I pushed him head first down the pipe and he fell through. He won't attack another woman.'

Feldrark stared with horror at her tale, yet when he thought to chastise her, he could devise no reproof. She'd merely given back what she'd suffered. But he determined never to give her cause to take revenge on him.

She'd crawled to the slaves' quarters and told the old crone to get food for Feldrark and the others before she'd collapsed on the floor.

They were all silent for some time after her account and Malarhah, exhausted and unrepentant after her ordeal but feeling safe and secure, fell asleep just as Myllthlan awoke.

'We'll have to wait for Malarhah's wounds to heal; at least until they're closed and won't bleed when she walks, before we can attempt our escape.'

'How long, Myllthlan?'

'She's young and healthy. Two or three days. If we're lucky.'

'Longer than I'd hoped, but we'll have to manage, I suppose. I just hope they remember to feed us. We'll have to keep Malarhah hidden until she's well enough to travel; if they see her on her feet they'll expect her to work regardless of any internal injuries.'

They turned to the scant provisions brought by the crone and shared them, wondering how they'd fare for the next few days. They would now have to make their escape attempt on poor rations and with no extra provisions to take with them.

Chapter 32

A RESCUE IN THE RAIN

*T*he party crossed the river on stepping-stones. Grahtl said a tribe of giants, chasing humans for food, had laid them down. The River Vobrah was wide but generally shallow and, so the story went, the giants didn't like wet feet. Whatever the legend, Tumalind was glad someone had spanned the water with long, flattish stones, allowing them to cross without having to wade or even wet their feet. Only the central portion, some forty paces across, was deep enough to have to swim if the stones hadn't been in place. It would've been difficult crossing with their packs, but they tossed these to each other before jumping the wide gaps.

On the far bank, she waited as the others crossed. Dagla Kaz looked across the water as he chatted with Jhonaht. 'Well, that explains why the road's so poor, at any rate.'

'Dagla Kaz?'

'No bridge, so no road transport for goods. You don't suppose we build roads for foot travellers, do you?'

'I hadn't given the matter much thought, Dagla Kaz, but you make sense. Perhaps it's bridged further upstream?'

'I doubt it. There's only Qlentz and Xythonl on the western coast between here and the Unnamed Mountains. Doubt it's worthwhile spending the money or labour, Jhonaht.'

Tumalind was curious. 'So, they do all their trade by ship, Dagla Kaz?'

He turned and smiled at her. 'You show a great deal of sense for a young uneducated woman from a small settlement, Tumalind. I could almost wish Ytraa hadn't Chosen you. I believe you might have the potential to become rather bright, given the right circumstances.'

His words made her head swim. That she might be seen as somehow special, in no matter how small a way, had never occurred to her. But she was unable to pursue the matter further as the rest of the party had made the riverbank and they set off straight away.

Grahtl set a good pace, stopping only for short breaks. Water was no problem as the track ran beside the river; another reason for their guide's hurry. A couple of hours before sundown, with the sky still clear and the day as hot as ever, he stopped and pointed ahead to where the road left the river to rise toward a forest. He explained they must keep the trees on their right and ignore the track, as brigands living in the forest sometimes ambushed travellers on the path. On the very edge of the trees there was a good chance these robbers, who were likely to be less active with the rains on the way, wouldn't notice them.

He left, to return home, and they set off into the unknown. Tumalind, anxious after her kidnapping and their brush with the pirates, kept her eyes on the trees. Nevertheless, the party moved quickly and didn't stop until the light failed, by which time they'd travelled a good league, were well above the river and no longer close to the road.

They'd walked all day without breaking to eat, foraging in wayside shrubs and trees for what fruit they could find. Grahtl and Tryonta hadn't hunted, so their first night on the edge of the forest was a weary and hungry affair. They slept without a fire, taking turns to keep watch. At sun up, Dagla Kaz led brief prayers. They breakfasted on berries and wild merphlion, growing on vines that climbed the tall trees into the canopy. The fruit wasn't as sweet as the homegrown variety but provided liquid as well as sustenance and they set off with their bellies full for the last leg to Qlentz.

The vanguards of the rain clouds had blown across the forest in the night and now stretched as far as the open horizon to their left; heavy, grey and threatening. As the day lengthened, their tabards clung to them, uncomfortable and sticky.

They walked quickly but in silence; anxious they wouldn't reach the city before rain began to fall. Four leagues passed underfoot with only the sounds of birds and the occasional scurry of small animals rustling from their path. Wendarah startled a long, thin, blue and black snake, which hissed at her before vanishing into the undergrowth. The air was heavy with the sickly sweet scent of zopoloah, its tiny flowers carpeting the entire area. It reminded Tumalind of home and Shoarhn but she couldn't recall why, until Dilanthas mentioned an antiseptic the midwives had used on her mother following the birth of her youngest brother.

A whimper of fear, so close it seemed almost to come from the party, stopped them, but they could see nothing. Just as they were about to set out again, the sound of a heavy beast rampaging halted in a thin scream of terror. Tarruss, Caarl and Phildrad drew their weapons and slipped into the trees. Within seconds, Tumalind heard a heavy creature trampling the ground and attacking the men. Dagla Kaz, Tryonta and Jhonaht formed a line with the Virgin Gifts behind them. Shouts, and another scream from a woman, came through the dense vegetation and then all was silent.

Leaves and branches shuddered and wavered as Caarl returned, sword bloodied and a gash, the length of the forearm bearing the weapon, bleeding onto his hand. He supported Phildrad, white and dishevelled, his tabard ripped. A rent pulsed with blood along a jagged line from above his hip to his inner thigh. Neither man spoke. The vegetation shifted again to reveal Tarruss, a woman draped in his arms, blood dripping from a slash under his eye, and his sword dripping gore. There was a brief threshing from behind him and then silence.

At once, Corphanda unrolled her pack and took out her herbs. 'Tear some strips of cloth, wide as your hand and long as you can. Do it quick or Phildrad'll bleed to death. Caarl and Tarruss, sit down. Come on; move. Don't stand there, gawping. One of you girls see to the woman while I look after these men. And someone pull some zopoloah for me'

Tumalind helped Tarruss lay the woman on the ground. Her bright cotton wrap was in shreds but her skin was only scratched. She was insensible. Tarruss stood by as Tumalind used the woman's rags, dipped in water from her carrier, to bathe her superficial wounds.

'Keep still, Phildrad!' Corphanda doused his wound with fresh-crushed zopoloah and water. Wendarah and Porryh ripped a tabard into strips for her.

'What was it, Tarruss?'

He looked over her shoulder into the trees, shaking his head. 'Terzet-horn. Biggest I've seen. Had her backed up against a tree. Toying with her. Never seen anything like it.'

'Is it dead?' Tumalind knew a wounded terzet-horn, with its three sharp horns and vicious teeth, was an awesome foe.

''Tis now. Phildrad…he, well, he just went straight at it! Never seen such courage. Had a blade through its eye when it gored him. I managed to pull the lass out the way, then it turned on me. Too quick for it, though. And Caarl stuck it in its throat. I sent them back and got another blow to its neck. It was threshing about when I left. Sounds like the bowelcreep's dead now, though.'

The woman stirred and Tumalind lifted her head onto her lap. 'Was anyone with her?'

Tarruss shook his head.

'Your turn, Tarruss. Let's get that cut seen to. Now, don't be a baby, it's only to stop infection. Is Phildrad keeping still? If he's not, he'll have me to answer to.'

The woman, pale and afraid, looked up into Tumalind's face.

'You're safe now. It's dead.'

It was what she needed to hear and she sighed with relief and began to sit up.

'Stay there for a bit. We're not going anywhere. Rest. You've had a nasty shock.'

The woman closed deep blue eyes and rested her head back in Tumalind's lap. Tumalind looked down at the loose, long tresses of copper gold, spread over her thighs in a shining fall. She was older than Tumalind but young still and had a childlike quality for all her voluptuary and maturity. Her body was firm but rounded as though well fed. The skin was lighter than her own, a pale honey colour.

'Thought I'd best get summat to cover 'er'.' Dilanthas held out her pale blue tabard.

'Can you stand?'

The woman looked up past Tumalind to Dilanthas. She suddenly seemed alarmed.

'It's all right. The men are busy. Put this on and you'll be fine.'

She frowned at the garment, until Dilanthas helped her. She was threading bronze pegs through kid loops when Dagla Kaz came over.

'Well, young lady. Are you unhurt?

She stood straight, head bowed, hands behind her back.

'I'm Dagla Kaz; leader of this party of pilgrims. Do you have a name?'

'Netrodyl, Paltrohn.'

'And where are you from, Netrodyl?'

'From Qlentz, Paltrohn.'

'Are you alone?'

'Yes, Paltrohn.'

'Are you hurt?'

'Just sore, Paltrohn, thank you.'

'We're on our way to Qlentz. Will you guide us?'

'As you wish, Paltrohn.'

Dagla Kaz gestured to Tumalind and Dilanthas to take charge of their guest. He returned to Corphanda who was examining the dressings on both Caarl and Phildrad.

Caarl told her to stop fussing. 'I've suffered worse in battle training.'

Phildrad, however, was cause for concern. The wound, in an awkward place to dress, was likely to open with each step. He'd also lost a good deal of blood and, though able and willing to stand, looked as though he might fall over at any moment.

Dagla Kaz shook his head and looked to Caarl, who approached the woman. She again bowed her head and placed her hands behind her back.

'Netrodyl?'

'Yes, Paltrohn.'

'Oh, I'm not Paltrohn. Caarl, please. How far is Qlentz from here?'

'A…it's a short walk, Palt…Caarl, Paltrohn.'

Caarl tipped her face up with his fingertips under her chin. 'We mean you no harm, dear. Don't be afraid.'

She wouldn't look into his eyes and seemed distressed that he looked so directly into hers, blushing and trying to turn her face away. 'Thank you, Palt…Caarl, Paltrohn.'

Like Dagla Kaz, Caarl was unsure what to make of her behaviour and went to discuss the best plan of action with the others.

'Netrodyl, I'm Tumalind. This is Dilanthas.'

The woman looked at Tumalind and smiled openly. 'Thank you for helping me.'

'What are you doing out here on your own?'

She broke into a wide smile of mischief. 'I ran away.'

'Who from?'

Wendarah's question seemed to give her heart. 'I was bad. I was; bad as can be. I wouldn't do it. He was going to strap me and put me in the basket for a day. A whole day! I wasn't that bad. It's not fair. He only does it 'cos I won't…anyway, I ran away.'

'What'll happen when you go back?'

'Happen?'

'Won't he punish you anyway? Maybe even…?'

'Punish me? I ran away. He can't punish me if I ran away, can he? He won't, will he? I mean, he can't. I ran away!'

'But you're going back?'

'Yes. He'll be sorry.'

Caarl came over. 'We're going to make a litter to carry Phildrad. Would you cut some thin vines to bind it with, Tumalind, whilst we trim some boughs?' He passed her a knife.

Netrodyl's eyes grew wide with admiration at the knife in Tumalind's hand. 'Sorry, Paltra, I didn't realize. Only you seem so young, if you don't mind me saying so?'

'I've eighteen cycles, just. Why are you calling me Paltra? I'm just plain Tumalind. How old are you?'

'Twenty-four summers. But the knife. He gave you a knife, Paltra. You must be senior woman.'

'No. Just a Virgin Gift. I suppose Wendarah, well, Kaz-Ca-Wendarah, really, is the senior woman, since she's a Village Priestess. But we…'

'Priestess? Women can be priests?'

'Women can be whatever they like, can't they?' Tumalind cut lengths from the vines, thinner than her finger and as long as she could make them.

Caarl and Tarruss hacked off stout boughs, trimmed them and laid them on the ground in an oblong as Tryonta chopped some into shorter lengths to form cross pieces. She took her vines to the men and helped bind the joints.

'You work with men?'

'We all do what we can.'

'They don't…I mean, don't they, well, look at you?'

'Sometimes. But let's just get this done so we can be on our way. We don't want to get caught in the rains, do we?'

'Rains?'

Tumalind pointed to the sky, growing darker and heavier even as they spoke. 'They'll be here tonight, I expect, and I'd rather be under cover before they come.'

'How do you know?'

'Oh, Jhonaht told us. But it's fairly obvious, isn't it? I mean, just look at the clouds.'

This, however, seemed no answer for Netrodyl, who continued to stare at Tumalind as though she was some exotic creature from myth and legend.

The litter complete, they padded it with sleepsacks and made Phildrad lie on it, much against his will.

'Try to walk with that wound, my lad, and you'll bleed to death inside a league. Do as you're told. And lie still. I'll have no arguments. I'm not wasting precious medicines on some daft man who doesn't know when he needs help. So, less of your complaints, and keep yourself still, or you'll know what for.'

'Is she your shaman?'

'Shaman?' Tumalind had come across the term in conversation with Baklan and understood it meant a mystic with healing powers. 'Corphanda? No, she's just a bossy fat old woman who knows a bit about healing.'

'I heard that, Tumalind. Don't think you're immune from a smack just because…'

'I've got a smack in hand, don't forget.'

'Just as well. Old indeed! You've used up your credit, so let's have no more cheek.'

'Whatever you say, Corphanda.' She turned to Netrodyl. 'She's all right, really. Just likes to feel she's in charge, you know.'

'I don't understand. You work with men, talk with them; you insult your shaman, you hold a knife like you've done it all your life and you're only a child, and a virgin. Why, even I'm senior to you! Won't they punish you?'

'Well, Corphanda's got a hefty smack if you're unlucky, but I've not done much to deserve even that, to be honest.'

'She's right enough. Young Tumalind's least of my worries if truth's to be told.'

'But what about respect?'

'I respect those who deserve it. Dagla Kaz, of course, and Jhonaht for his learning. I respect everybody, really, for different reasons.'

'But you talk with them, argue, even. This can't be right.'

'Well, it's the way I am, Netrodyl. The way most of us are, I suppose.'

Caarl, Tryonta, Tarruss and Jhonaht took a corner each of the litter. Dagla Kaz ensured everybody was ready again and they set off across the open ground beside the trees in the general direction of the city.

'I...is it alright to ask you, Tumalind?'

'Ask whatever you like, Netrodyl.'

The woman hesitated and then made up her mind. 'Why don't you use the road?'

'Our guide told us we might meet robbers.'

'Oh. Well, they're all dead now. Gret-Zudas sent out hunters and they came back with their heads on sticks. Gret-Zudas was fed up of them making the way unsafe. He wants to open it up, for trade. I know. I heard.' She said this as though party to some great secret known only to the powerful and seemed disappointed that no one was impressed.

'How far are we from the road, Netrodyl?'

She spoke to Dagla Kaz from behind. 'It's just a little way through the trees, Paltrohn.'

'How far? How many paces?'

'How many, Paltrohn? I'm sorry, I don't know.'

'You can guess, can't you?'

She became distressed. 'I...I'm sorry, Paltrohn. Please forgive me.'

Tumalind caught on. 'You can't count, can you?'

'Can you?'

She nodded, smiling. 'Is it just a little way? As far as we've walked, do you think?'

Netrodyl nodded.

'I think it's only a few dozen paces, Dagla Kaz. Shall I look?'

'Take Wendarah with you and don't go out of hearing. I can't have you injured by another terzet-horn, or anything else, for that matter.'

She and Wendarah returned a few minutes later to report that the road was, in fact, just four dozen paces through the trees and they'd get through easily even with the litter.

Netrodyl continued to stare at Tumalind as though she were some sort of superior being. 'You can count. No one but Gret-Zudas can count.'

'Oh, everybody can count, Netrodyl. It's easy enough if you've been taught.'

'But, what about the magic?'

'Magic?'

'The...numbers. They're magic.'

'Are they? I've never known any magic with numbers. Mind you, Jhonaht's a wonder with them sometimes. Now, he can add them together and all sorts. He's very clever, is Jhonaht. He discovered the Skyfire, you know.'

'Skyfire? The sky burns?'

'It will soon. Won't see it now until after the rains, though.'

'You know so much. A young virgin who counts and knows men things. I must be in a dream.'

'No dream, Netrodyl. I'm as real as you. Do you have a man in Qlentz?'

'Man? I am for the men, if that's what you mean. That's our purpose.'

This was such a strange idea that Tumalind was stumped for a response. She smiled and decided it might be better to let Netrodyl do any further talking. She might say something to upset the woman. It would be better to find out a little more about the customs and habits of her people before venturing any further opinions.

They walked along in companionable silence for a while. The track was easier going than the rough ground they'd had to use till then. They stopped to rest just twice, allowing the men to swap over the hands bearing the litter. Dagla Kaz took over from Caarl, as his wounded arm couldn't support it. Phildrad was very pale by the time they came out of the trees and saw the town up a shallow slope ahead. The road, which ran on to the coastal city of Xythonl, swept away through the trees to the northwest but a narrow, ill-made way led to the north, out of the band of forest and across grassland to Qlentz.

Just as they emerged, the first drops of rain, large heavy and warm, splattered them. By the time they reached the top of the slope, they were soaked to the skin.

A wooden wall of stakes surrounded the small circular town, but if there had ever been gates, they were no longer evident. A covered alcove, big enough to house a standing man, looked across the wide entrance from each side but neither was occupied. Rain had already soaked into the ground enough to cause water to run on the surface. They were forced to walk through small streams of mud and the collected detritus of the past few months.

Dagla Kaz called Netrodyl to him as they entered the deserted area just within the stockade. Tumalind accompanied her, as she seemed overawed by the High Priest.

'Where can I find somewhere for us all to stay, my dear?'

'You must speak to Gret-Zudas, Paltrohn.'

'Very well, take me to this Gret-Zudas.'

She dropped her head and seemed at a loss what to do.

'We're all getting rather wet and poor Phildrad, who I might add, saved your life a short time ago, is in danger of dying if we don't find somewhere soon.'

Netrodyl fell to her knees in the mud and placed her hands on the High Priest's thighs, her face down between her outstretched arms. 'I ask for the right to speak plain with you, Paltrohn.'

Dagla Kaz, as puzzled as the rest, took her arm and lifted her to her feet, though she still refused to look at him. 'Speak as plainly as you like, dear, but make it quick, please.'

At this, she looked directly at him for the first time. 'Gret-Zudas is leader. Forgive me, but you said I might speak plain; I don't know what you expect me to do. He makes decisions and says what must be done. I am only a woman and can do nothing. You must know I may not approach the house without permission.'

'Show us where we need to go.'

'Yes. That I may do.'

'Then, do it. And wait near by so I can ask Gret-Zudas to invite you to speak.'

She nodded and, keeping Tumalind close for support, pointed at the large building that filled the centre of the wide enclosure. The house was circular, with wooden walls and a steeply sloping thatched roof. Smoke issued from a loose-lidded hole in the top of the conical roof. An opening faced them and others were spaced at intervals around the walls.

Dagla Kaz began to move toward the nearest opening, the rest of the party following.

'Only men. Women mustn't go, please. The women must stay here. Please.' She seemed almost frightened by what she'd said, as if she expected some punishment.

Thoroughly fed up of the delays, and concerned about Phildrad, Dagla Kaz merely shrugged and led the men to the opening. As they approached, a tall thin man, of about his age, appeared and blocked it.

Tumalind couldn't hear what they said now that the rain was pouring hard but she watched Dagla Kaz gesture at them and at Phildrad. The man, clad from head to foot in a hooded, dark robe, called for Netrodyl, his voice surprisingly strong for one so frail looking.

'You must, please, stay here.' She ran up to the man and knelt.

They exchanged words and many gestures before the man nodded and pointed at the waiting women. Corphanda, growing increasingly irritated and concerned for her patient, strode across the muddy ground, determination in every step. The man held his palm out in a gesture clearly intended to stop her. Corphanda, however, was not so easily dissuaded.

Tumalind smiled as the little plump woman berated the man about the state of her patient. He looked at her aghast throughout and then turned without a word into the depths of the roundhouse. Within seconds, he returned, accompanied by a very tall, well-built man who looked at Corphanda with an expression so fierce most would've been cowed. She repeated her performance, gesticulating wildly at the sky and their party. The fierce man looked down at Netrodyl and asked a question. She spoke and he nodded, spoke with her again and then burst out laughing.

The men were admitted to the roundhouse with Phildrad on his litter. Corphanda, less than pleased, returned with Netrodyl. The woman led them to the rear of the roundhouse, taking a wide course so that they never approached closer than thirty paces or so. Out of sight of the gateway, the circular stockade formed the rear wall of a long narrow structure in the form of a parallel arc, built of the same materials as the roundhouse. It, too, was punctuated with openings and Netrodyl led the women inside through the nearest.

There were no dividing walls. Only women and very young children occupied the curved space, some in hammocks slung from roof beams, others squatting on the mud floor or seated on rush matting. Older girls played quiet games near the openings. There were no boys older than five. All looked up as the strangers entered and a hush fell at the sight of Netrodyl. Tumalind noticed some women wore a long wrap at hips or waist; others tied the garment under one arm to fall to mid-thigh. A few had folded their wraps to sit on or to use as a pillow.

An older woman, wrapped from underarms to ankles, approached Netrodyl and pointed at the tabard. 'What's this, Netrodyl? Have you no shame?'

Netrodyl struggled, trying to remove it. Tumalind helped and gave the tabard back to Dilanthas.

'Sorry, Mother. A terzet-horn ripped my bond. That woman loaned me it so I was covered outside.'

The older woman examined Netrodyl's skin, touching the cuts and scratches. 'Any other hurts?'

'No, Mother.'

She inspected the newcomers, who dripped on the hard mud floor of the women's house. 'You wear such things even inside?'

Wendarah moved forward and bowed to the woman. 'It's clear our ways and yours aren't the same. Our God, Ytraa, requires us to be covered in mixed company unless we're at prayer. I hope you'll understand that this is a sacred matter for us and that we intend no insult to your customs or your Gods.'

The old woman nodded and turned to Netrodyl. 'How came you by these strangers?'

Netrodyl said she'd disobeyed a man, whose name, given in very quiet tones, had those nearby gasping, and had run away.

'You ran away?'

'Yes, Mother.'

'You ran away?'

'I ran, Mother.'

'You ran away?'

'I ran away, Mother.'

To their surprise, the woman burst out laughing and took Netrodyl into her arms, embracing her with evident pride.

Netrodyl described how she'd been chased by the terzet-horn, trapped and then rescued from certain death by the men in the party. As she spoke, other women approached to listen and to examine more closely the tabards, plucking at them and lifting the hems.

'You blessed the men?'

Netrodyl hung her head. 'I was unable, Mother. But I'll gladly give all as is required.'

'See that you do.'

Corphanda could hold herself no longer. 'What's going to be done about Phildrad? He's in danger of …'

The older woman stared and stopped her in mid-sentence. 'The men deal with the men. You will not question the men.'

'Do they know what they're doing, though? I've precious little faith in men when it comes to looking after the wounded or the sick.'

The women gasped, shocked at this serious breach of some code of behaviour.

'I see we have many differences. We must talk and learn what we will from each other. Come. Remove your wet garments or you'll get rainfever.' Seeing them hesitant, she nodded. 'No man will see you, if that is your worry. They live in the roundhouse. We live here. Men never come here.'

'Sounds a bit boring. What do you do when you fancy a frowk?'

The old woman stared at Porryh, passed silent judgement, and turned back to Wendarah, who rid herself of the wet tabard. 'You, I expect, are the senior woman?'

Wendarah nodded.

'The rest may go with the women. You and I will share knowledge, such as we have.'

Chapter 33

Lodgings Found And Left

Dismissed, the Virgin Gifts and Corphanda followed Netrodyl to the rear wall where a small, smokeless fire burnt on a stone hearth, small sparks and hot air rising through a black gap in the roof. No rain came through this hole and Tumalind was intrigued to know how, but Netrodyl just shrugged when asked. Corphanda was reluctant to leave matters to Wendarah but they suggested she should wait until the priestess returned.

They draped their wet tabards near the fire over lines that ran from the rafters across the width of the room. Only Dilanthas bothered to replace hers with the driest from her pack. The others draped all their belongings along the lines to dry fully. The women from the town gathered to meet them and to examine the fabric, embroidery and fastenings of their tabards, fascinated by the strangers and their garments.

'So, going to tell us, then, Netrodyl? What do you do when you fancy a frowk?'

Netrodyl's admiration of Porryh's frankness was mixed with a touch of scorn. 'Such language isn't becoming for a woman, you know. But, to answer your question. If a man requires us, for any purpose, we wash and put on scent.'

Porryh raised her eyebrows.

Netrodyl continued, explaining as if to a rather backward child. 'We approach the roundhouse…'

'What do you wear, or doesn't that matter?'

'Scent; I said. Then we attend the man. Surely, you do this?'

'We're equal to our men, Netrodyl, not servants to do their bidding. We live in the same house, the same room with them if we're married.'

There were gasps and much murmuring at Tumalind's statement.

'Married? I don't understand what that is. But you really live in the same room? In the same house?'

'Families live under one roof; parents and children together. A husband and wife live in the same room, share a bed, wash and pray together.'

Netrodyl shook her head in amazement and was even more surprised at Tumalind's further explanations of marriage, husbands and wives.

'So, what happens when the man finally notices you, Netrodyl?' Porryh wasn't to be deflected.

'That's for the man to decide, of course.'

'How do you tell him what you want?'

'What the man wants he'll make clear. The woman will provide.'

'But what about what you want?'

'The man will tell her what he wants of her. And the woman will obey.'

'So, if he fancies a frow…wants to bed you, what then?'

'The woman provides for him, of course.'

'Where would that be? Outside, in the road, in this place, in the roundhouse, where?'

'The roundhouse, of course.'

A shout came from outside. Just a single word. 'Woman!'

The woman Netrodyl had called 'Mother' nodded at one of those nearby. She slipped off her wrap, ran to a wooden trough and splashed herself with water and then applied oil to her forehead, throat, breasts and thighs from a small jar at the side. She ran through the rain toward the nearest opening of the roundhouse.

Tumalind could see her, standing just outside the door, waiting with head down and hands behind her back. 'That's what happens when a man wants a woman?'

Netrodyl nodded.

'So, how does a woman get what she wants from this deal?'

Netrodyl shook her head at Porryh. 'Woman's purpose is to provide for man.'

Porryh gave a scornful grunt at that but said nothing, as the woman who'd gone out, suddenly returned and ran to Mother. Mother nodded and pointed her to their group.

The woman ran and touched Corphanda. 'You must go to the roundhouse, please.'

Corphanda felt her tabards, selected the least damp one, and struggled to put it on. The woman and Netrodyl both shook their heads.

'No. No. You must go now, as you are.'

Corphanda struggled with her fastenings until she was content. She collected her bag of treatments. 'Lead on, then.'

The woman looked across at Mother, clearly in a quandary at this odd behaviour. But Mother merely nodded. Corphanda left with the woman and dashed through the rain straight into the roundhouse.

'She didn't wait to be admitted.'

Porryh grinned at Netrodyl. 'That's Corphanda for you. Never stands on ceremony if there's a job to be done.'

'But how does she know what they want her for?'

'Well, with this lot to choose from, they're hardly likely to want to bed her, are they? Obvious they want her healing help for poor Phildrad.'

'But if they do want to bed 'er, Corphanda's not goin' to argue, is she?'

Tumalind grinned at Dilanthas. 'Only after she's seen to Phildrad. You know what she's like.'

It was dark by the time Corphanda returned, still wearing her tabard but also wreathed in smiles as if well satisfied with whatever had passed. She ignored their questions, however, and went straight to Wendarah who was still deep in conversation with Mother. They spoke, exchanging information and views with some laughter and occasional exclamations of outrage or shock. They were still talking when it was time for the evening meal.

Netrodyl led the others to sit elsewhere, whilst the women used the fire to prepare food, and then returned to do her share.

'Wouldn't like to live here.'

'Nor me. The women have no say at all, do they?'

'Jus' chattels; slaves, really.'

'They seem content enough.'

'Ay, 'appen cattle are content till they feel the blade o' the slaughterman.'

'They know nothing of the world. Yet the road runs, what, half a league away?'

'Always trying to work things out, Tumalind. They're just ignorant, that's all.'

'But how can they not know about the outside world? How can they stay ignorant?'

'P'raps their men keep 'em that way.'

'Well, that's obvious, Dilanthas. But how?'

'Maybe they don't let them meet anyone from outside.'

'They let them meet us.'

'Ay, but see 'ow they were? It was like they'd never seen other women. I reckon we only got in 'cos o' the rains.'

Netrodyl returned with two platters steaming with hot food. 'I'm sorry; I heard what you said. The reason you're here is because your men saved my life. We're in debt to you all.' She turned and went to collect two more platters.

'I think you're right, though, Dilanthas. Remember those two small alcove things either side of the gate? I expect they normally have men in them to stop strangers from coming through. Did you see the way Netrodyl peered inside them as we came in? They probably thought no one would be using the road in the rains and abandoned their guard duty. When we came through the gateway, you couldn't see the women's quarters at all. I bet that's what happens. The women never get to see any strangers.'

Netrodyl confirmed her suspicions. They were the first to stay in the women's quarters in living memory. They'd never met outsiders before, though the men frequently dealt with merchants.

'We'll not be too popular with the men, then.'

'I suppose not. I wonder what the women'll do?'

'We're about to find out.'

They looked up to find Corphanda, Wendarah and Mother approaching.

◆───◆◆───

Feldrark was finally convinced Malarhah had stopped bleeding. For four days they'd existed on poor rations, brought by a succession of slaves, as if they were an afterthought. Each time, Malarhah had hidden. They were hungry and in poor spirits by the night of the escape. But Jodisa-Li and Myllthlan had had plenty of opportunities to practice their route to the harbour so they could find their way in the dark.

Nervous, they were all determined to take what risks they must to get away and lead their own lives again. Feldrark's main concern, after the Staff of Ytraa, was how Aglydron might react. Okkyntalah had unwittingly given him reason to be anxious about this man who Feldrark considered a religious zealot of the worst kind.

Myllthlan and Jodisa-Li set off first, laden with sleepsacks rolled and stuffed with all their belongings. Shaulah went with them. They would untangle their boat from amongst the local fishermen's reed boats and await the rest of the party at the end of the jetty where they'd entered the town so disastrously, only eleven days before.

Feldrark, with Okkyntalah and Malarhah, set off in the opposite direction, heading first for the Galhta's tower. They reached their destination quickly and without incident.

'Where's the Staff?'

'Attached to the pillar at the southwest corner on the third level. You'll need a knife; it's tied on with twine.'

Okkyntalah unsheathed his hunting knife and handed it carefully to Feldrark in the dark, guiding his hand to prevent either of them being cut.

'You must be very quiet, Feldrark. The Galhta lives just below the calling platform.'

Feldrark nodded then remembered they couldn't see him. 'I'll be back soon.'

He climbed through the black night, rain soaking his skin and making the boards and supporting pillars slippery. As was customary, the Galhta had pulled his access ladder up. Only a determined climber could ascend the first two levels. Feldrark reached the second level after much slipping and silent cursing; found and lowered the ladder in readiness for his descent. Another ladder took him easily to the third level, where he orientated himself with the street and crossed the open floor on hands and feet to the corner Malarhah had indicated. He felt his way up the wooden support, seeking his precious Staff.

It was not there.

He knew Malarhah wouldn't lie to him. She'd be sure she was right before telling him where she'd seen the Staff. He felt again, carefully stroking each of the four faces of the pillar from the bottom to the top. It was not there.

Perhaps, in the dark, he'd become disorientated. He moved to his left along the open wall, railed more for strength than security. He searched that pillar and found nothing. Each of the four corner pillars was devoid of the Staff and when he returned to the first place he'd searched, he finally discovered the cut ends of twine high up. He descended again.

'It isn't there.'

'You felt all the way round, the full length?'

Feldrark didn't respond to the boy's inane question.

'They've moved it, Feldrark. Perhaps they move it regularly, in case you spot it. I never thought of that. The Galhta was here when I first discovered it and again when I came to check. Perhaps he saw me and decided to move it just in case. I may act the dumb slave, but he's wise and experienced.'

'What do we do?'

Feldrark snorted lightly. 'Obvious. We search the rest of the tower. Take the first two floors, Okkyntalah. But don't release the Staff if you find it. I must do that. Just let me know where it is. Malarhah, you stay here to pass on messages for us. I don't want you climbing with those wounds freshly healed.'

With that, he set off back up to the third level. Okkyntalah he left searching the ground level.

As all had to be done by hand in near pitch black, the search took precious time. Feldrark finally grew tired of the game. He reached the floor where the Galhta resided. It took some persuasion to get the man to release the information he needed. Once furnished with the Staff, however, the leader's usefulness ended and Feldrark killed him quickly and without unnecessary cruelty. He returned and passed Okkyntalah his hunting knife, blood making the blade sticky as it dried. He touched the boy's lips with his finger but said nothing.

'I have the Staff. Let's find Aglydron.'

Malarhah took them by touch and instinct through the black streets, rain soaking them to the skin with its warm wetness.

'This one.'

She remained, vulnerable and alone outside the door, as Feldrark and

Okkyntalah entered the house.

⋅ ⋅⋆⋅ ⋅

Okkyntalah could smell the ubiquitous burning incense; even see a faint glow from the earthenware pot in the corner. He gave his ears a moment to adjust to the muted roar of the falling rain outside. From his right he heard the breathing of sleepers. Two people. Feldrark kept with him by holding his shoulder lightly. Okkyntalah signalled they should drop to hands and knees and they crawled across the space, listening to locate the sleeping couple.

The doorway into the bedchamber was narrow and Okkyntalah grazed the top of his arm against the frame as he entered. He stifled the cry of pain as the rough wood took a length of skin from his arm. Feldrark was right behind him and gave no sign of his struggle through the gap.

Okkyntalah stopped at the side of the bed and reached out carefully with his fingers to locate the nearest sleeper. He discovered a smooth, slender ankle. It made the task more difficult, as the bed took up the entire surface of the floor apart from a thin space, which they currently occupied. They must silence the woman before attempting to wake Aglydron.

Okkyntalah had no stomach for the murder of a sleeping woman, no matter what was at stake. He spoke to Feldrark in tones quieter than a whisper. The Wharhll of Litkala agreed and, together, they placed their weight on top of the woman, Okkyntalah using a hand to gag her as he lay across her chest. She struggled and Aglydron awoke.

'It's me, Aglydron. Come; we must escape.'

'Chislanda? What's happening to…?'

'Aglydron! No time to explain. Help us bind and gag her. Then we must go.'

'Bind? Gag? What d'you mean? This woman's a gem, a jewel. She's shown me such…'

'Aglydron. I give you a stark choice. Either help us bind and gag Chislanda or I'll cut her throat. I have Okkyntalah's knife ready.'

'Who are…?'

'No time, Aglydron. We must leave. It's our only chance and we've little time. Help us, or Feldrark will do as he says. I don't want her blood on my hands. Do you?'

Aglydron seemed to weigh the matter for a moment and then come to his senses at last. 'Escape, you say? How? Whose idea is..?'

'Mine. Now help us or the woman dies.'

Aglydron was clearly torn. But he must know he couldn't stop what the stranger threatened.

'The mission, Aglydron. Remember why we're here.'

That worked. He spoke rapidly to Chislanda, assuring her they wouldn't harm her. They tore strips of cloth from the bedding and Okkyntalah released his hand from her mouth, warning her that any sound would bring instant death. The knife at her throat reinforced the threat and she remained silent as they gagged and bound her.

Working in the dark, it took longer than planned. Aglydron searched for his tabard and discovered it at last.

'Any food or drink in the house?'

He collected what he could find. Feldrark took the supplies from him as Aglydron knelt beside the woman's head and whispered in her ear. 'I'm sorry, Chislanda. I must go. I've a duty to fulfil. I'll remember you with love. I hope my seed grows in you and returns the respect you've lost. Farewell.'

The three men left the hut and found Malarhah seated by the door, holding Feldrark's precious staff tightly. He relieved her of it and, in silence, they moved through the rain-filled night as she guided them with whispers, attached hand to shoulder, like three blind men. They met not a soul on the journey and began to hope that their plan had worked better than they could've dreamed. Half way along the jetty, they met Myllthlan, wringing her hands and in tears with anxiety.

'You've been so long. I didn't know what to do for the best. Of course, I realize we must still go tonight, but I'm not sure she'll survive...'

'What's happened to Jodisa-Li?' Feldrark's question came before either Aglydron or Okkyntalah understood her anguish.

She hurried them forward as if terrified to stay in that place. 'She was badly hurt as she was trying to free the boat. I tried to help but couldn't get to her. By the time I got free from the other boat, they'd beaten her very badly and she was unconscious. If Shaulah hadn't helped fight them off, I think she'd be dead. I can't tell in the dark just what they've done, but she's seriously injured. I had to kill both the men to free the boat, I'm afraid.'

They reached the ladder and descended, one by one, Feldrark climbing down last. The first hint of light glowed in the east where the sun was rising to pale the dark rain clouds. It gave enough illumination to determine which way they should go at any rate.

'Cast off and get the boat under way. Whatever else we do, we must make our escape or die. I've killed the Galhta and Myllthlan has brought death to others. We must away, now.'

'The Galhta?' Malarhah's question was full of foreboding.

'I had no choice. We can't discuss it now. We must move. Go.'

Even as he spoke, a cry of alarm came from the harbour. Okkyntalah, determined to silence the fellow before he woke the whole town, found his bow and quiver, with its single remaining arrow. Aiming carefully in the rocking boat, he fired the shaft and felled the man.

'Well done, Okkyntalah. Away!' Feldrark organised the party.

They took to the oars and pushed the small boat into a sea calmed by falling rain and little wind. So hard was the rain that they needed to bail water from the boat; something Myllthlan had started whilst waiting. Okkyntalah and Feldrark took an oar each and Aglydron took the tiller whilst Malarhah and Myllthlan bailed.

'I tried to set the fire, Feldrark, but everything's so wet it wouldn't take. The most I managed was to make one of the boats smoulder by feeding hot coals from the slave kitchens into the bundles of reeds. I've little hope it'll catch, though. The men who followed me after I stole fire caught up with Jodisa-Li. I was trying to start the fires and didn't realize what was happening. She fought hard but it was so dark. I hope she isn't damaged beyond repair. I couldn't heal her in the dark and I didn't know what to do for the best.'

'I'm sure you did what you could, Myllthlan. Don't alarm yourself. We'll have a better idea of what we can do for her once the sun's up. At least the rains will stop them chasing us.'

Malarhah shook her head. 'Not if you've killed the Galhta. They'll hunt us. You've as good as killed their God. They'll never give up. Never; until we're all dead.'

Chapter 34

REST AND RELAXATION

Aglydron abandoned the tiller to make his prayers, reluctantly followed by Okkyntalah. The big stranger stood for a moment but made no obeisance. As the sky brightened with day, he bent over Jodisa-Li, prone in the bows, where Myllthlan had laid her. Aglydron, concerned he might lose the very purpose of his mission, moved beside him. Much to his concern, the stranger seemed personally anxious about her well-being.

'May I? Now I can see, I might have a better chance.'

They let Myllthlan examine the unconscious girl. She turned to face them, rain merging with tears to flow freely down her face. 'We haven't lost her yet, but she's barely alive. Whether it's the blow to her head or some other injury that I can't see, I can't tell. We must get her to shelter where she can lie still and peaceful if we're to have any hope of saving her. I'll do what I can in the meantime.'

'Land. We must make land.'

Aglydron could see logic in what this stranger said but felt disinclined to agree with a man who seemed reckless. A return to land would make them easier to discover. The dark young woman had said they were now the worst of criminals because they'd murdered the town's spiritual leader; they'd be hunted until they were caught. His experience with Chislanda led him to believe the girl. The Galhta was of supreme importance and their culture of vengeance would make them pursue the killers until his death had been repaid. At least the open sea gave them some chance of evading their pursuers.

Aglydron felt the stranger was a man of power and importance but thought he must put his point and not lose his leadership. 'No. We'll be easily caught on land. We stay at sea.'

'Do you want Jodisa-Li to perish, Aglydron of Muhnilahm? I desire her alive and well.'

'I don't know you, Paltrohn, though you seem to know who I am. I'm leading this expedition and so...'

'You may lead when I leave but whilst I remain, you'll find my word is stronger, by experience as well as status. I say we make for land, to the west. Even in this dismal light, it's possible to sail away from the sun until noon and toward it after that. Such direction is crude but places us in the right direction to return us to my home in Litkala.'

'If that's where you're from, you'll go alone!'

'So you think. I tell you, we're going to Litkala, and by the most direct means possible. Jodisa-Li will fade and expire if we don't…'

'And we'll all die if we do. I care more about Jodisa than you do; she's the reason for our mission. Without her, we'll fail. But there's no point sailing into certain danger…'

'Danger? Where do you suggest we go?'

'Anywhere but your home. They know where you come from, if I'm any judge. They know we're from Muhnilahm but Chislanda will tell them we're not going back until our mission's done. They'll expect us to make for your home. They'll be waiting for us on shore, ready to take us prisoner again or kill us.'

He nodded at Aglydron with respect. 'What you say makes sense. I allowed personal concern to cloud my judgement. However, we must make landfall or she will die. Where do you suggest we go?'

Aglydron was silent for a moment, thinking hard to keep the respect of this powerful man who was likely to challenge his every decision. 'We should sail east until noon, then turn north to land well away from Mipahnhil. My memory of the maps is that many rivers form the mouth of the River Sure and we should be able to sail up one of them, using the oars, and find somewhere we can shelter and hide while Jodisa-Li recovers.'

'It's hazardous, Aglydron; fraught with problems. The wind won't help and we'll have to row against the current of a swollen river. It also takes us toward the Mire of Rhoshe, which I'd prefer to avoid. But you're right. It's the best of our available options and it's the last place they'll think to look for us. I agree with Aglydron. How do the rest of you feel?'

'I'll go with whatever choice you two make. I've learned not to trust my judgement on this trip so far.'

'Spoken with humility and honour, Okkyntalah, though not entirely justified. You have the makings of a fine man. Ladies?'

'I know no alternative to Aglydron's suggestion, only that we must find a place of shelter soon; as a healer, my greatest fear is that the girl will die before we can give her the help she needs.'

'As a slave, I feel I have no say, but since you ask my opinion, Feldrark, I believe the east is the best way, for now.'

Without further discussion, Okkyntalah and Aglydron took an oar each whilst Myllthlan took the tiller and Malarhah continued to bail.

'You're not a slave, Malarhah, by the way. You're free to act as you please.'

'You're my master, Feldrark. I remain in your service, freely, as long as you wish it.'

Aglydron was pleased to have names for the two strangers. Their positions and reasons for being with his party could wait for now, but he must learn as much as he could when the opportunity arose. For now, it was enough that they work together. They could do nothing for the injured girl at sea. He was concerned that Feldrark cradled her head in his lap even as he bailed tirelessly. The strangely distant look on the big man's face puzzled him in this time of crisis. It was as if he were no longer with them but visiting a far off place.

Come noon, signalled by vague brightness directly overhead, they made a turn and headed for the unseen shore.

Malarhah spotted the darkness first and voiced foreboding. 'We're approaching land. Though it feels right for us, I believe it won't be as well for me as for the rest of you.'

Feldrark had come back to them and seemed unsurprised they'd found the land they so desperately needed. 'Your anxiety's understandable, Malarhah, but fear not. We're in this trouble together and we'll get through it together.'

'I said I'd die for you, Feldrark, and I will at need. But I'd far rather live with you.'

Feldrark placed a comforting arm about her shoulders. 'I hope and pray none us has to die, and I'll protect you with my life if need be.'

They spoke no more, for the shore grew suddenly clear, as they emerged into a space not subject to cloud and rain. The sky grew bright, sunlight sparkled on the water, and a light breeze helped them toward the land.

A strange landscape emerged. A low promontory, rocky and cloaked with trees of different types, protruded into the sea. On the west side, a wide slow brown river flowed. A small clear stream met the sea to the east. The headland stood, a peninsula with the broad wetlands, flat and featureless, disappearing into pouring rain to the east, west and north. Behind them, the sea vanished into the continuing downpour.

The rock was pale gold and craggy and, at the very tip of the raised hill the rough mouth of a cavern faced them, high above the sandy beach. Rough-hewn steps seemed to lead to this place and it was curtained, in part, by hanging vines of iasomia and another plant none of them could name.

There was no sign of life, but they had the impression that the place was inhabited.

'May Ytraa be praised! Sanctuary. We can hide the boat behind the trees in that small creek, and we can shelter in the cave. We can see without being seen. It's perfect.'

'Perhaps too perfect.'

Aglydron glanced at Malarhah and, seeing her eyebrows raised in surprise, followed her gaze to the approaching shore. An ancient crone stooped in the mouth of the cave, beckoning them.

'I fear that woman. She has my death in her mind.'

Feldrark tried to reassure her. 'She can't hurt you whilst you're with us. Besides, she appears harmless enough and even welcoming. See, she's coming down to greet us.'

'I don't trust a place of such calm and light when all around is dark and chaos. Perhaps she's a sorcerer.'

'Maybe she is. But we're here now and we need a place such as this if we're to save Jodisa-Li. I suspect your fear is no more than superstition.'

'Maybe it is, Feldrark, my saviour and my life, but maybe it is not.'

Aglydron, inclined to side with Malarhah, nevertheless accepted Feldrark's practical judgement.

⁜

Feldrark watched the old woman, a gentle breeze wafting rags about her bony, wasted frame. The same wind, absent as they'd ploughed through the rain, shifted long strands of dull grey hair against wrinkled skin on her shoulders and arms. Hooded, almost colourless eyes, fixed each of them in turn as the boat rode the shallow waves and ground on the sand.

'Malarhah's right. This woman isn't what she seems. But I believe she's good for us and that we would do well to treat her with kindness.'

Feldrark nodded at Myllthlan. 'I'd hope we'd treat any, who wasn't a stated enemy, with kindness.'

Okkyntalah leapt from the bows and pulled the boat up the sands where the waves no longer disturbed it. Without waiting, he stepped up to the old woman. 'Greetings, mother. We're sorry to intrude on your solitude but we have great need of shelter.'

The old woman looked him in the eye and nodded. 'Yes. I ask but one favour in return, young man. Will you grant my wish?'

'If it's within my power. What can I do for you, mother?'

She smiled, revealing gaps in her crooked teeth. 'I'd have you collect fresh water from yon stream and take it to the cave for me. My old hands aren't what they were.'

'Willingly.' He ran back down to the boat where the others waited. From the bottom, he collected the earthenware bowl they'd carried from the town with food for the journey and made his way to the stream.

Feldrark watched him flush the bowl out, fill it with clear water and carry it up to the cave. He returned to where she stood, halfway between shore and cave. 'Is there anything else I can do for you, mother?'

She smiled again and shook her head. In moments, she transformed from old crone to beautiful woman. Her hair shone like myllth, her rags were a rainbow gown and her face shone with the lustre of a goddess. 'Welcome to the ease that is my realm. Come, I will feed you, heal you, give you rest and make known that which is not known. I am Sha'ra, and you are not strangers to me.'

They left the boat.

Knowing what he must do, Feldrark took Jodisa-Li into his arms and carried her to the cave. Shaulah preceded him, her tail held high and wagging with a joy she hadn't shown for many days.

There was no ceremony. They formed their single file procession as if it were ordained and followed Sha'ra up the easy steps, Okkyntalah coming last into the cave.

'Lay Jodisa-Li upon the healing bench, Feldrark, Wharhll of Litkala, and I will see what may be done for her. Okkyntalah, pour your water over yon plants to refresh them. Take your ease all of you. You are weary, hungry and afraid. Here there is no fear, Malarhah. No eyes that are not mine may see what I do not reveal, Myllthlan. Those who hunt you will remain outside and may not penetrate my realm, Aglydron. They know not this place, for I reveal and hide that knowledge at will.

'In you, though there are mistaken beliefs and imperfect motives, I perceive your wish to do what is right, just and proper for the general good. In your hunters, I see a desire only for vengeance, a blood lust that seeks death and pain: revenge is never good reason for any action. Therefore, I choose to give you aid and to withhold aid from them.'

Feldrark laid Jodisa-Li on the cushions atop a solid stone platform rising from the smooth rock floor of the cave to waist height. Its sides, carved with relief representations of beasts, birds, fish and people in celebration, made the whole seem alive with joyful activity.

Sha'ra swept her arms about the interior of the cave, indicating the soft, welcoming settles and the table laden with fresh food and fine goblets filled with amber wine. They took their ease, comfortable and relaxed in the pervading harmony of this realm that seemed as natural as the sky and sea to them. To Feldrark, all seemed a natural consequence of their being in this place at this time.

'Myllthlan, you have skill with healing which I would have you share with me.'

She joined Sha'ra at the plinth and helped prepare Jodisa-Li and examine the girl's wounds, both women first washing their hands in a stone basin at the plinth's foot. Feldrark, confident all would be well, nevertheless neglected food and refreshment until Jodisa-Li was recovered, as he knew she must be. He stood and watched, close to the two women.

'It is here.' Sha'ra indicted a bloodied wound close to and behind Jodisa-Li's right ear. 'This is what prevents her waking. The rest of her wounds are nothing to a healer such as you, Myllthlan. See? Your fingers will heal the flesh here at her side and make whole again the organs beneath that were damaged.'

Watching as they healed her, Feldrark finally understood that this young beauty was more important to him than any other person in the world. More personally important than the political pawn he'd intended to make her. Myllthlan examined the gash in her side, previously hidden by her tabard and undiscovered in their haste to escape. Her fingers closed the gap and made the skin whole.

'Heal her other cuts and bruises, Myllthlan, whilst I bring the sleep from her and allow her to know herself again. For this is a skill you have not, a skill you will not acquire, until your own life is forfeit for the return of life to one I shall not name.'

Sha'ra placed the fingertips of both hands on Jodisa-Li's head, circling the injury as she closed her eyes and faced the sparkling ceiling of the cavern. Light played in the crystals there, shimmering and illuminating every part of the space with rainbow colours. Sha'ra's hair turned sparse and white, her gown faded as she withered to an age beyond the knowing of man.

Myllthlan touched and healed the numerous small bruises and abrasions Jodisa-Li had suffered. Feldrark was unsurprised to note Myllthlan no longer needed to sleep as she had previously after multiple healing.

The rest of the party, taking their ease around the cavern, seemed unmoved as Sha'ra dissolved into pale blue-white light, which flowed into and from the roof of the cave and curved around and into the girl's head. The light increased, expanded and enclosed the plinth and Myllthlan until all Feldrark saw was brightness without centre or form, shimmering as if full of heat and energy. He felt no fear or distress, understanding it was as it should be.

As the light decreased and faded into wisps of mist, so the plinth re-emerged with Myllthlan, almost luminous with health, and Sha'ra, now clad in pure white and with hair like silver, helping Jodisa-Li to her feet, her tabard as fresh and clean as her hair and limbs. The girl stood in wonder for a moment and then turned to Sha'ra who smiled and nodded as if in answer to a question. It seemed enough for Jodisa-Li who made a deep curtsy to both healers before she found Feldrark and melted into his welcoming embrace. He opened his mouth to speak but before he voiced his question her reply formed in his mind.

'I'm entirely restored. Have no fear. I'm back with you.'

He was momentarily stunned and then laughed as the knowledge came to him that he and she could always speak to each other in their minds.

'I thought I'd lost you, my sweet Jodisa-Li. You must know I love you.'

'That's as it should be, my love. It's what was always intended. I love you, also.'

'Of course. How could it be otherwise?'

She let him know that, when the time came, she would join with him and take her place beside the Wharhll of Litkala as his wife. Feldrark, conscious of her part in Aglydron's scheme, smiled as he advised caution but welcomed her acceptance with joy.

The company received Jodisa-Li back into their group and were overjoyed to see her wounds healed, so that she was whole again. They thanked Sha'ra, who merely looked at each of them until they understood that the healing had emerged from their love and concern for their companion and that she was no more than the focus of their wish that it be so.

They ate and drank and rested for the remainder of the day. Sundown, bright and full of coloured light, found them unconcerned that their prayers were neglected in favour of a different form of worship, in which they communed with the very earth and sea and sky.

Feldrark noted Aglydron's frequent stares in his direction, and at Jodisa-Li, and knew the man's concerns about the obvious connection between them would remain, regardless of Sha'ra's influence. But his own concerns were for the life and the love of this woman and he'd permit no one, no matter what their mission, to part her from him now he'd discovered that their love was true and mutual.

◆⸺◆

Aklon-Dji sat in the circle around the small fire and sang their songs, laughed at their comic tales and applauded their dances. In his mind dwelt the loss he'd felt earlier; a loss so connected he knew it must be his sister or his father who had gone. He said nothing to his companions and hoped his face betrayed nothing of his sorrow or fear.

Chellyth sat beside him, with Por-Kildu on her other side, and they supped their cups of the bitter, burning grog made from ibogaine nuts and flavoured with berries from the yurhtz. It was a heady mixture that rewarded the persistent drinker with a sense of euphoria that could last overnight. Aklon-Dji preferred it to the poorer wines on the island, as it rarely gave him the headache and lethargy they invariably left. Tonight, it had the added virtue that it clouded his misery and numbed his grief. Por-Kildu had perfected the mix, using just enough of the bitter berries to counter the cloying taste of the nuts but insufficient to cause the sickness associated with the fruit of the yurhtz. It said much about The Point that its most abundant plant was a bush with cruel thorns that bore berries of a hideous yellow that were just edible but induced severe vomiting if eaten in quantity.

'Lahntahl, Lahntahl, Lahntahl!' The cry came from a small group of men and women sitting at the opposite side of the flames and Aklon-Dji turned to see how

Chellyth would respond.

She looked briefly at Por-Kildu, who nodded. Rising to her feet, she bowed ostentatiously and signalled the man sitting with the hollow logs to beat the rhythm for her. It was a signal for three of the women to approach Aklon-Dji. He had no heart for this.

'I'm entirely restored. Have no fear. I'm back with you.'

There was no more than that. He thought it must be Jodisa-Li though he wasn't sure it was intended for him. Nevertheless, he laughed aloud and his sorrow fell from him. Quickly he selected one of the three, using a silly choosing rhyme and making them laugh. His chosen sat beside him as the other two returned a little disconsolately to their places in the circle.

'If our honoured guest is ready?' Chellyth's comically arch request brought laughter and Aklon-Dji, pointing to himself in innocent surprise at her accusation, added to the sense of fun.

The drum beat steadied to a slow sensuous, base throb, countered by a higher pitched trill of excitement, both echoing softly from the slope of the hill behind the settlement. Chellyth began her dance: the slow, erotic, final movement of the prohibited celebration of Tryhnn's victory over Mhortag, when she seduced him into watching her dance, as her adherents escaped his clutches and were able to hide until Ytraa banished him forever. The dance was explicit, rather than subtle, matching its message to the vulgarity of Mhortag rather than the subtlety of Tryhnn. Chellyth, however, invested it with her own authority, so that it was not cheap or demeaning but rather a celebration of the earthy sensuality of womankind. During the dance or, if they were capable of waiting, at the end, various couples slipped off to their private places.

Aklon-Dji waited for the dance to finish and allowed Chellyth to vanish into the dark with Por-Kildu before he let his partner lead him to the place she'd selected. As she towed him into shadow, a loud call came from the watchtower at the far side of the hill. Those still illuminated by the flames moved out of range of the fire and waited. A second call came, three shouts in quick succession. The people relaxed as they recognised the announcement of a friend. All who were able and not otherwise already engaged beyond interruption, returned to the fire to await the arrival of the newcomer.

Aklon-Dji felt disappointment in the grasp of the woman beside him. 'Patience. This is merely postponement, not cancellation.'

She squeezed his hand in recognition of his promise.

From the darkness emerged a tall, brown-haired man, travel-worn and exhausted.

'Delbon! What brings you to The Point?'

The man stopped at Aklon-Dji's surprised question, clearly relieved.

'Thank Ytraa you're here, Aklon. I thought they'd caught you!'

'They'll no catch Aklon-Dji; he's too cunning.' His escort stroked her palm along the length of his arm.

This seemed to be the general opinion but Aklon-Dji held up his hand so that Delbon could continue.

'There's a rumour going round that they've caught you and will be torturing you slowly to death during the next two sixdays. The talk is that until they execute you, they'll be using more subtle torture to extract the names of the Few from you.'

'Is there much panic?'

'Disquiet. You've chosen your people well. They don't scare easily. But I thought I ought to make certain they weren't telling the truth. I've been to all the settlements but nobody'd seen you since A'ahl in Morstahn and that was days ago.'

'I had to despatch some of their trackers. It was clear they had information as to my whereabouts, so I felt it prudent to spend a little time here. Rest, Delbon, then return and let them know the reality, would you? I will stay a little longer; there are things on my mind that I need time and peace to resolve. But I shall return to the mainland shortly.'

'In the meantime, Delbon, please be our guest. You know you're as welcome as Aklon amongst us.'

'No gifts this time, Chellyth. Had to set off in rather a hurry.'

'As with Aklon, Delbon, it's you we welcome, not your gifts. For now, though, I've just completed the Lahntahl, and Por-Kildu…'

'Enough said! Get back to the poor man. If there's a willing woman available after your performance, I'll join with her, once I've rested and had some of your disgusting grog.'

One of the women who'd wanted Aklon-Dji brought Delbon a cup to share. They sat before the flames with those who were unable or disinclined to join. Aklon-Dji touched his friend's shoulder with gratitude and allowed himself to be drawn into darkness again. Though, with so many other things on his mind, his attention was less than complete. It seemed to suffice, however and the lady relaxed afterward, happy to be with him. Relax: oh, that he could do that simple thing for more than a moment.

Chapter 35

Words Of Wisdom

Morning revealed Sha'ra, clad again in her rainbow, golden locks restored. Okkyntalah watched her summon Feldrark to a settle at the back of the cavern. The rest of the party breakfasted on fresh fruits and merphlion juice mixed with wine and spring water to revive them. Each, in turn, visited the clear waters of the stream, bathing where it pooled in a rock bowl to leave them feeling invigorated

Myllthlan took Malarhah to one side and spoke to her, quiet and serious. The former slave returned and grasped Okkyntalah's hand.

'Please?'

Her request puzzled him but he let her lead him to the plinth where Myllthlan had restored Jodisa-Li's body to better than its former state. With his help, the healer examined her internal wounds and completed the healing as the girl lay on cushions.

'If you wish, I might restore what was so cruelly stolen from you as a child.'

'You can?'

Myllthlan nodded gravely.

'Please. Yes, please, Myllthlan.'

The healer traced lines with her fingers, probed and finally kissed what she'd healed. Made whole again and with no trace of pain or discomfort, Malarhah asked Okkyntalah to release her legs. She rose from the plinth, embraced Myllthlan and kissed her in gratitude.

'I've only words to thank you, Myllthlan. If there are deeds I might do to show my gratitude, name them.'

'You're welcome to what my healing can bring. I need no reward other than that of knowing my humble attempts have been successful. Test your wholeness and let me know how well I've restored you. That will be thanks enough.'

Malarhah led Okkyntalah from the cave.

Sha'ra spoke with Feldrark, questioning him until she knew all of consequence that he knew himself.

'I have knowledge I'd share with you, Feldrark. Some may comfort you, some may cause you grief. I'll share it all or none, as you desire. But understand it tells of futures that may be or may not be and only you might determine which will happen, knowing not which will be but aware that your actions and those of no one else will direct what comes to pass. And know that nothing that is done is without cost. Will you hear what I know?'

'I'll hear it, Sha'ra, and know I will determine my fate.'

'Then know this: fire touches the nest of your heirs, yet they emerge unscathed by flame to inherit positions of power in a changing world, where all may be lost and rediscovered. The dark wood rises against the living and death swallows darkness in its slavering maws. Dark and light vie for glory on the road to fortune and the winner takes all life whilst the loser loses all there is to lose. Another challenges the time and finds, in tradition, reason to be wrath yet has no power but secret vengeance. Wisdom, in the form of another, finds a path in ways thought difficult and fraught with danger, and reaches a conclusion none could see, although the destination was as plain as day. Rejoicing meets with sadness and the joy that springs from greatness and nobility is met with rage at the futility of man's usurping what is rightly God's domain.

'You speak in minds with your beloved. When you leave my realm, reach out again to she who dwells alone and high. What was before not open to you is open now. Listen well to the words of the wise, Feldrark, for that wisdom is the fruit of honest labour, deep thought, sincere speculation, the gathering of many minds and, not least, compassion.'

Sha'ra rose and let the rainbow fall from her. 'Know that we are alone within this space and unobserved by those who wait. Know that I am yours. But know that, if you accept my offer, you must diminish when you leave this place and the future must be poor and incomplete for you and those you love. I would have you take me, even so. If you reject my gift, I will be removed from you forever.'

Feldrark looked upon her loveliness, which surpassed his vision of any woman he'd known. He knew she spoke the truth, that he could take her as his own and would experience a form of paradise. But he knew he'd damage everything else he held dear and she'd be his for only a short time, however long it may seem.

'You offer me a long moment in paradise, Sha'ra. And I'd take it and die a happy man if I alone stood to gain or to lose and if I felt not the love I know for another. I thank you for the honour of your offer but regret I must reject your gift. Farewell.'

Sha'ra let tears of sorrow fall unchecked. 'Your choice is wise, Feldrark. You love more fully than most men and are noble. I shall be no more for you and leave you as I am beneath the sheath I wear for those who know me not.'

Her hair grew thin, spare and grey. Her body shrivelled to bones wrapped in parchment skin. Her eye sockets hollowed but her eyes lost no brightness and retained their penetration of his soul. Rags of grey clung to her wasted flesh, barely hiding her withered sex and drooping dugs. He knew her to be old beyond the measure of man.

'Why?'

'Everything has a cost, Feldrark.' Even her honeyed voice had turned to dry leaves, rattling in a desert wind.

'I'm sorry, Sha'ra. Truly sorry.'

She nodded and faded from his sight. He walked slowly to the front of the cavern, which seemed bleak and unwelcoming now but Jodisa-Li was eager to commune with him and show her love.

He sat and ate in silence, though he gazed at her with love. He could share nothing of what had passed between him and Sha'ra; a barrier prevented her probing his mind for such information. He couldn't tell her, with mind or tongue, that he had no control over this exclusion and he watched her grow sad and puzzled by her inability to find what she sought.

As they spoke together of other things, in minds and words, Aglydron answered Sha'ra's summons and took his place beside her.

<hr>

Aglydron became aware once more, after a period of strange dreaming without sleep. He watched Myllthlan relax on one of the settles, talking with Okkyntalah and Malarhah, who'd recently returned to the cave together. But Sha'ra called him and he went.

Her hair was black as jet, shining with life and vitality. Her eyes, piercing his very soul, were blacker than night but bright with knowledge. She smiled but grew grave, her grey gown enclosing her in gloom as her face displayed serious concern.

'Courage and duty drive you, Aglydron of Muhnilahm. Such devotion to the letter of the law diminishes the man. Better to examine law, assess its proper value and then act in its spirit. It is the moral coward, the man of no imagination, who allows the letter of the law to master him. You might become a man of passion and great warmth, a man who loves as he is loved, for there is greatness hidden deep within you. I have other knowledge I'd share with you. Some of comfort, some of grief. I'll share all or none, as you wish. But understand it tells of futures that may or may not be. Only you can determine which will happen, knowing not which will be but aware that your actions alone will direct what happens. And know that nothing is done without cost. Will you hear me?'

'I'll hear, Sha'ra, and decide my own fate.'

'Age alone is no guide to wisdom. Words recorded on stone tablet or parchment roll are ever the words of man and never the words of God. Hearing with ears reveals less than hearing with soul and heart. Blind belief and faith may lead to death and destruction; belief and faith in self may lead to life and creation. Tradition dictates that all may be lost when wisdom pleads for tolerance and acceptance and is ignored. Opposing powers may both be wrong or both be right or one may have the good and the other the look of it. A wise man seeks beneath the surface, touches souls rather than ceremony and leads to glory by example. The bonds of slavery make the master servant to the captive. What occurs in life comes from the heart; knowledge of the scripts fits the reader for rite and ceremony and perhaps no more.'

'You speak in sayings I've heard before but only partly understand.'

Sha'ra shed her grey gown. 'As I reveal myself, Aglydron, so life will reveal truth for your growth and guidance.' She parted her legs and placed his hands as a cup beneath her fern, to catch the coins of gold she bore. 'Each will buy ease on your long journey, Aglydron. But, for every one you take, a companion will suffer pain or fear, sorrow or loss. Or you may place them back whence they came. Each intrusion will reduce and pain me, as I suffer in their stead and relieve them of what they would otherwise experience. What will you do Aglydron, recent lover of women and devoted disciple of Ytraa?'

His arms ached with the weight of coin he held. He looked on the woman who'd given birth to this wealth and knew he must hurt her. 'Do I destroy you, or only my vision of you, Sha'ra?'

She nodded. 'Wisdom is often shown more by the question than the answer. I have lived always as I am and will live so forever, but appearance may be reality or it may be a mask. More I cannot say. You must choose.'

He bade her lie down and slowly, gently and tenderly as he could, fed the coins back inside her, watching as her hair, skin and flesh aged and lost colour and lustre until she was a hag, ugly as death. The final coin seemed too large and he must force it into the dry divide and witness her pain and suffering or keep it and let one of the party suffer.

'Do I decide who suffers, or how, if I keep this last coin?'

'You choose neither. Your choice is only whether to keep or return the token.'

'Then I'll keep it and hope I suffer rather than my friends. I'll see you hurt no more.' He placed the coin in the small scrip at his belt.

She struggled into a sitting position, pain and age lying across her face and body like the scars of war and time itself.

'Why, Sha'ra?'

'Because much is priceless but nothing is without price. You shall see me no more.'

He bowed at her sacrifice and his loss and returned to his companions, knowing he'd spared them much but that Sha'ra had borne that suffering in their stead and they'd never know and he would never forget the hard lesson she'd taught him.

Jodisa-Li looked up to the back of the cave with surprise as Aglydron rejoined his companions. A call had come unexpectedly and she couldn't ignore its imperative. She rose and walked slowly to take her place beside Sha'ra.

The middle aged woman whose very posture and demeanour spoke of her role as mother, clad in homespun and with hair greying and tied modestly under a silk scarf, welcomed her as a daughter and bade her sit and take her ease.

Jodisa-Li, whose own mother had always been an unknown stranger to her, felt the warmth and comfort from this woman who'd restored her to life with what she recalled as little ceremony. 'What would you have me do, wise woman?'

'Do? I'd have you live your life to its fullest extent; to love and to live. I'd have you experience joy, pleasure, pain, fear, happiness, confidence, sorrow, ecstasy, cold, hunger, delight, wonder and, at the proper time, death. Jodisa, you are the principal cause for your companions falling under my influence. Had you not been near death and a wise woman not interceded on your behalf as you approached my realm, it's likely I'd have seen you pass without revealing myself. My gifts are scarce and must be used for justice and good. I may not give to the undeserving. But, having invited you into my world, forces and laws outside your experience require that I give everything I have to give to all in your party. You will always know this but they will remain ignorant and you will never tell them. Just as Feldrark cannot disclose to you what passed between him and me, so you and your companions will know only what I share with each of you, remaining ignorant of all that has passed between me and each of the others.'

'What would you know from me?'

'I know all there is to know of Jodisa-Li, only daughter of Dagla Kaz, High Priest of Muhnilahm. I know of your first love, of the real father of the child torn unformed from your protesting body. All that is in your mind is also in mine, since I had to be in your mind to restore you to life. I have lived your life, Jodisa, and know your dreams, your yearnings, your ambition. I have felt your desire, your hatred and your pain. I have heard your lies, your truths, your hopes and fears, your successes and your disappointments. All that you have felt has passed through me. All that you have been I know. Does that make you hate me, fear me, wish me gone?'

'You know it makes me humble and full of remorse for the wicked things I've done and can't undo. I can no more hate you than I can myself. And life has taught me one thing, if nothing else; that we, as people, are imperfect and can only hope to be true to ourselves. We are what we are, without excuse or blame. We grow or we decay according to choices we make with the gifts and faults within ourselves. We can be better than ourselves or worse. But if we're false to ourselves, then we're false to all and lower than the slime that coats the stagnant pond and denies its life. I wish I'd made better choices, been more generous, given more respect. But I am what I am and I've done what I have done. No regret for the past can change what's been. I ask not your forgiveness, Sha'ra, but your love, as I freely give mine to you, both in gratitude and in acknowledgement of what you are in this world.'

Sha'ra laid her hand on Jodisa-Li's shoulder and gifted her a smile of pride. 'I have no words of advice or caution for you. You are grown beyond your years. Not yet are you beyond error, and your nature still will make you do things you'll regret. But you have a heart that sits at ease and is steeped in the goodness of the world, in spite of your past and your father's influence. I have no doubt you will be good for those who serve you and for those you serve now and will serve in the future. I can tell you no more than you already know about yourself, Jodisa, but I have other knowledge I would share with you.

'Will you hear me?'

'I'll hear, Sha'ra, and know I will determine my own fate.'

'The trusted one is not always to be trusted and the enemy may or may not be a foe. The seeker of power may find defeat and death and the humble may be raised to glory. All who seek may find but all who find do not seek. The knowledge that spreads vengeance moves more rapidly than fire and is more deadly. The destination sought is not always where the journey ends. Some who would travel shall remain and some who would not go shall be made to take the journey. You may gain one and lose another on the way.'

'You speak in proverbs, Sha'ra, something like a village priest talking to the flock, though with much more depth. There's more behind your words than there seems. I must consider what you say in light of events, I suppose.'

Sha'ra nodded approval. 'I may give you something, Jodisa-Li. Will you have it?'

'That depends on what you offer and its price. You've already given me more than most can hope to gain; you gave me back a life I'd lost. I ask no more of you.'

'Yet I have the power to make your beauty last until you die, to make you changeless until death takes you at last.'

'At what cost, Sha'ra?'

'The cost is none to you.'

'But to another; you, perhaps?'

Sha'ra let the mantle fall and showed herself decrepit, wasted and haggard beyond recognition.

'I'll risk what the years bring, Sha'ra. Beauty may be pleasant on the eye of the beholder but its unnatural continuation may make the bearer proud, vain and impossible to love. I thank you for the offer of the gift but I'll not take it.'

Sha'ra changed her form and Jodisa-Li felt the veil lifted so that she saw her in all her female glory. 'Know then, as your reward for your wisdom and love, Jodisa, that I offered myself thus to Feldrark and he took me not, for he'd rather have another.'

Jodisa-Li embraced the woman, kissed her and returned to her companions.

Okkyntalah stared at her with open admiration as she passed. Myllthlan moved to take her place beside Sha'ra. Malarhah sat apart, gazing with wonder at Okkyntalah. Jodisa-Li returned to Feldrark, conversing with Aglydron at the cave mouth. As she grew near, she put out her thoughts to show him her approach. He broke off his talk to turn and look at her.

'If possible, Jodisa-Li, you've grown even more beautiful since your talk with Sha'ra.'

She smiled and made a small bow of acknowledgement. 'And you, Wharhll of Litkala, are greater in my sight even than you were before.'

Aglydron looked from Feldrark to her and she saw the fear in his eyes. Their love would destroy his mission and Jodisa-Li knew he'd do what he could to prevent them joining. She and Feldrark must be careful how they behaved with each other. To cloud and confuse him, she squeezed Aglydron's hand with gentle reassurance. 'All will be well, Aglydron. Never fear.'

Time seemed to dwell in curious phases in this place. She felt she'd been with Sha'ra for a lifetime yet she watched Myllthlan approach the extraordinary woman and it seemed but the blink of an eye till she was with them again in the body of the cave as Okkyntalah received the summons.

Myllthlan came to be with her and Feldrark and Aglydron, Malarhah choosing to remain alone as Okkyntalah spent time with Sha'ra. Jodisa-Li realised she was aware of aspects of their hostess that the others seemed unable to recall after their visits. She excused herself from the men and took the healer to one side.

'What did she say to you, Myllthlan? I know you helped in my healing and I'd like to know what she had to say about that. If you don't mind revealing it.'

'She pointed out that we have some qualities which match. Of course, she's older and my strengths and powers are nothing compared to hers. But I now understand I can heal beyond the skin. She said a strange thing, though. She told me my powers of healing will grow as I age and that, at the last, I'll bring life to one who's as near to dying as you were and, in that gift, I'll give everything. I think it means one day my healing will cost my life. She says my gift has limits. I'll be able to do much but some ills I won't be able to mend. All I can do for those is to give them rest until they feel no more pain. But where I can, I'll cure completely. She mentioned other things but those were private and I'd rather not talk about them.'

'Ah, those would be the things she says in riddles, I expect?'

'Yes. She phrased them in odd ways. But I'll tell you one amazing thing she showed me, though you won't believe it.'

'Tell me.'

'Sha'ra used her own body to display what dwells beneath the skin of woman and Aglydron's, for that which lies under man's hide.'

'I wondered why Aglydron had gone back. In fact I almost called him away because I thought he was intruding on your personal time with Sha'ra.'

Aglydron interrupted. 'There's something very strange about this place and that old woman.'

Myllthlan simply nodded. Jodisa-Li saw that they were already forgetting their experiences. For a moment, she dwelt on what had transpired between herself and Sha'ra until the memory seemed to drift and become fragile; something she could recall only as a feeling of joy and wonder.

In the cave, they took food together and talked as they waited for the young man to rejoin them.

Okkyntalah looked on Sha'ra, her long, straight copper hair flowing down across her shoulders to reveal the voluptuous young body beneath. Her face was the face of the woman he loved above all others, and as she studied him with those deep sad eyes of lapis lazuli speckled with gold, he saw the pain and hurt that Tumalind felt at her loss and knew that he looked on his love as she was at that moment.

He hung his head with sorrow and regret and the image faded. The feel of Malarhah, as she'd shared her delights with him under the sun, rose and faded as he felt the love and passion Tumalind promised. When he looked up, Sha'ra had resumed her seat beside him.

'Myllthlan restored Malarhah her rightful womanhood and I rejoice. You are alone, and young and full of that desire that some men feel strongly all their lives but especially in youth. Don't blame yourself for giving and receiving what pleasure there may be to share. I encouraged Malarhah to discover her new pleasures and you were her natural choice. Life is uncertain and opportunities for giving and receiving don't come along often. Take what comes your way, Okkyntalah, without shame or remorse, enjoy what life brings you and give pleasure where you may.

'But remember Tumalind. Remember she is virgin still and knows not that pleasure you enjoy with others. She has only her memory of you and that closeness you shared before events parted you. The thought of you keeps her alive and stops her heart from breaking. She lives for you, Okkyntalah, even though she is uncertain of your pursuit and intentions. Her love for you is endless and remains true. Don't desert her,

Okkyntalah, though all manner of beauty and delight in female form will come your way. She is for you as surely as you are for her. That is a truth I may proffer without fear of events.

'There is about you another quality which you have yet to recognize. You have the gift to see far, Okkyntalah; farther than is normal, even for the clear-sighted. You can see with the eyes of the hawk, the clarity of the circling buzzard, over the distance the oryol spots its prey. You have this gift but knew it not until now. Use it well and let your eyes inform your mind and give warning at need and hope when despair is near.' She told him then of other knowledge she wanted to share with him. 'Will you hear what I know?'

'I'll hear it, Sha'ra, and determine my fate.'

'Turmoil separates and divides even as togetherness at last is come. The hunter hunts again, alone. Murder, death and torture in the bowels of the earth pass time but purpose sees through all. The bonds of iron chafe and burn, the brand disfigures beauty and the user abuses what is in his power. But reward comes when love overcomes all barriers and finds truth. Joined, two are greater than the single ones and go beyond the realms of knowledge, seeking truth and justice. Home is changed beyond recognition and death waits to serve a promise given long before. But peace and justice, love and harmony are all the end that lovers seek and, finding it, will rejoice as one and make the many share.'

'I don't pretend to understand what you say, Sha'ra. Perhaps events will tell me. But I thank you for your warnings and your advice. I'll be true to Tumalind in my heart and I'll find her if I can and be hers forever when I do.'

'I have a gift I may present to you. Would you take it?'

'Is it freely given? For I've learned that sometimes what we're promised isn't what we get and sometimes the cost is greater than the gift is worth.'

'For you, Okkyntalah, there is no cost but that which you've freely given. The cost is mine in this. Would you have the gift on those terms?'

'I'd like to know what it is.'

'You are wise to ask, and your replies please me. You have grown, Okkyntalah and are no more a youth but a young man with the seeds of knowledge that may one day make you great amongst your people. I would give you myself, once, and only once and for myself. I have never known man and I would sample that pleasure that seems to drive so much of what goes on amongst the people of this world.'

'And that is all? And this will cost me no more than pleasing you and taking my pleasure?'

'It will cost you no more than that, and a memory you will never lose.'

'Will it harm my love for Tumalind?'

'What you feel for Tumalind may grow as a result, it will not harm that.'

'And this is all?'

'For you.'

'And for you?'

'Ah. You are perceptive Okkyntalah. You have an understanding of women that is not given to many men. You see beneath the surface now you've experienced our delights. Where once you worshiped blindly, you now respect and honour our knowledge that we feel driven every bit as much as you do. The cost, to me, and me alone, is my eternal want of you that will remain unsatisfied.'

'You know this and you still want me, just once?'

'I do. Will you pleasure me, Okkyntalah, knowing I will ever afterward be empty and unfulfilled in that place?'

'I can't make that choice, Sha'ra. I can be what you wish me to be for you but I can't decide whether that's what you want. If you need to make a sacrifice for reasons I can't understand, then I'll happily assist you, but I won't share your regrets and I won't accept responsibility for your sorrow at the loss. The choice, Sha'ra, is yours alone.'

'You have grown, Okkyntalah, and become even more desirable in my eyes.'

Chapter 36

ENLIGHTENMENT AND MYSTERY

Aklon-Dji hoped two and a half sixdays on The Point would be long enough to put his hunters off the scent and have them assume he'd gone to ground for good this time. He wondered if any of them even suspected he rested in the district most islanders believed was worse than Mhortag's bowels. He'd gone the first time, so many years ago, in search of Por-Kildu after his father had tortured and disfigured his friend for daring to question his authority.

Now, Aklon-Dji was making his way back to the mainland. He'd spent the previous day alone, communing with Ivdulon. It concerned him that he knew things of a life-changing nature but couldn't share them with other people, in case they thought him deranged. Hearing voices in your head definitely wasn't normal. The fact that Gadhallah had privately admitted to similar experiences, and blamed them for his heinous crimes, made Aklon-Dji less inclined to admit to his own ability to mindtalk, even though only a select few knew this detail about their religious leader. It was learning of Gadhallah's gift that had encouraged Aklon-Dji to reach out in the first place, finding Ivdulon in the process.

His conversation with Ivdulon had changed his concept of himself and his place in the world so fundamentally that it would take time for him to come to terms with his new status. He was a much smaller fish than he'd supposed. Still the fish of greatest significance on the island, but a minnow in world terms.

But it had been Ivdulon's disclosures relating to Jodisa-Li that had intrigued, alarmed and excited him.

'She's well, after a brutal attack that might've killed her if she hadn't had the good fortune to come under the influence of Sha'ra.'

Ivdulon hadn't revealed anything about the woman who'd saved Jodisa's life and sanity. But Aklon-Dji had the impression that Sha'ra wasn't mortal. She was some sort of other being; an entity residing outside the normal rules of life. Such an idea was so far outside his personal experience, though not beyond his imagination, that he was unsure how to respond to it.

'Yes, Aklon, there are things in this world that even I don't understand.'

He said this with a touch of irony that had Aklon-Dji smiling.

'Jodisa is in love with Feldrark, and he with her. If they manage to escape the

clutches of those who hunt them, they'll come to the city. I suspect they'll marry as soon as they can. Feldrark's always been able to mindtalk, of course, but he's now learned he can project further than he'd believed possible. Sha'ra helps people see things in themselves they were not previously aware of. Jodisa, as we suspected, can also project over long distances. I'd strongly advise against you contacting them for now. They're in extreme danger and your intervention could be catastrophic. Wait until they're in the city. Feldrark, though, may try to contact you himself. He was ever a law unto himself. Headstrong. I'm afraid I let slip your existence and he seems intrigued. I advised him to keep silent until he reaches the city but...Well, he goes his own way.'

He told Aklon-Dji a little about Aglydron and Okkyntalah and their place in the scheme of things and warned him about his father's unrecognized ability to mindtalk.

'This isn't advice, Aklon, but a desperate plea. Dagla Kaz has no idea he can mindtalk and must remain ignorant as long as possible. Years of hard work and organisation will be destroyed if he learns of his skill before I'm ready to reveal it. Many people, apart from you and your sister, will be in real danger and our plans and schemes will be set back years. I've plans for Dagla Kaz that will serve your purposes very well. But if he has even an inkling about mindtalk, my schemes will be ruined. You are but one tree in the forest, Aklon, and whilst you're a tall and magnificent specimen, the forest can exist and grow without you. If Dagla Kaz recognizes his place in that forest he'll set a fire that'll wipe out more trees than grow on your entire island.'

Aklon-Dji knew that Ivdulon only resorted to imagery of this sort when something was of great importance and he'd agreed to remain silent regarding these new players in the field. Although fascinated by the possibilities of talking with his sister, her lover and his father, he was willing to be patient. Things were moving rapidly and in more directions than even Ivdulon had envisaged. They were living at an important time in the world. Things were going to change and he, Aklon-Dji, was one of those who would effect those changes. He'd make sure they were for the better for as many people as possible.

The Scar rose before him: a sheer cliff towering to almost a hundred manheights at its peak and no less than thirty at its lowest point. It was considered to be unscalable and the authorities found it a convenient and effective bar to escape by those they banished to The Point.

He'd watched them, once, from the shelter of a deep cleft in a rising slope on the island side. The Holy Ones had brought a small group of prisoners, bound and linked together with ropes around their necks, clad in rough sacking for their journey. At the top of the cliff, they'd systematically stripped and raped them; men, women and youths, before placing a noose around the ankles of each in turn and lowering them head first down the cliff to the rocks below. The victims had a short time to get loose and then the rope was hauled back to the cliff top. If they hadn't escaped, the poor unfortunates were brought back up. The Holy Ones then simply cast them over the cliff, to fall to certain death on the rocks forty manheights below.

Of those who managed to free themselves in time, most would die within days as they were in poor health and bore signs of recent torture. The Point was no place for anyone not both very fit and very tough. The few creatures inhabiting the wild place were almost universally venomous in one way or another and even the birds were either carrion fowl or fierce hawks. It made a perfect natural prison for those who displeased the authorities, and served to frighten naughty children. 'You'll end up on The Point'.

Aklon-Dji knew the Scar and had no need to search for a route up. He checked, on his approach, that no one was in sight on the cliff edge above but still made his way by a circuitous route to one of the two places where, with care, he could climb. Delbon had left a pile of moveable rocks in place, knowing Aklon-Dji would soon follow. He used the regular system of ascent, clinging on with his fingertips as he kicked away the small pile of rocks beneath him before making the unaided climb. It was hard and dangerous work and he rested, once at the top.

From this elevation, the settlement wasn't visible. It could be seen from the highest peak, on those few days when the viewpoint wasn't shrouded in the almost permanent cloud which hung over it and watered the rain forest on its northeastern slopes. None of that rain found its way to the plain below, the updraught ensuring all moisture was carried back to the mainland side of the Scar. The smoke from the settlement's domestic fires was visible from the Scar. He thought of Chellyth and her man and the small group of people they led. Soon he'd set them free.

Aklon-Dji would visit his people, the Few, to show them he was still at liberty and not the rumoured prisoner of the authorities. But the real reason for his trip was to share succour with Shoarhn. He wondered how she'd view his revelations about her husband and Okkyntalah. For reasons he didn't investigate too deeply, he was convinced that she, at least, would accept what he told her of how he obtained such information. No doubt she'd think it marvellous and strange but he was sure she wouldn't find it incredible or him mad. Shoarhn would be the one to share his secret and, thereby, ease a little of his load.

⁕

Malarhah was waiting for her time with Sha'ra when Okkyntalah returned to the group. He took his seat beside her and allowed her kiss of gratitude. 'I know our saviour will bring me grief, Okkyntalah. And I beg you counsel me on my return.'

She left then to discover her lot. Okkyntalah remained where she'd left him and felt the wonder of his own experience with Sha'ra.

It seemed but a moment before the young woman returned, full of grief. She sat with him and looked deep into his eyes before she spoke.

'I must tell someone what passed between me and Sha'ra and she's given me but a spell to fulfil this need. Listen to me, Okkyntalah and know that none of the others will hear my words or even be aware of the passing of time. But listen well and without interruption for, once you speak, the spell will be broken and then we must all leave. Say nothing until I release you, please.'

He nodded, happy to do this for the young woman.

Malarhah told him how Sha'ra had sat huddled with a sadness even greater than that she'd detected on their first meeting. Clothed in black from head to foot and hooded so that only her face, painted with sorrow, could be seen, she'd welcomed her.

'Sit beside me, Malarhah and hear what I must say.'

'Do I have a choice?'

'You have a choice, Malarhah, but I have experience that may help you through the days to come and information known to only me.'

'Suppose I don't want to know? Suppose I'm happy in my ignorance and would live without your knowledge of what might or might not be?'

'I understand the reasons for your fears. I can't advise you in this, Malarhah. I can tell you what I know or not tell you. That choice is yours and you must make it, as I and your companions have made ours.'

Malarhah took Okkyntalah's hand in hers and he felt the anxiety in her grasp, saw the concern in her dark eyes.

'Sha'ra told me I won't forget, as the rest of you will. That much she could tell me for certain.

'I told her I saw sorrow in her and knew it wasn't for me alone. I'd seen that sadness when we first met and her own grief, whatever its cause, only served to deepen it. I saw no benefit in knowing what particular end I'm destined to meet, or when. I'd far rather live each day as it passes and let the fates take me when they will. Since I can't prevent what will be, I'd rather not know. And I asked if I might leave her.

'She told me that I was the only one who hadn't received her knowledge. To the others she'd offered gifts, which bore a price. To me she gave a gift without a price for me or herself because it sprang entirely from love. And love is a place without beginning or end and therefore can give of itself without loss. She gave me the mask of the carefree to wear for the rest of my days, as soon as we leave this place. She asked one thing in return. How could I refuse?

'She told me that when I left her, after this brief pause, she must go to a place without time or space or dimension, a place so far from our experience it's incomprehensible. It's a place of great torture for her and the longer we remain here, the more her influence will diminish, the more she'll suffer.

'The rest will believe night is coming. It isn't. I have to make them understand that we have the time from noon before us till this day closes with the fading of the moon. Will you help me, Okkyntalah?'

He understood her question released him from the need to be silent. 'If I can. Tell me how.'

'We have to go up the wide river that flows into the sea outside the cave. Once we reach the place of thorns, we'll be out of Sha'ra's realm and beyond her help. We may not return and I alone will remember her. The rest of you will recall only what she allows.'

Malarhah looked beyond Okkyntalah to their companions, eating and relaxing on the settles in the cave. 'We have to leave.'

He looked up at the darkness at the back of the cave.

Malarhah seemed strangely urgent, insistent. 'We must go now; straight away.'

As though in shock, they left the bare cave, a place they couldn't recall entering; Okkyntalah had only a faint recollection of what Malarhah had told him moments before. He pushed the boat into the gentle waves and took to the oars with Feldrark to move them past this strange place that had been nothing more than the hope of sanctuary.

As they passed the promontory into the already rising mist, they saw the mouth of a cave. But it seemed unwelcoming and not at all suitable for the girl's recovery. Malarhah urged them try the brown waters of the river that merged with the sea to take them inland, in search of a suitable landing place. As Feldrark protested they couldn't row far against the current, a breeze sprang up from the south and they hoisted the sail to catch it. The boat sailed against the current, slowly gaining headway and leaving the sea behind and, with it, the small patch of dry weather.

Jodisa-Li, curled in the bows, unwound, stretched and rose to her feet. 'Is there anything to eat? I'm hungry. Where are we?'

They cheered to have her back amongst them, though none expressed surprise at her recovery. Each of them kissed and embraced her in welcome.

'You were badly injured. Let me make sure you're properly healed.' Myllthlan examined her from head to toe and declared her free of injury and as perfect in body as a woman could be.

'As for food, I'm afraid you'll have to…'

'No, Feldrark, there's food here in plenty.'

Okkyntalah showed them the supplies and they fed on fresh fruits, concealed in strange skin bags amongst the water skins of spring water. Malarhah took the tiller as they tried to come to terms with this strange fortune that had restored Jodisa-Li and miraculously given them food and water. As they puzzled and found small unrelated glimpses of a memory too strange to comprehend, so Malarhah pointed to the west, where the mist had lifted and the rain cleared to give a short spell of bright warm sunshine. Beyond, a shadow drifted to the sky from the surface of the distant sea.

'What is it?'

'It's the fire you left in the reed boat, Myllthlan. It must've caught after all.'

Later in the day, Okkyntalah noted thorn bushes growing amongst the reeds on the flooded banks they sailed beside and knew, without knowing why, they were no longer safe. The rains began again.

Malarhah seemed more aware than the others. 'We must be careful now. Not only have we killed the Galhta and some citizens, but we've set fire to the town and it'll burn easily if the flames take hold. They'll douse the fire and then send their best hunters to find and kill us. The sooner we're away, the better.'

'How good are their hunters, Malarhah?'

'Oh, very good indeed. It'll take all our ingenuity to escape them. And they may send others to Litkala to await our return. We must take care at every step.' She spoke as if these things were of no matter.

'They'll never get inside Litkala.'

'Then expect them at your borders, Feldrark, if they haven't killed us by then.'

They looked at Aglydron and hoped his prediction was based on anxiety rather than foreknowledge.

'We'll get through. All will be well.'

Malarhah's confidence seemed out of place and Okkyntalah frowned at her. She shuffled to sit beside him and whispered in his ear, talking as if what she had to say was of far more import than their present danger.

'When Myllthlan made me whole again, she purged from me the fear and resentment, the loathing and rage I felt at all the abuse and use I'd had from the men of Mipahnhil. Okkyntalah, you've shown me what's possible. I don't delude myself that you love me or that you ever will. There's part of you I'll never have and it'll remain locked up until Tumalind releases it and makes you complete. But you've given me, along with pleasure I never knew was possible, self-respect and a sense of worth I thought was lost forever. You may not love me, Okkyntalah, but I love you and always will.

'Feldrark's my master and has always been kind to me. He talks of returning me to my home but I won't go back. My parents sold me into slavery fully aware of what would become of me but greedy for the price I brought. I won't return to haunt them. I'll serve Feldrark as willing servant all my life. He knows I'd die for him, though I'd far rather live for him; the days in Mipahnhil as his servant were the best of my life until I gained my freedom. I'll not forget such kindness. But it's you I'll always love, Okkyntalah.'

The wind blew steadily from the south for three days and took them upriver some thirty leagues. They stopped many times in the first two days as they moved through the Mire of Rhoshe, where the swamps were flooded with the rains and giant clumps of reed and thorn interrupted their progress. But they had no need to hunt for food.

'Where did we get these supplies? I don't remember collecting any food.'

Malarhah smiled. 'She said you wouldn't recall. That only I would have memories. Just give thanks, Jodisa-Li. I can't tell you what she would have remain secret to all but me. If I try, I'll fail.'

Something about Malarhah allowed Jodisa-Li to accept her answer, inadequate though it was. Their memories of the days since they left the sea were hazy and incomplete and, in several matters their individual recollections seemed so diverse that they could make no sense of them and were forced to abandon all attempts to find the reality.

'We're following the rains but they'll eventually pass away to the west. Whilst we're in the Mire, we're sheltered by the reed beds and thorn bushes from the flooding that makes the rivers treacherous. But the main river will be in flood when we reach it and I doubt this friendly wind will be strong enough to take us upstream when we get there. We'll struggle to cross the currents without travelling downstream a good distance.'

Malarhah said this in such light tones that they treated it as well meant but unreliable. She admitted she had little knowledge of boats or rivercraft and there was no particular reason why she should be better informed than the rest of them, apart from her long residence in the city of reeds.

But, on the third day after leaving the sea behind, they emerged from the Mire and into what they first thought was the Sure itself. The current was very strong and they made progress only with difficulty, taking to the oars again in order to move upstream. The land about them was mainly flat and featureless. The west bank of the river lay low but steep and much undercut by the swiftly flowing water. A dozen times, they tried to land but every time they sailed inshore, the overhang confused the wind and the current sent them downstream again. In the end, they decided to struggle on upstream as best they could until the land on the western bank grew shallow and landing was easier.

'Ytraa preserve us!'

Jodisa-Li, sitting as lookout in the bows, pointed and the others followed her finger, as the grey light of noon lay sullen on a huge expanse of turbulent water ahead. They had reached the confluence of their own smaller waterway with the main River Sure.

'Look at the current! We'll be swept downstream and end up back in Mipahnhil.'

'Please don't speak of that vile place, Okkyntalah.'

'He's right, though, Malarhah. We'd best find a landing place and rest for what's left of today and the night. In the morning we'll be fresh and can use the oars to help us cross that deluge.'

All agreed with Feldrark's suggestion and Jodisa-Li used the sail, along with help from the men on the oars, to reach the riverbank. There, in slack water against a softly rising bank, they lowered the sail and Okkyntalah and Feldrark jumped into the muddy water to pull the boat onto the waterlogged grassland that was now the river's edge.

The swiftly flowing Sure surged and roared its way across the plain. To the south, their smaller river flowed back into the Mire. North, lay slowly rising flatlands; grasslands that appeared empty of human life. Here and there, herds of large grazing creatures roamed and, overhead, the wide winged oryol hunted in disconsolate groups seeking stranded fish or carrion washed down by the flood. Eastward lay more grassland; flooded, marshy and unwelcoming. None of the far horizons was visible under the heavy but now spasmodic rain. They rested, creatures of the land, surrounded by water.

'There's no game here. Those beasts, whatever they are, would see me from a league away in this landscape and the marshes will have only waterfowl and I've no more arrows for my bow. I'll try to catch some fish.'

Their water bags were still well stocked with spring water that they now accepted must've come from the cave, though none recalled collecting it. The fruit and bread had all but gone with their last meal, so Okkyntalah's offer of fish was welcome. He dropped out of the boat and slowly waded upstream, seeking a likely spot.

Jodisa-Li watched him move away and found her admiration for the spirit and courage of the young man enhanced by his readiness to do all he could to provide for them.

'What are we going to do, once across the Sure?'

'If, as I believe, Aglydron, we're at the place where the Sure splits into its first great branches, then Shorrannon lies a dozen leagues upstream and we're some thirty five to forty leagues east of Litkala. The plain of Rophan-Ra is rich in game and I don't doubt we can catch enough to feed us. Jodisa-Li has her burning glass, Myllthlan her knowledge of roots and herbs and Malarhah's proved herself a good cook. We should eat well enough.

'Shelter's our real problem in this foul weather but the rains will end soon and, in any case, there's nothing we can do but use the sail for cover as we have so far. Once the sky's clear, it'll stay that way for a season. The ground will be wet underfoot and marshy in places but we'll travel easily and, once we're on the plain, there's cover. Unlike this eastern plain, the western side of the Sure is rich in grassland with plenty of wooded areas and lots of brushwood.

'It's barely inhabited, though there's rumoured to be a wandering tribe of herdsmen, who're supposed to live in hide tents and move from place to place with their animals. They're reckoned to worship the sun and make blood sacrifices, cutting the beating hearts out of their victims and offering them to Ulkhon in a bowl made from a human skull. It's said they live in their skin, which they decorate with strange cuts filled with mud to make raised scars. I'm inclined to think they're just creatures of imagination made to scare young children when they're naughty. We call them the Bruxa, but I've never come across them all the times I've ventured on the plains and I doubt they exist.

'I think we should cross the Sure as quickly as possible and then burn or scuttle the boat so no one...'

'Why not let it take its chances down the river, Feldrark? Perhaps the hunters from Mipahnhil will discover it and believe us drowned.'

'An excellent suggestion, Jodisa-Li. Yes, we'll do that. Then travel on foot to Litkala. From there, we can plan the next stage of your journey, Aglydron. It's plain you've no hope now of meeting up with Jodisa-Li's father and his party. You may as well have a rest and then we'll see what aid I can provide for the rest of your journey.'

'You're not going to Shorrannon for a beautiful wife, then?'

'I've regained the Staff of Ytraa and I believe it's only just and right that I take as my wife the talented and beautiful young woman who retrieved it.'

Malarhah managed shy delight at this announcement. Jodisa-Li, aware she must hide her amusement, gave the appearance of disappointment. Myllthlan seemed genuinely surprised but said nothing.

'Malarhah, then? I'm surprised, Feldrark. I believed you had your eye on Jodisa for your wife.'

'Aglydron, what man wouldn't want Jodisa-Li as a partner? Malarhah knows I find the young virgin extremely desirable but, now that my former slave's been restored to full womanhood and can enjoy the proper pleasures of joining, honour dictates I have her. She's beautiful, talented, devoted and loving.'

Jodisa-Li saw Aglydron's determined look and knew he'd continue to keep an eye on them to prevent her joining, thus destroying his pointless mission. She was eager to be in a safe place, under Feldrark's dominion and out of Aglydron's power, where she and her beloved could finally make the physical connection their minds had already made.

Chapter 37

Deception And Relief

'How long before we reach Litkala, Feldrark?'

'Without accidents or stoppages, we should cover four or five leagues a day. I hope to make it in just over a sixday. We're all fit and well again since that, that...you know, when we came across the...where we were...'

Malarhah smiled. The memory of something no one else could recall in detail seemed to amuse her.

'Okkyntalah's returning. He has food, look.'

Feldrark followed Myllthlan's gaze as the young man ran low along the slight rise in the ground that edged the river. His spear held three good-sized fish and in his other hand, he grasped a brace of waterfowl.

'He's a talented hunter.'

'One of the best on the island, Feldrark. Don't tell him, but I'm proud he's promised to my daughter.'

As Okkyntalah came closer, he raised his finger to his lips and pointed across the wide expanse of water to the west bank. Shading his eyes, Feldrark could see nothing on the far bank of the river.

'Hey, it's not raining anymore.'

'Quiet, Jodisa!' Okkyntalah climbed aboard. 'Sound carries well over water, so keep your voices down. It was your talking that distracted these two or I'd never have caught them without a bow.' He dropped two brightly coloured birds into the boat. Pointing across the water, he nodded at the far bank. 'They're from Mipahnhil. I recognize the reed boats; no mast or sail. They're obviously our hunters but I can see a woman with them. Do they send their women out, Malarhah?'

They followed his direction of gaze but none could see anything other than water, mud, cloud and rain.

'You're eyesight's better than mine, Okkyntalah; all I can see is the river bank beyond the flowing water.'

Okkyntalah frowned at him. 'They're plain as day. Two boats and a party of eight.'

'We'll have to take your word for it, Okkyntalah. The woman'll be Chislanda. She bears a double responsibility now. Aglydron may have filled her with new life but we've taken their Galhta. The others will leave you to her, Aglydron, if she's truly carrying your child. She must kill you or spend her life in shame and condemn the child to slavery.'

'Would they know so soon that I've made her pregnant?'

'Perhaps, perhaps not yet. The toadwives can tell very early. But even the chance of pregnancy would make Chislanda volunteer for the party. If she finds out later she's pregnant and someone else has killed you, her shame and the child's slavery remain.'

'I can't begin to comprehend the philosophy of those people. They declare life to be sacred, yet they'll destroy it if it falls outside their narrow definition of what should be. And even in that definition there's no sense or…'

'Yes, Feldrark. You may be right but this is hardly the time for discussion, is it? What are we to do?'

'It's obvious, Myllthlan.'

They turned to Jodisa-Li who made no effort to keep her voice quiet for her reply but then lowered her tone as she offered her solution.

'They're in two reed boats that have to be driven by oars, without sails. They're on the far shore, the place we hope to be tomorrow. But we want them here by then. So, let them know we're here. Let them "discover" us. They'll try to cross the torrent, get swept down into the Mire and be days paddling back upstream again. By then, we'll be across the river and half way to Litkala.'

Feldrark was impressed with her thinking but found a possible flaw. 'Suppose they just wait for us on the far bank?'

Malarhah shook her head. 'They won't. Jodisa-Li's right. As soon as they know we're here, they'll be forced to try to reach us, no matter how impossible it seems. It's their way. Once they've discovered us, we mustn't be allowed to escape or disappear again.'

'Suppose there are others; maybe on this bank?'

'That's not very likely. They won't devote too many to the hunt at any one time. Last time I experienced something similar to this, a couple of years ago, they waited for twenty-one days before sending the next lot. I thought it was stupid: the trail must've grown stale by then. But they brought one of their quarry back for public execution and the heads of the other two on sticks.'

'I think Malarhah's right. It's their good luck that they've managed to come so close to us. They must be expecting me to take you to Litkala. They'll be overjoyed when they discover we're here but they'll believe we're on our way to Shorrannon first. I made it clear I'd not take any of their own women, even if I could, when I returned home. And they won't consider Malarhah or even Myllthlan as suitable. Jodisa-Li they'll see as untouchable because of your mission, but they know I must take a wife. What choice would I have but Shorrannon? No, I believe we should make our presence known. If they don't set off to cross the river, at least we'll know where we stand, and the wind's still strong enough, with two of us on the oars, to outrun them if they try to follow us upriver.'

'We're agreed, then?'

After some hesitation, all nodded.

'I suggest we try to light a cooking fire.'

Feldrark frowned at Jodisa-Li.

'It'll signal our position and hopefully they'll see the smoke and then our sail and it'll tell them we're not aware of them. They'll expect to catch us by surprise.'

'A good suggestion, Jodisa-Li, but how do we start a fire? And what can we burn?'

All land within easy distance was waterlogged. No trees studded the ground and the only stuff that might burn was either part of the boat, their stores or the thorn bushes that Malarhah had warned them against touching due to their poisonous thorns.

'We've got to cross the river and we can't do it with them waiting there. We'll have to get rid of the boat after we've crossed, anyway. There must be bits of it we can burn now, and maybe some other stuff?'

Aglydron's suggestion made sense. There wasn't much. Coils of rope and twine, especially the tarred lengths, would burn well. The fishing spear would be a loss but was of little use for hunting on land. Two rough boxes and the canvas bucket with bits and bobs of fishing gear would make some flame and smoke.

'What about the sleepsacks? We can manage in our clothes for the journey overland.'

So, they gathered all they could. Malarhah suddenly plunged into the river and swam strongly to the edge of the fast current. She grabbed the fuel she'd spotted and returned, dragging a large branch, that half floated and was half submerged in the water.

'I know it's wet, but the other stuff'll dry it out and it'll burn with plenty of smoke. That's what we want, isn't it?'

Feldrark set about breaking and cutting it into manageable pieces, as Okkyntalah gutted the fish, plucked the birds, and skewered them on the fishing spear to cook them.

'I still don't see how we're going to start the fire, though.'

Jodisa-Li glanced at the sky and confirmed what she'd seen earlier. She took the earthenware bowl they used for cooking and emptied it of rainwater. She wiped it dry with a spare tabard from her pack. Taking several of the smaller bits and pieces they'd collected to burn, she placed these in the bottom of the container. The feathers and oily innards from the fish she placed around the small pile.

The rest of them piled the other combustible material on the nearby bank.

She took out her treasured burning glass and polished it on the same dry tabard. They scoured the sky and saw what she'd already noticed. A narrow strip of blue had opened on the western horizon, a patch of sky devoid of cloud. And the sun would soon enter this narrow band. The timing would have to be perfect.

She bent over the bowl, turning it so that the small pile of material was in the right place. As the sun dropped into the clear strip, she focused its rays on the driest stuff, her burning glass held still, and the bowl sheltering its contents from the wind. The sharp point of concentrated heat and light settled on the pile and she held her breath, watching and waiting. The boat suddenly rocked as someone moved to get a better view.

'Still!'

'We'd have been better off doing this on land.'

Okkyntalah's observation came too late, however. It was now or never.

They remained steady and Jodisa-Li focussed her burning rays again. A small plume of flame rose from the centre of the pile, wavered and blew out in the slight breeze. The thin slit of clear sky now held the whole orb of the sun as she again focused the rays. She held her breath again, concentrating on obtaining the most powerful beam she could. The pile began to smoke again. A tiny flame flickered in the bowl, licking at the drier stuff and catching the oily waste from the fish. The downy feathers caught and smoked with acrid fumes, catching her breath, but still she held her glass until the material caught and flamed strongly in the bowl. Confident of her fire, she held the flames close, her tabard in danger of catching light, and moved from the boat to the pile of material on the bank. Slowly, she pushed the bowl beneath the open pile of belongings.

The wet stuff of their fire smouldered and smoked as the small amount of dry material slowly caught the flames. It seemed an age before it began to roar but it did at last. Smoke blew into their eyes and steam hissed from the wet wood. But the heat grew intense enough to dry out the fuel in stages and make a proper fire at last.

They cheered and yelled at their success.

Okkyntalah turned his eyes from the flames and scanned the distant shore. 'Look. They've already boarded their boats. They're paddling towards us.'

Jodisa-Li strained her eyes to watch but, like the rest, she could see nothing of what Okkyntalah described. Perhaps, there, on the very edge of seeing, might be a suggestion of something slipping down with the current.

'How are they doing, Okkyntalah?'

'Use your eyes, Feldrark. The current's swept them downstream already. I've lost them. They'll be leagues away before they get across.'

Okkyntalah began to roast the fish and fowl over the fire.

'No, Okkyntalah. No one but you could see them.'

'I thought I saw a dark smudge, just for an instant. Then it disappeared.'

'Did you, Jodisa-Li? Why are you undressing?'

'I thought I'd set my tabard on fire.'

'Nearly did, didn't you?'

'It was a risk, Myllthlan. But it worked, didn't it?'

She finished her examination.

'Thanks for your good sense and mature judgement, Jodisa-Li. I'll not forget this sacrifice when we reach Litkala. You're not hurt at all?'

Jodisa-Li smiled at Feldrark and shook her head. 'Not a mark, see?'

He examined her closely, to Aglydron's outrage. But the man had the sense to say nothing.

Gathered in the boat again, the party sighed their relief and ate with real relish.

'Delicious, Okkyntalah. You'll keep Tumalind well fed once we swap her for the real Virgin Gift and take her back home.'

Neither Jodisa-Li nor Feldrark rose to the bait but they exchanged secret amused glances.

'Ever hopeful. How are you going to deal with his disappointment?'

'I've some ideas. I need to chat with Ivdulon first, but I think I have a solution. But don't you worry about it, my love; I'll have you for my wife once we're in Litkala. You're not going to Chalamamnon under any circumstances.'

They kept half the food to eat the following morning, wrapping it in a hide bag that Malarhah told them they'd acquired from the cave. They had no need to burn the fishing spear, after Malarhah's contribution from the river, and Okkyntalah cleaned the flesh, fat and soot from the shaft to keep it as an extra weapon.

Malarhah and Myllthlan took the night watches between them, as they expected to be least involved in the hard work of the river crossing. The men would be rowing and Jodisa-Li would control the tiller and the sail.

<hr>

The ten days they spent confined within the women's quarters in Qlentz, as the rains poured without ceasing, were the most tiresome Tumalind could recall. They saw nothing of the men and spent their time inside the women's quarters with little to do but educate them, gossip and idle away the time.

As abruptly as they had begun, the rains ceased. Once the sky began to clear, Gret-Zudas wanted them out of his town. What sort of legacy they might leave behind, Tumalind had no way of knowing but, for all his declared desire to open up the road to trade, Gret-Zudas had clearly not reckoned on the possibility of traders liberating his women.

They were escorted from the town by a large group of worried and disgruntled men, even before the sun had emerged from the dark clouds to dry the roadway. With the rains over, the town's men considered their debt paid.

To the north, the cloud was still heavy and threatening but Gret-Zudas assured them there would be no more rain in this part of the country for a long time. The wet weather would pass away to vanish in the Unnamed Mountains, leaving Balagaaq and Tohltaz dry as deserts.

The road through the trees was ankle deep in water, mud and rotting vegetation for long stretches. They splashed and waded along it, occasionally up to their thighs in muddy puddles but glad at last to be out of the claustrophobic atmosphere of Qlentz. Phildrad was much recovered, though he still limped and had insufficient strength to carry his own pack. Tarruss carried it for him without apparent effort. Caarl's sword arm bore a livid scar from elbow to wrist but he'd lost none of his strength and put his healing down to Corphanda's skill and her constant care of the three of them. Tarruss bore a short red crescent beneath his left eye that gave him a slightly fierce appearance.

Tumalind smiled up at the giant as she walked beside him. 'That battle scar might make those who don't know you very wary. They'll give you a wide berth, Tarruss.'

He glowered fiercely down at her, making her fear she'd said too much, then he lifted her off her feet and gave her a great hug, laughing at her fear. 'Didn't really think I'd be cross with you, did you, Tumalind?'

'You're wicked.' She laughed as he set her back on her feet. 'But I still think it gives you the air of a brigand.'

He touched it lightly with a fingertip and put on a serious face. 'Don't think it'll spoil my chances with the women, do you?'

'If I were free, and as long as Okkyntalah wasn't about, I'd have you in a trice.'

He shook his head at her. 'Thanks for the compliment, but I know you'll only ever be happy joining with that man you carry in your heart, lass. Would that you could have your wish. It makes me sorrow for you to think of you landed with some uncouth and unworthy foreigner.'

He'd say no more but his sympathy and tacit support made her feel warm inside.

The men spoke little of their time in the roundhouse but Tumalind gathered that only Tryonta had taken advantage of the free availability of the town's women. The others had considered such enforced service and provision beneath them and had found the domestic enslavement of the women difficult to accept. Tarruss and Phildrad had, apparently, made it abundantly clear to their hosts that they considered the treatment of the townswomen unacceptable and cowardly. And even Netrodyl's attempts to give herself in thanks for saving her life had been rejected because she had no real choice in the matter.

Corphanda and Wendarah had been the saviours of the girls' virtue. In a society where women were inferior and available, virginity earned neither admiration nor respect. Their men, however, had made it clear that any interference with the girls would result in the death of the man concerned. Gret-Zudas, apparently anxious to have as little trouble as possible, had issued a decree to his men to leave the girls unmolested. Wendarah and Corphanda, excluded from this prohibition and, novelties in the small town, had been much in demand. Both were heartily pleased to be traipsing through mud and away from the town after their somewhat public experiences in the roundhouse. Dagla Kaz praised them for their selfless sacrifice in this implicit bargain for the girls' honour.

'Bet Corphanda thought she was in the Garden of Delights with all that attention.' Tumalind giggled as she speculated with Tarruss.

'Heard that, young miss. I'll be marking your bum if you're not careful.'

'But you're right, Tumalind. I'll keep her in practice now I've seen how keen she is.'

Tumalind was rewarded by a wide smile of appreciation from her chaperone and knew the threatened smack was now unlikely: Corphanda had had her eye on Tarruss since the trip had started.

By sun up, they'd eaten and were prepared for the crossing. They made what prayers each deemed fit and took their positions in the boat. Jodisa-Li took her place at the stern, tiller in hand and all ropes controlling the sail within reach.

The rain had returned in the night and continued as they set out. The river ran dangerously high, flowing fast with large branches and even the occasional whole tree floating down on the flood, threatening to ram and sink their small craft.

At the point where the waters split into two, the current ran less swiftly, though the water was very choppy. The men were able to relax their efforts on the oars for a brief spell and Jodisa-Li let the wind take them through until they were about a third of the way across the river. But, once they drifted into the main stream, the current swept them backwards at an alarming rate. The tumultuous waters splashed over the sides and bows so that Malarhah and Myllthlan had no chance of rest after their night watches. Having burnt the canvas bucket and wooden goblets, they resorted to cupped hands to bail. Jodisa-Li turned the sail to cause as much wind resistance as she could and this slowed them down a little, as the men pulled and heaved on the oars, moving them slowly across the current so that the distant shore grew slowly nearer.

Feldrark, not on the oars for this leg, kept watch in the bows for floating debris that might sink them. Shaulah leapt up on the stern seat and sat precariously beside Jodisa-Li. She moved to let the dog lie down and make her less likely to fall overboard as the boat lurched and tossed on the fast moving water. When they were almost out of danger, approaching the calmer water a few dozen strokes from the shore, Feldrark yelled a warning.

'Tree bearing down on the left!'

Jodisa-Li, by deft handling of sail and tiller, saved the boat from being rammed and sunk but had to take them further out into the main stream again. They struggled back, Okkyntalah and Aglydron, on the oars, growing exhausted as they fought the current to drag the boat across it. As they made slacker water, they risked changing places. Feldrark took the oar from Aglydron, who bailed beside Malarhah. Myllthlan kept lookout. At last, the rain eased, making bailing easier. The clouds lightened and the landscape took on a brightness that brought its features into sharp focus.

As they were changing places, Okkyntalah pointed to the eastern bank. The hunters from Mipahnhil were close to the shore they'd just left and had spotted them. They hurriedly moved back across the torrent, intent on following, but when they reached the edge of the wild current, their light boats were swept downstream with no hope of battling across. In spite of their skill and determination, within moments, they were out of sight.

'They travel quickly. To have reached so far upstream after their crossing, they must've rowed like demons all through the night. They'll be a few leagues behind us but we must be on our guard. I'd hoped to reach Litkala without the need to fight, but we'll have to stay alert and prepared for attack.'

They made landfall, at last, finding a suitable place where trees overhung the bank and a small gravel spit had been washed out of the eroded side of the slope. As the others emptied the boat of everything they might need, Okkyntalah moved inland in search of food.

He'd been gone only a moment when Feldrark, checking the boat for the last time before making ready to push it back into the river, made an unexpected discovery.

'What's the meaning of this, Aglydron? Tell me how you came by it and make it quick, less I cut your throat!'

Jodisa-Li turned to see the cause of this sudden violent outburst. Feldrark, his face grave and threatening, stood in the stern of the boat. He held aloft the gem-studded myllth bracelet that Okkyntalah had removed from the body of the woman they'd found on the shipwreck.

Chapter 38

Night Watches

'You threaten bravely for a man with no weapon, Feldrark. What do you mean?'

'This! How did you come by it?'

'What's it to you? And what makes you think I came by it dishonestly? For all you know, I might've bought it, owned it all my life, might even have made it…'

'No, Aglydron. See!' Feldrark placed the bangle beside the one that circled his ankle.

Jodisa-Li knew he was wondering that no one had remarked on the piece before if they'd seen this other. She'd forgotten it in the rush of events; perhaps the same went for the others.

In the silence that followed, Okkyntalah crashed through the bushes. 'I don't know what's wrong with you two, but you've just scared off a brace of fat conies with your yelling. I was ready to strike when you frightened them away. Perhaps you don't want supper…?' He stopped as he saw the bangles. 'Ytraa's balls! They're a matching pair!'

'And unique. I ask again, how you came by this.'

'I've no idea why you're so angry, Feldrark. I came by the thing honestly enough. Aglydron's nothing to do with it. It adorned the ankle of a dead woman we found tangled in wreckage in the sea near Ylcrat. Oh. Feldrark; I'm sorry. You knew the woman…?'

Feldrark slumped to his knees and tears started in his eyes, the bangle gripped tightly in his hands. Jodisa-Li felt his grief well up. 'Dead? There's no doubt?'

'She'd been dead some time when we hit the wreckage. It saved Jodisa's life, and mine when I rescued her. The woman was decaying but still whole and pinned to the deck by rope and netting that had trapped her there. Those green orbs around the boat were attached to the netting and keeping the wreckage afloat. I cut her free and gave her the dignity of the sea. It seemed pointless to let her take that with her. We thought to sell it for food or other needs on our journey.'

'Was she…wounded, harmed, in any way?'

'She seemed whole; her skin unpierced. I don't know how she came to be trapped. Perhaps she fell or…who was she? We thought her of noble stock.'

'My sister, called Mythanpho after the serpent slayer. She was lost to us a month before I set out. We thought pirates or slavers had taken her but no one saw what happened. We didn't even know whether she'd been kidnapped, had fallen, or been taken by a beast in the forest. She went out on her usual ride and, though her guardians tried to keep up with her, she lost them as she did so often. This time, she never returned.

'Trapped, you say? This is sad news indeed. I pray she wasn't used or harmed; felt no pain or shame.'

'She still wore the bangle, and the shreds of clothing that clung to her were of rich weave. You've been away from home almost a full cycle, Feldrark, which means she was missing nearly as long before we found her. It's unlikely she was abused or held against her will all that time if they treated her with enough respect to let her stay well attired and allowed her to keep such a precious item. I think you needn't trouble for her comfort or safety, wherever she was bound and whoever she was with. I think it most likely she was honoured and treated like a noble lady.'

'Thank you for your words of comfort, Jodisa-Li. But, if that's the case, how was she trapped on board the ship when others presumably escaped?'

'I don't think we'll ever know. As for the crew, we can't tell. Hers was the only body; the others may have been washed overboard. Maybe she died before the ship broke apart in whatever accident befell it.'

'Perhaps. You give me some solace, Okkyntalah, but, as you say, we'll probably never know. My poor, dear Mythanpho, to have perished far from home, amongst strangers.'

'Strangers, Feldrark? I think a cycle away from home and still well and healthy suggests she knew at least one of her companions on the ship, don't you?'

Feldrark was thoughtful a moment and then nodded. 'She was so precious to me. My parents will mourn her loss when I return.' He held up the bangle. 'This is worth a thousand, thousand crowns but you found it in good faith, Okkyntalah. I thank you for its recovery, however tragic the news you bring with it, but it is yours, as finder.'

'No. It's clearly yours, Feldrark. Use it as seems right to you. Already you've given us more than its value in helping our escape.'

'As to that, we owe another for our escape. Without her help, we'd still be rotting in that shit-hole on sticks. And, as she's to be my wife, I freely ask that she wears this as proudly as my sister did.'

Jodisa-Li took a half step forward before his glance of warning stopped her. The move, unseen by Okkyntalah, caused Aglydron some anxiety. Malarhah, however, stepped up and let Feldrark open the bangle on a secret hinge and place it round her right ankle. 'Wear it in pride and duty, Malarhah, for this is a sacred symbol of the rulers of Litkala and carries more weight than mere monetary value. The wearer of this bangle will be obeyed absolutely wherever she may tread in Litkala and the citizens will defend her with their lives.'

'I am honoured by this gift and symbol of your regard, Feldrark. I will wear it as well as I may until life itself, or your displeasure, strips it from me.'

In spite of her feelings, Jodisa-Li allowed herself no sign of jealousy or anxiety over this display.

Okkyntalah was about to leave again on his hunting expedition. 'You're going to release the boat, Feldrark?'

'As we agreed.'

'I thought you had other ideas, Aglydron?'

Aglydron shrugged. 'No more than a thought. We might split up here and now. You and Malarhah, with Myllthlan if she wishes, go on to Litkala whilst Okkyntalah and I continue our mission with Jodisa by boat up river.'

'I thought we'd already decided we've no chance of catching my father? And we'd never sail up river in this lot. We'd have to wait for the rains to stop and the river to drop to its normal level. If we travel to Litkala, Feldrark might provide some aid for the rest of our journey.'

'Jodisa-Li's right, Aglydron. You can't row against the flood. Look what happened today. You'd be swept downstream to Mipahnhil. And how would we fend off the hunters if they attacked after we separated?'

Aglydron seemed defeated by the argument. Jodisa-Li knew he was anxious, in spite of Feldrark's stated intentions to take Malarhah as his wife.

'It was just an idea. But you're right. Go on, Okkyntalah. We'll deal with the boat.'

'Can you bear a companion, Okkyntalah?'

He frowned at Myllthlan. 'I'll be better alone. Why would you accompany me?'

'I'd like to gather some roots and herbs to go with whatever you catch, but I'd rather not wander alone in this strange land where we're hunted.'

'Come, then. But be quieter than the wariest rhaat if you wish to eat tonight.'

'Okkyntalah?'

'You too, Jodisa?'

'You wouldn't be safe.' Feldrark's concern was obvious.

'I've no wish to go hunting. I merely thought it might be better if he did two jobs in one. Look at where we landed the boat. Footprints in the mud and marks as we dragged our belongings onto land. It shouts out to those who hunt us that here is where we set out on foot. They'll track us easily, knowing this is where we came ashore. But what if Okkyntalah takes the boat a little way downstream, beaches it, and then hunts on his way back?'

Feldrark nodded. 'Excellent idea, Jodisa-Li. Will you do it, Okkyntalah? With your skills as hunter and tracker, you know how to disguise your return. They'll waste a day or more trying to discover our route.'

'Come on, Myllthlan. It'll be easier with two of us.'

They cast off and the river took them slowly downstream in the calm water close under the bank.

With the boat no longer a concern, the rest set about finding a suitable place to camp. They discovered a stand of low trees and bushes a few hundred paces from the river bank and cleared a small space beneath a pair of trees where they hoped to sleep partly sheltered from falling rain.

Aglydron hunted in the bushes. Feldrark collected kindling for a fire but gave up when he saw how wet everything was. Jodisa-Li and Malarhah helped for a short while, disconsolately adding twigs and fallen branches to the pile. But when Feldrark went to the edge of the copse so he could guide Okkyntalah and Myllthlan on their return, Jodisa-Li suggested she and Malarhah should search for fruit and berries. They found a small stand of wild, stunted cirera trees on the other edge of the wood.

'You'll surrender that when the time comes, won't you, Malarhah?' Jodisa-Li asked as they gathered ripe red and yellow berries.

'I may. Or I may not. You surely don't question Feldrark's intent, do you?'

'That's a strange reply.'

'How well do you think you can keep up the pretence, Jodisa-Li?'

'I'll manage.'

'Aglydron will get desperate if he suspects you and Feldrark are more than you try to appear. If ever I saw a fanatic, he's one.'

'I can act the part. Can you, Malarhah?'

'Perhaps I don't need to. Feldrark's publicly announced I'm to be his wife. Will he go back on his word? I've shared his bed. Have you?'

'It's me he loves, Malarhah, as you well know.'

'I love him. Do you?'

'I do. You agreed: you'd pretend so Aglydron and Okkyntalah would go along with the plan without suspicion.'

'I might let them in on the secret, Jodisa-Li. What will they do if they think their precious virgin's in danger of violation?'

'You won't do that, if you love Feldrark. They might try to kill him. As you so rightly point out, they're fanatical.'

'Aglydron is. Okkyntalah's different. But I still might keep Feldrark for myself. I have the right. For years, I've been subject to the whims and fancies of others. Used, abused, shamed and humiliated. I deserve some happiness, some joy, some respect, don't you think?'

'Feldrark will see you well settled and honoured when we reach the city. Don't try to steal him from me, Malarhah, you'll never win.'

'You think a woman with my past can't persuade a man over an inexperienced virgin, a girl who doesn't even know what it's about? I've serviced more men than...'

'I'm not a virgin. I've known a man. Oh, and don't think you can use that against me, either. Feldrark knows. And, as for Okkyntalah and Aglydron, they'll not believe you. I staged my virgin status so convincingly that they believe I'm intact. If you tell them otherwise, they'll ask if you heard it from me. I'll confess my attempted subterfuge and you'll look foolish. In any case, go ahead and tell them; if they decide I'm not virgin after all, they'll let me go to Feldrark.'

'Of course I won't try to convince them. But, Jodisa-Li, know we're in competition. May the best woman win.'

'You swore to serve him, Malarhah.'

'And serve him I will, all my life, and with pleasure now Myllthlan's restored me.'

'I'll not give him up!'

'Keep your voice down, girl! Do you want to bring our enemies down on us?'

'Don't speak to me like that, slave girl. I'm the daughter of the High Priest of...'

'I'm not a slave; Feldrark set me free. I'm the betrothed of the Wharhll of Litkala. You're just a child. Your father's nothing to me, Jodisa-Li. I don't respect your customs or odd religious beliefs. I was robbed of my own culture and god. Don't imagine your faith matters to me.'

'If you were in Muhnilahm, my father...'

'But I'm in Rophan-Ra, with the Wharhll of Litkala and here your father's just a man, and absent.'

'Feldrark will consider your behaviour blasphemous. He'll have you flayed and roasted alive.'

'Even you don't believe that, Jodisa-Li. Your little island group might accept those extremes but Feldrark doesn't. I've spent almost a full cycle with him and learned a lot about his beliefs. Cruelty isn't part of his creed. He believes in mercy and tolerance. Can you live as consort to a man like that, Jodisa-Li? I can.'

'He'll never take a partner who isn't a Follower.'

'Then I'll have to become one, won't I?'

A noise behind them startled them into silence. They sought in the shadows for its source. Shaulah, carrying a small coney in her mouth, pushed through the undergrowth back toward their encampment.

'This won't do, Jodisa-Li. We've nothing to show for our time. I suggest we forget our quarrel until we reach Feldrark's city. He'll no doubt make his choice there.' She took off her tabard as she spoke and Jodisa-Li searched the sky to see if the sun was almost down. It was difficult to tell but it didn't seem dark enough yet.

'You don't believe. Why are you preparing for...?'

'I'm not prudish like you. We need something to carry the fruits back, that's all.' She gave a mocking smile and laid the garment on the ground and, plucking sweet fruits from the trees, tossed them onto her tabard.

Jodisa-Li shrugged and they plucked fruit until Malarhah's tabard was heavy with it. Between them, they carried it back to the camp area. Aglydron had already returned and he gazed openly at Malarhah as they appeared and lay the food down. He continued to stare as she moved past him to one of the low bushes and peeled a few of the broad, flat leaves from one of the branches. Returning, she made them into a flat platter, crouching to transfer the fruits from her tabard. Shaking it, she replaced the tabard, all the while facing Aglydron.

'Aglydron doesn't share your worries about nudity, Jodisa-Li. I wonder why?'

'He's a man. He should be ashamed, ogling you that way.'

'Malarhah isn't a Follower and isn't likely to be, I appreciate her free display. She's pretty and, as you so scornfully point out, I'm a man. I hope to take some pleasure with her before we reach our destination.'

'Sorry, Aglydron. You'll have to make do with the view. I'm Feldrark's now.'

'But you show your body to other men?'

'My body's my body. It's what I was born with and covers the essence that is me. I don't feel any need to hide it. I'd happily be naked all the time if it weren't for Feldrark's quaint customs. In Mipahnhil, I followed their customs. They were clothed or naked according to status so I spent my time naked or as I was when we met.

'In Litkala, I'll fit in with Feldrark. I'm not ashamed of my natural state. I can do a bit about how I look, but not much. When I'm old, my firm dubbies will droop into the dugs of the crone and my fern will dry up and lose its appeal. I know I'll grow fat and flabby from too much food if I do too little work. I know I'll grow skinny from too little to eat and too much to do. My skin can be clean or soiled as I wash it or not. My hair can shine or grow dull. I'll smell horrid if I don't wash. My breath will stink if I don't clean my teeth. What I can do to keep myself attractive, I'll do. But I can't stop time and I know I'll be less appealing as I grow older...'

'You'll always appeal to me, Malarhah.' Feldrark appeared in the small clearing, followed by Okkyntalah and Myllthlan. He walked straight up to her and placed a gentle protective arm about her shoulders. But his eyes strayed to Jodisa-Li and, seeing his look, she was a little comforted.

'*Don't worry, my love, Malarhah's act is just that; a pretence.*'

'Did you manage with the boat?'

Okkyntalah nodded. 'It's part obvious, part hidden, as if we tried to hide it but were in too much of a hurry to do a proper job.'

'Okkyntalah made us make half a dozen journeys from the boat, across the mud. Each time we had to get back to the boat by jumping into the water a short distance upstream. He made me carry him for one trip to shore and then he carried me for another.'

'Should confuse them and convince them that a number of people got out of the boat where we left it. I also made a trip to some rocks I could see, half a league from the river. Left a few false clues there as well. With luck, we'll delay them by half a day or more.'

'Well done, the pair of you. Now, what's our fire queen at?' They turned to look at Jodisa-Li, following Feldrark's comments.

She was on hands and knees, spinning a thin piece of wood in a hollow on a larger block. Her pose made her face invisible to them and she was glad no one could see her surprised smile at his description of her. She blew on the end of the thin piece of wood, as the island guide had taught her; another of her father's lessons. Smoke began to issue from it. It took her some time and considerable effort, but eventually she had a small blaze going and the damp wood slowly began to catch, billowing smoke.

⁕

'Sundown!' Aglydron's warning, though the day was simply growing dimmer, had the Followers preparing for prayer as Malarhah stood by, an amused smile on her full mouth. She stepped over to where Okkyntalah lay prone, his palms flat on the ground beneath his buttocks, as custom required. Aglydron suspected she was up to no good but involved himself in his devotions. Finished, he looked again and saw the girl astride Okkyntalah so he'd look up and see her as he opened his eyes. Her act was a tease, since she'd no intention of joining with anyone but Feldrark, and, more importantly, an act of blasphemy.

Okkyntalah opened his eyes and smiled.

'What are you about, girl? You do sacrilege.'

'For you, Aglydron, perhaps. But I see no harm in what I do. I don't believe in your strange god. In any case, why do you men lie this way, Feldrark stand, but women make themselves so open to assault when they pray? It seems an odd posture for worship to me.'

Feldrark moved forward and placed a hand on the young woman's thigh, squeezing gently to persuade her to step away so Okkyntalah could rise and dress.

'Malarhah has no real knowledge of our customs and no belief in Ytraa, at present. She means no disrespect and does no harm, Aglydron.'

'Feldrark's right. But why do you pray in these odd ways? I'd have stood astride Feldrark if he did as you two do.'

Feldrark smiled. 'Let's prepare and eat whatever our hunters have provided, shall we? Then we'll sit around our fire and explain what we do and why until we've answered every question you wish to ask. Will that satisfy you?'

'Perhaps. Do you think the fire's a good idea? Won't it lead our hunters to us?'

'It might, if not for the darkness. They'll see no sign from their position. Even if they row their boats like demons, they'll still be many leagues downstream and by daylight we'll be on our way. We have the advantage that I know my own land very well.'

Aglydron was dissatisfied with the way the girl had got away with her blasphemy but he said no more. Instead he collected the brace of flightless game birds he'd caught earlier and showed them to the party.

'Kokos.' Feldrark named them. 'Very good eating. Birds with almost no brain but the most delicious breast meat.'

Okkyntalah had caught a large river fish, which no one could name but which looked much like the tonyina he'd caught in the sea. He also had a good-sized coney. Myllthlan contributed aromatic herbs and the purple swollen roots of a leafy plant she recognized as similar to one she'd cooked on Ylcrat. They congratulated each other on their ingredients for a feast and set about preparing the meal.

'I'll take first watch, if that's all right with everyone. I'm weary after my hunting expedition and fear I may fall asleep once I've eaten.'

They nodded at Okkyntalah and no one expressed surprise when Myllthlan offered to watch with him after she'd discussed the cooking of the herbs and roots with Malarhah.

'We need two pairs of eyes if we're to keep out of danger. I think we might take all our watches in pairs.' Feldrark suggested.

'It means less sleep.'

'I, for one, prefer less sleep and a good chance of survival, Aglydron.'

The party agreed and the pair went to the edge of the copse to find a suitable vantage point until they could be relieved and take their share of the meal.

The food was good and all were ready for relaxation afterwards. Picking cirera fruits from the leaves, they spat round stones into the fire where they burned with a sweet scent.

'Now, Feldrark, instruct me in the strange arts of your faith. I must learn or I'll bring shame to you when I become your wife.'

'There's much to teach, my sweet Malarhah, but first I'll answer your question about why we pray the way we do and what significance our nakedness and my posture has.'

'Looks undignified for the women, as well as making them incredibly vulnerable, and the men…'

'If you let me explain…'

'Sorry.'

'We expose our bodies so that Ytraa may see that we are what we are and that we wish to please Ytraa with our whole selves, hiding nothing from the God who created us. In Litkala, both men and women stand as I do, so that their sex is displayed and available. In Muhnilahm, the men lie flat and trap their hands so that Ytraa, as female, may join with them unimpeded. The women take up their position so that Ytraa, as male, may most easily join with them should that be Ytraa's desire.'

'Anyone ever seen Ytraa join with anyone?'

Aglydron broke the embarrassed silence. 'We don't talk of it. It's a private matter between Ytraa and Ytraa's chosen.'

'But has anyone ever actually seen it, not had it happen to them, but seen it happen to someone else?'

'Ytraa works in mysterious ways, Malarhah, my sweet innocent.'

This was clearly not enough for the girl and Aglydron tried to expand on Feldrark's brief comment. 'Ytraa can become a priest or priestess for joining during prayer. If that happens, the one chosen stays in position with his or her eyes closed until the blessing's over. Anyone seeing the joining has to turn away and wait for a signal that Ytraa's finished.'

'Sounds as if the priests and priestesses have a good job to me. They can have anyone they like and no one can complain.'

Aglydron held back his anger at her flippancy. 'It might seem that way to you, Malarhah, but priests and priestesses can do that anyway. They don't have a life partner. As representatives of Ytraa's holy essence, they're meant to spread their blessings to many.'

'It's different in Litkala. We have only a few priests and none of the Holy Ones that Muhnilahm boasts. But our High Priests do have the duties Aglydron describes.'

'Still sounds like an excuse to frowk anyone any time to me.'

'I can see it might seem that way to a stranger to the faith, Malarhah, but you must understand we worship on the basis of long held beliefs and traditions.'

'You're more patient with her blasphemy than me, Feldrark. If I was responsible for her, she'd be weeping for forgiveness by now.'

'What would you do to me, to have me weep, Aglydron? Beat my naked body till I bleed, like they did in Mipahnhil?'

'Beating the naked isn't allowed. Naked is sacred. You'd be hung upside down in a beating bag and whipped with thin sticks. How many lashes depends on your sin. For blasphemy, most priests would give sixty lashes and a half day hung up.'

'Approve of this barbarity, don't you, Aglydron? In fact you enjoy it.'

'Enjoy? It's not for us to enjoy or otherwise, Malarhah. I don't know why you'd think it is. We act on the laws of Ytraa. If Ytraa declares a punishment, we give that punishment on behalf of Ytraa. I don't enjoy causing pain but I make sure the sinner's properly chastised. A bit of pain and humiliation brings them back to the right ways.'

'It's odd. I've been exposed to two very different religions in my short life. One lot believes in some strange denizen of the sea and some fabled distant city of white stone that's supposed to be their stolen birth right, the other lot worship some three-sided being embodied in wood. Both lots punish wrongdoers with beatings and humiliation. There's talk of love, mercy and forgiveness in both but precious little evidence of it. I'm not sure I can adopt such an odd faith, with its hypocrisy and brutality but, for your sake, Feldrark, I'll try.'

'How very magnanimous of you, Malarhah.'

'Well, Jodisa-Li, when you love someone, you make an effort, don't you?'

Feldrark rose to his feet and helped Malarhah to hers before he embraced her. 'I think it's time we relieved Myllthlan and Okkyntalah so they can eat some of the food they provided, don't you?'

'Excellent idea, let's go and find them.'

'Er, Malarhah, Feldrark. I don't think you should watch together. You'll be distracted by each other and put us all in danger. I think you should watch with someone else.'

'You would say that! You're just jealous of our love, Aglydron. Well, I don't see why we should take any notice of…'

'I'm sorry, Malarhah. I think Aglydron's got a point. I'd find it difficult to keep my mind on the job and I think you would as well. I think it might be better, for the moment, if we were to watch separately.'

'If you say so.' Malarhah sulked at Feldrark's accommodation to Aglydron's wishes. 'I suppose I'd better watch with Jodisa-Li.'

'We can't have two women on watch together; we need a man's strength. But a woman's watchfulness and attention is of equal worth and we're better with two on watch. You know Jodisa's status, Feldrark. I trust you to be true to our beliefs and not to violate her. Will you watch with Feldrark?'

'If I must.'

Jodisa-Li's reluctance sounded genuine and puzzled as much as it pleased him. Perhaps there had been some falling out he hadn't noticed.

'We don't have any choice.'

'I'd be good and wouldn't distract you, Feldrark.' Malarhah wanted him with her, as there'd be so few chances on the road.

'You'd have every intention of concentrating but, now you're complete, I doubt you could resist. I know I couldn't, Malarhah. No. I think it better I watch with someone else.'

'Then, remember your promise, made in public, Wharhll of Litkala.'

'Feldrark's a man of honour, Malarhah. I believe he'll keep his promise to you and not violate the status of our sacred Virgin Gift.'

Jodisa-Li said nothing, simply waiting with a sulky expression on her face.

'Thank you for your confidence, Aglydron. Come, Jodisa-Li, let's relieve our watchers and allow them to eat.'

'With pleasure, Feldrark, my love. Can Aglydron really be so foolish?'

'Seems we've convinced him with our act and Malarhah's help. Let's go.'

Chapter 39

LOVE AND LUST

The condition of the road out of Qlentz made progress slow and Tryonta's hunting delayed them, so that they covered only two leagues the first day, reaching the western edge of the forest by nightfall. Nowhere was dry and they lit a fire only with difficulty and Phildrad's ingenuity. But, by making a wide platform of small branches and fallen boughs, they managed to keep clear of the muddy ground for eating and sleep.

As they finished prayers, thanking Ytraa for delivering them from the misery of the town, noises from the road startled them. Caarl held up a hand for silence, as they listened to the sound of someone or something splashing just beyond the edge of the clearing. He beckoned Tarruss to investigate with him. A scream of fear sounded before they returned, both grinning, with Netrodyl between them, splattered with mud from head to foot and exhausted.

She prostrated herself on the ground at the High Priest's feet.

He bent and coaxed her to her feet. 'You may speak to me plainly, my dear. What is it?'

She burst into tears and it was a while before she regained control, by which time the fire was hot and the evening meal well under way.

'I've run away, forever this time. Please take me with you.'

Careful questioning revealed she'd disobeyed the same man as she had previously, in the roundhouse. She'd dashed to the women's quarters, grabbed the nearest wrap and run most of the way to catch up the party. Although unlikely to be pursued, if they took her back, the townsmen would beat her every day for ten days and cage her each night in a prison of thorn branches, too small to stand or lie in.

'And if you return voluntarily?'

'I won't go back.'

'But if you do, of your own free will?'

'It's the second time I've run away.'

'And what does that mean, Netrodyl. What will happen to you?'

'The women won't let me back in the house and the men will ride on my back whilst I crawl round their house, every day. I won't be able to wash or make myself smell nice and they'll hit me with sticks.'

'Where would you live?'

She considered. 'Outside.'

Dagla Kaz shrugged. 'I've seen the peculiarly cruel nature of the subjugation of the women in Qlentz, Netrodyl. We don't need another member of our party, unless you have skills of use to us. But I'll not abandon you to your people. You'd better come with us as far as Xythonl. We'll decide what to do with you there, depending on your behaviour. But you must cover yourself properly and do as you're told. This isn't a journey for pleasure. We do the will of Ytraa and if you cause delay or disruption you'll be severely punished. Do you understand?'

She was about to fall on her face again in gratitude but he stopped her.

'Clean yourself up as well as you can and see if one of the women has something suitable for you to wear.' He turned away and left the women to take care of her.

Tumalind dug out her spare working tabard; the one she was embroidering.

'Put it away, Tumalind, you've done enough for her. Let me.' Wendarah gave her a deep red one with silver pegs and a waistrope of plaited blonde hair. They took her to a pool of water beneath a small fall in the swollen stream just beyond the trees. She washed as well as she could in the near dark.

'Tryonta will be glad, at any rate. But you're with us now, Netrodyl. We act according to the will of Ytraa, and you don't have to obey a man, unless you want to.'

'I must repay my debt of honour to those who rescued me, or be shamed.'

'They won't expect it, you know.'

'I must. It's the only way for a woman.'

'That's between you and them. Just make sure you do it privately.'

Netrodyl settled in well, her time with the women serving her well in the new life she'd chosen. Though what the future might hold for her, no one seemed to know.

It took them three more days to travel the eight leagues to Xythonl across country made marshy by rain and, in spite of Gret-Zudas' prediction, under frequent rain showers peppered with lightning and thunder. They spent the final night, dry at last, on a hillside overlooking the large port with the edge of the unknown city less than a league off.

◈⊰⊱◈

'I hoped Aglydron would suggest you came to watch with me. But I knew he'd be opposed if either of us suggested it.'

'We've no need of speech, Feldrark. *We can speak in our minds.*'

He stopped whispering. *'It might be as well not to make too much of a habit of it. Our silent communing will seem odd to anyone watching us.'*

'And Aglydron will watch us very closely. Still we can do this when others are present and without their knowledge, if we keep it short and to the point. I love you,

Feldrark. I never thought I would want only one man, raised as I was to enjoy any man I desired. But you've won my heart.'

'And I love you.'

'Malarhah's challenging me for you. I thought she'd agreed to...'

'Malarhah's a good player of parts. She's trying to make it more real for you and the others, to make it easier for you to act your part so there's no suspicion. When we reach the city, she'll renounce her claims. Trust me. I know. But she may wish to join with me on the journey, Jodisa-Li, now that Myllthlan's made her complete. She told me she's got her eye on Okkyntalah, once we're in the city. And I can't say I blame her.'

'Why don't we join, here and now, and then declare I'm not virgin? They'll have to accept it and there's nothing they can do. We can drop the pretence and join whenever we wish.'

'We're hunted and in danger, Jodisa-Li. We need all the allies we have to ensure our safe passage to the city. The hunters from Mipahnhil won't give up their chase: Malarhah's right. We'll be safe in Litkala but until then it's best we keep everyone on our side. In any case, there are ceremonial and traditional reasons for us to wait until the right time.'

'Don't you want to..?'

'You know I do. Right now, right here. You can feel it in my mind.'

'I want so much to ...'

'So do I. But we must wait, Jodisa-Li. The dangers are too great. I won't risk the rest of our lives together for one stolen night.'

'Sometimes I wish you weren't so sensible, Feldrark, Wharhll of Litkala.'

'I'll be as spontaneous and impulsive as you like when we're safe within the walls of Litkala. Till then, I'll be the stern and sensible leader I know will get us home alive.'

'Why did Aglydron allow us to watch together?'

'He's a simple man. Our act back there tipped the balance of his suspicions. He'll still be concerned about us but he's also convinced I'm a man of my word, which, by the way, I am. He's right to think I won't betray his trust in that way. But, once the journey's over, I'll have you because I want you and no amount of special pleading from him or anyone else will change that.'

'No sign of anything moving on the plain, or the river. I must sleep now, Aglydron. I'm weary beyond words.'

'We best all sleep, Okkyntalah. I'll wake you when it's our watch, Malarhah.'

'If you must.'

'Rather watch with Feldrark? But you know I'm right. You'd be distracted and we're in danger. Sleep now. We've got to be up early.'

'Just one thing, Aglydron; this Skyfire of yours: where is it? Why can't I see it through the clouds if it burns so fiercely we're in danger of going up in flames ourselves?'

'Don't mock, Malarhah. You're not under Feldrark's protection now. I'll punish any irreverence.'

'It's a simple question, Aglydron. Where is it?'

'It's only forty days since the Seer first saw it and told the High Priest. It came earlier than expected; bad news. It means great changes for all Followers. It's only a spark now, glowing low in the west. You can't see the sun through the clouds: why d'you expect to see the Skyfire?'

'What is it, exactly?'

'It's like a star with a faint tail. But it'll grow. It's the test of Ytraa and comes only once every two hundred and forty three cycles. Watch it and you'll see, when the rains end and the sky clears, every night it'll glow more strongly. When it fills the sky with flame, we'll feel the heat and learn whether we're worthy. Those who fail will burn; true Followers will be untouched in body but their spirits will be kindled with the love of Ytraa so their fire and passion will grow with every day they live in this world. When their lives are complete here, they'll join with Ytraa in the Garden of Delight above the sky, where everything is balm and there's no pain, no loss or hurt or sorrow. There, all is harmony and love and wonder as all join with Ytraa and become the One eternally.'

He was pleased he remembered the actual words of the village priest; it left him feeling more righteous and correct. This heathen, with her wicked ideas and her preference for Okkyntalah and Feldrark over him, needed to learn some respect.

'Frowking with God till the end of time? No wonder you behave yourself, Aglydron, if you believe that's your reward.'

It was too much. He grasped her hair and pulled her to her knees and swiped his hand back and forth across her face until she cried out in pain and fear. 'Wicked, wanton whore! How dare you mock the…?'

Okkyntalah pulled him off her as Feldrark and Jodisa-Li crashed back into the encampment to see what caused the noise.

'She spoke blasphemously of Ytraa and the Garden of Delight! I lost my temper. She deserved it. I'm sorry; I shouldn't have acted in temper. She should apologise to Ytraa. I never meant to…'

Feldrark took the weeping woman into his arms and comforted her.

'You're a bigot and a fool, Aglydron. Malarhah isn't a Follower. She's not subject to our laws. Fanatics like you are dangerous, especially when you make such judgements.

I would've explained her error but I wouldn't have hurt her. She should be treated as an innocent until she converts and learns the creeds and litany. If that's what she wants. How can we persuade others to become Followers if people like you behave so stupidly?'

Jodisa-Li's words chastened Aglydron, who felt foolish for his outburst, though justified in his assessment that Malarhah had been blasphemous.

Malarhah calmed in Feldrark's arms and, when he turned to deal with Aglydron, she put her hand on his arm to stay the blow he would deliver.

'I was in the wrong, Feldrark. I made the mistake of thinking Aglydron was a reasonable and intelligent man. I know now that he's a zealot and therefore as near mad as a man can be without being too dangerous to live. I'll tread more carefully in future. Don't fight him, Feldrark. We need to stick together if we're to get through this alive.'

'Hurt her, or anyone in this group, again, Aglydron and you'll feel my wrath. Curb your unnatural passions and try to apply the spirit of the law instead of clinging to the letter of it; or suffer the consequences.'

Feldrark's words hit Aglydron as though a physical force had struck him. He stood with his mouth open and his mind racing.

'You revive a memory, Feldrark, something someone else said to me in a…it was when we…I can't recall the circumstances but those words ring true, about the spirit of the law. I'm sorry, Malarhah. I let blind faith get the better of me again and forgot your true state. Your words were wicked and shouldn't have been said but you're not to blame. You're just an ignorant slave of heathen people and can't be expected to know better. I'll curb my passion for justice in future and give you the benefit of the doubt.'

'Such magnanimity; I hardly know where to begin to serve my penance for speaking my mind. I hope my conversion to the faith won't blind me as effectively as it has you, Aglydron. I'd feel diminished as a person to be so governed by hard rules that I could see no place for doubt or disagreement.'

'There can't be doubt or disagreement regarding Ytraa or the Lord Gadhallah.'

'Enough!' The sheer volume of Feldrark's command put a stop to the argument.

The silence that followed was thick with unspent passion and emotion.

Feldrark took Jodisa-Li to the edge of the small clearing. 'We'll watch from here. That way I can keep one eye on you, Aglydron, and use the other to look out for our enemies on the outside.'

When A'ahl wandered in off the dusty road, she came to a halt with her mouth open in silent shock. Shoarhn wasn't surprised; the sight of Wesdan Kaz joined with her, wasn't one A'ahl would expect. She retreated. Shoarhn willed her back; bored, humiliated and uncomfortable under his usage. Her friend stepped back into sight, feigned surprise at the presence of the priest and removed her tabard, as required in his company.

'Ah, A'ahl.'

She'd told Shoarhn how he loved to use that expression to her face.

'Nice to see you again. I'd pleasure you once more but you can see you're a little late.' He gave a telltale grunt of satisfaction and moved from Shoarhn, smacking her rump to show he was finished. He dressed, unconcerned for the state of the receptacle of his lust.

'Shoarhn's had the best of me for now, I'm afraid, though she lacks your appreciation of the joining we shared. I was considering honouring her as my consort but she hasn't the knack you possess of expressing the joy and delight I give all my partners. Still, her loss.'

He slapped Shoarhn's bottom again; much harder than simple male affection required. She refused to gratify him by yelling her displeasure or hurt.

'And I'll be leaving again in the morning. So much to do in the capital with Dagla Kaz away, you know.' He required no answer other than her smile of condescension.

'I came to ask if you'd like to eat with me tonight, Shoarhn. Assuming Wesdan Kaz isn't staying, of course?'

Shoarhn nodded, and rose belatedly from the table, glaring at the village priest but determined not to rub her stinging posterior.

'Oh, I shan't be staying the night, A'ahl; no point. I've other potential consorts to inspect and try out. Shoarhn's loss is another's gain, eh?'

Both women nodded.

'Actually, I'm rather glad to have the pair of you together; saves me having to ask twice. Tell me, do either of you happen to know the whereabouts of Aklon-Dji?'

'The High Priest's son?' A'ahl's voice indicated her utter disbelief.

'But he's a renegade.' Shoarhn made her statement one of obvious fact.

The priest scrutinised them. 'Indeed he is. You've not seen him, then?

'I imagine he must be on The Point with the other criminals and blasphemers.'

'And if he isn't, he should be.'

'Just so. I ask only because I'd heard he'd been seen in Morstahn.'

'Really? I'd better lock my door. Or perhaps you and I could stay together for a while, Shoarhn, until we know we're safe?'

'Excellent idea. I'll bring the boys round tonight. We'll spend a couple of nights at yours and then you can come to me. We'll be safer together, whilst we have no men folk around. You never know what a desperate monster like Aklon-Dji might do with a woman on her own. I've heard tell he's unbelievable in the way he deals with women.'

'What does he look like, Wesdan Kaz? We can keep an eye out and let you know if we see him.'

'Oh, you'll know him. Terrible, ugly string of a man. Just keep an eye out for any strangers. And let me know if he turns up. It'd be in your own best interests, you know.'

'In the best interest of everyone, surely, Wesdan Kaz?'

'Of course, of course. Well. I'll be on my way, Shoarhn. You'll be wanting to rest after your exertions.'

'Yes. I was rather hoping for the chance to recover. Thank you, Wesdan Kaz.'

'Well, perhaps, next time? Though, I must say, I'm used to a little more enthusiasm.'

'Not all of us are blessed with the ability to perceive the finer points of joining with a man so unique in the act, Wesdan Kaz, but my door is always open to the faithful.'

'Quite so. And you, A'ahl? Shall I see you next time I'm in Morstahn?' He groped with curled fingers.

'You'll have to make it soon, Wesdan Kaz. I'm not sure I'll be all that suitable for you in a couple of portion's time.' She thrust out her swollen belly. 'I'm two thirds to my time already.'

'Indeed. I'll collect the fruit of our congress. A sacrifice to Ytraa's service, you understand. Although, with Dagla Kaz on such a perilous mission, who knows, the child might serve as my heir. You never know.'

'As you wish, Wesdan Kaz. I'm merely a vessel to bring your seed to fullness.'

'You've both received greater pleasure than you've previously known but I'm afraid I must leave you now. I hope I haven't spoilt you for future joining. Still, a man such as me must spread his gift to as many willing partners as he can. I'll take my leave, for now. I'm staying with Diryss tonight and, though she doesn't yet know it, if she's as adept as you, A'ahl, she'll be returning to Chalamamnon with me in the morning.'

'Lucky Diryss.' A'ahl concealed her smile behind a hand pretending to stifle a non-existent yawn.

'Yes, we can't all expect such fortune. I hope she appreciates exactly what she's getting.' Shoarhn avoided looking at her friend in case she should burst out laughing.

'I'm sure she does. At any rate, she will once we've joined. Farewell, then, ladies. Until next time.'

'Goodbye, Wesdan Kaz.'

'May Ytraa bless you and bring what you deserve.' Shoarhn kept his just deserts inside her head.

'And Ytraa's blessings on the two of you.'

At last, he went and the two women relaxed.

'Ytraa's balls, that man's a creep!'

'How did you bear him all that time, A'ahl?'

'I closed my eyes and imagined I was with Caarl. It was horrible. Well, you've experienced his version of joining.'

'Yes. He makes even Aglydron seem like an accomplished lover.'

'He'd make a worm look like an accomplished lover.'

'What was all that about Aklon-Dji? Do you think he..?'

'He doesn't know anything. And neither do we. But we must tell Aklon-Dji next time we see him that someone knew he was in Morstahn.'

'Are we likely to see him soon, do you think?'

'You know better than that. He comes and goes as and when he can and will. Anyway, for tonight, you'd best bring the boys to me and spend the night. I don't want that creep hearing we did something different from what we suggested. I don't trust him and I don't want to fall under his suspicion.'

'But if Aklon-Dji comes and we're together…'

'We'll just have to hope he stays longer than one night or has energy to spare.' A'ahl laughed. 'Don't look so shocked. You know he spreads himself wide and far. I've as much right to him as you have.'

'It's just that…well; I'm rather taken with him, A'ahl. And I thought he…'

'You're not the first and you won't be the last. We all love him; who wouldn't? And, in his way, he loves all of us. You'll just have to be content with your share. I'll see you after evening prayers.'

Shoarhn watched her friend waddle off. She wondered if Aklon-Dji really would visit her again and whether he might love her more than he did the others. Might love her as she loved him, in fact.

Chapter 40

NEW FRIENDS AND ENEMIES

'How do you read the Skyfire, now you can view it again?'

Jhonaht was thoughtful. 'It brightens. Yes, it glows more clearly. I noticed as I pointed it out to Tumalind but she already knew its whereabouts and the names of many stars. She's clever. Shame to lose her to Choshinahm.'

'Indeed. Beautiful, too. But we cannot deny the will of Ytraa.'

'Perhaps not, Dagla Kaz, perhaps not.'

The High Priest was minded to put the astronomer in his place but he might know more than he was voicing. Dagla Kaz had no wish to open a dispute over the validity of the Choosing. But, he agreed with Jhonaht about Tumalind; she was a good young woman with intelligence, warmth and common sense as well as beauty. Perhaps a less gifted and plainer girl could have replaced Jodisa-Li. He shrugged. Nothing to be done about it now.

They were walking a wide, paved, tree-lined avenue between well-spaced, single storey houses leading to the market area of Xythonl. Open, prosperous and cosmopolitan, no one in the city noted their manner of dress as they had in other places. Here, people of different colours, beliefs, customs and apparel populated the streets.

Tall, dark men and women balanced on devices strapped to their feet, raising them two handbreadths off the ground. Tall, cylindrical hats of polished, stiffened hide perched on their bald heads made them appear giants. Others, with yellowish skin, were clad in moulded sheets of shining metal over chests, thighs and forearms.

The native people were much like those in Kamakq and similarly clothed, with the added refinement of a short, open jacket for men. Women wore flimsy scarves loosely tied around their necks, the ends only partly concealing their breasts. Here and there, skinny men and women crouched naked on the ground, begging bowls at their feet. Passers-by tossed in coin or handed them food, receiving muttered blessings in return. Nearing the dockland area, they saw others dressed in such outlandish ways that they gaped, open-mouthed.

A blind beggar, makeshift crutch under one scrawny arm to supplant the missing leg, cried out for alms and Tarruss stepped across to place a coin in his outstretched hand, receiving a terse acknowledgement for his trouble.

Here, in the business quarter, buildings were more crowded, roads less wide. Rows of open fronted stores displayed goods of every type, many so strange that the

Followers couldn't guess their purpose. Noise, smell, colour and confusion assaulted their senses.

Initially, Dagla Kaz had intended to replace their lost and damaged tabards but they found nothing of use. The nearest was a short jacket of similar design, with open sides fastened by a single peg but covering just shoulders and the top half of the chest. Some women sported this short tabard, their lower halves clad in strange garments covering their hips but clothing each leg in a separate tube and leaving their parts uncovered. After searching, they abandoned their quest and bought a length of silk with thread, so they could make new tabards.

'We'd best have some of that there white linen, Dagla Kaz. Can't tear up no more tabards to stop you men bleeding from sword cuts an' the like. Men. Allus getting themselves in trouble of one sort or another. Worse than children.'

No one reminded Corphanda that the men had received their wounds whilst rescuing a woman from almost certain death.

They stocked up on food, girba and other essentials for the next part of their journey, recognizing they would have to buy the girls ready-made new clothes when they found a place where other Followers dwelt.

'If such a place exists.' Jhonaht's scepticism was echoed by most, since they had so far met none.

This was no surprise to Dagla Kaz. He expected to find Followers at Kah-Labaz, where they were less devout and, of course, in Choshinahm, where some of the founders had returned with news of their epic journey, hoping to convert others to go to the island. There was Litkala, of course, but Dagla Kaz wouldn't have them as Followers after the Division. They would go via Kah-Labaz and obtain new clothing there.

Closer to the wharves, it became a trial keeping all members of the party in sight through the milling throng. Tarruss put an arm about Tumalind. 'Stay close to me. Don't want to lose you again. Not in this city of cutthroats and brigands.'

Supplies and needs collected, they made their way to the northern end of the city to find the road to Slophrahn. They needed an inn for food and to spend the night in some sort of comfort, before the next long walk across the land.

Their road quickly became obvious by sheer weight of traffic. They joined the dusty press slowly pushing out of the narrow streets of the dockland into the wider thoroughfares beyond. Carts, oxen and trains of mules moved north and south in such numbers it seemed the whole population was leaving the city and another moving in to replace it. Along with the traders, Dagla Kaz noted large numbers of men bearing arms and shields. At last, the going grew less crushed and they could look about again.

'What are those, Dagla Kaz?'

He glanced down at Tumalind beside him, her eyes full of eager interest.

'Camels, my dear. They raise them in desert areas where it's said they can travel many days without need of water. Something, I believe, to do with those humps on their backs. Ugly beasts, aren't they?'

'I like them. A bit ungainly, perhaps, but their eyes are so soft.'

He smiled indulgently; she reminded him of Jodisa-Li before she'd lost her innocence. 'They may look soft, Tumalind, but beware. Camels spit and kick.'

'How do you know so much, Dagla Kaz?' She put her hand to her mouth as if she'd said something out of place. 'I mean, I know you're the High Priest of course, but how do you know about other lands and other peoples?'

'I've travelled. Not many leave the island. Not many visit, either. But I've seen foreign lands, strange customs, unusual creatures. You, too, have seen odd and unusual sights, and sounds, and smells...' He stepped carefully over a steaming pile of dung and was amused by her mischievous smile.

'Dagla Kaz, may I ask you something?' Her sweet face clouded with doubt and anxiety.

He wanted to allay it. 'Please do.'

'What do you know of Choshinahm?'

'Well, my dear, I've certainly never been there. Too far. It's further north than Muhnilahm, of course. You've heard of the Equimark?'

'Yes. Jhonaht explained how the world's shaped like a magrana and the Equimark is a sort of imaginary line that goes round halfway down. I wonder we don't all fall off.'

'Indeed. No doubt the seers understand how we stay attached. I don't. But, yes, the Equimark divides one half from the other. Muhnilahm sits just a hundred leagues north of the Equimark and so is always very warm, like it is here. Choshinahm lies beyond a great range of mountains more than a hundred leagues further north. Although it's still warm, it's cooler than the island at some times of the year but warmer at others. Also, the mountains are very high. Much higher than any you've seen so far. When rain falls, it lands as a light solid and lays there, white and very cold!'

Tumalind frowned at him. 'I know I'm just a country girl, Dagla Kaz, but I was quite serious. You don't need to make fun of me.'

Her mild reproof again reminded him of his daughter. So strong was the likeness, he almost bent to embrace her. To hide his sudden confusion, he laughed instead. 'I'm not! It's the absolute truth, Tumalind. Really.' But it was clear she couldn't picture this strange phenomenon that he'd seen only once, in the Prolanq Mountains, as a young man.

'Well, if you say so, I expect it must be true. But I don't see how water can be solid.'

'If we pass through the mountains, you'll see it for yourself. And feel it. It's very cold. Have you ever shivered? No, I suppose not. You will if we go through the mountains.'

'Dagla Kaz, are we going to eat and rest today? Only my girls need refreshment and, tell the truth, so do I. There's a likely looking tavern. Should be room enough if we're quick. Shame to pass another by and not take advantage, don't you think?'

'Very well, Corphanda. It will do as well as any, I suppose.'

'Good job someone thinks of these things. Men. Heads in the clouds thinking of anything but what matters, I don't know. We'd all starve if we left it to them.'

Tumalind gave him a grin and his quick anger at Corphanda's rebuke died at once. He shrugged and grinned back at this intriguing and desirable young woman.

<hr/>

The night passed without further incident and Aglydron spent his watch with Malarhah in a silence broken only by nocturnal scratchings and squealings of small creatures and the single distant roar of a large cat. They roused the sleepers before sun up for a hurried breakfast of the previous night's leavings.

After prayers, they began their long trek, west of north, across the plains of Rophan-Ra. Two days and nights, sleeping under trees now the rains were less continuous, collecting fruits and roots along the unmarked way and hunting when possible, set them well on their way. But labouring through soggy ground under threatening and thundery skies lowered their spirits and led to irritability and disagreement. Myllthlan twice had to intervene to prevent Aglydron coming to blows with Feldrark over things Malarhah said or did.

On their third night, they reached the banks of a small tributary flowing north to south across their way. Unwilling to risk its turbulent waters in the dark, they camped where they were. Okkyntalah again supplied fresh fish and they slept well fed but fitful.

There'd been no sign of their hunters and, confident they'd put them off the scent by their trick with the boat, they kept single watches. Aglydron took the first and sighed his relief when the rain stopped again, the clouds dispersed and bright stars spangled the black above. Jodisa-Li relieved him, sending him to sleep on the patch of dry grass she'd vacated. In the early hours, he heard Feldrark wake Malarhah for the final watch and doubted their minds were on the group's safety.

But he woke later to Malarhah's quiet warning. 'I heard a voice just now. From the south. A man's voice; though I couldn't make out what he said.'

They skipped breakfast, alert for further signs. But there was only the gurgling river and wind sighing in branches above. With sunrise, the birds began their chorus and all chance of hearing other human voices drowned beneath that cheerful cacophony.

After a scramble down the bank, they began to cross. The water was deeper than it appeared and even Feldrark was forced to swim for a short stretch. Myllthlan stood up to her chest in the fast flowing stream, unable to take another step.

Okkyntalah returned for her. 'I'd forgotten your fear of water. Here, let me help you. Relax and trust me, Myllthlan, I'll not let you drown.'

He tossed their rolled tabards to Feldrark, waiting in the shallows. The Wharhll threw them to Malarhah, leaving his hands free should Okkyntalah need help. The boy explained that she must let the water support her body as he cradled her head and pulled her to safety. But fear made her struggle and sink. Okkyntalah touched ground again and reasoned with her but she couldn't relax.

Feldrark pointed, silently, at the bank he'd just left. Turning, Aglydron saw their hunters entering the shallows. One had a longbow already strung and let his arrow loose even as Aglydron watched. Okkyntalah ducked instinctively, pulling Myllthlan with him under the water as the arrow sped toward them.

He surfaced and dragged the spluttering woman up with him. She was thrashing the water in panic and he slapped her. She hadn't seen the hunters and when he pointed them out, she at once became resolute.

'Come to shore, Feldrark. You're a bigger target standing there.' Aglydron, in spite of their differences, had no wish to see him hurt.

Feldrark hesitated until Malarhah waded back to drag him away. Okkyntalah ducked again as a second arrow came his way. The bowman was good; the missile almost hit him. He cupped Myllthlan's chin in one hand and began to swim backwards with her floating above him. 'Stay as relaxed as you can. We'll cross quicker.'

She mastered her tension and her legs began to float toward the surface, making the task easier for Okkyntalah.

Under the far bank, the hunters, eight including Chislanda, waded toward him. The archer was already too deep to use his bow and Okkyntalah put on a spurt of speed for the shallows. He released Myllthlan once she could support herself.

'Get to the bank. Tell them to throw stones at them. I'm going after the archer.'

Before anyone could stop him, he'd plunged beneath the surface and was swimming to meet their pursuers. Myllthlan did as he bade her and stepped onto the western bank. At once, the companions plucked stones from the shore and aimed them across the water.

Aglydron had to curb their enthusiasm a little. 'Don't hit Okkyntalah!'

The cart lurched suddenly, bringing Tumalind back to the present. They were now well above the city, the huge ocean a great flat expanse of unbroken blue-green to the west, where it met the sky in a wide flat curve as far as she could see. Perhaps the world was round, after all. Dilanthas slept with her head on Tumalind's shoulder.

Four great oxen pulled the cart and, over their long curved horns, she watched the cart in front. There Tarruss, Tryonta, Dagla Kaz, Wendarah, Netrodyl and Phildrad sat in two rows, back to back, as they lounged on the small stepped hill of bales filling the wagon. The wagoner, whip in hand, sat up front with his armed assistant beside him.

They'd cleared the city crowds and bustle and risen to the plateau along which they would ride for the next few days. Ahead of the first cart, snaked a long camel train and, in front of that, a shorter line of mules with three more wagons ahead of it. Behind, another two of their merchant's carts followed, with a second camel train after them. And, strung along at regular intervals, pairs of mounted militiamen kept look out for brigands.

Progress had been slow up the climb, but they moved more quickly on the level. It was the change in speed, to a fast walking pace, that had brought her out of her reverie.

The tavern where they'd spent the night had provided good food, a refreshing bathe in clean water, comfortable beds in airy rooms and cheerful, colourful entertainment. Contributed by the parties staying overnight, the diversion, had been partly responsible for their ride. The merchant, taken with the girls' dancing, singing and playing, had invited them to accompany him on his trip to Slophrahn. His wagons had to go back anyway and were less than full. He'd travelled with four wagons, expecting a large consignment from some exotic land over the Southern Ocean, but had arrived to find only two thirds the quantity. What he was carrying, wrapped in hessian sacks, he wouldn't say. But it gave off a strangely sweet aroma and was evidently rather heavy, if the grunts of the men loading it were any guide.

'It's a new venture. Something I'll try out in Litkala and then Shorrannon. If it goes the way I expect, you're looking at a very rich man. Rich enough to tempt even lovely young wenches like you into his harem.'

They'd laughed, and explained they weren't available.

'Your men are giving you away? Don't they know, as virgins, if indeed such beautiful young women can possibly remain so, you're worth ten times any ordinary woman?'

Corphanda had explained the girls weren't for sale, at any price.

'Ah. You're their keeper, Paltra?'

'Don't you Paltra me.'

'I'll cut you in on the deal, dear lady. I could get a very good price indeed for these three. The one with copper hair's especially valuable.'

'If you want bed girls, you're prodding the wrong fern. They're sacred to Ytraa. They'll be swapped for other virtuous girls in Choshinahm. We never sell women at any…'

'Virgins in Choshinahm, dear lady? You'll have to be content with ten year olds, for you'll find none older.'

'D'you know of Ytraa? D'you know what I'm talking about, you silly man?'

'Lady, I know Ytraa and Tryhnn, Taniwha, Krakgragog, Vaarkil and Mythanpho, the Uhmbard and Uhmteld of Tohltaz and any number of other deities you care to name. But, if they worship Ytraa in Choshinahm, it must be in some backwater. I've sold and sailed, carted and hauled all round Lake Qonahn and never come across Followers. Litkala and Kah-Labaz, yes. But not Choshinahm.' He'd seen Corphanda's alarm, glanced at Tumalind and maybe understood her anxiety. 'Doesn't mean there are none, of course. They probably live away from the lake. Didn't I hear that Ytraa dwells in holy ground under the mountains?'

'The Groves of Ytraa, where the Godwoods come from.'

'Ay, that'll be it. The Followers must live up on the slopes, near the Groves of Ytraa. That'll be why I've not met them. I keep to main roads and big towns, you know.'

Corphanda had nodded wisely; satisfied her faith was of more value in this than his partial knowledge of the country. She'd returned to talk with Tarruss. Tumalind, however, was certain he'd modified his story simply to avoid causing antagonism and she'd decided to cultivate him in the hope of learning more about her final destination. So it was that, at her suggestion, and after some negotiation between Dagla Kaz and the merchant, they now sat on Ven-Gadla's carts, on a cheap ride to Slophrahn.

The sweet smell seeped from the sacks at her back and below her. The stuff was firm but cushioned the ruts and potholes. This road was by far the best they'd travelled, however; hardly surprising, given the amount of people, goods and animals using it.

She'd asked Ven-Gadla why he travelled to Slophrahn when Kamakq must surely be closer.

'You're a bright girl, Tumalind. I don't know where you're from, but you obviously aren't aware all the real trade's done to the west and the north. In any case, the road from here to Kamakq's impassable…'

'The stepping-stones. You'd never get carts across the river.'

'Exactly. Litkala and then Shorrannon are my first ports of call. Then to Kah-Labaz and Mehrrhyphrol and up to Aagtaz in the pass. Choshinahm, of course, around the lake where they have some very queer ideas, I can tell you. And then along the Old Merchants' Road, through the Earthworks to cross the desserts in Tohltaz. Dangerous place, especially for pretty young ladies. They'd have you in a harem quick as look at you. Spend your life dressed in a smile, a flower in your hair, and get bedded once in a blue moon. From there, I'll have to pass that blasted smoking mountain and on to Kah-Labaz and back home again.'

'It all sounds very exciting. Don't you ever go to Muhnilahm or..?'

'Oh, Mipahnhil, Ylcrat, Muhnilahm are all too backward, you know. Unsophisticated societies with no understanding of modern commerce.'

'We're from Muhnilahm, actually.'

'Are you? You are? I wondered, when your mother said you were Followers, but, well, folk from there don't usually travel. All I can say is you must be the exception that proves the rule. I've only been a couple of times; to Chalamamnon, but there was no interest. Whole place seems obsessed by Ytraa, prayers and frowkin', if you'll pardon my language.'

Tumalind realised she'd get more information from this man if she didn't argue so, biting her tongue, she continued to question him and learned a good deal about the country she was in and those through which she was destined to travel.

'And Choshinahm?'

'Big country. The lake alone must be nearly as big as Muhnilahm.'

Tumalind gave him a look that said she wasn't as daft as that.

'Seriously. Huge, it is. Takes more than a day to sail from one end to the other, half a day to sail across. And the fish! Never seen anything like them. Big as a house, some of them. I can see you don't believe me, Tumalind, but I'm telling you the truth…'

Corphanda had interrupted then, sending her to bed with the others, and she'd had no chance to talk with the merchant since.

The cart trundled on, swaying to the rhythm of the oxen, taking the road away from the ocean. Soon she could see outlying houses and long low buildings, set apart, where isolated farmsteads struggled to win a living from land constantly threatened by dense shrub and tall, reed-like grasses. The dust continued to rise but, from time to time, the sweet smell of some wayside flower helped the scent of the cargo to hide the stink of the animals pulling the cart.

The beasts grazing these fields were thinner than those nearer the city. The buildings were not so imposing. Poor farmers; eking a living too far from the city to sell their produce at reasonable prices. Eventually, even these last outposts of civilisation vanished and she was staring at unbroken walls of grass growing taller than she stood. They seemed to go on for league after league on either side and, with nothing to mark their progress, she stopped looking about and moved inside herself instead; reliving memories, toying with dreams, playing with hopes she had no real expectation of fulfilling.

She wondered what Okkyntalah might be doing, at this precise moment, as she drifted endlessly across the flat plain, thinking how long it seemed since breakfast and wondering how long it would be before they stopped. Unaccountably, she was assaulted by a sudden feeling of danger and anxiety about her love, as if something had harmed him. So strong was this feeling that it made her cry out in alarm and wake Dilanthas.

'What's up, Tumalind? Ytraa's cleft! You're pale as a cloud. Whatever's the matter?'

'I don't know. I was thinking about Okkyntalah and suddenly had a vivid sensation that he's hurt and in danger.'

"As it gone?'

'Sort of. I still feel anxious, but I'm bound to be worried after something like that. I hope he's safe.'

'Close, weren't you?'

'Close as you can be without joining.'

'Was 'e, y'know, I mean, did 'e know 'ow to meck you feel…nice?'

'Oh, yes. But I just liked being with him. Liked to walk in the fields with his hand in mine, loved to watch him making new arrows, loved the sound of his voice and the way he'd suddenly look up at me and smile. I miss him, Dilanthas, I really do.'

'Ay. Y'seem to feel it worse than me or Porryh.'

'Waste of time and effort. They're gone and there's no getting them back. Might as well forget them. They've forgotten us by now. How many days we been travelling?'

'I last saw Okkyntalah at the Choosing. The twenty-fifth of the tenth portion. It's the second of the twelfth now. Thirty eight days.'

'Frowkin' Mhortag! You know what day it is, even when we been travelling so long?'

'I like to keep track, Porryh.'

"ow d'you do it?'

'In my head. It's not difficult.'

'I couldn't do it.'

'Me neither.'

They talked for a while of something and nothing. Porryh had taken a shine to the armed guard on the wagon behind and, since she was at the rear of the row, she could look round and smile at him from time to time. He returned her smiles and occasionally mouthed rude suggestions that made her laugh out loud.

'He does know you're a Virgin Gift, doesn't he, Porryh?'

'I've not told him. Why should I?'

'Suppose he gets the wrong idea and…well, tries something?'

'Won't be a virgin then, will I? Won't have to go to frowkin' Choshinahm.'

Tumalind shook her head. 'Dagla Kaz would make you a blood sacrifice. You know he would.'

'Only if he thought I was to blame. Suppose I was forced? Couldn't blame me then, could he?'

'No. But Caarl would kill the man responsible.'

'Maybe.'

'There's no maybe about it, Porryh.' Caarl, seated with his back to them, reminded them he could hear even if they couldn't see him.

Tumalind was shocked Porryh would even consider risking someone's life just to get her own way. 'And what about Ytraa?'

'Oh, you! Trust you to go and mention something like that!'

'Eternity's a long time.'

'I know. I know. You've made your point. I just don't want to go all that way.'

Tumalind nodded. She continued to hope that something or someone would allow her to return to Okkyntalah. The merchant's information about their destination had only served to increase her anxieties.

Tumalind lowered her voice. 'Ven-Gadla says there are no Followers in Choshinahm, unless they live in the mountains.'

"Ow would 'e know?'

'He's been all round Lake Qonahn, Dilanthas. But he's never met a Follower.'

Porryh's whisper was hoarse with frustration. 'That's frowkin' marvellous! We're being taken all the way to this heathen land to frowk away our lives with some unknown Follower and there aren't even any there?'

'So Ven-Gadla says.'

'Have you told Dagla Kaz?'

'Not yet.'

Dilanthas frowned. 'Goin' to?'

'Probably. When I find the right moment. I mean, he won't be very happy, will he?'

'Rather you than me.'

'Shall I not tell him, do you think?'

'Oh, you tell him all right. You tell him.'

'But you wouldn't, Porryh?'

'He's got a soft spot for you. Come to think of it, all the men have. Why's that?'

'I don't know. Anyway, it's not true. They like us all.'

'No, Tumalind, Porryh's right. They like you best. It's 'cos you're not just nice, you're clever with it.'

'I'm not clever.'

'Jhonaht thinks you are. I 'eard 'im tell Dagla Kaz. Says you're as bright as Jodisa-Li. Jhonaht says you remind 'im of 'er, an' all.'

'Maybe that's why he looks at me oddly. It answers one question, anyway.'

'What's that, then?'

'Oh, nothing.' She was thinking that her similarity might explain Jhonaht's interest in her. The Chief Astronomer must have had a lot of contact with Jodisa-Li. If he had feelings for her, could she take advantage, maybe get Jhonaht to join with her? Would the High Priest kill him for taking her virginity? No doubt. So that was out. In any case, she didn't want to join with anyone else. But there might be some way she could make use of his interest.

In the meantime, she wondered if that surge of pain and anxiety had really meant Okkyntalah was in danger. Was he well? Would she ever see him again?

Chapter 41

THE FIRST KILLINGS

*O*kkyntalah struggled with his quarry as fast flowing water swept them downstream. The hunters waded the shallows, hoping to aid their companion, but the Followers threw stones to keep them from Okkyntalah and the bowman. Feldrark hit a man on the head, knocking him down. Jodisa-Li hit another on his shoulder. They backed out of range. Okkyntalah fought his opponent alone. When Feldrark made to go to his aid, the hunters used stones to keep him in the shallows, one hitting Myllthlan on her thigh.

Okkyntalah seemed to have met his match. Water, a constant element in Mipahnhil meant the hunter had been swimming all his life. He was as strong as the young man, but older. The fight went this way and that as each tried to drown the other. Both groups of supporters yelled encouragement or abuse, making ready to stone the opponent should he be victorious.

Both disappeared beneath the water and all grew silent as time passed with neither emerging. Feldrark moved forward as one of the hunters did the same. It seemed impossible that either man could live after so long underwater. The hunters began wading, intent on connecting with their prey. The Followers threw more rocks and they backed away again. In the stalemate, Feldrark turned and quickly splashed downstream, where Okkyntalah had pushed through the surface, gasping for air. He held the bow and the quiver with half a dozen arrows. But his arm was gashed; blood flowing freely. Covered by the others' stones, Feldrark helped Okkyntalah from the water.

Malarhah was distraught. 'Stop him bleeding, Myllthlan.'

But the healer couldn't perform her miracles under such conditions. 'I need something to bind the wound. Quickly!'

Without hesitation, Malarhah tore off her tabard, ripped a wide band from it and gave it to Myllthlan. She bound the wound tightly, unhappy at her inability to do the job properly.

For a while, little changed, as the hunters tried to cross and their prey kept them at bay with well-aimed rocks, often finding targets. Having lost their only bowman, the hunters finally withdrew out of range, huddling together to plan. The Followers gathered around Okkyntalah, congratulating his bravery.

Abruptly, the hunters moved upstream. Malarhah wrapped the remains of her tabard round her hips. 'For your benefit. I don't care.'

'Better we're not distracted.' Feldrark's timely touch of lightness lifted some tension and helped them concentrate again.

'What now?'

'They'll cross where it's narrower. We must move to high ground, where we can defend ourselves. Let's go.'

They ran to the wooded area cresting a low rise, a league or so ahead. As they approached the trees, their hunters emerged from a small copse a short way upstream. The Followers were spotted at once and the hunters approached quickly through knee-high grass.

In the trees, they gathered long, straight branches. Aglydron formed them into rough spears, cutting the ends to points. Okkyntalah's injury made the bow useless to him and he passed it to Feldrark. Myllthlan wanted to heal his injury properly, worried about blood loss. But the hunters were moving fast and he was more concerned to defeat them.

'Weapons are more important than healing for now.'

Her binding had reduced the blood loss and reluctantly she agreed. 'So be it.' She borrowed his hunting knife and fashioned a forked branch into a spear thrower and showed the others how it worked so they could do likewise.

Between them, they had only two knives, the fishing spear, two bows and six arrows, and their makeshift spears. Their hunters all had swords, spears with iron tips, and small leather shields. But they'd lost one of their number and another carried a head injury.

The Followers waited under the eaves of the small wood as their hunters closed on them.

'The woman will try to kill Aglydron.' Malarhah explained. 'None of the men will touch him unless she fails. That gives us an advantage, doesn't it?'

'In a way, yes. Aglydron can handle her. That leaves six for the rest of us to tackle. And we have the advantage of height and cover. Don't throw a spear until you're sure you can hit one of them.'

'We're not warriors, Feldrark.'

'Don't forget, Myllthlan, not just your life but ours depend on your willingness to kill, or at least disable them. Only one group can come out of this alive. They're attacking us: we're just defending ourselves. You killed in the town. If you can't kill again, then disarm and disable your opponent until one of us can finish him off.'

'I've no problem killing scum like these.'

'No, but you've only one arm at present, Okkyntalah. You'll have trouble simply defending yourself.'

There was no more time for talk. The hunters had spread into a long arc, covering a wide area. Those on the ends, one of them Chislanda, moved in, making for the trees before the Followers were close enough to attack. Aglydron challenged Chislanda, her thrown spear cutting his arm and her sword drawn to finish him off.

Feldrark let go his first arrow. It glanced from the raised shield of the hunter closest to him. No archer, he was stringing a second arrow as the man rushed at him. Myllthlan used her spear thrower to aim her sharpened stick at the man to the left of Feldrark's attacker. She hit him in the thigh, penetrating almost to the bone. He dropped his shield and fell, pulling out the makeshift spear as he did so. Blood spurted from the wound but he rose, took up his shield and moved closer to her.

Feldrark's opponent was close as he released the next arrow. Again, the shield saved him. Okkyntalah easily dodged the thrown spear of his opponent. He waited until his man was almost on top of him before he used the fishing spear with his usual accuracy. The enemy, arm raised to strike with his sword, was dead before he hit the ground, the blade entering his chest with such force it pierced his back. Okkyntalah grabbed the sword with his good hand. And then the other hunter was on Feldrark.

Malarhah fired her first spear, with the thrower, at the man closest to her but missed completely. His spear cut her shoulder and she dropped her thrower. Feldrark wanted to help her but he was fighting a swordsman, using only a stout bough.

The hunter closed on her, sword drawn. With nothing to defend herself, she ran forward, sidestepped her enemy and, stooping, grabbed a short, thick branch. Unwrapping the band from her hips, she circled the trees, keeping them between her and her pursuer. She tied one end of her cloth around the bough as she dodged tree roots. The swordsman chased and she stepped into open ground. Feet apart and knees bent, she swung the heavy lump of wood on the end of her makeshift rope. It whirred around her head, too fast for him to close on her.

Feldrark, concentrating now she could defend herself, warded off his opponent's sword strokes. Okkyntalah ran to Malarhah's aid as she backed up to a tree. He reached them, as her whirling stick hit the trunk behind her. The man who'd wounded her dashed forward and held the point of his sword against her throat, hesitating briefly at her nakedness. It was time enough for Okkyntalah to rush in and kill him.

She saw Feldrark's uneven fight. The hunter Okkyntalah had felled still clutched his sword. Wrenching it from his dead fingers, she rushed to help Feldrark. His defensive stick had been chopped to less than the length of his forearm and the swordsman was ready to strike. She yelled to draw the attacker's attention. He turned and swung at her, sweeping her blade aside with his sword as she ran at him. Feldrark's yelled warning was too late. Her momentum carried her onto the hunter's blade and he twisted it in her belly. She crumpled to the ground as Feldrark struck the man's head. He collapsed over her.

Disarming him at once, Feldrark finished him off with his own sword. Stricken at her injury, he dragged his foe clear and bent over Malarhah.

Okkyntalah moved to where Jodisa-Li was fending off one man, back to back with Myllthlan, who was fighting the man she'd wounded. Their swords parrying the women's flailing sticks.

They were in difficulties, but too far for him to reach in time. In moments one of them might be killed. Okkyntalah grabbed an arrow and strung it by biting the tip of the flight. Pulling back with his teeth, he took aim; confident he'd miss both women and might even hit one of the men. The arrow struck just below the right eye of the one fighting Jodisa-Li. He fell backwards. Okkyntalah retrieved his own dropped sword. Jodisa-Li leapt on her attacker, struggling to disarm him. Myllthlan, moving back, found the man's spear at her feet. She pushed the point into his stomach. Hesitating only a moment, she pushed it with all her force. He screamed. Jodisa-Li kicked her attacker's sword arm and scrambled to seize the weapon. Okkyntalah, reaching them, sliced his sword across the man's throat, splashing them with blood. He turned and finished off the man Myllthlan had speared.

Aglydron, cornered by Chislanda, was failing in the fight; his broken stick no match for her fierce sword.

The remaining male hunter closed on Feldrark as he bent over Malarhah. He'd been waiting in the trees, in case Chislanda failed to kill Aglydron.

Jodisa-Li shouted a warning. 'Feldrark!'

The big man rose from his position of grief and swept his captured blade round in time to slice the hunter's body, catching a cut to his wrist but spilling the man's guts as he fell. He slashed again, across his neck, killing him instantly.

'Myllthlan; come see to Malarhah.'

The healer moved swiftly to help, calling as she went. 'Aglydron needs help!'

Feldrark ran to aid Aglydron. Okkyntalah turned in time to see Feldrark corner Chislanda and disarm her with a swift blow from his sword.

Aglydron leapt from the tree and stood beside the woman. 'Don't kill her!'

Feldrark pointed the sword tip at her heart and nodded, indicating she should kneel. She did so, her chest heaving with the effort of the fight.

'Why should we spare her?'

'She carries my child.'

'Do you?'

Chislanda nodded.

'Get up! Okkyntalah, give her sword to Aglydron so he can run this murderer through if she tries to escape.'

The young man handed the weapon to Aglydron, who prodded Chislanda forward with the point in the small of her back.

They gathered round Malarhah who lay moaning softly on the ground, blood flowing freely from her wound.

Myllthlan was in tears. 'The wound's too great for my normal healing. I must bind it. Now! For pity's sake, give me something to stem the blood.'

Feldrark unclasped his belt to remove his tunic. 'We've nothing but...'

Aglydron stripped Chislanda of her wrap and Jodisa-Li cut it into lengths.

'It may already be too late.'

Okkyntalah, the fighting done, dropped to his knees, his world spinning around him. He heard no more as darkness took him.

The twins were finally asleep. Sounds of distant surf, breaking on the beach, leaked in through the window along with the scent from the carah-carah vine draped over the fence of the small paddock behind the house. The night with A'ahl had been fun and they'd spent the following day together, A'ahl returning to Shoarhn's house to help with milking and feeding the livestock. Now Shoarhn was alone again, tired after another long day. One of the cows had given birth and she'd spent the evening tending it and seeing that the calf was well. Aglydron would be pleased with the new young bull for their small herd; he was a sturdy little fellow, already showing his mother who was boss. Shoarhn had laughed as he butted his head into the udder to obtain his first milk. A real bull. They'd slaughter the old one for meat once the youngster matured.

The dark oblong of sky, bright with stars, marked the opening where soft air drifted into the room. Sitting with her arms enclosing her raised knees in the dark, loneliness descended. She frowned over Aglydron, missing him even though his greeting on his return would be perfunctory; his earnest desire, as always, to serve Ytraa. Shrugging the sorry thoughts off, she sought to ease her sadness with dreams of Aklon-Dji.

'Are you awake, Shoarhn?'

At first, she believed it was a trick of her mind; as if she'd somehow summoned him out of the very air. A small gasp of surprise escaped her.

'Shoarhn?'

He really was there. His call was soft but the window silhouetted him.

'Coming.'

The door opened onto darkness and she felt rather than saw him come in from the blank blackness of the night; the trees and hills cutting out the sky in that direction.

She closed the door and sought a lamp.

'Darkness, Shoarhn. And silence.' His whisper was soft but urgent. He put his hand over hers to stop her lighting the lamp. Arms about her as they listened to the night around them, he held her close and still.

She could hear soft surf and the close sound of his measured breathing, the rhythmic thud of his heartbeat. They seemed to stay so forever, the feel of his hands against her skin filling her with comfort and growing desire. But his hands were still, his arms unmoving.

'We may shift.' His whisper was barely audible, though his mouth touched her ear.

She led him to the bedchamber. He sat beside her, one hand holding hers, the other gentling her shoulder. Briefly, he kissed her mouth and touched his lips across her face until he could whisper again in her ear.

'A few more minutes.'

They sat, silent and unmoving in the dark. It seemed a lifetime, as they remained static and yet linked in some unspoken prelude to passion. Desire rose within her simply from his closeness. But he was still and listening.

'All is well. We can speak now.'

'Words aren't what I want.'

They lay together, after that space where time was meaningless, her head resting on his chest, his hands cupping her soft curves.

'I have news of Aglydron.'

'Oh?' She realized her lack of interest must show. 'You have?'

He laughed gently. 'He is a fool to make no effort to please you, Shoarhn. You are a woman of love and passion.'

'He'd rather please Ytraa.'

'Not himself, then?'

'Oh, no. Everything's Ytraa with Aglydron.'

'Not now.'

She was curious. 'What do you know? And how? Is he back on the island?'

He brought his free hand up and stroked her hair, following the contours of her head and fingering the tresses where they fell against her back and shoulders. 'The how must come first and you may not believe me, though it is perfectly true.'

'I think I'd believe anything you said, Aklon-Dji. I just know you only tell the truth.'

'To you, at any rate. I need a confessor and you are so full of generosity, warmth and trust that I could find no better. Aglydron is not back on the island. He was in

Mipahnhil until a short while ago.' He waited for that to sink in.

'That cesspit? What was he doing there...and how do you know?'

'Ah. The how. This will be hard for you to grasp, Shoarhn. Not because you are stupid or dull; you are far from either. It is difficult enough for me to understand and I am the one who experiences it.' He paused, his hands halting their sensual passage over her skin as he gathered his thoughts.

She knew he was trying to find a way to tell her something that may distress her. 'Just tell me Aklon. You know I love and trust you.'

It was enough. He kissed her mouth, lovingly and long. 'Thank you. Have you ever had that strange sensation when you know what someone is going to say? Seemed to know their thoughts before they spoke?'

'Happens with Tumalind all the time. Both ways. It's a bit disturbing when your daughter giggles, informing you that your mind's dwelling on a man other than her father.'

'Yes. Suppose you could do it at will? Instead of it happening just occasionally, when you were not expecting it, imagine it happening when you wanted it to.'

'I don't know what you mean.'

'I mean being able to talk to someone without speaking, able to hold a conversation, even though you are not in the same house.'

'You mean...but that would be fabulous. Being able to hear each other's thoughts and to send them as well. Is that what you mean?'

'You are truly remarkable, Shoarhn. Most people would find the idea so impossible they would reject it without consideration. You can see what a wonderful gift such a skill would be and so you accept it. You are good for me, Shoarhn, so very good.'

'And you can do this with Aglydron?'

'Not Aglydron. A very clever man called Ivdulon.'

'Not a name I know. Does he live in one of the other towns?'

He was silent for more than a moment.

'He lives in Litkala.'

Her gasp he accepted without comment and she found her tongue, at last. 'Litkala? But that's where the other Followers...'

'The ones we never refer to because they are so evil? Yes. It is their home.'

She took this in and it was clear he had more to say but would let her think before he gave her new information. He was patient with her, waiting for her to come to terms with what he was telling her.

'But, if he's from Litkala, how can he know about Aglydron in Mipahnhil?'

'Excellent! The fact that you are more worried about practicalities than about any prejudice is very encouraging. Mipahnhil is closer to Litkala than we are, of course, but they are still a good way apart. Ivdulon can communicate; we call it mindtalking, with others apart from me. One of them is Litkala's spiritual leader, a man called Feldrark, who was with Aglydron in Mipahnhil.'

'What was he doing there?'

'Do you know, Shoarhn, that is just one of the many things about you that makes me love you? You are more interested in what matters than in everything surrounding it.'

'You do love me, then?'

'I thought I had made that abundantly clear.'

'Yes. I suppose you have. Though A'ahl says you love all of us…'

'A'ahl. A good woman. Of course, I tend to choose only the good ones, so perhaps I live in a dream world when I believe that women are, by and large, better human beings than men. Anyway, Aglydron was in Mipahnhil because that is where the boat took them. He, Okkyntalah and Jodisa-Li are all well. What I know from Ivdulon is only bits and pieces since he is obviously more concerned about Feldrark than he is about the others. Though, it is interesting to learn that this Feldrark is rather smitten by my sister.

'It seems they were all trapped there but some slave girl helped them escape. I am not sure of the details but it seems Aglydron was required to father a child on some woman whose child died as they arrived there. I cannot say I understand it, really, but Aglydron had to make her pregnant and none of them could leave until he completed the job.'

Shoarhn laughed. 'That'll be a real task for him. He only frowks for Ytraa. And they're not Followers in Mipahnhil, are they? She'll have a hard time getting any joy out of Aglydron. I wish her luck, poor woman. But if he's prodding her fern…'

She moved a little and covered his mouth with her own. He made no protest.

Waking, still wrapped in his arms, she heard the boys squabbling in their room and warned Aklon-Dji they were awake.

'You want me to go?'

'I want you to stay. But will you be safe if the boys know you're here?'

'Tell them I am a friend from Pampahn. Tell them I am Phildrad; it is a common enough name and I know of a few who live there.'

'Breakfast?'

'Prayers first. It is best we behave as normally as possible.'

'You know I've the animals to tend…?'

'I will help, if I may? I want more time with you and I cannot have that if you are busy whilst I remain idle.'

'Oh, Aklon-Dji, why couldn't I have married you?'

He smiled and shrugged.

'Oh! There's something I should've told you last night. I'm sorry, I hope I haven't been stupid but I was so eager to have you to myself, I forgot.'

He looked serious and questioning but without threat.

'Wesdan Kaz asked A'ahl and me if we'd seen you. He'd heard you'd been here last time. I'm sorry. I really should've told you at once. I was so eager to...I hope I haven't...'

'Not to worry, Shoarhn. Had I known on the way here, I could have done something about it; I passed the unpleasant little bowelcreep on the road. Oh, worry not. I saw him and his tearful female consort. He did not see me. How I hate that man. I am glad you told me, though. Do you think he suspects either of you at all?'

'I don't think so. Perhaps you ought to ask A'ahl as well, though.'

'Even though you would rather I did not see her?'

'I don't own you, Aklon-Dji. I love you. But I understand that part of the way you keep safe is by being the way you are with your women. But come back to me tonight?'

'Shall we go to see her together?'

'Someone might be watching us. I don't want to do anything that'll place you at risk.'

'Good. You understand as well as I hoped you might. You go and see her. Tell her I am here and want to see her.'

'Aklon-Dji, I want you to know you can join with her, here, if that's what you need to do to keep safe. I'd rather have some of you alive than none of you, or have you in danger.'

'You will have as much of me as I can give. We shall breakfast. Then, why not send the boys to ask A'ahl to visit? I can help with the animals. I want to tell you a little more of what I have learned about Aglydron and Okkyntalah. More importantly, I want to explain the truth about Gadhallah, Ytraa and the Followers and why my father made me renegade. It is time you learned about the evil in this land and in our religion.'

Chapter 42

HEALING, BURNING AND LEAVING

*M*yllthlan rose up from her patient and stood, bereft and grief stricken. 'I can do no more. She's beyond my help.' She turned and Feldrark enclosed her in his arms to show she held no blame. Jodisa-Li felt so proud that his concern for their healer should overcome his great grief at Malarhah's loss.

'But I can, and must, look after Okkyntalah, or our brave young warrior will die from blood loss.' Quickly, she started her healing, stopping the blood from his wounds before he lost more, and beginning the process of joining the sliced flesh and skin together again.

He came to and turned to look at Malarhah. 'Leave me. I'm fine.'

She let the lie go unchallenged, for now; his need to part properly from the girl greater than his need for further physical healing. Okkyntalah rose to his hands and knees and crawled to Malarhah. He bent and kissed her lips. She managed to curve them, pale and dry, into a smile for him. No words were needed between them and he moved away again quickly, to Myllthlan, so Malarhah wouldn't see how weak he was.

Myllthlan closed the gaps precisely and breathed life into his flesh to preserve him.

Jodisa-Li knelt to bind the wound at the top of Malarhah's arm, though she knew it was pointless. Only she heard the soft words from the young woman's lips. She bent closer to understand what Malarhah had to say.

Her soft breath came in short gasps as though each caused her pain. 'Was only show, Jodisa-Li. Feldrark's yours. Always was. Take bangle…now…whilst I live to give it.'

Jodisa-Li looked up at their faces. 'She wants me to have the bangle. What am I to do?'

Aglydron shook his head in misery, knowing it was hopeless. 'We can't ignore her dying wish. Take the bangle.'

Feldrark nodded his agreement and Jodisa-Li struggled to undo the hidden clasp until he knelt beside her and helped. Releasing it, he placed it round her ankle and clicked it shut.

He moved closer to Malarhah so he could hear her words. 'Love you, Feldrark… rather die… than… cesspit… Thank… loving me… and chance…' She closed her eyes as if keeping them open was too much effort.

They gathered about her. Okkyntalah, almost healed, and Myllthlan prepared to wait.

Chislanda began to move a little away but Aglydron saw her and used the remaining strip from her skirt to bind her hands and feet together after he forced her to the ground. She lay silent and resentful as they clustered round their fallen companion.

'No worms… Burn me.' Malarhah said no more.

Myllthlan placed her fingers at the girl's throat, bent and kissed her forehead and then moved back and stood. She shook her head, tears wetting her cheeks.

Aglydron, contrite because of his treatment of her; Jodisa-Li, regretful of her suspicions; and Feldrark, aware she'd received her wounds protecting him; all took their leave of the brave girl who'd made their escape from Mipahnhil possible. Okkyntalah, having parted with the living girl, wouldn't revisit her corpse and turned away to hide his grief.

Aglydron untied Chislanda and hauled her to her feet with her long hair. He shoved her into the open, away from the shelter of the trees. 'You die or live by my word, woman. It's well for you that what I started as a duty, you made a delight. You frowked as though you cared. And now you want to kill me and my companions. It makes no sense. You say you worship life but you risk death and danger to kill. I don't understand you.'

She stood defiant and proud, staring at him, saying nothing.

Aglydron slapped her face and then dropped his gaze in shame. Jodisa-Li approached and held him, understanding some of what he felt amongst the blood and death. He tried to master his emotions in her embrace and pulled away, his face a picture of confusion and distress. In those brief moments, Jodisa-Li saw beneath the mask he wore and understood that this man was frightened by his own capacity to love. Had she time and opportunity, she felt she might release him from his fear of being vulnerable to loss, but now wasn't the place or moment and she let him go with words of practicality instead.

'Bind her arms behind her, Aglydron, though not as harshly as you did when I was in the boat. And allow the binding at her feet to let her move but not escape. We've other duties to perform before we decide what should be done with this evil woman.'

They scoured the wood for fallen branches and built a pyre on the open ground east of the trees. Malarhah's broken body they laid reverently on the mound and prayed to Ytraa that she might take her place in the Garden of Delights because, although no Follower, she'd saved their lives and acted always in their interests. As flames slowly consumed wood and flesh, Jodisa-Li, inspired by Malarhah's courage and selflessness, was reminded of the legend of Vaarkil and Mythanpho and sang a short lament.

'In times before time began,
When men and women were Gods,
Then did the great hero, Vaarkil
With Mythanpho, his woman, his love,
Defeat the vile serpent, Na-Dagun.

But those heroes so strong and so true
Lost their lives as they battled the beast.
And they lie neath the mountains of Geldakq
Till their people again have great need

Oh, great was the mourning
And many the tears
That the people did weep on that day.
And long the lamenting
And deep lived the grief
Of the people they saved that great day.

Chislanda, her face streaked with tears after the lament, remained where Aglydron had placed her. He released the tie at her ankles and freed her wrists. Tying the thin rag around her hips, he let the loose ends fall in front, in mockery of a garment. 'That's your status now, Chislanda. Go back to your cesspit and tell them what happens to them as come to kill us. Tell them we won, even with our poor weapons. And, now, we've got the swords and spears you meant to use on us.'

Feldrark stood tall and fierce before her. 'Warn them, woman, to send no more to hunt us. All the power and might of Litkala is with us. You will not defeat us. Go, before I would have you die.'

'Wait. What should we do with your fallen?'

Chislanda glanced at Myllthlan oddly, as if her question surprised her. 'They failed. Let the carrion beasts devour them. They're nothing now.'

'You do no honour to your dead?' Feldrark was amazed.

'They who fail deserve no such honour.'

He clenched his fists and stared hard at her. 'Then, leave us. Return to your cesspit and live in your filth. Come no more into my land, Chislanda of Mipahnhil, for if we meet again, you will find death at my hands.'

Chislanda drew herself up tall and faced them. 'You send me shamed, alone and weaponless, without food or water, over strange lands. But I'll find Mipahnhil and tell what was done here. When we return, as we will, we'll kill every last one of you. We'll destroy the thieves of Litkala. And my blade will slice the flesh of Aglydron as surely as the river cuts through mud.' She turned and walked down the shallow slope toward the river and, not looking back, but pausing as she reached an odd collection of standing stones a short distance from her track. Feldrark watched, curious about her exploration of what seemed no more than random rocks. But, as the party prepared to go about their business, they heard her cry out in anguish. The woman fled the scene as if pursued by some demon.

Feldrark couldn't ignore this strangeness and followed her route down the slope until he reached the rocks. Jodisa-Li came after him. As they approached, it became clear that, far from being a random collection of stones, this was a collapsed monument of some sort. Great uprights supported what had once been a huge stone roof to some strange and crudely built edifice.

'What caused her fear, do you think, Feldrark?'

He glanced at Jodisa-Li and pointed to the only thing he could identify as the possible cause. On the face of one of the interior stones, protected from wind, rain and sun, was a strange and oddly disturbing device. Carved into the rock face and coloured with faded red and blue pigment was a stylised figure. Clearly female, it held an odd power that hinted at something malevolent.

'What is it?'

'I've no idea, my love. I've never seen the like.'

'It frightened Chislanda.'

'Scared her. Or, maybe meant something to her that caused her real anguish. Had we time, I'd follow her and ask, but we have too much else to do and no time to waste.'

They left the site to return to the others, but decided they would say nothing of their discovery.

When they gathered with the rest, they fended off questions, saying they could not tell what had alarmed the woman.

'Will she return with others?'

Feldrark nodded. 'I'm sure she will, Jodisa-Li. I let her live only for the sake of Aglydron's child. But it's likely we'll not be free of her or her people until more death teaches them they can't win. Let them send whatever force they will against the city of Litkala. A hundred thousand couldn't storm that citadel. If they choose to feud until the end of time, they'll always be the losers.'

'Are there any more injuries amongst us, now we've honoured our dead?'

Myllthlan wanted to know.

She'd dealt with the cuts the others had sustained during the fighting and now turned to complete her work on Okkyntalah.

Feldrark glanced at Jodisa-Li. *'As ever, my love, full of surprises. Thank you for your acknowledgment of Malarhah's bravery.'*

'She saved your life, Feldrark. How could I do otherwise?'

'You'll be so good for me.' And, to the others, 'We must rest and eat. But not here. Not in this place. Aglydron has made sure they're all dead; a wounded beast is the most dangerous. We'll leave here, now the pyre has burnt down, and camp for the remainder of the day some distance away to relax after what we've been through. Come. Let Myllthlan do what she may to aid Okkyntalah's full recovery. We'll all gather at the far side of the wood, to the west. Do not be long. Evening falls fast.'

Okkyntalah and Myllthlan, following her brief rest after the healing, caught up with the others as they reclined on the grass beyond the trees.

Aglydron rose at once to examine his wounds. 'You work miracles, Myllthlan.'

Only pale scars remained, one running from shoulder to elbow and another from wrist to halfway up his forearm. Okkyntalah, relieved at the completion of the healing, and feeling his strength returning, smiled and flexed the strong muscles to show that his arm was intact.

'I'm but a healer. It's what I do and what I am. The wise woman…I forget. There was a cave…' But the memory went as quickly as it arrived.

Feldrark picked up a spare scabbard attached to its broad leather belt and handed it to Okkyntalah to sheath the bloodied sword he still carried. He passed him the bow and the half dozen retrieved arrows in their leather quiver.

'You've shown more skill with this than the rest of us. I understand we all owe our lives to you in one way or another, Okkyntalah. When we reach Litkala, I'll find a way to properly reward you for your courage and quick thinking. For the moment, please accept my heartfelt thanks.'

Okkyntalah was mildly embarrassed and muttered a soft reply, aware of Myllthlan and, to his surprise, Jodisa-Li staring at him with open admiration.

'You saved me, Okkyntalah. I can do little to thank you but behave in obedience for the remainder of our journey together.'

'I, however, may find a way to give substance to my thanks, once the sorrow's subsided and we find rest and solitude. For the moment, accept this token.' Myllthlan kissed him softly.

'You owe me nothing, after this.' He raised his healed arm. 'But I accept your gratitude. Malarhah did as much, and paid far more than me. I'll miss her cheerfulness, easy service and companionship.'

'You've proved yourself a man today, Okkyntalah. I'll try to remember that, next time I find reason to rebuke you.' Aglydron clasped a hand to his shoulder in token of friendship and gratitude.

'Will you carry this, Myllthlan?' Feldrark held out another sword, sheathed in its decorated leather scabbard.

She took the weapon and examined it. 'I'd rather save life than take it, but sometimes the need to kill is more urgent than the need to heal. I'll carry it until that need ends.'

'Come, let's find somewhere we can take our ease and eat, well away from all the blood and death that lingers here.'

They each took up their spears and shields and followed Feldrark, his Staff in place of a spear for him, as he led them from the scene of their loss and their victory.

Okkyntalah no longer felt prey to the anxiety of being hunted like a wild beast. And, but for his grief at Malarhah's death, he travelled with a lighter heart than at any time since escaping the town on stilts. It must be many days before Chislanda could return to Mipahnhil to raise a new hunting party. Indeed, she might never arrive home, bereft as she was of the means of survival.

⁕

The three nights and days with Shoarhn were the happiest Aklon–Dji had known in many cycles. She pleased him as a partner. But, more than that, she fed his spirit and eased his heart, offsetting the horrors of the murders and other actions he must take in the name of the Cause. She refreshed and reinvigorated him and he left her only with great difficulty.

Explaining that he must go again, for her safety as well as his, was more difficult than it should have been. 'I want to settle down and live with you for the rest of my life.'

'I think I might be able to put up with that. Why so worried, Aklon?'

'I am used to enjoying the love and pleasure of many beautiful and willing women. I swore never to allow myself to be involved emotionally. My life is too unsafe, my situation too precarious to sustain such a relationship. But you have found something in me that no other woman has reached and I respond to you in a way I never have before. It is hard to leave you.'

'But you will leave.'

'Only because I will do us both the most good that way.'

He kissed her tears and vanished into the night and waited to kill, if he must, after loving so completely. But fortune was with him this time. No one emerged from the shadows to track him and he concluded his presence in Morstahn had remained secret. He set out on for Chalamamnon; there to discover what he might about events. On the way, he would mindtalk with Ivdulon and find out how things stood on the mainland, and ask for further news of Jodisa-Li.

He considered the information he'd given to Shoarhn and smiled at the way she'd received it. Her response to the adventures of Okkyntalah and her husband had been mixed, with more concern shown for the boy than the man. It pleased him that she felt that way about Aglydron, who seemed a pious and rigid fool.

Her shock and horror, at learning the truth about Gadhallah, were no more than he'd expected but she'd repaid his faith in her by accepting all he said. It was so good, so refreshing, to be able to explain all he knew without any sign of the doubt that many displayed. It wasn't that Shoarhn was gullible or dim; simply that she knew him so well she could tell he was truthful. He loved her. And now, as well his care for his own safety and future, he found himself burdened with care for her. It was a burden he welcomed in spite of the extra weight. Her love made the changes he planned more important but also more personal. It was no longer a matter of conscience alone. Now it was something to strive for to make life better for Shoarhn and him as well as for everyone else.

And the start of that journey was coming soon. Perhaps the murder of Wesdan Kaz was due at last. He would talk with Ivdulon and then decide. For, on that decision rested the fate not only of Shoarhn, the Few and himself, but of his entire nation.

Feldrark led them over ground that fell away for a few hundred paces and then rose slowly again as they left the wood behind and trod a broad grassy slope, patched with scrub. From time to time, as they had throughout their journey, they had to skirt patches of marshy land made impassable by the rains. But their progress was good and they made the crown of the rise in mid-afternoon. From there, the ground fell away abruptly in a steep, scrub-covered escarpment down to a small open forest. Beyond the spread of widely spaced trees, Feldrark could see the glint of water, where two small tributaries flowed to join the larger River Dash. That waterway emptied into the Sea of Llahkan close to its junction with the Shylnah Sea. Having hunted there previously, Feldrark recognized the place at once. Travelling from the city as far as the foot of the ridge, he was familiar with this part of the country but had never ascended it or approached from the east before. It seemed they must spend a night here as the sun had gone down as they walked.

Morning saw them rise early and hungry. Blackened with the smoke and ash of Malarhah's pyre, bloodied from their battle, clothes ripped and stained, they made a sorry sight. But their spirits rose with the sun and they were ready to travel.

'If you look to the horizon, you'll see a line of blue-green. There lies the edge of the great Greenreald; the forest that covers the bulk of the peninsula on which the city of Litkala stands. With Ytraa's help, we'll be in the city in four days. Indeed, if we push hard, we might make the road itself by sun down.'

'We should rest, Feldrark. Our hearts are as weary as our legs and I, for one, don't want to carry on today.' Myllthlan's plea was heartfelt.

'Let's rest as we agreed. The road can wait 'til tomorrow.'

Feldrark glanced at Aglydron and then looked out, gazing beyond the haze on the horizon and glimpsing the peak of the solitary mountain, on the slopes of which lay his beloved city. It had been too long since he'd left that place and he wished to return, in triumph, with the Staff of Gadhallah intact and his beautiful wife-to-be on his arm.

Jodisa-Li smiled at his thoughts. *'We all have our different hopes, my love. I understand your wish to be back home, but be patient.'*

'I'm eager to show you to my people and my parents, Jodisa-Li. I long to lie with you and make you my own.'

'You will. Patience, love. Do nothing that will arouse their suspicions. Aglydron's already conscious that I wear the bangle you gave Malarhah when she was to be your wife. We need some tale to put him off the scent if he asks what you'll do about a wife now.'

'You're right, Aglydron. We all need rest. See? There's a small clearing in the forest, there. Let's make for that, find food and eat and sleep away the rest of this sorry glad day.'

He turned to survey his land from this vantage point he had not previously visited. To his surprise, he noticed three more stands of rocks, similar in form to that which had so bothered Chislanda. At another time, he must investigate these and discover who had made them and why. But not now. Now was the time for the return to home, hope and glory.

The descent was more awkward than perilous. They were lightly laden, having few goods but their water bags and the weapons they'd acquired. The sun was still high in a sky now cloudless, when they entered the clearing.

After a brief rest and a drink to refresh him, Okkyntalah left to hunt game and Aglydron set off in another direction to try his hand with his newly acquired spear. Myllthlan and Jodisa-Li sought roots, herbs and fruits and Feldrark collected wood for a fire as he ensured the ground was free of lumps and rocks that might disturb resting bodies.

They ate well on the zwahan Okkyntalah had killed with a couple of arrows.

'Was the bird alone, Okkyntalah, or did it have a mate with it?'

'I saw only the one. Why?'

'Zwahan mate for life and it's considered very bad luck to kill one of a pair. But if there was no other in sight, I imagine this is a solitary male not yet mature enough to gain a mate.' Feldrark praised his skill in securing the bird and remarked on the fine black plumage of its neck and the red feathers of its crest, these being prized in Litkala as decoration for women's costumes.

Okkyntalah gathered the feathers in bunches and tied the loose ends with short lengths of fishing line he cut from that still wrapped around the shaft of the fishing spear. 'Never know; I might be able to sell them for useful coin in Litkala.'

Feldrark smiled more encouragement than he felt. How would the young warrior react when he learned Jodisa-Li wouldn't be completing the journey?

They supplemented the plentiful meat from the bird with a small blue-skinned hog that Aglydron had speared, and more of the nutty sweet purple roots Myllthlan had dug up with the point of her sword. Fresh sage and wild mint added to their enjoyment and Jodisa-Li's discovery of ground-loving wild blueberries finished off the meal. Shaulah had the hog carcass and spent her time gnawing noisily on bones from which she'd stripped the remains of the cooked flesh.

They sat around the cooking fire not for its heat, as the sun gave that freely, but for the sense of comradeship their shared situation brought. They talked quietly amongst themselves of Malarhah. A few more tears of grief mingled with bursts of laughter as they recalled, and Jodisa-Li mimicked with an accuracy that surprised them, the slave girl's peculiar way of speaking when they'd first met her. As the sun lowered toward the horizon through the well-spaced trees, they made their prayers and then prepared for sleep, Myllthlan volunteering for the early watch.

'I'll wake Okkyntalah to take over from me.'

Feldrark watched the healer move away from the camp and set herself on a high point overlooking their resting place. He saw Okkyntalah follow her with his gaze and found himself hoping the young man might find comfort in the woman's embrace. Perhaps she might even become Okkyntalah's consort when he discovered that Tumalind must be forever beyond his reach.

Chapter 43

Discussion, Tales And Awareness

*O*n their third day with Ven-Gadla, Tumalind watched the road draw parallel with the River Fleet and follow it. They travelled through wilderness; an untamed deserted landscape of low hills and wide valleys. Dense in places, the bush gave cover for wild beasts. Once, the carts shuddered to a halt as a huge horned creature, with a hide like thick bark, emerged suddenly and ambled along the road for three or four hundred paces before turning and splashing into the river. Some of the flies that swarmed about the beast's rear end came instead to bother them. Tumalind longed to splash in the river herself.

'Aye, lass. Pretty as a flower, bright as a star you might be, but it'd no stop crocs teckin' a munch on your lovely flesh, nor leeches clinging on that soft skin an' growin' fat on your blood; mekkin' you sick.' The driver told her.

So, she'd made do with the shallow stone baths they found outside the scant wayside inns. Spaced roughly a day's journey apart, they sheltered amongst dotted farmsteads where the bush was tamed and stout stockades kept grazing animals from straying and partly protected from fierce predators. They looked hard places to earn a living; wild, dangerous and lonely, but for passing travellers. The inns were mostly comfortable, not too clean, and served food that filled a space without the mouth-watering flavours of Phildrad's cooking. All had wells at which they replenished their water skins for drink as they journeyed under a sun that sometimes threatened to consume them.

They arrived at each inn just before dark and set out again with the rising sun. Dagla Kaz wanted to make up lost time and Ven-Gadla's only religion was trade, which meant time was money. The carts moved a little faster and for longer each day than the party would have managed on foot, so they saved effort and gained time.

They'd followed the river for three days when they reached a ford. Wide and shallow, the water flowed around the wheels of their wagons as the oxen hauled them across. The armed guard sat astride the leading beast to keep watch for crocs so he might use his long spear to deter attacks. The cart lurched along the uneven riverbed as the driver picked his way amongst rocks and ridges. Ahead, the first wagon was already on dry land when their own came to a jarring halt. A wheel had lodged in a narrow rut, hidden by silt. The oxen couldn't shift it because of the weight of the load.

Two at a time, the passengers dropped into the stream and were escorted across by the armed guard from the wagon ahead. Tumalind, enjoying the cool water with Dilanthas, followed Corphanda and Phildrad across. Dilanthas had to raise the hem of her longer tabard to keep it dry. On the bank, waiting for Porryh and Tarruss to join them, they checked each other for leeches and were happy to find none. A sudden yell of dismay made them look up to find Porryh sitting with water up to her neck. Tarruss pulled her back to her feet just as the guard jabbed his spear at a croc lurking nearby. Porryh dashed the rest of the way, heedless of her splashing, and arrived at the bank soaked from head to foot.

The whole party stood in a circle around her; the men with their backs to the centre as Corphanda inspected her for leeches. She was free and reluctantly replaced her wet tabard to dry in the sun. Tarruss was examined in similar fashion and Phildrad found a red blob on his calf. He was about to pull it off when Ven-Gadla stopped him.

'If you pull it, it'll leave the head behind and go septic. Best to let it feed and drop off by itself.'

Tumalind allowed curiosity to get the better of her and watched the small creature swell and then drop off, leaving only a tiny mark on the giant's muscular leg. He looked up, straight into her eyes and surprised her with a cheeky grin instead of the disapproval she deserved. Blushing at her naughtiness, she turned away with a smile.

The drivers waded back and forth with the hessian sacks until their cart was empty, the guards keeping watch. Other parts of the travelling caravan passed by; a broken line of wagons, mounted riders and guards, exchanging mocking banter with the driver of their stranded wagon. Once unloaded, they lifted the wagon free and the oxen pulled it onto dry land without damaging the wheel. The final camel train passed as the men reloaded the wagon and made checks of each other and the beasts for leeches. By the time they set out again, it was clear they wouldn't make the next inn before nightfall. The militia leader detailed a group of five guards to remain until they could catch up with the main caravan, which would wait for them just one day: safety in numbers being the watch-word out here in the wilderness.

Game was plentiful on the plain and Tryonta and Tarruss killed a large antelope and a senglar with huge, curling tusks that could gore a man to death. Phildrad found herbs and roots and performed his usual magic so that everyone ate their fill. They sat surrounded by Ven-Gadla's four wagons, positioned in a rough open square. The oxen grazed, tethered on the grass, and the fire kept wild beasts at bay as the party ate a late supper with their guards happily joining in the feast.

Rested and replete, they sat on warm dry ground and talked as crickets screeched their shrill song into the black night. Dagla Kaz asked a question Tumalind had considered from time to time. 'We'd thought to make our trip along the coast from

Kamakq but were warned against, because of the Wormstalls or something. Do you know anything of the place?'

Ven-Gadla nodded sagely. 'Natives go all quiet on you when you asked?'

Dagla Kaz nodded. 'One was positively aggressive.'

'I can tell you why. Though I'm not sure it's a tale for a night out in the open.'

'So, there's a real reason for their fear? I'd put it down to superstition.'

'Superstition. An odd idea, don't you think? I intend no offence, Dagla Kaz, but isn't all religion just regulated superstition? All these ideas that try to answer the unknowable are much of a muchness, aren't they?'

Tumalind watched anger knit the brow of the High Priest, but the merchant grinned wickedly and gripped Dagla-Kaz's arm in friendship.

'No. Didn't think you'd agree but, I'm just an ignorant heathen, so perhaps you'll excuse my disbelief?'

Dagla Kaz relaxed and gave the man a wry smile. Ven-Gadla filled his long, white pipe with a pungent mixture, lit it amidst clouds of blue smoke and puffed contentedly a few times as he collected his thoughts.

'The Wormstalls. An experience not to be forgotten; nor repeated. You know, a real body of folklore's built up over time, mostly by folk who've never set foot there. But it's become part of the legend that it brings ill luck even to mention the name. Just by saying "Wormstalls of Glahynne", you're supposed to invoke some sort of dire…'

'Easy to mock, Merchant Paltrohn, but I for one ain't listenin' to no tale o' that place. I'll be about me guard business, if you'll be excusin' me.' The burly old soldier in charge of their small group wandered off to mount a patrol around the perimeter of their camp.

'See? Even hardened warriors like him aren't immune. Me? I've been there. Seen it. The fear's all in the memory and I've no doubt the evil of the place is confined within its borders and poses no threat to us.' He paused to take a deep pull on his pipe. 'Be about five years ago. I was trading copper ore from Kamakq to Slophrahn and the ship I'd chartered let me down; looked like it would sink if you put a single bale of kapok stuffing on it. I had the buyer with me and he wouldn't wait for another ship so I had to cart it up the coast. Sixteen wagons; driver to each and a couple of armed escorts. Don't need much protection for ore.

'Anyway, we made good time, though there's no real road and we had to detour to get round outcrops of rock and the odd swamp. But we were going according to plan and I was confident we'd make it to the port in time.

'Hadn't reckoned on the Wormstalls, had I? Like you, I thought it was all just native superstition. Couldn't get a hand from Kamakq itself and had to get help in from the ships. All extra expense. Still, I'd made a deal. That's what makes me known the world over as reliable. I deliver what I promise.

'We came on the Wormstalls in early evening. At first, I thought I was seeing things. Great lumpy casts, full of boreholes and buzzing with ugly black flies, covered the plain as far as you could see in all directions. It was a maze for the wagons, I can tell you. There was an odd smell: something I couldn't identify at first; unpleasant and discomfiting. And the wind, such as it was, died as soon as we reached the place.

'I'm not a man to waste time, so I pushed on through. They're like those things you see in wet sand, left by globworms. Except these were huge; some, three or four manheights high and two or three manlengths broad. And solid. Hard as stone. The men and oxen were unsettled but there seemed to be nothing actually living in the area and I put the disquiet down to the strangeness of the place. It was very quiet; even the buzzing insects seemed muted unless they flew right by you. No birds, which, given the number of flies, was odd.'

'After a while, any noise felt like an intrusion, unwelcome at that. We were all quiet and subdued as we wound our way through. Darkness slowly fell but there was nothing other than this uneasy feeling to stop us moving on. The smell grew stronger as the light faded. Earthy, like and tinged with the sickly sweetness of decay. Sort of filled your chest with its stickiness and cloying so you felt you couldn't get enough air.'

He pulled on his pipe, enjoying his tale but recalling some of his fear. Tumalind shuddered a little and felt the need to look behind her, though she knew her anxiety was silly.

'A driver near the front of our column let the queerness get to him and yelled at the night to stop what it was doing. His voice died, like something had swallowed it. That's when we noticed how even our footsteps and the rattling of the wagons were all muted, as if we were travelling through thick fog. Night was clear as they come. Stars shining and a thin crescent moon; you know, low and sickle shaped.

'Well, whether it was that yell or something else, I don't know. But from behind us came this hint of slithering and sliding. Like something soft dragged across the ground. There were shadows of movement in amongst the casts but nothing you could name. The oxen were really spooked and started to pull and strain in their yokes.

'Then, came this great burst of silent wind. Never experienced anything like it. So hot and swift, it was like walking through flames, only not so clean, if you know what I mean. And a stench of decay and rot so foul it made you retch. But still you couldn't see anything.

'One man took fright and leapt off his cart and ran into the darkness. There was the faint whisper of his footsteps disappearing, then this sucking sound and a muffled scream, cut short. Well, you can imagine, the rest of us were scared by now. What with the queer feeling and the smell and the almost silent sounds and nothing to see to blame it on. I called them all together and we gathered on top of a wagon as the slithering and sliding went on around us. The shadows moving but never showing what might make them. One of the oxen rattled its traces and then went silent. Then the foul stench came over us again.

'We stood together on that wagon as the night grew blacker. The stars went in and the moon sank below the horizon and left us in total darkness. We had wood to make a fire and I always carry my flint box. But we daren't get down off the wagon and we couldn't light a fire up there with us standing and sitting so close.

'Three more times the stench came, twice so powerful I thought I was doomed. The buyer was standing right next to me and I was sure he'd gone in that last blast of foul air. It was then I recognized it: the very stink of death; the odour of decaying corpses: no more, no less. That foul unholy stench filled your nostrils till you thought you'd drown in it.

'The night seemed to go on without end. The wagon never moved, although the oxen struggled quietly in the shafts. And that was queer. Beasts usually make a noise if they're alarmed but they were quiet, like they knew whatever was out there was attracted by noise. We stood through the night, back to back with blackness surrounding us. Two more men went. Just the foul, hot stench, a sound like something sucking and then silence. It was the smell and the darkness that got to you more than anything else. Not knowing what was out there and if you'd be next to go.

'At last, dawn began to come up and the sky lightened over the sea all those leagues behind us. The shadows vanished. Five men were gone; four from the wagon, mind you. One was my buyer. Luckily I had the price in my scrip already. And another ox had vanished.

'Here's the odd thing. We never saw anything. Nothing. But the straps on the oxen's yokes were complete and fastened and not a shred of clothing or a sign of bone or blood did we discover from man or beast. There was nothing. No tracks along the ground. Just two empty harnesses and five missing men. Even the smell of death had gone by morning.

'I can tell you; we pushed on through like we were chased by demons. Funny thing, we were almost out of it already, had we but known. When we turned to look, after we were clear of those stacks, the sun was shining through behind us. You won't believe this, but solid and unwholesome as they were, none of those stacks made any shade. Not a shadow to be seen. And there, on the outer edge, a new stack had formed, steaming and soft and vile with putrefaction.'

They looked about them in the darkness as if fearing the mysterious beast, the unseen power, might be out there waiting to devour them.

Dagla Kaz spoke first. 'And you really caught neither sight nor sound of this evil?'

'If it hadn't been for the missing men and beasts, I'd have put the whole thing down as a nightmare.'

'Perhaps the men went off with the beasts themselves, you know, untied them and went off into the night.' Jhonaht looked for answers, as always.

'If they did, they left no tracks in the soft dust and made no sound. And why would they refasten the traces before they went, I wonder?'

'I don't like things unexplained. There must be a reason.'

'There's a reason, man of learning, but what it is I'll never know. And nor, I guess, will you. I'd not go back that way for a fortune. If you feel that curious, Jhonaht, make the trip yourself. You'll not get me to return.'

'Have you any idea what it might have been, Jhonaht?'

'None, Tumalind. There are things in the world that defy explanation. What holds the Moon up in the sky, for instance? What power keeps the sun alight? What makes rain fall?'

'Some would say Ytraa does these things.' The High Priest's remark came with a little venom, as if Jhonaht had questioned the power of Ytraa.

'I don't say Ytraa doesn't. But that still doesn't answer the question "how", does it?'

'Start asking questions like that, Jhonaht, and you'll soon be questioning the existence of your God. That's how I started.'

'But you have a God, Ven-Gadla. You worship trade.'

'No, Lass. I just make my living that way. I worship nothing.'

'And what happened to your copper ore; the stuff the missing buyer had paid for?'

He grinned at Tumalind across the dying flames. 'Ay, lass, you're a canny one. I sold it to his rival. Double profit; made some recompense for the lost beasts and men. Had to give their folk something for their loss. I look after my workers, you know.'

Tumalind could see there was no point in pursuing the argument on moral grounds so she tried another tack. 'But, Ven-Gadla, if you don't believe in Ytraa or any other God, what do you think happens when you die?'

He smiled indulgently. 'Trouble with promises of a fabulous afterlife is you don't get the most out the present. You see, Tumalind, I believe this is the real life. It's what we do here and now that counts. There may, or may not, be an afterlife, who knows?

Followers, as I understand it, believe there's a sort of celestial garden where everything's wonderful and no evil exists and that death takes you into this garden where you frowk for eternity. Sounds pleasant enough. But it's what you have to do to get there that worries me. I mean, you're the most beautiful maiden, ripe for learning the joys of love and togetherness with the man or men of your choice. But you're stuck in the middle of nowhere on your way to a strange land with strange people who you'll have to serve for the rest of your life. Seems a big sacrifice to me. And, suppose, just suppose, there is no Garden of Delights. What then, eh?'

Tumalind looked to Dagla Kaz for guidance but he was staring into the embers of the fire with a distant look on his face, as though he'd chosen to hear no more blasphemy. She'd get no help there. And Jhonaht had already left to study the stars from the edge the campsite.

'In the end, it depends what you believe, doesn't it? I believe in Ytraa and the Garden of Delights. Maybe, if you believe in things they're true for you and if you don't they aren't.'

'That may be so. But think on this, pretty lass: something created us, and all the other things in the world. Most people call that something God and give their god a name. Yours is Ytraa but there're many others, believe me. Suppose this creator; that's my preferred term, suppose this creator designed and made us all. Do you think it likely that he or she, for we can't know whether this being has a sex; is it likely they'd want to see us all die and fade to nothingness? Can't see it, myself. My own feeling is we're likely to go on in some form or other. Else, what's the point creating us in the first place?'

'I shouldn't listen to you, Ven-Gadla, you speak blasphemy. In any case, we can't know the answers, can we?'

'Well, my pretty, there's one way to find out. And we all will. But I'm in no hurry to discover that truth just yet.'

'Neither am I.'

This seemed to signal the end of the night's activities and they made their ways to their sleeping places. Tumalind watched Netrodyl take Tarruss by the hand and lead him to her sleepsack beneath a wagon. Tryonta looked put out, until Wendarah either took pity on him, or else felt the need for company in the absence of Dagla Kaz's attentions. She found her mind back on Okkyntalah and wondered, for the thousandth time, what it would be like to lie with him. Sleep was a long time coming.

Aglydron announced morning after their night in open forest passed without incident. Enough meat remained for a cold breakfast and they set out in good heart, aiming for the road that Feldrark told them led through the Greenreald. Should they lose

Feldrark now, they'd need no guide: the mountain on whose slopes the city was built was an ever present beacon on the western horizon, rising into clouds that seemed to shroud it in the mornings.

'Mount Vaherht, how good it is to see you tower above the sweet plains of home. Soon we'll gather in the city on your ancient slopes and rest within your shaded halls and bathe our travel weary limbs in your limpid pools.'

Jodisa-Li gazed at Feldrark, love shining clear in her eyes. Aglydron knew he might lose her to this powerful man but felt incapable of preventing it. He put his faith in Ytraa, praying fervently for a solution and trusting all would be well. But his anxiety remained; a practical concern untempered by faith.

Around mid-morning they came upon the first of the streams they'd seen from the ridge and welcomed the chance to wash their skin, their tattered garments and their weapons free of the blood of battle. They took their time, men and women finding separate spots, not far apart, to bathe and refresh their spirits as well as their bodies in cool clear water, already settling after the rains.

Okkyntalah speared a red-bellied trout, which Feldrark identified as very good eating, and Shaulah amused them with her energetic pursuit of a large swift green granota, which hopped and dived frantically in its efforts to escape. She eventually planted her front feet on the creature and bit off its head before devouring the whole thing in a few gulps.

They cooked the fish over a quickly kindled fire and ate it at once. By late afternoon, they'd reached the road and followed it, heading for the city of Litkala. Paved and wide enough for them to walk abreast, the road was free of weed, washed clear of dust, and in good repair. A wide strip of cleared ground ran at either side.

'More difficult for ambushes. A gang of labourers, convicted criminals and paid, free men, shift up and down the road, repairing it and keeping it fit for travel. This time of the year, we're likely to meet merchants coming out of the city but it's too soon after the rains for anyone travelling our way, unfortunately; we might've begged a ride otherwise.'

True to Feldrark's prediction, a small group of merchants, their wagons loaded with blocks of white, sharp stone, sacks of every colour of dye, flat, mysterious sheets of some material they couldn't see through its cloth wrappings, and dyed, tanned hides, passed them, leaving the city. They were unescorted and greeted Feldrark like a friend, clearly both relieved and pleased to see him. One even offered to turn around and provide transport back to the city. But Feldrark declined gracefully and sent him on his way, thanking them all for their trade and the kind offer.

Three uneventful days of purposeful marching brought them across the open plain and through the wide dense Greenreald. For Aglydron, the question of Jodisa-Li and Feldrark was never far below the surface and it rose again as they came out of the trees at last. Soft rolling hills lay before them, where many crops grew and animals grazed to feed the city.

Feldrark stopped as the setting sun blazed orange flames from the smooth flags of the road ahead. Innumerable feet and the iron shod wheels of many wagons had worn the stones to a shine and made shallow ruts to lead the way to a city that lay out of sight on the west-facing slopes of the mountain, rising in solitary and awesome splendour before them.

The big man held the Staff in both hands, his arms outstretched above his head, and knelt with one knee on the road, his head bowed.

'I am returned to my land. I am come home to the land that bore me. I am restored to my place in the world.' He remained silent for a moment before rising. 'Come with me into my realm and I will feed you, give you wine to drink, make you merry with rejoicing.'

It seemed to Aglydron that Feldrark altered and stood proud, taking on the mantle of a leader of his people. They walked with him, Jodisa-Li by his side and the others behind, as he strode the paved way.

'We won't enter the city tonight. It's too far to walk in comfort. But there's an inn, The Wanderers' Joy, where we can eat good wholesome food, cooked and served for us, drink fresh sweet wine in cups the like of which you've never seen, bathe in clean hot water and sleep in soft clean beds for a change. Are you with me?'

An eager 'Yes!' came from the others, but Aglydron's doubts about the Wharhll and Jodisa-Li kept him quiet. Nevertheless, they marched forward enthusiastically, eager for a meal cooked by someone else and served at a table, a warm bath and a real bed.

It was only as the hostelry came into view, below a low rise, that Aglydron finally grasped the reality of the situation. Feldrark had no intentions toward Myllthlan. So why was he so eager to return home, having lost Malarhah, if he didn't intend to take Jodisa-Li? But, before he could challenge him, workers leaving the fields and returning home, spotted them. Some gathered in a knot and approached quickly, their grim faces signalling determination to be tough with these vagabond strangers who approached so well armed at fall of evening.

Feldrark held up the Staff as they came near and, one by one, the dozen or so men recognized this symbol and then their leader and dropped to one knee in supplication.

Joyous cries of, 'The Wharhll!', 'The Wharhll returns!', 'Feldrark is come home!', filled the air. One man ran back to the fields and another to the inn to announce the news. Soon, country folk lined the road, cheering the return of their beloved spiritual leader and marvelling vocally at the beauty by his side.

Aglydron knew then that his mission was lost. Amid great rejoicing and glad tidings, he alone was downcast and defeated. His suspicions had been well founded. Feldrark would take Jodisa-Li for his wife. Of course, he would. It had been obvious from the start, but faith and desperation had allowed him to believe it wasn't so. He fell behind the rest, unable to partake in the universal joy and merrymaking, and came to a halt in the road as the sun crossed the horizon.

Mechanically, his spirit broken by this irreparable end to his mission, he made his prayers apart from others. When they were done with worship, he remained alone as people crowded Feldrark and Jodisa-Li into the inn. Okkyntalah and Myllthlan, caught up in the excitement of the crowd, were close behind.

Aglydron stood without hope on the road in a strange land and knew he'd failed Ytraa. It was impossible for him to defeat Feldrark. He couldn't battle an entire city where every citizen would readily lay down his or her life to defend the Wharhll. Jodisa-Li was lost to him, lost to the mission. Lost to Ytraa.

The Skyfire would consume the world for its wickedness and it would be his fault. He'd never reach the Garden of Delights and would die and be no longer. He would become a spirit without home or substance, a wisp of awareness, feeling pain, loss, hunger, and despair but unable to control his destiny, bereft of all means of sharing for eternity. Aglydron crumpled to his knees and, head in hands, wept.

Chapter 44

Rejoicing And Dreams

The force of the gathering propelled Okkyntalah, Myllthlan, Feldrark and Jodisa-Li into the inn. Their host welcomed them with a simple gesture: he bellowed at the top of his voice.

'Quiet! Give me peace so I can speak with the great man.'

A sort of silence descended, but merriment remained on faces. Recognized as part of Feldrark's party, and therefore sharing his glory, Okkyntalah and Myllthlan were respectfully bustled into the area they cleared to give Feldrark and Jodisa-Li breathing space.

'You honour us with your arrival, most worthy Wharhll of Litkala, Keeper of The Truths, Holder of the Secret Knowledge, Guardian of the Staff of Ytraa. What may we do for you and your guests?'

'You speak well, Landlord. For the moment, we require only food, drink, the means to bathe, preferably in hot water, and clean soft beds for the night. Do we ask too much?'

'Sire, you ask for what is easily provided. Is there other service I may give?'

'Thank you, Landlord. I would ask that one present bear a token of truth to my honoured parents, the Kiral and Kirallah, to inform them of my return with the Staff and this most beautiful young woman, a jewel bearing the name of Jodisa-Li, to be my wife.'

At this, there was such prolonged and loud cheering that Okkyntalah felt obliged to join in, his mind failing to recognise the full implications amidst the clamour and jubilation. As it settled, a young man with eyes scarcely able to leave Jodisa-Li, stepped forward, dropped onto one knee, and finally stared determinedly up into the face of his lord.

'Sire, I beg the honour, for the sake of your gracious lady. May I carry the joyful news to the Kiral and Kirallah?'

Feldrark unstrapped his jewelled scabbard and placed it in the man's outstretched hands. 'Take your reward. Then carry the news, fast as you may.' He turned to Jodisa-Li and spoke softly. She took a pace forward and let the man embrace her and kiss her cheeks.

He bowed very low to her and then to Feldrark. 'The Kiral and the Kirallah will hear the finest news to grace our proud city in many a cycle!' And then he was gone, the crowd parting to allow him through.

Feldrark took Jodisa-Li into his arms and kissed her full on the mouth, sealing his intent to have her as his chosen partner. That kiss finally brought home to Okkyntalah the significance of what was happening. Feldrark was quick to forestall any trouble he might cause, placing a firm hand on his shoulder and turning him to face the crowd so that he could see the adoration there and be aware that challenge was pointless.

He bent low and spoke softly. 'Fear not for your Tumalind. Impossible though it seems, I've a solution to your problem that doesn't involve Jodisa-Li. And, remember, I'm the equal of your Dagla Kaz in the world and his superior here.'

Okkyntalah's mind spun with conflicting ideas and wishes. He wanted to deny the man Jodisa-Li, wanted to take her from him, but he wished him well, and wanted to see Jodisa-Li allowed her life of freedom and love with this great man.

It was then that he noticed Aglydron was missing. He asked Myllthlan. 'Where is he?'

She shrugged and shook her head, caught up in the joy and adoration greeting Feldrark's return. 'He was with us on the road but I don't think he came into the inn.'

'Feldrark, Aglydron's missing.'

The Wharhll nodded, beckoned a man and spoke a few words. The man left, gathering others as he went.

'Landlord. We hunger, we thirst, we stink! Can you remedy this?'

The landlord held his nose as he looked at his lord. 'Sire, a man stinks regardless of rank, and rank is your stink, Sire.'

Everyone laughed and it seemed the formalities were over. The landlord led the travellers through a narrow corridor to the bathhouse. Steam rose from a large round wooden tub set half into the stone floor of the room, as a servant poured fresh boiling water from a large vessel. Wooden benches lined the walls and an iron brazier burned scented coals and resins, giving the place a clean, refreshing odour.

'What of Aglydron?'

'Before you, he recognized that I mean to take Jodisa-Li as my wife. But only now does he fully comprehend the truth. He's deeply distressed. My people will bring him and I'll relieve his mind, as I have yours. Come; let's bathe away the stench of battle and travel.'

Without further ceremony, he stripped and stepped into the hot water. Jodisa-Li and Myllthlan followed as naturally as if they were alone. Shrugging his resignation at events over which he had no control, Okkyntalah entered the water.

The landlord had vanished, closing the door behind him. A young man and woman, clad in tunics of pale blue linen trimmed with yellow, entered with piles of fresh soft towels in bright colours, which they placed on the benches. They took from the top of each pile small round tablets of scented soap and passed these to the guests in the water. As they were handing them out, Aglydron entered reluctantly, the men behind him making it clear he had no choice. They closed the door but their voices remained outside. He wouldn't be allowed to leave without Feldrark's permission.

'Join us, Aglydron. I've a solution to your problem. Believe me, once Jodisa-Li and I are joined, there'll be a way for you to complete your mission and to satisfy the needs of both Ytraa and Dagla Kaz. Trust me, Aglydron. I have the means to do as I say.'

Aglydron looked doubtful and Okkyntalah had to confess he could think of no way in which this promise could be kept. But Feldrark sounded genuine. For a while, Aglydron stood breathing the scented steam and trying to decide what he should do for the best.

'I believe Feldrark's found a solution, Aglydron. I'm giving him my trust, will…?'

'Why should I note the opinion of a boy, a verigreen with..?'

He was about to remind Aglydron of his earlier words but Feldrark spoke. 'Only three days ago, Aglydron, you remarked how Okkyntalah had grown to become a man. Does your attitude to his maturity vary according to the degree of his agreement with you?'

He shrugged an apology at Okkyntalah and stepped into the tub.

Relaxing, no one noticed when their shabby clothes disappeared. Only when they left the water and dried themselves, did they discover fresh clean clothing lying ready for them.

There was some confusion about which outfit was which and Okkyntalah made them laugh, trying on a pale fuchsia tunic intended for Myllthlan. Feldrark added to their laughter as he struggled to wrap a short, flared yellow skirt around his broad waist before passing it to Jodisa-Li and helping her match it with the tasselled sleeveless red jerkin that left her midriff exposed. Aglydron looked on in silence but his disapproval was ignored.

⁕

Relaxed and refreshed, Jodisa-Li led them from the bathhouse. Feldrark dismissed Aglydron's escort party with kind words of gratitude and sent them to mingle with the rest of the people. As Feldrark entered the big room with her, a spontaneous cheer went up. At his lead, they all bowed their appreciation of both welcome and clean clothing.

Cool wine awaited them, in shiny clear goblets that showed the colour of the liquid inside. They intrigued Jodisa-Li. A scrubbed wooden table, where they were seated in a row, faced the floor of the inn with its scattered settles and round tables with surrounding hard-backed chairs.

Feldrark summoned the landlord and spoke to him in a voice clearly intended to reach all present. 'Take account of your expenditure, Paltrohn, and let me have it in the morning. I'd not see you ruined for your hospitality tonight.'

'Sire, the joy of your return is reward enough. Any case, these folk won't hear of your paying a leather dorltah. They're all chipping in, so I'll not be out of pocket.'

The crowd murmured their agreement.

'You keep a hostelry as good in fact as in reputation, then, my friend?'

'Ask the customers, Sire. I'd not presume to tell you this is the finest inn the realm has ever known, hosted by the most accomplished landlord and his lady.'

Another murmur of assent.

'I like a modest man, landlord. Perhaps you'll pass a similarly unbiased opinion on my choice of wife?'

'*Stand and turn on the spot, my love. On the chair, if you dare, so those on the floor can see. It's all part of the custom.*'

'*This skirt's very short, you know.*'

'*I know. What you need is an awareness of your beauty mingled with the modesty of a maiden and the confidence and poise of a dancer. I'll explain later. Trust me. You can't be more admired at this stage, for showing what those carefully selected clothes will allow, without exposing more.*'

'*Very well. For you, even if it makes me feel like a prize cow at market.*'

'*A valid point, my love, but I'm powerless at present to change the traditions of long centuries, no matter how much I might wish to.*'

Jodisa-Li stepped back from the table. 'You wish to see the riches your Wharhll brings to Litkala?' Her question, though aimed at the landlord, she addressed to the assembly, crowding close against the table.

A great yell of raucous ascent went up.

Jodisa-Li raised the edge of her skirt to expose the top of her right leg. 'Is this what you wish to see?'

'More!'

'More?' She stepped lightly onto her chair and raised the other side. 'This, then?'

'More!'

'Yet, more?' Carefully rotating, so that all in the room could see her, she lifted her arms over her head, so the bottom of her jerkin rose to hint at the lower curves of her breasts.

Feldrark's expression of pride and admiration gave her the courage to remain on show a little longer and speak to the crowd. 'Perhaps this, then, is enough for you? For surely what remains is for the eyes of Ytraa and my lord Feldrark alone. You have seen the delights your Wharhll discovered on his travels. Such beauty is not easily won. Be proud of your Wharhll and see what pleasures he will take to his bed. May you have as much joy in the knowledge as we shall have in our joining and sharing.'

The crowd cheered loudly, clapping their hands, whistling, shouting their admiration. Jodisa-Li stepped unhurriedly down to the floor, with Feldrark's helping hand, and inclined her head to the landlord. Bowing low and nodding his appreciation, he backed away to the bar. With all the grace she could muster and without hurry, she sat next to Feldrark.

'*Perfection, my love. I couldn't have expected as much even from a noblewoman native to the city. You've won their hearts and you'll be the talk of the city by morning. You'll be much loved and admired and your well-chosen words and perfect display will go down in legend; made into song. I haven't the words to express my gratitude, pleasure and surprise at what you've done tonight. I hope to show you those and my great love tonight when we will, at last, share a bed.*'

'*Tonight? We may join before the public ceremony?*'

'*Not only may; must.*'

'*Tradition?*'

'*You have it.*'

'*I'm growing to like your traditions, Feldrark. Though some are a little demeaning.*'

'*Tomorrow will be difficult. Before the people, we'll remove from each other the old clothes we'll wear to approach the ceremonial platform and, after joining, we'll dress each other in finery befitting our status.*'

'*We have a similar ceremony on Muhnilahm. A public declaration of a private pledge and a demonstration of our real love and commitment; joining before Ytraa to declare our faith and determination to be as Ytraa made us. But, at home, the first joining of maidens and bucks of the right age happens in public, though only the parents of those couples witness it. Here, you say we do it before the entire population?*'

'*After tonight, not a soul will miss the ceremony. All the young men will be in place before sunrise, to get the best view of you.*'

'*And the young women, of you, no doubt.*'

They had to break off their silent communication as the landlord returned bearing a silver goblet full of clear liquid burning with blue flame. He knelt on one knee and passed the cup to Jodisa-Li. For a moment, she stared at the offering, unsure what she should do. Feldrark gave no help. He kept his thoughts to himself and she knew she was being tested.

The goblet felt cool, despite the fire, and she brought it close to her face to test the heat. It was warm but no more and she assumed she must drink the liquor as it flamed. Raising it first above her head for all to see, she brought the cup to her lips and drank a draught, discovering the spirit warmed her throat. Feldrark's smile told her she'd exceeded expectations again and, when she passed the drink to him, the whole company cheered.

He drank and placed the goblet on the table, still flickering with blue flame. 'See? My chosen one, who knows nothing of our customs, is brave, courageous and wise as well as beautiful. What more could we wish from the woman who will sit beside me for life?'

The crowd called out their acclaim and then, as if at a signal, parted to settle on the various seats. A small and rather grubby boy came shyly and anxiously through their moving ranks to stand beside Jodisa-Li. He carried a single deep-blue bloom from the carah-carah vine, its colour echoing her eyes. He bowed and held the flower up to her.

Taking it, she inhaled the sweet scent and placed the flower behind her ear before she bent and lifted him to sit on her thigh, facing her. 'Thank you, little one. That's the finest gift I've ever received. I'll wear it tomorrow for the ceremony and you shall come with us through the city, if you wish.'

'I'm mucky, Paltra; I don't wanna shame thee.'

'We'll be ragged too, young 'un, you'll not shame us. Are your parents here?'

He pointed at a young couple, smiling with pride in the corner. Jodisa-Li beckoned them over. 'Would you honour us with your son as our page tomorrow?'

'Our Pettaklon wait on the Wharhll?' The boy's mother looked at Feldrark with awe.

Feldrark nodded.

'"Twould be an honour more'n we can put in words, Paltra.' She turned to the boy. 'You make sure you do as you're bid, lad.'

Pettaklon nodded vigorously.

'Good, that's settled then. And when we're ready, you'll hand us the new clothes.'

'Ooh, Paltra, I'd be that honoured, that I would.'

'Landlord, would I ask too much of you to let this fine young gentleman, Pettaklon, be bathed, fed and bedded in comfort for the night, please?'

'For you, most worthy lady, it'd be all pleasure. Come on, lad, let's get you washed and then put some food in you, shall we?' And he took the boy by the hand.

Before he left her lap, Jodisa-Li embraced him and kissed his cheek. The lad touched his face and, as he was led away, turned continually to look at her as if she were some sort of miraculous being. He was still staring over his shoulder as he disappeared into the corridor to the bathhouse. His proud parents returned to their seats, where friends plied them with drink.

'And, to her other qualities we now add compassion and generosity of spirit. A perfect choice, I believe. What say you?' Feldrark took her hand and brought her to her feet again.

'Perfect!' The acclamation nearly took the roof off and it seemed to end one stage of the proceedings. Food and drink became the centre of attention for all as they set about the serious task of filling their bellies. The various meats, white, red or dark, were tender and succulent in their pungent and aromatic sauces. The roots, roast, boiled, crushed or raw, filled the mouth with flavour and texture. And the leaves were crisp and tasty. Wines, fragrant and light, or smooth and dark with mystery, were of a quality Jodisa-Li hadn't experienced.

'What's this, Feldrark?' Myllthlan held her goblet up for his inspection.

'It's a light, pale wine we make from…'

'Not the wine. The cup. What's it made of? I can see right through it.'

'I'm glad you asked, Myllthlan, I was wondering about it, too.'

'Ah. Glass. We have a reputation in Litkala for the best available. Do you like it?'

'It's…it's extraordinary. Where does it come from?'

He smiled at her and then turned to Jodisa-Li, his eyes twinkling. 'You'll not believe me when I tell you we make it from sand. There! I knew you wouldn't.' He turned again to Myllthlan. 'Perhaps you'll tour the city before you leave with Aglydron, if that's what you propose, and see the glass works. Then you'll believe me.'

Jodisa-Li looked across the table to find Aglydron watching them closely. Feldrark had told the fanatic he had a way to solve the problem of their marriage but she knew he had no such plan. Later, he intended to discuss the problem with Ivdulon and his father.

'We'll come up with something to satisfy even Aglydron. For now, my mind is all on you and the coming night.'

It was that anticipation and Ivdulon's extraordinary ability to mindtalk that had kept Feldrark from contacting the seer during the last days of their journey.

'I've no wish for the sage to interrupt us.'

'Such intrusion might not be welcome.'

The night and their chance to be alone together couldn't come soon enough. She looked at Feldrark and saw love shining in his eyes. Love for her. Something she'd known only briefly once before; but the sorrow of that episode was not for now. It was time for joy and laughter, and for love again.

The company, now full of food and wine, clamoured for a tale or a song, a dance or some other entertainment, demanding that the strangers give the first performance.

'Okkyntalah, you sing well. Will you give us a ballad?'

'I've no instrument, Feldrark.'

A slender young woman, demurely dressed in the white, blue-trimmed tunic of a maiden, golden hair in braids to her waist, stepped from the crowd. She carried a U-shaped lyre, framed with pale bukva inlaid with fine bands of ebony and ivory. Plucking and strumming the strings as she approached, she tested for tone and tune.

Okkyntalah pulled his chair clear of the table for her to sit. He bent and whispered in her ear and she nodded gravely and played a few bars of lilting melody. Okkyntalah stood behind her with his hands resting on the back of the chair.

'Not the best choice for a night of rejoicing, but something that should be done, I think. And, at short notice, all my poor mind will deliver.'

Silence descended until the melody of strings filled the room with familiar tones and chords. Okkyntalah sang softly, until his confidence grew and swelled his voice to fill the space. He composed stanzas to a popular folk tune, which the girl played at a haunting tempo.

'Born in the sands of Niphralon and
Torn from her mother's breast,
Malarhah, the dark-skinned beauty
Was early put to the test.

'Captive and sold into slavery
Long before youth formed her frame,
Slave to the barbarous city on stilts
Malarhah was destined for fame.

'She fooled all her captors and lords
With pretence that she understood not
And she bore all the shame and the usage
Until Feldrark discovered her lot.

'She it was discovered the Staff.
And guided the captives from death.
Malarhah did love her lord Feldrark,
And for him breathed her own last breath.

'Beautiful dark-skinned Malarhah
Shall live in our hearts evermore,
For she saved the Wharhll of Litkala
And died that he might reach his door.'

Okkyntalah's song, delivered more with affection than scholarship, captured the hearts of the crowd, who then wanted to know more about the heroine. Jodisa-Li, moved by his sincere eulogy, rose and, with many glances at Feldrark, told Malarhah's tale. When she'd done, the crowd called for Okkyntalah's song once more and the lyre player joined in. A third rendition had the song on the lips of all but the most inebriated or dull-witted.

Jodisa-Li smiled with joy at Okkyntalah. 'Thank you. Your tribute will ensure Malarhah lives on in Litkala.'

He nodded his acknowledgement and embraced and kissed the musician, thanking her for her clever improvisation. Blushing furiously, she tried to hide amongst the crowd until Feldrark called her back.

'What's your name, child?'

'Linlyss, Sire.'

'Are your parents here?'

'I've no parents, Sire. I'm sixteen cycles and can speak for myself, if that's all right?'

'It is. Will you play for me and Jodisa-Li, tomorrow?'

'I'll do my best to please you, Sire, and your beautiful lady. I'll be scared, but I'd be that honoured, I would.'

'So be it. Be ready to depart shortly after sun up. Do you live nearby?'

'My bed's over the stables, Sire. The landlord and his good wife have provided for me these past ten years. If they'll let me, I'll be on hand for your departure.'

Feldrark called the landlord and spoke, apparently satisfied with his answers. 'Good. All is settled, then. Will not some of you provide a little entertainment before we go early to our beds so the morning finds us rested?'

There was raucous and ribald comment at that suggestion but the crowd had enough respect for their Wharhll and his lady to accede to his wishes.

The local bucks and maidens made space between the crowd and the royal party. Accompanied by Linlyss and a boy tapping a small drum, they danced the shinsninarah, a local celebration of fine weather and sunshine, tunics flying as they spun and kicked high. Linlyss and the drummer sang traditional lyrics describing the dance for the audience.

It was a fitting end to a merry evening and the party went off to comfortable beds full, content and ready for a night of sleep in comfort, without watches.

Observed by Aglydron and Okkyntalah, Feldrark took Jodisa-Li to a separate room. Any lingering hopes of her completing their mission would be gone by morning. Jodisa-Li spent a moment wondering how the Wharhll of Litkala could possibly help their mission to continue with any meaning. But Feldrark soon took her mind off everything but joy and happiness.

⊕ ··· ⊰⊱ ··· ⊰⊱⊸

Tumalind, alone on her sleepsack, thought on Okkyntalah. The feelings of pain and danger had passed but she felt a sadness that seemed to be from outside of him, nothing to do with herself or Okkyntalah but something he felt for another. She wondered what these sensations could mean, for she was convinced they were real and connected with her love.

Just as she was dropping into sleep, she heard Netrodyl moan with pleasure and she awoke again. What was it like to lie with a man, what would it be like to take Okkyntalah into that sacred place? Would he still want to join with her now that he'd joined with another after the Choosing? He must be fulfilling Ytraa's decree, joining as and when he could. But who pleasured him, who received his pleasure? Such thoughts made her loss more acute and she was long awake in the vibrant night of the dark plain.

Ven-Gadla's disturbing tale returned as she listened to the sounds about her; oxen stamping and snorting as they grazed, cicadas screeching, ash and embers settling in the fire. Closer, Dilanthas slept; her breathing shallow and slow. Porryh snored softly. Corphanda giggled at some passing fancy in a dream. These friendly sounds vied with the soft slithering of some unseen creature, snake or creeping thing, too close for comfort. But there was none of the tension, none of the unholy stench Ven-Gadla had described in his story.

Sleep gathered her into dreams at last. She travelled a dark land pocked with deep, black pits that issued smells of death and wailed with sorrow. Something unseen stalked her as she stepped with care along soft, damp ground. A hot, harsh breath blew her into a deep, dark pit in which her dreamer's sight had her see courses of huge stone blocks forming hexagonal walls. Naked and defenceless, she tried to scream, as she saw the floor of the pit rushing to meet her, its surface all wide, gaping mouths with sharp pointed blood-stained teeth, and lidless eyes lusting for flesh. One mouth, a lipless hole lined with vicious teeth, was devouring another woman, her upper half already lost within its jaws.

Tumalind was falling, falling, falling with nothing to stop her and no one to save her from certain death. A swift blackness opened between the jaws and she felt the sharpness of teeth on her shoulder. And, at last, a scream escaped her.

Chapter 45

LITKALA

Sodisa-Li bathed, dressed and breakfasted in a dream; memories of Feldrark enfolding her in a cocoon of warmth and pleasure she was reluctant to shed. Only on the road to the city did she realise she was wearing the shabby, stained, but now clean, tabard she'd worn as they approached The Wanderer's Joy. Feldrark wore his leather apron but with the sword of their vanquished enemy replacing the empty scabbard he'd sent ahead.

He smiled at her, love and wonder still deep in his eyes. *'Back from the land of dreams, at last?'*

'If that's dreaming, give me sleep forever. I'd live in such all my life.'

'Me too, were it possible. But now you're down from the clouds, there are things you must know before we reach the city. I've no wish for you to seem unschooled or ignorant simply because I've not taken the trouble to forewarn you, especially after your inspired actions for the people last night.'

'Your words seem full of foreboding but your tone is light. Tell me what I must know, my love. And, unless there's reason for the wagoner to be excluded, can we use our voices? I love the sound of yours. We should keep mindtalk for when we're separated and for private words in the crowd, lest we lose the means to speak to each other.'

'As wise as you're beautiful. The driver of the horses will hear little and repeat nothing. I know him well. Know why you're back in your old clothes?'

His sudden reversion to speech caught her off guard and she giggled at her surprise. 'You said something of it last night, before other things claimed our attention.'

'Yes. I thought it better to leave matters of state; I couldn't concentrate on less vital things with you before me.'

'Will I always be as important as I was last night?'

'Always. Though sometimes I may act in ways that make it seem otherwise. Like your father, I'm a leader and have calls I can't ignore or, sometimes, even delay. I hope you'll understand, especially as, after today's ceremony, you'll often be in similar situations.'

'I'll try. But ignore me and I'll take my pleasure from a servant or a passing man of...'

She could say no more with Feldrark's mouth clamped over hers and his hand questing. He persisted long enough to gentle her into a state of pleasant anticipation before releasing her.

'Wicked man! How can I resist when you do such things?'

'I rather hoped you wouldn't be able to.'

'You'll pay for that.'

'Gladly. Name your price.'

'Nights forever in your arms, days always by your side.'

'Done, at least as much as our duties will permit.'

'Come on, then. List what I must know. I can delay it no longer. The city looms and I'd like to concentrate on my new home. Tell me all I need for today. The rest can wait until we have more time.'

Feldrark took her through the events of the day and detailed her duties at each stage, the levels of respect she should convey and be prepared to accept, the nature of her responses to ceremonial questions. There was much to learn and she wished to shine for him and save him embarrassment, so they had reached the city walls before she was satisfied that she'd absorbed what she'd need to get through this day.

She remained silent, allowing all he'd told her to coalesce in her mind so it might seem second nature to her when she had to perform her part. Satisfied, as much as she could be, she relaxed a little as the wagon took them under overhanging walls high above. Now she could take in the wonders of this place that would be home for the rest of her life.

Briefly, she felt a pang of loss for the island of her childhood, the careful stern and demanding grooming from her father, the ease of having someone take her decisions. All that was gone and soon she'd be Feldrark's partner, helping him lead his people; people who would be hers as well. But all that was too much for now. Let the city take her, let it overwhelm her senses as its master had last night; let it show her what it was, let it surprise and delight her, shock her, make her laugh or cry; let it make her gasp or disappoint her with what it had to offer.

'It will do all that, but I hope the disappointments will be few, the tears less and the delights no less than those we shared last night, though of a different type.'

'Nothing will match what we shared last night, Feldrark. Except tonight and every night to come, I hope.'

'I hope so, too, my love.'

Leaving The Wanderer's Joy a little after sun up, Okkyntalah gazed at the rural scene before him with its neat cultivated fields, orchards, meadows and vineyards. The wagon, hauled by a pair of chestnut carthorses, rolled easily on four iron-shod wheels over the paved road, cushions reducing the vibrations from the hard surface as they moved at a slow trot toward the city. Rested and content after a night in a comfortable bed with Myllthlan, his mind had cleared and his heart was untroubled now that Feldrark had promised Jodisa-Li's new status would be no impediment to their sacred mission.

Okkyntalah shot a glance at Aglydron, sitting ahead of him on the gently swaying wagon and fretting over what he still saw as their problem. He shook his head and relaxed; there was nothing they could do about it anyway. Travelling behind the impressive wagon transporting Feldrark and Jodisa-Li, he smiled at her simple display of beauty on the previous evening. Beside him, Linlyss sat in silent contemplation, leaning back against the slatted wooden support, her lyre in her lap. He could smell her soft female scent and noted the lithe limbs of the young woman.

Myllthlan shared the wide seat with Aglydron and Pettaklon, now clean and groomed. The adults, other than Feldrark and Jodisa-Li, were dressed in finery that had appeared, as if by magic, from the city overnight.

Okkyntalah assumed Linlyss was thinking about the music she'd play before the Kiral and Kirallah; a daunting prospect for one who'd led a sheltered rural life. He placed a hand on her arm and, as she turned in question, smiled encouragement.

'You'll do fine, Linlyss. No need to be anxious.'

'I'll do me best.'

'Play the way you did last night and they'll love you.'

She gave him a smile of gratitude.

'Where is everyone? I expected a crowd to see Feldrark and Jodisa off to the city.'

'What? An' miss the ceremony? They were all up long afore the sun. They'll be with the rest when we get to the city. They'd never've kept up with the wagons. They'd only get the leavings of places if they'd waited.' She shook her head in surprise at his ignorance but smiled indulgently before she went back to staring at the scenery.

He followed her gaze, slightly to the right, and examined the solitary peak, soaring from the plain ahead. From here, the city was hidden by the bulk of the mountain. Much of it would still be in the shade, but already their own shadows were shortening, as the sun rose into a sky almost as blue as the carah-carah flower Pettaklon had presented to Jodisa-Li. He noticed she'd placed it, slightly wilting, behind her ear again.

The left edge of the lower part of the mountain seemed unnaturally sharp and straight and he shaded his eyes to see what caused this strange illusion. He realized, with amazement, that the steep slope was straight because it was artificial. A huge wall ran up the slope of the mountain reaching to a wide flattened area a little under halfway up. At this distance, some three leagues from the city, he could just make out what appeared to be towers set at regular intervals into the wall. Rising vertically from the steeply angled mountainside, they formed a toothed edge as each length of wall ran horizontally from the top of one tower to a point halfway down the next.

'Does the wall surround the city?'

Confusion furrowed Linlyss' face, making her look comical. 'You can't see no wall from here! No one can see that far.' And she screwed up eyes, paler than the sky, and squinted toward the city. 'You must've been here before.'

'Never. Does it?'

She looked at him again. 'Can you really see the wall?'

He nodded.

Her expression changed to open admiration, brightening her eyes and giving her face an appealing innocence that slightly disconcerted Okkyntalah. 'If your heart an' soul see as well as your eyes, Okkyntalah, you're right unusual.'

'I have hunter's eyes.'

'I like their colour, and the way they look at me.' She blushed just enough and gazed at her lap, giving her admission veracity.

'They like looking, Linlyss. You're worth the study.'

That had her blushing more and she covered her confusion by staring ahead and concentrating on his question. 'Yes, the walls go right round the city in a great big half circle at the bottom of the mountain. Then they go up the sides in straight lines until they nearly join, just under the lake. There's a short bit up there with a gateway in the middle. That's where the Red Rill comes out the Upper Lake and runs through the city.'

'Does the mountain have a name?'

'We all call it Hollowtop, 'cos of its great wide basin, half way up. That's where the Upper Lake is with its water, red as rust. Tastes foul: you'd as soon drink horse piss. But the real name's Mount Vaherht.'

They were silent for a while, both taking in the landscape around them, verdant and lush after the rains.

'Do you know the city well?'

'I been three times. For the rites, you know.'

Okkyntalah assumed all Followers progressed along the same lines from childhood to youth to adulthood. He'd visited the Plain of Ytraa three times; as a boy approaching youth, as a young man coming into adulthood and as prospective husband to Tumalind at the first joining. But Linlyss, still without a partner, should have been only twice. 'Three times?'

'Once for the climb from childhood, when you have your first bleeding, well, not you, of course, only girls.' She chuckled. 'Then for the choosing and again for the proving, like.' She said this as though he must be a fool not to know.

'The first and the last I understand. But what's the choosing? Selecting a partner?'

'Why, no. It's when you decide what you're going to be, to do in life, of course.'

'Ah. We do that in the village, not on the Plain of Ytraa.'

'There aren't no villages.'

'Of course.'

'What's the Plain of Ytraa?'

He described it, telling her about the Godwood and the Skyfire and the reason for their journey.

'Skyfire? Godwood? You talk in riddles, Okkyntalah. And Jodisa-Li ain't no virgin. Not after last night. You can't take Jodisa-Li away from Litkala. No one'd let you.'

'I know that. She can't go with us. Feldrark says he's found a way to make everything right again, and I expect he has, though I don't really see how. We must have a virgin to replace Jodisa but I don't see how he can just select someone to take her place when she was Chosen by Ytraa.'

'If the Wharhll says he can, he will. What's this 'ere Skyfire? Sounds a bit scary.'

'You should be frightened. If we don't appease Ytraa, Ytraa will let the Skyfire scorch the whole world and burn all those who haven't been faithful. Don't you know anything?'

'Might ask you the same. That's just a story to frighten the children. I mean, no one actually believes it, do they?'

'I do. Aglydron does. Jodisa and her father, the High Priest, do.'

'Yeah? So, when's this Skyfire thing coming and what's it like?'

He explained, and Linlyss was silent for a while. 'Well, Okkyntalah, all I can say is I hope you're wrong. Here, we can either keep to the strict rules of Followers or go our own way. There's some in the city who aren't Followers at all. They pay the God-tax so they can live here, like, but not everyone in Litkala's a Follower in exactly the same way. I decided I'd go my own way. 'Course, I'm still virgin, but only 'cos I've not found a lad I'd like to pierce me an' stay with me awhile, like; yet. Till I met you, like.' She turned away, embarrassed by her own boldness.

'Lived with the publican for long?'

'My father left Mother just after I were born, seems. She died: some say she were killed, when I were six. Publican and his wife took me in.'

'You speak of them as though they were nothing special. Don't they treat you well?'

'For a servant, yes. Never beat me, like, and he's never tried to force himself on me the way some might. But I work. I worked right from the start. No work: no food. And I've always slept in the stables. They make it sound like I'm their daughter but I'm just a skivvy. I'd like to go where I'm appreciated. Somewhere I can have a life of my own.'

'Away from Litkala?'

'P'raps. Anywhere I'd get a chance to do summat with my life.'

'You play very well. Do you enjoy that?'

'It's kept me going, really. If I feel low or angry, I tell the Lyre and let it sing for me. And I've earned a few dorltahs with it.'

'Do well today and you could find yourself in demand.'

'Playing in people's houses at namings and joinings and that? I don't know as I want that for the rest of my life.'

'What do you want?'

'Don't rightly know. Excitement. Fun. Adventure.'

'You'd find plenty of adventure if you were with us. We've had enough adventure to last a lifetime. And we're not halfway to our destination yet.'

'There's an interestin' idea.'

'Think again, if you think you can tag along with us.' Aglydron's sudden interjection reminded them he was there, and listening.

She waited for Aglydron to face the road again before she stuck out her tongue and crossed her eyes in a gesture that had Okkyntalah gleefully outraged.

'Still want your prod in my fern afore today's out.' Her whisper, warm in his ear, had him stroke her thigh in answer.

For a while they travelled in mutual silence. Okkyntalah, lost in thought, looked at the landscape with outward eyes whilst his inner eye saw futures and hopes, losses and wants.

'What's that, Linlyss?'

Their wagon had followed Feldrark's onto the crest of a rounded hill and the lie of the land now allowed them to see more of the city. They were closer to it and more features became visible.

Linlyss followed the line of Myllthlan's pointing finger. 'One of the watchtowers. There's four. One each end of the outer wall and one each end of the inner. Should see the other one at this end in a bit.'

And so it was. A second tall tower rose from the plain, behind the first, the line of the high outer wall cutting across it. At this distance and angle, it was impossible to judge how high or how far apart they were but Okkyntalah was impressed by the suggestion of great size and strength in the structures. They stood stark and white above the general lush green of the countryside. And then the road took a final long slow descent, in a wide northerly sweep, to the flat plain, so that all they could see to their right was the mountain, white and grey and dotted with patches of black and brown earth, grass and small copses of elegant trees.

Once on level ground, the road turned again to run under the mountain so that the sheer steepness and nearness of the slope hid all trace of the city for a time. They had travelled a full league before the sloping wall came back into view and now it was a sight to impress even the most jaded senses.

Okkyntalah followed the stepped line of sharp white wall as it climbed the slope to the top of its reach. Even from this distance, over half a league, he could see how massive were the blocks, how impregnable the walls and towers. It was even possible to make out the tiny figures of people; soldiers he supposed, moving along the horizontal surfaces that were the tops of the stretches of wall between the smaller towers. He estimated the height of these towers at between eight and ten manheights and the distance of the span from one to the next at around the same measure. The structures were so much a part of the mountain that they seemed to grow out of the very rock.

'By the Core! That's not possible.' Myllthlan's lapse into her abandoned past exposed her sense of utter disbelief as she tried to take in the sheer size and wonder as the larger towers came back into view. 'Men can't have built this. It must've been built by gods.'

Okkyntalah matched her amazement, but in silence.

'There's only one God, Myllthlan, as I've instructed.' But even Aglydron couldn't remain unmoved by the spectacle and there was no conviction in his rebuke.

'I s'pose it's pretty amazing when you first see it. Don't they have nothing like this on your island, then?'

'I've known only mud brick houses and one stone building. I've never seen anything like this. It must've taken dozens of cycles to construct, hundreds even.'

'They say it were built in the time afore men, by a race of beings that died out for lack of suitable food. Any rate, it were standing, just like it is now, when the Followers came and found it, deserted. All they had to do, they say, is clear out a few wild animals and the weeds and plants as had grown inside the city and do some repairs. The drains and things was blocked, like, an' they didn't know how things worked. But they gradually got everything going and the city's been more or less the same for about a thousand cycles.'

'You seem to know a lot about it for a country girl.'

'I've 'ad schooling. Everyone's done schooling, ain't they?'

'Depends what you mean. We learn about Ytraa and history; you know, Vaarkil and Mythanpho and Gadhallah and the Skyfire. That, and whatever trade we decide to do.'

'Oh? We was learned about lands nearby; Rophan-Ra and Kabalyt and Niphralon, and Balagaaq and Tohltaz over the Unnamed Mountains, you know? And then we done history of Followers and the Great Division and all the terrible stuff as made Mhortag's Dread, Ytraa be blessed.' She made a curious gesture, crossing her arms over her chest and placing her palms flat against her cheeks. 'And the boys, they done stone dressing and glass working and tanning; the girls they done gardens, wood working, charcoal making an' dyeing, like. That's how they keep the city repaired and looking fine as it does.'

'Our island has thirty five thousand souls, you know. Chalamamnon holds ten thousand: they live in houses; some built of brick with thatched roofs.'

Linlyss was less impressed than he'd hoped. 'They say more'n hundred thousand people live in the city. It's built with stone from the mountain.'

He was genuinely interested and she told him what else she knew of her homeland.

Rising in steep slopes to over two thousand manheights, in the shape of a rough cone, the mountain stood in splendid isolation at the tip of the broad peninsula. To the northeast, small low hills created a sparsely wooded hinterland where game and wildfowl provided sport for those who wished to hunt. To the east and south, was the land they had crossed; the food basket of the city. It provided all the meat, grain, fresh fruit and vegetables needed within the walls. West lay the wide Sea of Llahkan, almost landlocked but for the narrow straight between southern Rophan-Ra and the easternmost tip of Kabalyt.

Okkyntalah thanked Linlyss and turned again to the two huge watchtowers that had made Myllthlan exclaim so graphically. They were colossal, huge, enormous, beyond the imaginings of men. He tried to measure them but lost track after a hundred manheights and guessed they rose another twenty before they raked the sky with their strange indented tops; the regular pattern of rise and fall there puzzling him. The stretch of wall between them ran some thousand paces and rose in a sheer face for a dozen manheights. At the top, the stonework protruded outward for three paces in a lip that turned and hung in a vertically curving wave, making the wall almost impossible to scale. Every so often, square openings pierced the angle between the wall and this overhanging lip.

'What're the holes for?'

'Soldiers squit through them, of course. Though, they do say they're meant for pouring things onto anyone trying to get up the wall.' Linlyss said this as if she couldn't believe anyone would even try.

The road widened slightly and the land on the right narrowed to no more than a strip of grassland, kept short by the grazing of small animals with dark woolly coats.

'What are they?'

'Them's just ovellah. Stupid as they come, but good eating. Had some of that last night, you did. The dark meat. Tender and succulent with a real good taste. My favourite is ovellah. And their coats pull off every year and can be turned into cloth.'

To their left, open woodland with widely spaced ornamental trees masking the orchards and crop fields beyond, had given way to a narrow and steep rocky decline that dropped into the clear waters of the sea. With little wind, the surface was an undulation of long, shallow waves that broke softly against the unseen cliff below. Not a single boat was at sea. The fishermen and merchants had given up this perfect day for a sight of the Wharhll and his new woman.

They travelled now hard under the city wall, so that the overhanging lip cut out the sky immediately above.

'Is this the only approach to the city?'

'You can come by sea, but you got to go through that dock thing over there. It's got great big walls an' a gate. It's real narrow and the fishermen often don't bother an' leave their boats in the dock outside the city.'

Aglydron turned round to Okkyntalah and made a sweeping gesture to take in walls and road. 'That lot from Mipahnhil can't get at us in the city. An army of thousands couldn't breach that wall.'

'Nobody can. City's impre… impregnant…'

'Impregnable. I expect it is.'

Linlyss' irritation at Okkyntalah's gentle correction subsided at his smile of kindness. 'Never could say that word.'

'Why would you? You've no wish to be impregnable have you?'

She considered for a moment and then, understanding, landed a good-natured slap on his arm. 'Naughty!'

'Given the chance.'

She grinned encouragement at his whispered response and shifted as close as she could. 'I'll give whatever you're willing to take.'

He stroked her thigh again through soft silk and felt the warmth of her. As soon as the opportunity arose, he would delight in teaching her some of the lessons he'd learned from Malarhah and Myllthlan. She'd clearly be a willing pupil.

———

Tumalind woke, trembling, with Dilanthas crouching over her in the dawning light. Her shoulder hurt and felt numb. The girl was looking at her with concern. Beyond,

Phildrad stood with a long rope-like object hanging from his hands. He dropped it as soon as their eyes met and fell to his knees beside her.

'Lie still.' He put his mouth against the skin of her shoulder and sucked so hard that it hurt. As others gathered round her, he pulled away and spat. Sucked again. Spat again.

'Striker. Kill a healthy man in a day if it's not treated.' Ven-Gadla held the dead snake. 'Must've turned over on it in her sleep. Wouldn't normally attack. Have to get her to the nearest inn, soon as we can. They'll have something for bites. I'll unload a wagon; load it on the others. She and Phildrad can go together. Very brave man, but unwise. Still, you may have saved her life. Need to get them both there quick as possible if we're to save them.'

'I'll go with them, as guard.' Caarl's voice reassured her a little.

She tried to rise. Found she couldn't move. Frightened, she tried to call out. Found she couldn't. The scene around her faded. Brightened. Pulsed in and out of shade to brightness. Shapes blurred. Mingled. She was lifted. Carried. Around her the air was thick. Smoking darkness. Oven hot. Sounds of moving people came and went. She was lowered. Another rolled against her. Trembling. Hot. Tense.

The ground rumbled. Lurched. Sweet scent cloyed every breath. Voices clamoured for attention. Crawled over her. Dazzled her hearing. Words swam. Tasted salt and sour. She must sleep.

Blackness filled her ears. Her mouth. Her nose. Noise covered her eyes. Swirled with colours. Shadows. The world spun. Dizzying. Air too thick to breathe. Drowning her. Heart pounding. Hard. Slow. So hot. So cold. So weary. So weak. And darkness. Darkness…

Chapter 46

Entering The Realm

'Enjoy this entrance to your new life, Jodisa-Li, my love. Enjoy this experience. There's no place like the city of Litkala.'

She gave herself over to sensation and smiled as she dwelt on what she'd shared with him in the night. But this was a time for now, not for memories she would relive soon and for the future to come.

The sea washed calm and inviting on her left, small ripples reflecting morning sunshine, seemeeuws diving and squabbling over some morsel one had scavenged. To her right, the wall rose, marbled here and there with the slightest hint of aquamarine and veined with fine threads of red and gold. Solid, it climbed to curve overhead. Before her lay the paved road, patterned now in checks of black, pale grey and white.

'Who built this wonder?'

'No one knows. It was devoid of human life when we arrived. Only a few fierce medvjed; huge, sabre-toothed bears that roam the forest, and some stripecats, prowled the upper city. There are many signs of a cultured civilisation but no graves or records. It's as if the people simply vanished. Perhaps some plague took them, though there were no bodies, no bones, even, when the Followers came. I don't suppose we'll ever know. But we owe a debt of gratitude to whoever they were. They left a city we've been proud to restore and maintain. And we've added our own refinements over the years.'

'What are those holes for, up there?'

Feldrark explained. 'I imagine some have a special purpose today.'

She followed his gaze; the gap they approached issued a gentle rain of white and pink, which, as they passed below, proved to be sweet smelling petals. This evidence of what they could expect in the greeting made her smile with pleasure at the thoughtfulness of such soldiers.

'Threlepsis flowers: they signify welcome. The fishermen's women make scent from them and wear it when their men come home from sea. Probably hides the stink of fish!'

'And I thought you were romantic!'

'Oh, I am, I am.'

She stroked his thigh. 'You'll do for me.'

The wagon reached the corner watchtower where the road made a sharp turn, almost at right angles, so it could follow the outward curve below the mountain's foot.

But Jodisa-Li, for all her determination to take in all the details of her new home, found her mind taken back to her night with Feldrark.

She closed her eyes, recalling intimate details and reliving an experience beyond her expectations. That Feldrark had been equally transported by joy was an additional pleasure. Time passed, as she dwelt content in that past until, behind her, she heard cries of admiration and surprise and opened her eyes again; her travelling companions were impressed. Feldrark laid a hand gently on hers, sending a thrill through her along with the comfort of contact in these new, strange and wonderful surroundings.

Turning into the straight avenue leading to the gateway, they passed between triple rows of sculpted trees running in straight lines on each side of a highway, which was here broader and split in two by a continuous trough. Their wagon took the right hand road and Jodisa-Li became entranced.

'Those trees, their crowns are perfect spheres; are they artificial?'

Feldrark shook his head. 'Natural.'

Their multitudes of tiny, pink flowers contrasted with dark, russet leaves. The trunks, straight and coated in deep, rich bark of rust red, shone as though polished. Small bright birds of blue and green, in twittering flocks, played amongst and between the branches.

In the troughs grew tall green plants with pliant foliage shaped like spears and shining in the sunlight. Their single stems bore many of these long leaves and were topped with vibrant yellow blooms in spherical sprays. The surface of the road no longer gave the rhythmic click-clack it had when wheels had passed over uniform paving slabs.

'The sound's amazing. How does it do that?'

'See how the road's formed from small blocks of stone making complex patterns? The wheels play a tune according to the blocks they pass over.'

Squares within squares, concentric circles, spirals, chevrons, zigzags and diamonds paved the way toward the gate in red, blue, green, black, white and grey. Each variation in colour and pattern subtly altered the tone as the wheels crossed, playing a complex harmony to accompany the ride.

Closer to the gate, the two halves of the road split apart to border a small, oval, rippled lake of deep clear water, stained rust red.

Jodisa-Li gasped. 'What's that? I've never seen anything like it.'

'Wonderful, isn't it? I confess; I still find it intriguing. We call it the Fountain; a name Ivdulon devised. Sounds better than "spout", which is what it used to be called.'

In the very centre, it rose five manheights before it curved according to the gentle breeze to fall in a shower to disturb the surface and spread gentle ripples toward the decorated low wall bordering the lake.

They followed the road beside the water to the gateway with its soaring spires. Here, at last, they came upon the first citizens. A score of urchins played an elaborate game that involved chasing, jumping over one another and touching each other with a small stick that constantly changed hands. Young enough to play naked, the boys and girls were nevertheless unsupervised and seemed absorbed in their game. But, as the wagons approached, they stopped and formed two equal lines, one either side of the road.

Their wagon halted and reached the first two, who looked up at Feldrark and Jodisa-Li.

'Who wishes to enter the great city of Litkala?' asked the girl at Feldrark's side.

'I, Feldrark, Wharhll of Litkala, wish to greet the Kiral and Kirallah and bring them news that I return with the Staff of Ytraa,' He raised the staff above his head.

Jodisa-Li turned to the boy beside her. 'I, Jodisa-Li of Muhnilahm, daughter of the High Priest, Dagla Kaz, wish to enter with the Wharhll, to make him my husband, greet his people and make them mine also. Take token of our goodwill.' From a small bag, brought by the wagon driver, she tossed each child a gold coin.

After catching their tokens, each bowed formally. The wagon moved on and stopped at the second pair. The ceremony was repeated until all were furnished with gold.

'They look exceptionally well fed and clean for street urchins.'

'We have no poverty. No one goes without. These orphans live in a communal home with widows and widowers to care for them and have the same rights and privileges as everyone in the city.'

Jodisa-Li thought of the poor starving street children of Choshinahm who fought for every scrap of food. 'You put my island to shame, Feldrark. It's a wonder to me that a society so large can care for its poorest members. I approve.'

As they'd approached the gates they had slowly closed and a wide, long drawbridge, unseen from the road, had been raised. Jodisa-Li was surprised to see that the water of the lake spread through the gateway, lapping the walls of the towers on either side so that it was impossible for the wagon to go any further.

'The water's three manheights deep and sharp pointed spears of stone lie hidden just under the surface. No man or animal can cross and expect to live. In fact, without the drawbridge, the bears and stripecats wouldn't have got into the city when it was abandoned.'

Feldrark touched her cheek softly and stepped down from the wagon. Jodisa-Li became aware of the quiet that had fallen as she stood beside him and took his hand. The growing sound of many voices, muted by the city walls as they approached, was now still. Only the sibilant fountain, twittering birds, soft sighing breeze and distant caress of surf on sand broke the silence.

Sweet blossom mingled with the scent of the sea and a strange spicy aroma that touched the tongue and brought juices to the mouth.

Feldrark cupped his hands around his mouth. 'I am returned. Feldrark stands at the gate and begs entrance. The Wharhll of Litkala is come home and wishes to appear before his people, his Kiral and his Kirallah.'

A hidden female voice, strong and clear, replied from within. 'What price will the Wharhll pay for entrance?'

'Service to my Kiral and Kirallah. Service to the people of Litkala. Service to the city and the state.'

'What proof have you that you are who you say you are?'

Feldrark took the Staff and held it by the end, vertically above his head in his right hand. 'I return the sacred Staff of Ytraa. I bring the fairest woman in the world to be my bride. I come in clothes I wore when I left many portions past.'

'Who are these that accompany you?'

'The fair lady by my side is Jodisa-Li, daughter of Dagla Kaz, High Priest of Muhnilahm. She is a paragon of beauty, wisdom and kindness who will be my wife. Aglydron, Myllthlan and Okkyntalah are travelling companions who have aided my return and bring honour to the city by their visit.'

'Return to your wagon, he who claims to be Wharhll of Litkala, and wait on our decision.'

'How can they see us?'

'See the carvings either side of the gate, the ones that look like eyes?' Feldrark pointed as he helped her back onto the wagon and then climbed up to sit beside her again.

'I see them.'

'The black spots that form the pupils are spy holes. Each member of the Citizen's Forum will view us.'

'What now?'

'We wait on their decision.'

'They'll let us in, though, won't they?'

'It's their decision. Only once has the Wharhll been denied access, and, to tell the truth, he deserved no better.'

The drawbridge slowly lowered until it lay flush with the surface of the road and provided a causeway over the water to gates that remained closed.

'The wagons will come forward.'

Without waiting, the driver urged the horses forward and they moved onto and across the drawbridge to stop five paces in front of the gates. The other wagon followed. From behind the heavy wooden gates, studded with massive iron bolts and rivets, came the murmur of impatient voices; thousands of them. A man's voice called something they could not make out and the crowd chorused agreement. A low chanting began and rose until Feldrark and Jodisa-Li could hear the words as they waited in the shadow of the gateway.

'We want Feldrark.'

Something caused the chant to falter and lessen until it failed and a grumbling silence returned, out of which the female voice sounded from behind the gate.

'We are content that you are Feldrark. We agree that the lady is most beautiful. But these others, these strangers; who guarantees their good intentions and behaviour?'

'My liberty is forfeit should any of them fall foul of our laws. I stand as their surety.'

The gate opened out a discreet distance and a woman emerged, followed by a man. Both wore the common dress; simple, sleeveless tunic to mid-thigh, wrapped across the front opening and belted with a chord at the waist. Each carried a wide garland of mixed flowers. They placed one round the neck of Jodisa-Li and the other round Feldrark, as the pair remained seated. The man and woman returned through the gate.

From within, the woman's voice, loud and clear, addressed the crowd. 'Know that Feldrark, Wharhll of Litkala, enters the city with his chosen, Jodisa-Li of Muhnilahm and with them, travelling companions worthy of honour. Greet these our lord and lady and their friends; welcome them.'

The gates swung wide toward them, revealing the huge crowd in the space within at the same time as they revealed Feldrark and Jodisa-Li to the throng. A huge roar of greeting met them, as Feldrark and Jodisa-Li rose to their feet on the moving wagon to acknowledge the welcome.

'*Look at their faces. They love you already.*'

'*It's you they love, Feldrark. I'm just your chosen. You're the source of respect and admiration.*'

'*After last night, and everyone here will know of it, they'll love you, Jodisa-Li. Love you for your humility, compassion and courage.*'

She raised her hands in greeting as the wagon moved slowly past the ranks of faces lining the road as far as the inner gateway, almost a thousand paces ahead. 'I thank you for your gift and your welcome.'

'*That was well done, my love. Well done indeed.*'

'*For you, my love, for your honour and respect.*'

They stood, feet slightly apart, inner legs touching and forward of those on the outside for balance, holding hands and waving with their free hands, as the wagon rolled forward at a steady pace.

Slowly, the adoration of the crowd extinguishing her anxiety as the focus of so many eyes, she and Feldrark progressed. Approaching the inner gateway, she now saw the path of steps leading to the palace and the raised platform where their joining would be made before Ytraa. It was a ceremony she both welcomed and dreaded. To be the focus of so much attention at such an intimate moment. Just she and Feldrark, public and elevated, joining in passion for all to see.

✦ ⸎✦⸕⸎

Aglydron struggled to control himself as Jodisa-Li and Feldrark entered the city. Their last chance of redemption threatened, he forgot for a moment that she was no longer virgin. Beside himself, he rose to leave the slowly moving wagon.

Okkyntalah grabbed him. 'She's lost to us, Aglydron. They'll kill you if you interfere. We must be patient and wait for Feldrark to tell us his plans for our mission.'

'What's wrong, Aglydron? Don't like to see a woman enjoying such adoration?'

Aglydron sneered at Linlyss. 'What I like or don't doesn't matter. My care is with my Virgin Gift and her…'

'Cept she ain't no virgin, is she? So what you going to do now, Aglydron? Get yourself another virgin to take with you, eh?'

'Is that what Feldrark plans, Aglydron?'

'If it is, he's a fool. Ytraa must choose the Virgin Gift. We can't take just any virgin girl. Else, why are we bothering to replace Tumalind?'

'Because she's my chosen and I…'

'That's your reason, Okkyntalah. Not mine.'

'Perhaps I could go instead of Jodisa-Li?'

'You? What makes you think I'd want to take a…?' He stopped, seeing amusement on her face. 'It matters to me, girl. Even if you think it's a joke.'

'Don't jump in the furnace! I never meant nothing by it. Too stiff by 'alf, you are, Aglydron.'

She turned away, dismissing Aglydron and staring at events around them. Morose and at a loss what he might do about his insurmountable problem, Aglydron withdrew into himself and passed the journey through the lower city deep in introspection and despair.

✦ ⸎✦⸕⸎

In a high, isolated cleft in the cliff overlooking the broad plain round Chalamamnon, Aklon-Dji could rest a while and think; safe in the knowledge that no one could creep up on him unobserved. His constant round of anxiety, risk and danger, was interspersed with all-too-brief intervals of comfort and togetherness like that recently shared with Shoarhn. Even those, however, were rarely without their costs and he was always conscious of the danger his people faced simply by contact with him.

He sat in the shadows of the shallow cave and gazed over lush green plains to the sea. A sea made dark by heavy thunderclouds that poured their storm onto the port below, lightning searing restless waves with momentary brightness. Across that sea, to the west, lay Litkala and Ivdulon in his high tower. He tried to picture the place where the wise man lived, recalling the images of the city that Ivdulon had shown him, spread out below his tower. But much of what he'd seen was alien and he felt he knew little of the scale or sophistication of the city.

Ivdulon's ideas, however, indicated a man with education and knowledge far greater than anyone else he'd come across. If Followers of Litkala were even remotely like this sage then they had much to offer that was good. They clearly couldn't be the barbarian heretics his father labelled them. And now, Jodisa-Li was to become involved with their leader, perhaps marry him and form an alliance. It was desperately important that she form that alliance with him and not with their father. Ivdulon said the city had a population of a hundred thousand. An army from there could easily defeat any fighting force the island could muster. Aklon-Dji wanted that force on his side, not with the Holy Ones and Dagla Kaz.

'Are you hearing me, Ivdulon?'

'Ah, Aklon. You catch me when much has happened. I've a great deal to impart and can spend time with you. Ask your questions first, if it's safe for you to do so, and if you're properly sheltered from that storm. Then I'll pass on news I believe you'll find both surprising and welcome.'

Aklon-Dji asked his questions and found, as always, Ivdulon's knowledge and advice worth the waiting. Ivdulon reported Feldrark's return with Jodisa-Li and their forthcoming wedding, filling him with great joy. That, however, was not all. He learned of their escape from Mipahnhil and of Okkyntalah's bravery. The skills of the healer from Ylcrat greatly impressed him. There was much to learn and some previous ideas to be changed. But Ivdulon saved his greatest piece of news until last.

'Reach out to your sister, Aklon. I've contacted her and witnessed her intelligence. Try to contact her, though not just now, or for a day or two: newlyweds, you know? I think you might be surprised. Like you, she was unaware of her skill but she's developing fast and shows every sign of being a Gifted, like you. Few who mindtalk can cover the distance you and I achieve but Jodisa-Li will be one. Try her and see. I've not told her of our contact. I leave that intelligence to you.'

Aklon-Dji watched the storm pass out to sea, wondering what he should now do. That he must contact Jodisa-Li if he was able, there was no doubt. But how to introduce himself and what to tell her? Her feelings and sympathies were closer to her father's than to his. He would speak to her of inconsequential things before deciding what to tell her. And whether to confide in her regarding the Few, the Cause and his plans for the island.

Chapter 47

TRUTHS AND HALF TRUTHS

*O*kkyntalah refused to let the vexed question of the Virgin Gift distract him from what promised to be a most enjoyable day. It was out of his hands, anyway. He left Aglydron to his dark musings and concentrated on the swirl of people, sights, sounds and smells around him.

Their wagon was halfway across the wide flat space between the two gated walls. They travelled a road paved much like that approaching the outer gate, except that here the patterns depicted leaves, flowers and stylised trees. A parallel road, packed with rejoicing citizens, lay at the other side of the shallow stream of red water that flowed between them in its stone-lined course.

People had gathered on both sides, from outer gate to inner. Over the heads to his left, Okkyntalah saw a wide expanse of grazing land, dotted with herds and flocks of domesticated animals. There was no fencing.

'How do they keep the animals under control, Linlyss?'

She glanced his way. 'Don't know.' And then stared out the other way.

Behind the crowd on that side, another, wider expanse of grazing land stretched away. This was devoid of animals and seemed no more than a very large flat meadow, speckled with white flowers and dotted with single examples of the elegant trees they had passed on the way in.

Linlyss suddenly turned and expanded on her two-word answer. 'The ceremonies take place on the meadow, there, see? Some poor culls must've spent last night and this morning shifting the animals and clearing up dung so folk can join on the grass without getting it all over them.'

'They join out here?'

'Course! When Feldrark and Jodisa-Li show themselves to Ytraa, way up there in front of the palace, everyone else'll do the same, won't they? And when they join, everyone else'll do the same down 'ere, 'cept those as live in the upper city, like. They'll be on their roofs or in their gardens. We've been getting ready for it since Feldrark left. After, there'll be a right celebration for everyone. All the food and drink's given by the Kiral and Kirallah. There'll be singing an' dancing an' bonfires an'…oh…all sorts of lovely things.'

This was similar to what Okkyntalah expected on Dagla Kaz's return to the island with the Godwood. The day, it seemed, was destined to be even more enjoyable than he'd expected. He might even get to join, in the name of Ytraa, with the lass beside him.

'I might get myself pierced.' She put her hand on Okkyntalah's leg and stroked under his tunic. 'Yes. Something fine's gonna get stuck into me before the day's done.'

If Aglydron heard her, over the cheering crowds, or the ribald comments of those close by, he chose not to respond.

Okkyntalah, feeling rather exposed and conscious of smirks and leers on faces nearby, gently shifted her hand so the tunic separated her skin from his. 'For a virgin, you certainly know how to raise a man's expectations.'

'Oh, just 'cos I ain't made use of one, don't mean I can't prime a prod.'

They pulled up behind the leading wagon, in front of the open gateway to the upper city and Okkyntalah used the distraction to deflect her from her pleasurable teasing as he took a good look around.

The inner sides of the city walls were lined with stepped buildings. Houses rose to six tiers, each level slightly shorter than the one below and each showing doorways and windows open to the city. Steps climbed between each house from ground level to the roof of the fifth layer, which was also the floor of the sixth, dividing each building from its neighbour, missing only the final tier, which ran as a continuous block along the top.

'People live right under the walls?'

Linlyss smiled with pleasure at the strain in his voice as he tried to turn her mind from carnal intentions. She was kind, understanding his plight in the presence of so many people and moving her hand to rest just above his knee. 'Yes, Okkyntalah. The bottom bit along the wall facing us is mostly shops. They live on the level above. Then there's their workers and families. The top houses are just two rooms, where the soldiers live. The other walls are the same, 'cept the bottom ones aren't shops, just houses.'

Feldrark and Jodisa-Li dismounted from their wagon and were conducted through the gateway by a young man, amid loud cheering and applause.

A young woman approached and bowed formally to Aglydron. Okkyntalah noted the gold headband that took her blonde hair away from her face and the gold band around her right wrist, studded with bright gems of brilliant red. Her tunic of fine silk shimmered with a multitude of colours as she moved and the high hem was fringed with finger-length strands of golden thread that shone in the bright sunlight.

'Please come with me.'

Her voice was at once soft and commanding and Okkyntalah wasn't surprised when Aglydron obeyed her. He and the women followed. Their wagon was turned end to end with the one Feldrark and Jodisa-Li had left, forming a barrier across the open gateway after the party had moved through into the upper city.

'If you would step onto the lifting seat, please.' Again, the elegant woman's voice gave instructions they felt compelled to obey.

She invited them to take seats on a strange, wheeled device. Feldrark and Jodisa-Li were already standing on a similar cart in front, prepared for the ride up the steep ramp rising toward the palace. Normally, Okkyntalah would have resisted travelling on such a dangerous looking contraption but the woman's voice was so persuasive that he took his seat without demur. The large rear wheels were on long shafts and the front ones small, so that the wagon remained horizontal as it was dragged up the steep slope that they now began to ascend. Flights of simple steps lined each side of the slope and these were lined with people from the upper city. Their tunics were finer and the people themselves taller and more elegant than their counterparts in the lower city.

Halfway up, Okkyntalah gazed over the heads of admiring citizens to the houses that occupied the stepped tiers. The bulk of the city spread below them; a great wedge between its towering walls. A walkway fronted each tier, giving access to all the buildings along its curved length. Some houses took up wide swathes of the ledges on which they were built but others were more modest. All, however, stood at least two storeys high and some, three. Their flat roofs were adorned with gardens, or with sitting areas dotted with tall, elegant plants in round coloured pots and, on the nearest of these roofs, more parties of citizens gathered to greet them. Many of the homes had gardens where flowers and fruits grew and fountains played. Coloured vines climbed the stonework here and there, adding colour and variation to the fine veined white stone. All, on this hot clear still day had their doors and windows flung wide open.

'Aren't they worried someone'll steal their treasures?'

'Steal?'

'Pinch, take…' He saw her frown of incomprehension. 'You really don't know what I mean?'

She shook her head, golden locks brushing her fair skin so that he was suddenly lost in her. Her eyes shone with the knowledge that she'd captured him but she said nothing for the time being, and he wondered at her caution.

'It's taking something from someone else, without their permission. The way you've just stolen my heart.'

'No one'd do that. We only accept what's freely given or been earned. It's a terrible thing to take what's not yours. And if I've won your heart, Okkyntalah, it's 'cos you've let me believe it's there for the winning.'

He knew she told a version of the truth and it troubled him, deeply. What of Tumalind, his promised and beloved? Had the time of absence made him love her less? Had his fun and frolics with other women made his heart less full of Tumalind? The questions answered themselves as the very thought of her conjured her in his mind, bringing her alive, filling his whole being with a desire for her so strong it drowned out all else. And he was suddenly clear about why he'd neglected her on his journey. His need and want and love for her was so overwhelming that her inaccessibility had forced him to close his mind to her. If she was no longer available for him, if he could no longer have her, he must make it so she no longer existed; he must deny her very being or lose his sanity in his unfulfilled want of her.

The abrupt and powerful gathering of his true feelings made his head swim and he recognized that his want of Linlyss and the others whose bodies he'd enjoyed was no more than the natural carnal desire of a young man denied the company of his true partner. His heart belonged to Tumalind still; and always would. If, and here he gulped to hide tears that might so easily betray him, if she were denied him, he would have to try to forget her. But he knew, no matter what happened, he would love his Tumalind until he died and beyond, until he no longer existed.

Linlyss stared at him as if his thoughts were etched upon his face, as if she heard his voice telling her the truth. 'And now I've lost you, just as quickly.'

'You never had me, Linlyss. You only had my prod. I'm sorry.'

'You're not mine. Never will be, will you?'

'That's right. I'm Tumalind's and always will be. The rest's just desire and lust. I'm stuck on frowking, Linlyss. I'd frowk you now and three or four times every day if I could. But, soon as Tumalind appears, I'll leave you flat, and never even look at you again.'

She was silent as the cart climbed ever up and passed the cheering folk, the waving hands and banners, the grand houses of the noble families who lined their route. In all this joy and jubilation, these two, who each believed they'd found love, had discovered it wasn't what they thought.

Linlyss was first to break their lonely quiet. 'You're honest, Okkyntalah. Too honest. Truth is, I never a met a man I wanted till you come along. And I still want your prod to be first in my fern, even if you'll never love me. Will you, Okkyntalah? Will you still be the one to turn this girl into a woman?'

It was only frowking. Joining for Ytraa; without any other meaning. Like he had with Myllthlan and Malarhah and the women in Mipahnhil and, suddenly unbidden, the memory of the professional woman of pleasure who'd given herself in Chalamamnon came to mind. Frowking for Ytraa, but not with her; she'd been all about pleasure. But that was what they all meant; if he was honest. Ytraa was no more than an excuse; he wondered if such thoughts were blasphemous, but he couldn't deny them. They were all nothing more than fun and pleasure and maybe comradeship in a world full of uncertainty. And here beside him sat a girl desperate for his attention. 'Try and stop me.'

She smiled but there was now the darkness of the woman bruised and, though she tried to bring the brightness back, she could no longer show him that delight and want she'd expressed for that short spell when she'd believed his heart could be hers. He saw this and knew he was powerless to change it. Knew he'd take her when he could and spend himself in her, give her pleasure, give her joy and take her heart and never, ever give her his, never be to her what she wanted him to be. Knew he'd enjoy her fresh delights each day and night for ten or twenty years and drop her like a broken spear as soon as Tumalind came back to him. And knowing, knowing she knew, he'd do it still.

Their hands touched, fingers squeezed, as they signalled their recognition of the truth, their acceptance of what they were alone and what they would be to each other. And then the cart came to a halt and events overtook and surrounded them.

Okkyntalah watched Feldrark and Jodisa-Li step from their lifting seat and stand together at the foot of the final flight of broad, curved steps leading to the platform where the palace stood, exclusive in its raised location. He and Linlyss led the others to the same steps and gazed about in admiration. On either side of every step stood a child; alternate boy and girl. Each held a spray of small purple flowers. As the Wharhll and those with him began to mount the steps, the children moved closer and, stripping the small flowers from their stems, tossed the petals at the feet of the party. The sweet scent of the crushed flowers lifted their spirits as they climbed. The children sang out as they stepped past each pair.

'Greetings, great Wharhll of Litkala. Greetings Jodisa-Li of Muhnilahm. Greetings true friends of the Wharhll.'

At the top of the flight, they came to the edge of the royal platform with the palace in front of them and the long, straight fall of the Red Rill tumbling down the quarried face of the mountain behind it. A group of men and women, perhaps two hundred strong, waited in silence. Feldrark motioned the rest to remain where they were as he strode toward the centre of this serious gathering. Two people stepped forward: the man tall, broad shouldered and clean-shaven, his face an older version of his son's. The woman dark skinned, like Malarhah and very beautiful despite the passage of the years. The Kiral and Kirallah, dressed identically in long tunics of gold, fringed at the hems with delicate strings of jet beads and tiny pearls, and girdled with fine ropes of woven myllth, moved a few paces toward their son and then stood together, waiting. Though no signal was made, the crowd fell silent, leaving the city quiet but for the distant sound of the falling rill and the closer twittering of birds in the palace gardens.

Feldrark walked slowly forward and halted, three paces from them. He dropped onto one knee and held the Staff aloft in both hands, stretched out toward them. 'I am returned with the sacred Staff of Ytraa. I place it, once more, into your care.'

The Kiral and Kirallah stepped forward together and grasped the Staff in one hand each. They moved back with it in their hands and, without seeming to examine it in any way, passed it over their heads to an official, wearing a black tunic, who returned to his place a little behind and to the left of them.

'I am come back bearing the most glorious and beautiful woman the world can offer after my most beloved mother, the Kirallah. May I present this incomparable wonder to my Kiral and Kirallah for inspection?'

The royal pair nodded just once. Feldrark took three steps back, turned, and held his hands out to Jodisa-Li. She approached, head held high, and took her place beside him. At a silent command, she then stepped forward and stood where Feldrark had stood, in front of the Kiral and Kirallah. They gazed at her and walked around her from opposite directions until they were back where they started. Feldrark came to stand at her side again.

'This woman was without child when you took her?' The Kirallah's voice was clear and stern in tone.

'Unprompted, she confessed the destruction of a love child, torn early from her belly before it knew life. Her own father, Dagla Kaz, the High Priest of Muhnilahm, killed the father of the child, without her knowledge or consent. She would have born the infant but her father deprived her of that choice and made her act the part of a virgin afterwards.'

Some quality of the rock face surrounding the platform magnified the sound so that their words were heard in every part of the city. In return, the response, a confused cry of indignation and distress, swept up the tiers from the people to fill the space.

Okkyntalah felt a physical shock at this revelation. He turned to consult Aglydron who seemed so affected by this announcement that he almost fell where he was, such was his outrage. The Kirallah held up her hand and silence returned.

'We deem this tragedy no fault of the woman. A love child is no sin. Its removal before birth is wicked, when against the will of its creators, and those responsible should be punished. No blame is attached to the woman in this. She is undiminished in our eyes. Has this woman joined with you and given you delight?'

'With passion and love declared and demonstrated, she has joined with me and given more delight than I could dream possible. She is beautiful to behold and a wondrous partner in love.'

'Will this woman live with you, will she bear your heirs and do the duty bound to one who would partner you for life?'

'This woman will forsake her home, her father, and the mother she knows not.

She will give me all the heirs I could desire. She will do what is required of her for city, state and family and never leave my side.'

'Do you love this woman?'

'With all my heart and all my soul and all that I am and all that I possess both now and in the future I love this woman.'

The Kiral then spoke to Jodisa-Li, his voice deep, strong and full of gentle power. 'Tell the realm your name, woman who would take the Wharhll and be his partner till he breathes no more.'

'I am Jodisa-Li, heir and daughter of Dagla Kaz the High Priest of Muhnilahm, and I make it known to all who hear that I now relinquish all I own and all I might have come to have in power and possessions to become, with willing heart, the lifelong partner of the Wharhll of Litkala.'

'Do you love our son?'

'I love him with every facet of my being. I love him with my heart, my soul, my mind and my body. I love the Wharhll of Litkala, Feldrark, my lord with all that I am and all that I have been and all that I will become.'

The Kirallah moved a step to stand with the Kiral. Together they spoke for all to hear. 'Feldrark, son and heir to all this realm, know that we accept the woman of your choice and name Jodisa-Li our son-daughter and welcome her into our realm, our home and our hearts.'

A huge cheer rose out of the city at this and the noise of celebration was allowed to continue unabated as the formal part of this first ceremony ended.

Feldrark at last embraced his mother and father and they in turn embraced Jodisa-Li. Okkyntalah saw the Kirallah make an involuntary start, her face registering shock, as she took Jodisa-Li's hand and glanced down at the bangle around her ankle. The lady made no comment, however, only glancing first at Jodisa-Li's face and then at Feldrark's. He, in turn, simply nodded and closed his eyes, briefly.

The Wharhll then introduced the rest of the party to his parents, giving brief accounts of their parts in his return and including the story of the loss of Malarhah. He spoke softly to the Kiral. The official holding the Staff moved forward at a silent command. He nodded at some words unheard by the others and approached Linlyss and Pettaklon. 'I understand you, young lady, are to play for the ceremony?'

Linlyss nodded and kept her gaze to the floor.

'And you, young man, are to tend the Wharhll and his partner during the joining?'

Pettaklon looked seriously at the man. 'Yes, Paltrohn.'

'Good. Then please come with me.' And he detached them from the group and took them toward the palace.

Okkyntalah watched the young woman go obediently with the man in the black tunic and wondered what they intended for her and the boy.

'Don't be anxious, Okkyntalah. They go to prepare for the ceremony, nothing more.'

Feldrark's words of reassurance were comfort enough for the time being and he smiled and waved encouragement at Linlyss as she turned to glance at him before she disappeared into the palace.

'What happens next?'

'We eat a little, drink a little. The sun's past his mid-point and everyone's ready for food. Then we perform the sacred joining.' Feldrark nodded at the high wooden platform standing a little way back from the edge of the stone stage. 'Up there, where the entire city will witness our becoming one in the sight of Ytraa.' He turned to Jodisa-Li and took her hand. 'Come. Let's put food inside us and prepare for the end of our lives alone and the beginning of our lives together.'

❦

'Tumalind?'

That was her name.

'Tumalind?'

Yes. Someone called her. She must open her eyes and see who.

Lightness. Brightness that hurt. Slowly, then. Better through half closed lids. Still bright but bearable now. A shape, dark against the brightness.

'Tumalind, wake up.'

So thirsty. The shape moved, came close. Hung over her so she could smell food and fear. The world started to spin and she breathed deep. Found the air no longer thick. She panted; the air helped her grow still again. The spinning stopped and the brightness was sky and blue. The shape was Corphanda. Corphanda bending over and holding her hand.

'Tumalind, come back, my child.'

She turned her head and saw them all at prayer. How odd they looked. She recalled something she could not quite fix but knew she should look away.

'Tumalind. Can you hear me?'

She nodded. Tried to speak. Her mouth so dry. Something hard and damp touched her lips. She opened her mouth. Liquid touched her tongue. Swilled her mouth. Swallowed.

'I had a dream…'

'She's back. She's come through. Ytraa be praised!'

The shape that was Corphanda moved back a step and Wendarah, fresh from prayers, came and looked on her. A smile lit the pretty face of the priestess as she stared down at her.

'How do you feel?'

Her fingers were numb. Her feet felt far away and not connected. She tried to get up but there was no strength in her and she moaned with the effort.

'What…? Why am…? But words were too hard to find.

Dagla Kaz moved and was close to her, his hand on her forehead. 'How do you feel, my dear child?'

'I…Where are…my…feet?'

He lifted her leg and raised it so she could see her foot. Her skin flowed down the leg across and up to her eyes without a break. She tried to turn, to hide herself but found no power in her muscles.

'She's still feverish.'

'That's to be expected. It'll go.' A strange voice; unknown but confident. 'She'll need to be kept cool until it does. I want none of your silly rules forcing her to be covered. Unless the fever escapes her quickly, she might not recover her movement.'

'It will be so. Can she travel?'

'It's best she rests today.' The confident voice sounded in charge. 'Sleep now, my beauty. Sleep and rest.'

'So thirsty.'

Water came again and filled her mouth until she swallowed. Someone else was in danger.

'Phildrad?'

'Phildrad's fine, my lovely. He's back on his feet already. You sleep now.'

Sleep came quickly.

There was a man. He bent over her, stroked her parts with his fingers. Handled her where only Okkyntalah's gentle touch had been. Moved legs she couldn't control and pushed at her. She couldn't move. She didn't want this. Her eyes opened. She saw the man and knew him. He was a man she didn't trust. A man she didn't like. He would invade her. Intrude where no man must go. He was ready to move above her; would rape her. She felt terror. Felt revulsion rise within her. Fought against helplessness that kept her limbs from shifting to her aid.

'Tryonta!'

The call that was almost a scream left her. Filled the room. But the effort of the cry was too great. Had they heard? Darkness drowned her.

Chapter 48

AN ENDING AND A BEGINNING

Jodisa-Li happily accompanied Feldrark into the palace, out of the midday heat. The sibilant splash of water from many small fountains increased her relief as he led her across the hall and into a spacious, light dining room. Wide platters of many types of food crowded the long table, making her mouth water. Low settles hugged the walls. Young men and women in palace colours waited, eager to serve.

The Kiral and Kirallah entered as Jodisa-Li and Feldrark spooned food into wooden bowls and filled glass goblets with pale blue-green wine. The Kirallah approached and knelt to examine the bangle round her ankle. She spoke to Feldrark. 'What does this mean?'

'Your mother doesn't mindtalk?'

'Look at her eyes.'

Jodisa-Li saw deep brown pools of concern and recalled what Feldrark had told her.

'It's better explained by those who took part in it, Mother. It's not a happy story and now isn't the best time but it must be told so you're not in doubt. Timing won't alter the sorrow of its end.' Feldrark sought and found Okkyntalah, standing near the table, trying to persuade Aglydron to eat. He signalled a serving girl to bring the young man over.

Okkyntalah told the Kiral and Kirallah about the shipwreck. He was more diplomatic than he'd been with Feldrark. The questions from the parents were no easier than Feldrark's but Okkyntalah's answers were more circumspect. He clearly felt he'd let the family down with his sparse information and Jodisa-Li again found herself re-appraising him.

Through her grief and loss, the Kirallah put him at his ease. 'You were kind to release my daughter to the sea, Okkyntalah. And you did well to remember all you have about a stranger in such difficult circumstances. I thank you for telling the tale, even if it breaks my heart. I never blame the messenger for the message. Know that you are blessed in our eyes and have earned our gratitude.'

Okkyntalah bowed, uncertain how to respond. The Kiral and Kirallah each touched him on the shoulder in token of thanks, releasing him from the duty. They moved a pace or two apart from the others, summoned the man in the black tunic and spoke with him in earnest.

'We'll announce Mythanpho's death tomorrow, following the festivities, Feldrark. Much time and effort has been put into the celebration of your return and joining. It would be inappropriate to mar the joy with news that must cause the people great sorrow.'

Feldrark nodded. 'Thank you, for myself and for Jodisa-Li. Today will be ordeal enough for her, without the added burden such sadness would bring. She's brave and true to her faith but she doesn't welcome the public display.'

'Have you schooled your companions in the way it must be? Their culture may make them unable or unwilling to participate. And we may need to make arrangements for some, if they're to witness the ceremony.'

Feldrark clapped a hand to his forehead. 'Thank you, Mother. I've neglected to pass the full details on to them, forgetting their ways may be different from ours.'

The deep sorrow and grief that enclosed the Kirallah, was quickly replaced by genuine concern for Jodisa-Li. 'No wonder the poor girl's anxious. She probably thinks you're to give a performance to the entire city. Put her out of her misery, Feldrark, and allow your lovely bride to relax.'

Jodisa-Li felt real warmth for this lady who had the grace and humanity to care about the distress of a stranger. Feldrark beckoned a serving lad to bring Aglydron and Myllthlan to listen to what he had to tell them all.

'I'm sorry; I took it for granted you'd know what will happen after we've eaten. But your customs may not be like ours. Everyone present at the ceremony of our joining must also join. You can't attend otherwise. Do any of you want to be absent or need a partner?'

Aglydron took Myllthlan's hand. 'This ceremony shouldn't be. Unless it's true that Jodisa-Li had a child.'

'I swear before Ytraa it's true, Aglydron. I tried to tell you but…'

'So, our mission was in vain, after all. I'm sorry we dragged you halfway across the world on a fool's errand.'

Jodisa-Li accepted his apology with a nod.

Aglydron turned to Myllthlan. 'Would you honour me, before Ytraa?'

'The honour is mine, Aglydron.'

Okkyntalah looked put out. 'Like Aglydron, I feel deprived of our mission, but I won't miss the ceremony. I don't know where it leaves us, or how I'll regain Tumalind without…'

'Peace. I promised you all will be well. Your mission will go ahead as planned. Trust me. Tomorrow you'll have proof. Let me say this, just to rest your spirits. Ytraa moves in ways we can't understand, but we do well to read signs we're sent. Consider; had you not taken Jodisa-Li, I'd still be in Mipahnhil without a bride. Ytraa has purposes for us and we don't always know what they are. Time will reveal the solution.'

He said this with such conviction that Jodisa-Li wondered whether he'd already consulted others on the matter.

Okkyntalah brightened. 'Since I can't have Myllthlan, I'll ask Linlyss.'

Feldrark frowned. 'I'm sorry; I hadn't realized. Linlyss is to play for the ceremony and is already in the music chamber high above us, so her music will be heard over the entire city. It's a part for which she'll be generously rewarded.'

Okkyntalah made no effort to hide his disappointment.

Feldrark nodded his sympathy. 'Let me see what I can do. Will you accept a partner if I find one?'

'I suppose I must if I can't have the one I prefer.'

Feldrark spoke softly to a serving girl. She giggled, studying Okkyntalah openly before returning to the gathering.

The group ate, drank, relaxed on the settles and spoke with the Kiral and Kirallah in the easy atmosphere of the informal meal. The serving girl reappeared with half a dozen young women. They surrounded Okkyntalah and two took a hand each, persuading him from the room, followed by the girl.

Jodisa-Li moved closer to Feldrark. 'What goes on, my love?'

'A small selection process so Okkyntalah and his potential partner may meet.'

'Sounds less than sacred.'

'The better pleased each is with the other, the more enthusiastic, and therefore sacred, will be their joining before Ytraa, don't you think?'

'Sounds a thin excuse for wanton behaviour. How will he choose from such a bevy of lovelies?'

'They'll see each other separately for a short spell. The serving girl will stay. She'll tell the one he chooses for the ceremony. Which, by the way, will start soon. Still nervous?'

'Not as I was before your mother made you explain it wasn't to be just you and me, performing before thousands.'

'Tens of thousands; almost a hundred thousand, in fact. Sorry, thoughtless of me. We'll disrobe first and cover up last but, once it begins, I doubt we'll even be noticed. Young Pettaklon will take away our old clothes and bring new tunics. He won't be joining.'

'Obviously not, at his age. What'll happen to him afterwards?'

'If he does well and he wishes it, we'll take him into the palace to learn a trade or become a royal servant, if his parents approve. Otherwise, he'll go home with a full purse and the envy of his peers.'

'Better than the life he was leading. Must I lose my flower for the ceremony?'

'Everything. We must be as Ytraa made us. Even the bangles must be taken off for this one time.'

Okkyntalah returned, beaming, with a young woman who looked mightily pleased with herself.

Jodisa-Li wasn't surprised she was a redhead with blue eyes. *'I understand Okkyntalah's charms, my love, but who is she and why is she so pleased?'*

'One of the few unwed daughters of the nobility. They vie for such chances. His song at the inn last night and courage in defending us against the murderers from Mipahnhil will have spread all over the city by now. Okkyntalah's a hero. The girl's standing in the city will be enhanced by association with him.'

'News travels fast here, then?'

'Very. It's said that the Kiral yawns at noon and by mid-afternoon they're asleep in the furthest fields.'

Jodisa-Li laughed. 'I'd best be careful what I say and do, then. I've no wish to be the cause of panic in the orchards because I've found a worm in my merphlion.'

Feldrark took her in his arms and embraced her. 'The city will soon love you almost as much as I do. Come, my love. We are called.'

The man in the black tunic, now partnered by a rather squat blonde woman in unblemished white, beckoned the company into the bright sunshine again. The ceremony was about to begin.

❦

Aglydron, relieved after the pressure of the past few sixdays, now knew he could've done nothing to prevent this union. Ytraa preordained it. He and Okkyntalah were but instruments of their God.

Feldrark and Jodisa-Li went up the steps of the platform with the man in black and the woman in white. Aglydron went with the remainder up a wide, sweeping stair onto to a long, deep balcony. This overlooked the city and the platform, which thrust out immediately below. Their balcony, some six manheights above the level shelf of rock housing the palace, was without a barrier. The witnessing couples spread along the length according to some pre-set pattern. The Kiral and Kirallah motioned Okkyntalah and his partner, and Aglydron with Myllthlan, to stand either side of them. Their view was excellent.

Aglydron watched a frown of condemnation flash across the face of the Kirallah. He followed her gaze to a stunning young woman in a tunic open to the waist, exposing most of her ample breasts and so short that her fern was barely concealed. She was in animated conversation with a young soldier, whose eyes never left her cleavage. Aglydron sneered, sympathising with the Kirallah's censure.

The man in black raised his arms and a hush descended on the city below and, more slowly, on the balcony. Beside Aglydron, Myllthlan, kept his hand in hers and stood so that their arms touched. It was a contact he welcomed and he relaxed at last.

He stared at the whole wide wedge of the city and wondered at the perfect, parallel arcs of the lower walls, the harbour and its canal leading to the docks within, the raised lake of clear drinking water, the flat meadows, tiered houses and regular streets. Nothing he'd experienced had prepared him for such a sight and he was overwhelmed by the scale and majesty, the mastery of design and planning that had made it possible.

But he wasn't left to gaze for long. The man in black spoke, his voice carrying down to the plains of the lower city and resounding behind him to those on the balcony.

'I, Patradko Kaz, elected High Priest of Litkala, do this day proclaim the return of our Wharhll, Master of the Holy Tablets, Keeper of the Secrets, Holder of the Staff of Ytraa, to our midst.'

A great cheer rose from the crowd and the High Priest indulgently allowed it to settle.

'He brings a woman of great beauty; Jodisa-Li, of Muhnilahm.'

At Feldrark's urging, Jodisa-Li stepped forward and raised her hands above her head, palms facing the people. She stood at the very edge of the platform and bowed three times before retreating. The crowd gave another huge roar of approval.

Patradko Kaz waited a few moments before he signalled for quiet. 'Know you that Feldrark has passed through legend, fire, flood and battle to return this day. He has known and trodden Mhortag's Dread and escaped that fearful place unscathed.'

An involuntary gasp rose from the people and many, including those on the rooftops of the upper city, crossed arms over their faces to ward off evil.

'Feldrark has travelled the plains of Rophan-Ra, where the wild Bruxa hunt. He has sailed the wide waters of the turbulent River Sure and been made captive in the heathen city on stilts, Mipahnhil, where for the whole of time the people have hated all who occupy this city. There, he lay with hundreds and fathered many offspring, as required. But, liars and cheats, as they ever were in that cesspool, they kept not their promise to restore to him the Staff of Ytraa and release him. It was there he met his companions; the beautiful Jodisa-Li, Myllthlan the healer, Aglydron of the sacred mission and Okkyntalah the fearless.'

Another great cheer from the crowd arose as, at the Kiral's bidding, Aglydron, Myllthlan and Okkyntalah stepped to the edge of the balcony.

'There also, he befriended Malarhah, the brave and faithful. The Lay of

Malarhah, composed and sung by Okkyntalah only last night, tells of the lovely slave girl who gave her life for her master. All must know the Lay before this day's end. For it was Malarhah who discovered the Staff of Ytraa, though it was moved before Feldrark could retrieve it and he had to search again. Feldrark led the companions out of that sewer on the mud and, with courage and daring, brought them home. Malarhah laid down her life to save Feldrark, as they fought the foul hunters sent to kill them. Many and great will be the tales of their battle. Know that Feldrark has shown great courage and skill, returning with the Staff of Gadhallah that is now the Staff of Ytraa.' Patradko Kaz suddenly held the Staff in his hand and showed it to the people, who cried out in joy at the sight. 'And, true to his quest, he returned also with the woman that he will wed today before all; Jodisa-Li, the beauteous and compassionate.'

Jodisa-Li bowed once more. Cheers greeted this proclamation and the High Priest allowed these to take their course as he held the Staff for Feldrark and Jodisa-Li to touch. As mysteriously as it had appeared, the Staff vanished.

Patradko Kaz stilled the people with a gesture. 'Hear all. Hear now the promises made by Feldrark and Jodisa-Li as they prepare to become one in the eyes of Ytraa.'

A lilting run of harmony from plucked strings issued softly from the mountain behind them, the notes hanging in the air and slowly dying in the lower city. Feldrark took Jodisa-Li's hand and they stepped to the very edge of the platform and faced each other.

'Make now your promises, one to the other, and know that your words bind you together for life more strongly than any chain, more closely than your joining skin. Nothing may cut bonds you make now but the ending of life itself.'

Feldrark, taking her hands in his, dropped to one knee and looked up into her face. 'Know that I love you this day and all the days I have yet to live. Know that I will be true to you and will love no other, will join with no other, will cast my seed in you alone. Know that I am yours from this moment until I breathe no more. Know that all I am is yours, all I have is yours, all I do is for you and for our people. Of my own free will, I hereby share with you the riches, authority and duty of my office. Take me to be yours for all time, Jodisa-Li, and accept my love as a gift without cost to you.'

Jodisa-Li raised him to his feet before she knelt. 'Know that I love you now and tomorrow and tomorrow without end. Know that I will love no other, will join with no other, will take no other to my heart, my body or my soul. Know that I will harvest your seed and nurture the life Ytraa may send us. Know that I am yours as you are mine. Of my own free do I hereby relinquish all claims of office, birth and inheritance I hold from Muhnilahm. All I am is yours, all I have is yours, all I do is for you and for our people. Take me to be yours for all of time, Feldrark, and accept my love as a gift without cost to you.'

Feldrark raised her to her feet again and the couple faced the balcony and spoke together. 'We pledge to one another for the span of our lives. We pledge our union and our lives to service of you, our people.' They turned and made the same declaration to the crowds.

The Kiral and Kirallah then spoke across the space, so that all could hear. 'Feldrark, son of our love, and Jodisa-Li, son-daughter, we accept your pledge and bless you in the sight of Ytraa. Join now, that the people may witness you are one and may never be put asunder.'

Jodisa-Li and Feldrark faced the people. 'As we join before Ytraa, we give thanks for our love and ask Ytraa to bless the fruit of our loins, and that Ytraa may permit us long life and good health together.'

The crowd gave back their response. 'Ytraa be praised. As you join before Ytraa, so we do.'

Jodisa-Li and Feldrark undressed each other. Pettaklon collected the discarded clothes and ran out of sight, as Feldrark knelt to remove their bangles. They faced the balcony as, led by Patradko Kaz and the woman in white, those assembled prepared each other. Jodisa-Li and Feldrark then faced the people as the whole populace made ready.

When all were displayed to Ytraa, each couple kissed and indulged in love play as they saw fit. Aglydron found Myllthlan willing and passionate, investing more fun, energy, enjoyment and skill in their joining than the sacred ceremony demanded. He found nothing distasteful in her passion and, although unprepared for such delight, was quick to adapt and was soon lost in the act as he had never been before in public.

After joining, Aglydron allowed Myllthlan to settle, wondering at such shared pleasure: more even than with Chislanda, who'd given such delight and shown him how joining could be more than mere physical release. He'd chosen Shoarhn for his partner but had never pleasured her like this nor allowed her to please him as Chislanda and Myllthlan had. He resolved to accept what Ytraa provided and not to be so pious that he missed the wonders of joining.

When ready, Myllthlan rose and helped him to his feet. They dressed each other and waited. Custom required a quick sweep of those around him. Okkyntalah and his partner remained joined. Influenced by his experience with Myllthlan, he smiled at their enthusiasm.

Patradko Kaz and the blonde woman completed their devotions but awaited Feldrark and Jodisa-Li's pleasure.

Aglydron surveyed the city and noted, as the Kiral and Kirallah rose beside him, that all the people now waited, their eyes on one another and only occasionally straying to the wooden platform. Cries of delight signalled completion.

Once all were clothed, the woman with Patradko Kaz raised her arms for silence. 'I, Rrildyss Kaz, elected High Priestess of Litkala and all its dominions, declare Feldrark and Jodisa one in the eyes of Ytraa. The garments of their old lives are gone. They will don raiment of office and begin their lives anew.'

This announcement astounded Aglydron, as only one High Priest or Priestess reigned at any one time on Muhnilahm.

Pettaklon solemnly mounted the steps and stood a little way behind the pair, his outstretched arms bearing the garments each would wear.

Feldrark took the fresh flower of the carah-carah and slipped it behind her ear. He placed the tunic of fine white and gold silk, edged with blue and fringed with strings of tiny jet beads and pearls, on her body. The waistrope, plaited from gold and silver thread bound with circles of jet, Feldrark looped about her narrow waist. From the platform, he collected her bangle, held it up to the crowd and those on the balcony and placed it about her ankle. The confused muttering at this was quickly subdued.

Jodisa retrieved Feldrark's bracelet, held it aloft and fastened it about his ankle. She placed the fine tunic of pure white, edged with gold and fringed with strings of tiny pearls, on her husband's body. The leather belt, trimmed with gold and studded with precious stones, she fastened about his waist.

The couple kissed, embraced with love and stepped back from the edge of the platform as Patradko Kaz and Rrildyss Kaz moved forward with the Staff held between them.

'All who have joined and celebrated coming together as one, have witnessed before Ytraa the uniting of Feldrark and Jodisa. Let none try to put them asunder. May they dwell as one in mutual pleasure, love, respect and righteousness all the days of their lives to come.'

The crowd responded. 'Let it be so.'

'May Ytraa bless them with heirs.'

'Let them have children.'

'May Ytraa bless them with long life.'

'Let them live long.'

'May Ytraa bless them with health and vitality.'

'Let them have good health always.'

'May Ytraa give them wisdom to judge with justice.'

'Let justice and wisdom live in their hearts and minds.'

'May Ytraa show them the value of compassion.'

'Let compassion ever guide them.'

'May Ytraa instruct them in the virtue of duty.'

'Let duty be their watchword.'

'May Ytraa reward them with the love of Ytraa for evermore.'

'Let Ytraa so love them, as we do love them.'

From above and behind, strains of music floated down as Linlyss played her lyre to introduce the other musicians. A sweet ballad, performed by the Sacred Singers, filled the hearts of the listeners with joy and warmth and serenity. When the air was done, Linlyss struck a lively tune, as drumming and the piping of high-pitched horns, echoed round the city walls. To this accompaniment, Jodisa and Feldrark slowly descended the platform and walked to the foot of the wide staircase, leading to the balcony.

The Kiral and Kirallah, signalling Okkyntalah, Aglydron and Myllthlan to follow, stood at the head of the steps, as the couple climbed. The wooden platform was swiftly removed so that no barrier stood between the crowds below and those on the palace balcony. The Kiral and Kirallah kissed Feldrark and Jodisa and gave them personal messages of good will. All members of the royal party followed suit.

Okkyntalah held Jodisa in a close embrace and kissed her cheeks. 'I can tell you now, Jodisa, I'm glad for you that you're not a Virgin Gift and I'm happy you've found love with Feldrark. But I wish we could've…'

'Thank you, Okkyntalah. Believe me, until Feldrark, if we could, we would've...'

Aglydron found the informality and frivolity difficult but, determined not to cast a shadow on the day, took Jodisa's hands and kissed her cheek. 'I never wished you harm, Jodisa. But I had to do what seemed right. I'm sorry I hurt you.'

To his surprise and slight consternation, Jodisa took him in her arms and held him close for a moment. When she released him there was brightness in her eyes that spoke of unshed tears. 'Thank you for stealing me away from the luxuries and contentment of home, Aglydron. Had you not been so determined to put right the real wrong my father did, I wouldn't have met my true love here. Ytraa moves in curious ways, ways we can't always understand. But I truly believe that what has happened here today was meant to be and that Ytraa approves.

'The Followers of Muhnilahm and Litkala have been divided for hundreds of cycles. Today a bond has formed between them that may grow to heal the wound. I fulfilled my mission as Virgin Gift, Aglydron, but to Litkala instead of Choshinahm. Feldrark will provide you with another girl to take my place and form another link, this time between Litkala and Choshinahm, so that all Followers will be reunited. And you, Aglydron, will be Ytraa's instrument in that union.'

He was so overcome by this assessment of the situation, so full of joy and exultation at what seemed a true appraisal of what had been done, that he picked up

Jodisa and swung her round, laughing and shouting until she protested that he must put her down again.

He placed her lightly back on her feet and straight away took Feldrark's arm in his hand as the other man clasped his arm. They pledged friendship and trust. His heart was lighter than it had ever been.

Myllthlan stood before Jodisa, placed her healer's hands under the tunic and on her flat belly and closed her eyes. She moved her hands up to cup the girl's breasts. 'You'll bear well and with ease, Jodisa and give enough milk to sustain your children. When the time arrives to harvest Feldrark's seed and grow a child within you, let him lie above you, raise your hips on a cushion, and lie a while after joining. That way you'll take his seed to that part of you where it will grow.'

The two women embraced and Myllthlan moved on to Feldrark. Aglydron was shocked as Myllthlan placed her hands beneath Feldrark's tunic and took his manhood in her hands and cupped his love fruits. Despite his initial shock, the Wharhll allowed her to do what she would.

'Your seed is strong and full of life, Feldrark. You'll father the heirs you desire and they'll be strong and full of health. Learn first to live with Jodisa, to love and honour her, before you plant the first seed in her to grow.'

She withdrew her hands and embraced him, kissing his cheek as he recovered from her intimacy and pecked hers. 'Thank you, Myllthlan. I'll try to remember that.'

The rest of the party gave their blessings and goodwill to the couple and gathered with the Kiral and Kirallah until all had finished. With music still playing, Feldrark and Jodisa descended to the waiting lifting seat, now decorated with flowers and furnished with many bags of gold dorltahs for the crowds in the lower city.

'They'll not return until the evening celebrations are due. You and your companions are at liberty to relax and explore the city, the palace or simply take your ease. The Kiral and I will take a dip in the royal pool. You're welcome to indulge in the luxury of cool clear water to wash away the heat of joining.'

Aglydron consulted Myllthlan, Okkyntalah, and the smiling girl holding his hand. The refreshing pool was most appealing.

Feldrark helped Jodisa onto the lifting seat and squeezed her hand in token of her anxiety as she faced the steep slope they would descend together. 'We've travelled thus ever since we took over the city, Jodisa, my love. Never has a seat failed. We renew the pulling ropes every year. Now, if you'll excuse me, I've an urgent task to put to Ivdulon.'

'Relegated to second place, behind matters of state, already? I think I might ask for a formal separation.'

'I'll set the wheels swiftly in motion.'

As he spoke, the lifting seat began its descent and they both laughed as Jodisa clutched Feldrark for security.

'Too swift for me, my love!'

He smiled and signalled his contact with Ivdulon.

'You do me no pleasure by missing my wedding, Ivdulon.'

'All that thrusting and sweating. Not for me, young man.'

'I need you to do something, urgently. See my bride?'

'I see a face of womanhood difficult to ignore.'

'There's another, who looks much like her, I'm told. I need you to find Tumalind and encourage her to the city, as soon as you may. She travels with Jodisa's father, somewhere between Litkala and Niphralon, though whether by sea or land we don't know.'

'I think I see where you plan to go with this, Feldrark. It's fraught with danger. And I doubt the girl holds any sway over that fool High Priest anyway.'

'But you'll do what you can?'

'How could I not? I'll retire to my roof and cast a seeking spell in the hope I can locate her. If she's unaware of her gift, I must be circumspect or she might suffer the same fate as that foul usurper, Gadhallah. We can do without a repeat of such madness.'

'Your concern is worthy but unfounded. Everything I know of the young woman says she has a kind spirit and warm heart. Selfless and caring rather than self-obsessed and grasping like Gadhallah.'

'Then I hope your plan will see her rewarded rather than exploited.'

'As to that, it's too early to say and too vital to neglect.'

Chapter 49

A Visit To The Tower

*F*eldrark and Jodisa needed rest and refreshment on their return to the palace. They'd distributed coin to every citizen and received, even if at a distance, their loyalty and affection. The timing of the banquet, due to start after prayers, should have given them time to bathe and relax together but that wasn't to be.

The Kiral had mindtalked with Feldrark about the Skyfire that Aglydron had described in glowing terms. He now awaited their return.

'Can't we mindtalk with Ivdulon on this, Father?'

'We might. But I'd rather speak with the old reprobate face to face; perhaps look at any figures and records she's made. In any case, I suspect I've an unknown listener to my conversations with Ivdulon and I'd prefer to keep this between us, for the moment.'

This was serious and unwelcome news to Feldrark and he gazed with concern at his father when they met in the palace.

'Come, I've need of your opinion on this matter.'

Feldrark turned to his new bride and shrugged his resignation. 'I'd hoped to spare you duties this early, Jodisa. But matters of state call us.'

'I'm called, too?'

'We are one, now, in every sense of the word that can be understood.'

'I see. Tell me, Feldrark, am I really needed on this particular call?'

'Not needed. Traditional, but no harm will come of it. Are you tired?'

'A little. And I want to be at my best for tonight's celebrations.'

'Indeed. Relax in the pool, my love and I'll be with you as soon as I can.' He kissed her and watched her saunter down the high white corridor the Kiral had used to meet him.

'I'll be unclothed soon. Are you certain your meeting can't wait?'

'This involves my father and matters of state, my love; I must do my sworn duty, as must you in future. But I hope to be with you before too long.'

The Kiral set off in the opposite direction and Feldrark followed reluctantly, casting occasional glances back at the swaying figure of his wife.

'Yes, Jodisa is very…erm…but you have your whole lives together. I didn't want to say anything in front of her. In fact, if you hadn't released her, I might have had to make the suggestion myself, with her father being High Priest. I've good reason to believe the Skyfire our visitors are so bent on following must be false. Ivdulon will no doubt confirm it.'

Feldrark was minded to let him know that Ivdulon had already said as much but, since the wise woman hadn't told the Kiral herself, he felt it better to say nothing. 'She's not still up in her…?'

'Where else? The woman spends her life up there. I sometimes think she must be mad but there's no doubting her knowledge and predictive powers.'

'I hate going up to the observation tower.'

'I'm none too keen myself, Feldrark, but needs must. I warned her and she's sent the Riser down for us.'

Feldrark grunted his displeasure as he strode purposefully through palace rooms and corridors with his father, acknowledging salutations, bows and curtseys from servants they passed, all busy preparing the evening feast. From the back of the magnificent building, they walked the short distance through trees and flowering plants, across water gardens, to the foot of the sheer cliff that loomed unbroken up the mountain. The Kiral stepped to the very edge of the steeply angled chute that carried the Red Rill, paced seven strides to his left and smacked his palm against an almost invisible square indentation in the rock face. A stone door swung slowly outward, revealing a small chamber containing only a stout wooden door in the far right hand corner.

Feldrark and the Kiral entered and the stone door closed behind them, the only sound a soft grating as it caught tiny grains on the floor. Once sealed, the room was blacker than the darkest night. They waited: a faint sliding sound alerting them to the dim glow of light that now marked the open door in the corner. Feldrark followed his father up the steps beyond.

'Jodisa is unaware of our suspicions concerning the Skyfire?'

'I've said nothing of them.'

'Just as well for the present. She'll find it difficult to credit her father's deceit or incompetence, whichever it is, and it'll be better if she gets to know of such things gradually.'

'It's not as straightforward as that, Father. We speak in minds.'

The Kiral stopped dead in his tracks so Feldrark collided with him.

'Really? I mean; just suggestions or full comprehension?'

'Just as you and I are talking now.'

'You understand the significance of this, of course?'

'You must've noted her eyes. Why do you think I took such trouble to secure her?'

'Of course. I'd assumed it was mere coincidence. Do you love her?'

'I could do no other, knowing what exists between us. But, yes, I love her, Father. I love her physically, which is very easy, as you've seen. I love her spiritually, and I love her as a fellow mind-talker. She's neither pure nor unblemished, not even very nice at times, but she's an extraordinary young woman and I'm proud to have her as mine.'

'That's just as well, in the circumstances. It puts an entirely new light on the whole business, though. She'll have to be told, of course.'

'I know. But preferably not until that fanatic Aglydron and his friend Okkyntalah are out of the city. By the way, I need to find a way to persuade that young lyre player, Linlyss, to serve us by volunteering to be their replacement for Jodisa. Any thoughts?'

'From what your mother tells me, I suspect it won't be difficult. What's likely to be more of a problem is getting Aglydron to accept her and his continuing role.'

'I've already made a start on that, with Jodisa's quite coincidental help. I've a scheme that should help us, involving Pharah-Li. I think I can pull it off.'

'Risky. She's unreliable and contrary as they come.'

'Precisely why I selected her, Father. Ah, the dreaded Riser.'

Having ascended a long zigzagging flight of stairs, illuminated only by reflected sunlight, they stopped before an oblong opening. The edge of the chute and the Red Rill, running swiftly down its smooth, angled face appeared through the gap. No more than a very short stone corridor with sides, roof and floor slightly taller and wider than a doorway, its length was just three paces.

'This is the bit I hate most.'

Feldrark nodded. 'I find the initial descent worse.'

They plunged into the small space and stopped with their backs against the left hand wall. At once, the small open-sided room began to slide down the mountainside in line with the Red Rill. It gathered speed at first but when they'd dropped six or seven manheights, it slowed to a smooth halt. They were now almost back at the foot of the steep channel, though neither of them took the trouble to look. The wall of the passage down which the chamber had dropped, closed the open side through which they had entered. The chamber halted briefly before it began to rise again, accelerating until it reached a steady speed, exceeding the pace of a fast runner.

Feldrark and the Kiral kept their eyes on the floor, neither willing to watch the Red Rill flashing past them.

'Best warn Patradko Kaz to keep the boy and girl apart. In fact, we'd better do that as soon as we're out of this vile contraption. The pair seem eager as conies to mate.'

'True, Father. That lad's got an appetite for joining that puts even me to shame. And she's as hot for him as any wench I've come across.'

'An unfortunate metaphor, Feldrark. But, seriously, I wonder if it's such a good idea to use her as the substitute, under the circumstances?'

'She's ideal, because of her desire and because she wants adventure. I overheard Okkyntalah telling her she'd get plenty of that with them. He's certainly not going to put up a fight against her. It's only Aglydron we've got to persuade. Pharah-Li will convince him our choice is for the best.'

'Wish I had your confidence.'

'Not a serious issue ultimately, Father. I'm really only concerned for Jodisa's sake. I've a soft spot for Okkyntalah; in fact I owe my life to the lad but there are more important issues here than personal considerations. If we don't succeed with Aglydron, we'll have to send them off by themselves on their quest to find their own High Priest, though I admit I'd really rather not do that. If they'll take Linlyss, or some other willing virgin or even virgins, both sexes, from the city, we'll give them a reliable guide. There's a good chance those persistent hunters from Mipahnhil will eventually track them down. With a guide, they should be able to either evade the scum or deal with them the way we did with the first lot.'

The Kiral gazed at his son with a mixture of respect and resignation. 'You've come a long way in the last year, Feldrark. I said farewell to an innocent, principled dreamer and I greeted an experienced, pragmatic statesman on your return. You'll do a creditable job when you succeed me, as long as you never lose sight of humility and compassion. And, I have to say, I'd rather not have that hypocrite, Dagla Kaz here in the city if we can avoid it.'

Feldrark wondered should he tell his father of his intervention on that issue. Too late now. He could only hope some obstacle had prevented Ivdulon's contact with Tumalind.

The chamber approached the top of the chute and slowed to a halt. An inner opening appeared as it came to rest and the two men left the chamber quickly, with relief. The Kiral thrust his palm against a small square of stone, sticking out of the wall next to the exit, and pressed it flush. The Riser, locked into position, remained available for their descent.

They climbed another zigzagged set of steps and emerged on the flat plain that sliced into the face of the mountain. The Kiral immediately set off along a narrow footway, leading to a rock ledge that overhung the city. Bulbous beneath the protruding end, this flat-topped spur held a round tower with a domed roof.

'It's a long time since I stood here. Permit me a moment?'

The Kiral nodded. 'I'll wait with Ivdulon in her observation tower and get her to send a message about Linlyss, bearing in mind my unknown listener. From what you've said about the hunter lad, he'll be frowking her at the first chance. Don't stay too long in contemplation, Feldrark. The wedding feast can't begin without the bridegroom.'

Feldrark nodded absently, lost in the scene before him. The city and land spread in spectacular glory below him; meadows, orchards and fields of the hinterland rippling away like a gigantic patchwork bedcover. Northwest, the low headland pushed its round nose into the calm Sea of Llahkan. Over that sea, where the sun would soon set, a dark line showed on the far horizon, over thirty leagues to the foothills of the mountain ridge that divided Kabalyt from Balagaaq. He'd intended to send Malarhah back home there, if she'd lived and had wished it. He allowed himself a moment's grief at the loss of a constant, loving and loyal companion.

Turning, he fancied he could see the break in the horizon to the far south that marked the narrow straight where the Sea of Llahkan met the Shylnah Sea. He shuddered at the memory of Mipahnhil. Had the hunters from that foul place learned their lesson or would they return to haunt him? Perhaps Chislanda never made it back home; they'd given her little enough aid. He shrugged with indifference he didn't truly feel, in an attempt to put away the thought.

A further turn and he looked out over the eastern fringe of the Greenreald, the remainder hidden by the man-made plateau in front of him. He took the few steps toward the central lake and marvelled again at the workmanship, forethought, and sheer energy that had gone into constructing it. Over five hundred paces from shore to shore in a perfect circle, the lake stood still and glassy in the windless air. Deep: the lake had a bottom, despite rumours and tales of the city folk. But it had never been sounded. It was certainly deeper than the three hundred manheights that separated the flat ledge from the lower platform holding the Palace. He knew this because just once, during a period of intense drought many tens of cycles ago, the level of the lake had dropped until the water no longer ran through the city.

The chute that bore and fed the Red Rill, miraculously engineered with multiple locks and dams, allowed the level of the lake behind to drop, opening successive gates to permit the stream to continue to flow. The stream thus always ran at the same rate. But this one year it had failed, as the level of water in the lake dropped to that of the Palace grounds. Still the bottom of the lake hadn't been visible and no one had dared descend the sheer sides to test the depth of the remaining water. But they had discovered, then, what coloured the water. The sheer cylinder, cut through the white crystalline stone that formed the city, bore a patch of dull red mineral, about the size and shape of three men standing one on top of the other and leaning at a crazy angle. Just above the lowered surface, pitted and rough where the water had slowly dissolved parts of it, it scarred the perfection.

Now, so soon after the rains, the lake was full to the brim, constantly topped up by snow melt from the heights above, where the peak, permanently coated with snow and ice, stood hidden by cloud. The overflow from the rains drained through an occasional stream that followed the outer wall and rejoined the Red Rill somewhere beneath the palace platform, augmenting the flow until the level of the lake settled.

The water flowed through the city, cleansing it of waste and watering gardens and greens on its way. The fall provided power to the Riser and to draw drinking water up as high as the palace from the artificial lake, The Fresh, in the lower city. No one had yet discovered the mechanism that worked this miracle. But, in the year of the drought, when the Red Rill stopped, so the water cisterns feeding the Palace had emptied and the Riser had stopped working, leaving the Court Astronomer to die of starvation. The Fresh hadn't been exhausted even in that year; its crystal clear water rising from an inexhaustible spring in the bottom of the artificial lake.

Feldrark shook his head at puzzles that had often exercised his thoughts. They were not burning issues; unlike the topic that had brought him to the mountaintop on his wedding day. He followed the wide, flat path alongside the channel feeding the Red Rill and round the edge of the lake and out to the observation tower, perched so precariously over the city.

'Feldrark, my boy! Good to see you back. And has your pretty wench proved warm in bed and cool in the kitchen?'

They had long since given up trying to make Ivdulon conform to normal protocol. Feldrark, having known her since his childhood, having in fact been taught a great deal by this woman who knew so much, was used to her total lack of ceremony.

'I've returned with the Staff intact, the most beautiful and willing young woman a man could want and a handful of tall tales to tell by the fireside in your cool domain. Why you stay up here where it's always chill, I'll never know, Ivdulon.'

'It's my element. The air is clear. There are no sounds but the calls of seemeeuws on the lake and ravens in the northern crags. I can think up here. A woman can't form ideas amid all the chaos and noise down there. Order. That's what I need to use my brain. Order. It'd do you no harm to spend some time up here, young man. A little more probing with your mind and a little less poking with your prod. That's what you need.'

'If you think I'd swap a moment with Jodisa for a week with you, Ivdulon, you're a dreamer.'

'Jodisa-Li; daughter of the high priest of Muhnilahm. It explains a few things.'

'What do you know, Ivdulon?'

'More than you suspect and less than I would. So, has reason overcome tradition and superstition at last down amongst the herd?'

'You've been up here too long, Ivdulon. The citizens have long accepted the time's ripe for reconciliation. We've been quietly working away for the last few years, especially since I suggested to Father I should include Muhnilahm on my list of places to seek a wife. We can't go on forever warring with a people we haven't met in fourteen hundred years or more. I'd set our people thinking, long before I left. Of course, there's still prejudice in some areas but it's general and diffuse. Thanks to you and those who preceded you, Ivdulon, our very philosophy tends away from fanaticism and extremism.'

'You've grown, Feldrark. The year away has developed your mind more than I ever could.'

'A full cycle of idleness with nothing to do but frowk every woman who came begging me to father a child. After a while, the novelty wears off and the mind and soul seek other diversions. Your reasoning and Father's statesmanship, combined with Mother's compassion and creativity, all moulded together whilst I was held captive. I'd done the groundwork before I left and the people were so pleased to have me return with the Staff and a beautiful bride, they were in the mood to overlook her origins. Jodisa doesn't quite know it yet, but the final and real breakdown of prejudice is entirely her doing. Her beauty, grace, compassion and carriage have won their hearts. They love her as one of their own already.'

'This lady I must meet.'

'Come down with us. The wedding feast's tonight.'

'And get drunk and have some hot-prod stuck into me for his own gratification? Not me. Bring your beauty up to see me when you're tired of frowking her.'

The Kiral laughed. 'I thought you wanted to meet her?'

Ivdulon shook her head in despair. 'Never seen the attraction in all that grunting and thrusting, myself. Where's the satisfaction? An instant of physical release gone in the blink of an eye. No. You'll get bored soon enough. Bring this paragon to me and let me see whether her other delights can change my mind.'

'I might let you into her mind, once we're through the first flush of our passion.'

'Does she have control and reach, yet?'

The Kiral shook his head. 'You amaze me, Ivdulon. What else do you know that you haven't told me?'

'It's clear someone's listening to your mindtalk, Sire. I've to be careful of what I release to you. I'm unsure yet of the identity of the intruder. But, as for the girl, I've suspected she could mindtalk ever since her brother told me about her eyes and an incident that otherwise defied explanation. Of course, he wanted to try her at once but I managed to dissuade him. She's made a couple of involuntary contacts with him; once when she was drowning and again when she'd been reclaimed from a near fatal blow to the head.

'Feldrark won't recall Sha'ra; she's very careful who she allows to remember her but I was aware of their contact. It was Sha'ra who opened your mind to the possibility of spanning greater distances. It was a while before she recovered from her giving but she's back to normal again now. Though her sortie to help heal Tumalind, being well out of her own realm, has rather taken it out of her. A wonderful mystic, Sha'ra; willing to put herself in danger for us mortals.

'By the way, Feldrark, I made only light contact with that young woman. She was too weak, before Sha'ra's intervention, to stand full contact. But I managed to plant the idea of Litkala in her mind. I imagine she'll try to get Dagla Kaz to come in this direction if she can.'

Both the Kiral and Feldrark stared at the Court Astronomer with confusion and respect. It was the Kiral who spoke, however.

'You've ever been a mystery, Ivdulon. I know nothing of Sha'ra and clearly there's more here than you've told us. But that, despite its fascination, must wait for now. We're here on specific business. Those who travelled with Jodisa claim the Skyfire's on its way. We all know it can't be. When's it really due?'

Ivdulon scratched her head. 'Today's the eighth of the twelfth portion of cycle 1457. Their astronomer's an idiot if he can't see it's not the real thing.'

'Perhaps just not as gifted as you, Ivdulon.'

'Humph! A child of ten cycles with one good eye can tell you it's just a small irregular that'll probably never return. It'll get a bit brighter before it fades but it was never going to be the Skyfire. Don't the fools know their dates? Don't they know what cycle it is? Can't they add up? Still believe the sun spins round the world, no doubt. Fools. The Skyfire's not due until next cycle, when, by the way, we're going to have to warn the populace not to be alarmed, since this visit's likely to be fairly spectacular; maybe even as fiery as the encounter so misused by that charlatan Gadhallah. We all know it signifies nothing but the return of a singular wanderer, but common folk are superstitious of such things.'

'That's my area of concern, Ivdulon, and I'll deal with it as and when necessary. Superstition's a dangerous quality to fool with. When's the real thing actually due?'

'Fifth day of the second portion's the first time I'll see it, Feldrark. Another three or four sixdays before it's visible to the naked eye. I reckon this false flame'll die well before that but by then even the most dim-witted dunderhead will have realized it's not the real thing.'

'Thank you, Ivdulon. You've confirmed our suspicions. Now; coming down with us to get that underused fern filled or are you stopping up here to gaze through your instruments at pretty lights in the sky?'

'Don't you mock my stars, young man. Big as you are, you're not beyond a good belting round the buttocks. Royal blood or no royal blood, I'll…'

'Don't bust your bosom, Ivdulon. The lad's only tugging your toe. Come on, Feldrark, the old greycurl's obviously planning to have a surprisingly good time with some particularly seductive numbers.'

'And you! Don't think your title will stop a strap striping your royal bum!'

Feldrark and the Kiral each gave a mock bow to the Court Astronomer and backed out of the lower chamber of the tower, hands held protectively over their posteriors.

'No respect. I get no respect.'

Father and son laughed and returned to the Riser to make their descent to the Palace in time for the celebrations.

Chapter 50

JOY AND DISQUIET

*F*eldrark and the Kiral greeted Patradko Kaz as he entered the antechamber with Linlyss, fearful and subdued, in tow.

'Don't be anxious, my child. I'm sorry to keep you from your friends but you'll understand in a little. You're far from being in trouble, I promise.'

She bowed her head at the Kiral but said nothing.

'First, I wish to thank you for your contribution to the joining today. Your playing was exquisite and lent the ceremony a touch of magic and an air of grace that we all appreciate. I wish to reward you.'

His father nodded to Patradko Kaz who handed her a small drawstring bag made of kidskin, beaded in red, yellow and blue, containing a quantity of gold coin.

'My reward is your appreciation, Sire. That and the opportunity to play before an audience of taste and sophistication.'

They regarded her quizzically. 'They said your speech was coarse and uneducated....'

She dared a smile, which, as they were all eager to encourage it, quickly turned into an impish grin. 'Sire, like all who play or sing, I have a way with words and style of voice. I can be a lady or, if it mecks yah larf, I cun be as cawarse as yah laikes, matey.'

The Kiral and Feldrark laughed delightedly. Patradko Kaz gave a thin smile.

'Nevertheless, young lady, we'd be honoured if you'd accept this token of our appreciation.'

She tossed the purse in her hands. 'If I can earn this with a wooden instrument, what might I earn from those foreign sailors with the one between my legs?'

The High Priest looked outraged but, though Feldrark and his father tried to look stern, both failed hopelessly under the influence of her mischievous grin.

'We have to be serious, now, Linlyss.'

To their surprise, she nodded and became alert and attentive.

'What you've just suggested is the last thing we want. You're still virgin, aren't you?'

"Fraid so, Sire. Only just found a man as I'd like to do the honours, see?'

'We know. Can you keep a secret?'

'As well as any man, better'n most women.'

'We have a task for you. Difficult; perhaps even dangerous. You may never return to the city and might live the rest of your life in a foreign land.'

Feldrark thought his father was a little too honest at this stage but it seemed to be the right way to treat the girl.

'What you want me to do; it's important, like?'

'Vital. I can't explain it in full detail tonight, but I'll tell you all you need to know in the morning. At least until we speak again, however, it's absolutely essential that you remain virgin. Can you manage that?'

She considered. 'Won't be easy with Okkyntalah close by. He's as hot for me as I am for him.'

'We know. In one sense, that's why we've chosen you for the job. But, for now, can you make that promise?'

'I can, but I can't vouch for Okkyntalah. What if he takes it into his head I'm just teasin' when I refuse him? He knows I'm eager; I told him so this afternoon. He might not take no for an answer. Then what do I do?'

'Leave the young man to us. We have ways to distract him. And, to make it easier, you'll remain as part of the musical entertainment for the evening. I'm sure you'd love to accompany the Tryhhnarmahl, wouldn't you?'

'Who'll be dancin' it, Sire?'

'You've seen it before, of course?'

'Few times. There's a plain stick of a lass makes a stab at it at the Inn once in a while. I'm usually too deep in mucky pans an' that to watch but I've sneaked a look once and there was another time the lyre player was in his cups and the landlord made me play instead.'

'So you've never seen a performance by an adept?'

'Onny those at the Inn, Sire.'

'What did you think?'

'It's a pretty tale, and sad. But the bit at the end…that's just wonderful, that is.'

'Can you follow the mood of a dancer?'

'Happen I can. It's a question of watchin' an' matchin', that's all, I reckon.'

'Good. Do a good job and there'll be more of that for you.'

'I'd do it just for the honour, Sire. For you an' the Kirallah an' your beautiful lady, Feldrark, Paltrohn.'

'Look on the money as a bonus, then.'

The Kiral nodded at the High Priest.

'Thank you, Sire. I feel mighty honoured.'

Patradko Kaz led her from the private chamber.

Jodisa felt refreshed after her lazy swim in the great Palace pool. Stone ledges below the surface of the water all round the oval gave support. She'd lain for a while and then sat on a lower shelf with just her head above water. Servants had passed her sharp wine and spiced savouries as she relaxed, alone in the wide body of water.

When she left the pool, a girl barely a year her junior, had gently towelled her dry before urging her to a low table covered with cushions and soft cloth.

'You'll appreciate the effects of a massage to take away the tiredness of the tour, I think, Paltra.'

A tall, gaunt man with a hide dark as ebony, caressed her with scented oil, warmed in his huge hands, and massaged her entire body without a word. His hands performed such magic on her muscles and joints that she left the table feeling fresh, alive and full of vitality. The girl wiped her skin free of excess oil, as the man left. Bald and hairless, clad in a small leather apron, he seemed an unlikely figure for the duty and Jodisa wondered how a man was allowed to work as he did.

'No parts, Paltra.' The girl neither lowered her voice nor giggled and the man gave no sign he was concerned. Jodisa, accustomed to ribaldry or shyness around such things, tried not to show her surprise. She'd question Feldrark later.

'But what hands!'

'They call him the Spiritman and he's much in demand. I hope you don't think me forward, Paltra: the Wharhll himself asked him to work his magic.'

The girl wrapped a soft towel around her, leaving her exposed from the navel, and indicated she should follow her. Jodisa shrugged and walked through the open side of the pool area into a patch of light from the setting sun, past banks of cultivated flowers, and onto a wide terrace at the side of the Palace. A small group of women, including Rrildyss Kaz, gazed as the sun sank into the sea. Following the High Priestess, without a word, they slipped out of their tunics, allowing them to fall at their feet. They faced the dazzling orb, palms on the backs of their heads and feet a little apart.

Jodisa tugged the towel free and took up her normal prayer position. With reason to thank Ytraa, she took longer than normal to commune with her God. Finished, she discovered the other women as when she'd begun but with eyes open, waiting. Aware how easily she could make a bad impression, she said nothing, merely nodding as she rose to her feet and signalled the serving girl who was in the same attitude as the others. The girl approached.

'Have I something to wear?'

The girl nodded and walked off, giving no indication whether she should follow. Rrildyss Kaz, evidently feeling sympathy for the new woman in their presence, gathered her companions to surround Jodisa to protect her from unlikely stares.

The girl reappeared, carrying a clean white tunic, and helped Jodisa to dress. Rrildyss Kaz waited until all were clothed before she covered herself. Scandalous in its brevity and design, the tunic the girl brought bore tailored slashes front and back, edged with fine myllth thread, leaving little to the imagination. Belted with a waistrope of pure myllth thread plaited into a fine cord, the tunic fell so that the hem barely covered her.

'This can't be right. Raise my arms and I'll be on show to all and sundry.'

'The Wharhll was most definite, Paltra. He gave it me himself.'

Rrildyss Kaz smiled. 'Seems, for this night, you remain an item of curiosity and pride. As the herdsman shows his best breeding bull to all, demonstrating his ownership of such a fine beast, you're displayed to show how well the Wharhll has done in catching a beautiful bride. And you are beautiful, Jodisa, very.'

'And the Wharhll? Is he to be similarly on show, as my prize?'

'That's a matter for you, Jodisa. He has a sense of fairness that I'm sure would respond to such a suggestion. Certainly, I and the other ladies would raise no objections.'

'What about the law that defines naked as sacred?'

'Well, you're not really naked, are you? In any case, as I'm sure the Wharhll has made known to you, here in Litkala we're less concerned about such strict adherence to ancient customs from a time before the full truth was known.'

'You tread dangerously close to sacrilege, Rrildyss Kaz. Are your views those of the majority?'

'Patradko Kaz, the Wharhll and I are as one on the matter, with a few minor quibbles. But, surely, he's discussed this with you? He certainly led me to believe there would be no difficulty with you over such issues when we talked last night…'

Jodisa frowned at the High Priestess. 'Last night Feldrark was with me. He never left my side and we slept but little, being together for the first time. How could he talk with you?'

Rrildyss Kaz inclined her head in a soft bow and gently persuaded her along the terrace, out of earshot of the other women. The serving girl followed, carrying the bangle and a heavy collar made of many fine myllth bars studded with scores of precious gems, to mimic the rays of the setting sun.

'I'll finish dressing the Wharhll's bride. You may go about your other duties.'

The girl, though clearly in awe of the High Priestess, looked to Jodisa-Li for her agreement. Jodisa nodded and gave her a quick smile of reassurance.

Rrildyss fastened the bangle about her ankle and then stood behind her and draped the heavy collar around her neck where it lay around her throat and across the firm rise of her breasts where the wide V of the tunic's opening exposed them. *'Can you hear me?'*

'So, you speak in minds. I suspected as much, but Feldrark made it clear I must take care with the skill and who I reveal it to.'

'I'll have to have words with him, leaving you unprepared. I don't know what he was thinking of, not to inform you, my dear, there's much for you to learn. Still, I expect he's had other matters on his mind.'

Jodisa detected the humour in her thoughts. 'You speak informally in minds?'

'We all do.'

'All?'

'There are a few of us, Jodisa. Mindtalk makes each of us a part of the others and each of the others a part of ourselves. You're a member of a select few, now, and need to learn the ways and customs that govern us. But now isn't the time or place; the other women are puzzled by our silence. You'll have to speak to Feldrark about that. Now, shall we go in and find him and see whether he needs persuading to change into something as daring?'

'Please lead on, Rrildyss Kaz, I look forward to his reaction to my request. Do you think I could mindtalk to him without being close?'

'Some can span great distances. It takes practice. Why not try?'

'Feldrark?'

The two of them sauntered from the terrace into the relative darkness of the Palace. The other women followed at a discreet distance. Servants were lighting lamps, candles and torches so that shadows filled some corners and flames reflected from glossy surfaces of polished stone. Rrildyss Kaz took her along wide corridors and down two broad flights of shallow steps to the Great Hall at the very heart of the Palace.

'Feldrark, can you hear me?'

'Jodisa! Not in trouble, are you, my love?'

'No. But you are! What are you wearing?'

'Ah. I know it's not very dignified but it's been the custom for...'

'Dignity isn't the issue, Feldrark. I'm happy naked. I've a good body and don't mind displaying it. But I'm yours now and I assumed you'd wish to have me to yourself, aside from the insult to Ytraa, of course.'

'Only for tonight, my love. And, of course, I'll wear something equally revealing. I'm in my dressing room now. Where are you?'

She told him.

'Return the way you came, up the first flight of stairs, turn right into the corridor and then right again. I'll be waiting, so make sure you're alone.'

'I'm going to Feldrark. Make my excuses, will you Rrildyss?'

'Phenomenal! You've learned to switch so quickly and to reach so soon. You may turn out to be a Gifted. Go, have your pleasure, but don't forget we can't start ours without you!'

'I'll be back as soon as circumstances permit.'

'Or as late as they require.'

They exchanged smiles and Jodisa turned and walked purposefully up the stairs. She heard Rrildyss Kaz call the gathered folk to silence.

'Sorry; there will be a short delay as the happy couple examine certain possibilities in private. I'm assured they'll be absent only as long as is necessary to come mutually to a conclusion.'

Jodisa giggled as she heard the general laughter of approval echoing along the corridor behind her. One man's voice was ribald as he observed. 'If this afternoon's any guide, "short" isn't the operative word, Rrildyss Kaz.'

Further laughter from this followed her into the room but was silenced by the closing door as she saw Feldrark, waiting for her.

Time ceased to have meaning but eventually she returned to the here and now. Still smiling, both from what she'd shared with Feldrark and at his teasing her over the clothes he'd first offered as a joke. Dressed now in the outfit he had really intended for the evening, she felt proud, confident and resplendent.

Her white silk tunic dropped from its fine shoulder ties to her knee at the left, to mid-thigh at right. A single piece garment, which Feldrark had slipped over her head, the front bore an embroidered design echoing her floral tattoos. Although her skin was just perceptible beneath the sheer fabric, the design covered her so she felt neither displayed nor exposed, but enhanced by the garment. On the seat, a dragon curled in sleep, its tail snaking to the hem in elaborate coils and its head resting in the small of her back where the fabric ended. Another dragon breathed fire over her front. The colours and style matched her tattoo precisely and she wondered at the skill of the work completed over such a short period. Sleeveless, and with a deep curving neckline, the gown was trimmed with finely stitched myllth thread in interwoven curving bands.

The heavy neckpiece almost filled the space exposed, allowing a glimpse of her cleavage. Filigree bangles adorned her ankles, beneath the bracelet of state, triangles of bejewelled gold gauze resting on the bare skin of her feet. A plaited band of gold and silver tied her hair in a loose fold at the back of her head to display the rest of her floral tattoo. On the second finger of her right hand she wore a band of polished myllth set with a finely cut ruby. A delicate waistrope of plaited blonde hair coiled with myllth circled her waist, emphasizing its slenderness and the womanly shape of her hips.

She studied Feldrark in his wrap of deep red silk that lay against his thighs. The material, sheer as her dress, crossed at the front in a double thickness to veil his manhood. The front was edged with coiled myllth thread and a small emblem of silver over his left hip depicted the Tree of Life. Open at his chest, it was belted with a broad strip of polished hide, buckled with myllth and studded with a dozen emeralds and rubies. The seat of his robe bore two fighting bears in exquisite embroidery. Around his neck, on a fine chain of myllth, hung a large tear of jet, enlivened with a single bright ruby. His feet were bare, but for the bangle of state, and the second finger of his right hand bore a ring matching Jodisa's. She looked at him with love and pride and knew she wanted to be with this man forever.

As they made their way to the assembly, she ran through the words he'd taught her, hoping she would remember them.

'I'll try to avoid mindtalk tonight, my love, unless I see you in need of guidance. We make a formal greeting to Mother and Father and then the fun can begin for all.'

She let him lead her across the wide open space of a floor of polished white stone inlaid with a delicate and intricate mosaic of flowers, trees, wild animals, men and women, gods and goddesses in a pageant depicting a feast with food, wine and dancing. The workmanship was exquisite and she wondered how long it had decorated this floor.

Feldrark followed her gaze across the space. 'It was here when my ancestors arrived. If nothing else, it shows that the builders of this wonderful place were human, even if they were all extraordinarily beautiful.'

'And not in the least modest.'

'Who'd want to hide such beauty?'

The hall grew quiet at a signal from Rrildyss Kaz.

'*Please stand beside me as we greet the Kiral and Kirallah.*'

He addressed the assembly. 'Most worthy servants, noble people, mighty Kiral, compassionate Kirallah, High Priests of the realm of Litkala, you have honoured Jodisa and me with your acceptance of our marriage. Now we are wed and joined before Ytraa and the people, we stand before you to make our pledge of loyalty. *Speak the words with me, Jodisa.* We do solemnly swear before Ytraa and all those people present, to serve the realm of Litkala with honour truth and duty for all the days of our lives until we breathe no more. We declare our love for you, our Kiral and Kirallah, our devotion to our people and our loyalty to the realm for this day and all the days that follow.'

Their voices echoed softly from the walls until they faded into silence.

'*Well remembered and delivered, my love.*'

'We welcome your love. We accept your service. We acknowledge your loyalty to us and to our people. Know that you are one and are blessed and loved by us and by all this realm.' The voices of the Kiral and Kirallah whispered from the walls and fell to silence.

No one moved. No one made a sound. Through the windows and open arches, the sea could be heard washing the distant beach and, below, the murmur of the crowds awaiting the announcement to allow them to indulge in a night of utter frivolity.

Rrildyss Kaz stepped to the outer wall of the hall so she could look out over the city. She turned and accepted a flaming torch from a serving boy and girl, so that she held a brand in each hand as she stepped to the edge of the balcony. 'Let the rejoicing begin!'

A great cheer came up and was followed by distant sounds of people in song, music filtering from below. She returned the torches to the servants and came back into the hall.

In the centre of the vast space, she raised her hands above her head and clapped three times, the sharp smacks slapping the walls and tapping away. Young men and women entered, carrying trays of food and wine. Clad in skirts of multi-coloured silk strips, varying in length from a handbreadth to an armslength, and attached to a fine band around their waists, they swayed in rhythm to music from the group playing in one corner. Beneath the open skirt, a plain white band of white circled hips with a black fabric strip hiding private parts. The girls' breasts snuggled under plain white bands of silk. All walked proudly and with ready smiles as they set their burdens on the tables and waited for guests to summon them to serve.

Rrildyss Kaz waited for movement to cease and raised her hands again. 'Let the feasting begin. Let the dancing commence. Let the music play. Let the contest start.'

At once, the guests moved to settles and cushioned benches distributed around the walls, leaving the central space available for groups to congregate or for those who wished to dance.

Jodisa and Feldrark sat with the Kiral and Kirallah accompanied by Aglydron, Myllthlan, Okkyntalah and the girl who'd partnered him in the ceremony.

'Try not to mention Linlyss, my love. I'll explain later on. She's with the musicians and happy to be so.'

Jodisa inclined her head in acknowledgement.

'Linlyss is engaged for the evening, so I've persuaded this divine creature to be my partner. This is Stellanyl.' Okkyntalah introduced her to his friends and only Aglydron looked askance at him.

Serving boys and girls, between fourteen and sixteen cycles, approached to ask what delights they wished to try and then rushed off to collect food and drink almost as if their lives depended on returning before the others. The boy who arrived first, with a goblet of pale golden wine and a platter of mixed savoury delicacies for the Kirallah, was rewarded by her tearing the longest strip from his skirt. He bowed and enthusiastically sought his next opportunity to serve.

'What goes on, Feldrark?'

'The one who loses all the strips first, wins. The prize is much sought after.'

'And it is?'

'For a boy, to become my personal attendant. A girl, to become yours.'

'Why can't there be one of each?'

'An excellent innovation! Mother, Father, Jodisa suggests we have two winners, one of each sex. What do you think?'

'The simplest ideas are always the best.' The Kirallah signalled Rrildyss Kaz and passed on the message.

Within moments, everyone in the hall knew of the new rule and the boys and girls adapted their behaviour accordingly, competing by gender instead of against all others.

'Won't they cheat?'

'Would they cheat on Muhnilahm, Aglydron?'

'Some would.'

'Our system of education and fairness discourages such behaviour.'

'Doesn't your free attitude to nakedness make people more likely to take advantage of each other?'

Feldrark thought for a moment. 'There hasn't been a rape or even an assault in Litkala in living memory. Can you boast the same for your population, a third the size of ours?

Aglydron shook his head. 'I can't. But we follow the rules of Ytraa.'

'No. You follow your rules of Ytraa, Aglydron. The differences between us stem, as you know, from the Great Division. It's my belief that it's well past time to heal that divide.'

'Great Division? Never heard of it. What is it?'

'My people don't know of it, Feldrark. Only the Holy Ones and the High Priest are aware of what happened.' Jodisa tried to keep concern from her voice as she relayed this to her lover and husband.

'I see you have something to learn, Aglydron. I'll gladly teach. But not now. Tonight's for celebration, fun, enjoyment. Let's celebrate. The morrow will be time enough to learn what split Follower from Follower.'

<hr/>

'Wake up, Tumalind. Wake up.'

She opened eyes on Corphanda with the dull grey of a thatched roof above her. The sunlight streamed through a window and she knew she lay uncovered on a bed.

'It's all right, Tumalind. There's no one else here. How do you feel?'

She tested her fingers and discovered cloth beneath them. Her feet moved when she willed it. She moved and her body let her rise to a sitting position. 'I…feel…I feel all right, I think. I'm hungry!'

Corphanda helped her into her tabard. 'She's well again. Wants to eat.'

Four of the party came in at once; Dilanthas hugged her, tears in her eyes. Dagla Kaz examined her and held her hand, his mask of anxiety washing away with relief. Tarruss nodded at her from the doorway and then removed his bulk to let Caarl in. The rest of them came in one by one and expressed their relief at her recovery.

'Had us worried, you did. I thought I'd lost my inquisitor. I'm delighted you're back with us.' Jhonaht was the only man who bent and kissed her and, though the kiss seemed more than simple friendship, she believed it was right that he should. He looked on her with different eyes and saw her not as a woman to join with but as someone whose curiosity acted in some ways like his own.

Tryonta appeared at the doorway and she recalled a disturbing memory. 'I dreamed that Try…someone was about to invade me and I could do nothing to…'

'It's all right, Tumalind. Tryonta explained he arrived just after you called him. I was here straight after. You'd been dreaming and we soothed you back to sleep again. I've sat with you ever since, in case you had another nightmare.' Corphanda's reassurance was edged with a glance that hinted at her distrust of Tryonta.

Tumalind was sure nothing had happened to her, in view of Corphanda's statement, and that nothing would as long as she was around.

They ate after the greetings and congratulations. Phildrad served her food and she took his hand and kissed his cheek.

'Thank you, Phildrad. I believe you saved my life.'

'Well worth the saving. World'd be a poorer place wi'out you in it, Tumalind.'

'Thank you again. Are you fully recovered?'

'Fully. Which is more'n can be said o' the snake. It's fitting you eat as much as you do on this occasion.'

'Why's that? What special properties have you bestowed on this particular meal, Phildrad?'

'You're munching the beast that tried to put an end to you.'

'Well, it's very good to eat.'

'Better to eat than be eaten by, I think!'

They laughed, but from the corner of her eye, Tumalind was aware of Tryonta watching her with even more carnality than she'd seen previously. She knew he'd been about to rape her and that only Corphanda's timely arrival had stopped him. But now he had the idea in his head, would she ever be safe with him again?

Chapter 51

A PROMISE MADE, A PROMISE KEPT

Aglydron lay awake: heat, the eroticism that closed the Tryhhnarmahl, and his lack of a partner, preventing sleep. The dance-induced desire thrust images of Chislanda into his mind and he dwelt on the beauty and generosity of this woman who'd given herself so completely in pursuit of a child. How could she now be so determined to kill him? And why did she come to mind, why did her absence make his heart heavy, when he rarely even thought of Shoarhn?

He wondered also at Myllthlan's disappearance from the hall after the celebrations. Knowing her devotion to him, he could think of nothing that would separate her from him voluntarily. And why had Okkyntalah been denied the company of Linlyss? He'd no liking for the coarse girl, though her playing had impressed him; she had a real talent for music and he couldn't deny her ability to draw out the emotions of her listeners. The applause had been loud, long and fully deserved. But why had she simply vanished from the feast without even approaching Okkyntalah?

He couldn't rest from these thoughts. At the window, he pulled back the heavy drapes and pushed open the wooden frame with its sheet of glass. It fascinated him. He'd seen glass as ornament and in use for small containers in the city. But to see it used to keep wind and sound from entering the room, shutting out the unwanted whilst allowing in the scene from outside, was amazing. The serving girl who'd guided him to his room had promised to show him where and how it was made. Dark and quiet beyond the window, it was long past the middle hour.

The air outside felt no cooler and there was the heaviness of a coming storm. Close by, the constant whispering of the falling Red Rill irritated more than relieved him. From the opposite direction, came the distant sound of waves. And, somewhere in the lower city, made small by distance but still clear, the raucous singing of drunk and happy revellers returning home, was interrupted by a moment's silence, then outraged male laughter and a woman's laugh of delight. The images conjured did nothing to dampen the want aroused by that supremely danced final movement. And here, in this permissive city, he was alone.

A soft sigh came from where the door lay in the darkness behind him. Perhaps it had been opened and then closed again. Certainly, the air moved and softly stroked his skin. He turned, but the darkness in the room was absolute. He listened, waiting, convinced someone had entered.

'I see you are awake, Aglydron of Muhnilahm. But are you alone?'

Her voice was young and soft with promise but he formed no picture of its owner.

'I am; who wants to know?'

'May I let your fingers, lips and tongue inform you?'

'I'm by the window.'

'The night sky silhouettes your masculine shape, but I want the softness of your bed.'

He heard her lie on the coverings and sigh with desire.

'Is there a lamp so we can see as we share pleasure?'

'See with your fingers, tongue and lips.'

He moved across the cool stone floor and felt her hand on his wrist and hip as she led his to her warm body.

With the first glow of morning paling the oblong of the window, she left, a mystery still. She'd shown him more in darkness than he'd ever learned in the light with any other woman. But, before he could share the slumber of satiation with her, before light displayed her visual delights, she retreated to the solid darkness by the door, a vague hint of loveliness seen only in silhouette passing the dim window.

'We may join again, Aglydron of Muhnilahm, but I wasn't supposed to be here this night. The scheme dictates that you stew in want until the end of the coming day. Tell them nothing of my visit. But remember, when they mention your reward for agreement, I'm part of it. Not in dark and secret, but in light. Don't disappoint me. Already I would have you again. But, as was to be the way for you, I now must wait all this long day until we join again in joy.'

'What scheme?'

'I know only what I've told you because I heard things I shouldn't.'

The door opened and closed and she was gone. Even though he hurried to catch a glimpse of her, she'd vanished into shadows and he looked out on hard stone and empty walls.

◆ ══╼◦╾══ ◈

Okkyntalah was alone when Aglydron appeared in the dining room for breakfast. Myllthlan remained absent. The serving boys and girls, once more in blue and gold, fed and tended them.

The lad who'd won the evening contest entered, still full of pride and wonder at his luck. 'Paltrohns, my master would meet with you, after the midday meal, in his chambers. Until then he bids you explore as you will.'

He was gone as suddenly as he had appeared. The servant who'd shown

Aglydron and Okkyntalah to their separate rooms came in and Aglydron nodded at her.

'We've to be in the Wharhll's chambers after noon. Will we have time to see the glass being made?'

'We will, Paltrohn, if we set out at once.'

'Call me Aglydron; I'm not used to titles. I'm just a farmer.'

'And I'm a hunter. Call me Okkyntalah. What's your name?'

'Horsylth.' A lithe girl with small breasts and long thin legs, fair-haired with hazel eyes set in a plain face enlivened by her ready smile.

The three descended to the lower city on a riser and passed through the inner gate, where an armed guard issued Okkyntalah and Aglydron with metal tokens on chains to place about their necks.

'You'll not get back inside without, so don't lose them.'

They followed the girl through the long arch under the inner wall, into the lower city. Above, the sky was building cloud for a storm. Aglydron was buoyant and seemed full of energy.

Okkyntalah was sure he knew the reason. 'Good as that, eh?'

Aglydron looked quizzically at him.

'The woman you shared the night with?'

'Yes. Yes, it shows, then?'

'It shows.'

Aglydron didn't sulk, shout or remonstrate with him but smiled at his confusion and, taking Horsylth's hand, indicated she should lead them to the place where the miraculous glass was made. Okkyntalah shrugged and followed. Let him keep his secrets if he must.

The streets, now he could study them at ease, surprised Okkyntalah with their cleanliness. At home, the roads were of dirt and gave up great blinding clouds of dust as wind and feet disturbed the surface. Here, the white shiny stone stayed smooth and clean as sweepers constantly removed the detritus of the huge population. He watched one with his wooden barrel set between two wheels and his broom made from some sort of reed. The man wet the broom from a small container at the foot of the barrel and deftly stroked rubbish onto a flat shovel. He dropped the waste into the barrel, used a cloth on the end of a stick to dry the area, and moved on to the next patch.

From the gate, they walked beside the inner wall, lined with its tiers of houses, towards the area he'd spotted from their cart. The masts of ships identified the small dock. All around them, people went about their daily business, occasionally noticing the strangers in their midst and saluting them with an open hand held palm outward and sideways over their chins. Okkyntalah watched for Horsylth's response, but she made none.

'Should we make a gesture in reply?'

'The correct response is so.' She curled her hand into a loose fist and touched it, thumb uppermost, under her chin.

'But you don't respond?'

'As a servant of the royal house, plainly marked by my tunic, I'm neither expected nor required to respond, lest my duties for the royal family be interrupted or delayed.'

They had walked as far as the end of the plain where the animals were grazing.

'How are they kept from straying, Horsylth?'

'It's something to do with breeding, I believe.'

'Have you always served the Kiral and Kirallah?'

'I was born in the lower city. Over there, in fact.' She pointed to the houses rising in steps against the inner side of the outer wall. 'My mother deals in animal hides. My father, sisters and brother live in the house above the shop and warehouse. There, the one with the sign of a hide painted in brown, white and black.'

Okkyntalah followed her pointing finger and identified the shop. On the roof above, he could see a couple of small children playing a game, crouching over something on the floor between them.

'You send money home to help the family?'

'I have no money and they need none. We serve the palace for the honour.'

'How long will you serve?'

'Until I'm wed. If my chosen declines, I'll spend my life in the Palace and partner guests as and when required.'

'You seem quite happy to accept that role.'

'I'm honoured and I'll willingly serve, if that's what's meant to be. But I'd rather wed and raise my own family. We may see my chosen in the harbour, if I'm lucky. He's a fisherman, with his own boat!'

They walked now beside the low wall of the inland harbour, where several small boats and a number of larger vessels nestled against the stone wharves. All were far more sophisticated than the boat they'd stolen. Horsylth suddenly leapt on top of the wall and ran a few steps ahead before she remembered herself and waited for them to catch up. Her impatience was clear, however.

'That's his boat. There! Do you see him getting ready to go out to sea?' She waved and a man on one of the smaller boats waved back and shouted across the still water.

Okkyntalah looked up at the glowering clouds and shook his head. 'Is he wise to go out when a storm's gathering?'

Horsylth nodded but continued waving. 'He says the best fish are caught under the rain. He won't go far from the outer harbour. He'll be safe.' She stopped waving, brighter for the sight of her beloved, and led them toward one of the large buildings Okkyntalah had assumed to be warehouses. He noticed, now, the shimmer issuing from the open door, windows and roof.

Intense heat hit them as they approached. The girl stopped and took three pairs of flat wooden boards from a pile, giving them a pair each. She fastened hers to her feet, showing them how to use the leather straps attached, and raising her a thumbslength off the ground. The strange devices were uncomfortable but surprisingly light to wear and Okkyntalah wondered at their purpose. Horsylth took a large metal ladle from a hook, attached to an open water barrel, and soaked herself, liberally, from head to foot. She handed it to Aglydron. When all three were dripping wet, tunics clinging like second skins, she led them, clomping on their wooden shoes, into the building.

Okkyntalah thought he'd entered a nightmare. The heat was almost unbearable and the din, deafening. A small group of men, naked but for thick, wooden-soled leather boots up to their knees and odd cups of leather strapped over their ears, was engaged in a variety of tasks that had no meaning. On a gantry above, lads and lasses walked, constantly sprinkling water on them from buckets, avoiding the flaming pits of white-hot coals. Some men were shovelling what looked like sand mixed with a dark powder into a thin, flat, oblong space carved into the top of a shallow slab of stone. Others used scrapers and flat boards to level the mixture already filling another. And yet others hauled on chains attached to another slab as their colleagues pushed it with long stout poles until it was sitting directly over one of the pits of flames. They left that slab in place and lowered a great metal cowl down over it using chains depending from the ceiling. Then they raised a second cowl from another slab atop a different fire pit and drew it into the body of the vast space, where it was left to rest with others. This last slab shimmered with a sheet of red-hot liquid.

A tall, blond man approached and signalled a lad to follow with a bucket of water to keep them all wet. He made no effort to speak but gestured to them to follow him across the floor to the cooling slabs. As they approached, Okkyntalah realized each had a sheet of clear glass resting in it and the last placed was now cooling so that the red liquid changed even as he watched. He understood, from the man's gestures and the evidence of the process that the sand mixture was now glass for use in glazing windows.

The blond man took them to another part of the huge building. There he showed them a perforated but enclosed container half filled with the molten liquid; a white-hot fire pit beneath. A group of women, clothed in sweat, worked together beside it. One took a long metal rod, dipped it in the liquid and spun it rapidly until a red-hot blob gathered at the end. She handed it to another, who rested the rod on the edge of a heavy wooden bench where she continued to spin it, blowing down what Okkyntalah realized must be a tube and expanding the blob into a large bubble. She returned the piece to the heat from time to time and, using metal tools, produced a wide fine-stemmed goblet, which she detached from the rod and placed with others on a wooden tray. Horsylth, flushed with heat and clearly anxious to leave the building, placed her mouth close to their ears and asked if they'd seen enough. Nodding her thanks to their guide, she led them from the building.

'Amazing!'

Okkyntalah smiled at Aglydron's look of disbelief and then realized he felt just as astonished. Horsylth took them to a small shack just outside the doors and dredged three large tankards of beer from a barrel within, handing one to each of them. To Okkyntalah's delight and surprise, she emptied her own in a few draughts, quenching her thirst in the same way as a farmer fresh from the hot fields at home. He followed suit and watched Aglydron drain his more slowly.

Horsylth belched loudly and gave a little giggle before she led them the short distance from the building to the harbour where, without ceremony, she slipped off her tunic and jumped into the clear water. They followed and delighted in cooling after the oppressive heat of the workshop.

Okkyntalah was surprised at Aglydron's lack of dissent but welcomed this change in him.

They dressed in garments still damp in the humid heat and she led them behind the large buildings into an area housing a multitude of smaller workshops and other working areas. As they rounded the glass-making workshop, they came upon pile after pile of charcoal.

'Fuel for the furnaces.'

They went with her past smiths working different metals; making everything from iron beams for construction work to the most exquisite delicate jewellery. They passed carpenters making doors, window frames, furniture and toys. She took them past the aromatic houses where fish hung smoking over bark from the kiral tree, past the stinking works making tallow for candles and rendering animal fat for soap and other products, past the animal pens where ovellah, cabraxah and horned cattle waited patiently for the slaughterer's knife. They saw corn mills driven by waterpower and, finally, she took them into a large area of wide shallow circular ponds, all different colours. Here, men and women, skin splashed with various hues, trod on leather skins in the dye tubs, pressing and working the tints into the skins.

'This is where they colour and tan leather. My father's part owner of the trade; it's how he met Mother. We sell leather all over the world.' She spoke with great pride and Okkyntalah, mind reeling from all he'd seen, began to understand how undeveloped was his own culture.

'How do they get the colour off their skin?'

Horsylth smiled and nodded. 'A good question. The dyes wash off as they are at present. See the small running fall over there? They stand under it and wash off the dye every so often. Once they've worked them thoroughly into the skins, they take them over there, where they use some horrible, smelly stuff, mixed with piss. It's traditional for visitors to add to the supply.' She indicated a low wall and behind it they found a low trough where all three made their donations.

'Thank you. It fixes the dye and stops it being washed out. I don't know much about it, to be honest. My father threatened to make me do that.' She pointed to the people treading the skins. 'But I don't think he really meant it. He just wanted me to do something useful. I was relieved when I was chosen to serve in the palace.'

They exited from behind the wall to pass a foul-smelling pit. Aglydron pinched his nose. 'What is that?'

'Pigeon pooh. I don't know how or why, but mixed with other things, it makes the leather very soft and supple. I'm just glad I don't have to do that.' Horsylth pointed to where a young man was treading hides in a shallow vat full of the stinking mixture.

She let them gawp and stare awhile, taking in the many different processes going on about them; the noises and smells and actions of the varying trades.

'We must set off back to the Palace if we're to arrive in time for your meeting with the Kiral.'

'Do you know what the meeting's about, Horsylth?'

She smiled. 'If the Kiral hasn't said, it's not my place to do so.'

'That's hardly an answer.'

She blushed at Aglydron's tone and nodded. 'You're right, Aglydron. I don't know why the Kiral wants to see you. Please forgive my silliness. I saw how my fellow citizens impressed you with their arts and skills and I wanted to impress you by pretending intimacy with the Kiral that I don't really have.'

Aglydron, to Okkyntalah's surprise, put an arm about the girl's shoulders and gave her a reassuring hug. 'Your good service, your way of speaking and your knowledge all make you impressive, Horsylth. You're good enough for us.'

She smiled up at him and relaxed again. 'Thank you, Aglydron. You're not as uncultured and barbaric as we've been led to believe, are you?'

'Is that how you see us?'

The girl turned to Okkyntalah and bowed her head. 'I'm sorry if I offend. I meant only that the stories of the Great Division portray Followers in Muhnilahm as coarse, uncouth, ill-educated and brutal and that you and Jodisa aren't at all like that. It seems the stories aren't as accurate as we were once told. Perhaps that's why the Wharhll's been trying to persuade us all to open our minds and be prepared to discover that your people are…better than we've previously believed. Certainly, as ambassadors of Muhnilahm, you three have shown the stories to be entirely false. Everyone I've spoken to is ready to accept the changes the Kiral and Kirallah propose.'

Before Okkyntalah or Aglydron could reply, a great flash of lightening crackled across the sky over the sea, bleaching shadows for an instant and leaving frozen images in the mind's eye in reverse colours. It was followed at once by a huge roll of thunder, echoing and resounding from the walls and buildings in a deafening peel of raw sound.

'We must return to the Palace at once. Hurry, or we'll be drenched.' She almost ran ahead and they were forced to stride quickly to keep up with her.

'It's only rain, Horsylth. Why the hurry?'

She made a wry face, embarrassed. 'To tell the truth, I find thunderstorms very frightening. I don't like to be out in them.'

The rain hadn't yet reached them but it was plain in the sheets of waving grey that issued from the dark clouds over the sea. When it came, it would be a torrent and they were happy to rush with her to be under shelter.

They reached the inner gate as the vanguard of the rain spattered them with heavy drops that dotted their tunics with large spots, cooling the heated skin beneath.

'Shall we make it up the slope before the real rain comes, do you think?'

'Absolutely not. But the rain will last too long for us to shelter in the guardhouse and still arrive in time for your meeting with the Kiral. It seems we must take a soaking.'

'Are there no covers for the carts? For the rainy season?'

She stared at him in astonishment. 'That's a brilliant suggestion. I'll tell the Wharhll of it as soon as I see him, and let him know you suggested it, Okkyntalah.'

The two carts for the upward journey were already full of citizens anxious to get home before the rain set in. Horsylth went to the one at the front and spoke quietly to the passengers. They looked around at Okkyntalah and Aglydron and, without protest or demur, three passengers disembarked and gestured them into their places. Horsylth urged them forward, for they were unwilling to seem to be taking advantage.

'You've important business with the Kiral. He mustn't be kept waiting.'

They reluctantly took their places on the crowded cart and nodded their thanks to those who'd made room as they moved into the shelter of the guardroom by the gateway to await the return of the carts.

Lightning split the darkness beneath the cloud and another peel of thunder rolled and rumbled over the city. Rain fell in earnest. Everyone on the cart was quickly soaked, their silks clinging. No one seemed concerned and Okkyntalah tried not to stare as he noticed the citizens' indifference.

He concentrated instead on rivulets of rainwater forming streams and waterfalls as they drained rain along channels and hollows made for this purpose. The water was clear and clean except where it flushed hidden detritus from obscure corners. And, looking over to the raised reservoir of drinking water, he noted that much of the drained rainwater from the upper city was channelled into it along a narrow stone trough that sloped to its surface. A team of people stood either side of this trough, holding fine nets across the flow and extracting leaves and other objects before they fell into the water supply. The exercise was just another example, for Okkyntalah, of the organisation and mutual spirit of concern that prevailed in this city.

Aglydron put a comforting arm about Horsylth and held her in a protective embrace. She resisted slightly at first but huddled gratefully into his body as soon as the thunder roared overhead. Okkyntalah was puzzled but pleased by the change in his companion. Perhaps the rest of their mission would be less fraught with unnecessary disagreement.

They arrived back at the Palace, dripping and cooled, to be greeted by servants with fresh towels and clean dry tunics. A light meal, with neither Myllthlan nor Linlyss present, followed. Servants then conducted them through the wide airy passages of the building to Feldrark's private chambers for a meeting they both faced with a mixture of curiosity and foreboding.

Chapter 52

Learning The Truth

'Why would I keep you here against your will, Aglydron? Your argument makes no sense.'

Okkyntalah was also puzzled. 'I agree with Feldrark. It doesn't make…'

'Quiet, boy.' He turned to Feldrark. 'Your blasphemy and your denial of Ytraa's great message make no sense either. I don't know what you're about, Feldrark, but I know when I'm being taken for a fool.'

'How can you accuse me of trickery or bad faith? I've offered you practical help to fulfil your mission. But I'd be no friend if I sent you into the wilderness, knowing you were following last month's spoor. I tell you this Skyfire isn't true. It's a false sighting; what's known as an irregular. And it's not the first. I can't help the ignorance of your astronomer, Aglydron, but I trust my own implicitly. In fact, why not come and get the information from the dragon's mouth, as we say?'

Aglydron seemed about to protest against even this suggestion.

Okkyntalah wondered whether he should again state his real concern; to rescue Tumalind. Falseness or otherwise of the Skyfire made no difference to him. 'What do you have to lose by seeing the astronomer, Aglydron?'

'Alright. Let him show me his proof.'

Feldrark sighed with relief. The argument had been going back and forth with no development for too long.

'Come; Ivdulon won't come down. In any case, you'll need to be up there to understand the proof.' He led them from the chamber and past his sleeping quarters.

Jodisa put her head around the door. 'Where are you off to in such a hurry? You promised me your undivided attention this evening.'

'You shall have it, my love, as soon as I've persuaded this stubborn man of the truth about his wretched Skyfire. In fact, come with us. Ivdulon wants to meet you and we can catch two fish on a single spear.'

Feldrark led them past kitchens and stores to the cliff. He found the link-stone and explained what their route entailed. Jodisa poked her head out of the opening as the stone carrier lifted them toward Ivdulon's domain.

'Amazing! How does it work?'

Feldrark raised his eyes to his brave, bright bride. 'I've no idea. But I wish you wouldn't hang out like that. It's over three hundred manheights to the ground.'

She drew back in and stood next to him, her eyes still on the scene rushing past. Okkyntalah, torn between daring to emulate her adventurous spirit and needing to copy Feldrark's study of the floor, noted Aglydron's fear; he was white, hands gripped into tight fists and eyes shut.

The device slowed and finally stopped and they climbed to the surface. Feldrark gave them a few moments to collect their wits and gaze on the city, as the sun dropped slowly toward the horizon. He pointed to the thin dark line in the southwest and put an arm about Jodisa. 'Over there my mother was born.'

He turned to them. 'Ivdulon has no use for ceremony, no appreciation of rank or position, and can be quite blunt; rude and very personal, in fact. Please don't let this distract you. One other thing you should be aware of; Ivdulon has a deformed foot. Please, I beg of you, neither stare at it nor refer to it in any way.'

They followed him along the wide flat path to the squat cylindrical tower with its strange domed roof.

'Is it safe?'

Feldrark grinned at Aglydron's fear as he saw the building perched on the end of the spur of rock. 'It's been there for as long as the city, as far as we know. And the city's been standing for ten thousand cycles, if Ivdulon's calculations are correct.'

This piece of information slowly insinuated itself into Okkyntalah's mind, where it merged with all the other strange, impossible information and scenes he'd experienced here.

The door was open and Feldrark neither knocked nor made any announcement as he led them inside. The room, as circular inside as the tower was outside, was furnished with a wooden bedstead, softened by a stuffed mattress with a woollen throw crumpled on top. A single wooden chair with a rush seat stood near a large wooden table covered in scrolls, sheets of parchment bearing strange symbols and designs, and complex items of metal and glass construction that had Okkyntalah fascinated and bewildered.

A strange wooden device, with three tall, sloped legs and a flat board, stood against the wall opposite the doorway. It held a picture of a woman's face; Okkyntalah recognised it as the Kirallah with the city in the background. He'd seen nothing like it in his life and approached to look more closely. The walls were decorated in likenesses, some of faces, others of bodies, unadorned. The three of them stared open-mouthed. An open stairway spiralled up the inner wall to disappear through a dark gap in the ceiling above their heads. Of the tower's occupant, there was no sign.

Feldrark shouted. 'Ivdulon! I've brought you a couple of candidates for persuasion, and my lovely bride.'

'Tired of her lubricious delights already? You told me I'd never see her if I decided to wait until you'd grown weary of frowking her.'

Feldrark glanced shamefaced at Jodisa but she only grinned. Aglydron appeared outraged, but held his tongue.

'A man has to rest from such delights, from time to time, Ivdulon. Are you coming down or are we to conduct the whole of this conversation via the stairs?'

'Keep your finger on her fern. It takes time for brains and learning to descend to the plane of the mundane.'

'You let your astronomer talk to you this way, Feldrark?'

'I did warn you. Anyway, such brilliance and talent can't be constrained by convention, Aglydron.'

Ivdulon ambled down the stairs, plain grey tunic swaying. Okkyntalah was merely surprised at the dark skin, short, black curly hair and eyes of lapis lazuli that seemed to pierce everything they discerned. But he was amazed that Ivdulon was female. Heavy, buxom and tall, she was not a woman for joining. Glancing swiftly and then looking away unseen, he noted the ugly deformity they'd been warned not to mention.

Ivdulon ignored him and Aglydron completely and only nodded briefly at Feldrark as she approached Jodisa and walked round her three times, examining her like a farmer buying a breeding bull.

'I apologise, Feldrark. You weren't exaggerating. The lady is exceptionally beautiful, clearly gifted and undeniably as desirable as can be. I approve.' She faced Jodisa. 'This young whelp has captured your heart, young lady. Give me time and I'll capture your mind and show you ideas and thoughts even your dreams have never touched. Will you give me a little of your time, when you're both resting from thrusting and puffing?'

'Only my mind, Ivdulon?'

'Physical attributes are of passing and aesthetic interest; I might make a picture of you, if you'll permit?' She waved in the general direction of the pictures on the walls. 'Your mind; the thoughts, dreams, plans and schemes, the knowledge and experience you hold are what excite me. I feel far off thoughts, distant dreams, strange beliefs within you and I wish to search for the treasure that undoubtedly lies hidden. May I?'

A flash of surprise passed across her face and turned into a smile as she nodded at this strange woman. 'You may. I'll come to see you again soon, I promise.'

Ivdulon nodded back and turned her attention to Aglydron and Okkyntalah, whom she scrutinised as if they were strange creatures from a dubious place. 'So! You're not prepared to accept the word of the Wharhll?'

'I am!'

She raised her eyebrows at Okkyntalah and stared at him without blinking for a few moments, making him feel as though he'd been stripped to the bone. 'Good.' She turned her attention to Aglydron. 'You, then, know the stars better than Feldrark? Know the movements of Wanderers and Rovers more accurately than Ivdulon?'

Aglydron, clearly uncomfortable, didn't quail. 'I know our Holy Astronomer on Muhnilahm said this is the Skyfire. I know the High Priest of Muhnilahm accepts his word and I know the Choosing's been done and the mission to Choshinahm has set off.'

'Ah, a man who cares more for the letter than the spirit of the law; some would say that's foolish. Well, Aglydron, your astronomer's a blind man with a hollow stick for an observerscope. And your High Priest's a charlatan or a fool, I don't know which…'

'He's my father, Ivdulon.'

'The siring of perfection, Jodisa, is no guarantee of either intelligence or ability in the sire. You may have inherited all that's good in you from your mother. But your father is mistaken, of that I'm certain.'

'It might be better to show them the proofs, Ivdulon.'

She nodded at Feldrark and strode to the table where she delved amongst scrolls and parchment until she found what she sought. 'There! There's your proof. Clear as air, obvious as a ship at sea.' She pointed to a pattern of circles, ellipses, dots and strange symbols that meant nothing to Okkyntalah. Judging by his reaction, they were equally incomprehensible to Aglydron. Jodisa, however, stared at them with more interest than curiosity.

'You don't understand?'

'Ivdulon, there can't be more than a handful in the city who'd begin to understand your charts. At least explain what they mean.'

Ivdulon took a deep breath and, with the air of one forced to explain the need for water in the desert, began to interpret her chart. He listened intently, but Okkyntalah was quickly out of his depth and saw this was true of Aglydron. Jodisa, however, seemed to have some understanding of what the woman was telling them and even put forward a couple of questions that made Ivdulon glance at her with respect before she answered.

'So. You can see that this faint spark isn't the Skyfire. It'll no longer be visible by the twenty-first of the first portion of next cycle. The true Skyfire'll appear to my observerscope on the fifth of the second. Of course, if you wish to wait until then to verify my observations, you're welcome to come back up here and see it for yourself.'

'What's an observerscope?'

'An intelligent question at last! Come with me, young man. And fetch yon disbeliever with you.' Without waiting for agreement or acknowledgement, she climbed the stairs.

Okkyntalah followed quickly and Aglydron tagged along reluctantly with Jodisa making up the rear. They emerged into another circular room, with the dome for its ceiling. Standing in the centre of the floor was the most peculiar device Okkyntalah had ever seen. It consisted of polished metal tubes, rounds of glass and an extraordinary hollow mirror all attached to a stand fitted with wheels and toothed levers and rails in what seemed a deliberate pattern but from which he could divine no purpose whatever.

'Observerscope. Designed and made it myself. Well, had it made.'

'What does it do?'

For answer, Ivdulon approached another strange device attached to the wall of the tower. She consulted this tall metal instrument and nodded before she went to a small alcove set into the wall opposite. They could hear her move something heavy and a small section of the roof slowly opened on the sky. To their consternation, the entire room then began to move slowly round until the pale quarter moon was visible in the space against the deepening evening sky. Ivdulon moved to the complex apparatus in the centre of the room and turned handles and wheels. 'There. See reality at last.'

Okkyntalah placed his eye as directed and saw only brightness at first. But his eye quickly accommodated and, after a few moments in which he puzzled over what he saw, he moved backwards, unable to come to terms with what had assailed his vision. Even with his hunter's eyes he'd never imagined that the Moon might be covered in mountains and valleys. But that was what he'd seen. It was too much. He had to let his mind and sight come into single focus again, for his mind said the Moon was a flat disc that varied in colour, shape and luminosity but his eye now declared it a sphere bearing ridges and strange circular vales.

Aglydron looked and was fascinated, beguiled, rendered speechless. At last, he let Jodisa observe. She seemed more impressed than amazed, as if she had some prior knowledge of what she might see. Okkyntalah, needing to reinforce his brief impression, took a second look and stayed with it longer this time.

Overcome by this revelation, they returned to Feldrark, sprawled on the bed, perusing one of Ivdulon's parchments.

Explanations seemed unnecessary but Ivdulon answered unspoken questions. 'Yes, they are mountains and valleys; odd, I'll admit. Yes, the Moon is a ball floating in the sky, just as the world is. And, yes, the Moon spins round the world as the world spins round the Sun.'

This was blasphemy, but Okkyntalah couldn't argue against this extraordinary woman who spouted such things with no concern for the teaching of ages. Aglydron still appeared dazed, or he might have railed against this new wisdom. Ivdulon gave them more facts and some figures and sent them on their way. Okkyntalah, head reeling and beliefs damaged, felt in need of spiritual support.

As they descended in the gloom of the Riser, Feldrark asked Aglydron. 'Believe me now? This spark is not the true Skyfire?'

'No one could argue against what Ivdulon's just shown us. I don't understand a tenth of what she said but I know I've just seen what I was taught was a flat disc to be a solid ball. I saw it. If our astronomer doesn't know that and, if…'

'He does, Aglydron. My father told me years ago.'

'Does he have a thing like that?'

'No. His tired eyes and an ancient observerscope about as long as my arm, that's all. But he worked it out about the moon and told father. I'm sure Ivdulon's right. It all makes sense and, if nothing else, there's the timing. Even I knew this Skyfire we're following was too early. Father knew it wasn't due until sometime next cycle, though he was uncertain of the true date. But father hasn't an Ivdulon to sift the false from the true and, with the information he had, he was bound to go ahead with the Choosing.'

'Ivdulon worked out all the sightings, past and future, using some weird numbers in her head. I showed her our secret books and her historical dates tally exactly with those in the books. If she says the Skyfire's due on the fifth of the second, then that's when it'll come, I promise you. She knows all the risings and settings of the moon, the sun and the wandering stars with complete accuracy.' Feldrark said all this in the most matter-of-fact manner that none of them could imagine disagreeing with him.

They reached the ground and walked back to the palace.

'Our mission's a waste, then. Dagla Kaz will soon know he's wrong and he'll take the Virgin Gifts back to Muhnilahm. We might as well…'

'He won't Aglydron. He may delay his arrival in Choshinahm, but he won't return to Muhnilahm. He'd appear a fool and, in any case, he's already well on his way. No. My father won't turn back. The Virgin Gifts will still go to Choshinahm. Tumalind is still lost to you.'

'She's not. I'll follow alone, if I must, to bring her back.'

'Not alone, Okkyntalah. You've been faithful to the purpose, for all your youthful tricks, and I'll not desert you now. In any case, we must still right the wrong. Though I don't know how, now that Jodisa's beyond our reach.'

Feldrark put up his hand to signal patience and led them back to his chamber. Servants brought wine and food.

'Your father knew about the Moon but never told us. Why?'

'If you'd been told, without Ivdulon's observerscope, would you have believed?' Aglydron grunted.

'The Moon being what we now know it to be makes no real difference to our beliefs; but casts doubt on the truth of others. Had Father told Followers on Muhnilahm, with no proof to back up his denial of such long held beliefs, he'd have lost the trust of all and done Ytraa great disservice. No, Aglydron, he did what he believed was best for Ytraa and best for Followers. Like Feldrark, if he'd had the benefit of Ivdulon's instruments, he would've told others, knowing that doubters could be shown and would then pass on the truth.'

Okkyntalah, ready to be persuaded, wondered what argument and proofs Feldrark would produce to show he could replace Jodisa as Virgin Gift and remain within the strict rules of the sacrificial journey.

'What, exactly, is your objection to having Jodisa replaced as Virgin Gift, Aglydron?'

'She was Chosen by Ytraa. We can't replace her with another virgin just because it suits us, or rather, you. In spite of what Jodisa said to me after your wedding, I'm not sure you have the power to do anything.'

'I've no wish to argue on that, Aglydron, or to remind you that Jodisa never was a suitable choice in the eyes of Ytraa.' He leant forward and placed a comforting hand on her arm. 'My lovely bride wasn't virgin at the Choosing. Ytraa couldn't have Chosen her. It's my belief that something else happened, which we'll discuss in a moment. First, let me ask you, Aglydron, why do you take the Virgin Gifts to Choshinahm?'

Aglydron used the holy words. 'The Virgin Gifts from Muhnilahm form blood links with Followers in the land of our ancestors, reminding those people of their debt to Ytraa. Virgin Gifts return from Choshinahm to join with us and mingle their blood with ours.'

'You may find that difficult now, but that's another matter. The purpose of the Virgin Gifts is to spread unity amongst Followers, you agree?'

Aglydron nodded.

'Aren't we Followers? Why should Litkala be excluded from this mingling of blood? Leaving us apart from other Followers goes against the express wishes of Ytraa.'

'I don't have the law and books of secrets, Feldrark. I know nothing to stop it. Yet, Dagla Kaz never mentioned Litkala when he announced his pilgrimage to Choshinahm.'

'Doesn't that strike you as odd?'

'We were told that Followers from Litkala, I'm sorry, Feldrark; that they're cruel and vile and not worthy of the name. We know now that's not true. But I'm just a common Follower. I don't make decisions. I leave them to the High Priest, who knows better than me.'

Feldrark clicked his fingers and Patradko Kaz and Rrildyss Kaz came into the room as if by magic.

Okkyntalah caught a look of mild reproof on Jodisa's face. Feldrark returned one of amusement and she nodded. Okkyntalah wondered what had passed between them.

'High Priests such as these two?'

Aglydron seemed about to protest but, confused, he merely hung his head as if the problem was too difficult for him to solve.

'You accept that Patradko Kaz and Rrildyss Kaz are High Priests in the mysteries of Ytraa?'

'Of course!'

'Good. Then their interpretation of this unusual situation must be as valid as that of Dagla Kaz. More so, since they are two and he is one.'

'I can't deny that.'

'Tell these two brave men from Muhnilahm why it's right for me to have Jodisa and how we might replace her with another.'

Patradko Kaz nodded but it was Rrildyss Kaz who explained.

'Jodisa is no common Virgin Gift. I've ascertained that never has the High Priest's daughter been Chosen. Jodisa has described for me, in great detail, the nature of her selection and the way in which you two, and you alone, were given the means to detect what seemed a falsehood.

'Consider; Jodisa appeared to be properly selected, yet her father, a man of impeccable record, seemed to overrule that choice and selected your daughter, Aglydron, your promised, Okkyntalah, instead. A young woman who, I understand, is remarkably similar to Jodisa in looks. You, by your own admission, unschooled and inexperienced, nevertheless manage to steal away the High Priest's daughter and, facing many risks and perils, land on the tiny island of Ylcrat. There, you arrive precisely when the fire mountain springs to violent life and, by the choice of the leader of those heathen people, you're given a guide who turns out to be a gifted healer. Myllthlan later proves vital in keeping Jodisa alive when she's seriously injured.

'In the course of your long journey to put the error right, you come, seemingly by chance, and after many adventures, on the Wharhll of Litkala, who is in search of a bride. You're given help, almost at once, to escape the evil city, even though Feldrark was unable to escape before you arrived, and you're led by events to Litkala. On the way, you're attacked by vicious hunters and escape with only one of your party killed. Did coincidence kill the only person who might challenge Jodisa's claim for Feldrark's affections?'

Okkyntalah couldn't keep silent. 'I see! I see it, now. You're saying it was Ytraa who made these things happen. It was Ytraa's will that we took Jodisa and set out to follow Dagla Kaz, so we could bring her to Feldrark and unite Followers in Muhnilahm and Litkala.'

'It certainly could be interpreted that way.'

Aglydron was determined to be unconvinced, however. 'Malarhah wasn't the only one who might've been Feldrark's bride. What about Myllthlan?'

Feldrark nodded. 'Myllthlan would be first to acknowledge there's little but affection between us and that, pretty as she is, she's no match for Jodisa. Also, she's older than me. It's fundamental to the duties of the Wharhll that his bride be accepted by all as beautiful. And long tradition holds that she be younger also.'

'You accept there are clear signs of Ytraa's hand in what has so far been described, Aglydron?'

'It might be so.'

Patradko Kaz put the tips of the fingers of both hands together and placed them under his chin as if in deep thought. 'We have, thus far, seen that events have allowed a linkage of Muhnilahm with Litkala, forging a bond between the communities and making unity more likely. The remaining Virgin Gifts with Dagla Kaz are destined to link Muhnilahm and Choshinahm. One link of the chain remains unmade: what could be the perfect circle to reunite all Followers is still breached.' He was silent as the others pondered this. Just as Okkyntalah was about to state the solution, he stayed him with a gesture, glancing at Aglydron with expectation.

'If Jodisa's replaced by a Virgin Gift from Litkala, the circle will be whole. We'll have done a service for Ytraa that'll reunite all Followers!'

'Exactly, Aglydron. You take a girl from here to replace Jodisa. When you see the broader picture, you can understand the mysterious ways in which Ytraa works to bring the Followers together again.'

'But how can we Choose a substitute? It's never been done before.'

'Ytraa, we believe, has already shown us. Will you hear our reasoning?'

Aglydron nodded, his full attention on Patradko Kaz.

'All of us have come to the same conclusion. Okkyntalah, we're sure, will agree with us. Only you, Aglydron, remain to be convinced. It's our belief that your reward will be the greater if you find yourself able to agree with what we've concluded.'

A flash of eagerness passed across Aglydron's face but he said nothing.

Patradko Kaz continued, staring intently at him. 'A peculiar event occurred on your arrival. Okkyntalah was inspired, why we cannot tell, to compose a song, a lay in memory of Malarhah. He called for someone to accompany him. Although mature and experienced musicians were present, only one person stepped forward. We can't know what caused a previously shy and unknown young woman to put herself forward in this way but the conclusion that she was divinely inspired seems, to us, obvious.'

Aglydron's previous aversion to Linlyss surfaced. 'That girl's had a craving for him ever since she set eyes on him.'

Patradko Kaz nodded. 'That may be. But her selection by the Wharhll, to play at the ceremony, was made in ignorance of this mutual attraction. Her exclusion from the feast, except as a musician, was made by the Kiral, again in ignorance. Imagine the natural consequences of this passionate pairing at the conclusion of the Tryhhnarmahl. Already wanting each other, the dance must increase their desire. Yet, by chance, or perhaps by divine intervention, they were unable to join. Linlyss remains virgin, against all probability. Is it not the case, Okkyntalah, that you actively sought the girl to join with you at the wedding and again at the evening feast and were prevented by the innocent actions of those without knowledge of your mutual attraction?'

Okkyntalah nodded enthusiastically. 'But if Linlyss is to be the substitute Virgin Gift, it'll be a great test of her strength of will and mine. We'd both love to join and we'll be long on the road together.'

'Your honesty does you credit, Okkyntalah. You're proving yourself a mature and thoughtful young man as well as a brave warrior and excellent hunter. But does not Ytraa demand sacrifice, testing, to show the true mettle of Followers? To select an unknown or unattractive girl would be simple but to Choose Linlyss tests both of you, and Aglydron as your mutual guardian. Succeed, and you will glorify Ytraa the more by your strength and self-sacrifice.'

'Does the girl agree to be the Virgin Gift?'

'She volunteered as soon as the question was put.'

Aglydron's face showed relief. 'We must accept what Ytraa decrees. When you said you'd solve our problem, Feldrark, I didn't believe you. And you couldn't have done it like this without help and guidance; it must be the will of Ytraa.'

'I made my promise more in hope than expectation, Aglydron. I intended to try to persuade you in a way I hadn't, at the time, determined. But, I readily admit that the solution given us by Ytraa is far better than any I could've devised.'

Jodisa stood and held out her hand for Feldrark. 'I believe this meeting's over.'

Feldrark rose and embraced her. 'Patience, my love. Aglydron and Okkyntalah will be gone soon. We've arrangements to make and then, I promise, I'll be yours exclusively.'

'Don't be long.'

'Most can be done by Patradko Kaz and Rrildyss Kaz but some things I must do.'

She frowned at him and left.

Feldrark led them to the main hall, where, to Okkyntalah's surprise, the Kiral and Kirallah met them to celebrate a farewell feast.

'It's a shame you have to leave after such a short break, but I know you must, if you're to catch your High Priest.'

Okkyntalah assumed Aglydron had told the Kirallah that they wished to be on their way, and it suited him. Their two nights and days in the city had been useful and entertaining but he wanted to find Tumalind.

All the guests present were due to depart with them the following morning. He was vaguely doubtful about the selection of Linlyss and it felt as if they were being hurried on their way. But he could think of no reason for either suspicion. Both Linlyss and Myllthlan were present, so he would ask them about their part in the scheme. The morning, it seemed, would find them back on the trail.

Chapter 53

Departure And Arrival

Their departure from the city was such a contrast to their arrival. Quietly, almost, it seemed to Okkyntalah, like deviants escaping, they left the city and set off under the wall toward the fields and forest.

Pleased to be on his way, he was anxious not to lose complete track of Dagla Kaz by delaying too long. He was eager to find Tumalind as soon as possible.

A small group; Jodisa, Feldrark, the Kiral and Kirallah bade them farewell, along with the wife and children of their guide, Sondukal, who led the packhorse. There was also the family of Stellanyl, whom the Kirallah had selected as companion to Linlyss and partner to Okkyntalah, so that his lust for the virgin might be quenched to some extent.

Instead of their colourful celebratory garb of the wedding day, the senior members of the farewell party wore gowns of drab grey down to their ankles, marking the death of Mythanpho. The ordinary citizens had grey sashes around their hips. The whole departure was subdued and the travellers were pleased to leave the gloom behind.

Feldrark gave some final advice. 'Make for Shorrannon. From there, you'll have to go your own way, depending on what you discover of Dagla Kaz. If he's sailing, as Jodisa believes, he'll pass through that city. I suggest you follow the Sure, avoiding the Grave Mounds, as far as Lake Mistahn. She tells me he mentioned a possible visit to Kah-Labaz. Whether you go is up to you, but I advise you to avoid the great mire that lies north and east of there.

'You'll have to enter at least the very western edge of the Great Forest, to stay clear of the mire, but you should be through the trees in a day. You don't want to be in there at night. Beyond that point, I'm afraid I'm rather hazy. But, if you keep close to the river, you'll reach Mehrrhyphrol. Once there, get local advice about travel over the Mountains of Geldakq, through one of the passes. Otherwise, you'll have to go right up to Aagtaz to get into Choshinahm. Good luck and may Ytraa be with you.'

They exchanged embraces just beyond the gate and the party set off, well before noon. Their horse, a gift from the Kiral, carried large panniers and a basket copious enough to leave them free of all but their weapons. All wore practical travelling clothes of hardwearing silk and wool mix in plain colours or the island tabards. In the panniers, spare clothing and a special ceremonial tunic for Linlyss to wear at the giving, was folded along with their sleepsacks. They had food for some days, a small amount of wine, and water in one metal and several skin carriers. Feldrark had furnished Aglydron with a hundred gold coins to buy goods along the route; gold respected in all countries, whereas myllth, although more precious, was not always recognized further north. The walking was easy on the paved road and they faced no danger in the cultivated fields and orchards of the realm.

At the Wanderers' Joy, they spent their last night in beds and Linlyss made her farewells to the innkeeper and his wife. To her surprise, they were quite generous to her, giving her a small purse of silver to add to the gold she'd received from the Kiral. They gave the party good rooms and a bath, fed them, and wouldn't take a dorltah. And, in spite of their slight misgivings, they allowed Shaulah the shelter of the stables again and fed and watered her as a welcome guest.

Feldrark's return had brought increased custom from the city and surrounding lands, as word spread that he'd slept at the inn on his way home. And the news that Linlyss had learned to play the lyre whilst living under their roof had brought further promises of visits from the wealthy. They'd done well out of the business and expected to continue to do so. It was easy to replace a lost serving wench; in fact, they'd already done so. They made no apologies for their past treatment of her but wished Linlyss well in her new situation.

That night, Aglydron spent with Myllthlan and Okkyntalah with Stellanyl.

'So, what do you think of the High Priest's daughter, Okkyntalah? Is she as wicked as they say?'

Okkyntalah was puzzled.

'Pharah-Li. You spent last night with her.'

'Oh! Is that who she was? She never said, just dragged me to my room and got on with it. Tell the truth, Stellanyl, you're much more my type. She's a bit, well, you know, selfish. Very beautiful, I don't deny, but she demands too much. You're much more generous and straightforward. I feel I know where I am with you. She told me she was supposed to be with Aglydron last night; some sort of reward for something or other. I wasn't really listening, to be honest. But she didn't feel like another night with him; said he was boring.'

'Poor Aglydron; Pharah-Li must have done something special with him the previous night and he was expecting more of the same. They say she can drive a man mad; has some very strange ways with her. Anyway, I'm glad I'm back with you.'

'Me too. How do you feel about journeying to Choshinahm with us?'

'I do what the Kiral asks, Okkyntalah. I've no one special in the city and, who knows, I might find a lifelong partner on the road. It's a bit of fun, anyway, especially if you and I are together. And I've always longed to travel.'

'I hope you're ready for a bit of discomfort and adventure. We've a long way to go and most of it on foot. There'll be dangers, new people, different customs, weird foods…'

'Sounds wonderful.'

⸰ ——⸱—⸱—

They set off from the inn immediately after breakfast the following morning and soon reached the end of open countryside to follow the well-paved way through the Greenreald. Aglydron was curious about a small party of men and women in a clearing just beyond the road.

'Fuel for glass making, mostly.' Linlyss was friendlier to him now they were on the road together. 'Men cut the trees, lasses turn the wood into charcoal and plant new 'uns to take their place, Aglydron. Never run out that way, see? Teck trees from small patches all ower the forest, they do, so's not to meck any on it too open, like.'

Hot and humid under the canopy, they were at least out of direct sunlight and able to make good progress. They met a group of merchants; a dozen or so with packhorses, on their way to the city. Sondukal asked about the road ahead and whether they'd come across any difficulties on their way from Shorrannon. But they'd made the journey without event, barring a close encounter with a large roaming bear that had stolen some of their food before they'd chased it off. Sondukal recommended they spend the night at the Wanderers' Joy and they parted company to continue on their respective journeys.

'Are there many such strangers who visit the city, Sondukal?'

'Merchants, mostly. Bring in luxury stuff; gems, fine woods an' jet. Trade for glass, whitestone, dyes an' leather.'

'Are they all Followers?'

'No. Followers all live in Litkala.'

'What of those from Kah-Labaz and Choshinahm?'

'Ah, well, mebbie. But we do precious little trade in that direction.'

Aglydron was sure there was something behind this remark but he felt it wiser not to pursue it until he knew their guide a little better.

'Are there really bears out here, Sondukal?'

The tall man turned and looked down seriously at Stellanyl. 'Not just bears, lass, but medvjed with great pointed fangs and claws to teck your 'ead off; stand high as three men; that's what I call a bear. Then there's serpents, manecats, long-noses, zirafa, stripecats, wild oxen, senglar, an' the rest. Don't none of you go running away wi' the idea this is a safe place to venture. It's wild country, this. We 'ave to stick together.'

Aglydron wondered if their guide was teasing the girl from the city. 'Feldrark didn't say anything when we crossed the plains. He did mention the Bruxa, though.'

'Feldrark's a hunter. Wise an' kind. 'Ad his reasons for not saying nothing, no doubt. P'raps thought you'd be squittin' on shadows. Mind, Bruxa need watchin'. They'll strip off your flesh soon as look at you.'

'You've actually seen them, then?'

'No. But I've known plenty as 'as.'

But, for all his warnings, they met neither animals nor other travellers and settled down in a small clearing at the edge of the road to spend their first night in the open. To Linlyss and Stellanyl this was a novelty and they carried out their set tasks with enthusiasm, though a little nervousness, when told to gather fallen wood in the trees nearby.

Sondukal soon had a fire roaring well enough to boil water and brew tlathan to drink with their evening meal. They left the horse, a grey with white feet and a white blaze, hobbled to forage for grass in the trees. Since the likelihood of rain was remote and the night warm and windless, they decided against erecting temporary shelter and settled around the fire to sleep. Shaulah, happier away from the confines of the city, was enough of a guard to warn them of approaching danger, though Sondukal seemed confident the fire would keep away animals and they were still too close to the city to worry about the Bruxa.

'Live on the plains. Got a thing about trees, 'ave Bruxa. We'll not see 'em till we're out the Greenreald an' then like as not, neither.'

After the meal, Okkyntalah and Linlyss gave a short rendition of a well-known song about a fisherman who caught a mermaid in his nets and fell for her but ended up as supper for a whale. To their mutual surprise and pleasure, Sondukal sang a bawdy comic song, which Stellanyl accompanied on an instrument made of wooden pipes attached to a bladder made from the cured and softened stomach of an ovellah. Her Skinpipes made a sound with the haunting quality of a flute mixed with the clarity of a horn. Linlyss, delighted at this surprise accomplishment, invited Stellanyl to play a duet with her. To everyone's astonishment, especially Myllthlan's, Sondukal pulled her up to join him in a lively dance to their music. When night fell, they went happily to their sleepsacks, alone or with a chosen companion, tired but content after their first full day's walking.

As soon as Aklon-Dji made contact, he withdrew. His timing had been a little askew and he had no wish to intrude. Whether she'd even been aware of him was debatable, in light of the sheer ecstasy he'd briefly sampled.

It was much later that he tried again; only to repeat the previous experience at a slightly earlier stage. He smiled to himself. They had, after all, only just got married.

Early morning, with the sun enough above the horizon to assume the end of prayers, he tried for the third time and found her in relaxed contentment.

'Your timing could be better. I thought you'd be able to do this when I realized the telltale sign. How are you, you wicked reprobate?'

'*Are you in a fit state to do this? I was never one to spy on or view others, you know.*'

'*Oh, we finished a while ago; Feldrark's bathing. It just takes a time to return to earth after... anyway. Yes, I'm in a fit state to talk now. How did you know?*'

Her immediate acceptance and total lack of surprise was surprise enough for him. He explained his first faltering contact with Ivdulon and Ivdulon's contact with Feldrark.

'So, Feldrark knows about you? Hasn't said a word to me. I'll have to have words with him about that.'

'*He might not know. Ivdulon is perfectly capable of keeping secrets. However, to the point, dear sister, I am curious to know what happened to you and how you got where you are. The last I knew of you was when I discovered you had been stolen away from the house. Apart from the incident when I was in the sea with you whilst you were drowning, of course.*'

She acknowledged his part in her rescue and thanked him. As the sun rose higher, they chatted freely with each other, the way they always had in spite of deep religious differences. Eventually Feldrark came into the conversation and then Ivdulon joined in so that they had to employ some rules to avoid confusing one another. It transpired that Ivdulon hadn't told Feldrark much of his contact with Aklon-Dji, so Jodisa quickly forgave him with a public kiss, which signalled a break in their contribution to the conversation.

'*Newlyweds!*'

'*I heard that, Ivdulon. One day you'll discover the delights, then see how you feel.*'

'*Shall we leave them to it, Ivdulon? Clearly, they are more interested in less lofty pursuits.*'

'*Hark at the arch-lover of Muhnilahm, who's had more women than the most dedicated Holy One! Anyway, I don't agree with your definition of lofty if it excludes what Feldrark and I are doing. But, I'm...oh, I'm going now....*'

'*Women! Beautiful creatures but so distracting.*'

'*Perhaps, Aklon, but not always. I think it sensible for me to reveal my gender to you, since you'll learn of it soon enough now you're contacting Jodisa. I am female.*'

Aklon-Dji was silent at this news; he tried to decide whether it mattered and concluded it didn't.

'But why did you keep it secret from me, Ivdulon?'

'Our initial contact made it clear you thought I was male. With little real understanding of your island culture, I couldn't be sure you weren't prejudiced against women, the way so many less developed cultures are. Afterwards, when it was clear it wouldn't matter to you, the subject never came up. I didn't intend to deceive you and I hope you won't take offence at the lack of clarity.'

'None at all. In fact, it is rather fascinating. In a way, I suppose I must have some residual prejudice, since I automatically assumed that your logic and sheer genius meant you were a man. Another lesson learned.'

They spoke for a while longer and agreed to return to the wider ranging talk later on. Ivdulon explained how Jodisa had impressed him with her understanding of his charts and calculations. Her main concern had been her father's response to the false sighting when he discovered it for himself. The tenor of the conversation with her and Feldrark led Aklon-Dji to believe that he'd found a new ally and that his sister might well be ready to come over to his way of thinking.

The most important outcome of the contact was that Aklon-Dji decided the time had come to remove Kaz-Ca-Wesdan and, thereby, set off the landslide of change. He had no love for killing but the man was already acting like a despot, punishing folk for no good reason and roughly taking any woman he wanted just because he could. If left in place, he'd soon have some poor unfortunate put to death and, knowing his meanness and cruelty, it would be by painful means. No, it was time to set the Cause in motion and the acting High Priest's death would make a fine starting point.

Would Ytraa let him change the way they worshipped? Or would the real Skyfire, as the priests and Holy Ones predicted, burn up all who failed to travel in the ways dictated by that foul disciple, Gadhallah?

Now was not the time for such doubts. He shrugged and turned to start what would begin the war for freedom. The old Skyfire was going. But the new Skyfire was on its way.

⋄ ⋙——⋘ ⋄

The enforced rest, following Tumalind's brush with death, had caused a delay Ven-Gadla wasn't prepared to accept.

'I'm working to a tight plan, Dagla Kaz. The ship I've chartered in Slophrahn might wait an extra day or two if necessary, but it'll cost more.'

So it was that they found themselves driven across the last ten leagues rather more quickly than they might have wished. Comfort was less important to the merchant than money or time and he urged the oxen forward at a pace that took them to the port by the evening of the ninth day after they'd left Xythonl.

Dagla Kaz had already discussed his plans for a crossing with the merchant but one aspect of that journey wasn't to his liking. He was determined not to visit the city of Litkala, Ven-Gadla's port of call.

'Slophrahn to Litkala's near enough thirty leagues: in fine weather with a fair wind it'll take a day and a night.'

Dagla Kaz, consulting his map with both Ven-Gadla and the ship's master, proposed they sail a little way further up the northern coast of the Litkala peninsula and the Followers be landed on the shore where convenient. He offered enough compensation to persuade the merchant to consider the detour.

'What's wrong with Litkala, Dagla Kaz?'

'You're a good man but you're a heathen, Ven-Gadla. There are doctrinal conflicts between Followers in Muhnilahm and those of Litkala. I'll not go into detail. Let it be enough for you to know that we're not friendly. We haven't communicated since the Great Division, several hundred cycles past. There's deep enmity between us and I'd hesitate to place my people in the danger they must face from the wicked, perverted and violent people who inhabit that city.'

'I've been to Litkala many times. Never felt less than safe or welcome. They're as civilised a bunch of folk as I've ever come across. Cultured, sophisticated, liberal minded. And they don't ram their religion down your throat, like some. Mind you, they make you pay a hefty tax if you live there and don't worship like them. Perhaps they've altered in those long cycles and there's nothing now to fear between you.'

'Tumalind suggested more or less the same, though where she gets such ideas I can't imagine. And it may be so, Ven-Gadla, but it's a risk I can't afford. I'd rather hazard the open country than dare the city with so few of us on such an important mission. If we can be landed on the coast, we'll make our way across land to Shorrannon on foot.'

'Seems a shame. I'm staying in Litkala only a day or so, to sell a bit of this consignment, then I'll be on my way with another wagon train to Shorrannon. It would ease your journey if you stayed with me.'

'And you could spend more time gazing desirously at my Virgin Gifts, I know, and frowking with Netrodyl. But, disappointing as it will be to both of us, I daren't risk Litkala.'

The ship's master knew a place they could put the party ashore using the small rowboat and the deal was made. They would set out on the tide that night.

'Oh, Dagla Kaz, have you no mercy? We've been travelling for days without a proper rest. Why can't we spend a day or two here afore we cross another sea? My girls are in need of pampering. Poor Tumalind's still recovering, though she never grumbles, bless her, and Porryh's got a touch of fever. They can manage if they've got to but we should stop a while.'

'Sorry, Corphanda. We lost time through the rains and our troubles with the pirates. We've a chance to make that up and must be on our way. I can't afford further delay. In any case, Ven-Gadla must be on his way on the boat. We do the will of Ytraa. Time isn't ours to use as we will.'

The crossing was uneventful, except for the transfer from ship to row boat in the growing dawn of their second day at sea. The waves were choppy, rather than high, and made it a perilous shift from one moving surface to another. Only Corphanda, however, missed her footing and fell into the water, to be rescued by the sailors, amidst great hilarity. She thanked them for saving her life and then lashed them with her tongue for their cheek about her bobbing in the waves like a cork.

The shore was no more than a few hundred fathoms distant but the journey across that short stretch was uncomfortable and wet, with the wind forcing waves hard against the bows of the small boat and splashing the company.

A team of four sailors rowed the boat hard up the beach so they could at least step on to dry ground. But, for all that, they set off on the next leg of their journey dispirited by the wetness of salt water on their clothes. Corphanda demanded a stay, so she and her girls could change into dry tabards.

For the rest of that day and the whole of the next, they walked in a land teeming with game and with gruesome signs of wild beasts living off that meat. To begin with, their route was bordered on one side by the coast and on the other by a deep forest but they left the sea behind quite quickly to be replaced by a narrow stretch of grassland. Dagla Kaz decided not to explain why he kept them out of the forest. He had no wish to stray into the region he'd heard of as Mhortag's Dread.

On the night of the second day, they camped close to the trees and ate off Tryonta's hunting, cooked as always by Phildrad. After the meal, Jhonaht took Dagla Kaz to one side and pointed to the sky in the west.

'I see the Skyfire. What of it?'

'I hesitate to confess this, Dagla Kaz, but I'm no longer certain that it is the Skyfire. It should be mightier by now, yet it remains little more than a spark. I'm deeply concerned.'

Dagla Kaz was silent for a while. 'It's happened before, that the Skyfire didn't grow as it should, but was still the Skyfire. What makes you feel this isn't as it should be?'

Jhonaht shrugged. 'It's less bright and isn't moving in the right direction. See, it should be rising higher, moving to lie between the Eyes of Ytraa, yet it moves more slowly and towards the Hunter's belt.'

'This may not be the evil news you dread, Jhonaht. If it proves a false sighting, it merely means we're on the road to Choshinahm sooner than we should be. It gives us more time to make our destination and return.'

'But what of the Choosing, Dagla Kaz? Doesn't it throw that into doubt?'

'Only amongst the learned. And only you, Kaz-Ca-Wendarah and I in this party have that knowledge. As for those on the island, I've little doubt that Wesdan would want to make capital from such an error, if he knew of it, but he'll avoid making too much fuss in case the people turn on him in my absence. I'll say nothing of it to our party, if it turns out to be a false sighting; shall you?'

'Not a word shall pass my lips, Dagla Kaz.

'Good. We'll say no more for the moment, at any rate. Watch and keep me informed. I may still have you skinned and roasted on our return home, of course.'

Jhonaht smiled a sickly smile that revealed his misgivings about Dagla Kaz's real intentions. His fear and uncertainty suited the High Priest perfectly. *'Keep them all in fear; it helps you control them.'* The voices: ever-present now, they were some comfort in his loneliness. They returned to the party but, for all his declared indifference, Dagla Kaz did not sleep easy. It seemed the false Skyfire would soon be gone. But the real Skyfire was yet to come.

HERE ENDS BOOK ONE OF A SEARED SKY

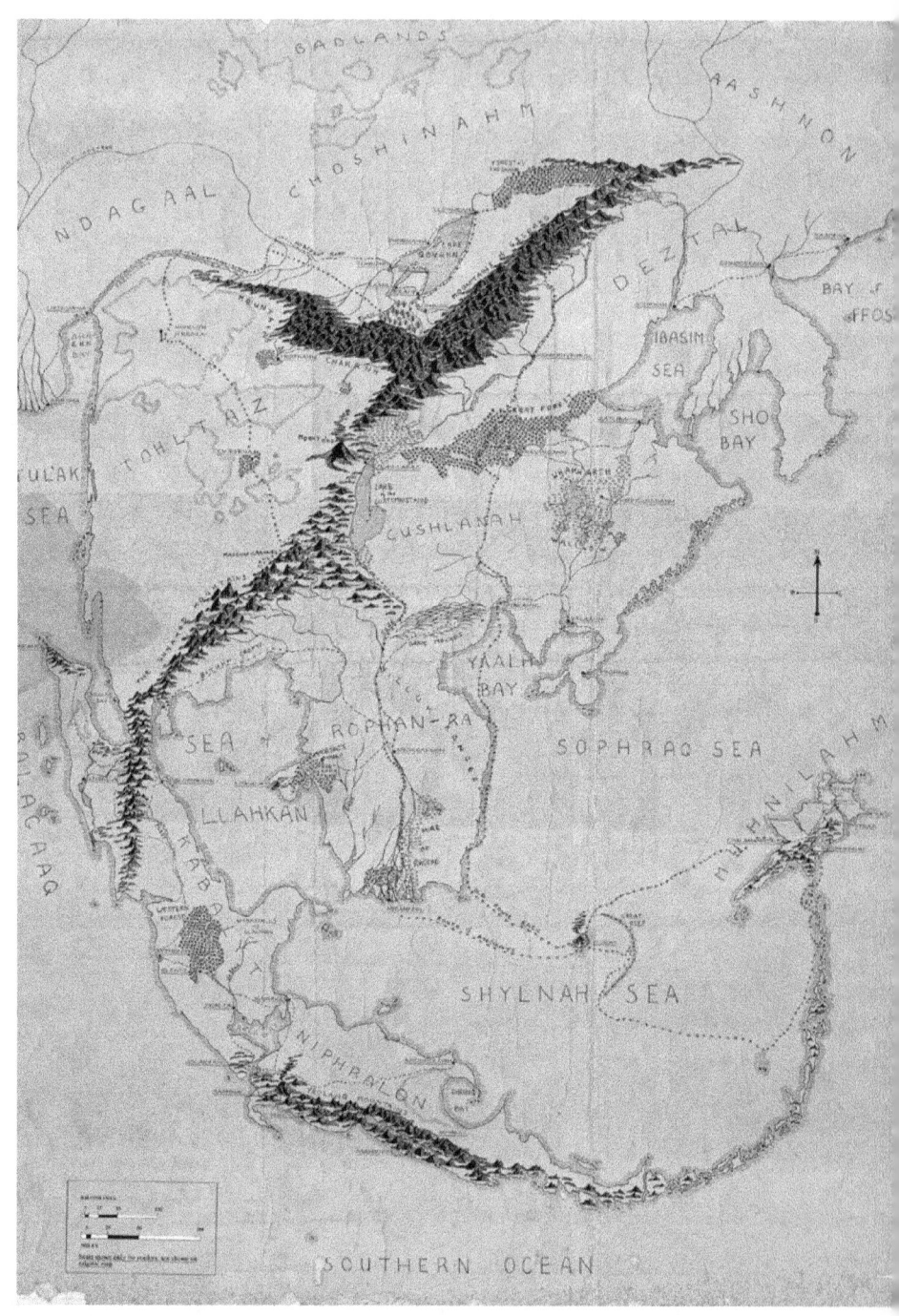

ABOUT THE AUTHOR

Stuart Aken is the author of other works of fiction. To explore these, please visit his blog at;

stuartaken.blogspot.com

Stuart loves to interact with his fans so please go and find him down on his various social media sites and say hi;

Tweet with him on Twitter
@StuartAken
Like his author page on Facebook
facebook.com.StuartAken
Join him on Goodreads
bit.ly/StuAkenGR
Pin with him on Pinterest
pinterest.com/stuartaken
Add him to your Google circles
bit.ly/StuAkenGPlus
Stumble with him on Stumbleupon
bit.ly/StumbleAken
And link with him on LinkedIn
bit.ly/StuAkenLinkedIn

If you've enjoyed this book, please tell your friends, and maybe find the time to place a brief review where others can discover what you think.

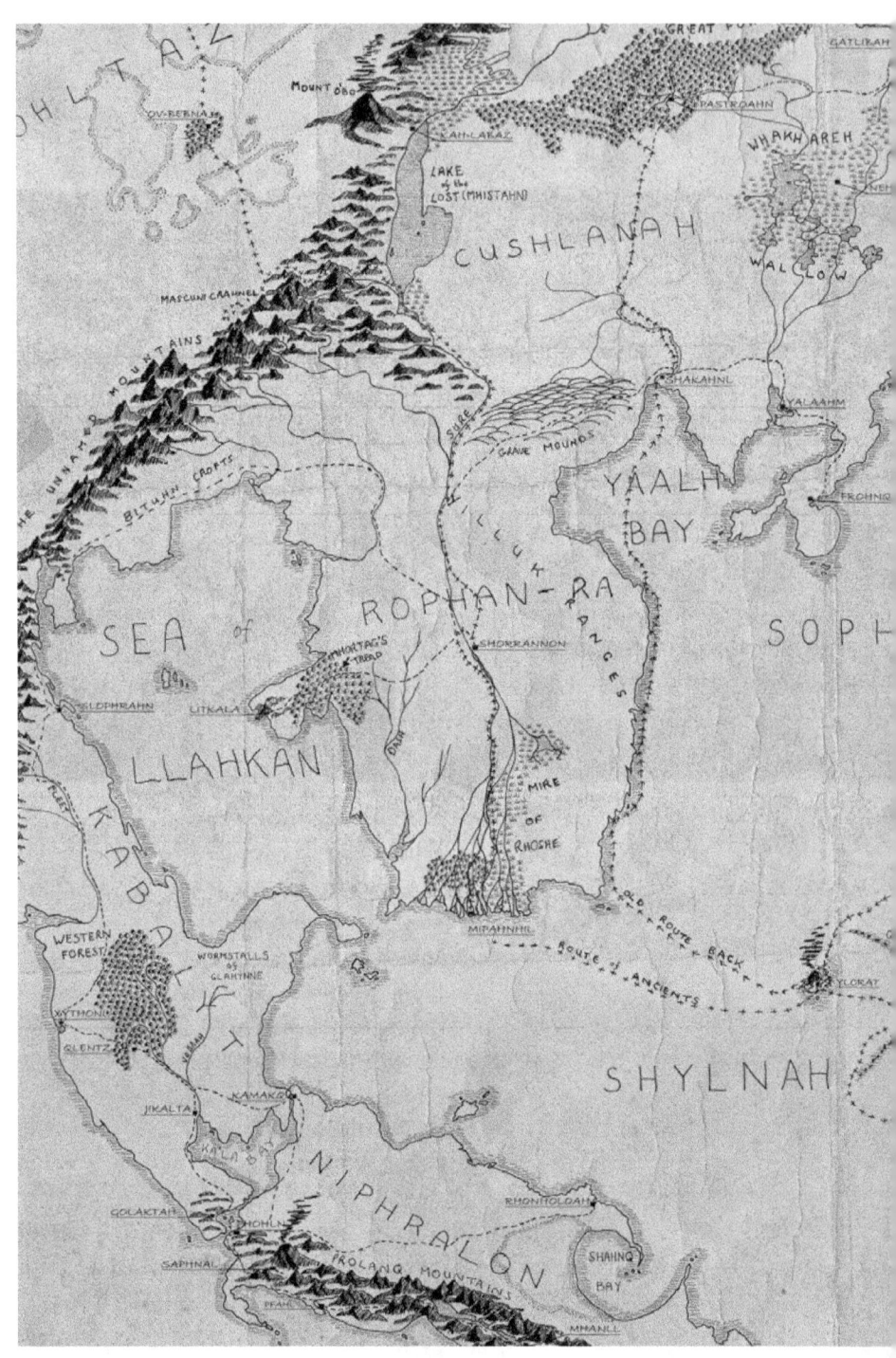

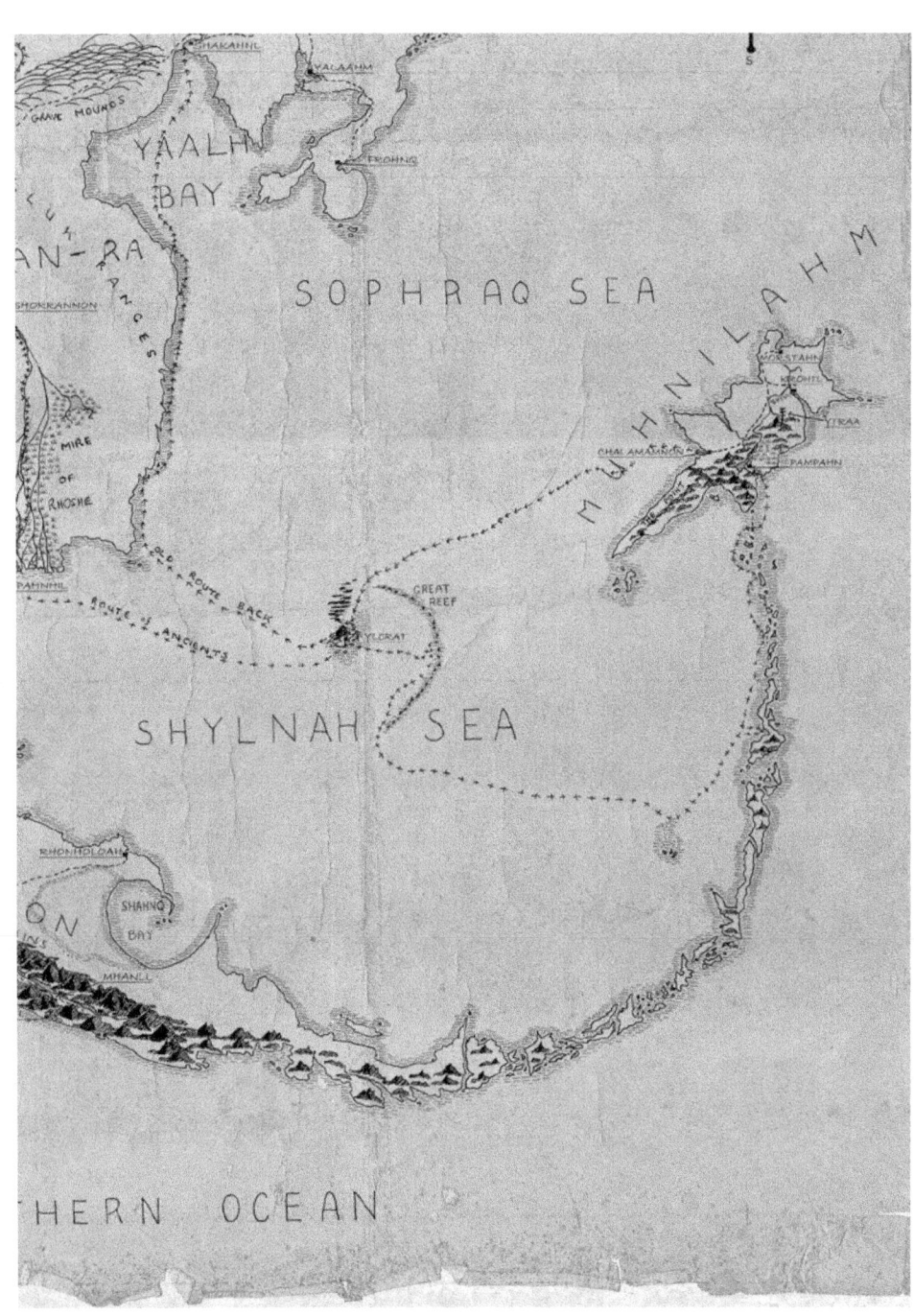

528

Characters in Alphabetical Order

Main players:

A'ahl is a young woman, held as consort by the village priest, Kaz-Ca-Wesdan. She is Caarl's wife and lives in Morstahn, Muhnilahm.

Aglydron is a pious Follower who chases the pilgrimage. He is Tumalind's father and Shoarhn's husband and lives in Morstahn, Muhnilahm.

Aklon-Dji is Renegade and an outlaw with a price on his head. He is Dagla Kaz's disinherited son and Jodisa-Li's brother and was born in Chalamamnon, Muhnilahm.

Baklan is captain of the ship, Nupraxyss, and hails from Kabalyt.

Caarl is the senior soldier on the island of Muhnilahm and accompanies the pilgrims as expedition leader and guide. He is A'ahl's husband and lives in Morstahn.

Chellyth is a young woman who leads the criminals and outcasts living on The Point, Muhnilahm. She and her husband, Por-Kildu, are known as The One.

Chislanda is a bereaved mother from Mipahnhil, Rophan-Ra. Her husband is Doklas.

Corphanda, a tubby widow, looks after the original Virgin Gifts on the pilgrimage. She comes from Pampahn on Muhnilahm

Dagla Kaz, the supreme ruler and High Priest of the Followers on the island of Muhnilahm, leads the pilgrims on their mission. He is father to Aklon-Dji and Jodisa-Li and is based in Chalamamnon.

Delbon is one of Aklon-Dji's trusted colleagues. His partner, Choryssa, is a soldier. He is a resident of Krohtl, Muhnilahm.

Dilanthas is a shy original Virgin Gift from Krohtl, Muhnilahm, who is Chosen to go on the pilgrimage.

Diryss becomes consort to village priest Kaz-Ca-Wesdan when he goes to Chalamamnon, Muhnilahm.

Doklas, a citizen of Mipahnhil, Rophan-Ra, is Chislanda's husband.

Feldrark is the spiritual leader and Wharhll of Litkala, Rophan-Ra. He is the only son of the Kiral and Kirallah.

Franorahl, a greatly respected highly skilled tattooist, lives in Chalamamnon, Muhnilahm.

Grahtl is a native from a village in Kabalyt, employed by Dagla Kaz as a guide in this savage land.

Gret-Zudas is the leader of the tribe who inhabit Qlentz in Kabalyt.

Horsylth, a Palace servant in Litkala, Rophan-Ra, is a young woman with a fisherman for a partner.

Ivdulon lives alone in a tower overlooking Litkala, Rophan-Ra. She is a wise woman, astronomer, inventor and mindtalker.

Jeklyzhon, a sailor on the Nupraxyss is named only in death.

Jhonaht is the astronomer from Krohtl, Muhnilahm, who announces the arrival of the Skyfire.

Jodisa-Li is heir apparent to Dagla Kaz, a beautiful and spoiled young woman from Chalamamnon, Muhnilahm, and sister to Aklon-Dji.

Kaz-Ca-Charrohn is the sexually demanding female Village Priest from Krohtl, Muhnilahm.

Kaz-Ca-Porlesah is the female Village Priest from Pampahn, Muhnilahm, who befriends Aklon-Dji.

Kaz-Ca-Uldrad becomes the male Village Priest in Morstahn, Muhnilahm, when his predecessor is promoted.

Kaz-Ca-Wendarah is the ambitious Village Priest in Chalamamnon, Muhnilahm and consort to Dagla Kaz on the pilgrimage.

Kaz-Ca-Wesdan, the predatory Village Priest in Morstahn, Muhnilahm. He becomes deputy High Priest in the absence of Dagla Kaz.

Lasdilyss is carer to her husband, Phildrad's, elderly parents and lives in Pampahn, Muhnilahm.

Linlyss is a volunteer Virgin Gift from Litkala, Rophan-Ra.

Malarhah, a slave girl in Mipahnhil, Rophan-Ra, befriends Feldrark.

Myllthlan is a gifted Healer from the island of Ylcrat.

Netrodyl is a wayward young woman rescued in a forest near Qlentz, Kabalyt.

Ni-Dehla is a female pirate leader from Niphralon. She is Ryglan's sister.

Okkyntalah is a brilliant hunter from Morstahn, Muhnilahm. He is Tumalind's betrothed.

Patradko Kaz is the male High Priest from Litkala, Rophan-Ra.

Pharah-Li, the spirited daughter of Rrildyss Kaz in Litkala, Rophan-Ra, has designs on Dagla Kaz.

Phildrad, a superb cook from Pampahn, Morstahn, is required to go on the pilgrimage. He is Lasdilyss' husband.

Por-Kildu is a much-scarred man who, with Chellyth, leads the criminals and deviants on The Point, Muhnilahm, as The One.

Porryh is an original Virgin Gift taken on the pilgrimage. She is troublesome and determined to change her status. She comes from Chalamamnon, Muhnilahm.

Ryglan is the male pirate leader from Niphralon. He is brother to Ni-Dehla.

Rrildyss Kaz is the female High Priest in Litkala, Rophan-Ra and is Pharah-Li's mother.

Shaulah is Okkyntalah's faithful hunting dog.

Shoarhn is a farmer in Morstahn, Muhnilahm. She is Tumalind's mother and Aglydron's wife.

Sondukal is an experienced tracker and guide from Litkala, Rophan-Ra.

Stellanyl is an attractive unattached young woman selected to accompany Okkyntalah on the mission from Litkala, Rophan-Ra.

Syylvah, a nymphomaniac informant who considers herself Aklon-Dji's lover, is married to the useless Wurrt in Chalamamnon, Muhnilahm.

Tarruss, a gentle giant of a man, taken on as guardian for the pilgrimage, comes from Krohtl, Muhnilahm.

Tryonta acts as Dagla Kaz's trusted and feared henchman and comes from Chalamamnon, Muhnilahm.

Tumalind, an original Virgin Gift forced to go on the pilgrimage, is Okkyntalah's betrothed and Shoarhn and Aglydron's daughter from Morstahn.

Ven-Gadla is a helpful merchant from Kabalyt.

Yatukon is the masked leader from Ylcrat. He is endowed with magical powers.

Mythical and Legendary Characters, and Titles in Use:

Caboceer: the native people originally inhabiting the island of Muhnilahm.

Dji: title of recognised male heir to High Priest.

Gadhallah: Revered Founder of the Followers, born in Choshinahm.

Galhta: title given the male leader of the people in Mipahnhil.

Holy Ones: a sect of extreme Followers who have some powers over the general populace.

Kaz: title identifying the High Priest of the Followers.

Kaz-Ca: title of lower level priests to the Followers.

Kiral: title of the male civic leader in Litkala.

Kirallah: title of the female civic leader in Litkala.

Krakgragog: the savage God of the Fire Mountain on Ylcrat.

Lesythemis: legendary daughter of Mythanpho and Vaarkil on Lake Qonahn, Choshinahm.

Li: title of recognised female heir to High Priest.

Mhortag: the Devil, as accidentally created by Ytraa, according to Gadhallah.

Mythanpho: possibly legendary heroic figure and Vaarkil's wife on Lake Qonahn, Choshinahm.

Na-Dagun: legendary double-headed monster of Lake Qonahn, Choshinahm.

Pah-Llon: possibly legendary adopted father to Vaarkil of Lake Qonahn, Choshinahm.

Paltra: general title of respect for senior women.

Paltrohn: general title of respect for senior men.

Poliphri: possibly legendary mother to Mythanpho in Choshinahm.

Sha'ra: a mysterious Goddess, residing on the coastal margins of Rophan-Ra.

Skyfire: the name given to a celestial sign (a comet) that presages doom for those who fail to Follow to the letter of the law.

Taniwha: a cruel sea God worshipped and feared by sailors.

Tihldha: possibly legendary adoptive mother to Vaarkil on Lake Qonahn, Choshinahm.

Tryhnn: kindly Goddess of open water.

Ulkhon: the Sun God and reputedly Mythanpho's father.

Vaarkil: possibly legendary hero found in Lake Qonahn, Choshinahm, and Mythanpho's husband.

Valorysta: Poliphri's mother in Choshinahm.

Wharhll: title given to the spiritual leader in Litkala; traditionally male.

Ytraa: Supreme God of the Followers as determined by Gadhallah. This being is man, woman and God combined and is credited with creation of the world.